LOVE IS A WOUND

BOOKS BY WORTH TUTTLE HEDDEN

Wives of High Pasture

The Other Room

Love Is a Wound

Love
is a wound

WORTH TUTTLE HEDDEN

CROWN
Publishers, Inc.
New York

This is a work of fiction.
The characters are my creations; their motivation, their actions,
and their dialogue imaginary.

"Love is a wound within the heart, and if it may not win its way out, it is an ill that lasts long, because it comes of nature."

Guizemar, in *Marie de France*
(*Translation by Edith Rickert*)

For Mark

PART ONE   ORA 2

PART TWO   ELLEN 164

PART THREE   DAVID 327

PART ONE
ORA

CHAPTER I

1

. . . OH, I DON'T KNOW, I DON'T KNOW, I DON'T KNOW. HOW OR why it happened as it did, I don't know. Some of it so clear, some so mixed up. If I could just straighten it out in my mind, the days and the hours in a row like the beads in that "Rosary" Cindy plays and sings, maybe I'd have something to fall back on times like this. But they all keep coming up here, asking me how I feel and I can't make any sense of it and explain it so they'll understand.

Begin that Easter Sunday twenty-five years ago. Nothing much'd happened then but enough to make me feel different. Every bit of me, body and mind, fresh and strange like an old dress I'd turned and made over to feel and look like new.

Was Easter Sunday, April 13th, 1884. I can see the date, black on white, above the numbers of the hymns on the golden oak board the League had presented. I can see the leaf-shadows on the white walls of that little old Bayport church and I can hear the twittering in the live oaks and the outspoken Amens in the pauses of his sermon. Seemed there was a new tone in his voice that day, even when he pronounced the benediction. The words were the words I'd heard him repeat many a Sunday since the first of January, but the voice and the gesture were certainly different. That day he held out his arms after the Amen till I'd counted ten beats of my heart, his eyes all the while pulling on the eyes of the congregation like the moon on the tide, so no body turned to the aisles, no hand reached toward another's nor wafted a fan. But when he stepped from rostrum to chancel those Bayport people moved from their pews in orderly rows like the breakers on a calm day, overlapped in the center aisle with a swishing of skirts and a murmuring. Hats and bonnets eddied around bared pates, ribbons and lace around solid black shoul-

2

ders, like foam around driftwood, then hurried toward the altar, toward his eyes and his smile, and his welcoming hand.

I stood still, only my fingers trembling a little on prayerbook and fan.

"Surpassed himself today, didn't he, Ora? Hasn't been holding out his arms like that after he's pronounced the benediction. When he first came, he hurried through whole Order of Service like a piece he'd memorized for school. Reckon he realizes we're not going to turn our backs soon's he's said *Amen* and's being as reverent as he wants to be. You excuse me?"

Miss Marmie Hughes sidled past, stumbled over a prayer stool, grasped the pew's back, and reached the aisle upright.

"Nuisances. No business keeping thum here now, half these people never using thum," the Major muttered along ahead of me, poking with his cane, pushing each worn velvet-covered stool under the pew in front.

I had to inch along too. I opened the gauze silk fan Ellen'd sent me from Savannah and waved it to and fro, screening my eyes from other eyes, wanting no other voice to hush the voice that still echoed like a conch's song in my ear. Wished I'd heard a few of his words though. The text or the summation. Something I could repeat to him, show him I'd got an especial message from the sermon. I'd meant to listen. I'd heard "The Lord is in His holy temple, let all the earth keep silence before Him. . . ." Then I'd slipped over to the parsonage and out to the kitchen and I'd told Aunt Merry she needn't turn down her mouth that way just because I looked in the chicken-pot. And I'd told her hereafter I'd make up the bed. No negra's ever been known to make up a bed right. All the quilts pulled up to the head 'sthough white people are as scary as colored. . . .

"Come long now, Ora. Way's clear."

"Oh! Thank you, Major."

"Pleasure, Ora. Always a pleasure smoothing the path for the fragile and the fair."

"Fair, sir?"

"Certainly you're fair. Fair as you're fragile. Fragile you can't question. You're a southern lady, ergo, you're fragile. Deny that, you wreck this sorry scheme of things entire. Wouldn't do that now, would you, Ora? Wouldn't leave southern gentlemen worshiping before an empty pedestal, protecting an illusion with our hearts' blood?" Silver knob of his cane

3

nudged my elbow and his eyebrows drew together like a long white caterpillar hunching for the crawl.

"Why I don't know bout that, Major. Fraid I don't feel much of a southern lady—not the way my mother did."

"Tut, tut, must never admit that, Ora. Never in this world. Mustn't be literal, you know. Leave facts to the Yankees. Facts their stock in trade. Ours . . ."

Charlotte and Mary Sue fluttering and whispering at the end of the line back there. Wanting to be the last again.

"That's true, Major. It certainly is. True's Mistuh Humiston's sermon this morning. Now how'd the text go?"

"Sermon? My dear young lady, that was no sermon. That was a lawyer's brief declaimed by a stage-actor. Taking the Resurrection Scene and proving beyond the shadow of a doubt Christ rose from the dead! Putting those sixty Roman soldiers on the stand, making them testify against themselves. Smartest legal trick I ever witnessed. Why, I saw every last one of thum cowering there before him. 'If you were asleep, my fine fellow, how did *you* know the body was stolen? And who stole it?' Yes, ma'am, he's right—if I'd printed such a story of grave-robbery in *The Argus* I certainly would've lost subscribers! Yes, made me think right seriously this morning of giving up my pew at St. James's—hardly ever get to Wilmington over Sunday any more anyway—and join you Southern Methodists. That is if I thought your bishop'd hide a young orator like that under a pile of oyster shells here for more than one year. Feel like joining you every time I get hot under the collar bout that *Northern* Methodist preacher up there in New Hampshire."

"What's about him, Major?"

"Said—and it was printed in a filthy abolitionist sheet—said the rebels ought to be taken by the nape of the neck and held over hell till they squealed like cats. Stated, furthermore, meant spiritual death for Northern Methodists remain united with the foul Southerners."

"Mistuh Humiston says we must forgive our enemies, Major."

"All I can say for him that respect is, he's cognizant of all we've got to forgive. Illiterate you've had in this pulpit past four years was a scalawag, ever I saw one. Twenty years ago last Wednesday your grandad and I laid down our swords with Johnston—"

"Major, look a there! Miss Parker Piver on Easter Sunday! Did you ever! You excuse me, I think I'd better speak to her."

"Your servant, ma'm." He pressed his knees against the pew

4

and let me by but his lips folded in and the goatee bristled.

Now I've done it! Now he won't say to Mistuh Humiston, in the post office or somewhere, "I tell you, sir, Miss Ora Fanning's fine a young lady's there is in this county. Father a Gentleman Private, contracted consumption in Elmira prison, sent home to die. Mother went into decline too. Left Miss Ora an orphan when she was six years old and look what she's done for her brothuh and younger sistuh!"

I just did get to the aisle in time to catch Miss Parker's black calico sleeve. "Good morning, Miss Parker. How're you today?"

Black shoe-button eyes blinking beneath a black sunbonnet, sallow skin crumpling in a ragged-toothed smile. "Morning, Ora. I'm all right, I reckon." She stood on tiptoe and hissed in my ear. "Tell you the truth, I feel real old, old's I must look, this graveyard get-up."

"Oh, no, Miss Parker! It's just right for church. I was going to tell you how nice you look in black." Now summer visitors won't be laughing behind their fans when she comes in a dress made of old lace curtains and a hat trimmed with fresh flowers that wilt before the second hymn.

She clawed at the streamers of my Leghorn and tittered in a nasty way. "La, child, look at you! All decked out in blue for that cock-of-the-walk up there."

I drew back. It's what I get, trying to be Christian to her. She's more than forty and still loony bout men. Lots of wives with little children lost husbands blockade-running and haven't made disgusting sights of themselves ever since. Still, if I had been going to marry Mistuh Humiston tomorrow and stumbled over his dead body on the beach . . .

"Get off your high horse!" She flapped a black cotton glove at me. "You girls can't fool me. Maybe you pull the wool over *his* eyes, all your putting on sanctified ways here lately. Men were made to be fooled and one of you'll get him mighty soon. You mark my words. Sat by my fire, winter time, talking bout me casting aside my earthly garments, preparing for the heavenly ones. Wisht I'd started then and there. Me here last Sunday, most penitent sinner *he's* brought to knee, and he hasn't set foot my place all week!"

"Miss Parker—"

"Come on. Out with it. You know any tricks I don't?"

"I—well, I was just going to say, I'm president of the League now you know. Supposed to help him keep track of pastoral

5

calls and things. I'll ask him to go see you right away and pray with you."

"Now that's real clever of you, Ora. Have to eat humble pie, rather have a Fanning dish it out than anybody I know. Started down there to ask him myself but saw some, gabbing and carrying-on, I don't want to be mixed up with." She looked back at the chancel and clutched at my wrist. "Look a yonder now? You see that head? That face? La, he's a beautiful man. A beau-ti-ful *man!*"

"Why, Miss Parker!"

Miss Tempy Williams came between us. "Parker, those fryers you left on my back porch were biddies. Coonie said made her feel right mean wringing their toothpick necks. No wonder you didn't knock for your money. Now you can just wait for it till next Saturday."

Miss Parker bent over, reached in her deep skirt-pocket, and I saw Charlotte and Mary Sue, three pews back now, laughing and talking to the Major and Cousin Sweetviolet Rutland.

"Put my last copper in the collection plate," Miss Parker said, shaking her little old man's purse upsidedown.

"Not sure I've got forty cents." Miss Tempy fumbled in her reticule.

Miss Parker held out the purse and waited.

"Thank you, Tempy. Williamses always did put up a poor mouth."

"Get along with you." Miss Tempy waved her away, sighed, and shook her head. "Last time Parker came to church in black, Ora, it was English lawn trimmed in 'blockade braid' Hollis'd brought her his last trip. She looked mighty pretty. How're you?"

"I'm right well, thank you, Miss Tempy. How're you today?"

"You look it. Saw you come in church in that new Easter dress and hat. Glad to see you've made something for yourself at last. It's more than that though. Kind of alertness in your face I never noticed before. A looking-*out*. Always did think, feature for feature, you're prettier than Ellen. Been sparkle you've lacked. What've you been doing to yourself?"

Dreaming all day, lying awake all night, forgetting to eat, not hearing Old Lady's scolding, not answering Buddy's questions, plucking petals off all the daisies as far as I can see, sunlight and moonlight, believing the He Loves Mes well's the He Love Me Nots.

6

Had to answer Miss Tempy's question now, though, surely as once I'd had to bound North Carolina or recite the list of its governors. "Why, I've been house-cleaning, mending, preserving strawberries, and—"

"Doing a little visiting with Reverend 'Adonis.'" Miss Tempy's long upper lip lifted, showed the edges of her strong white teeth, and I knew she'd smiled. "Saw you going in Annie Wescott's gate with him last Sunday after church. Don't fluster. I approve. Never did think ministers, specially young handsome ones, should go calling alone on ailing ladies." She pushed those steel-rimmed spectacles in place across the high bridge of her nose, then pointed that forefinger at me. "Here's your assignment till class meets next time, Ora Fanning: You whip up a little self-confidence and hold to your colors. You were born and bred to be a preacher's wife. If you won't be a school marm."

"Why, Miss Tempy! I never thought of such a thing! I'm president of the League you know, and Mistuh Humiston thinks the League—"

"You're a human woman too, aren't you, spite of your virtues? And here's a sentence you're to copy a hundred times on your slate: The business of youth is to find its mate. If it can. In the South this decade that's no idle pastime. Not enough of either sex to go round. Look at all the old maids in this town, loony one way or another. I'm the only sane one. If I had my way up there at Raleigh, I'd order a canvass of all counties and even up the sexes of marriageable age in each community. Give nature half a chance. But this legislature! Railroads, railroads, railroads. Who's going to run thum and ride thum, if the few babies got born during the war grow up spinsters and bachelors?"

"I hadn't thought—"

"Then answer me this: When's Ellen coming home?"

"Writes it'll be around middle of May but who knows what Ellen's going to do?"

"Hope and pray it'll be soon. Mercer's been down in the mouth here lately. She doesn't answer his letters."

"Why, you know Ellen, Miss Tempy. Never stopping long enough to mend a stocking or tack up a hem. Parties and picnics and clambakes and moonlight sails!"

"Well, I just hope and pray there's no young whippersnapper down there cutting my nephew out. That's one marriage I'm counting on. Ora Fanning, stop looking every which-a-way but at me. I'm not asking you to name Confederate victories order

7

of their strategic importance. I'm asking you if Ellen's found a better man—thinks she's found a better man in Savannah than Mercer Williams?"

"If she has, Miss Tempy, she hasn't written us." There. That's no story. She hasn't called Mistuh Stephen Clay a better man than Mercer.

"All right. Take your place at the head. Where's Benton this morning?"

"Said he felt mighty tired. Set out onion plants all day yesterday. I persuaded him to stay home and rest, even if it is Easter."

"Um-m, better persuade him to pop the question to Mary Sue, let her do your worrying. If there's any to be done. That boy's working too hard. Your father gave his life for a Cause but a farm's just a farm—two for a penny round here yet. Bring Reverend 'Adonis' round to see *me* next time. I'll give you both some good advice and scuppernong wine. Never like to serve one without the other."

"Why, thank you, Miss Tempy, I certainly will. I mean—that is—"

"Didn't know you blushed, Ora. It's becoming. Keep it up." Old black taffeta seemed to catch a sudden breeze, filled like a mainsail, and bore her off up the aisle.

Charlotte swooped at me. "Teacher's pet, teacher's pet, always were and ever will be! What's the old gray mare quizzing you on today!"

"Charlotte! Mary Sue! Why I thought you'd gone up long ago!"

"That's a story, Ora. You've been watching us like a hawk."

"I made Charlotte wait for you, honey. Two of us together might keep her from shocking Brothuh Humiston pink." Mary Sue slipped her hand in my arm. "What was Miss Tempy talking to you so long about?"

"Just inquiring bout Ellen and Buddy."

Charlotte tossed her head, little pink plumes on her fancy new hat dancing. "Talks just battle of the sexes to me. Told me every single time she saw me—till the Reverend 'Adonis' came —I ought to marry the Major, since I'd let Mercer slip through my lines. Imagine going to bed with that old goat. Wouldn't help repopulate the South anyway. He couldn't get either his other nannies with kid, don't know how—"

"Charlotte, you hush! You've shocked Ora white."

"She tease you bout Mistuh Humiston—now?" I almost said *too*.

8

"Did, till I told her that man-god hadn't got to be twenty-six, -seven years old without being nabbed and *I* had sense enough to know it. You just wait. When he comes back after his 'rest at the old home' in August, we'll have some stuck-up pris in the parsonage to go calling on."

"Then I'll tell you right now I'm not going with you, Charlotte Berry!" Mary Sue squeezed my arm. "I'm going with Ora and make a good impression. He said right there on our porch the other night, said Miss Ora Fanning's the most consecrated young lady he's ever met in his life. Said she's the ideal pastor's aid." Mary Sue clapped her hand over her mouth. "Should've saved that for a last-go-trade! You remember, Ora, you owe me one now, hear."

"I'll keep my ears open." I hoped it would be a compliment from Buddy, too. I couldn't tell her the one thing he'd said to me about her way last December. Said he liked that little Mary Sue because she didn't seem to care a bit she wasn't pretty-pretty. Said he might want to marry her some day. Now, if others didn't tell me more than Buddy does, I wouldn't even know he goes to see her every time he drives in town.

"Come on, you all! Old Sistuh Wendel's let go of him at last." Charlotte's hand, brown where her lace mitt stopped, all that deep sea fishing she goes at like a man, grabbed my free arm way it grabs the tiller in a storm, pulled forward, pulled back. "Who in the name of saints and little fishes 's got him now!"

"Silly, that's that northern woman your Cousin Winnie's been expecting. You ever see such elegance in all your life! Wonder if all the other boarders left. Miss Winnie said she didn't give a hoot if they did. Said this Mrs. What's-her-name's going to pay her more than a houseful of home folks. Look, come on, she's backing off."

"That's just her bustle twitching, see which way the wind blows," Charlotte laughed and said.

"Well, she will be gone time we get up there."

"Ah," she was saying, "then we'll have a little talk about it, shall we?"

Her words, clipped off short, seemed to fly about the quiet church. Then a swish of dark green silk, a smell of violets, a condescending smile, and she'd swept past us, her face so shadowed by dark green lace straw I couldn't tell whether she was thirty or forty, pretty or ugly.

9

"Who's the Queen of Sheba?" Charlotte thrust her hand at Mistuh Humiston.

"Sh-sh, Miss Charlotte. Hasn't your mother taught you to refrain from personal remarks within fifty feet of your subject?"

But he's smiling. He likes Charlotte's bold ways.

"Come on, out with it. Who is she?"

"Mrs. Layton D. Baker. From Philadelphia, Pennsylvania. Came yesterday to spend a few weeks at Miss Winnie Swain's. Her husband's in the state on railroad business. She seems an earnest, devout—"

"*Brothuh* Humiston!"

"*Miss* Charlotte. Remember the scriptures: Man looketh on the outward appearances but God looketh on the heart."

"And who're you, pray!"

"Charlotte Berry, be ashamed yourself! Talking to Brothuh Humiston like he was just anybody."

"It was a fair retort, Miss Mary Sue. I deserved it," he said but he looked hacked and the clock under the slave gallery ticked loud, ticked five times, before he held out his hand to me.

I dropped my fan and prayerbook, passing them from right to left. Didn't know whether to pick them up or shake hands first, and when I'd decided to put out my hand first, his wasn't there. He was shaking hands with Mary Sue.

Charlotte turned away. "I'm going over to the organ, see what Miss Daffy-Taffy thought she was playing for the offertory."

". . . inspired sermon this morning, Brothuh Humiston. So sorry Mama had to miss it. Might've given her some comfort. Papa fell twenty-one years ago today, you know, and she just couldn't trust herself to come out even on Resurrection Sunday."

"Yes, these anniversaries are sad, Miss Mary Sue. But you give your mother my text and ask her to meditate on it. I'll call tomorrow and we'll find consolation."

"I certainly will, Brothuh Humiston. Thank you ever so much."

"Miss Ora." His hand clasped mine.

Tell him what consolation the sermon gave you, an orphan. Tell him you're sorry Buddy had to miss it. Tell him . . .

"Mistuh Humiston, do you think you'll have time or opportunity to visit Miss Parker Piver some day real soon? I spoke to her this morning and she seems upset you haven't been this week—since her conversion."

"I'll make a point of it, Miss Ora." He leaned over the chancel rail, lowered his voice, though Mary Sue'd followed Charlotte. "Fact is, I don't like going there alone. Poor soul's such a talker. Could I persuade you to help me out again? After dinner today? If you can give up your siesta for the Lord's work."

"I'd be real glad to. After three o'clock that is. Old Lady wants to get off early, go see some of her grandchildren baptized, so I'll have to wash dishes." Now Ellen wouldn't've said that.

But he didn't seem to think any the less of me. "We mustn't interfere even with the misguided Baptists! I'll drive out around three then. Oh, by the way, this Mrs. Baker came to Bayport—to pass the time waiting for her husband to complete his transactions—because her mother was an old friend of your grandmother's—"

"Grandma's!"

"Of old Mrs. Evans, that is. Asked if I could tell her why Miss Winnie seemed doubtful about her calling at Brookside. Told her I'd speak to Mrs. Evans' granddaughter. Excuse me, Miss Ora. *Step*-granddaughter. If you'd been alone there in the aisle, I'd have introduced you, asked you to explain—"

"Oh, Mistuh Humiston, I'm so glad you didn't! I hardly know what to say. Maybe Buddy—"

"Don't let it distress you. You and I will talk about it when I come out."

He was smiling down at me the way I'd seen ordinary men smile at Ellen. As though they liked to look at her. I walked up the aisle to the door, feeling his eyes following me, feeling a tingling along my spine, feeling all pulled together, feeling safe.

"Ora, honey, you drop us at the Garrison corner?" Mary Sue asked.

"What in the name of saints and little fishes was he talking to you so long about?" Charlotte's black eyes were out on stems.

"Oh, several things," I said carelessly.

❖

I leaned over Mary Sue and tucked the laprobe in around Charlotte's pink ruffles.

"New?" Charlotte pinched at it.

"Half of an old bedspread I dyed with sumac and fringed." I shook the reins. "Get up, Madam."

Mary Sue's arm slid along the seat back and her hand squeezed my shoulder. "I declare, Ora, you're the smartest

11

thing in this world! Mama thinks so too. Was telling Brothuh Humiston the other night Benton owes half his success with the farm to you."

I love you, Mary Sue, I love you. You'll make Buddy a mighty good wife. You're almost pretty here lately, freckles, kinky hair, and all.

"Why, I don't know about that, Mary Sue. I try—"

"Ora," Charlotte broke in, "you come in with Benton when he comes to see Mary Sue after dinner, and les us go sit on Cousin Winnie's veranda. Such a fine view of the sound from there."

"Why, I—"

"Now what're you up to, Charlotte Berry? Tell me or I'll shake it out of you." Mary Sue squirmed around and got her hands on Charlotte's shoulders.

"Stop it! I'm sitting on the edge of nothing. I'm not up to anything." She folded her hands in her lap, bowed her head. "Except my soul's salvation."

"Lord knows you need to be up to that. But I don't see how sitting on Miss Winnie's veranda's going to help your soul."

Charlotte made her bold black eyes wide and innocent as a little baby's. "By her shuttered parlor windows? Hearing Brothuh Humiston's resonant voice exhort another 'earnest, devout' soul?"

"How do you know Brothuh Humiston's going to call on that Mrs. Baker after dinner?" Mary Sue asked.

"How do I know how crabs copulate? By remembering what the Bible tells us bout male and female and by using my eyes."

"Charlotte, I don't believe I can go with you today," I said.

"Why not?"

"To tell you the truth, I've got a previous engagement." I slapped the reins and Madam clomped along a little faster.

"To do what? Rub Miss Ryder's head or the cow's belly?"

"To make a pastoral call with Mistuh Humiston. On Miss Parker."

Charlotte whooped.

"Now I reckon you won't want to view the sound!" Mary Sue tittered.

Charlotte leaned over and patted my wrist. "It's all right, Ora. I'll do what I can to save your reputation, honey. Every single, solitary time I hear somebody say you've taken up with that old whore, I'll remind thum you're president of the League

12

and have to help *Mistuh* Humiston, you call him, look after the nasty stinking fish he catches in his net. Nice, clean, sweet-smelling ones he takes care of all by himself. Honestly, I will, Mary Sue be my witness."

"Ora, don't you mind Charlotte. She were half as conscientious as you are—"

"I'm not minding Charlotte." I heard my voice cool's a cucumber, way I'd always wanted it to be when Charlotte teased.

"Whoa, Madam!" Her big hands closed over mine and she pulled us up short. "There comes my lost love!" She turned Madam in, to the long grass between road and sidewalk. "Mercer Williams, you come here," she called.

"Why, Charlotte Berry!" Mary Sue gasped.

Mercer strolled from the shade of that old Garrison wall, lifted his new straw hat, and held it in his blunt-fingered hands, twirled it lazily. "Morning, Charlotte. Miss Ora. Mary Sue."

"Why weren't you at church, Sinner?" Charlotte reached for the hat, balanced it on the finger tips of one hand, and spun it like a top.

"Tell you the truth, Charlotte, I had the best intentions in the world but Aunt Tempy insisted I stay in bed this morning and get my beauty sleep." He ran his fingers through his sand-colored hair and grinned like a negra, his square teeth showing and his sand-colored mustache stretching thin.

"Yes she did! Listen, Mercer, look here, when you going to take me to the shoals?"

Mercer screwed up his face and squinted at the sky. "Lemme think now."

"If you tell me one more time you haven't got that old wreck fixed—"

"She fixed! She fixed!" Mercer jumped back, caught his hat before it hit him. "Had Roscoe working on that aft rigging all day yesterday. Soon's I get her caulked and painted. And, oh, yes, that rudder—"

"Oh, stop your hemming and hawing! What's the matter with you? Ora knows what she'll get if she blabs to Ellen."

Mercer's eyes, keen and gray when you got a look at them beneath the heavy lids, fixed on me. "Miss Ora, you hear from Ellen this week?"

"Not a word, Mercer. Reckon Cousin Sudie keeps her mighty busy running round."

13

"No news, good news, Mercer," Mary Sue piped.

"Reckon maybe that's right. Well—" He bowed and walked backwards toward the shade again.

"I'll give you one more week!" Charlotte called. Then, as I pulled Madam's nose from the grass, sighed, "Lord, I love him."

"Charlotte Berry, you shameless hussy!"

Charlotte turned her head languidly toward Mary Sue and her eyes beneath the frilled black bang were kind of soft and lustrous in a way I'd never seen them. "Why shouldn't I say it? Everybody knows it." She sat up straight. "What they don't know, I've loved Mercer Williams ever since the time he pried that crab's claws loose from my big toe, rest of you shrieking and hopping about and doing nothing."

❖

"Get up, Madam. Take me home fast's you can, please, m'am."

Bayport might be Goldsmith's Deserted Village right now. To a stranger's eyes. But I can see everybody like "Here's the church and here's the steeple, open the door and there's the people." See them plainly as I see the pin oaks and the poppies and the phlox. I can look right through the chinaberry trees and the mimosa, beyond the gates and the conch-lined paths, the verandas and the shutter-doors, straight down the passages to the dining rooms. They're all eating chicken and talking about the sermon and Easter clothes and Mistuh Humiston. . . .

Charlotte must feel light's a feather inside now, saying a thing like that right out. Everybody knows it nothing! Why, several've said to me Charlotte couldn't have thought much of Mercer, letting Ellen cut her out that way. And she went right on being loud and boisterous and staying friends with Ellen. I felt right sorry for her just now. Yes, sorry for Charlotte Berry! She didn't say another word after that. Except "Thank you, Ora," when I dropped her and Mary Sue. And she went ahead of Mary Sue through the Garrison gate and started cutting across the enclosure, still ahead. Wish I could've told her maybe Ellen's got a suitor in Savannah she likes more than she likes Mercer. They say when a man's been jilted, he marries the next girl he meets. Mercer wouldn't have to go off to Wilmington or anywhere looking for a girl. Charlotte'ud be right here waiting.

Certainly don't have to worry any more now about Mistuh

14

Humiston's liking Charlotte even if she does make him laugh. Been a little daft anyway thinking he'd consider a big bold girl like Charlotte, I don't care how handsome she is. Miss Lucy Berry's just wasting all the chicken-and-dumplings and apple pie she invites him to eat. I should've got *my* beauty sleep last night instead of twisting and turning every which-a-way, worrying about Charlotte and Bessie Davis and Claiborne Faircloth. He wouldn't want a fat, calf-eyed wife like Bessie and I don't believe the Faircloths would let a preacher, even Mistuh Humiston, the like of which they've never seen, be attentive to Claiborne if she should come home and stay all summer and try to add him to her string. Couldn't've helped worrying last night, though, nor any night all week. Any more than I could help that sick feeling in my stomach when Charlotte said there'd be a pris in the parsonage to call on soon. Charlotte's mouth's no prayerbook. If she'd said it *after* he clasped my hand harder and longer he's ever done, asked me to go out with him again, looked at me that way, I'd've laughed in her face. He's too honorable a man to do that and be engaged to a girl up the country. . . .

Major just getting home. Must've stopped in the Judge's office for a nip now Doctuh Willie don't let Joseph keep it in the house. Looks mighty feeble, hobbling along like that. Up that old path, bricks laid in a pattern now you see, now you don't. Used to try to find it, waiting for Grandpa and the Major to finish fighting the war again. There's Joseph running to help him up the steps, take him to the dining room. To that bleached mahogany table. Sit him down in front of Dido's chicken-bogged-in-rice.

Hear Grandpa now, "Who cares the Yankees did contaminate every table and chair and bureau? They couldn't spoil the Gallaway darkies. Kemp didn't have to scald *them* and dip *them* in lye make them fit for use again. They're right there in their natural color ready to do for him way they've always done. Wasn't for empty pockets, Kemp'ud be much of a southern gentleman he ever was." And I can see Miss Ryder cut her eye at him, green-black and hateful.

Now there's something'll make Mistuh Humiston laugh, I tell him bout the Major's having all his furniture dragged out to the back yard and scalded like hogs after the Yankees left his house. Certainly enjoyed my telling him bout Cousin Ida Rutland's boiling every piece of Ida Belle's baby clothes after that

15

Yankee private fumbled through the drawers looking for silver. "Up the country," he said, "we weren't so squeamish. I ate both my Easter eggs that fellow in Stoneman's outfit handed back to me, time I was telling you about, and didn't get a stomach-ache either."

Well, even Yankees are human, I reckon, and a black-haired blue-eyed boy-child, beautiful's he must've been, could pull at their heart strings way such a boy, grown, can at a woman's. . . .

"That's all right, Madam. Didn't mean to pull on the reins like that. You just take your time through this sand stretch, way you always do."

❖ ❖ ❖

Buddy threw away the sweetgum twig he'd been chewing and took hold of the slack checkrein. "Whoa, Madam. Give a lady time, can't you?"

He's trimmed his mustache. His neckline looks a little ragged, though. After dinner, I'll get at his hair again.

"You feel rested?" I gathered up my skirts and stepped from footrest to ground.

"Ought to. Been lying out there on the pine needles breaking the Sabbath quietly."

"How?"

"Just using my head for a change. Wondering if it wouldn't be smart to turn half the place over to Irish potatoes. Mistuh Brax Davis telling me yesterday they're going to ship thum from Wilmington two, three times a week here on."

"But, Buddy—"

"We'll go into all the pros and cons tomorrow. Hear a good Easter sermon?"

"Mighty good. Everybody going on bout its being the best Resurrection sermon they ever did hear. Major told me he'd feel like moving his membership from St. James's and joining us Methodists if he thought the bishop'ud let Mistuh Humiston stay out his four years down here." I watched Buddy's face.

"He won't. Get a man like the parson in the Conference, bishop'll make the most of him. Put him here just for practice this year. Whoa, Madam." Buddy reached over the wheel and handed me my prayerbook and fan. "You better go on in and put on your Cinderella rags. Old Lady's been banging pans last half-hour. Go long, Madam."

"Buddy, wait a minute!" I began untying my hat streamers.

16

"Buddy, Mistuh Humiston asked me to go with him to make a call on Miss Parker Piver. Bout three o'clock. You think it'll be all right?"

"You say you'd go?"

"Yes. That is—"

"Then why're you asking my permission?"

"Oh, stop your teasing! You know how people talk bout Miss Parker. But she's converted now. Came to church today in a black calico dress and sunbonnet."

Buddy whistled. "What a man!" He looked at me solemnly. "I won't worry bout your making a bosom friend of her. And I don't blame the parson for not wanting to go there by himself."

"Well, then—but I'll be back time to get your supper." I stepped through the break in the boxwood.

"You don't have to think about that tonight. I'm invited out."

"Mary Sue's?"

"Yes." He pulled his handkerchief out of his jeans pocket and mopped at his flushed face. "Look here. Just had an *i*dea. Why don't you invite the parson to stay and eat cold chicken here? Then you drive in to service with him, come home with me?"

"Why, I can't do such a thing's that, Buddy! I'll be here by myself."

Buddy threw back his head and laughed. "He's a gentleman. Besides, who's going to know?"

"Why, everybody. When they see me driving in with him and know you're at Mary Sue's."

"You stop thinking bout what you think other people think and think about yourself. I swear, you're the—now, Sistuh, don't pucker up. I'm not mad with you. Just use your head. How can anybody know Old Lady and Lucille and Slippy're not all here? Miss Ryder and Vin, whole passel of thum for that matter. Slippy will be here, milking time. How you expect to get—"

"Oh, Buddy, I forgot to tell you! That northern woman Miss Winnie's been expecting has come! Was at church all dressed up like a picture in *The Queen of Fashion Magazine*. Now wait a minute, that's not what I had to tell. She told Mistuh Humiston her mother was an old friend of Miss Ryder's and she wants to call at Brookside! What'll we do?"

"Let her. She won't do it but once."

"Buddy, we can't do that! What'ud she think of you and me,

17

we meet her? Seems to me only thing is, suggest she write Miss Ryder a note, ask if she can call. Miss Ryder'll never answer it and it'll all blow over."

"Now that's as graceful a solution of an awkward problem as I ever heard. Don't know why you had to ask me. Just go long now, or you won't get any rest before you have to go out again."

Buddy smiled at me and I had that safe-and-sound feeling for a second time that day. He looked right handsome in his way, standing there, sun glinting the brown in his hair and mustache, making his light blue eyes bluer. Reckon Mary Sue thinks he's handsome all the time, skinny as he is. . . . No, Mary Sue, I wouldn't try to keep him from marrying you. It was just such a shock, coming that way from Buddy out of a clear sky. No. Out of a mottled gray December sky. Out of a nor'easter. Struck me as hard as the wind was striking those old magnolias. Pulled and tore at me, left me a heap on the floor, clutching the bed clothes, stuffing them in my mouth to blot up the sobs. *My* brothuh. Ellen's other parent. To be with me when she was married and gone. *My* farm. *My* house. Little Brookside I had helped him get back from those Henshaw carpetbaggers, gone. Gone to you because you didn't seem to mind you weren't pretty-pretty. But it's all right now, Mary Sue, it's all right—I said that Easter Sunday.

On the other side of the hedge, in the Sunday silence, I stooped and tucked a shoot of mignonette in among the upright stems and suddenly had a thought about Ma I'd never had before. Ma wasn't always a head on a pillow, two thick brown braids, two enormous brown eyes, two thin cheeks with rosy splotches, two bony hands hot to the touch. When she set out this herb garden, she was as straight and healthy and alive's I am this minute. Must've stood right here on a hot April weekday morning, brushing dirt off her hands they say were as soft and white Ellen's are now, lifting one to shade her eyes to see Pa and the negras way off over there making a rice gate. She wasn't worrying bout her three little orphans then. Didn't even know we were to be. She was thinking about herself and Pa. . . .

"Miss Orie."

All I could make out was a blob of white turban in the black cavern beyond the kitchen door but I certainly heard the reproach and the pleading, the indignation and the long-suffering in Old Lady's tone and I went up the back steps in a hurry.

18

That's right, Mistuh Humiston. Miss Ryder's no blood-kin atall. That's why we all call her Miss Ryder. She didn't like being a grandmother, we were little, not even a *step* one. But, as I was saying, after Grandma Evans died, Grandpa didn't know where to turn. He'd made a lot of money with his rice, and Grandma, they say, was always after him to take things easy—there was only Ma to leave it all to. So he began selling off his slaves, many's he could to planters in the county, some to agents coming all the way from Mississippi. And—"

"Cruelest part of the whole system, breaking up families like that, sending—"

"Why, Grandpa was gentle's a kitten. He wouldn't have separated mothers and children."

Mistuh Humiston threw away the sweet betsy I'd crushed between my fingers and given him to smell. "Maybe *he* sold them intact, but those agents had no human feeling. They cared about nothing but money and put them on the block one by one. One of the rascals came to our place once. Father met him with his cowhide, told him if he ever set his horses's hoofs on his land again, he'd kill him quicker than a blacksnake. He would have too. When Father was mad for righteousness sake, he was— But I'm being 'interruptous' again, as Old Abe Lincoln said about the fellow." He leaned back against the cushion. "You were saying—"

What had I been saying? How could I remember, he sitting two steps below me, his head on a level with my knees, his face turned up to mine, waiting, expectant?

"Well— Where was I? Oh, yes. When Grandpa got down to not more than he needed for light farming and house servants, he took Ma—she must've been sixteen or seventeen then—and went down to Savannah to visit the kin Sistuh Ellen's visiting now. And there was this handsome widow come up from a lonely plantation in Florida husband-hunting. Or so Aunt Cleo, Cousin Sudie's mother, used to say about Miss Ryder. Anyway, she got poor Grandpa. Now, Mistuh Humiston, what're you laughing at?" I laughed too.

"Got poor Grandpa! You'll excuse me, Miss Ora, but—"

I nodded graciously.

"—just struck me funny, an unworldly young woman like you being so perspicacious. Please go on."

"I reckon I was still quoting Aunt Cleo. But I can remember how Grandpa was ever under Miss Ryder's thumb. So I expect that was the way of it. She was nigger-rich and he land-poor. She brought a boat load of blacks up with her. Old Lady says there were more than a hundred, counting the Hunchback, the No-eared Jacob, and the blind singing girl, Himalaya."

"Why, Miss Ora, why? Why did she own them and why did she bring them up here? I've pondered that question since Mrs. Evans' peculiarities were first mentioned to me."

"To show thum off, make folks talk. Same reason her father, they say, used to go to auctions all over—Georgia, Alabama, far's Louisiana once—buying up bargains in deformed negras. Every summer, they say, he'd invite people from miles around to a barbecue and circus, have The Monstrosity Family play at tournament and dance and carry on. I reckon he had plenty cruel Spanish blood in him. Miss Ryder didn't get those eyes of hers from English ancestors. They're the strangest eyes. When she's mad, always make me think of the underside of a breaker in a storm—black shot through with green. When I was a child, I'd run right out in thunder and lightning many's the time to get away from them."

Sympathy made Mistuh Humiston's eyes blue as indigo. "Ah," he sighed, "once the devil gets his hold on a character, how he clings to it! Punishes it in this world and in the world to come. Time or two I've driven past Brookside, I've been struck with all that rich soil going to wild artichoke and plantain and all these poor darkies begging work of everybody but old Mrs. Evans." He slapped his knees hard. "Miss Ora, when will you take me there? I'm going to bring that soul to Christ if it's the only thing I accomplish in my pastorate here!"

I didn't know where to look or what to say.

His jaw relaxed and the line of his mouth was as sweet as it was strong again. "Don't be ashamed, Miss Ora. Or alarmed. I faced a panther once and her skin warmed my toes many a cold night. I've got even better ammunition for an atheist. All I need's a good sight. Whenever you think—"

"I'll certainly do my best, but that may not be much. Maybe you've heard no preacher's been admitted to Brookside since our mother died there."

He nodded. "Yes, and that you Fanning children weren't allowed to go to Sunday School or church. And that those little twin boys there now are being brought up heathens."

"Oh, no, sir! That's not so. Buddy and I have thum over here real often, read Bible stories to thum. And they're going to school in the fall if I have to take thum myself every morning. They're bright boys, spite of their mother's being poor white trash. And you mustn't think Buddy and Ellen and I were raised heathen. Grandpa used to read the Bible to us—Miss Ryder never paid any attention if we weren't under her feet. And taught us catechism and responses from Grandma's prayerbook. Very one I carry now. He and Grandma were staunch Episcopalians."

"So you still carry the prayerbook. Oh, I like it, Miss Ora. Like to see you walking in church so demurely, clasping it. Wish more would. Should've left them in the racks when Methodists took over the church, instead of storing them in attics. Till we get more hymnals, they'd come in handy for responsive reading. Miss Ora—"

"Yes, Mistuh Humiston?" He's going to tease me! Mouth twitching a little, way Buddy's does when he gets ready to. I flicked at an inchworm, measuring the edge of my knee ruffle, and missed. He shot it off like a marble, laughed that little laugh of his would've been a snigger any other man did it.

"You call me *Mister* Humiston because you feel I haven't quite grown to 'the cloth' yet?"

"Oh, no, sir! I don't know quite why, just seems I began that way." I couldn't tell him it was because when Ellen came, she'd laugh at my calling a suitor *Brothuh*.

"Thought it might be because of your Episcopal background."

"May be. But it's just a habit any case. If you'd prefer—"

"No, no. I like it. Now don't you ask me why. May be every other parishioner, old and young, calling me 'Brother'—may be the 'Mister' makes me feel— In short, Miss Ora, may be I'm still a little worldly!" He lifted one hand, slim and white as they say all gentlemen hands used to be, and shaded his eyes against the band of sunlight slanting up through that cut-out in the magnolia branches. "Must be nearly six—" The other hand reached in between the buttons of his Sunday coat, pulled out the gold watch, snapped open the case. "Twenty to! Miss Ora, you're a Lorelei!"

He slipped the watch back in his pocket, got to his feet. But he didn't turn to help me to mine. He turned his head to the

21

right, gazed over the young green of the orchard to the old green of the pines pressing against the sky.

My hand was at my throat as though it could steady my voice. I said, "Mistuh Humiston, could I persuade you—that is, if Aunt Merry doesn't come back Sunday nights—no, of course, she doesn't. None of thum do. Maybe you have a previous engagement. I just thought—"

He turned around and laughed down at me. "Miss Ora, are you getting ready to invite me to stay for supper?"

"It won't be much, just Old Lady's chicken, and some strawberry cake."

"And a glass of sweet milk?"

"Why, yes, sir. Listen. There's Slippy clattering the milk pans out there now. You can have as much as you can drink, cold or warm."

❖

I set my plate on Grandma's big hand-painted waiter behind us on the edge of the porch, wiped my fingers on one of Ma's damask wedding napkins and looked toward the west. "Sunsets like this always make me think of a quilting-bag turned upside down on Heaven's floor," I said.

He laid down his fork and the bite of white meat, turned his face toward mine. "Now that's as apt a simile as I ever heard! An observant housewife's mixture of the practical and the sublime, but beautiful nevertheless." He looked again at the sky above the pine tops. "Yes, makes me see Mother and kin leaning over the half-finished quilt, suspended waist high from the ceiling hooks in the family room at the old home, floor strewn with scraps of all shapes and hues I wasn't allowed to touch. You have a real sense of analogy, Miss Ora, and that, I've heard or read somewhere, is the mark of a good mind."

"Why, I don't know about that, sir." I made a little triangle out of the big triangle of my folded napkin. "I've read all the books I could get my hands on but there haven't been many. Before I'd learned my ABC's Miss Ryder'd used Grandpa's library to start fires. Grandpa'd belonged to one of those English book clubs before the war. And I reckon you've heard how the Yankees took Miss Tempy's and the Major's and the Judge's libraries, and everybody else's, for that colored school they set up in the church?"

"Miss Tempy was telling me, just the other day. Seems a pity

22

they couldn't've been collected again. Understand that school lasted only two months or so." He looked at me inquiringly, then laughed that little laugh. "So you can blush at Low Country squeamishness! Your cousin's baby clothes, the Major's furniture you were telling me about. I see. Those books were contaminated."

"They were all torn to pieces." And I can't tell you why! Shame you didn't see those carriage sheds those negras used for gardenhouses! "Let me get you another glass of sweet milk, finish up your cake." I started to get up.

"No, no, Miss Ora, sit down. You'll have me too groggy to preach."

He dipped his spoon in thick cream, strawberries and sweet crust. As his head bent over, I stole a glance at the trim line of his sideburns. At the dark hair brushed back. At the curly ends behind his ears he couldn't brush flat. At one ear, just the right size and close to his head. At his nose, straight and well-formed but with more flesh on it than I'd thought, wider nostrils. It's his eyes, deep blue and set in deep like that and far apart, and his clean-cut lips, just full enough. . . . No wonder he has no mustache!

"From all I hear about you, Miss Ora," he said suddenly, looking up, "you wouldn't've had time to read, in the best-stocked library. Sister Ives, I think it was, was telling me how you've tried to take a mother's place with your brother and younger sister. You must've had your hands full."

"Particularly after Grandpa died. When I was eight. Then I had to wait on Miss Ryder and Vincent, my step-uncle though he's not much older than Buddy, as well as cook and sew and wash for Buddy and little Ellen. Used to get up at daybreak in winter, work till time to start to walk in town to school, and work again from time I got home till nine or ten o'clock at night many's the time. Old Lady wanted to help but Miss Ryder wouldn't let one of the Fanning negras near the house and she said I couldn't go to school I didn't pay for our keep."

"Miss Ora—" He laid his fork across his empty dessert plate. "I know there's more bitterness on your tongue than in your heart, because you couldn't harbor such resentment there and be the Christian you are. Maybe, if you can remember when you speak of your past, that God's purpose was in it all, it'll help you."

"Yes, Mistuh Humiston. I want to. I try to." The darkening

parlor, kneeling together, his arm pressing mine— "I expect I need your prayers too."

"You shall have them, Miss Ora."

He lifted his plate and I started to get up.

"No, no, don't bother. I'll set it here with yours on the waiter, for the time being. Just a few minutes more to enjoy this quiet scene." He rested his elbow on the step behind him. "Don't look so woebegone, Miss Ora. Peace will come to you some day —I'm sure of it—as, I was telling you driving along, it came to me with my conversion. Came in a sunset much like this. Three years ago. A stillness as in the dawn of creation. Then, suddenly, a light. A light not of this world. The landscape that'd been bright, suffused with brilliance. The rock at which I prayed, grayer. The grass around me, greener. The mountains in the offing, bluer. I raised my eyes, searching the sky. There was no sky. There was only Light. Light no mortal can describe. Infinite Light and infinite peace—God's living presence."

His face, as he turned toward me, was full of light, his eyes shining as though a lamp'd been lit behind polished panes. They didn't seem to see me. I felt like I wasn't there.

"And God's own peace. The peace that passeth understanding. I knew I was one with God, then, henceforth, and for-evermore."

Down in the marsh beyond the brook the first frogs croaked and a whippoorwill called from the thicket behind the quarters. In the branches of those magnolias sparrows twittered sleepily and katydids shrilled all around.

"Listen," he said, but not to me. "All God's lesser creatures praising Him. They sing praises in the twilight of the dawn and of the eventide. . . . Early this Easter morning I worshipped with them. In that dense tangle of jungle foliage and bloom, along the shore road beyond the wreck of the—of that blockade runner—what's its name?"

"The Rattlesnake. You didn't go beyond it!" Now I was with him, in time and space, fearful of his safety, way out there alone on the road to Halcyon.

"No. I was far enough from the haunts of men. Hearing a halleluiah chorus by a hidden choir, glimpsing soloists in brilliant reds and blues and yellows. Even the waves of the receding tide soughed softly of God's awful might and curved in continuous obeisance before Him. And over their offering of delicate white lace on His terrain, sea-swallows soared and

24

dipped in reverence, and black-headed gulls laughed their praise of Him. Even the skimmers, running hither and yon on the sparkling sand—"

"Miss Ora, you excuse me please. I'm agoing long now do I want to get back next meeting call."

You jinni! You soft-stepping, dusk-colored, slippery, sliding, "interruptous" jinni! "All right, Slippy. Good night."

"Good night, Miss Ora, Reverend."

"Good night, sir." Mistuh Humiston lifted his hand exactly's he would've to the Judge or the Major!

"Sir!" Grandpa's old felt, almost on Slippy's head, fell at his feet but he didn't stoop for it.

"I said, 'Good night, sir.'"

"Yessir. Good night, *sir*." He started down the path, turned back and picked up his hat.

"Oh, by the way"—Mistuh Humiston got to his feet—"you have time to bring my turnout around? We've got to get to meeting too."

Slippy stared at him. "Hit right there, *sir*." He pointed to the hitching post. "Knowed you had to be going, church time. Wind's just right tonight, I heerd the first bell minute ago, *sir*."

❖

I pressed the palm of my hand in the hollow of the cushion at my side, soon's Mistuh Humiston's back was turned, and its warmth made me shiver. I held my breath, heard every hoof-beat, every turn of the wheels, on the crushed shells of the drive. When the dirt of the road muffled the sound of his going, he was with me again.

Standing there two steps below me, holding his hat in his left hand, saying, "It isn't your missing my second sermon today disappoints me as much as my missing—remember what another David said? Psalm fifty-five, fourteenth verse, 'We took sweet counsel together, and walked into the house of God in company.' But there'll be another time for that." Leaning over me then, his hand on my head, saying, "Don't sit too long in the night air."

In all my life nobody'd ever spoken to me in just that tone, commanding me tenderly to take care of myself. For myself. Not for the good my taking care would do them. Not even Buddy. Never, never, never.

I wanted to call to him to wait for me. Tell him I wasn't too

25

tired after all. What had got into me? What had I been thinking of? Yes, I know. But driving with him through the dusk, nobody living but him and me, the world going round on four
shining wheels, would have made up for later. For the lights, the
people, his awareness of them and their possession of him. And
I would've had the drive in with him to go over in my mind
driving home with Buddy. Might've got up my courage and asked
Buddy how many times he called on Mary Sue before he proposed.

If I hadn't tried to ask him to stay for supper just when I did,
this cushion would be puffed up again and on the parlor sofa.
I would be wandering about the house, setting the lamp down
here and there, wishing I had asked him, and never knowing
he wanted to stay as much as I wanted him to. After all, I didn't
actually ask him. He asked himself. Only my preliminaries
came tripping to my tongue. I was just thinking out loud. Why
couldn't I've been as natural when it came to going to church?
Have let him manage that as he managed the picnic on the
steps?

He insisted on going out to the kitchen with me after he suggested eating in the sunset. He wasn't any help—what man
could be?—but I loved his hindrance, standing there in the
doorway between kitchen and entry, leaning against the
jamb, his hands in his pockets, not looking a bit like a preacher.
Taking in the scrubbed table and floor, the chopping block,
the new wire screen on the corner safe, the blackened stove, the
polished copper pail, the smooth-bottomed pots. Saying he supposed all kitchens were pretty much alike no matter what section of the country they were in. Only thing he missed from
ours was fruit, cut up and drying on big slabs of oak. "In
April?" I asked, and he laughed and said, "My mother'd be
ashamed of me."

And I worrying, all the way to and from Miss Parker's, as
to how I could persuade him to stay long enough on our
veranda to ask him to stay for supper, beneath all he was telling
me, confiding in me, about his giving up the law for the ministry. I heard every word he said, though, and I murmured
something now and then to let him know I heard. Said I felt it
was so noble of him to've given up a promising career for the
church.

He interrupted me mighty quick. "I didn't give it up, Miss
Ora. It was taken from me. God called me as surely as He called

26

Samuel. I had no choice. It was such an experience as there're no words to describe. I heard His voice and within an hour I was back at the camp meeting I'd left in a tumult of spirit, kneeling with other sinners from near and far, giving my heart and soul to Him, dedicating my life to His service. All that was of the flesh was forgotten, cast aside like an outworn garment. I arose from my knees a new man. Such rejoicing you never heard. Such shouting. Old men hobbling on canes. Mothers with babes in their arms. Whole families, simple mountain people, deaf all week to the sermons and the pleading, then seeing the evidence of God's hand on me, pouring to that improvised altar under the stars, shaking my hand, begging *me* to pray with them. Not a one there but had witnessed my departure less than three hours before. Watched me mount my horse, a few yards from the circle of benches, and gallop away, making no effort to hide my scorn. But the voice of that aged saint preaching from a pulpit stump—*God's voice preaching through his*—went with me. The faster I galloped, the louder and more insistent it became. I lost all sense of time and place. My horse took me home. I slipped from the saddle, strode past the kin and friends awaiting my return from they knew not where. Strode past them as though they weren't there and on, to a boulder on a hillside I'd always made for, child and boy, after a fracas with my father. There, after two hours or more of prayer and supplication, God revealed Himself to me as surely as ever He did to the saints of old. Then and there all worldly ambition vanished. All pride in the petty triumphs of my three years at the bar—and I'd had some in spite of the oldsters who would've restrained me. Damning me because I refused to live in the past. Their past. How useless had been my struggles against the wall of bitter memories they'd erected! How foolish the solace I'd tried to find in the society of my contemporaries! In a flash I saw the Truth. I'd been depending on mental and moral human strength alone and I'd been going at wrongs I would right hindpart-first. The Democratic Party, the Confederacy, the State of North Carolina, this nation, other nations, heathen lands, the world, are but group-words for people and in each person there is a soul to be saved from sin. Peace on earth and good will toward men will never come, Miss Ora, until each individual soul has given his life to Christ. . . ."

"Pick um up, child, pick um up. They'll get you there you

pick um up. You Jesus' little lamb now. Don't need to stumble and fret. Can fly like a dove now you minded to."

Old Lady bringing that little rascal of a Joel home with her again. Well, I can find something keep him out of mischief if he stays round tomorrow.

I waited till they'd passed the gate, for Mistuh Humiston to go on, but he was in church now, far, far from me in spirit and in fact. I had just the memory of his hand on my head and I had "But there'll be another time for that." For taking sweet counsel together and walking into the house of God in company. Next Sunday night? Maybe prayer meeting Wednesday. He could send a note out by somebody passing or ask Miss Taffy to put one in our pigeonhole at the post office Slippy or Buddy would pick up. Or he could just come along bout five o'clock any day, knowing he'd be invited to stay for supper.

3

"What're you doing out here in the heat of the day?" Buddy slipped from the saddle and reached in his side pocket.

No note! A note would be in his breast pocket. "I thought maybe there'd be a letter from Ellen. Last one came on Tuesday and I just couldn't lie down till you got back."

He mopped his face with the blue bandanna. "Nope, nothing at the post office. Now, Sistuh, don't look like that. Ellen's with kin having her a good time. Way you act, you'd think she was off down there among strangers pining for a home she couldn't come to if she wanted to." He pulled the sack of seed potatoes from Jezebel's back. "Where's Slippy?"

"He's been hanging round waiting for you. Said you told him—"

"I did. Got to get these things eyed. And set out, rain holds off till dark. Sistuh! Wait a minute. Two messages for you. One, I met Ace panting away down there by the gate. Miss Ryder wants you, soon's you can get over there. Seems she's got a headache and the boys are driving her crazy."

"Buddy!"

He threw back his head and laughed. "I swear. You'll never learn you're free. Bad's they say good darkies used to be when 'freedom come.' You don't have to go and it's time Miss Ryder realizes that. Even if you can't. You're not bounden to her for

28

anything any more. I sent back word you're otherwise engaged this evening."

"You want me to help with the eyeing?" Better to do that than walk from one end of the house to the other and back again. Picking up my sewing, putting it down. Getting out quilts to air, folding them away again.

"We-ll—" Buddy looked at the east, at the clouds thickening and curdling like clabber. "Your nimble fingers would certainly be a help but I doubt if the Parson knows why an Irish potato's got eyes. Only thing he learned on a farm was how to sit a horse. I grant you he knows horses and what to do with thum. Oh!" He slapped his forehead. "I'm daft. Forgot to give you message number two: Parson's coming calling. Met him in front of the post office. That is, he was caught there under that northern woman's parasol. Funniest sight I ever saw. When I passed and tipped my hat he looked at me like I was long lost kin and started backing away but the parasol kept following. I went on inside and when I came out he was still backing, parasol still following, lady still talking. I examined every one of Jezebel's shoes and when I finally mounted, there he was at my elbow and the lady tripping off up the street faster I ever saw a lady walk before. These Yankees!"

"What time's he coming?"

"Long bout five he said to tell you. Said Mistuh Newt offered him a horse and buggy for the evening and he couldn't think of any better use for it today than a drive out to Little Brookside. If we wouldn't be inconvenienced by a visit. I told him nothing could give us more pleasure. Said I'd be busy till dark but would enjoy his company at supper. He said he hadn't counted on an invitation to supper but if it was safe to accept one extended by me, he'd be delighted to do so. Yessir, we bowed and scraped like all get-out. Old Lady still in the kitchen?"

"No, but your dinner's in the oven keeping warm."

"I mean, don't you have to plan something special for supper?"

I shook my head. "It's shad roe and scrambled eggs and big hominy. Talking at League meeting last week somebody said they'd had that for him and he'd passed his plate three times. Quite a coincidence his coming tonight."

"Seems so, and that's a fact." Buddy turned quickly and

slapped Jezebel's rump. "Get along to the stable and find Slippy."

Jezebel lifted his nose and clumped away. Even a stubborn mule did as Buddy advised.

"I'll set you a place on Ellen's potting table," I said as he followed me through the hedge gate. "See—there under the crêpe myrtle. Get a little breeze that spot. I had Lucille stack all Ellen's flower pots under the edge of the house. Had Slippy move that old table from under there. Be right nice for summer meals, picnic style, won't it?" Better than the front steps in a Sunday twilight.

"Um-m, if Ellen doesn't miss her table. Now don't you bother bout me there today, though. I'll try it, when I have time to eat like a gentleman. You go on upstairs and get your rest."

"Well, if you think you can manage—" I stood hesitant in the triangular shadow between the house and the kitchen ell.

Buddy strode past me to the kitchen stoop, tapped my shoulder lightly. "Put on that same frock when you get up," he said.

"Why, Buddy! This is a calico morning-dress!"

"Fits you mighty pretty." He opened the kitchen door and closed it behind him.

Standing on tiptoe in front of my looking-glass I saw what Buddy meant about this dress. Saw my face turn right red. To think of his noticing my figure!

I spread my hands at my shoulders, brought them down slowly over the buttoned bodice to my waist. Trim, if I did say it myself. Ellen's face is a lot prettier. It's more than the sparkle she always has. It's her honey-yellow, wavy hair, her dark eyebrows and lashes, her eyes turning from gentian to violet blue according to her mood, and her fair skin. But Ellen's almost flat here. If she didn't sew those ruffles on her chemisettes, have me put frills and lace on her summer dresses, loops of braid or grosgrain ribbon on her winter, it'ud be noticed. People might say, "Ellen's prettier but she hasn't got the fine bosom Ora has." I don't know. I don't know. Nobody I know of ever's said Ellen's nose isn't as straight and aristocratic-looking as mine. Or that her lips are fuller and less lady-like.

Wouldn't bother Ellen if anybody did say such a thing. Time I took her to task about those ruffles, told her Ma'd be sorry to see her puffing herself out like that, shamming, she just laughed and said Ma'd worn hoops hadn't she, and everybody

30

wore bustles now. That's the only trouble with Ellen. She takes everything in a light and airy way. There's just no persuading her to be serious about anything. I marry Mistuh Humiston . . .

I pulled a chair close to the window and spread my dress over it. Breeze would take out what wrinkles there were. Otherwise it looked as fresh as when I'd put it on this morning. The little bitty sprigs of flowers as purple, the background as green. I believe I'd have put it on again even if Buddy hadn't said what he'd said. It's going to be cloudy rest of the day whether it rains or not and Mistuh Humiston's never seen me in work-a-day clothes. A preacher's wife should look neat at all hours, all the coming and going there is in a parsonage. . . .

> "My soul be on thy guard,
> Ten thousand foes arise,
> The hosts of sin are pressing hard
> To draw thee from the skies."

Hum it, Ora. Hum it over and over and over again. Just because they haven't got you yet's no sign they won't.

My knees felt as shaky as when Buddy told me he was coming. I got out of my stays finally and laid them across the footboard of my bed and slipped into my wrapper.

If Buddy'd been five minutes later, I'd have been down at the gate when Ace came. How'd I know Buddy was set and determined to get those potatoes in today? Thought, since he was in town, he'd go sit on Mary Sue's veranda till it got cooler. Didn't once think of his bringing me a note from Mistuh Humiston till I saw him reach in his pocket. I thought it might be Lieu or Cap. "Just a minute, my man," I could hear him call out, there in the post office, "you're from Camilla Plantation? Wonder if you'd mind dropping this note at the Fanning place on your way home." And if I had been there when Ace came, I'd be at Brookside right this minute. Be laying horse-radish leaves soaked in vinegar on Miss Ryder's forehead and listening to her tirade against Jefferson Davis, Abe Lincoln, and Vin's cooking. No, I couldn't have taken the chance Ace's getting a whipping just because I hoped for a note. Buddy would've suspected where I was and come for me, but I'd have been hot and tired. . . .

And Miss Ryder would've come right along with me. Sat

there in the parlor, at the supper table, mocking me, making me feel little and mean and of no account. I couldn't have heard a word Mistuh Humiston said, for her:

"Don't count your chickens before they hatch, my girl."
"Laugh before breakfast, Ora Fanning, you'll cry before supper."
"Brag's a good dog but Steadfast is better."

She's here now. . . .

Get out of my room, Miss Ryder! Get out! I won't have you in here again. I've been rid of you for two weeks. I haven't seen you. I haven't even heard you. I haven't had one single nightmare. I've been happy. For the first time in my life I've been happy the way girls're supposed to be. Happy, I tell you!

Yes, I know. I don't have to tell you. You knew. Your green-black, black-green eyes see everything I do. Those diamond studded ears hear everything I say. Everything's said to me. You know everything's going to happen to me. You knew Mistuh Humiston was coming to see me. That's why you sent Ace for me today. You didn't have a headache. You just had to think up something keep him from asking me . . .

Shut up, Miss Ryder, shut up! I *will* count my chickens before they hatch. I've done it many's the time and I'd always've been right hadn't been for you. I know a good setting-hen from a bad one. I can tell a warm egg from a cold. You were *not* in church with me Sunday morning. You were *not* on the veranda steps with me Sunday night. You were not there because I'd forgotten you. Ha, so you're not everywhere, seeing everything, hearing everything. I haven't said a word about this to you or anybody else.

You heard me tell Ellen that time I was going to be Portia in Miss Tempy's Scenes from Shakespeare so you made me get soaked to the skin hunting for your old sick cow just so you could wrap red flannel around my throat, make me swallow coal-oil and sugar, and tell me not to count my chickens. You ever did eavesdrop on me so you could quote a saying and scare me out of getting whatever it was I wanted. You never did that to Buddy or Ellen.

But you can't eavesdrop about Mistuh Humiston and me because I'm not going to say a word about it until we're engaged. After what happened Sunday any girl but me'ud be checking

32

linen for her dower chest, not walking the floor this way shouting *you* down. And I won't have to do it much longer.

Very first thing I do after we're engaged I'll let Mistuh Humiston drive me over and I'll wear my Easter dress and hat, carry my fan, be such a lady's you've never seen me. And we'll walk right in wherever you are, however you look—you'll look a mess in that old black Mother Hubbard with diamonds in your ears. And you'll have to admit Mistuh Humiston's everything Buddy told you he was, not a namby-pamby, pussy-footing, nincompoop hypocrite like all the other Methodist preachers you've ever wiped your feet on. When he tells you there is a God, you'll shake in your boots for your sins. And when he says "let us pray," you'll pray. My, how you'll pray! You'll get down on your knees and you'll grovel and whimper and thrash around and beg for mercy like the poor slaves you used to put the whip to. That blue-black hair of yours you won't tell the secret of will be straggling to your waist and you'll wipe the sand from Mistuh Humiston's shoes with it and plead *his* forgiveness. But he'll tell you only Christ can forgive sins and you must show Him a contrite heart. So then you'll hobble on your knees to where I'm standing and beg me to forgive you all your meanness to me. I will, Miss Ryder, I will. And then you'll call the twins and Ace and ask them. And poor Vin. Because you'll remember that winter of '66 you nearly let your own son starve with the rest of us before you'd swap those diamond earrings to the Yankees for something to eat. Then you'll slush through the swamp to Aunt San Dosia's —oh, you'll have to begin begging her when you're a long way off or you'll be scalded to death with that water she's kept on the boil for you all these years for what you did to her Josie. 1884 minus 1863 equals 21. Twenty-one years! It'll be hotter than that sugar-syrup you made Aunt San Dosia dip her hand in once. It's all going to happen, Miss Ryder, when I-take-Mistuh Humiston-to-call-on-you.

Oh, yes, I'll take him. You just wait. You were wrong once about me and now you're going to be again. You said Buddy and I'd never get this place back. You didn't know what the Judge knew about the deed. And you thought Cousin Ida and Cousin Sweetviolet 'ud be as mean about Ma's furniture and things as you were about Grandma's. Even when you knew others were helping us, you kept coming up behind me, not making a sound. Making me jump and spill whatever I had in my hands, with your hissing in my ear, "There's many a slip twixt the cup and the lip." But we didn't freeze to death cooking outdoors or sleeping on bare floors. Then you said Buddy'd never make us a living, farming here by himself. You didn't know Old Lady was just biding her time to bring Slippy and Lucille home with her. So, you see, you were wrong about every bit of it. Just as wrong as you're going to be about my dying an old maid.

❖

Heavens and earth, idea Mistuh Newt lending him that brand-new buggy today! It's certainly getting christened. With water and mud. But he's dry as toast in there, those buttoned-down curtains.

Um-m, driving on to the stable. That's right. Wonder if he's got his umbrella. One out there, hanging on a peg by the harness rack, Buddy or Slippy remember it. Hope he doesn't "sir" Slippy again. Slippy'll get on to it he's not being corrected. Almost did Sunday night . . . I'm as good to negras's I know how to be but I believe in keeping them in their place. People took that sermon about the Brotherhood of Man all right because he stuck to Christ's teachings way over there in Jerusalem or somewhere and didn't once mention this county but if he goes round town saying "sir" to colored, he'll hear about it. May be different up the country where he says there're not so many of them but it won't do down this part of the state. Subject ever comes up between us, I'll just have to tell him how far he can go practicing what he preaches. Don't believe I can stand it everybody doesn't like and admire him.

I let the curtain fall in place, picked up the hearth broom and swept the hearth again. So glad it rained so I can have him in the parlor again. Time he made his first pastoral call, end of February, he sat there in the platform-rocker, Buddy and I there on the sofa. He talked about the differences between the mountains and the seacoast. Said the easy-going ways we have down here were a little hard to get used to. Said if the people weren't so friendly and hospitable, he'd feel a stranger in a strange land. But said he liked living in his "Little Parsonage by the Sea," as he always called it, heading his letters. I lost a lot of what he said. I was nervous as I could be, being in a room with him, even if he did seem as far away across the hearth as he does in the pulpit. I never once thought that some day I'd sit

34

on the sofa with him—well, what could be more natural today? He didn't look at our Family Album that day. Never thought I'd be glad, a preacher called, Buddy wasn't around to carry on the conversation. La, the times last fall I saw to it Slippy made a fire in here for Ellen and Mercer, never dreaming . . .

"Miss Ora! Ah, this is nice on a dreary day!"

He came toward me, hand out stretched, and the broom fell between us.

It's not bad luck, Miss Ryder! It's not! It's the way slaves used to marry. *I* stepped over it. "Why, Mistuh Humiston! I saw you drive in and was waiting to open the door for you."

"I came in the back way. And Old Lady did the honors. Took my hat and *um*brella, even insisted on wiping off my shoes."

Pull on your hand a little. He's still just your pastor. Cling when . . .

"That old soul's a treasure, worth her weight in gold. Now that measurement can't be fair to her, can it? She seems to have shrunk a little again, got a little smaller since I saw her last."

He let go my hand but he smiled kind of wryly.

"I was describing Allen Brothers' new turnout to her. She said, 'You the preacher. I got to believe but I ain't seen nothing like what you say since this freedom come.' You saw it? Most up-to-date vehicle yet put on the market by the Cobb Carriage and Wagon Factory in Wilson. Yankees don't look out, Tarheels'll beat em at their own game." He picked up the broom, hung it on its hook, and took a stance, his back to the fire. "Buttoned in behind those waterproof curtains, looking out through isinglass windows, reins coming to your hands through a slit with a protecting flap over it, felt as snug as I used to feel when Mother tucked me in the trundle bed. No, people haven't seen anything's new as that around here since before the war. Quite a little crowd at the livery stable to see me off. Brother Fanning out there said Allen Brothers were after some free advertising, offering that buggy to me on a rainy day. I said no, I didn't think Brother Newton Allen had such an *i*dea in mind, just suggested I take this new one when I stopped for the one I usually *hire*. I hope I haven't upset your domestic schedule calling this way on short notice? Seemed to me I should be social, having the loan of a turnout."

"Oh, no, Mistuh Humiston, not atall. And I'll give you an official invitation now to stay and take pot-luck with us."

He laughed that little laugh I couldn't bear to call a snigger, said, "Knowing I can trust the pot in this house, I accept with pleasure. Please sit down now and make me feel at home."

"Oh, I—" I sat down on the sofa.

"Unless you'd be willing to brave the weather between house and stable, and take me to call on old Mrs. Evans?"

"Why, I'm afraid we couldn't go there today, sir. Miss Ryder's suffering with one of her headaches. We had word from there a little after dinner time. Thought I should go over and keep the boys quiet, but Buddy told me you were coming to see—us, and I—"

"So I've kept you from an errand of mercy. By the way, I happened to meet Mrs. Baker yesterday down town and passed on to her your suggestion about a note. She said, 'Why, of course, I'd never thought of calling without writing first and presenting the compliments my mother would have sent were she still with us. As a matter of fact,' she went on, 'I should not have thought of making the first call at all if Miss Swain had not implied that Mrs. Evans is too feeble to go out.' So we've— what're you laughing at, Miss Ora?"

"Your rendering of the northern dialect. It's fine's I ever heard."

"Come by it naturally, those paternal ancestors I was telling you about. So, you see, you and I have nothing to worry about for the time being. Nothing later, once you've gained admittance for me at Brookside."

He sat down beside me then, got up again immediately, poked and pushed Slippy's three logs out of place. "Pshaw!" he growled.

I had to laugh again.

He looked at me over his shoulder reproachfully. "Do you think that's kind?"

"I wasn't laughing at your efforts. Was the way you said 'pshaw.' Like Buddy says a bad word when things don't go to suit him."

He hung the poker on its hook and lifted the tongs.

Reckon I shouldn't have said that. And I've heard Ellen say you shouldn't laugh at a man, just with him. Was funny though and his being so talkative and fidgety today makes me feel easy. Spite of the way my heart's beating.

"There! One thing I can do about a house is make a fire burn. Even Father has to admit that." He hung the tongs over the

36

wrong hook, rested one elbow on the low mantelpiece, and smiled down at me. "So you detected the impatience in my mild expletive. No point in changing the word if I can't change the tune?"

Smile again. Please smile again. I don't know what to say. You shouldn't ask *me* what's right or wrong. "Why, I—why, a minister has to be human once in a while, well as the rest of us. I wasn't taking you to task."

"Ah, but you should have, Miss Ora. I need a guardian angel to check me on little sins I forget to mention in my prayers." He looked at the fire, back at me. "I'm striving for perfection, Miss Ora. For that state of perfect grace Christ promised if we would but be born again. I have been born again. At times I've thought I had perfect grace. That evening on the hillside, at the altar in the grove, and for weeks afterward, I was as sinless as mortal man can be. Above all temptation. Closing my law practice and consigning to a rival the most lucrative case I'd had were mere matters of form. It took no courage even to face Father, for what is an earthly father's disappointment compared to our Heavenly Father's command—and understanding?" He glanced down at his slender, long-fingered hand dangling over the embroidered trumpet-flowers of the velvet mantel-cloth. "I felt not a twinge of regret bidding farewell to old companions whose ringleader I'd been. Nor"—he looked straight at me— "to the worldly young lady I'd determined to make my wife— when I'd mustered the courage to ask for her hand."

A tremor went all through me. I couldn't help or hide it. Could only hope he hadn't noticed. How could he have, his eyes fixed on mine? The lids stretching, the pupils widening till I seemed to see nothing but blue. I pressed my arms to my sides. Wait, wait. When he's here at your feet, his head on your breast . . . Don't look away. Oh, *don't*. But I couldn't stand it. And I couldn't spring at *him*, spite of every muscle's pulling.

I felt my eyelids flutter. Felt the pain of my nails cutting into my palms and watched my hands drop like weights in my lap, one lax on the other. I tried to look up at him again but my lids too were weighted. I felt like I was smothering and tried to draw a breath.

"Yes, Miss Ora, you may well sigh for me."

Then I heard the clink of the tongs again.

Why those little summer-logs are nothing to get hold of. His hands are shaking too. Now he's got it. Now he's putting it just

37

where it's needed. Between the two back ones. They're about to burn in two. The seat of his pants is shiny. Aunt Merry's pressing cloth is too thin. One cuff is a little frayed. It's an old pair he wears on rainy days. There is a man. *Voilà un homme.* Here is a woman. *Voici une femme.* Here is the little poem. *Voici le petit poème.* Learn the poem. *Apprenez le poème.* It is not difficult. *Il n'est pas difficile.* It is very easy. *Il est tres facile.* . . . Ma's old bonnet box. Her school books from St. Mary's in Raleigh. The attic at Brookside. Raining like this. Ma's slate. Pencil tied to it with a frayed red ribbon. I wrote and wrote. Sentences I liked . . .

"Oh! Yes, sit down, do, Mistuh Humiston. What did you say?"

"I said you're a very sympathetic young woman. But you mustn't waste your sweet sympathy on that sentimental episode in my life. Now I know it wasn't lack of courage restrained me. It was God's own hand. His eye was on me, too blind then to see the Light I saw so soon—two days after my last effort to propose."

His arm stretched along the back of the sofa, the tips of his fingers almost touching my shoulder. If only I could slide the least little bit. I tried. My limbs tensed but the horsehair was like glue.

"Miss Ora—"

"Yes, Mistuh Humiston." I managed to raise my eyes.

"You're deeply interested in the church?"

I swallowed. I nodded my head. "I've tried—to do my share, since I've been free to do as I liked. That is, on Sundays. During the week, when little Ellen's home—"

My voice just died away. Maybe I'd made no sound atall. He didn't seem to've heard me. He was staring at the hand that clasped his crossed knee as though he was counting the black hairs on its back. Just enough of them, I noticed, to make it a man's hand.

"As a matter of fact, I've been surprised and heartened by the enthusiasm I've found among all you Bayport young women. It's mighty encouraging to a new pastor—a green pastor—I can tell you."

He's not cracking a smile! He doesn't even suspect. If he could've heard old Brothuh Kenway for four years rant and rave about "Bayport's devil-ridden young people," never coming to evening service in summertime, sailing or driving too far away

38

to even hear the bell, he'd *know*. Charlotte going on last League meeting bout Brothuh Humiston's self-conceit! She knows no more about his character than she does about his love affairs.

"But of them all, it seems to me, you alone have the serious, dedicated manner Christian effort demands. Your enthusiasm, I feel, springs from a deeper source. A truly spiritual source. It will be lasting. Miss Charlotte, Miss Mary Sue, Miss Bessie—the most active among you—will lose interest when they marry and have family cares, whereas you're already accustomed to finding time for the Lord's work while you do a woman's. You know what I think makes the difference?"

He looked up suddenly and his face was alight as it'd been Sunday, telling me of his conversion. Made me feel dizzy, like going up too high in one of Slippy's grapevine swings, and I shook my head more to get rid of that feeling than to answer his question.

"I think it's because you gave your heart to God when you were old enough to know what it meant. Coming to Him—"

"I joined the church five years ago this Easter. 1879. Year we moved back here. I was twenty." Now why'd I have to tell him that? Makes me an old maid already!

"I know. I looked up your—the date in the church register. And coming to Him as you did, after your upbringing at an infidel's hearth, you felt His power and His glory. Felt His infinite love overwhelm and envelop you, even as I felt it after my *willfully* sinful youth."

I tried to remember feeling all that. Feeling anything, in my soul. Could still feel the clammy clasp of Brothuh Kenway's hand. Could remember being embarrassed holding out my hand to Miss Tempy when 'twas Mercer's she was groping for through her tears. Could remember being proud of the white lawn dress I'd made from first material Buddy'd ever bought for me.

"I don't mean to imply, Miss Ora, that I was one of the devil's prize flock, worldly as I was. I'd been brought up by a devout mother. Suppose I might say I was a Christian, as some define the word. Negatively. Doing no real harm, doing no real good either. I thought only of temporal success and I planned only for it. I wanted the veneration of this world rather than life everlasting in the world to come. I had lofty political ambitions because I wanted to see justice done, but out of my office I wasted my time, enjoying the status of 'eligible bachelor.'" His lips twitched. "Used to scan the Social Notes of *The Cataba*

Commentary for the sight of my name: 'Our fellow-townsman and popular young bachelor, David McCall Humiston, Esq., has returned to our midst from a visit to his esteemed parents at Humiston Hill.' Such self-pride as that, Miss Ora, must be incomprehensible to one of your modesty. I can't believe you've ever felt the slightest impulse to sin, inwardly or outwardly."

"Oh, but I have, Mistuh Humiston. There's been times—"

"Little selfish exhibitions of will, maybe. Nothing wicked. I'm confident of that. In any case, you know the ecstasy of surrender to God's will—heart and soul, mind and body. You know it, even if God doesn't intend for women to serve Him in just the way he intends for men. His plan for women is different. They are the mothers, the wives, the comforters, the upholders of the faith for and in men. I'm confident you, too, understand the divine purpose in our lives."

"I—try to, sir. With you to guide me as my—pastor—"

"And friend. Add that, Miss Ora. Always your friend if not" —he slipped two fingers between his collar and his throat—"always your pastor."

The hand that had been on the sofa back was in my lap, covering both of mine. The fingers stretched and their tips pressed hard on one of my palms. A bloodless line across his knuckles. Black hairs thicker at the edge of the white cuff . . .

It's gone! He's gone! He's standing there at the center table. He's opening the Album.

I cleared my throat, delicately's I could. "Bring it here, Mistuh Humiston. Let me introduce you to the members of our family."

He sat down again and opened the Album on his knees, turned the pages slowly while I, my shoulder just brushing his, mentioned the names of dead uncles and aunts and cousins, some killed on the battle field, some who'd passed on in hospitals, some stricken, time the yellow fever epidemic hit the county in '63. He thought Buddy favored Grandpa Fanning, thought he detected a resemblance between me and Cousin Ida Rutland, tintype made when she was being courted by Cousin Clem. Told him that couldn't be, flattered as I was, because Cousin Ida was related only by marriage. Said it was Cousin Clem then, and he was certainly a handsome young man, that picture taken in his captain's uniform last time he was over from Fort Fisher, before he was killed in the siege. Told him I didn't think he was right there, either, because Grandma Evans'

40

family, the Rutlands, were supposed to have some French blood, way back, and we children all tended toward the fair like the Fannings. Laughed out loud when I told him Miss Tempy used to tease us, saying Ma'd married beneath her because the Fannings didn't come over from Yorkshire, England, till 1790 and the Evans and the Rutland families, like the Williamses, had been among the first settlers at Old Charleston—before the town site was moved on down to South Carolina.

"Now, there's Ma," I went on. "Wasn't she a beauty! Brunette like *her* mother, they say. Shame no one of us—"

"Why, your hair looks dark in this photograph and I can see a resemblance between you and her I don't detect between her and your sister here—this *is* Miss Ellen sitting in the chair you're standing behind?"

"Yes. Buddy took us to Wilmington have that taken, three years ago. You look closely, you'll see Ellen's facial expression is a lot like Ma's. And you can't see how pretty Sistuh Ellen is from that likeness. She's not smiling and her bright coloring doesn't show up."

"That may be," he said, "but there's more of the spiritual in your face and that, to me, is above mere prettiness." He closed the Album, rubbed his hand over the pansies appliqued on the maroon plush. "Now I wish I had the Humiston-McCall gallery here in as compact a form. I have a feeling you and my mother and sisters would take to one another. Bishop doesn't read me out for another pastorate another year or two, I'll try to persuade them to visit me in The Parsonage by the Sea. Be a treat for them to see the ocean. Expect though, my two youngest sisters, Lucinda and Elspeth—she's named for our mother—will be married and gone down to Mississippi before the year's out, if Father doesn't continue to discourage two young admirers they became acquainted with visiting in Asheville last summer. How you'd love 'The Land of the Sky,' they call it now! The invigorating climate, the clear air. You'd be surprised how much more you can accomplish in a day up there. And you and my sister Kathy and my brother Maxwell could climb High Brighten. That's the lowest peak near us but the view is splendid."

"Wouldn't you go too?" It came out without my thinking, coquettishly, way Ellen might've asked Mercer.

"I'd ride but I'd be there. And if you got tired, I might—what's that?"

41

I laughed and said that was the warning bell for supper and if he'd excuse me, I'd go see if Lucille'd taken hot water up to the company room for him.

❖

Oh, yes, you did, Miss Ryder. If it hadn't been for you, making me afraid of my own shadow, I might've got the first refusal over right here in this room this evening. When he stood there on the hearth looking at me that way, was you made my eyes waver. When he pressed his hand over mine, you made me sit there like a stone. You're the old witch in the fairy tales Cousin Sudie told us that time. Every single time she said "old witch" I saw your green-black eyes and your high, skinny nose. But it all came out right for the princess in every one of them and you'll see. . . . The princess was Ellen because Ellen had blue eyes and golden curls. I was the Good Fairy who took care of her. But I'm the one the prince has come for so I must be the princess now. In this story. Ellen has her own. All you've done, Miss Ryder, is put off the happy ending a little. Because if it hadn't been for you, sneaking in here when I wasn't noticing, the way'ud be clear for my saying "yes" the second time he asked. All I had to do was to keep on forgetting there was anything in the world but his eyes pulling at mine like a magnet. Just mine. I wouldn't have had to spring at him. In another second or so, my body would've left the sofa, slowly, easily to meet his, moving toward me. His feet would've crossed the rug and his arms would've reached for me. Right there, between the center table and the ladder-back chair, we would've come together. . . .

Yes, it was all your fault for making me believe I couldn't have what I wanted, ever. Making me act cold and indifferent when what I wanted was there for me to take. I heard Charlotte say to Ellen last summer talking there in Ellen's room bout Bessie Davis letting that drummer from Lynchburg, Virginia, that Mistuh Gibson, slip through her fingers. Said a girl's got to know how to egg on a man without his knowing what she's doing. Said every daughter's mother knew how or she wouldn't have a daughter and if the daughter's as dense as Bessie, a mother should teach husband-catching when she teaches rolling-and-whipping and Battenberg lace. Ma didn't have time to teach Ellen and me anything. Didn't need to teach Ellen. Since she was a little thing she's known how to get what she wants,

42

even from you, Miss Ryder. Wouldn't be a bit surprised if she's taken that Savannah fellow she wrote about from some girl down there with no more trouble, far as anybody could see, than she took Mercer from Charlotte. And I reckon that poor girl loves her as much as ever too. Ma didn't need to teach me, if you'd let me alone. I'm not dense. I know. I just can't act. My body knows but my mind holds me back. It's plain as my hand now. You did something to my mind worse than you ever did to a poor black's body. Because of you, what my body told me today I couldn't listen to. But I knew. I knew my body was made for more than to be fed, and washed, and dressed. Knew it had a life of its own. It wanted to spring at Mistuh Humiston —at Mistuh Humiston's body. He's not all mind either. Mind and religion. His body strains at the leash too. He was feeling all that I was feeling. And he'll show you, when he's ready, that you can't . . .

"Sistuh!"

I jumped.

Buddy laughed. "You in a trance? Sitting there staring at the fireplace, eyes big as saucers."

"Was just trying to decide whether to get Lucille at the soap making tomorrow or finish turning out the closets."

He closed Grandpa Fanning's big old law book with a bang, laid it on the table, stood up and stretched. "Don't care what the Parson says bout my being better off never having got to the Law, I wish I could've. Wouldn't feel so lazy and good-for-nothing all the time if I could sit at a desk, walk back and forth to the courthouse, lean against a tree and air my opinions. Wouldn't've hurt my morals either. Here in this county we don't get so all-fired hot under the collar bout politics way they do up where he comes from. We low countrymen know how to take things as they come. Know they're going to change give thum time. And not through 'the saving of individual souls' either, my way of thinking. What men invent 'sgot a lot more to do with it. Look at—"

I looked at Buddy and tried to hear what he was saying.

"—the cotton gin back there in '28. Heard Grandpa Fanning say once slavery would've been done for without a war, that fellow Whitney hadn't come down here with his inventive genius. And if the Parson thinks there's not intimidation and bribery and fraud wherever there're politics, whether it's to keep the darky from voting or some other poor man somewhere else— You're not listening to me for all that rapt expression. Les go to bed. Be morning before I get rested." He took the shovel from the hook and began scattering ashes over what fire was left. "May as well have Lucille sweep and blacken here tomorrow. And put up that pretty fan-screen Ellen made. Won't need any more fires till fall, almanac be trusted. And I reckon it can. Walked out with the Parson, wouldn't have believed there'd been such a rain storm. All the stars out—"

"What were you and he doing so long out there?" I stepped to the table and put my hand on the wick-screw.

"Answer that question euphoniously I'll say it was such a fine night we took a little stroll down to the gardenhouse."

"Buddy!"

"Well, you asked me. Then we took the buggy curtains down. Be kind of chilly going through the low road, but he said he wanted to watch for the moonrise. Reckon he's a right romantic fellow for all his talk about the evils of politics and the glories of religion. Listen, Sistuh—" Buddy came to the table, ran a finger nail in between the ridges of the chenille cover. "I didn't mean to monopolize the conversation at supper and in here too, but you didn't seem inclined to talk much and—"

"That was why. I wanted you to. And you won't if you can get out of it."

"Then that's all right. But I'm sorry I said was getting late and I had to get going early at those potatoes. Must've made him think I was hinting for him to go, way he jumped up and said he had to. All I wanted to do was leave you the parlor."

"That's all right too, Buddy. Did tell me, when he came downstairs before supper, he wanted to talk bout the League's having an ice-cream social, raise money for the new hymnals. But we'll be going in to prayer meeting tomorrow night and I'll get a few words with him then maybe." I turned the wick down.

"If that's all you had to talk about—here, don't blow out the lamp till I get the candles."

Well, what if he didn't? He'll pick a better time for it. Might be, he'll write a letter: "Dear Brother Fanning, May I have your permission to pay my addresses to your sister with the intention of asking her hand in marriage? I—"

"Sistuh"—Buddy held the china candle-holders close to his chest and the flames lit his face from below, making it look

44

broader and fuller, his mustache thicker—"I've got something to tell you."

"Yes, Buddy." I tried to lift my hand to take my candle, but it was trembling so I had to hide it in the fold of my skirt, and just wait.

He set the candles down. "Been thinking bout telling you ever since Sunday night but thought I might's well wait till Mary Sue set the day. The exact day. What're you smiling at?"

"At your news." At you, mistaking a grimace for a smile. "Might've known, way you were talking tonight, you had something on your mind you mighty pleased about."

Buddy laughed and rubbed his hand on the back of his neck in a shamed kind of way. "Yes, when the Parson said shad roe was something he'd have to tell his family about when he goes home in August, I realized we'd have to set our wedding day before or after his vacation. So I asked him out there what part of August he'd be away. Said that depended. On what, I asked. On the Lord, he said. Said he'd learned to leave matters most concerned him, personal matters, in the Lord's hands and wait patiently for 'that still, small voice' to direct him. I laughed and said reckoned I was too much of a sinner for the Lord to take such interest in my affairs and since I had to manage them myself—"

"Why, Buddy!"

"Was all right. What I like bout him, he doesn't try to ram his beliefs down your throat. Just seems to go on thinking and doing what's right for him, and you can take it or leave it. He laughed too. So then I said maybe the Lord wanted me to tell him he was to be here first part of August to tie the knot for Mary Sue and me. Said he'd accept that, then, as a divine command, and congratulated me. Mary Sue wants it that time so we can have a kind of honeymoon here before haying. That be all right with you?"

"It's kind of sudden. You hadn't even told me you'd proposed."

"Hadn't till Sunday night. Just asked her to name the day. Best way of doing it I could think of."

"And she named it right off, just like that!"

"Why not?"

"Why, nothing. Only I've always heard a girl should say 'no' twice before she says 'yes.' "

45

"No foolishness like that bout Mary Sue. Said if I hadn't come out with it, she'd have asked *me* before long."

"When'd you speak to Miss Callie?"

"Didn't. She'd gone to bed. But I reckon she knew it was coming, spite of her trying to act surprised—act like she'd been surprised Mary Sue waked her from a sound sleep to tell her. Kissed me and carried on like she's mighty pleased. You pleased, Sistuh? You love Mary Sue, don't you?"

I nodded. "She'll make you a fine wife, Buddy."

"And you and Ellen a fine sistuh!"

"I don't expect Ellen'll be here long. This place'll be too dull for her now. I think somehow it'll be Savannah and that Mistuh Clay for her, no matter if she does break Mercer's heart."

"Well, we can't tell about any of that yet. But it's not so mighty important how long Ellen's here." Buddy picked up his candle and came round the table. "Ellen keeps us lively, but you, Sistuh, keep us alive." He put an arm around my shoulder. "I don't want you stepping off till Mary Sue knows the ropes, you hear me?"

4

When Buddy helped me, then Mary Sue, down in the hitching circle beneath the pin oaks, we heard the organ's first notes. Still holding on to Buddy's hands Mary Sue cocked her head that birdlike way she had.

"Listen. Miss Taffy's feeling fine tonight, coming down hard with her hands and feet both." And she hummed "The Day is Gently Sinking to a Close" like Miss Taffy was playing it, with a see-sawing sound.

I crossed the drive between grove and church, walking slowly, giving Buddy and Mary Sue a minute alone, and craning my neck to get a glimpse of Mistuh Humiston behind the chancel. But all I could see were the heads of people nearest the windows. Didn't matter. After prayer meeting, if he accepted Mary Sue's invitation, I'd be close to him on the Ives' veranda.

Buddy grasped my elbow just as I reached the outer row of First Settlers' old tombstones. "Hey, wait a minute! We'll feel kind of timid tonight going down the aisle by ourselves."

"Silly," Mary Sue said 'sthough she said Darling, "I haven't told a soul but Mama yet."

46

If Buddy hadn't been holding my arm, I think I'd have stumbled in the vestibule, such a weakness went through me at the sight of *him* standing so tall and erect by the little table he used for Sunday School and prayer meeting. He had to be looking straight at us but his face was a blur to me, like the face of the sun when you try to focus your eyes on it.

"Sit in our pew," Mary Sue whispered.

By the greatest effort, I separated Miss Callie's widow's bonnet from the other widows' bonnets dotting the mass of flowers and ribbons, slipped in and stood beside her. She didn't lift her eyes from her hymnal, just pointed a black-gloved finger at the beginning of the second stanza and I sang:

> "Our changeful lives are ebbing to an end;
> Onward to darkness and to death we tend;
> O Conqueror of the grave, be Thou our guide;
> Be Thou our light in death's dark eventide;
> Then in our mortal hour will be no gloom,
> No sting of death, no terror in the tomb."

Mistuh Humiston lifted his hand and Miss Taffy broke off the prelude to the third stanza and played the *Amen*.

I could see his face now. It looked older than it had last night, somehow. He's tired, I thought. His mouth is stern. Sterner than I've seen it in the pulpit on a Sunday. He looks like he's going to preach. Prayer meetings 're supposed to be just inspirational.

He waited patiently till the swishing of skirts, the shuffling of feet, the thudding of hymnals in racks had ceased, then stepped around the table, stood between it and the chancel rail, and stared at us. Silently. He turned his head a little to the right, his eyes moving from Miss Taffy at the end of the front bench near the organ, back, pew by pew. Then a little to the left, from old Dummy Sayer in the amen corner, back, pew by pew, to me, and beyond. Pityingly. Accusingly.

I never heard the church so still. Stiller than last Sunday when he'd paused after the benediction. Prayer meeting congregations were smaller but I didn't remember ever having heard the clock tick during a service before. I wanted to turn my head, see how Buddy and Miss Callie were taking this. I held it as straight as Miss Tempy in front of us held hers. As all in front of her.

"I asked that you stop with the second stanza of the 'Nacht-lied,'" he said finally, "because I should like the awe-ful warning of its words brought home to each of you as potently as they were brought to me in the past fourteen hours."

It's his usual voice. Even, quiet. He did stand on our hearth twenty-four hours ago. Sit on our sofa . . .

"Since taking up my pastorate in Bayport last January, I have been at many a deathbed in town and county—the old, the young, the middle-aged—and I have learned much sooner than I had expected to, to accept God's will whenever and wherever I see it manifest. To see the light in death's dark eventide. And, more blessed, to help the bereaved to see it.

"But on this brightest of spring mornings, the world of na-ture washed clean after yesterday's rain, there was no light. For me, for the victim, for the bereaved. I can only pray for you and with you that God's reason for permitting the Devil to be the Conqueror of the new grave dug today will, in His good time, be clear. Ah, you need not look from one to another, question-ing. The new grave is not in your well-tended cemetery. Look at *me*. I alone among you, the stranger, the uninformed, will not shake my head in ignorance. In self-imposed ignorance of the fate of a fellowman.

"Before dawn this morning I was awakened by a violent knocking on the parsonage door. When I had mastered that feeling of panic that comes with the first clang of the fire-bell in the night, I groped my way down the passage to the front door. In the wavering light of a lantern I made out the figure of a half-grown mulatto boy. Through chattering teeth—though he was well clad—he asked me if I were the preacher Aunt Merry worked for, 'one who used to be a lawyer.' Then would I come with him to Halcyon Plantation, 'Mistuh Adrian' was dying fast and needed me. He assumed I knew who Mistuh Adrian was and I did not question him."

I felt Mary Sue start and heard Miss Callie draw in her breath. Every neck in the left side pews twisted and craned and Miss Callie half rose from her seat, sat back again.

"Becky Rankin's got to her," she whispered to me, then leaned over and touched Miss Tempy's shoulder. "Stop him, can't you?"

"How?" Miss Tempy whispered back.

". . . pointed to the hitching post and I could just make out two horses there. I got dressed in record time.

"Borne so swiftly by that fleet-footed mare through the awakening world of nature, along the shore road where in Easter's dawn I had worshiped God with His lesser creatures, it was hard to believe I sped 'onward to darkness and to death.' Several miles beyond the wreck of The Rattlesnake—some of you men in this congregation could tell me the exact distance—my guide turned to the right and I followed. On to a road once so well-bedded, time and hurricane tide have not been able to corrode it. And hence to an avenue of oaks, tall, lordly, standing—I thought on my return beneath them—like sentinels." He lifted his chin and the light of all the swinging lamps seemed to reflect the blue of his eyes. "Like sentinels who, given another chance, would fall before they surrendered.

"Having noted, in the sky's first glow, the young darky's good clothing and the sleek coats of the mounts," he went on 'sthough he was having a private conversation with each one of us, "having felt the vigor of the one I rode, the healthy leather of saddle and bridle, I was not surprised to see, as we galloped into the open, a stately white mansion. It *was* a mansion. Though following the lines of most of your comfortable homes in this section, there was that extra length and breadth in its structural beams, that extra depth in its double verandas, and that extra thickness in the pillars supporting them, that made this house more than a substantial dwelling. As we drew nearer, the sun, just above the sound's horizon, gleamed on the fresh white paint of entablatures and pedestals and threw into shadow the extra deep depressions between the flutings."

He looked down at the Bible on the table, touched it with his finger tips, looked up as though to catch us unawares.

"Travelling from the mountains in bleak December, through the Piedmont section, down through the coastal plain to this southeasterly tip of the Old North State, I saw once flourishing plantations, proud mansions, devastated by raiders or by the neglect inevitably following in the wake of war. And saddened by the sight of such useless waste, I felt anger in my heart and prayed silently for the charity to forgive. God heard me. Instantly He answered me, in a paraphrase of Christ's own words, 'Forgive them, my son, for they knew not what they did.'

"They knew not what they did, those Union soldiers. They were strangers in a strange land, blindly obeying the commands of Sherman's officers. But *you* knew, you people of Bayport and of this county." He looked at the Bible again and his voice rang

49

out as though he shouted the words through its cover. " 'Do ye indeed speak righteousness, O congregation? Do ye judge uprightly, O ye sons of men? Yea, in your heart ye work wickedness; ye weigh the violence of your hands in the earth.' You were not mercenaries in the Union Army. With malice aforethought you free men of this county, under cover of the white robes of the Klan and the black robe of a winter's midnight, did create the devastation and commit the atrocity that in an April's sunrise, eleven years and three months later, chilled my body and revolted my soul. And you 'Christian' women of this town and of this county, accessories before the fact, under cover of quilts and of the sheets left you, did aid and abet these felons. You knew the watchword:

> Thrice hath the lone owl hooted
> And thrice the panther cried—

You must have heard it that January night, echoing eerily through your quiet streets and lonely roads. You too—I beg your pardon. I am not in the courtroom. It is not I who sits in judgment."

He lowered his voice. "I wish only to lend you my eyes that you may see the horror that I saw this morning. To do that, you must ride with me along the bridle path. It begins—some of you will remember—at the junction of the shadowed avenue with the crescent-shaped drive which curves in front of the mansion, skirts the open lawn and the rose garden, and leads to the stables about two hundred yards in the rear. You must dismount with me, hand the bridle to the bright-faced, sad-eyed boy who stands there waiting to receive it. You must then turn with me. And turn in the expectancy of viewing at closer range a noble work of man, nobly planned. Now you must see with me.

"A little child builds half a house with his alphabet blocks, loses interest in his project, and wanders off to play at something else. A man buys lumber, hires carpenters and masons, loses his money, and leaves a timber skeleton to rot. But never have I read of, heard of, or"—he glanced over our heads at the clock—"until fifteen hours ago, seen *half* a house finished to the minutest detail and in perfect repair.

"The cloudburst God sent in the early morning of January the eleventh, 1873, to mock your usurpation of His vengence,

50

cut through the flames you had kindled like a knife through butter.

"Half-burnt timbers have fallen off, jagged edges have been smoothed by time. Roses, growing from soil enriched by ashes, climb to the cornice of what was once the parlor's front wall— as pretty a wallpaper as I ever saw. Oh, you'd never suspect, focusing a telescope on that white façade from a pleasure boat on the sound! The vine encircling those three long windows is so carefully trimmed no tell-tale tendril can show through. The carpet in that floorless room, intricately woven of smilax and honeysuckle in shaded tones of green, pale yellow, and white, is such as no money could buy. A hedge, clipped true and smooth, follows the line of vanished walls on the west and north. Where were pianoforte, sofas, tables, and chairs, all flowers native to your clime bloom. Bloom from this soil sweetened with wood ashes as I've never seen flowers bloom before.

"Could I have approached from the rice swamp, the front walls and the walls of the two rooms whose wide doors open on half-a-hall would have been but a background for my lady's garden. Approaching as I did, finding a garden where rooms should have been, the shock was not lessened by the sight and the perfume of dew-drenched blossoms rather than the sight and the stench of blackened clapboards, broken bricks, and crumbled plaster which, in all logic, should have been there— left where they had fallen to nurture all the rank weeds native to your clime.

"The shock was not lessened. Because—led by a courteous, soft-spoken mulatto woman down the length of that half-a-hall and into a four-walled room—I could not look at the broken, shrunken, scarred effigy of a man propped on a mound of pillows in a mammoth bed, and say, 'How merciful that you are blind!' I could only quote under my breath from Psalm—"

It wasn't a shriek and it wasn't a scream. It was more like the sound of a length of homespun torn in a hurry. It began but it had no beginning and it ended when it ended, no tag end of sound left.

I heard it and I saw Mistuh Humiston's body stiffen, go rigid as old Jake's did when the lightning struck him. Then his head began to turn like it was set on rusty hinges. Turned toward the right in short, jerky movements.

Miss Tempy jumped to her feet. Miss Callie squeezed past

51

me. Buddy leaned over and whispered to Mary Sue and me to "keep calm now," and followed them to the aisle.

I must've been staring at Mary Sue 'shard as she was staring at me and she said what was on the tip of my tongue, "Oh, what'll people think of him!" Then indignantly, "They said she'd outgrown those fits, long ago."

"Prayer meeting is dismissed," Mistuh Jim Berry's voice boomed from somewhere near the organ. "Please leave quietly by the center aisle."

I stood up, stood on my tiptoes, but I couldn't see Mistuh Humiston in the confusion. Everybody moving from pews to aisle like sandfiddlers, one step forward and two back, saying something to whomsoever was behind or trying to see what was going on down there on that front seat. Everybody but that Mrs. Baker. She was walking straight toward the door, looking neither to the right nor to the left, 'sthough she considered all this a family affair she had no right to be in on. Spite of my agitation, twas then I got a good look at her—white linen dress with accordian pleating at throat and wrists, little white hat that showed her auburn hair and brown eyes. Her skin looked like a girl's but she must be thirty-five years old, at least, be Miss Ryder's friend's daughter.

"Ora, look yonder! Wouldn't you know she'd get into it!" Mary Sue grabbed my arm, pulled me to the end of the pew.

"What? Where?"

"Charlotte! Crossing in front of the chancel now. Been with Brothuh Humiston get water and a towel from the parsonage. Honey, you're shaking like a leaf. Don't be upset. They won't tar and feather him."

"Don't know why we shouldn't, Miss Mary Sue, dragging up a thing like that. Adrian Spier wasn't any better than a 'venomous, shabby, scrubby, scurvy cattle of a scalawag.' "

"Why, Mistuh Alex, you—"

"Don't pay any attention to him, you all," Miss Mary Dade said. "Been married to me thirty years and still's not over Taffy's jilting him."

Mistuh Alex winked at us and rubbed a hand over his bald spot.

"We ladies'll take care of our pastor any case, won't we, Mary Sue, Ora?" Miss Mary said and pulled on Mistuh Dade's arm. "You come long with me, Mistuh Dade. No time or place you be settling old scores."

52

"You all see Miss Taffy fall over?" Bessie Davis' full-moon face spoiled my view again. She giggled. "I declare it's been as tittilating's a stage play Mistuh Gibson escorted me to in Wilmington."

She turned her head to see what she could see and I wanted to tell her if a man'd been as attentive to me as Mistuh Gibson was to her and left town without proposing, I certainly wouldn't go round recalling places I'd been with him.

"Course it's mighty sad and everything but it's just like the Judge was saying to Mama and them over there. Said it's salutary sometimes, having old buried sins dug up and aired, takes thum off our conscience. Cousin Lucy had herself a time though calming Cousin Jim Berry down. He was mad's a hornet. Said this town's *too* good, a preacher has to go way back eleven years to find a sin. Course they say Cousin Jim and Mistuh Alex were ring leaders . . ."

"Yes, ma'm, she's come to," Buddy answered somebody's question over his shoulder, then spoke to Mary Sue and me over Bessie's. "Sistuh, you walk on to Mary Sue's. I'll be along. Miss Callie and I're going to take Miss Taffy home in the buggy, soon's the church is clear."

❖

"Thodike Stevika! Radical plan
    Must yield to the coming of the Ku Klux Klan,
    Niggers and leaguers, get out of our way,
    We're born of the night and we vanish by day."

"Bet you don't know the next verse."

"Bet you a cent I do."

"Les hear it then."

Mary Sue turned around. "You boys hush. Some people on this street are in bed and asleep. You better hurry up home and study your lessons."

"Shucks, Miss Mary Sue, we don't have to do that tonight," one of them said. "We met Miss Tempy going in prayer meeting. Shook hands with every last one of us. Said she was mighty glad to see us out."

"That's the truth, Miss Mary Sue."

"Well, be quiet anyway."

"Yesum."

"I don't reckon she's glad now," Mary Sue said, as we walked

53

along. "It's a pity they picked tonight. That's the crowd Brothuh Humiston's been working on to join the church. Now they'll think everybody's mean—"

"Go on or take a dare! Miss Mary Sue's not your ma. She can't whip you."

Mary Sue whirled again.

"Ignore thum. They're just trying to tease you." I pulled her around. "I don't reckon Mistuh Humiston'ud feel like coming to your house now even if you'd had a chance to ask him."

"No, he must be mighty tired. And kind of sick. That Halcyon business is only thing people don't talk about, or he'd have known better than to do what he did tonight."

❖

> "No rations have we but the flesh of man
> And love niggers best—the Ku Klux Klan;
> We catch um alive and roast um whole
> Then hand um around on a sharpened pole;
> Whole leagues have been eaten, not leaving a man—
> And went away hungry—the Ku Klux Klan."

"I never heard that verse!" I started in the Ives' gate.

"I don't reckon any other lady ever did." Mary Sue stood there, waiting. "Good thing they didn't follow Mrs. Baker out. She'd think everything Northerners say about us is gospel truth. I'm going to give those sorry boys a piece of my mind." They came opposite, and she darted at them like a mad, ruffled-feathered bantam hen. "You Tom Bradley, stop right here!"

I went on up the walk. Mary Sue loves Buddy, I thought, in her way but other things're as real to her as ever. Buddy just takes some of her thoughts and feelings. Buddy's not Mistuh Humiston.

I pulled a rocker from behind the smilax festooning the corner of the veranda but I couldn't sit down. I felt like I'd been running and I wanted to run again. A little breeze fluttering the leaves of the live oaks in the yard fanned me and cast moon shadows every which way on the oyster-gray of the street. If only Mistuh Adrian hadn't died today, Mistuh Humiston would be right here this minute . . .

The Ives' old tabby rubbed against my skirt. I stooped and picked her up. Squeezed her. Pressed my lips on her neck.

"Why, Ora, I thought you hated cats!" Mary Sue ran up the

steps. "Come help me fix the lemonade. Then we can sit down with Mama and Benton and hear about poor Miss Taffy."

In the passage she hung our hats on the deer's antlers, whirled about, and hugged me like I'd hugged that fishy-smelling cat. "Oh, Ora, I'm so happy! Spite of poor Miss Taffy and everything." She giggled, "I couldn't even be stern with those bad boys. Not like they deserved. *I*dea their memorizing that nasty stinking old rhyme. Said they found it in the Bradley's Bible. Reckon you can't expect any better, poor white trash Mama says they were before the war."

❖

"Good night, Ora. Come soon."

"Thank you, Miss Callie, I certainly will. You come."

"I certainly will. Make Charlotte drive Mary Sue and me out real soon."

Buddy waved his hat to Mary Sue and Miss Callie at the gate and Madam picked up her feet.

"Buddy, you have much trouble getting poor Miss Taffy in the buggy?"

Buddy laughed. "Knew you've been on pins ask that—"

"Well, I couldn't get a word in edgewise, way you all were talking wedding. Wouldn't've tried to, after what Miss Callie said about putting 'the whole unpleasant incident' out of her mind for the rest of the night. Miss Callie's mighty positive about things."

"No, no more trouble with Miss Taffy than putting a bird back in its nest. She's light's a feather, all skin and bones."

"What'd she say and do when she came to?"

"She moaned some, then all of a sudden sat up straight, pulled loose from Miss Callie, and tried to take the reins out of my hands. Reckon she wanted to turn round and go back. Kept saying, 'He didn't tell me how Adrian died. I've got a right to know *how* he died.' Miss Callie tried to quiet her—had to hold her hands so I could drive. Made out, after she lost consciousness, that the Parson'd gone on to describe a peaceful passing. Then Miss Taffy got real mad. Madder I've ever seen her, somebody raises the roof bout her mixing up the mail. Blamed everybody in the county for not telling her how he'd been suffering all these years. Wouldn't believe Miss Callie's telling her nobody knew. Don't know who Miss Taffy thought could've known except the darkies and just try to get anything out of

55

them! Miracle enough the Parson saw what no human eye—white human eyes—been allowed to see. What beats me, though, is how the place's been kept up. Mistuh Adrian had enough master-craft workmen—more than the Parson saw—but where'd he get fresh paint? Or the money to buy it? Mistuh Jim said, standing there talking while the ladies were fussing over Miss Taffy, said could be, some of those smart darkies'd found a way through the swamp to Shallotte. Bound to do some trading even on a self-sustaining plantation like Halcyon. Judge laughed and said they might still be using U.S. Treasury bonds. 'Buffalo rations.' Grandpa, though, never believed Mistuh Adrian was a Buffalo. Said Hell didn't have that much fury for a southern turncoat."

"Where was Mistuh Humiston, all this going on?"

"Standing there by the organ with Miss Tempy, looking 'sthough he felt a fool's cap on his head. Didn't even rouse when Mistuh Jim quoted, loud enough for him to hear, definition of a scalawag 'an *intelligent* Methodist minister' had given. You know, 'a scalawag's a white man thinks he's no better than a negra and in so thinking, makes a correct appraisal of himself.' "

I held my breath but Buddy didn't say another word. Wasn't much consolation for my fears in the town's being as quiet and dark now as on any night I'd ever seen it after ten o'clock. We'd sat a long time on the Ives' veranda. Men could've met and disbanded long ago. We passed the Dades' house and on to our road before I managed to ask whether Miss Taffy'd been all right when they'd left her.

"Meek's a lamb, that what's-her-name put her hands on her."

"Caledonia?"

"That's right. Kind of funny, come to think about it, Miss Taffy making a bosom friend of a darky woman for the past twenty-five years after breaking her engagement and her heart because she wouldn't marry a man who'd—get up, Madam!"

I almost laughed at Buddy. What'd he think girls talked about all the time? Sugar and spice and everything nice? Mary Sue'd surprise him before long. Living in town, even nice girls heard things, put this whisper-above-their-heads with that one, and time they pinned up their hair, knew as much gossip as their mothers did. And they certainly loved to pass it all on to Ellen and me.

"Well," I said, "Caledonia's not just *any* darky woman."

"You know that tale?"

"Bout Mistuh Adrian tying his calling card with ments of the Season written on it round Caledonia's neck w̲ a red ribbon and a sprig of mistletoe and sending her and her papers to Miss Taffy, Christmas of '53? Course I know it."

"I didn't. Till Miss Callie said tonight Caledonia was the only present Miss Taffy's had from Mistuh Adrian she didn't return with the betrothal ring. Must've loved each other on sight, those two, way they take on now. Would've thought Miss Taffy'd been away two months stead of two hours."

"Yes, say they're all in all to each other."

Madam's hoofs plodding through the sand stretch made a scratching sound. Pine needles hissed in a breeze too weak out here to stir a leaf. Back in the thicket an owl hooted who-who-whoo*re* you? I shivered.

"Cold?" Buddy took the reins in one hand, reached across my lap and tucked the robe in around me.

"No. Was just that lone owl. Buddy, what'll Mistuh Humiston's dredging up that old story do to him? You think people'll keep on going to hear him preach? Or want him sent back here next year?"

"Well—you had your answer back there talking bout Miss Callie's not wanting to hear any more about it tonight. They'll all put it out of their minds. After a few days and nights. They'll *talk* it out. Preacher got up in the pulpit ten, 'leven years ago and hinted he knew there was a Klan in this county, he'd've gone and gone fast. And I don't know where. But times've changed. Tempers've cooled off. Take more than the telling of an old story—even way he told it—to make Mistuh Jim and a few others concerned do more than rant. To tell the truth, I felt mighty sorry for the Parson, way—"

"Oh, Buddy, we all did!"

"I don't mean that way. You ladies were embarrassed for him. He made a social error. I'm sorry for him because after all he's seen and felt today, all his praying for guidance—bet he was on his knees right up to time the bell rang—after all the thinking it must've taken to make that tale come out way it did, after all that, nothing and nobody's going to be any different. Fellows warming the benches on Davis's porch and at the livery stable'll do more talking than chewing and spitting a few days, ladies'll take pound cake and syllabub round to Miss

57

all upset, but Mistuh Jim and Mistuh
n't ask him to pray for their immortal
itted one occasion the Klan acted down
ch'll be crowded next Sunday, everybody
athbed scene he got stopped on tonight. After
ust jog along same old way."
he'll bring it up again Sunday then?"
They'll all be disappointed. Miss Tempy walked to
nage with him before we got away. And she'd've told
hi out what I've said. Miss Tempy and I, we know Bayport. Buddy shook the reins and Madam trotted. "Can't make
out whether it's his inexperience or his godliness, but what he
knows about ordinary humans wouldn't fill a chinquapin shell.
Reckon he needs a good wife mighty bad."

5

I smoothed and flattened my petticoats, still warm from the
iron, and in spite of all the starch, got them in my second
drawer, and looked about for something else to do. My bed!

That Lucille! No use trying to teach her to set things down
gently. Clothes, dishes, or big, pink-bottomed feet. I slipped
my hands beneath the counterpane, patted and plumped up the
featherbed. Maybe Slippy got past the house and to the stable
while I was telling Lucille once more how much starch to make
for the little washing there was when Miss Ellen's away.

I looked from the east window again, went back to Ellen's
room and looked from her west window, down the drive. Back to
the passage, to the shutter-door between our rooms, out on the
upstairs veranda. Certainly had had to work hard get Buddy
and Slippy to cut that limb out of the old magnolia at the east
end. Was worth it, though. Now its rain-drenched leaves wouldn't
slap like hands on my front panes in a storm and now, leaning
over the banister rail, I could see a stretch of road this side the
brook.

Back to the head of the stairs.

Old Lady and Lucille talking on the back porch, no louder
than chickens clucking, as continuous and sleepy-sounding.
Should go down and stir them up, taking all morning to shell
a mess of garden peas and iron a few clothes. No use trying to
hear what they're saying. Not yet. Slippy's the only wire con-

necting them with town negras this morning. Them and their grapevine telegraph!

I took two steps down, two up again. If I'm there when Slippy comes and if he has no message for me—I went down the hall to the company room. Better come in here when I feel like cutting out Buddy's nightshirts. Mess it up so I can clean it again. La, any night now Mistuh Humiston might get caught in a thunder storm out here. Have to sleep in the four-poster. Then there'll be more to do than drop the hand towel in the clothes hamper, empty the not-dirty water from the slopjar.

I crossed the passage to Buddy's room. Now just look at those socks! Folded and ironed flat 'sthough he never wore a hole in heel or toe. I put away the shirts, patted and plumped *his* bed. Bed he and Mary Sue'd be sharing before long. Like Slippy and Lucille . . . No, no, stop it now! Blessed are the pure in heart.

In my room I got my darning bag and pulled the little rocker close to the window. Every time I lift my eyes I'll see the tip of the steeple, old weathered shingles gleaming like pewter above the treetops.

Maybe he's back from the post office now, sitting in his study, trying to think of something good to say funeralizing Mistuh Adrian. Why, I couldn't get a message from him this morning! What've I been thinking of? He didn't say when the burying would be but even those negras can't keep a body above ground more than twenty-four hours, this heat. And he's certainly got enough on his mind, writing the eulogy of a man took the oath of allegiance and got a Yankee chaplain to marry him to his slave concubine, then flaunted her in the faces of crippled soldiers couldn't get honorable license to marry girls who'd loved and waited. Say he dressed that woman in calico when it was thirty dollars a yard. Maybe Mistuh Humiston doesn't know all that. Oh yes he does. Now. Miss Tempy would've told him last night, explain all the excitement.

Reckon he's right hard on his socks too, all the walking he does.

Well, Miss Ryder, there's one thing I can say for you. You saw to it I learned to darn neatly. Making me slush through the swamp every summer morning to Aunt San Dosia's cabin till I did. Never could decide whether I was more afraid of moccasins going or of zombies coming back. Oh, but she told me more than tales of living dead men on that island where she was born! Told me what went on on your father's sugar plantation. And she told me about *you*.

"Don't want nothing her got. Nothing her had she hand on fitten for hogs to eat," she used to say and she'd throw the rotten sweet potatoes or the maggoty rice you'd sent out of that hole in her back wall. "Her wont no bigger than you is now and her ustuh hang round the quarters of a Sunday morning, big old black eyes out on stems uhpeeping through the cracks the chinking done fall out of. Little old ears uhglittering with little bitty diamonds and laid back like a mule's, uhseeing and uhhearing what no white child—black child neither—got any call to uhsee and uhhear. Then uhrunning on them shiny black shoes all tied up with red ribbons faster a snake can slide on she belly to tittle-tattle to that devil-man her call Pa-Pa. Then uhdancing out again, behinst and before him, all round, uhgiggling and uhwriggling when him tickle she neck with the shred end of a cowhide. Say, 'Which a one, baby?' Laugh out big her say 'Josie!' 'Not Josie!' him say and take out him big old gold watch, uhlook at hit, uhshake he head. Say, 'No, no, baby, you uhfooling Pa-Pa. You uhjust uhtrying to tease your Pa-Pa. Make he *real* mad. You better run play with your dolls. You too much a baby-child yet know what you uhtalking bout.' Then uhbending over and uhlistening her put she little old dimpled arms up round he old bullneck uhwhispering. Uhstraightening up, old crocodile face red's a beet, old turtle eyes mean-black, uhtipping to Josie's big cabin—same's him lay the gals out in, him got gentleman company, uhsaying 'wenches like wines, sir, not all sweet to all pallets, ha, ha.' Uhtipping up to the door, uhbusting in, uhdriving poor Bright Angel, uhdragging poor Josie stark naked. Uhtying um up together, uhcalling, 'Now you see dancing, baby. Stand back, stand back. Pa-Pa don't want to hurt you.' "

And the fire under that big boiling pot would hiss with her spit. "Come a day I'm uhgoing to get she, little gal and old woman, all to once. Uhgoing to cast my spell. Uhgoing to take she back every year of she life. Uhgoing to lash she one for every day, every hour, every minute howsomeever many they is in every year. And when I gets she back, away back to that devil man's youngun, I'm uhgoing to take that water uhbiling in that pot, mix hit with some lye . . ."

60

My darning gourd hit the floor with a hollow sound and I was quivering all over, way I used to in that rotting old cabin and in nightmares still, my head shaking from side to side trying to rid it of memories like Madam's of flies. But memories kept coming back too.

Aunt San Dosia's droning hushed sometimes by the buzzing of young negra women. Coming on scorching hot mornings, from as far away as Camilla, to swap a bag of goose feathers or a pan of chitterlings or froglegs for that gray, rank-smelling mess in a cracked chamberpot on the hearth. Aunt San Dosia's withered hand dribbled it from a rusty spoon into a little bitty newspaper cornucopia carefully as Mistuh Flowers Westcott doles out asafetida and quinine from his shining glass jars with gold lettering. Sometimes I caught words slipped loose from the buzzing. "Mought be since last full moon." "He pay no more mind to me I was a turnip." But I couldn't make heads or tails of why they wanted the nasty, stinking stuff till Charlotte told us bout their cook's getting rid of her unborn baby, then going after another love-potion to . . .

"Miss Orie!"

Now what do I care whether the peas are cooked by themselves or with rice today? Everything tastes the same to me here lately. Very idea her calling like that instead of coming on up! Cousin Sudie says untrained negras are a reflection on the mistress. Not much I can do when Ellen's here spoiling Lucille but while she's gone, I can make a start. If I'm going to be mistress of the parsonage, all and sundry dropping in . . .

I went to the head of the stairs. "Yes, Lucille?" That's it. Quiet and dignified. And patient.

"*Miss* Orie, where you?"

"Right here. At the head of the stairs. You should come up instead of calling me like that."

"Yasum. They's a letter for you."

I started down, drew back in a kind of dancing step. Kept my arms at my sides. "Bring it up, please."

"What you say, Miss Orie?"

I cleared my throat and tried again.

"Yasum."

A turtle could do it faster. "Lucille, hold up your skirts and you won't trip so."

"Yasum." She held the letter in one hand, her skirts in a

61

bunch in the other, but her bare feet came down on each step like it was a hot stove. "Slippy say Miss Tempy Williams—Miss Tempy she holding the post office this morning—say Miss Tempy Williams say hit from Miss Ellen. Say tell you she want to know what's in hit. Reckon when Miss Ellen coming home? Would pleasure me to see her, yes, ma'm! Reckon maybe Miss Ellen writ it down here when she coming?"

"I don't know what Miss Ellen's written till I read it," I snapped.

Lucille ducked her head and giggled, "Now that's the truth, ain't it? Here 'tis. Mind I waits—?"

"You go straight back down and put on your shoes." My arm, reaching for the letter, felt like it was weighted down with iron.

"Lord, Miss Orie, nigh a hour till dinner time."

"Do as I say, Lucille."

"Yasum."

❖ ❖ ❖

I sat down by my window again. How could I've hoped when I knew perfectly well . . . I opened my hand and stared at the crumpled ball had been Ellen's letter. A letter from my baby I'd done that to! Why, I had no more recollection of doubling my fist round it that way than I'd had of opening the scissors that time and slashing her sailor-dress. What does come over me? "I can't believe you ever felt the slightest impulse to sin, inwardly or outwardly," he said. Oh, if he only knew, if he only knew. But I didn't feel an impulse. Either time. Didn't feel anything. Was done before I knew it, both times. It wasn't premeditated, as they say in the court house. So maybe he and God'll forgive me.

I straightened it out letter-shaped again, laid it on my knee, and smoothed out the creases best I could. It wasn't much good. Not good enough for Buddy to see or read it. Ellen's pretty script not even and flowing, bold and free, as it used to be on her slates Miss Tempy'ud hold up for all to admire. Looks more like the copy I used to try to make of it, down on the floor with the candle after Ellen was asleep.

I started for Ma's pearl handled letter-opener in her lap-desk on my table, sat back and opened the flap with my little finger. No use being neat about it now.

Dear Sister and Buddy,

But it was *addressed* to me.

Dear Sister and Buddy,
    You will just have to forgive me for not writing more often and I'll forgive you. I haven't had a word from home in more than two weeks.

Oh, baby, I tried and tried. Ma's desk is full of beginnings. But I couldn't write about Mistuh Humiston and my feelings and it's been hard enough to have to *talk* about something else. . . .

It's all right now, though, because I am coming home sooner than I had expected to. Cousin Louis has to go to Charleston on business, leaving at five and a half o'clock next Friday morning and I have decided to travel that far under his protection. *I* think I'll reach Bayport safely but to hear Cousin Sudie, Cousin Louis, and a few others talk, I'll be annoyed, insulted, and molested by evil-minded men the whole way, if not abducted, murdered, or carelessly caught under the wheels of an on-coming locomotive.
    Now this is not one of my "sudden notions." I've been thinking for some time that I could not stay out my visit because there is something I must make up my mind about and I cannot do it here—there's hardly time to change my dress between social engagements.
    Of course Cousin Sudie is imploring me to stay but to tell you the truth, she's the one who makes it hard for me because she is so sure she knows what is right for me. But I have to decide about this "for my own individual self," as, Buddy, you used to say. So be sure to meet me on Saturday's boat. Sister, you come too if you can get away. If you want to see me as much as I want to see you, you will be there on the pier. But please don't either of you tell anybody in town that I am coming Saturday. If you drive to the pier by the cemetery road maybe nobody will see you. I want a few days at Little Brookside peaceful and quiet before I see Mercer or anybody.

I must close now because Mr. Stephen Clay is coming to escort me to Bonaventure Cemetery to see Cousin Louis's grandfather's tomb. He's buried facing South instead of East because he died in disgrace. He committed suicide because he could not decide whether to be loyal to King George or to fight with the Colonists. Mr. Clay says it is very important to make up your mind about things before indecision drives you crazy.

Love to all at Little Brookside,
Your devoted Ellen

I read it through again but there was no more to be got out of it. It was just like Ellen, not coming right out and saying this Mistuh Clay wanted to marry her but she couldn't decide between him and Mercer. I could see her sitting there biting her lip all the time she was writing, holding back what anybody else would've come right out with. I just didn't understand it. Time she'd mentioned him before, she'd said Cousin Sudie had pronounced her a Reigning Belle because Mistuh Stephen Clay, the best catch in Savannah, was showing her marked attention. I'd certainly thought she'd be writing us any time now that she was engaged to him.

What more does Ellen want than social position and wealth? He must have both if he's the best catch. Buddy's always said Ellen would have to marry money to be happy, all the things she wants, but that I'd make a tramp industrious and well-to-do. I don't know about that but I do know I could make even a preacher's salary go a long way. . . .

Why, it's Mercer bothering her! She must love him. Not like Charlotte says *she* does. But a little. She doesn't want to come home with everything settled and give him a shock. Ellen ever was a tender-hearted little thing. Seems to me, though, it would be kinder that way. Like Buddy's cutting the moccasin poison out of Ace's leg. Quick, before Ace had time to think how it'ud hurt.

Oh, well, Ellen never did tell anything till she had to. She'd rather be deceitful than hurt anybody's feelings. Look at the way she acted about Mercer. She must've known long before anybody else did that Mercer was easing away from Charlotte but she pretended, first time he came out here without Charlotte, that she was as surprised as Buddy and I were. Reckon it's selfish of me, but I can't help being relieved Ellen's not already engaged. Or not ready to admit it. I'm the oldest and I should be married first. . . .

"Sistuh!"

I ran to the stairs. "Yes, Buddy, I'm coming."

"What's this bout a letter from Ellen?" He started up.

"Don't you tramp stable-dirt up here! I'll be right down. Soon's I wash for dinner. You better, too."

When I came out on the back porch, Buddy flung the hand towel on the rack and held out his hand.

"You'll have to wait till it dries out." I dodged his slap at me. "I dropped it in my basin, I was in such a hurry, but I can tell you every word she said. Important thing is, she's coming home day after tomorrow—Saturday's boat!"

Lucille set the last vegetable dish on the table, untied the cord of the flyfan, and stood behind my chair. But when I'd served the plates, I took it from her.

"*Miss* Orie, what you trying to do now?"

"I'll handle the fan. You go—"

"How you do that and eat your dinner same time?"

"I'll manage. You go eat yours. I want you to polish silver and brass today. Miss Ellen coming home, we'll be having a lot of company."

"Lord, company ain't what we're going to have round here, come Saturday. Crowd ain't neither. Two's a company, three's a crowd, say. What we have, Miss Ellen home—" She threw up her hands and shuffled to the door, shaking her pig-tailed kinks. "Reckon all folks likes to hear her laugh and talk and go on, same's I does."

"Lucille, where's your turban?"

"Hit here, ain't it?" She put her hands to her head, bent over laughing. "Can't remember my head and my feet same time seem like."

"Remember next time."

"Yasum."

"Come on, Sistuh. That's not important. Tell me what Ellen said. Every word now." Buddy leaned toward me, over the expanse of table, his hands still beneath it as though food was of no importance at all.

I waited till Lucille had crossed the entry. When I'd finished the verbatim account, he laughed.

65

"Same romantic little Ellen. She should've lived awhile ago, when rivals duelled for a fair lady's hand."

"Funny this Mistuh Stephen Clay hasn't written you for permission to address Ellen."

"Probably spoke to Cousin Louis. More point to that, Cousin Louis being acquainted with him."

"You don't think Mercer'll be heartbroken?"

"Oh, Mercer'll feel down in the mouth week or two, lose interest in his shrimp. Masculine pride be hurt a little bit. Then he'll beat the same old path to Charlotte's veranda. Mercer's smart in business but he's lazy as the next one otherwise. Look how he drifted from Charlotte to Ellen, Ellen gave a little tug at his moorings."

"Why, Buddy! He jilted Charlotte for Ellen. Everybody said—"

"Everybody never knows anything. Don't you think for half a minute Ellen wasn't at the helm. Oh, nothing that you or I or anybody could see. Only Mercer." Buddy picked up his fork and touched his peas-and-rice. "Ellen was getting worried. No prospect in sight but that pusillanimous evangelist and tract-vender."

I laughed now. Laughed at Ellen's saying she'd die an old maid before she'd marry a preacher or a book-agent. Just wait till I introduce Mistuh Humiston!

"—and Claiborne's offerings not being able to see a poor farmer's sistuh as a likely match. Why, if Ellen'd had the least *i*dea that mattress factory up there in Norfolk was going to pay me enough cash for Spanish moss to get her what she needed for the Savannah visit, she'd never have let her liking for Mercer go as far as it did."

"You think she's fond of Mercer then?" I tried a bite of calf's liver.

"Um-m. Ellen's not a heartless coquette."

Not even any taste to *that*. "Yes, Ellen ever was tender-hearted."

"But she craves the things of this world, as the Parson'ud say." Buddy crumbled corn-bread, frowned down at it. "Hope, though, she's not thinking of setting her wedding day till spring. Don't know how I could manage a trousseau before then, even with your knack of making silk purses out of sows' ears. Maybe she'll be willing to wait, she hears about *my* romance and about—" Buddy broke off and looked at me with a glitter in his eye.

I reached for the bell.

Buddy took a toothpick from the holder. "Parson coming out this evening?"

"Why, no. Not that I know of."

He snapped the toothpick in two. "He'll be here."

The bell tinkled again, louder than before, and I set it down carefully.

"Oh, I haven't been withholding information! Word of mouth information. I just know if I'd been through what he's been through past thirty-six hours, I'd make a beeline for Mary Sue and—"

"Didn't think you was noways ready for dessert yet." Lucille shuffled to the table. "Slippy and me was having us a picnic kind of out there. Ain't neither one of you eaten enough keep a bird alive. You going to hear from Mammy, she see these plates."

❖

I folded a clean nightgown and laid it under Ellen's pillow, spread out the pillowshams Ellen'd embroidered in blue forget-me-nots. Ellen's never been able to sew a seam straight but give her embroidery hoops and some colored thread and she's smart as anybody with a needle.

I reckon I've spoiled her. She was such a little bit of a thing when Ma died, closing her fingers tight on mine like she was saying, "Sistuh, you'll take care of me, won't you?" Reckon it's my fault she takes all I do for her for granted. An older sistuh like me who seems always to give, never take, is exactly like a mother. And I've heard Charlotte and Mary Sue and the rest talk enough to know a mother's not any great shakes in a grown daughter's life.

Won't make any difference now though, her not knowing the first thing bout running a house, marrying so well. I don't want to scare her about her trousseau, telling her—well, far's that's concerned, I can sew for her as well in the parsonage as I can here.

Telling her! Telling her! Telling her what? That I know he is going to propose?

"A bird in hand, Ora, is worth two in the bush."

Shut up, Miss Ryder! Let me think.

That's what's given me this empty feeling in my stomach ever since I read her letter! I was so sure I was going to be able to tell her soon's she got here I was engaged. Thought Mistuh Humiston had two, three weeks to get up his courage. Or hear God's voice, if that's what he's waiting for. Then I'd have some importance in her eyes soon's she saw me. I'd be a person, not just hands and feet for her. But I can't tell her I know he loves me. Can't describe that look in his eyes or anything makes me know. And if Buddy was attentive to Mary Sue six months before he popped the question, there's no telling how long—why, I didn't see anything of Mistuh Humiston by myself till early in March when the roads were good and he began making calls out this way, stopped here to chat or to ask directions. Still, he's worked fast, as Buddy'ud say. Hasn't tried to disguise his feelings when we're alone and many's the time, after service and at a League meeting, I've caught him looking at me in a way I can't describe. Unless it's the way we all look at hats in Miss Belle's window, wondering which one would be becoming. . . . And if Buddy didn't think any the less of Mary Sue accepting his hand first time he asked, I reckon Mistuh Humiston wouldn't of me. I've heard Miss Lucy Berry say that in an emergency like the war when time was short, it was considered proper for a girl to say yes right away. A Methodist preacher's time may be short too.

Maybe he's coming to propose this evening! Hush, Miss Ryder. Buddy knows more than you do. Buddy's always right. Buddy said he'd be here. Buddy thinks he's going to propose any time now. He wouldn't tease me if he didn't think so. If we lived in town, everybody'ud think so. Buddy must've told Mary Sue. If Mary Sue gossiped like Charlotte, it would be all over town by now. I wish I didn't feel so much older than Ellen's friends. Three years 're not much but I can't be confidential with them and I certainly wouldn't try to be with Bessie Davis.

If I don't go with Buddy to meet Ellen, maybe he'll tell her on the way home! Then when she sees me, she'll—oh, no, she won't. She'll have to see Mistuh Humiston before she'll realize I'm something more than her handmaid.

But it's going to be mighty nice having her in this room again. It's been right lonesome going to bed and getting up without her. No walking back and forth across the passage or talking from room to room. Be mighty nice, even if I can't kneel at my window every night and say my prayers to Mistuh

Humiston—say my prayers, then *think* of him just two miles away as the crow flies. Across two wood lots, a pasture, and the marsh. "Sistuh," Ellen'll call, "answer me. Why're you so quiet? What're you doing in there?" Maybe I could close my door, say there's a draft on my neck. If I could close it first night she's home, I could close it every night. Every night till I'm engaged to marry him. After that, I can show how I feel about him. If I want to blow out my candle and kneel by my window in the dark, I can come right out and say that's what I'm doing. She'll be quiet then. Or she might say, "Well, I don't blame you. I'd be dreaming too if I was going to marry a man like that." Because I don't care how grand this Mistuh Clay is, he can't be . . .

"Miss Orie, whichever room you in?"

"Miss Ellen's, Lucille." Barefoot again. I didn't hear a sound. I stepped from the bed to the window and began ruffling the white lawn curtains.

"Lord, Miss Orie, what you finding to do in here? I cleaned hit up yesdiddy like for Miss Mary Jesus. Musta felt in my bones Miss Ellen were coming."

"Just fluffing these curtains a little. You got them starched just right."

"Yasum, I does right well when—Lord, hit do look nice. Come a day, I'm aiming to cut me some pretty flowers outuh seed catalogues and frame um up on me and Slippy's wall." Lucille rolled her big eyes, purple-black as her skin. "Miss Ellen do know how to make a room pretty, I declare she do." She raised her arms, bent over, laughing her big laugh. "A sin and a shame Miss Ellen ain't never seen hit look this-a-way, ain't it? Come Sunday morning, curtains be looped back every which-way let in air. Trunk be in the middle of the floor, clothes spread all over. Reckon how long take her get unpacked so's you can put away? What she going to do when she marries up with Mistuh Mercer, don't have you to do for her, I declare I don't rightly know."

"She'll have to learn, Lucille." Lucille was right understanding about some things. "Why were you looking for me?"

"I clean forgot, talking sociable! Mammy tell me ask you, you want hominy and guinea eggs for supper. Mistuh Benton he like um and he eating like you or a humming-bird one here lately, seem like we oughtuh tempt his appetite."

"Well, Lucille, you know I never did have much appetite."
Wonder if Mistuh Humiston likes guinea eggs.

"You telling me! That way you keeps so slimlike and pretty-figured. Miss Ellen don't watch out what's girl-plump's going to be woman-fat and all her pretty dresses'll get rump-sprung. Mammy say this morning, 'Who'ud a thought a puny child like Miss Orie'ud grow up to a fine-looking, up-standing woman?' You remembers time we was little, Slippy he tug and he pull getting me in the grapevine swing, you come long he think he got to tug and pull get you in. First thing we knowed, you and him was both on the ground!"

"Stop your laughing now and tell Old Lady guinea eggs and hominy're all right. She might make some tipsy cake, tell her, with that sponge layer left from dinner. That'll be a nice surprise for Mistuh Benton." For Mistuh Humiston too, invited to take potluck again. "You go on now. It'll take you the rest of the day to do all that polishing, this heat."

"You talking! Sweat been pouring off'n me out there powdering bricks. Howsomever, powder's ready and I got the silver laid out. Time that's shined Slippy'll be here with the ripe tomatoes for the brass. Funny, ain't it, Miss Ellen noticing silver and brass right off if hit tarnish, then raising them pretty eyebrows and saying, 'What mess?,' you asks her when she aims to pick up that-a-one in this room? That Miss Ellen! It'll certainly pleasure me to see her."

"Miss Ellen's mighty particular bout putting her best foot forward, isn't she? What can be seen must be just right. She's not a bit like me. I want things nice for my own satisfaction."

"Yasum, you two don't favor none noways. Remember time—?"

"No time to remember now, Lucille. You get along to your work."

I'm as bad as Ellen, running on like that with her and it just won't do making a boon companion of any negra, even our own.

"Yasum, reckon I better. Got to get out there my cabin before dark and make up Slippy's and me's bed. Done put the featherbed out to sun this morning."

The shamelessness of her! Talking right out like that bout the bed she shares with Slippy. Least she can do is *pretend* she sleeps with Old Lady. Started it in their teens, old shack at Brookside, they didn't have money for a license, but there's no excuse now, Buddy handing Slippy his ten dollars every month, Old Lady and Lucille their three, if we have to go hungry. All right having that preacher of theirs say some words over negras living to themselves, but living right here in our yard, Lucille and Slippy should get a courthouse license and be married right. Can hear Miss Ryder, huddled over a dying fire, calling me from something else she'd told me to do. "Ora, you run down to the woodshed and tell that bitch and mongrel stop that sniffing and climbing, and bring me some logs. They can get thum a lot quicker than what they're going to get if they don't watch out."

They certainly haven't been watching out since we've been back here and why Lucille hasn't had a baby I don't know. Time I heard Old Lady taking her to task about it—'sthough there're not enough pickaninnies in the world!—Lucille asked her if she didn't remember how Slippy nearly died with the mumps time all we children had thum. Old Lady said, "Might be, was a fact masters used to put slave-boys in quarters by themselves, mumps come round." I don't understand how mumps . . .

Lieu or Cap! Only a Camilla horse makes a lively clack-clack like that!

I leaned from the west window, drew back just in time. I stumbled over the rocker and clutched at the bed-post, my knees like water, my heart thumping till I thought I couldn't breathe. This early!

Then, somehow, I was in my room, fumbling in my wardrobe, trying to get my hands on my checked muslin. Found it finally and dropped it on the bed. Too many hooks down the back. This old pink cambric's clean if it is mended. . . .

"Sistuh, you come down? Par—Brothuh Humiston's here."

6

What did Buddy say about it, Mistuh Humiston?" I pleated my handkerchief in new folds. I wanted to dip it in that goblet of cool spring water and wipe his flushed face.

"Laughed and said that's one gift horse you can look in the mouth!" He leaned over and set the goblet on the flower stand behind us. "And I haven't done it. Come, let's go do it now!" He half rose from his chair.

"You sit still." Just like I spoke to one of the twins. "You're hot and tired. You've got plenty time to inspect that mare's teeth."

He sat back. Except for his own full set, strong and white, his wide smile was an eight-year-old boy's. "I have your permission to keep her then?"

"Why, Mistuh Humiston, I—I hardly know what to say. What right have I to give you permission a thing like that?"

Elbows on his knees, he leaned toward me. A grown man's face now, serious and intent. Don't move, Ora. Don't let your eyelids flutter.

"It's just this—ah, Miss Ora, when you fix your clear gray eyes on me, so honestly, so steadfastly—" His eyes faltered, fixed on his hands. He laced his fingers, pressed his palms together. "It's just this. Masculine opinion, that of my board of stewards, will be approximately what Brother Fanning's is: the laborer is worthy of his hire. If the hire happens to be a blooded mare, I'm fortunate. Lawyers are accustomed since the war to accepting anything in lieu of cash. Brother King had me in his office the other day showing me a bureau an old fellow in the country had given him for drawing up a will. Said it was brought over from the old country two hundred years ago. Sister King wouldn't have it in the house so he'd had it set up in the yard. Comes in mighty usefully for his briefs and documents. Pointed out its fine points with such enthusiasm I had to quote Matthew five, twenty—"

"Matthew five, twenty?"

" 'Lay up for yourselves treasures in Heaven—' Why're you smiling?"

"At you. A horse is even more perishable."

He didn't smile. "But I've had my temptation out with my conscience. On my way here. There in that glade where you showed me the first spring flowers when I stopped by in March. An hour ago I turned in there, dismounted, got on my knees in the ferns, and asked my heavenly Father to tell me whether it was my old besetting sin—my love for fine horses— or my earnest desire to increase my usefulness in this county prompted me to accept—rather, to delay refusal of this gift." His face lit up, that way it had. "He answered me, Miss Ora. As clearly as I am speaking now. Oh, why will people fret and chastise themselves when by going to God in prayer, they can so easily understand His will!"

72

"How did God answer you, Mistuh Humiston?"

"Even as He opened the mouth of the ass so that she spoke unto Balaam. I pleaded for a sign that my motive was above reproach and instantly my—*the* mare neighed and nudged my shoulder with her mouth." He sat up straight. "So, you see, all I need now is your approval."

I reckon I just stared at him.

"You're wondering why I need that when I have my Father's. I want the approval of my congregation in temporal matters and I feel I can have it through you." He reached for the goblet, took a sip of water. "Often those who do not go to God habitually for guidance are skeptical of the evidences of His direct answers to prayer. If I confided in others as I have confided in you, said that I know God wants me to accept this gift, I might be called a sophist. On the other hand, what the men and women of my church think of me would have no weight if, first, I didn't know what God thinks. God expects us to use our best judgment even when our conscience is clear. We must avoid the appearance of evil. You're an influential young woman, Miss Ora—"

"Oh, Mistuh Humiston, I don't know—"

"Then you're a too-modest one. I hear your praises sung on every side. If you think the source of my gift will nullify the good the use of it would accomplish, please say so and I will take it back to Halcyon before sunset." Lips narrow with renunciation, eyes wide, beseeching.

"Why, if you put it that way, I feel—I think you need a horse for your errands of mercy just as much as Doctuh Willie needs one for his."

"Yes." He nodded but he didn't seem convinced.

"I feel it's more of a gift from Heaven than from Halcyon!"

That was it! It's me he's looking at that way. It's me! Who am I to cause his countenance to shine? Where am I? Come back, Ora, come *back*. He's getting up. He's standing close and I can't . . . oh . . . oh . . . oh . . .

"Then I accept it! Come, let's christen her! Just enough water left in this goblet for a sprinkling." I felt his fingers brush my hair light as a moth. "I've no feeling of irreverence, Miss Ora. We will consecrate her to the work of the Kingdom. And we'll call her Esther. Certainly she's found favor in my sight even as another graceful dancer did in King Ahasuerus's. You must be godmother."

73

I got to my feet somehow and he took my arm.

"They told me her name is Trixie but that'll never do for a consecrated steed. I said I'd have to change it—though at the time, of course, I didn't know that I'd keep her. Just agreed, since they insisted, I'd ride her home. Save young Adrian a trip after the funeral."

"That was the first you knew of it—that they were giving her to you?"

"Yes, though I should've guessed what was in their minds yesterday morning when I wrote the will. When I took the pen I'd been guiding for the old man's signature—"

"He leave everything to those negras?"

"To his family, Miss Ora. But as I was saying"—still holding my arm, he stopped in our walk to the gate—"when I took the pen from his palsied fingers, he asked me—almost with his dying breath—what my fee was. I assured him there was none. Couldn't be one, legally or morally. He protested as best he could. Shook his head feebly and tried to lift those limp arms. Young Adrian bent over him and whispered in his ear. Such an expression as I wouldn't have believed possible in a blind face came over his. 'Yes, yes,' he whispered, 'do that, Son.' And no more was said about a fee. Then, when we returned from the family's burial ground and had had some refreshment, young Adrian led this beauty, groomed and saddled, from the stable."

He handed me the goblet, opened the gate, stroked the beauty's neck, laughed aloud when she turned her head and munched at his shoulder.

"Preacher in a frock coat riding such an animal would've caused some amusement in town had he been seen. Miss Ora, I ask you, did you ever see such coloring? A shade lighter it would be gold."

"She's mighty pretty. Nobody atall see you?"

"No. Fortunately it was dinner time. Only Aunt Merry running to the gate as I dismounted. Threw up her hands and said, 'Praise the Lord, now we *is* folks in the parsonage!' "

"How did she know it was yours? Though, of course, they know everything."

"Why, I hadn't thought. Some of the darkies from town must've told her. A wagonload came out for the funeral."

"Halcyon negras and their children. Lots of thum live in town now. Nobody saw you riding out here either?"

He shook his head. "I changed my clothes quickly's I could to

74

take advantage of the deserted streets. I wanted you to be the first—there, there, Esther, if Miss Ora has some lump sugar, maybe she'll give you some. But first, we must have our ceremony."

He took the goblet from my hand and I shaded my eyes to see who in the world that could be driving in at the big gate in the heat of the day.

"Now, Miss Ora, if you'll stand here—who is it?"

"I can't make out. Miss Callie and Mary Sue maybe. They said—" My hand groped for support, slid off Esther's slick hide.

He was aiming the water at my face. I clutched his arm. "No, no, I won't swoon. It's just such a—surprise."

"Who is it, Miss Ora?"

"Miss Ryder," I whispered.

Seemed to me then I was standing off to one side watching something didn't concern me. Ace perched on the rim of the front seat like a blackbird on a rail, sleeves of Grandpa's old alpaca flapping like wings when he flapped the reins over poor old Cleopatra's backbone. Little wooly bullet head thrust forward, eyes set straight ahead like he was having his picture taken. Wreck of the victoria opposite me now. Miss Ryder, erect, keeping her balance on the broken springs of the back seat, not an inch of her touching the moth-eaten brown padding oozing like sores from the scaly gray-black leather. Ruffled black parasol not wobbling, sun shining through its holes holding the same spots on her black net over black taffeta I'd taken the hoops out of years ago. Black hair piled so high it almost hid the silver Spanish comb. Earrings glittering.

"Stop, boy." In the shade of the magnolia she collapsed the parasol.

"Why, Miss Ryder—" No use. Was a gasp, not a welcome.

"Why indeed at this hour?" She set the tip of the parasol exactly in front of her on the bare boards, clasped her black gloved hands on the mother-of-pearl handle, fingers curled to hide the worn tips. She bent forward from her corseted waist, head and shoulders still erect, eyes taking me in from tip to toe, flicking them at Mistuh Humiston hastily pulling Esther in close to the fence.

"I expected to find you taking a siesta, to be announced by Lucille, and to wait in your cool parlor for you to make a proper toilette." She sighed and shook her head. "One never knows the routine of these smaller places." She laughed lightly.

75

"This reminds me of the faux pas I made soon after coming as a bride to Brookside and guests arrived unexpectedly. Senator Guthrie of Georgia, his wife, two charming daughters, his body-servant, three maids. I was dressed for dinner—and so were the turkeys. The embarrassment was in the lack of pallet material and company rooms. Never, my dear child, shall I understand how your grandmother managed with only two adequately furnished! Because, you understand, I well knew the Senator and his lady had not shared a room in fifteen years. Here, I thought, is where—"

"Miss Ryder, won't you come in?"

She arched her black brows. "Now you're forgetting one courtesy in remembering another, aren't you, child? As I was saying, here, I thought, is where I take the bull by the horns. Lapels, rather. And I did. (In the long run, I've found, it's always the shortest way.) The Senator no sooner perceived my distress than he rushed, so to speak, to my rescue. 'Dear lady,' he said and patted my shoulder, 'trouble your pretty head no more about it. My man prefers the companionship of his kind in the quarters and my younger daughter's waiting-girl the bare floor just without my chamber door.' She looked upward, fore-finger on thin purple lips. "That, I believe—"

"Mrs. Evans, I haven't had the pleasure—"

"Hush, young man, whoever you are. That, I believe, is a paraphrase of a line in a poem entitled 'The Raven,' by Edgar Allan Poe. The Senator was a gentleman of the old school. In every way. And he knew literature. I, alas, have not been able to peruse my favorite authors in recent years. Two generations of children at Brookside destroying a library that was balm to my soul. Boy, back the victoria. That will give me more shade and Cleopatra *some* protection from the lively hoofs of Young Lochinvar's superior steed. Where is the Fair Ellen?"

"Why, Ellen hasn't come home yet, Miss Ryder. She's still in Savannah."

"Then why is this gentleman—?"

All of a sudden Cleopatra backed of her own accord and Miss Ryder bounced like a jack-in-the-box. Mistuh Humiston stepped to my side, touched my arm, whispered, "Ask her again, to come in."

Mistuh Humiston with me, I walked forward boldly.

"Miss Ryder, won't you come in?"

"Thank you, child, but I must drive on, now you've kept

76

me here talking so long. I am driving in to Bayport to call on the daughter of an old and dear friend from whom I've received a charming note. Mrs. Layton Davies Baker she is. Perhaps you've heard of her arrival. She is stopping, alas, at that mediocre boarding house on the sound. Would that I could offer her the hospitality to which her mother was accustomed in her youth. Yes, a dear girl she was though a resident of Philadelphia. After our school days together there, there was nothing she loved so much as spending a winter in Florida with me, enjoying—relishing, rather—the blessings of slavery. In the last letter I received from her before her untimely demise, she reviled Old Abe as vehemently as ever. Remarkable vocabulary for a well-born and well-bred girl—her parents had been slave-owners up there, you understand, years earlier when the north was civilized."

Mistuh Humiston snatched at the pause, stepped closer to the sagging running board. "Mrs. Evans, I've been awaiting an opportunity to—"

"Ora, you may present this impatient young gentleman."

"Why, this is Mistuh Humiston, Miss Ryder, the new pastor in Bayport."

Mistuh Humiston held out his hand. "This is a pleasure, Mrs. Evans, I've long been anticipating." His hand dropped to his side.

Because Miss Ryder kept both of hers on the parasol handle and managed to look into his eyes, on a level with hers, as from a great height. Silently. Mistuh Humiston's face flushed with more than the heat. I didn't know what to do or say. I looked down the drive for a sight of Buddy, but not a thing stirred in the quivering sunlight.

"If this were twenty-five years ago," Miss Ryder said finally, drawling out each word even slower than usual, "and you came to my place to preach meekness-on-earth and treasures-in-heaven to my blacks, I would permit you to come to my dining room through my front door. I would see that a table was set for you and a master's dinner served to you. Obviously you were cut out to be a gentleman whatever happened to the finishing." She glanced at Esther. "I would order your mount, though she were just plain horse, unsaddled and fed. It is not April, 1859. Today I would not let you crawl through my stable gate. Disguise yourself as a gentleman if you will, you pull no wool over my eyes. You're still a namby-pamby, pussy-footing, nincompoop hypocrite of a Methodist preacher, preaching—"

77

"Madam, I will not stand here and listen to such an insult."
His fists clinched.

"—preaching myths no white-skinned animal should befoul
his ears hearing. Fear made men invent gods, my father used to
quote from one of the bards, and self-conceit made them claim
kin through a make-believe celestial bastard—"

"Drive on!" Mistuh Humiston shouted to Ace. "Drive on, I
say!"

Ace jumped, rubbed the reins over his eyes.

"—not worthy the superstitious imagination of the dullest
black beast on my plantation. The first of your line of namby-
pamby—"

Mistuh Humiston leaped around the front wheel, snatched
the whip from the socket, and brought it down on Cleopatra's
ribs.

Cleopatra plunged forward, headed for the stable. Miss
Ryder's back bent suddenly 'sthough her spine had been broken,
and she collapsed against the mangy cushion.

"I can't tell you how sorry I am you've been so insulted," I
said to Mistuh Humiston's back when I could say anything. "If
I'd had any *idea* she was coming—why, she hasn't dressed up
like that and gone out since the first Decoration Day barbecue,
when Pa's George, and all the other body-servants went to war,
were invited to have their own table and she tried to wreck it."

But he wasn't listening. He was standing there flicking the
air with the whip and watching the victoria turn on its battered
wheels in front of the stable. As it neared us again, he strode
out to meet it.

"Boy, take that whip." Miss Ryder, erect again but half
turned, was pushing padding back into the scaly leather with
her forefinger, as daintily as a lady in a boudoir threads ribbon
through eyelet embroidery. She didn't even look up.

Mistuh Humiston held the whip just out of Ace's reach.
"Madam," he said solemnly, "I'll call your soul to account for
your blasphemy if it's the only achievement of my pastorate in
this county."

Miss Ryder looked past him, bowed and smiled at me.
"Thank you ever so much, Miss Fanning, for your hospitality.
It was such a pleasure finding you alone and at leisure. The ice
was delicious. You must give me your recipe. I shall expect a
return call quite soon, you know. Boy, take the whip the fellow's
trying to give you. Good-bye, my dear."

Mistuh Humiston turned from the drive, his hands thrust in his pockets. He didn't even raise his head to glance at Esther or stand aside at the gate for me to go through first.

On the veranda he picked up his wide-brimmed straw from the banister rail, looked down at it. "Miss Ora, I must beg your pardon for my display of temper."

"Oh, no, Mistuh Humiston! I should beg yours for the insult you received from a—a family connection."

He shook his head and his eyes, meeting mine, were tender. There's no other word for it. "I see now that the note of bitterness I detected in your voice here last Sunday didn't spring from personal animosity. You, too, are horrified by the evil in the heart of that handsome woman. Let us join hands in solemn covenant that together we will save her soul from eternal damnation."

I placed my hand in his and after the first strong clasp, he held it, solemnly, tenderly.

"Must you go?"

He nodded. "But if I had my choice, I'd sit here till dusk. The memory of our communion on these steps last Sunday— and by your fireside last Tuesday—has sustained me through the trials of this week. This evening I'd hoped—" He broke off, looked down at our clasped hands. "I've come to the conclusion, Miss Ora, that perhaps God doesn't always make His wishes known as unmistakably as He did for me today in the case of Esther. It may be that if He doesn't say, 'stay thy steps,' He is directing us forward. Certainly the urge to come to you today seemed stronger than my own will. But now"—he smiled ruefully, gave my hand a final pressure—"I'm too depressed by spiritual burdens—the direct knowledge of atheism added to that of cruelty in professing Christians—to think of temporal happiness. And I must go and make my peace with Miss Taffy Hines."

"She'll forgive you. And when she has, you'll find nobody's going to resent what you said in prayer meeting."

"I'm not afraid of their resentment, Miss Ora—if only they'll ask God's forgiveness and walk uprightly hereafter. Promise me that you'll think of me till we meet again—Sunday about three?"

I nodded.

"And pray for me?"

"Oh, I will, Mistuh Humiston, with all my heart!"

79

CHAPTER II

1

SATURDAY AFTER DINNER I FINISHED ICING THE POUND CAKE and set it in the corner safe. Everything I did that day turned out just right. Happiness must spread from your heart to your hands just as misery does, making you do right as misery makes you do wrong.

I left pots and pans for Old Lady to grumble over, took my kettle of bath water from the stove, and tiptoed across the damp, clean entry floor. Lucille was on her knees at the upper end of the porch now, scrubbing and humming, and I could hear Old Lady in the chicken yard shooing at the two fryers she'd had her eye on all week. Going up the stairs, I hummed, too, and not about getting to Heaven when I died. I couldn't be happier if I were there already. I had waked up in the morning feeling that Miss Ryder, appearing in the flesh Thursday, had exorcised her spell over me and could never frustrate me again.

I didn't even care if Old Lady had noticed the way I felt and acted today. "What's got into you, Miss Orie, flitting here, flitting there, like a bird in springtime? Must be old she-devil didn't upsot you none uhdriving up here unexpectedly. . . . Yes, *ma'm*, we sees her and we hears her. Lucille come uhrunning from the parlor where she uhpolishing andirons. Say come quick, want to see old Miss Noah in the old ark. We peeps through the shutters and we opens our ears. Lord, the preacher he got him a temper, ain't he? Pleasures me to bear witness when the soft-spoken uhrise up in righteous wrath. But he ain't uhgoing to pre-serve *her* soul from the everlasting fires. And Miss San Dosia might's well go on to her re-ward. She ain't uhgoing to get her re-venge in this world. Devil he uhsaving Miss Ryder for heself. . . . No, ma'm. I shame for you uhthinking that. Ain't never eavesdrop on my white folks' personal affairs, never 'low my children do hit neither, ain't uhgoing to begin now. Soon's we sees you and the preacher come up the

80

path, I comes back to my work and Lucille she go back to hers. Courting's a mighty skittish business. Now she got him, now she ain't. Don't do to . . . Go long, Miss Orie, he got town full womens talk church doings to. But I ain't asking no questions so you don't need tell me no lies. You just keep a good holt on yourself till he ask you *one*. Like what you did, you used to hold on to your Ma's tit she think you done had enough. Say to me, 'My baby look puny, Old Lady, but she got strength of character. Won't give up till she got what she wants.' . . . Yes, ma'm, they was her very words. Took my ease in um many a time, Mistuh Benton he get dis-courage bout uhgetting this place back."

❖   ❖   ❖

Tired pacing back and forth across the upstairs veranda, straining my ears for the sound of buggy wheels, I finally pulled a chair close to the banister rail and sat still.

Suppose it rains tomorrow and we can't sit down there in the summerhouse! We'll have to sit in the parlor and unless Buddy does tell Ellen Mistuh Humiston's calls are not pastoral, she'll think she must come and help entertain him!

He said in prayer meeting once God answers every sincere request if it's in keeping with His plan for us. He didn't say whether you would've got what you asked for if you hadn't prayed, or whether God might overlook little things that mean a lot to you—like sunshine instead of rain—if you failed to call His attention to them. "If we mortals could see the celestial chart," he said, "we wouldn't feel rebellious when all our prayers are not answered. Our Father in Heaven is like the father of a big family of children on earth. To give one child that which his heart craves may deny another something that is more important at the time."

But who would want it to rain on a Sunday in spring?

My hand drooping over the rail brushed against a wilting magnolia blossom the color of sour cream. I drew it back like it had been burnt. Miss Ryder used to say I was making it up, saying I remembered when Ma died. Said I'd just heard them talk bout Grandpa's laying Ma out in the parlor with magnolias around her head. I was nearly eight then and I saw her with my own eyes. Nobody told me bout the two three-penny pieces on Ma's eyelids or that her cheek felt as cold and smooth and waxy as a magnolia petal. I remember creeping in the parlor while they all were on the veranda waiting for the preacher. I didn't want to touch Ma but I had to. How could Miss Ryder know about my going to sleep every night I was a little thing with my hand on Ma's face? Because that was while we were still living here and Pa was off fighting.

And I remember trying to sleep with her after she got sick and we had to move over to Brookside. One night when the wind was whistling through the bare scaffolding of Miss Ryder's Folly like it'd found a big harp. A big harp in that music room ell Old Abe didn't let her finish. She pulled me from Ma's bed just when my fingers had found that little brown beauty-spot and were spreading to cover her hot cheek. Miss Ryder's hands squeezed my ribs and she held me up high like Slippy held a lizard. "Now what're you trying to do—get consumption too and give me more trouble?" "Let her stay, Mother," Ma pleaded, "I'll breathe the other way." That's the only memory I have of Ma's voice, sweet and low and tired. I don't remember any more but I don't think I stayed. Expect I was dumped back in bed with Ellen in the room at the end of that long dark passage I'd never been brave enough before to feel my way through. But I know it's all true because I asked Grandpa once if Ma had called Miss Ryder "Mother" and he said, "Yes, she did. Would've taken more than Miss Ryder to make Sally forget *she* was a lady."

Minute I touched Ma's cheek there before the funeral I wished I hadn't. Every day I've lived since I've wished I hadn't. Ma wasn't dead to me till I touched her. And when I heard Cousin Sudie say, time she came to visit a month at Brookside and stayed two days, that Sally'd been "cut off in her bloom," I saw a big wilting magnolia, not Ma. Now when I see a wilting magnolia, I see Ma dead.

No use to tell Buddy any more what a torment these trees are to me and beg him to cut them down. Took me long enough to get that one limb out. He says I should remember how Ma loved them, how Ellen loves them now. Mistuh Humiston doesn't like them though. I asked him last Sunday whether there were trees up the country as beautiful as most people think magnolias are, and he said, "Yes, more beautiful. Cedars and oaks don't shut out the sky as these big, close-growing leaves do." You'd think after this past week I wouldn't let them get to me this way. . . .

Chair rockers were still clack-clacking when I got to the top of the stairs. I lifted my skirts in both hands and ran to the bottom and out the back door. Old Lady and Lucille were

82

coming from the kitchen carrying on like Christmas. Slippy left Jezebel or Jacob one in harness way down by the barn and came loping to the carriage block. Madam came trotting in the other direction and the blue teal feathers on Ellen's new hat bobbed and fluttered.

"Whoa, Madam!" Buddy looked like Christmas morning too, when he had a present for everybody.

"Sistuh! Old Lady! Lucille!" Ellen was waving both hands, her reticule and a pink-striped candy bag, as though she was just in sight.

Slippy circled the buggy. "I here too, Miss Ellen. Lemme hist you down." He rubbed his sweaty hands, color of underdone cornbread, on the sides of his jeans and reached right up to Ellen's armpits, swung her over the dashboard and the block, and set her down in front of me.

"Sistuh! I declare I've never been so glad to see anybody in all my life!" And she hugged me like she meant it.

"Ellen, baby, it's been so long!" I hugged her as hard as I could. Oh, it's good to have her again. Better than having the house neat and Buddy to myself. Better than being the only hostess. My baby to listen to, talk to, scold, and pet. Her neck smelled like white phlox in the sun.

"Well, don't cry about it," she laughed. "I'm here now. Where's your handkerchief? Here, take mine."

I had to let her go and when I'd wiped my eyes and looked up, the candy bag and the reticule were swinging at the back of Old Lady's twiggy shoulders.

"I brought you peppermint sticks! All the way from Charleston! Must be glued together now."

"Knowed my child would have something-nuther her Old Lady!" She twisted and wriggled like a happy pup. "You ain't plump's no possum no more! Musta not fed you no victuals down thataway."

"Plenty, only it wasn't your cooking and I couldn't eat much." She whirled around to Lucille. "Now you stop looking so down in the mouth, you hear? Your present's in my valise."

"*Miss* Ellen," Lucille reproved, and swung Ellen's hands back and forth, laughing big. "You nough of a present for me and you knows hit. Lord, what I care for whatsomever you mought bring me, I got you to feast my two eyes on?" She looked over Ellen's shoulder. "Slippy honey, you take aholt that big old grip Mistuh Benton histing out and put hit on the steps, hear?"

"Buddy," I called, "who's bringing Ellen's trunk?"

"Uncle Ram. Get here before morning maybe."

"Doesn't matter"—Ellen turned around—"I don't need any clothes tomorrow. I want to sleep all day."

"Thought you had to think," I said.

"I'll just dream."

"Twirl round like that onct more, honey," Old Lady mumbled, a peppermint stick in her mouth like a snuff-brush. "I wants to see thum new shoes. 'Miss Pig she run on little high heels, Miz Cow she bounce along.'"

I stepped over to Buddy. "Any news in town?"

"Plenty. Didn't stop anywhere but the post office. So many in there had a time leaving a message for Mary Sue with Miss Taffy—"

"Miss Taffy!"

"On the job again, busy and muddled as ever. Told me the Parson's not only the best minister Bayport ever had but the only one worthy the cloth anywhere. Here, you Slippy! Let Lucille have that valise and you come take care of Madam."

"Yasuh."

"You finish hoeing the okra?"

"Nearly bout."

"I'll finish it. Feel cramped sitting so long." Buddy took off his coat and handed it to me. "Halcyon business stirred up more talk than I heard about yesterday. Seems Mistuh Jim Berry called a secret meeting of the stewards Thursday morning and they drafted a letter to the Presiding Elder—wait a minute now. It wasn't sent. And you'll never guess who stopped it."

"Who?"

"Miss Ryder. Yes, sir, she smelled a rat soon's she got in town, everybody on the green like court week. Found out what the excitement was about and went on a rampage, trying to get the Parson tarred and feathered. Said she could tell thum just where to find him. . . . You don't get that look off your face, I won't tell you another word. . . . That's better. Well, she cleared the air like a thunder storm. Anything she was for, every man was against. Then they got to laughing bout last time she was in, raising Cain bout George and them being at the Decoration Day barbecue, and forgot all about the Parson. Anyway, nothing happened."

"What happened to the letter?"

"They tore it up, I reckon. Miss Taffy said they must've felt

84

getting the Parson out of town by legitimate means would class thum with Miss Ryder riding him out on a rail. And the Parson called a stewards' meeting last night and evidently got thum in hand. Miss Taffy even described the mare Halcyon gave him. Said it must be one of that Kentucky breed Mistuh Adrian was partial to. What a man! The Parson, I mean." He started toward the stable.

I called him back. "Buddy, you tell Ellen bout Mistuh Humiston?"

Buddy laughed. "Did my best to, but she wasn't much interested. Couldn't see a namby-pamby making such a stir, even revealing the truth about Halcyon."

"I mean—oh, never mind."

Ellen called from the steps and Buddy walked on.

"Yes, baby, I'm coming."

"You mind bringing up my hot water? If I don't let Lucille take my valise up, she's going to open it right here and get that Pinky Pack."

"I'll bring your water."

"Pinky Pack! Miss Ellen, you didn't bring me no Pinky Pack! You mighty good to me, always was, but you didn't bring me no Pinky Pack!" Lucille snaked about, bare toes blotching the broom marks on the hard earth near the steps. "She hadn't ought to fool me thataway, ought she, Miss Orie?"

"She 'hadn't ought' to bring it if you're going to dip snuff around the house."

"Won't dip a lip full no where's but on Slippy's and me's stoop come sundown, Miss Orie. Likes hit best that time uh day, seem like. Slippy he take out his pipe, I—"

"Come on, let's take it up," Ellen said. "Pinky Pack's in the very bottom. Didn't want it to be seen if I opened my valise on the train."

Lucille bent over but had to laugh before she picked up the valise. "Lord, Miss Ellen, you remembers the time you and me got aholt Mammy's snuff-box and—"

"You hush and go on upstairs." Ellen opened the shutter-door, calling over her shoulder to me to hurry with her bath water because she was bursting to talk.

I hadn't had time to ask Buddy whether he'd told Ellen about him and Mary Sue, whether Ellen'd told him about Mistuh Stephen Clay. Well, she could, if she would. Really hadn't needed to try to ask him whether he'd told her bout Mistuh

Humiston's attentiveness to me. She'd no more seen *me* than if I wasn't there. In her eyes I was still just Sistuh, waiting to do for her. Really wouldn't have made any difference if Buddy had told her. If she's so sure Mistuh Humiston's just another namby-pamby preacher, she wouldn't've expected his attentions and intentions had made me over new. . . . That was one time Buddy was wrong, saying the talk in town wouldn't amount to anything! Suppose Miss Ryder hadn't gone in, there's no telling . . .

"You scald yourself, you don't watch out." Old Lady hopped to the stove. "Better let Miss Ellen wait than—"

"Oh, no, I won't, Old Lady. Not today!" I leveled the kettle and hurried upstairs.

❖

"Sistuh, what in the world am I going to put on?" Ellen stood in my doorway, in chemisette and petticoat. "I didn't have room for a dress in that valise and I know I didn't leave anything here I could possibly wear."

"I'll find you something, baby." I dropped the length of Nile green watered silk I'd been fingering on my bed, followed her across the hall, and went to her wardrobe. "Here's your old blue lawn I washed and mended."

"Thank you." She pulled it over her head and looked down at it. "Thought I told you to give this old thing to Lucille."

I laughed. "You did but I see you're putting it on. I was saving it to get a little extra work out of her. Just occurred to me the other day you'd be needing something cool minute you got here, so I—"

"Need a lot more than I've got all the time. You should see how some of those Savannah girls dress, spite of all the talk bout the price cotton's bringing." She moved to the bureau and began unpinning her hair.

"Baby, you shouldn't complain that way. Buddy's doing all he can for us and now that he'll have another to feed and clothe—"

"Sistuh! I meant to tell you first thing I'm as happy about him and Mary Sue as he says you are."

"I'm mighty glad he told you. What I said just slipped out."

"Told me! He could hardly wait for me to get in the buggy. But—" She looked down at the hair-brush in her hand. "Well, I'm not so happy about you. I mean, you mustn't think you've got to marry a backwoods Methodist preacher just so you can have a home of your own—in a long string of little old ramshackle parsonages. Because—"

"Why, where'd you get that idea? Mistuh Humiston hasn't proposed to me." I stooped for the towel she'd thrown at the rack and missed. "If Buddy told you he had—"

"No, he just said the new parson had been attentive here lately. Said he'd called twice this week." She turned back to the looking-glass and drew the brush down the length of her waist-long hair.

Such indifference! Just wait till she sees him tomorrow, and I tell her I'm engaged to him! I had to laugh. "Buddy's got marrying on the brain," I said quickly. "Mistuh Humiston came out Tuesday, I think it was, to talk about a League social. I wrote you I'm president now. He wants to raise money for new hymnals. And Thursday was to ask me to use my influence with the ladies bout his accepting that Halcyon mare. Buddy tell you about all that and Miss Ryder's—?"

"Um-m. Wish I could've seen that encounter. He must be putting his foot in it all the time. Poor Miss Daffy-Taffy. But what can you expect? Buddy says he comes from the mountains. Sistuh, will you look at my brush? Looks 'sthough I've been brushing the hearth with it." She held it out. "My hair's stiff with cinders. Hasn't one speck of color left. If I don't sleep all day tomorrow, I'll wash it." She began twisting it in a rope. "I'm glad it's just Buddy's imagination about my sistuh's being interested in a Methodist preacher. Because I want my home to be as much yours as this is. And I know several well-to-do widowers in Savannah."

I turned my back and began sorting the hodge-podge she'd dumped from the valise to the bed. "So you think an old widower's a better match for me than a young bachelor?"

"*Old* widowers! Why the two I'm thinking of aren't more than thirty. One of them, Mistuh Jefferson Clarke, lost his young wife in childbirth. Left the sweetest little year-old boy you ever laid your eyes on. You'd make him a wonderful mother, besides getting—" She must've seen my face in the looking-glass, way she jabbed the last hairpin in the new kind of knot she'd made on the top of her head and spun around, "Why're you staring at me like that? Never saw such a mixture of emotions on *anybody's* face!"

"I've just realized what you've said. '*My* home in Savannah.'"

87

I dropped the cashmere shawl half folded and came around the bed. "That means you've decided already! You're going to accept that Mistuh Clay's hand!"

She laughed. "And all that goes with it!"

"Oh, baby, I'm so glad." I put my arms around her, drew back to fish for my handkerchief in my belt.

She put her hands on my shoulders and held me at arms' length. "So glad or so sorry, cry-baby?"

"Both, I reckon." I dabbed at my eyes and smiled. "Glad if you've found the right one, sad at the thought of losing my baby."

"You won't lose me, goose. I've just been telling you. You'll have to teach me to run that big old house down there—old Mrs. Clay's an invalid and they say the servants've taken over. Then, if I'm as good a match-maker's Cousin Sudie, I'll have you married to Mistuh Clarke in no time and we'll all live happily ever after. In Savannah! Come on, les go down." She stooped over the bed. "Where'd I put Slippy's pipe?"

"In your bedroom slipper. And Buddy's shirt linen is there by the bolster. You tell Buddy you're engaged to be married?"

"Couldn't. I wasn't when I was talking to him." She straightened up and a shaft of sunset light made her cindered hair look like dull gold.

"Now, Ellen, what do you mean by such a statement's that?"

"I'm not trying to tease you, Sistuh. Honestly. I wasn't sure I was going to accept Stephen Clay till I heard myself invite you to visit me in Savannah! Well, believe it or not, it's the truth." She balanced the folded linen on the spools of the footboard, stretched her left arm, cocked her head to one side, and surveyed her spread fingers, soft, white, with dimples instead of knuckles. "The ring's sapphires and diamonds. His grandmother's betrothal ring. Came from Paris. Fits too. Like Cinderella's slipper, Stephen said."

"You bring it with you?"

"Sistuh, the very *i*dea! I couldn't when I hadn't said yes. Now I wish I had. But, you see I was right, thinking I had to get away to be sure. Expect I've known ever since I left Savannah, though. The farther I got, the more sense all Cousin Sudie and Cousin Louis said seemed to have. But I'm glad I came just when I did—we'll need every minute between now and next April to finish filling my Hope Chest and make my trousseau."

"You won't be married till next April!"

"Of course not. Savannah'ud be shocked blue at less than a year's engagement." She lifted the linen, put it down again. "Good thing too. It gives me time to let poor Mercer down easy, bless him, before Stephen comes to pay his respects to Buddy and you. He wants so much to know you after all I've told him. And I didn't tell him half. You know, if we were still living in all that dilapidation at Brookside, why, I don't believe I could've let him press his suit as I did. I'd've been ashamed for him to come visit, spite of all Miss Ryder's past elegance—must go over and thank her, though, for teaching me the etiquette of the *haute monde* when I used to play lady. But I don't care how little Little Brookside is, we live the way we were born to live and I'm not ashamed—"

"That's what I've tried to do, baby. Give you something of what you'd had, hadn't been for the war and Pa's and Ma's dying."

She came and put her arm around my waist, squeezed me. "Now maybe I can do something for you! That's it! Smile. And come on! I want to tell Buddy."

❖

"Sistuh, why don't you blow out your candle? I think I heard a mosquito just now."

"I'm going to, baby, right now. I'll have to get Slippy put up the canopy frames Monday, summer's coming mighty fast this year."

I blew out the candle and sat down on the floor by my window. Mistuh Humiston seemed far away, all the to-do of Ellen's arrival distracting my thoughts. But after a while, the moon shadows began to take shape and I found the church steeple.

"Sistuh?"

"Yes, baby."

"I just thought—you're not planning to go to church my first Sunday home, are you? That preacher coming out here after dinner, you'll have all the religion you can take for one day."

"Why, I was, baby. I thought you were going to sleep all morning."

"I wish you wouldn't go. If you do, everybody'll ask about me and what can you say but that I'm home? And if you do that, Mercer'll be right out here and how'll I have time to wash my hair and write to Stephen?"

"Mercer hasn't been to church much recently."

89

"Oh, you'll see him, way you said you did last Sunday. Even if you don't, Miss Tempy'll tell him."

"Yes, that's so. I did want to be there tomorrow, though, in case there's more said about the Halcyon business. Buddy says church'll be crowded."

"Buddy can tell us about it. People in Bayport must be famished for something to talk about. In Savannah old people're the only ones still get excited about the war and everything. Promise me you won't go."

"All right. You go to sleep now." Just as well to stay home and be fresh and rested when he comes.

"Then I'll get my letter to Stephen signed and sealed and Buddy can drop it at the post office when he goes to Mary Sue's. And I'll give him a note to give Miss Tempy, evening service, to give Mercer. I'll tell Mercer to come out Monday. I've decided you're right—I should get it over with soon's possible and clear the way for Charlotte to console him."

"I know I'm right, baby. Nothing's harder than waiting, whether it's for something good or something bad."

"I wish you could tell me something about love. I don't know whether I love Stephen or Mercer. Wish there were two of me so I could marry thum both."

"Why, Ellen!"

"I do. I was so glad to be invited to Cousin Sudie's because I thought I could make up my mind about Mercer there. Then I had to leave Savannah to make up my mind about Stephen. Every time I'd get a letter from Mercer—'Dearest Ellen, I am well and hope you are the same. It has been mighty cold—or rainy or warm—up here. I wonder how it is down there. I received an order for another barrel of shrimps from The Yarborough House in Raleigh—or somewhere—today. Business is picking up every week. I hope Miss Taffy will have a letter for me tomorrow and that it will tell me when you are coming home. It's mighty lonesome in this old town without you. I must close now as I hear the supper bell. Yours devotedly, Mercer.'

"I declare, Sistuh, they were all like that. And every time I got one, I could hardly wait to see Stephen. Then before another one came I'd begin to see funny old sleepy-eyed, wide-awake Mercer." She laughed. "Now I can hardly wait to read my first love letter from Stephen! If his notes requesting permission to call are an indication, his letters'll be mighty romantic."

"Baby, you call him 'Stephen' right to his face?"

"Not yet but I shall—soon as we're formally engaged. When we're alone, anyway. I think it's prissy calling the man you sleep with 'mistuh.' "

"Why, baby!"

"Well, that's what you do when you get married. Didn't you know?"

"You hush such talk now and go to sleep. You need your rest after all that travelling."

"Same good old Sistuh, looking after me. Well, good night."

"Good night, baby."

Wishes I knew something about love! Same good old Sistuh! I bowed my head on the window-sill and asked God to take all the impatience I felt toward Ellen out of my heart and make me worthy of His goodness to me and of Mistuh Humiston's love for me.

2

Sistuh!"
  I turned back to the bureau for a last look at my hair. Not so drab. More the color of a field mouse than a house one. Must be that pinch of baking soda I'd put in the rinse water. If the hairpins'll just stay in . . .

"Sistuh!" Not so loud but more excited.

"I'm coming."

I peeped in Ellen's room. Still in the straight chair by her west window, feet on the highest rung. But she was bent over her lap-desk now like she had her monthly pains. Her pen was between her teeth and she was holding the curtain back.

My hand was on the banister when I heard her bare feet pattering. I turned around. "Ellen, you should be ashamed, nightgown open all the way—"

"It's not your preacher!" She tossed her head to get her hair out of her face and pulled her gown together. "It's a stranger! A tall, handsome *man*. On a gorgeous bay. Must want to ask the way to Camilla. May be Claiborne's new suitor from Edenton. No, couldn't be. She wrote me she wouldn't get home till this coming week." She gave me a little push. "Make haste before he gets to the veranda. And take a long time telling him whatever he wants to know. I want a good look at him. Sistuh, stop that laughing and go on *down*!"

91

"You're so funny, baby. It *is*—" No. Let her *see*. "It's a fine way for an engaged girl to be talking."

"You hush and go on!" She ran back to her room holding the gown up around her knees.

I took my time. I had to get my face straight.

His shadow blotted out strips of sunlight on the passage floor and the strips radiating from his long silhouette quivered with his knocking on the shutter.

"Why, Mistuh Humiston! Come right in. I didn't dream it was you this early! I was just coming downstairs to see if there was a slice of my pound cake left for you to taste."

"I hope so, Miss Ora." He held my hand and he looked at me, at my hair, at the black velvet ribbon in a love knot at my throat, and he didn't smile. "I had an apology ready but hearing that you've been thinking of me, I wonder if I need make it. Or am I flattering myself?"

"How can I tell if you don't make the apology?" My voice light and coy.

"Then I'd better. I missed you at morning service and that so multiplied the hours since Thursday, I thought I was due a little subtraction. One thousand hours minus one-half hour leaves nine hundred, ninety-nine, and one half. That the answer you get?" He smiled, just a little.

"The subtraction's correct at least." I laughed a little. "You must've been good at arithmetic in school."

"Only by virtue of the hickory stick."

"You mean you were whipped for sum inadequacy?"

"Sums, subtraction, fractions, plain and decimal. By my master at the academy and by Father at home. More often than I care to remember. Let's not remember now." He released my hand, dropped his hat on the chair by the console table, opened the shutter-door. "Come, let's walk to your brook. Must be a hallowed spot there where those blue flowers grow. Where I can forget spiritual thrashings as well as the other—the less painful kind." At the top of the steps he took my arm.

"I hoped you had already forgotten last week's troubles. Buddy told me how impressive your few words about it were this morning, those Baptists and Presbyterians there hoping for more excitement. And the gallery full of negras. I wish I could've heard you. But Sistuh Ellen came home yesterday and—"

"That so? I was relieved when Brother Fanning told me you

weren't ill but he didn't say why you were not in your pew. Let me see now if I can repeat my exact words for you." He stood still in the path, half closed his eyes, then lifted his chin as he did in the pulpit when he wanted to drive home a point. " 'I came to you to preach the gospel,' I said. 'To me, the gospel is the traveller's guide for the soul's journey to Heaven. It can attain life eternal by only one route through this temporal and transient world of the flesh, a route our Lord and Savior has marked with His blood. If, while I am your pastor, I fail to point out to you deviations from the path of righteousness, neither you nor I shall ever see our destination.' "

"Oh, Mistuh Humiston, that was just right!"

"Yes, it seemed best after my triumph at stewards' meeting to make a conciliatory explanation."

"Could you tell me just a little something about that? I don't want to seem prying but—"

"I took the initiative, both in calling and conducting the meeting. I told them that unless they stood behind me in this thing, I would ask the Bishop to fill the Bayport pulpit for the remainder of the year and make me an itinerant. Then I reminded them that church dues were paid up for the first time since 1860, membership increased by five souls, and church attendance usually at capacity. I said if 'aye' were their vote, they could signify by kneeling with me and asking God's forgiveness for past sins."

"And they did!"

His lips twisted. "They knelt. I'll feel satisfied about their penitence only when each of them has knelt with me individually." He led me on toward the gate and even his step seemed triumphant. "It was my first encounter with a Board and I came out victorious! I feel I've won my spurs and it's a portent for the future. I will not have laymen interfering with freedom of speech from my pulpit or with freedom of action in my daily life!"

He followed me through the gate. "Oh, Mistuh Humiston," I said, "we mustn't leave Esther here in the sun!"

He snapped his fingers. "Father's always said my head was too much in the clouds to remember a creature's comfort." He started to the hitching post, turned his head. "Today, though, the trouble's not with my head. Or maybe it's there too." He stepped back to me. "I forgot to ask whether Brother Fanning's home. I wanted a word with him if it's convenient."

"Sistuh!"

Ellen's voice. Ellen's in Savannah. Ellen's up there at her window. Mistuh Humiston's looking up at her. I hope she's not showing her navel.

"Sistuh, you're not going to walk without your hat!" Ellen's glittering head framed in the white curtains she clutched at her throat, face shining too, not a speck of rice powder on it. "Wait, I'll throw it down to you. Or had you rather take my parasol?"

"I don't need anything. We're just going to the brook."

"Oh. Then you don't." But she didn't draw back. She smiled as though she was dressed and on the veranda. "Aren't you going to introduce 'Brothuh' Humiston to me?"

"Why, yes. Ellen, may I present . . ."

I don't know whether I went on with it. It didn't matter whether I did or not, because Ellen was saying how glad she was to meet him at last, after all she'd heard about him from Sistuh and Buddy. And he was bowing and smiling and saying it was a great pleasure for him to meet the renowned Miss Ellen Fanning.

I'd never felt so proud. Ellen taking on so about a possession of mine! I reached back over the fence and picked a Cape jasmine, smelled it, and held it out to him. Something from me to him. A present, with love from Ora.

"Yes," he was saying, his head at an angle, his hand shading his eyes, "from all I hear, Bayport in general and one young man in particular have been eagerly awaiting your arrival. What's this?" He looked down at the jasmine I held in front of him.

"Don't you know? Smell it." I held it close to his nose.

He shook his head. "I see it and smell it in every garden down here but botanical names elude me."

"Shame on you, 'Brothuh' Humiston! You'll have to learn them. People in the Low Country . . ."

"We call thum Cape jasmine, some say gardenia."

But he was listening to Ellen, politely.

". . . love their flowers like their children. Imagine a pastor forgetting a parishioner's name!"

"Put it that way, Miss Ellen, I see I shall have to make an effort."

"Wear it in your lapel." I handed it to him.

"Why, Sistuh! He'll look like Oscar Wilde with a sunflower for a boutonniere!"

94

"Who's Oscar Wilde, baby?" I asked patiently.

Mistuh Humiston handed the jasmine back to me. "The odor's too cloying. You wear it for me." He looked up at Ellen. "And why did he wear a sunflower?" He fingered his lapel.

"He's an English author whose stories are shocking Savannah. I don't know why he wore a sunflower."

He extracted a pin and handed it to me. "Habit I acquired from Judge Kinkaid of the Circuit Court. Always said producing a pin for a lady's need was as good as Cupid's arrow for piercing her heart."

I almost pierced mine pinning the jasmine over it.

"Why did you say this author wears a sunflower, Miss Ellen?"

"I said I didn't know. Maybe a girl dared him to. Would you take a dare from a girl, 'Brothuh' Humiston?"

"Brothuh" Humiston. What had got into Ellen?

"Depends on the dare—and the girl who makes it," he laughed and said.

"Then I dare you to pick a magnolia and wear it!" Ellen thrust out her hand, tatting on her nightgown cuff showing, and pointed at the tree behind him as though he'd never seen it.

"To the brook?" He shook his head. "Wait until we come back."

"All right," she said, and laughed. "I'll have one ready for you. Don't stay too long."

The curtains fell together but before Mistuh Humiston had unclasped Esther's halter, Ellen was calling out again. To ask if she could give the prettiest horse she'd ever seen a lump of sugar.

"I'll thank you for her, Miss Ellen," he answered, not looking up. "You'll find her in the shade of the stable."

We walked on down the drive, Esther's chin at his left shoulder.

He broke the silence when we were opposite the hedge. "You were right about Miss Ellen's picture not doing her justice. She's certainly 'the fair Ellen.'"

"You see! But I must apologize for her, appearing at her window that way. Ellen never stops to think, anything she wants to do."

"She was thinking of your comfort and she wanted to meet her pastor, wasn't that it this time?"

"Maybe so. That reminds me. I started to tell you, when you asked about Buddy—he went upstairs for a nap before time to go to Mary Sue's. He'll be awake, I expect, time we get back."

"On second thought, I don't believe I'll trouble him today. Was just a little matter of—that can wait." He reached up and stroked Esther's nose.

"I hope you're planning to stay for supper—keep Ellen and me company?"

He stopped still. "Now, Miss Ora, why didn't you ask me before? When I was out Thursday? Whoa, Esther."

"Why, I—I had so much else on my mind. I didn't think. I just hoped—"

"I wish I could. Not being sure you would invite me, I accepted the first invitation I received after service this morning. Mrs. Baker's. For clam stew at Miss Winnie Swain's. I wouldn't have, except for the fact that I'd promised to call this week and, as things happened, couldn't."

"Miss Ryder didn't make her call either, Buddy said."

"No, she seems to have forgotten her social obligation when she reached town." He spoke as though it'd all happened a long time ago. "But don't think I've forgotten her soul's salvation! That remains the most urgent item on my official agenda. When I'm sure I can control my temper in the face of her blasphemy, I'll leave it to you to choose an auspicious date and we'll 'crawl through her stable gate.' "

Not in the clothes I'll wear! "I'll certainly do my best."

"Where shall we tether Esther?"

"The other side of the stable. By the watering trough. She can munch the grass there."

"Think Miss Ellen can find her?"

"She should be able to—if she hasn't forgotten her way about the place."

"She came home sooner than you expected? I don't remember your mentioning—"

"Yes, we didn't know till we had a letter Thursday saying she'd be on Saturday's boat. Right here, Mistuh Humiston—there's a stake there to your left. By that wild sunflower."

He laughed. "You making a pun? Thursday," he repeated, and snapped the bridle clasp. "That was the day I came out, so full of my own affairs, I didn't give you an opportunity to tell me your good news." He gave Esther a final pat and joined me on the path that wound between back yard and open pasture.

"I wouldn't've told you anyway. She asked us not to tell anybody till she'd had Sunday to rest."

96

He laughed again, that sniggering laugh I didn't find attractive. "Miss Ellen's the last person I'd think needed to use Sunday for rest. Is she always so lively?"

"Ellen's right lively all the time."

"Tell me—maybe I was mistaken, thinking I detected a touch of levity in the way she said 'Brother.' Or was I right?"

"Why, I expect you were. At least, I never heard her call a preacher 'Brothuh' before. Always said that was old woman talk. I've been wondering whether she called you that because she thought she might's well get used to— Why, do look at Buddy's okra field over there! He's raising okra this year to sell to a paper mill in Atlanta."

"Um-m." He stopped and stared at the newly planted black soil as though there was something to see in it. Then, when I started on, "Miss Ora, you sure the sun's not too hot for you? Thoughtless of me to've suggested the brook. Your veranda's always cool."

"Oh, no, Mistuh Humiston, I'm not at all hot. And soon's we cross the stile down here, we'll be in deep shade."

❖

"No bluebells here, Mistuh Humiston. Blue flags. I wanted to surprise you. Aren't they as pretty?"

"What's that? Oh, yes. Yes, they are." He drew a deep breath, fanned at his face with his hands, there under the weeping willow.

I wasn't a bit hot. I felt I'd floated along. Floated to this spot where all time seemed measured by the gurgle of water around the cypress stumps. Here on the sun-flecked sand he stood beside me and there was no other time, no other place. No remembering and no repeating. No doubt. No fear.

"Blue *bells* and blue *flags*," he said. "Sounds like a celebration. I can remember those two, at least. Prove to your sister I know the names of a few flowers." He glanced down at the clean white sand. "Shall we sit here a little while and get our breath? Wait. I'll spread my handkerchief for you."

We sat there quietly, I don't know how long. I didn't try to patch up a conversation with piece-talk. I knew now there was nothing to be nervous about when a silence fell between us.

This his voice, low, hesitant, questioning.

"Why, I don't know, Mistuh Humiston. I'd need some time to think about it. It's so sudden, your asking me. It took me by

97

surprise . . ." A voice from over yonder giving the answer I'd practiced to the question he would ask! Only lack of breath had stopped me. "That is, your asking me *that,* I mean—will Miss Ellen marry young Mercer?" I wanted to put my face in the sand. All I could do was put my hands over my mouth, turn my head the other way.

He was laughing! Out loud!

I wanted to run through the flags and the cat-tails. Jump in the brook. Stay there face down till I was drowned. I couldn't move a muscle.

"I'd no *i*dea you had such a sense of fun, Miss Ora." He laughed again. "Such an answer to an impertinent question takes the prize for tact."

I laughed then. My knees drew up and my head went down and *I* laughed till tears choked me.

He slapped my shoulder lightly. "Come, come, Miss Ora. A humorist shouldn't laugh at her own wit."

I found my handkerchief, dabbed at my eyes, drew in my breath till it scorched my chest. "I just—can't help it, your question struck me so funny."

"Not the question. My asking it. It was rude and you've answered it as it should've been answered."

"*You* mustn't apologize. It's I—"

"No, no. It's none of my business—till Miss Ellen taps at my study door to fix the date. I asked only because she seems too young to be thinking of marriage."

"Why, Ellen'll be twenty-three in November."

"That so? She looks a mere child. I was wondering whether Miss Tempy might be overanticipating—saying to me the other day it's a shame that I've conducted the usual number of funerals in Bayport but haven't officiated at one wedding and she hoped that would be remedied when Ellen Fanning came home and married her nephew." He picked up a pebble and threw it at a dragonfly hovering over the water. "Yes, it's plain Miss Ellen hasn't had the responsibilities you and Brother Fanning've had. I expect she keeps Little Brookside very gay—and you very busy."

Ellen visiting in a parsonage! House full of young people and he trying to write a sermon!

"She won't much longer now, Mistuh Humiston. Ellen is going to be married but not to Mercer. That's why she came home so unexpectedly. She wants to let Mercer down easily before she announces her engagement to a well-to-do young man in Savannah, Mistuh Stephen Clay. Seems he can give her all her worldly little heart craves. Oh, don't frown that way, sir! You mustn't misunderstand my little sistuh. She's not avaricious and she's not a coquette exactly. It's just that she hasn't got the deep feeling that I—that I'd like her to have. She's always wanted so much more than Buddy and I can give her. But she doesn't want to hurt Mercer either. That's why she didn't want him or anybody to know she came yesterday. She wanted time to break the news to Mercer gently."

His fingers played over the sand, found another pebble and spun it over the water. "Look at it scoon! I haven't lost my old skill. . . . So Miss Ellen's engaged to a young man of means."

"Yes, but please don't mention it. I wouldn't have, except that I don't want you to think hard of her when the news gets around. She'd never given Mercer her final word."

"I couldn't believe a sister of yours would act dishonorably. As for my mentioning it"—he smiled wryly—"I can't resent your doubt of my honor after my impertinent question of a while ago."

"Oh, Mistuh Humiston, les forget all that!"

"It's a covenant! But just one more word to explain my rudeness—in addition to my surprise at Miss Ellen's extreme youth—or the semblance of it—I had a selfish motive. I was wondering whether another nuptials to be solemnized would cut short my vacation in August."

"Ellen's won't. She says Savannah'ud be shocked at less than a full year's engagement and she'll need—"

"I've no patience with such fashionable rules and regulations! Once the troth is plighted, the sooner God joins together the better. Life is too uncertain." He brushed his hand in front of his face but I couldn't see any insects. "Let's get back to high ground, Miss Ora. If you're rested. There's a miasma in these low places that confuses and oppresses my mind and spirit—as though God's voice can't penetrate the thick foliage." He got to his feet, held out his hands to me.

As I grasped them, our eyes met for one second. His were as blue as the flags and as troubled as the gurgling water. He lifted me to my feet but released me so quickly, hadn't been for the sand my heels dug into, I would've fallen back. So close now. As close as when we sat on the sofa Tuesday, and as far away as when he's in the pulpit and I in a pew. What had I done? He stepped aside for me to go ahead. I was glad to. Grass over last summer's path moved back and forth like seaweed but I didn't stumble and by the time we came to the stile, I'd blinked my eyes dry.

"Look at the dutchman's-breeches! They look like—like—" But I could think of no simile. They were just common little yellow flowers.

"Where?" He looked around the horizon.

"There. In the grass at your feet. Why, I—I never saw so many."

"Oh. I was looking for a clothesline." He didn't laugh. He stooped and picked two, added them to a short-stemmed flag he had in his hand. "When I go to the old home, I'm going to press every flower I can find and bring them back to you ladies here. With their names attached." He laughed then and jumped the stile, laid his flowers on the top step, and held out a hand to me.

"Be interesting to see them," I said, on the other side. "Must be lots up there we don't have down here."

"We haven't got the variety you have in this Gulf Stream climate but what we do have, you can see. Everything's wide and open in the valley below Grandfather and Blowing Rock mountains. Sometimes—today, for instance—I feel that I'm in a foreign country. In my native state. So much green. No blue distances."

"The Major said once that travelling all over during the war, he was real surprised he felt more at home along the coast in Georgia and South Carolina than in the western part of North Carolina. Seemed to bother him." Now that scrap fitted in, conversation had to be pieced out!

"Expect it would. It's a sad thing every state has to be a kingdom unto itself, bickering and fighting every other for its rights." He stood still and his eyes brightened. "Miss Ora, you've given me a sermon theme! 'No Surveyors in God's Kingdom.' Can you picture an angel with a measure and level dividing Christians in Georgia from Christians in Pennsylvania? I'll make these old die-hards a laughing stock, you just wait! What's all that laughing and shouting about?" He parted the artichoke stalks along the fence and looked through to the back yard. "Old Lady has visitors, I see."

"Has thum every third Sunday regular as clock work. Her grandson and his family from Shrimp Hollow—below Miss Parker Piver's." Suddenly, saying Miss Parker's name, I felt a little better. What if he hadn't got the question out today? He was closer to it than he'd been last Sunday.

"That must be the crowd I said 'howdy' to on the road. Long walk for those parents carrying toddlers and for those other little feet. I would've taken the least one up with me if I'd known they were coming here." He stepped back to the path. "Speaking of Shrimp Hollow reminds me I haven't spoken to Sister Hughes about the condition of those cabins down there. I understand she owns them and it looks to me as though those rotten stilts they rest on 'll be washed away the next bad storm. The loss of life would be terrific."

"Well, you know they say a negra's got nine lives like a cat and if I were you, I'd take my time bout a thing like that. Miss Marmie's mighty touchy and her assessment for the pastor's salary's—" At the sight of his face I broke off.

"Please, Miss Ora, I know you're being satirical but I don't like your implying even in jest that I'd let fear of receiving my full salary stop me in doing my duty."

His tone was as kind as it could be but I'd never felt so rebuked. My eyes smarted and we rounded the corner of the hedge without another word.

"Why, that's Mercer's turnout down there at the hitching post," I said. "Now, how could he've known Ellen's home?"

But Mistuh Humiston was peering over the boxwood. "Look at Miss Ellen teaching that least one to walk!"

"That's it, honey," Ellen was saying as we came in the back yard. "Let go your mammy's hand now and come on." She sat on the bottom step holding out her arms and Mercer sat on the one above, swinging a child's faded dress on one finger and grinning like a Cheshire cat. Ellen shouldn't sit like that in a narrow skirt. I can see her stockings above her shoe tops.

Then I looked around and I couldn't believe my eyes. That pickaninny didn't have on a stitch! I didn't know what to do or say.

"There he goes!" Mistuh Humiston laughed out loud.

"Hush!" Ellen called, not turning her head. "Come on, honey. I'll catch you. That's right!"

"Mistuh Benton Rutland Fanning" went hurtling toward her, arms balancing and his little peter wagging like a tassel on his fat black stomach. He tottered but Ellen caught him, lifted him to her lap—lap of that blue lawn I'd pressed so carefully for her! "There now, you've done it! You're as big and smart as your name!" And she hugged him like he was white.

"Sure does thank you, Miss Ellen." Beulah got up from her squatting. "Seem like I couldn't of waited much longer get Mistuh off'n my shoulder."

"Yes, ma'm," Welly said, strutting round like a black cock. "You done uhkept your word sure nough. Say time you went away, we hist Mistuh round till you come home so's he won't get the bowlegs like the rest done got, you'd learn him to walk yourself. Howdy Miss Orie. Mistuh Preacher."

"Lord, I ain't seen the preacher here!" Beulah ran over and snatched Mistuh's dress from Mercer's finger. "Here, Miss Ellen, you give me that he-child. Lemme cover he's nakedness."

Lucille and Slippy and the whole ring of children burst out laughing but Mistuh Humiston just smiled and said he hoped the parents would never have any more than that to be ashamed of.

"Bye, Mistuh." Ellen ran her hand over the kinks emerging from the neck of the dress Beulah was pulling on him. "Next time you come we'll have a race, hear?" She started toward us, turned around to Mercer at her heels. "Oh. Mercer, go get me that magnolia—there in that tumbler on the banister."

"Now, Miss Ellen," Mistuh Humiston protested. "I didn't say I'd take your dare in front of an audience."

"You don't have to." Ellen looked up at him pertly. "We'll go to the veranda. I just came out here to put the magnolia in water and found Mistuh crawling around in the dirt."

"Then I'm ready." Mistuh Humiston bowed.

"Baby, how did Mercer know you were home?"

"He didn't. You should've seen his face when he came walking back here looking for you or Buddy. Came to find out if you'd heard from me again." She tucked a hand in my arm, whispered in my ear, "Don't you leave him alone with me."

"Now where is Old Lady, all her kin about?" Mistuh Humiston, still smiling, was gazing about the yard.

"Oh, she's in the kitchen getting us some refreshment. I thought you and Sistuh 'ud be thirsty after your walk. What are those wild flowers in your hand?"

"A flag and a pair of dutchman's-breeches," he said triumphantly. "For you, Miss Ellen."

"Why, thank you, sir. You're very kind." She thrust the stems through the lace of her fichu.

"Here's your magnolia." Mercer held it out.

"Oh thank you, Mercer." She flaunted it at Mistuh Humiston.

"What's all this about?" Mercer asked.

"If you'll excuse me just a minute," I said to Mistuh Humiston, while Ellen was laughing and explaining, "I'll run upstairs and see if Buddy's awake."

"Certainly, Miss Ora. But please don't disturb him on my account."

❖

Time I reached the top of the stairs I knew I'd been daffy thinking I could disturb him on my own account. What could I say? "Buddy, Mistuh Humiston said when he came he wanted a word with you but now he says not to disturb you. Buddy, I don't know what to think. I'm sure he had intentions when he came but he didn't go through with them. I can't make him out. He hasn't been a bit like himself today. I thought he was worried, somebody as worldly as Ellen living with us, but I explained about her being engaged and it didn't seem to make any difference. Oh, Buddy, I'm so disappointed!"

"Now, Sistuh, stop your sniffling. You think a man asks a girl to marry him as easily as he asks for a goblet of water? He hasn't been courting you more than a week. Look how long it took me to get my courage and I've known Mary Sue all my life."

I heard him so plainly I stood still in the passage listening, but there wasn't a sound from his room. I tiptoed to mine.

But that's exactly what he would've said if I *had* gone in there.

I dampened my washcloth and wiped my face, patted on a little rice powder, smoothed my hair, and ran down the stairs.

"You Slippy, Welly, one, come open the shutter-door," Old Lady was calling, "I got my two hands full."

"I'll open it, Old Lady."

I took the waiter from her. "You go back and enjoy your company. I'll serve the refreshments."

". . . the very *i*dea, 'Brothuh' Humiston!" Ellen was saying. "A magnolia's a beautiful tree. They say in Savannah you can't have a romance without a magnolia tree. A girl may say 'no' three times but lure her under the magnolias on a moonlight night and she's yours forever."

103

"Sure that's hearsay? To my ears it has the ring of direct testimony."

I pushed the waiter against the shutters and Mercer opened them. "Let me have that, Miss Ora. Looks mighty heavy."

"Thank you, Mercer, but I'll manage if you'll just hold the doors."

Ellen and Mistuh Humiston were standing at the banisters, their backs to me. I set the waiter on the balustrade at Mistuh Humiston's elbow. "You see, I've kept my promise!"

"What's that? Oh. Several slices of pound cake! Well."

"Don't pour the grape juice, Sistuh, till I decorate 'Brothuh' Humiston. Stand there, sir."

He stood at attention, his hands at his sides, and Ellen, on tiptoe, tried to push the thick stem through the lapel buttonhole.

"Ellen! You'll stretch that buttonhole!"

"Let me help." Mistuh Humiston spread the cloth from underneath.

"There! No, wait. I'll have to pin it. Losing it's no fair." She took a long white-headed pin from beneath her fichu. "Little trick I learned from you today," she said. She fixed the pin and stood away. "If Oscar Wilde could see *you* now, he'd never strut again!"

"Who's Oscar Wilde?" Mercer asked.

"How long must I wear it?"

"Till it wilts of course. I'm going to vespers this evening to admire you from afar." Ellen whirled around to me. "Sistuh, serve the cup and les drink to an ordained dandy."

"Ah, but I can't force this stem through the buttonhole of my Prince Albert," Mistuh Humiston said and shook his head. "Besides, the contract'll be null and void once I remove your pin." He followed Ellen to the chairs in front of the sitting-room windows.

"Miss Ora, who is Oscar Wilde?"

"An English author Ellen heard about in Savannah. He's said to wear a sunflower for a boutonniere. Here, hold these cake plates while I fill the goblets."

"Oh." Mercer brought it out full and round. "I thought he was one of those Savannah fellows." He took the two plates. "Miss Ora, how many beaux you reckon Ellen had down there?"

"You better ask her, Mercer."

"Won't do any good. She'll throw me off way she did when I

104

asked her why she didn't write me she was coming home yesterday."

"Mercer—" I felt so sorry for him I wanted to say something to prepare him for Ellen's news but there wasn't a word I could say. Then I thought, why Ellen's preparing him for it! Ignoring him, taking on so over Mistuh Humiston.

"What were you going to say, Miss Ora?"

"You take these over there." I set the goblets on the plates. "I'll bring yours and mine."

"Yes, I should've said evening service instead of vespers," Ellen was saying. "I'm afraid I haven't been a good Methodist lately, Cousin Sudie being an Episcopalian. But I loved driving past Christ Church. It's so old and— Oh, thank you, Mercer."

"Yes, it's very historic," Mistuh Humiston said. "John Wesley preached from its pulpit in 1735. Thank you, sir."

"Why, he certainly did! They say there's a plaque set in the wall commemorating it. I declare if I'd known I was going to meet you, I'd have had Ste—the carriage stop and I'd have gone in and *touched* the pulpit for you."

I handed Mercer his plate but he nearly dropped it pulling a rocker around for me. I didn't want to be drawn into another conversation with him. "I'll sit right here, Mercer," I said and took the straight chair next to Mistuh Humiston.

"Oh, excuse me, Miss Ora." He half rose. "Have this rocker."

"Sit right still. This is all right."

Ellen held up her goblet. "Here's to the—" She shut her eyes. "I want a rhyme.

> Here's to the parson who dresses so well
> He wears a magnolia in his lapel!"

It just came. It wasn't much but they all laughed and Ellen looked surprised. Looked at *me* surprised over the rim of her goblet.

"Miss Ora"—Mistuh Humiston leaned a little toward me. "You make up a rhyme like that on the spur of the moment, I'll have to bring my autograph album for you to write in."

"Now you've warned me, I'll have to—"

"Oh, do that, 'Brothuh' Humiston! I have a new one to fill, given me when I left Savannah. I'll save the first page for you."

"That's a promise! When may I—?" He looked off into space. "This next week I've got to go to Wilmington for the District

105

Conference. Three days, Monday to Wednesday. Get back on the afternoon boat. Rest of the week I'll be busy catching up on the lost days. The week after's clear—" He snapped his fingers. "Miss Ora, we haven't set the date for the League social!"

"Then what in the world were you and Sistuh talking about all afternoon? I thought that was—"

"*Afternoon?*" Mercer pushed to the very edge of his chair. "When's that?"

Ellen made a face at him. "After dinner. From after dinner till six o'clock's *afternoon*. From after supper till midnight's *evening*."

"Then it's morning," Mercer said. "No night in Savannah?"

"One, named Ste!" Mistuh Humiston spluttered grape juice and had to use his napkin.

" 'A humorist doesn't laugh at his own wit,' " I reminded but he didn't hear me.

Ellen turned from Mercer to him, tilting her nose in a superior way. "Puns're out of fashion, 'Brothuh' Humiston. I'm surprised at you. Besides, I don't see the point in yours." She sipped her grape juice indifferently.

"I see it!" And Mercer went on to explain. "You said something a while ago bout somebody named Ste stopping the carriage at that old church. Fellow name that 'ud be a *black* knight though." He checked his laugh to look down his nose at Mistuh Humiston.

But Ellen laughed. She leaned over and handed Mercer her empty goblet. "Mercer, you're smart." She hitched her rocker closer to his. "More ways than one. Tell me about shrimp. How many barrels did you sell last week?"

Mercer's heavy lids lifted and his gray eyes gleamed. He got up and set the two empty plates and goblets on the balustrade, pulled his chair forward till its rocker touched Ellen's chair. "Had bad luck after the rain storm Tuesday. It's like this in the shrimp business, Ellen . . ."

"Why, Mistuh Humiston! You haven't touched your pound cake!"

He looked down at his plate. "I'll remedy that right now, Miss Ora, while you and I get on with our business. When shall we have the social?"

"I'd thought of a week from Friday, first Friday in May. There'll be a moon then again and the Garrison green'll be mighty pretty."

106

"That's a fine time and a fine place! I believe in beating swords into plowshares—using an abandoned parade ground for the furtherance of God's work. Shame that sturdy old white building itself hasn't been put to some peaceful use. Town library or a county academy."

"Yes, it should be," I agreed. "Then will you tell Charlotte to notify League members of a call meeting? Reckon after prayer meeting Wednesday—"

"But you'll see Miss Charlotte at evening service, Miss Ora."

"Why, I can't go to service tonight, sir. Buddy'll have Madam."

"You certainly can go!" Ellen whirled around in her chair. "You'll ride in with Mercer and me! I've just invited him for supper."

"But, baby, two's a company—"

"Makes no difference. You stayed home this morning to make company for me. Mercer and I'll be only too happy have you make a crowd for us, won't we, Mercer?"

"We sure will, Miss Ora," he said gallantly as he could.

"Speaking of supper"—Mistuh Humiston got up and I hurried to relieve him of his plate—"I must be going on to mine, or I'll be eating and running."

"Oh, must you?" But Ellen stood up too. "Buddy hasn't gone yet. And I haven't given your Esther that sugar lump!" She put her hand on her cheek, aghast. "Suppose I run get it now, and meet you out there?"

"Yes, do, Miss Ellen. We mustn't disappoint Esther."

3

I didn't sleep much better Tuesday night than I had Sunday or Monday night and when I did I had a bad dream. I dreamt I was being married to Mistuh Humiston but it was all wrong, not legal, because Old Lady's preacher was officiating and Mistuh, stark naked, was—no, no, I couldn't have thought a thing like that, even in my sleep—Mistuh was just *carrying* the ring on a wilted magnolia that he had in his *hand*. And when that negra came to "Do you, Ora, take this man to be your lawfully wedded husband, to love, serve, honor, and obey, to live with him in sickness and in health, and forsaking all others, to cleave thee only unto him so long as ye both shall live?" his loose jaws

107

moved and his thick purple lips opened and shut but not a word came out. I waited till he had tried three times, saying the words to myself as he tried to form them, then, instead of the "I do" I wanted to bring out clear as a bell, I whispered, "I don't know, *sir*. I need some time to think about it. It's so sudden—" all that awful rigmarole I hadn't even thought of after I'd understood Mistuh Humiston had taken it for wit. But the whole church full of people heard my whisper and laughed in tune, looking down at new hymnals with flag-blue covers as though they were singing.

Wednesday morning I felt good-for-nothing but I laid out the pattern on Buddy's new shirt linen and pinned it in place. Then I unpinned it, tied it in a roll, folded the linen, and gathered up *The Farmer's Journal* I'd spread on the sitting-room floor. No use trying. My fingers were all thumbs this morning. If I should spoil one of his wedding shirts it would be too bad. Buddy's wedding shirt. No doubt of that. All settled and sealed. Mary Sue and Miss Callie out here yesterday asking Ellen what material Savannah brides were using for second-day dresses. When Mary Sue decides on hers, Miss Callie will stick the scissors in silk or near-silk without a qualm. All I can do with that Nile green watered Cousin Sudie sent me is rub my hand over it and wonder. . . .

> "When a shy little hand you're permitted to seize
> With a velvety softness about it,
> Do you think you can drop it with never a squeeze?
> Well, maybe you do—but I doubt it."

Ellen hummed a little, went on:

> "When a pair of red lips are upturned to your own
> With no one to gossip about it,
> Do you pray for endurance to let them alone?
> Well, maybe you do—but I doubt it.

> "When a tapering waist—"

I stepped to the window. "You out there this damp morning with no shawl around you? You'll catch your death, baby."

She looked up from the straw mat she was kneeling on, and drops of wet dirt dripped from the old kitchen fork on her clean gingham. "It's warm. Going to be a hot day when the fog clears. What're you doing in there?"

"Thought I'd cut out Buddy's shirts but decided I'd better measure his neck first. You noticed he looks thinner?"

"No. It's natural if he is though. Working as hard as he does *and* in love." She bent over the forget-me-nots again.

"When a tapering waist is in reach of your arm
With a wonderful plumpness about it,
Do you argue the point twixt the good and the harm?
Well, maybe you do—but I doubt it.

"And if by these tricks you should capture a heart
With a womanly sweetness about it,
Will you guard it and keep it and act the good part?
Well, maybe you will—but I doubt it."

First time I'd heard her sing it straight through and it sounded mighty cynical for an engaged girl.

I went on upstairs to get one of my checked aprons, then followed her voice around to the other side of the house, to her phlox bed.

"I'm having the best time! All I could do at Cousin Sudie's keep from getting right down on my knees with her Ben. I told her a flower gardener was one thing I *didn't* want. She said when I got a place as big as hers I'd want more than one but 'I doubt it!' "

"Buddy's got Slippy hitching up to go to town for some fertilizer. You want him to drop your letter at the post office?"

She looked up innocently. "What letter?"

"Why the letter to Mistuh Stephen Clay—one you've been writing on since Sunday?"

"No, I don't. It's not finished." She thrust the fork in deep, caught it in a root. "Drat it!"

"Baby, that's not ladylike. What do you mean saying you haven't finished it? It's sealed and addressed."

I saw her teeth bite at her lower lip way they had when she wasn't going to say what she wanted to say. Or while she thought up words to say something different.

"You've been picking up my room again! How'll I ever get over having two, three maids around if you spoil me like that? I wish you'd give me a little time to learn I mustn't stroll out of the house right after breakfast."

109

"That's what I'm doing, trying to help you out for a few days till—"

"Making my bed and emptying my chamber pot won't help me. I'll be pretending I think Lucille does it."

"You don't want Slippy to take that letter then?"

She poked the white root string down in the furrow she'd made. "No. I've got to write it over again. I blotted it." She laughed, "I sealed it up right fast, pretended I hadn't seen it. I had, though, and Mistuh Stephen Clay's mighty critical. Neatest man you ever saw in your life. Always after me about some piece of carelessness, way you are. 'Little lady, you'll crush your sash sitting on it. Little lady, hold your skirts away from the wheel. Little lady—' "

"That what he calls you—little lady?"

"Um-m."

"It's might sweet. He must think you're mighty sweet, giving you a hand-painted fan and a velvet, gold-bound autograph album."

Ellen sat back on her heels, pushed the hair from her forehead with her crooked arm, and laughed. "He's in love! Remember when that bitch Vin used to have was in heat and the dead rabbits and moles and things the Henshaws' feist used to leave on the back steps? Same—"

"Ellen, hush! Why, you're as bad as Charlotte. Very *i*dea your saying or *knowing*—"

"It's natural, isn't it? Anything that's natural is interesting. To me at least. There's Slippy now!" She twisted around. "You Slippy!"

"Whoa, Jacob." Slippy started to jump out of the wagon. "Won't aiming to go 'thout your letter, Miss Ellen. Miss Orrie she told me."

"Don't get out. I haven't got a letter to mail. Just wanted to tell you not to come back without stopping at the post office."

"No, ma'm. Get up, Jacob. Road your ladder now." The wagon rattled past.

"You expecting another letter today?"

"I certainly am. Said he'd write one a day till I said 'yes,' then two a day."

I reached out and pulled a yellowed leaf from a stalk. "Baby, how long had you known him before he proposed the first time?"

"Heavens, I don't remember. Sistuh, will you look at that coral-colored phlox, twice as big as it was last year. It's my favorite. Cousin Sweetviolet gave it to me." She began digging around it gently.

"When did he speak to Cousin Louis?"

"Sometime in February, I think, so he must've proposed first soon after that. He's a perfect gentleman. Don't worry. Well, that'll have to do for today. I've got to write my hospitality letter to Cousin Sudie. She'll think I've forgotten my manners." She got to her feet, began pulling off the old black kids she wore to protect her hands. "What're you going to do in that apron?"

"Thought I'd help Lucille with her soap-making soon's she gets the hopper pan out."

"Sistuh, do don't—" She put her hand over her mouth. "There I go, using that double affirmative again! Thought I'd been laughed out of it in Savannah. Sistuh, *don't* start that nasty stinking business this morning. I want Lucille to press my white dotted swiss. I haven't got another thing to wear this evening."

"Well, I reckon it can wait. We're getting mighty low on laundry soap though." But I'd be all tired out fooling with it. "I'll let her do my Easter dress too. I got it wrinkled sitting around in it that evening."

"Why'd you do that?" Ellen stooped, picked up the pad and fork.

"I told you Mistuh Humiston was here."

"Oh, yes. After you called on Miss Parker."

"How'd you know that?"

"Oh, Charlotte was just laughing Monday bout his being so conceited he thought he had to have protection when he called on ladies—or Miss Parker. Said Lord knew he needed it, calling on Miss Parker. You think he's conceited?"

"I certainly do not! Charlotte's just mad because he hasn't asked her to visit with him."

Ellen laughed. "I can't imagine Charlotte Berry making a pastoral call! Hasn't he paid any attention to Charlotte atall?"

"Not that I know of. But I know Miss Lucy's invited him to supper time and again. Can you imagine Charlotte a preacher's wife?"

Say it, baby. Say you can't imagine anybody but me. Say you don't believe what I told you bout his seeing me only about church work. I didn't mean for you to believe it after you saw him with me. I was just afraid to brag.

"Well, he's a *man* too. Maybe he thinks he could tame the

111

wildest. But I'm glad he's not interested in Charlotte. I'm counting on her to heal Mercer's wound."

"Oh, she will, baby!" And I went on to tell her about what Charlotte had said Easter Sunday.

Her eyes looked like big violets and her face got pink as her dress. "Sistuh, that's the best news I ever heard in my life. I knew it'ud work out eventually but it's wonderful she'll get busy pulling Mercer out of the dumps right away. If you'd told me that before Sunday—doesn't matter though. I'll tell him this evening." She groaned, "But now there's that supper at Miss Tempy's to be gone through with! Why didn't Miss Lucy give us her invitation first?"

"Because you didn't give her a chance Sunday night, darting all over the church, shaking hands with everybody. Was your fault, speaking to Miss Tempy before you spoke to Miss Lucy. Mercer laughed and said it'ud've been easier if you'd stood in the chancel with Mistuh Humiston."

"Mercer's foot in the band-box! Well," she sighed, "can't be helped now. I'll get through with it some way, I'll tell Mercer on the way to prayer meeting and Miss Tempy'll forgive and forget soon's she knows it's Charlotte after all. All Miss Tempy wants is *a* wedding. Maybe she'll get her fill—two this summer."

"Two?"

"Um-m. Charlotte says Mistuh Humiston'll bring a bride 'home from the mountains.' Come on. Lucille'll be slipping off to her Pinky Pack." She started around the house.

"Charlotte says!" I was shaking all over I was so mad. "What does she know bout his plans? He doesn't even know himself till God tells him."

Ellen turned around then, eyes shining. "He *that* conceited? Thinking God has time—why're you looking so mysterious? *You* know God's plans?"

"I just know that Charlotte doesn't know everything," I said and walked on ahead.

She caught up with me. "Mistuh Humiston tell you he's *not* engaged to be married?"

"He certainly did. He said there *was* a girl up there he'd been attentive to but he didn't propose to her because God's hand restrained him. All right, laugh. It was just before he was converted. That was a confidence, baby. Don't you repeat it."

"Of course I won't. But it's a good joke on Charlotte." Then she looked straight at me. "So 'Brothuh' Humiston confides in

112

you about more than his soul? No wonder you were so long at the brook Sunday."

"He says he finds me sympathetic," I said, lifted my skirts, and went on up the steps. "You find Lucille," I called back, "I'll get our dresses."

"I've found you sympathetic too," she laughed and cut across to the kitchen, singing that other song she'd learned in Savannah:

> "There's the tender girl,
> And the slender girl,
> And the girl who says her prayers,
> There's the haughty girl,
> And the naughty girl,
> And the girl who puts on airs.
>
> "There's the tulu girl,
> And the 'fool you' girl . . ."

Tender. Slender. And I say my prayers. I hummed the tune as I ran upstairs.

❖

Buddy and I must've sat in the buggy fifteen minutes that day waiting for Ellen, and when she finally came, she was holding her letters between her teeth, both hands behind her fussing with the bow of her sash.

"Get in, baby. I'll tie your sash when we get to the Berrys'."

She handed me the letters and lifted her skirts. The envelope addressed to Mistuh Stephen Clay was certainly thicker than it'd been when I'd seen it on her lap-desk after breakfast and I mentioned it as we drove away.

"I had to copy it over," she said, "so I wrote enough to last him three days."

Buddy said he was mighty glad he was near enough to Mary Sue not to have to write letters and asked Ellen what Mistuh Clay could find to say to fill two love letters since she'd left him less than a week ago.

"Oh, the farther south you go, the warmer men are," she laughed. "His letters are mostly compliments. I'm the fairest flower of the southland. My leaving Savannah made dreary winter of lush summertime, roses are fading and lilies droop."

"Don't know how I'm going to get the work done this summer if I have to send Slippy to the post office every day."

"I'll go myself. You and Sistuh're such stick-in-the-muds you've forgotten I've always gone in town three or four times a week."

Buddy didn't say anything till we'd clattered over the bridge, then he spoke solemnly, "Ellen, maybe it's none of my business —yes, it is too. I'm the head of the family and I've got a sympathetic feeling for Mercer. You tell him right away, you hear?"

"She's going to, Buddy. Tonight."

"Oh, I don't know, Sistuh. Maybe it'ud be easier for him if I just let him get the *i*dea gradually. You know, fix it so he and Charlotte—"

"Now, Ellen, you're just trying to get out of doing something's disagreeable to you. Thinking of nobody but yourself. You tell Mercer tonight or I'll tell him for you."

We both stared at Buddy. His face was flushed and his teeth clamped together till his mustache bristled like the Major's.

Ellen tried to laugh but the sound was more of a choke. She put her hand to her throat. "Being engaged's made you mighty stern," she said.

"Time somebody was, you playing the role of the heartless belle."

"I'm *not* that!" She flared. "It's just that as soon as I've told Mercer, it'll be all over town I'm engaged to somebody else."

"But, baby, why should you mind when the somebody else is Mistuh Clay?"

"It'll be all over town anyway," Buddy said, "your getting letters every day. You don't think Miss Taffy'll keep your secret, even if your traipsing to the post office every whipstitch causes no comment?"

Ellen sighed. "No, I suppose not, this gossipy little old town."

"Sistuh and I were saying, waiting for you, that you'll probably want us to make a formal announcement for you most any time now."

"When I do, I'll tell you. In the mean time, *please* don't either one of you say anything about it." She folded her hands and sat back against the cushion.

"Women, women," Buddy said to Madam's back.

"Baby, suppose somebody *asks* Buddy or me one?"

"Nobody but Mary Sue'ud ask Buddy. Anybody asks you, you say why of course Ellen had attention in Savannah but you don't know that there was a particular suitor. I won't keep

114

Bayport on pins and needles long. I just want a little time to—to have my romance all to myself." She moved her shoulders impatiently. "Now, for heaven's sake, les talk about something else."

But no one of us said another word till we were on the edge of town.

"Buddy! Stop a minute. There's Aunt Merry!" Ellen leaned over the side of the buggy. "How're you, Aunt Merry?" she called.

Aunt Merry set the little clothes basket down on the grass at the roadside and her squat body waddled like a duck's to the buggy. She ran her hands down the sides of her white apron, grasped Ellen's and pumped them up and down.

"Lord, Miss Ellen, you is prettier than ever! Ain't she, Miss Orie, Mistuh Benton?" Her big bosoms heaved and sweat trickled from beneath her white turban down into the wrinkles of her big black face.

Before I knew what I was doing, I was reaching for her hands.

"Lord, this *am* a sociable time, Miss Ellen she come home," and she pumped mine too.

"Who're you washing for now, Aunt Merry?" Ellen asked.

"Why, Aunt Merry's *cooking* for Mistuh Humiston, and washing too, aren't you, Aunt Merry?" Tucked in under that piece of white homespun that covered the basket, the shirts he wore, the underwear that clove to his skin, the sheets he slept between.

"Who else? Say to me Monday morning he uheating his breakfast-strip I fries crisp for him, say the younger Miss Fanning were home again. *Miss* Fanning I say. You means Miss Ellen. She my grandbaby. So to speak, I say. My daughter Sarah she wet-nursed Miss Ellen, time her pappy so sick her mammy's milk dried up. You see her next time, I say, you tells her I'm uhcooking for you, she'll run in tell me howdy. Say he certainly would do that. But now I is uhseeing you by happenstance and it a mighty pretty sight. You come anyway, honey. Gets mighty lonesome to the parsonage, no lady to talk to all the day long." She ducked her head and laughed. "Ask him why don't he get him a wife. 'Aunt Merry,' say, 'a preacher's gotuh be mighty careful uhchoosing him a helpmate, it gotuh be God's choice too,' say. I tells him I always heard-tell marriages was made in Heaven but he the first man I *ever* knowed believed hit." She laughed till her nose was flat as a flounder. "Yesum, I's on my

115

way take him his wash right now. He so clean seem like I don't have to do nothing but rinse um and twist um and hang um on the line. Want to see too do he want a little something to eat after his boat ride. Don't seem like I de-serves my pay come Satday, he in-vited out like he is."

She paused for breath, Buddy lifted the reins, and we had to drive on without my learning any more than that he liked bacon fried crisp.

"I wonder," Ellen mused, "why a man like Mistuh Humiston ever went into the ministry."

"Why, he had a call, baby. You should hear him tell about it."

"He's sincere all right," Buddy said, "but if he couldn't stand politics, it *would* be the ministry, call or no call. The Parson's got to have a stump."

At the beginning of High Street Ellen began waving or bowing to this one and that one, white and colored. She wanted Buddy to stop again so she could tease the Major, hobbling along for his mid-week call on Cousin Sweetviolet Rutland. Buddy told her she could do that next Wednesday. Today he wanted to attend to his business and get to Mary Sue's time for supper.

"Sometimes," Ellen said, "I think women should be as mean as they can *be* to men—when they get a chance, way men can be to women. Look at him toddling along there, as sure of his welcome as he was in his strutting days! Why doesn't he marry the old soul and be done with it!"

"Some say he proposed the Wednesday after Miss Letty died but Cousin Sweetviolet said if she couldn't be first or second choice, she wouldn't be third. Others, she never wanted to be anything but his affinity, talk about flowers and birds over her willow teacups every Wednesday, whether he was bachelor, married man, or widower."

"I've heard all that but I don't believe a word of it. Was the Major who—"

"You girls stop your gossip now," Buddy drew up in front of the post office and handed me the reins. "I'm going cross to Davis's. Hitch Madam at the Berry's post. Mary Sue and I'll get her after supper, take a little ride maybe. See you at prayer meeting."

"No, Buddy. Hitch her here now," Ellen said. "I want to run back and speak to Miss Belle and Sistuh'll have to mail my letters."

"Baby, you can drop thum in the slot on your way."

She gathered up her skirt. "Please you do it, Sistuh. Miss Taffy'll decide I've been away five years instead of five months, tell me a lot of mothy old news."

"Wait, baby. Look at Buddy, walking like he's all tired out. All he's done this morning was ride through the swamp spotting moss. You say you haven't noticed he's thinner so I didn't tell you I've heard him coughing. Several nights here lately."

"Sistuh, you're always imagining sickness. Remember how you rushed me in to Doctuh Willie's last September and all I had was a bad cold? Stop your worrying. Buddy's all right."

"Well, maybe so. I hope so."

From the post office steps I looked at the courthouse clock. Twenty-five minutes past three. If we'd been a little bit slower, the boat would've docked and Mistuh Humiston might've been coming straight to the post office to pick up his mail.

I lifted my skirt and tiptoed across the tobacco-stained porch. No use my getting involved in conversation with Miss Taffy either. I didn't know what to say to her after last Wednesday night.

There wasn't a soul in sight but I heard Miss Taffy's voice at the back door, wispy, no louder than the flies' buzzing around the day's accumulation of spit on government posters tacked every which-way on the dingy ceiling-board walls. Only thing Grandpa ever said about Reconstruction without a bad word was that that negra postmaster kept the place fit for a gentleman to enter.

I dropped Ellen's letters through the slot and turned around fast as I could. I'd reached the door when Miss Taffy called, "That somebody from Little Brookside?"

"It's me—Ora, Miss Taffy." I went back to the window. "How're you today?"

She ducked her head to drop Ellen's letters in the bag again, then her little tiny face, wrinkled and white as unironed linen beneath the taffy-colored hair, was thrust through the opening, and her great big brown eyes blinked at me. "Broke my new spectacles when I fainted last Wednesday night. Old ones hurt my eyes. All I can do to wear thum when I have to sort the mail. I hear Ellen's home."

"Yes she is, Miss Taffy. Came Saturday."

"Thought she'ud've been in, pick up her love letters herself. Tell her to come see us at home. Caledonia and I always enjoy her company."

117

"I certainly will, Miss Taffy. I know she wants to come mighty bad. Well, I must be going on now."

"Wait a minute, Ora. Got something for you."

No, he couldn't have. How could he? It would've been in the morning's mail if he had. I watched Miss Taffy put on her spectacles and bend over a long white box on the table by the back door. Invitations! Barbecue at Camilla! Claiborne's home then.

Finally Miss Taffy pulled three clear out of the box, held them up close to her eyes in the sun streaming through the open door, nodded, and brought them to the window. I held out my hand but she laid them on the pine slab and kept hers, fragile and blue-veined, pressed on them like an iron.

"Lieu just brought these to the back door. Never forgets to come round the back way on any errand beyond the jurisdiction of the United States Government. Smart darky. And more like his father every day he lives. Even has that cowlick Jeff Faircloth used to try so hard to brush down flat. Shame Jeff got that bullet in his heart before he could get home and sire another son. That one would've been named General. Got that yellow Daphne with child with every rank he attained. Amelia Faircloth ever been able to do arithmetic, she'd never invited visitors to the quarters to admire all those 'cunning tots' Daphne named Lieutenant, Captain, Major, and Colonel. Amelia never forgets manners, though. Look at that." She lifted her hand as though she had a fly under it. " 'Miss Fanning, Miss Ellen Fanning, Benton Fanning, Esquire,' and every one unsealed with 'Courtesy Miss Tabitha Hines' written in the lower left hand corner." She flattened her hand over them again. "You the first to receive your invitations so I'm going to let you be the first to hear the truth about this county. Because I'm going to speak it from this day till I breathe my last. If people'ud been honest and faced facts when I was young, I wouldn't be here now, in this public place no lady should be in, forced by law to speak civilly to some I wouldn't've wiped my feet on other days. Old Diogenes' lantern shone on one honest man and on one only those days and I should've looked over his shoulder and recognized that one instead of listening to my mother, grandmother, aunts, and cousins. Now it's too late, I know it wasn't Adrian Spier's *sin* horrified thum. Was his *honesty* about his sin. And the least I can do for his sainted memory is be

118

honest myself and proclaim the dishonesty of all who scorned him."

She leaned as far as she could across the slab and her voice was a scary kind of whisper. "I'm making me an *honest* genealogy of county families and when I've finished it, I'm going to tack it right up there by the boat schedule—see there behind you?—where it's too high for scum to spit on but low enough for those concerned to read. Now that you're here, maybe you'd like to see the notes for my chart." She fluttered back to the table.

I picked up the three little envelopes but before I could move, she was back again with pad and pencil. She turned some pages covered with her spidery handwriting and muttered, "Dade, Dew, Dickey, *Evans*. Here we are!" She rubbed her hand over the clean page to flatten it, held her pencil ready to write. "What I need to know, Ora, is whether that Slippy of yours is your step-uncle or your first-cousin-once-removed. Sometimes he comes in, I see your grandfather. Goes out, I'm positive only John C. Evans, Junior, could slide stead of walk. If you'll be so good as to settle this little matter for me, I'll be ever so much obliged." Her blue lips smiled way they did when she asked me how many postage stamps I wanted.

"Why I—I'm afraid I don't know, Miss Taffy. I've never heard —that is, I don't *think*— But I must be going on now. Thank you for the invitations. Good-bye." I walked backwards fast.

She waved her hand languidly. "Never you mind, Ora. I'll find out for you and post it right there where I showed you."

Ellen had unhitched and was in the buggy holding the reins. She didn't look at me. Just asked what in the world had kept me so long, as though she was the only one Miss Taffy ever talked to, so I decided to save my news about Miss Taffy's going crazy till we got to Charlotte's. Wouldn't have had a chance to tell her anyway after she saw the envelopes addressed in Miss Amelia's hand.

❖

I held in till all the excitement about the barbecue cooled down a little and Charlotte asked me why under the sun I hadn't made Miss Taffy give me the Berry and Ives invitations.

"Because I couldn't think," I said and went on to say Miss Daffy-Taffy was real crazy now and told them what she was up to. They listened without a sound but when I'd finished, they all laughed. I said they ought to be ashamed to laugh at a serious thing like that, said when Mistuh Humiston came for supper I was going to tell him and get him to stop her. But they poohpoohed me.

"Miss Taffy'll forget all about it before she finishes it," Charlotte said. "You'll be the first and the last to hear about it maybe. Lord, if we got het up every time Miss Taffy goes on a tear, we'd be in a constant stew. Remember the time she told everybody she saw she was going to give a fiftieth birthday party for Caledonia as a reward for her long and faithful service? Said she was going to serve all Halcyon darkies herself from her crested china with her grandmother's sterling? Nobody ever heard another word about it." Charlotte began pouring lemonade from a silver pitcher, all frosted with springhouse coolness.

"Thank you, Charlotte." Mary Sue spread a tatting-edged tea napkin on her lap and took her goblet. "But the reason they didn't, Charlotte, Mama told Caledonia and Caledonia stopped her. Told her she'd rather have the party in the kitchen as usual because those Halcyon darkies had lived to themselves so long they wouldn't know how to behave politely. I expect there're a lot of ways Caledonia's protected Miss Taffy we'll never know about."

"Yes," I said, "I was just thinking—thank you, Charlotte, this looks mighty refreshing—I was just thinking when Mistuh Humiston brought it all out in prayer meeting, how every negra in the county's known all these years—"

"You know," Ellen laughed, "when Buddy told me about it all, *I* thought the new preacher was just a poor mountain boy who didn't know any better than to talk about a thing like that in public! He certainly 'rushed in where angels fear to tread,' didn't he?"

"Maybe there was method in his madness. Benton says men think more of him because he showed he wasn't afraid to speak his mind and he gave thum something to talk about besides crops and the weather." Mary Sue quoted Buddy as though he wasn't our brother. "And Mama says it was as good for our souls as a dose of calomel is for our bodies. Says it purged us of spiritual impurities and started us out healthy on the road to Heaven."

"I heard Papa tell Brothuh Humiston"—Charlotte sat forward in her chair—"was a good thing he did go out to Halcyon.

120

Said if he hadn't and such a will's that came up for probate, those bastards might've been suspected of murder."

"Charlotte, Mistuh Jim didn't say 'bastard' in front of you!"

I didn't see why Ellen had to repeat that word. I frowned at her but she didn't notice.

"He certainly did but he didn't know it." Charlotte held her goblet toward the parlor window behind us. "I was crouched right in there. Last Thursday night. I blew out the lamp like I was going upstairs, then put my ear against the shutters. Always did love to hear men talk when there're no ladies present. You can learn a lot you never dreamt was in the English language."

"What else did they say?" Ellen's rocker was on its tips.

"Well, Brothuh Humiston told Papa *he*'d called a stewards' meeting for Friday night. If he knew about the secret one Papa had already had, he didn't let on and I don't see how he could've, he wasn't seen round town all day Thursday. Anyway, he told Papa he thought the best way to meet any trouble was head-on. Said he wanted to make his position clear before there was a lot of gossip. So Papa asked him what his position was and he said then about what he said in his sermon Sunday, about his duty as a pastor. Then he said he'd have gone off with that boy Wednesday morning if Mistuh Adrian *had* lived in sin with that 'kindly woman.' Papa growled like a dog—Lord, I could see the bristles fairly rise on his neck—and asked Brothuh Humiston if he'd call a marriage legal between a white man and a *white* woman that'd been performed by a Yankee chaplain on a license issued by Yankee interlopers to a sworn traitor. Brothuh Humiston said no matter how it had been done, it'ud be recognized as a common law marriage by now. Papa laughed kind of gently—way you do at somebody daft—and said the courts in Heaven wouldn't recognize any kind of marriage between a white and a negra any more than the North Carolina courts would. If you all think Brothuh Humiston can't get as mad as any of the rest of us, you should've heard his voice shake when—what're you smiling about, Ora?"

But she didn't give me chance to say and it was just as well— I thought then—because I couldn't've told those three why he was out home that day.

"—When he asked Papa what he knew about legal precedents in Heaven. Papa had to back down then, of course. Said they'd argue that point another time but the one thing he *was* sure about was that that buffalo had no *moral* right to leave all that

121

property to negras when the least he could've done for the pure, sweet girl whose heart he'd broken was leave it to her. Brothuh Humiston said he understood Miss Taffy had enough for her needs and that Mistuh Adrian *was* morally right in providing for those two boys instead of adding them to the ranks of ragged, starving darkies the North'd *willed* to the South." Charlotte threw back her head and laughed. "Maybe Brothuh Humiston didn't know it, but he'd said the one thing could pacify Papa. Was like sticking a sugar-tit in a bawling baby's mouth. Papa started sucking on it, and first thing you know, was asking Brothuh Humiston to kneel in prayer with him and crave pardon for his having taken vengeance in his own hands that time. Yessir, Papa's bad as one of those Roman Catholics in Wilmington, sinning, getting pardon, and—" She left her voice in the air and craned her neck to see around the moonvines. "Will you all look who's lifting her feet daintily over the roots in the sidewalk!"

"Who?" Ellen jumped up and peeped around the vines. "Oh, that Mrs. Baker. She's really *bon ton*. I want to meet her. Sistuh, les us call! After all she's a kind of family connection, we want to claim her."

"You do, you'll be ostracized too," Charlotte said. "She'd kept her nose in her own oats-basket, Mama and all of thum might've called but—"

"What's she done?" Ellen and I asked together.

"Went round town yesterday—Mistuh Josh King, the Judge, Miss Tempy and all—offering money and second-hand books to start a library. In the Garrison. For the good of the community. Everybody's mad as hornets. What does she think we are?"

"Miss Tempy wasn't mad, Charlotte," Mary Sue said. "*She* said food and clothes for the *mind* didn't reek of belated Yankee charity. Said way nobody's called or invited her to their homes, how can she know what we are? Said soon's Coonie gets her parlor curtains washed, she's going to invite her round for scuppernong wine so she won't go back up North with the wrong impression."

"I want to meet her," Ellen said again. "Put on all my airs and talk Savannah fast's she can Philadelphia."

"She's fast more ways than talking!" Charlotte said. "She paints!"

"Charlotte!" I gasped right along with Mary Sue.

Charlotte primmed her lips way Miss Lucy did and wagged

her head. "It's a fact. Cousin Winnie saw a little bitty jar labeled 'Rouge' on her bureau. I'll go with you, Ellen, Ora won't. Maybe she'll show us how to use it, we get old."

"Well, if nobody suspected how she gets that nice complexion till Miss Winnie saw the jar, I don't think she should be condemned for it," Mary Sue said. "And I'm not even sure she's fast. It's just because she's too dressy for her age people talk."

"I know how we can find out," Ellen said. "If Claiborne rides over before the barbecue, I'll ask her to invite Mrs. Baker. Miss Amelia 'ud love showing off Camilla to a Northerner and with all the out-of-town men there'll be—"

"Um-m, she'ud concentrate on Brothuh Humiston. And you ask me, he'ud love it. His engagement doesn't get announced before she leaves town, she'll ruin his reputation, chasing after him way she does."

Ellen cut her eye at *me* and I smiled at *her*.

"Charlotte, you're silly." Mary Sue got up and put her goblet on the table. "Nobody but you even thinks Brothuh Humiston's engaged and even if he were, Miss Taffy says Mrs. Baker gets a letter from her husband every day she lives."

"She does that, I'm certainly going to paint and dress to the gills, keep my husband devoted—I get one." Charlotte looked at Ellen and her eyes were like black grapes ready to fall from the stem. "Who're you getting so many letters from? Miss Taffy told *me*—"

"Charlotte Berry, you're the most impolite—"

"Mary Sue Ives, the height of impoliteness, they say, is to tell somebody else *she's* impolite. Hasn't Mama told you that?" But Charlotte was still staring at Ellen and the grapes had a sheen on them. "Were they from the same man? Miss Taffy said the 'calligraphy was masculine' but she couldn't be sure—"

"You don't think I stayed in Savannah nearly five months and had no attentions, do you?" Ellen managed to smile and bite at her lip the same time.

"Not attentions I'm talking bout. *Attention.* Who is he? What's his name? Has he cut Mercer out?"

"May I have a little more lemonade, please?" Ellen held out her goblet.

Charlotte lifted the pitcher, set it down again and drew it back on the bamboo table. "Not a drop till you tell me."

Ellen looked down at her empty goblet, then up at Charlotte, and the expression on her face made me right proud of her, it

123

was so serious and so kind. "Charlotte," she said, "I've never been engaged to Mercer, so how could any other man cut him out?"

Charlotte's hand fell from the pitcher and she looked down as though she didn't know what had become of it.

Mary Sue fluttered and said she just had to go, Benton coming for supper, and soon's Charlotte'd come back from walking to the steps with her, she asked Ellen if Mercer knew what'd happened to him.

"Not yet, but he will tonight," Ellen said. She bit at her lip and her eyes were wide and innocent-looking. "Nothing's happened to Mercer though, Charlotte. Mercer's just wanted a little variety. Don't *look* that way. It's always been you. And, well—I see now I just wanted a suitor. Why, if I hadn't gone to Savannah and discovered he wasn't the man for me, he'd have had to jilt *me!*"

Charlotte jumped up, stooped over Ellen's chair, and hugged Ellen hard. "Not a word of truth anything you say, honey. But Ora be my witness, you've said it and I don't have to be honorable any more!" She lifted her hands above her head, twirled about, and her face shone like a new silver dollar. "Lord, what a hussy I'm going to be!"

Ellen laughed. "You don't have to be."

Charlotte leaned over and shook Ellen's shoulders. "I *want* to be and don't you spoil it, Ellen Fanning! You're out of it—as of after prayer meeting tonight. And you let him down hard, hear? Hard's you can! I want to use every feminine wile I ever heard of to lure him back. I'll—" She sat down. "But that's my business. Tell me about yours. When're you getting married?"

"Next—"

Ellen frowned at me. "I don't know yet."

"You're engaged though?" Charlotte persisted.

"Well," Ellen stretched her arms lazily and smiled. "I think I'm in love."

"Same thing. He hasn't a coon's chance of escaping." Charlotte inched her chair closer to Ellen's. "Tell me about him."

"Well, he's right good-looking and—oh, everything I've ever dreamed of in a man."

"Then why're you waiting? Stop that smirking and tell me, or I'll get it out of Ora." Charlotte turned to me.

Ellen stopped smirking and sat up straight. "Sistuh, don't you do it! Sistuh and Buddy have their orders, Charlotte, and you

124

take yours. If I hear one word about my engagement, I'll know exactly where it came from and I'll never speak to you again."

Charlotte blinked, looked at me, and shook her head.

"Baby wants to enjoy her romance all to herself for a while," I said and just then Miss Lucy pushed open the shutter-door, waving her palm leaf fan and asking Ellen to tell her all about her trip, now she had time to sit in the cool and listen.

But Ellen had hardly begun charming Miss Lucy with her facts and fancies before Mercer clicked the gate latch.

Charlotte jumped up. "Come on, Ellen, les go meet him. You excuse us, Mama."

"Why, Charlotte, I should think you'd let Ellen go alone," Miss Lucy reproved and raised her eyebrows significantly.

"Oh, I want Charlotte to go, Miss Lucy," Ellen said, grasped Charlotte's hand, and they ran down the steps.

Miss Lucy sighed. Then she turned to me. "Ora," she said, rocking and fanning again, "I hear you've been seeing something of Brothuh Humiston lately, your League work, and I don't want you to repeat this, mind, but I'm curious to know whether there's one word of truth in what Charlotte says bout his being engaged to marry a young lady up his part of the country. I just ask because I thought he might've mentioned or hinted at such an intention to you—Charlotte refuses to say where she got her information, just insists she *knows* it for a fact—and if he *is* planning to bring a bride back here, we ladies'll be busier than bees, in August, getting the parsonage shipshape, and I'd rather begin—" She leaned over and parted some leaves with the edge of her fan. "Talk about angels you hear their wings flap! There he is now and Hattie's slow as molasses. You excuse me, Ora, I'll have to go see if she's got the fritter batter made." She paused by my chair. "He hinted at or mentioned any such thing to you?"

"He's not engaged, Miss Lucy. He told me."

She beamed at me, turned away, turned back. "Look at me, Ora Fanning."

"Yes, m'am."

"Was just the heat, I reckon, thought I'd detected a blush." Her gray eyes were motherly. "I won't pry, Ora, but I want you to promise me if there's anything to Tempy Williams' notion that he's more interested in you than in League work, you'll tell *me* before you tell another living soul, even your own brothuh and sistuh."

125

"I—give you my word, Miss Lucy."

She tapped my head lightly with the fan and bustled across the veranda.

The shutter-doors closed behind her and I felt weak all through. Whether was chagrin or relief that I hadn't told her there *was* something to Miss Tempy's notion, I didn't immediately know. Was both, I reckon. But holding myself there in the chair, hearing his laugh down there at the gate, I put out of my mind Miss Lucy's motherly feeling toward me, no matter how much I'd wanted to put my head on her big bosom and cry out my impatience at the waiting. Because her motherliness toward Charlotte was a lot stronger. She was still foolishly angling for a son-in-law while she steeled herself to be as gracious toward me, if I had the luck to catch Mistuh Humiston, as she'd been toward Ellen when Ellen'd taken Mercer right off Charlotte's hook. Gave me a lift, though, just knowing the old people saw me as a likely Mrs. Humiston. Pity Ellen and Charlotte never would till I told them it was to be. They'd got too used to my being just Sistuh who'd never had a beau.

I went to the balustrade and peeped through the vines at all four of them at the foot of the Berrys' lawn, laughing and talking. I couldn't hear all they were saying but enough to know Ellen was telling Charlotte about his taking her dare bout wearing that nasty stinking magnolia and I could see he was smiling. I reminded myself he was man as well as preacher and liked being taken on over by a pretty girl but I was a little ashamed of Ellen carrying on that way with her pastor and mighty glad I'd told him she would be living in Savannah before she'd told me not to. I wanted to get down there too but no greeting or remark I could think of to make at the end of that long path all by myself seemed just right.

Finally, when Ellen started off with Mercer, Charlotte called out to Mercer to tell Miss Tempy *she* was coming to have supper with her real soon and laughed out big when Mercer answered politely that Aunt Tempy'd certainly be glad to hear it.

❖

In spite of Charlotte's being on such a high horse, laughing and talking and making Mistuh Humiston laugh, all the way up to the veranda, he paid no attention to her when he found me there, placidly rocking, and wafting a Japanese silk fan to and fro. He said it was a pleasant surprise finding me a fellow guest and Charlotte had to sit quiet as a mouse for once when he took the chair next to mine and began telling me all about the District Conference. Said they'd reviewed the history of Methodism because it was just a century ago John Wesley'd permitted the Methodists in this country to separate from the Church of England. Said it would be amusing if it hadn't been brought out in connection with the seriousness of the coming Prohibition fight, fact that the early circuit-riders hadn't chosen celibacy but had had it forced upon them by the prohibition against their supplementing their salaries—sixty-four dollars a year—by the distilling and sale of hard liquor.

He said a lot more but was all I could do to pretend to listen, wishing so hard that *Charlotte* would stop pretending and go on in the house. She didn't budge till Mistuh Jim, fat and sleek's a porpoise, puffing and blowing with the heat, came out and said he'd been instructed to invite us in to the evening repast.

At the table he began pouring the white wine, said he reckoned even a preacher before prayer meeting could take a glass of this thirty-year-old vintage for his stomach's sake. In spite of all Miss Lucy's clearing her throat, trying to catch Charlotte's eye, and finally crying "Charlotte!", Charlotte went right on telling about how the Yankees had searched the place looking for Papa's famous wines and never did find them because they were hid under the *summer*-house. Miss Lucy laughed heartily then but Mistuh Humiston not knowing *garden*house was the real place, just smiled politely, then said solemnly he would take a glass tonight but that it would probably be his last, if he put his name on the list of active workers for Prohibition as the Presiding Elder had urged them all to do.

After that, not even Charlotte could get a word in. Mistuh Jim said a law against the sale of liquor was as much a denial of human rights as a law taxing property owners for the free education of white trash and black. Mistuh Humiston asked him if he were for the Federal Government's coming in then. Mistuh Jim's face got red's a beet. He thumped the table and said that was a subject he couldn't discuss adequately in the presence of ladies, was just a damn Yankee trick, a Trojan horse attempt to force mixed schools on the South and he'd burn in hell before—

"Ora and Charlotte," Miss Lucy said, pushing back her chair, "les us repair to the veranda till Mistuh Berry recovers from his choleric attack."

Charlotte didn't move and Miss Lucy and I pulled in our chairs again because Mistuh Jim was apologizing, saying the ladies and the preacher could have the floor the rest of the meal. Hattie came for the soup plates and Mistuh Humiston complimented her on her fish chowder but before Miss Lucy had finished assuring him the clam fritters Hattie was serving wouldn't give him indigestion, if he was subject to it, Mistuh Jim was off again. On Prohibition. Said he didn't care what anybody thought of him, he'd always been mighty grateful to the Republicans and negras for voting it down in '81. Said he wasn't ashamed to admit he'd gone to Wilmington to hear a negra speak against it—it was a damn good speech too even if it had been written by a white Radical and was full of that slop bout negras going back to slavery if Prohibition won.

I could see Mistuh Humiston was having a hard time keeping his temper but he did it, just asked Mistuh Jim mildly if he'd heard what they were saying in Wilmington now, that the Radicals were scaring out the negra vote again by the same method, telling them they'd go back if Grover Cleveland was elected president. Mistuh Jim said they'd never get him or any other Democrat to a mixed rally on that issue, so couldn't go around bragging again about "breaking down racial barriers." Just wait till those blacks in Wilmington got too big for the breeches the Radicals had made for them, native wets and drys would band together, ditch the whole Prohibition idea, put blacks in their place, and the South'ud be fit to live in again.

"Brother Berry," Mistuh Humiston said, "I've found a touchstone for Christian character I hope I shall remember to use throughout my ministry.—*If a man—or woman—has the Christian's attitude toward darkies, he has it toward everybody and everything.* Just let me leave that thought with you while we talk about something of more interest to the ladies than politics."

I don't know how Mistuh Jim took that mild rebuff, I was so busy trying to think of something I could do, show I was as Christian as anybody toward colored.

". . . a real thought to dwell on, Brothuh Humiston," Miss Lucy was saying, "but I'm proud to say you can rub that touchstone on any member of your congregation here and you'll find a streak of pure gold far's darkies are concerned. Cousin Winnie

128

Swain was saying here the other day that Mrs. Baker said she'd never believe another word up North bout the way negras are treated in the South, said 'Why, some of them live next door to your best families!' Speaking of course of those who live in the old quarters on several town lots here. Cousin Winnie said she told her they made mighty good neighbors too, always ready to lend a hand any emergency. Yankees'll never understand our ways of life, will they?"

"Not unless we help them to, Sister Berry. And speaking of Mrs. Baker reminds me—I met her in the post office just after I'd opened the little envelope Miss Taffy handed me inviting me to a barbecue at Camilla Plantation, and she laughed and said she could match it, and showed me hers. I presume—"

"Why, how does Amelia Faircloth know Mrs. Baker?" Miss Lucy looked at Charlotte but Charlotte was punching me in the side and didn't notice.

"I can tell you," Mistuh Humiston said. "Seems the Faircloth son who's in Raleigh, in the interest of the proposed railway from Tennessee to the coast, is a great admirer of Mister Baker and hearing—"

"Wasting his time," Mistuh Jim grunted. "Northern capital'll all go to financing feeders for the north and south lines. We'll never get a seaport in this state."

Mistuh Humiston nodded at him but went right on. "Hearing that his wife was visiting Bayport, Mister Faircloth wrote his mother, asking her that Mrs. Baker be invited."

"Oh, I see," Miss Lucy said, "and I'm pleased as Punch. Now she'll understand—"

"That's my point exactly!" Mistuh Humiston put down the dessert spoon he'd taken up. "She'll realize Southerners harbor no ill feeling. And that brings me to what I started to ask at the beginning of this conversation—I presume, of course, that you and your family will be going?"

"We certainly will. Camilla barbecues're annual affairs we all look forward to."

"Then would you further the good work Mrs. Faircloth's begun and invite Mrs. Baker to drive out in your carriage? She seemed concerned as to how—"

"Why, we've always taken Tempy Williams with us and this year I'd looked forward to having *you*. Another gentleman to keep Mistuh Berry company."

"Why, Mama," Charlotte reproved, "if Brothuh Humiston

129

didn't want to ride Esther, he'd hire a turnout and escort Mrs. Baker himself. Isn't that so, Brothuh Humiston?" Charlotte looked at him her teasing way.

Mistuh Humiston took a sip of water, tapped his lips with his napkin.

"That's a fact." Miss Lucy nodded vigorously. "Now, sir, you think no more about it. I'll send Hattie round first thing in the morning with a note. Riding out, I'll get it across to her tactfully's I can how we ladies feel bout her charity library notion."

"Sister Berry, I feel I should explain—"

Miss Lucy held up her hand. "Not another word about it, Brothuh Humiston! If I can't forget my prejudice long enough to do my pastor a good turn, I should be ashamed myself. You have more peaches and cream, Ora, Brothuh Humiston? . . . Then, girls, les us get ready for prayer meeting. Won't do to make Brothuh Humiston miss the bell."

Coming downstairs ahead of Miss Lucy and Charlotte, I found Mistuh Humiston alone on the veranda, hat in hand, gazing over the lawn at the lightning-bugs sparkling in the twilight.

"Oh, Miss Ora," he said, stepping forward, "I hoped I'd find the opportunity for a word with you. Just occurred to me when I received the Camilla invitation, it would be a fine occasion to try Esther in harness—if her godmother'll consent to ride behind her with me on Saturday."

4

Saturday morning I got dressed and down to the veranda before Ellen. Mistuh Humiston hadn't seen my dark green linen, new for last year's barbecue, and several had told me it was just as becoming as it could be. I had the coat I'd made for Ace on my lap, ready to be sewing on the last button when Mistuh Humiston should come up the steps. "Why, Miss Ora," he'd say. "What're your nimble fingers busy at now?" "Just a coat for Ace out of an old one of Buddy's I've turned and made over," I'd explain. "I felt so sorry for the poor little fellow, wearing that moldy old thing of Grandpa's." And Ace would come running up the drive just as we started to the buggy. . . .

Meantime, I'll be gracious and forgiving, say, "Why of course, sir. I understand. All work and no play makes Jack a dull boy." Still I was mighty curious about what explanation he'd make, saying there in the vestibule after prayer meeting he'd have to deny himself the pleasure of the fishing trip in order to get caught up with his work before Saturday, then going off with that crowd early Friday morning—Ellen said Mercer had thrown pebbles at the Berrys' windows to wake her and Charlotte. When I said I couldn't go either because I had some sewing to do, he'd nodded like he was commending me for putting duty before pleasure. Ellen said if it was her white duck skirt I had to finish before Saturday, she'd try to do it and let me go, because she'd been on so many water excursions lately she didn't care whether she went on this one or not but Charlotte told her it'd been her idea and she'd have to come if she went to Camilla in silk. I reckon she wasn't putting on that generosity, though, way she did her best to finish that skirt herself, singing at the sewing-machine like it was a piano all day Thursday, just speaking to me when she made a mistake I had to straighten out. . . .

"Sistuh—" Ellen opened the shutter-door, stopped whatever she'd started to say, said, "Why in the world're you sitting there holding Ace's coat? Give it to Old Lady. He'll come round the back way, he comes atall."

"I have to sew on the last button. Do want him to have it wear to meeting tomorrow." I reached for my thimble and threaded needle.

"Let it go a minute and look at the hang of this skirt." Ellen pivoted and the stiff skirt stood out, showing her little sensible-heeled shoes—if she'd been on her feet as much as I had, she'd wear a number three too! "On the left side, where I had to take that tuck in the hem."

"It's all right. Have to do for today if it wasn't. It begins to sag, I'll fix it next week." I looked her up and down. "That's a right nice outfit for a picnic—white shirtwaist and skirt, black sailor hat. But what'll they say bout your sistuh?" I pulled the thread through the cloth stretched on my knee, and glanced up. Why, you haven't even seen me! What did you think I was, sitting here seeing you? "Mirror, mirror, tell me true . . ."

"What'd you say? Oh you look nice too. Green's your complementary color. Goes with your eyes. That natural straw's all right, now you've taken that bow off the band."

"My eyes green? I've been told they're gray."

"They're green when you wear green. Gray with other colors maybe. Look up a minute. Um-m, they're pretty, Sistuh. Big and lustrous." She walked to the edge of the steps. "Somebody's coming!" She ran to the other end of the veranda, leaned over the banister to see beneath the magnolia. "It's Mercer!" She ran back. "Sistuh, what'll I do? I *told* him I was going with the Berrys. Sistuh, listen. You tell him I haven't begun to dress yet. Tell him you've got to stop at Brookside for something. To leave that coat! Say you'd rather not wait for Buddy because he'll have to wait till the Berrys drop Mary Sue here. Ask him if he'd mind starting ahead with you." She was at the shutter-door.

"Baby, wait! I can't do that. I'm going with Mistuh Humiston."

I couldn't help laughing at the expression on her face. I'd heard of mouths opening in astonishment. Ellen didn't seem able to close hers to speak. She backed in between the shutters just as Mercer called "Whoa" at the gate. "You sure?" she asked between the cracks.

"I certainly am! I thought you heard him say to me, walking out of church the other night, he'd be here round ten."

"How could I—Mercer and Charlotte talking fish! I thought he was going horseback. Maybe taking a buggy, he meant both of us!"

"He meant *me*. He asked me at the Berrys. Didn't mention you. Said he wanted to—"

"Oh, drat your old League business!" The shutters closed without a sound.

"Morning, Miss Ora." Mercer came up the steps, looking the way he'd always looked, coming for Ellen. If she'd told him what she should've, she hadn't made him believe it!

"Good morning, Mercer. We've got us a fine day, haven't we?"

"Sure have, Miss Ora. Couldn't be better. Warm enough be out doors, cool enough eat plenty of pig. Ellen ready?"

"Why I—I'll have to go see, Mercer. She—"

The doors opened and Ellen walked out as perky as a cuckoo on a clock. "Mercer! I didn't believe a word of what you said bout coming for me! I declare I never was so glad to see anybody in all my life!" She swung her reticule to one side and held her skirt out wide. "You imagine my squeezing in between

Miss Tempy and Mrs. Baker in *this*? Sit down a minute. It's early yet."

Now how can she make a man look like that just for her convenience! Whatever it is. I don't know, I don't know . . .

"Tell the truth, Ellen, I'd like to get started, go round by Ship's Folly maybe. Such a nice day, seems a pity not to make the most of it."

"I don't think it's making the most of it bumping over that old road, see that rotten hulk up on stilts. Channel's not a bit deeper it's ever been and no ghost crew's going to be trying to launch that ship in broad daylight, that's what you're hoping for," Ellen teased. Then sweet as pie, "Come here and take this rocker and tell me . . ."

"Miss Orie, you got Ace's coat ready? He out here for hit. Run acrost the field. Say eff'n he don't get right back Miss Ryder say she skun him so's he can't wear hit nohow." Old Lady's face between the shutters.

I looked down. The button was on. I bit off the thread. "Here, take it." That's the way things've ever gone with me. Plan and plan, nothing's ever worked out right.

"You ain't uhcoming see how hit fit? All that work, then you act like it won't something for Ace get him a new coat onct in a life time."

"Yes, I'm coming." May as well as sit there with Mercer and Ellen, look like a bump on a log, Mistuh Humiston drives up.

But I didn't see Ace in that coat till a long time afterward. Wish I'd never lived to see him then. Oh, if I could've only known what I was making it for. . . . No, no, no. Not yet. It hasn't happened yet. Was just Buddy's calling down before I got to the back door, asking where his socks were, kept me from seeing Ace that morning.

I gave the coat to Old Lady and went to the foot of the stairs. "They're in your lower drawer, Buddy, right-hand corner, where they always are. You better hurry. Mary Sue'll be here before you're dressed."

"Tell her to wait for me, hear? I'm kind of set on taking her today."

I got to the front door, heard wheels on the drive, before Buddy called out again he couldn't find a single, solitary pair. I went upstairs. Wouldn't hurt a bit making Mistuh Humiston wait. I'd always been *too* ready.

I had to laugh, Buddy standing there all dressed but for his bare feet. He was laughing too. "Got you this time! Always hoped I'd catch you not knowing where something was."

I found the socks finally, still in my darning bag, and mated two without holes.

"Parson'll be mighty proud, helping you out the buggy, in front of everybody today," he said as I handed them to him.

"Why Buddy, thank you. I wasn't sure—"

"*Be sure,* Sistuh. That's all you need."

I felt sure, stopping at the foot of the stairs, waiting for Ellen to call *me*. I went on to the shutter-door. The voices were in the drive!

From the veranda I saw a horse's head not Esther's behind Mercer's buggy. The laughing and talking were back there. One of the voices was Mistuh Humiston's. I walked slowly.

That morning last May when Buddy and Ellen and I'd got in the buggy to drive to the barbecue was warm like this, with a good breeze whipping up creamy clouds. Everything else was different. Mercer hadn't been out here without Charlotte. Buddy hadn't begun to pay particular attention to Mary Sue. I didn't know a man named Mistuh Humiston was living. We were the family we'd been for four years. If Buddy and Ellen weren't satisfied I didn't know it. Was enough for me then having Little Brookside, a home of my own. Not passing it on my way to town on a winter's day, that watery feeling in my stomach at the sight of the sagging gate, the weeds, the rags of Henshaw wash on the line, the newspapers stuffed in broken panes. I was sure Ellen'd marry some day, I didn't know who, but thought Buddy and I'd live on here and Ellen's children 'ud be like our grandchildren coming for Thanksgiving and Christmas. Why, yes, there was a young man at Camilla *that* day following Ellen around. Came from Edenton or New Bern or somewhere. I can remember thinking maybe he was the one but she never heard from him again and if she minded, we didn't know it. . . .

Ellen sitting in that new buggy with Mistuh Humiston, Mercer standing, one hand on the shaft!

"Oh, Sistuh, you forgot the autograph albums too!"

"Why, I didn't know you wanted thum. Good morning, Mistuh Humiston."

"Good morning, Miss Ora. You'll excuse my not getting out. Afraid to trust this strange horse."

"Sistuh, you mind getting thum? Mine's on the parlor table."

"Why, I didn't forget thum, baby. I didn't know you wanted yours." What would Mistuh Humiston think I was, Ellen's errand girl?

"That's right!" Ellen said. "Was yesterday we all promised to bring our albums."

"I'll get thum, Miss Ora," Mercer said.

Mistuh Humiston flicked the whip at a fly on the strange horse's neck.

"Why aren't you driving Esther?" Ellen didn't make any move to get down and I just had to stand there.

He smiled in a shamed kind of way. "Esther's never been in harness. We learned that at the livery stable this morning. I'll tell you about it while we drive along. I need your sage advice about your godchild."

"What're you talking about, Sistuh's godchild?" Ellen tilted her head to look beneath her hat brim at Mistuh Humiston.

"Why, I rode Esther out the day I got her. Wanted Miss Ora's advice about keeping her. And we had a christening ceremony—that is, we started to have one but Mrs. Evans came by, as I was telling you yesterday."

"Now if I'd been here, you could've had your ceremony. As I was telling *you,* I'm the only one can handle Miss Ryder. She's like a biting dog. If you let her see you're afraid of her—oh, thank you, Mercer! Now if you'll help me out of this elegant vehicle—"

"Remember, Miss Ellen, your pastor has first claim on the first page!"

"Of course, 'Brothuh' Humiston." Ellen put her hand in Mercer's. "You must think I'm a heathen Chinese to forget a promise like that, I declare you must!"

❖

"Yes," he said, when we'd turned in the stable yard and had waved to Ellen and Mercer standing where we'd left them, "I went on the excursion after all. Got through more work Thursday than I'd thought possible. Was my first experience deep-sea fishing and more profitable spiritually than materially. I didn't catch even a minnow but I understand Christ's parables and the disciples as never before. Physically enjoyable too. The sound was a little rough and I feared seasickness. Young Mercer knows how to handle a boat, however, and I felt no discomfort." He laughed that sniggering way. "Beginning to think he knows how to han—how to manage a young lady too. I happened to overhear him ask Miss Ellen to drive with him today, heard her tell him, very distinctly, she'd accepted the Berrys' invitation. But there he was. And Miss Ellen apparently acquiescent."

"There's no understanding Ellen," I laughed and said. "When he drove up she was beside herself. Ran behind the shutter-door and begged *me* to go with him. When I told her I was going with you, she popped out and told Mercer how glad she was to see him! Makes me feel mighty sorry for poor Mercer. She said she'd tell him Wednesday night—left fork here, Mistuh Humiston."

He pulled on the reins. "Tell him she's engaged to this Savannah fellow?"

We bounced in and out of that hog wallow by the chinquapin grove and Mistuh Humiston's hat between us on the seat fell against the dashboard. I picked it up and held it in my lap. "No, just that she can't marry *him*. And till she does tell him about Mistuh Clay, he won't take her seriously." Then I repeated what she'd said bout enjoying her romance all by herself for a while.

He brought the reins down hard on the chestnut's back. "Then Mercer can't be blamed for being persistent. Miss Ellen's got no right to think only of herself in such a matter." He gave me an inquiring glance. "Maybe I, as her pastor, should have a little talk with her."

"Oh, no, please, Mistuh Humiston! She's got no *i*dea you know about Mistuh Clay. I'd never've told you if I'd had the slightest *i*dea she was going to be secretive about it."

"But you're sure she *is* engaged to him?"

"Oh yes. I mailed her acceptance Wednesday myself. Now tell me about—" I was tired talking about Ellen but he broke in.

"Don't be distressed, Miss Ora. Your confidence is sacred. I appreciate it more than I can say. It gives me an insight to Miss Ellen's character I couldn't otherwise have had. They say all's fair in love or war, so I'll try not to judge her on her lack of entire frankness with Mercer. On the other hand, I'm sure I'd consider her a very frivolous young woman—even though she's your sister—if you'd hadn't assured me that beneath her gayety she knows her own mind. That's an admirable trait in either a man or a woman, particularly when it's a matter of choosing a life partner." He took the whip from the socket and touched the new horse's rump, though she was pulling through the sand as only a county horse could. "From my observation and experience, I've come to the conclusion that choosing a wife is man's greatest ordeal. Only Adam had the luck of having no choice." He replaced the whip and settled back against the sleek cushion. "As I think I've mentioned to you, in the glow that followed ordination, I felt I could be a celibate, accepting the logic of Paul's statement in his letter to the Corinthians that the unmarried, dedicated man careth for the things that belong to the Lord but the married for the things of the world—because he would please his wife. Now, after only five months as an active pastor, I'm convinced Paul would agree with me in my conclusion that it is not meet the *dedicated* man should live alone—if he will but achieve, through prayer, the strength to *please God first*."

My fingers tightened on the brim of his straw and I held my breath.

"A bachelor pastor, Miss Ora, is like an insect without antennae. Of all men, it seems to me, he needs a helpmeet. See how I've depended on your womanly understanding and advice this past month. Without it—" Suddenly he turned toward me. "Take off that hat, Miss Ora. I want to see your clear gray steadfast eyes."

My fingers shook so, I knotted the strings trying to untie them but when I finally looked up into his eyes a chilled numbness went all through me. He wasn't getting ready to propose. He was still wondering, after all his tenderness to me, whether I'd be a "becoming" wife. He didn't love me. Not as I loved him.

I tried to look away but I couldn't and I saw the blue appraising stare change slowly. Saw the muscles in his throat tighten above the black string tie. Felt his fingers touch the back of my hand. Heard his words as from the treetops above us. Knew that he waited as I waited.

"Ah, Miss Ora, where *is* the still small voice I listen for? The authentic voice of God? Others mimic His, confuse me. There can be no other explanation. You'll bear with me?"

"Yes, Mistuh Humiston."

Yes and yes and yes and yes, Mistuh Humiston. A day, a week, a month, a year, any way, every way, till death do us part. But listen harder, Mistuh Humiston. God will speak. I *am* the wife for you. Now you know I know it. You saw it in my eyes.

137

They've said yes. My lips'll never have to say no. Not even once. I'm yours. No pride left. No modesty. There shouldn't be, when *I* know. God's been telling *me* all this time. Why, God's been waiting to speak through me!

White sand and green leaves blazed gold and emerald. "In a light not of this world. Infinite light. Light no mortal can describe. God's living presence." I wanted to shout and I couldn't whisper. I wanted to fly and I couldn't move. I opened my lips but no sound reached him. I lifted my hand but I couldn't touch his sleeve.

But I was seeing the profile of his face all the while and suddenly, against a blue disc of open sky, it was like a medallion in its perfection and seemed to make a silent harmony. He hears it, feels it, knows it. Wait, wait, wait! Wait, I say, on the Lord.

I put on my hat and leant back and after a minute or two, he said, as he might've said if nothing had happened between us, or had happened on another day, or between two others, "What would you say if I told you I've about decided to swap Esther for Bonny here?"

Same old road veined with oak roots on either side. Juniper, wild grape, sour gum. Leaves just plain green in an everyday light. There's the bridge over the big brook. There're the red cedars and the mimosa Grandpa planted. There's the high arch over the carriage entrance, misshapen and broken under the weight of ivy. There's the foot-gate I was miserable coming out of, late for school, miserable going in. . . .

"Miss Ora, you dreaming? Ah, I see. We're approaching Brookside. Miss Ellen was telling me yesterday the happy times you three had here as children. The variety of wild flowers you used to pick to make penny-shows—that what you call them? Digging a hole, lining it with flowers, covering it with a piece of window-glass and sand, charging a penny for a view and brushing off the sand." He smiled in what he thought was an understanding way.

"I don't remember seeing a penny after Grandpa died. Negra children paid a sweetgum twig or a turkey feather. But that was one of Ellen's games. Buddy and I were kept too busy have time to play. Drive fast after we pass the bridge, sir. Miss Ryder may be watching for me—sent word by Ellen Thursday, Buddy drove her over after supper, the twins were getting bad colds and she wished I'd come amuse thum."

He clamped his jaw and reached for the whip. "She'll not

138

stop you this morning," he said above the rattle over the planks.

No sign of life atall. Just that space at the gate wide enough to walk through showing somebody lived back in there. Honeysuckle festooned between the trees, curtaining the remains of the rose garden and growing as tight as winter underwear over the bones of that music-room ell. Very sight of it made me shiver.

"Some day next week you'll drive over with me? Maybe I'll sleep more soundly once I've brought an atheist to her knees and a fear of Almighty God. Miss Ellen thinks maybe she'd better come with us."

Ellen kneeling in prayer! Miss Ryder at Ellen's feet! Ellen had nothing to forgive. "Mistuh Humiston, you and I were going to—"

"Talk about my horse-trading! Another of your gentle admonitions, reminding me I promised to leave the date of that call to you. I asked you back there what you thought of my swapping Esther for Bonny *and* this new buggy."

I had to smile. Why, he's not a grown man yet. Buddy used to look at me way he's looking now, waiting for my praise when he'd got a moccasin skin from Slippy for a hummingbird's nest.

"You're amused. Think I'm fooling. You know how I love Esther. That's the crux of the matter. When I accepted her I did so in the sincere belief I'd use her only for the Lord's work. These past few mornings I've found myself hurrying through my scripture reading and prayers just to mount and ride before breakfast."

"But you must have *some* pleasure."

"Not if I perjure my soul with worldly pride." A saint's face now. An *old* saint's face slipped like a mask over the greedy boy's. "An all-weather buggy'll be more appropriate and useful to a pastor than a saddle horse. Useful for funerals, for carrying the testaments and tracts I distribute in the country. Brother Newton declares he'll keep Esther for his own use mostly, hiring her only at County Tournament time to a lover of horse flesh. Only thing makes me hesitate is fear of hurting those boys at Halcyon."

"But Mistuh Humiston, they're only—" I caught myself just in time—"boys."

"Yes, Miss Ora, they're only boys. Seventeen and eighteen. But my father hurt my pride when I was seventeen more than he ever had before. If they were grown men I'd hesitate. Because they're darkies. I wouldn't want them to be disappointed in one of their first contacts with white people. I expect best thing I can do is ride out there and explain my situation. Must go out one day soon anyway. Young Adrian's ambitious to go to college. Mister Adrian prepared him well and I think that institution northern missionaries set up in Wilson's the place for him. Education's the only solution—"

"Mistuh Humiston! We took the wrong turn back there! Don't know what I was thinking of, letting you turn right at that grove of pin oaks."

"You were thinking of my problem. Anywhere up here we can turn?"

"Um-m, Jeb Johnson's place."

"That the Johnson who lost his young wife in the winter, just before I came?"

"That's the one. They say Jeb lives by himself now."

"You think, as many seem to, if he'd gone for Doctor Willie when his wife told him to, she and the babe wouldn't have died?"

"Why I—I don't reckon anybody knows the right of it." Mighty bold even for a preacher, talk right out to me bout a thing like that.

Before we got back to the fork we could hear the Major's cracked voice:

". . . So jump on the wagon and we'll all take a ride."

"Let's let *him* jump on ahead. Never did like being pushed from the rear." Mistuh Humiston pulled over to the left under a screen of low boughs.

The Judge's trap. Miss Letty's black umbrella and Cousin Sweetviolet's old yellowed lace one bobbing up and down on the back seat.

"Come all ye sons of freedom
And join our Southern band.
Oh, wait for the wagon,
The Dissolution Wagon,
The South is our wagon . . ."

Mistuh Humiston peered up into the branches. "I agree with you, sir."

"With whom—the Major?"

140

"With that nuthatch up there saying 'art, art' sarcastically. Even I can carry a tune better than that."

Soft sound of other hoofs and wheels in the sand, then Ellen's voice. "Mercer, you're making that up! I didn't say that. I said I wanted to be sure . . ."

"Hasn't convinced him yet, has she?" Mistuh Humiston laughed and said, and slapped the reins. "Get up, Bonny."

When Bonny's nose was poking at the back of Mercer's buggy, Ellen leaned way out and looked back. "Why, 'Brothuh' Humiston, where'd you come from?"

"Earth's my home and Heaven's my destination!" he called. "Tell your driver to speed up!"

"Now you're caught," I said. "Slowed down in front and pushed from the rear. I hear the surrey coming."

"That's so. Just thought we should keep an eye on young Mercer. Be too bad, he gets desperate enough to kidnap Miss Ellen before the barbecue."

"Why he can't do that now! No other roads between here and Camilla," I laughed and said.

❖

No, no, no, I don't want to remember that day at Camilla. Smell of barbecue and Brunswick Stew makes me sick even now. I didn't see Mistuh Humiston to speak to from time he helped me down at the foot of the long white steps (ones I'd thought led straight to Heaven first time Grandpa'd brought me out there) till we all got *in the surrey* to go home. Wasn't his fault I know. His last words to me were, "Now, Miss Ora, let's forget all care today and enjoy ourselves to the utmost. I want to see all the historic sights you said you'd show me." And just then Miss Amelia'd come hurrying from the barbecue pit on the left and Claiborne, with a crowd, from the belvedere on the right, and they'd encircled us, laughing and talking and introducing.

Sight of Claiborne's brunette beauty and cool perfection always did make me feel tacky, so I slipped off soon's I could and ran upstairs to the bathing room. I didn't fool around, though, turning on hot and cold water way I'd always done. Wasn't ten minutes before I was back on the veranda, and there was nobody around but Miss Amelia and a peg-leg old gentleman, so much white hair and beard his head looked like the great big power puff I'd just used. I started down those long wide steps on a slant, to keep out of sight, but Miss Amelia must've been watching for my shadow. She turned around before she could've heard my step.

"Why, Ora Fanning, you dear child!" she called and fluttered her hands at me. "Come here this minute. . . . I want to present Colonel Harper from New Bern. He's just been insisting I find a pretty girl for him. Now you two find a cool spot and make yourselves right at home while I . . ." Voice and hands fluttered away to greet another carriage full and I had to take the arm that old man offered. Had to sit between him and the Major at the table while they fought the Battle of Gettysburg with salt cellars, pepper shakers, knives, forks, spoons, and toothpicks, on the cloth in front of my plate. While Ellen and Charlotte and Mercer and Mistuh Humiston were having them a fine time up at the head with all those out-of-town people.

If Mistuh Humiston hadn't asked the blessing on all that food everybody but me seemed to enjoy, nobody would've known he was any less worldly than those other young men in sack coats and string ties. Some one of them must've teased him about his "r's" and he must've said what he'd said when I, and others, had mentioned them, that he'd come by them honestly because his paternal grandfather had been a Connecticut *Yankee*. Sound of that word, the Colonel's and the Major's ears perked up like setters', there was a lull in the battle, and I could hear Mistuh Humiston explain again how his grandfather'd come South in 1800, married a Carolina girl, bought slaves, and sent his son off to our cavalry on his own favorite mount. Everybody clapped, battle raged again, and all I could do rest of the meal was watch him laughing and talking.

When we got up from the table, Buddy and Mary Sue hurried around from their side and rescued me. But Colonel Harper was so long-winded, complimenting Buddy on his "lovely sister and most attentive young lady he'd ever had the good fortune to talk to," we were just the cow's tail of the tour Claiborne and Ellen seemed to be conducting to the pirate's cache on the river bank, the spot where the gold-handled Spanish swords had been dug up, the hole in the smokehouse wall a cannon ball from Fort Fisher had made, the wing of the house the Yankees had used for yellow fever and smallpox cases. How it happened Ellen and Mrs. Baker walked through the Exotic Gardens with Mistuh Humiston between them, I with Colonel Harper, I don't know. Just know I couldn't escape from the tiresome old fellow any more than from a bad dream. Nor hurry him up to make it a party of five. Ellen and Mrs. Baker darted like hummingbirds from plant to plant, sticking their noses in blossoms, breaking off bits of the japan all-spice and tea-olive leaves to hold under Mistuh Humiston's nose till they had it twitching like a rabbit's and I crept along at a snail's pace listening to a tale I'd known all my life about the ne'er-do-well Faircloth who'd run away to sea and brought all this "rare flora" from the Orient as a peace offering to his family.

When we got past the Chinese chestnuts at last, the other three were nowhere in sight but Lieu or Cap one was going about the lawn ringing a silver dinner bell and waving everybody up to the west veranda. The Colonel's old bones creaked bowing from the waist to me. He thanked me for the pleasure of my company, assured me that the doors of Holly House or some such place would be wide open should I ever visit New Bern, and "released me with reluctance to vie with my fair contemporaries in cutting Cupid's symbol from Miss Flower Abernathy's birthday cake, a surprise he, as a fellow house-guest, had been cognizant of all along but which he had kept a secret until this moment, as I could testify should the occasion arise in which his honor as a gentleman might be questioned. I must go right along now, not allow his physical disability, the result of no matter how glorious a cause, delay my participation in so momentous an augury for the happy future I so eminently deserved."

I hurried fast's I could without seeming to hurry, up, up, up that long flight of steps, stopped behind a pillar on the front veranda to catch my breath, then walked in a don't-care kind of way around the corner of the west parlor.

I the last. The cake more than two-thirds gone. Charlotte'd cut the coin, was biting it between her big white teeth, laughing around it. That other visiting girl was prancing up to this one and that one, giggling, pointing to the little bitty thimble on the tip of her little finger, saying, "Who'll teach me to sew a fine seam?" Mary Sue was feeding Buddy the frosting from her slice, and as I tried to get around the table to them, my sleeve brushed the back of Mistuh Humiston's coat. His head was bent toward Mrs. Baker's and she was saying something about a wife's gracious social manner being a great asset to any man. I was mighty glad I'd been gracious to her, Miss Tempy'd introduced us there by the steps.

143

"Why, Ora, honey, where've you been? Benton and I looked everywhere!"

"Who hasn't cut?" Claiborne called out, waving the cake-knife. "Still two full slices left and the ring's in one of them. Bessie Davis, you haven't!"

"And Ora, Claiborne! Here she is!" Mary Sue gave me a little push.

"Mary Sue, I really don't care—"

"Ora Fanning, of course!" Claiborne turned just as Bessie held out her hand and put the knife in mine. "You cut and take the slice falls to the right. All you all watch now, here's the county's next bride. Steady now, Ora."

I felt hot and outsized and the knife slipped, clicked on something. I laid it down and lifted the ring from the crumbs on the silver plate. It was a wedding band but it was brass.

"No fair, Ora," Bessie squealed. "You'd cut straight it would've been in my slice!"

But nobody paid her any attention. Claiborne threw her arms around me and kissed me. "Let me be maid of honor, Ora, hear?" And that was everybody's cue to offer felicitations, ask who the lucky man was, when the happy day would be. I heard Ellen say to one of the strange young men who was shaking my hand, "My own sistuh and she hasn't told me a word!" Then another hand was clasping mine but if *he* said anything I couldn't hear it above Flower Abernathy's, "Mistuh Humiston, isn't it a shame? *My* birthday and I've got no hope of being industrious, rich, or married!"

"Look, Ora, lissen!" Charlotte and Mercer were between him and me. "You don't mind if we change things around going home, do you? We all want to take the surrey, let Mama and them have the buggies. Be lots more fun. We can sing and—"

"It's all right with Brothuh Humiston, is with you," Mercer cut in.

❖   ❖   ❖

When Doctuh Willie stopped us at Brookside and I had to get out, Mistuh Humiston handed the reins back to Mercer and walked with me to the gate. But all he said as he shook my hand was "You'll be in my thoughts and my prayers, Miss Ora, rely on that."

It's just that we don't need words between us any more, I thought, going up those old sagging steps with Doctuh Willie.

144

Going up the steps of the jail with the jailer. Look at our getting off at Camilla. He didn't say, "I'm Miss Ora's escort today. I'll drive and she'll sit in front with me." When the surrey came up, he simply took my hand and helped me up on the front seat and Ellen and Charlotte and Mercer had to get in the back. And all the way between Camilla and Brookside he'd been as quiet as I was. He'd smiled a lot at the singing and foolishness going on behind us but I don't remember his making a single remark.

5

It was scarlet fever all right and both boys had it. Pretty bad, I thought. I stayed at Brookside eight nights and seven and a half days and I'd never left it. I wasn't Miss Fanning of Little Brookside. I wore her clothes Buddy brought over before church that Sunday but I was Miss Ryder's orphaned scapegoat, clenching my fists behind my back when she bothered to speak to me, answering meekly.

First thing she said was, looking me up and down after Doctuh Willie'd gone, "Quite the lady, are you not? Pity you've been too engrossed with your toilette lately to do your duty by your little step-cousins. If you could've thought of someone save yourself, they wouldn't have run away to play with their maternal white trash cousins and contracted this loathsome illness, and you'd be free now to continue your recessive pursuit of that sanctified firebrand who has won, if not wooed, your maidenly heart. . . . Oh, yes, he has, Ora Fanning! I saw that the minute I saw you two together. I've been clairvoyant since childhood and you've ever been one of my most rewarding subjects. I had to restrain my laughter here the other evening when Ellen said how glad she was you were taking an interest in church work because it gave you something to talk about more interesting than housework. But you'll never get him, my dear. You'll be silent when you should speak, step backward when you should step forward. You always have stumbled over your own feet and you always will."

I didn't stumble over them then. I turned on my heel and went upstairs, my head as high and my shoulders as straight as hers could be.

Buddy came back early Monday morning with a message from Mistuh Humiston. Should the committee go ahead with the

145

plans for the League social Friday night? Said he'd prefer it postponed unless I could be sure of release by then. I told Buddy tell him to go ahead. Everybody knew who was to give what refreshments and if I had to stay here more than two, three days, I'd be taken out headfirst. Buddy said he'd come nurse himself before he'd let a thing like that happen to me.

Except for the smallpox case I'd nursed in this very back room, the twins were the sickest children I'd ever seen, spite of Doctuh Willie's saying they had a mild case of the fever. They were as grateful for every cold cloth I laid on their scorching foreheads, every cup of cold water I held to their parched lips, every stroke of my hand on their aching backs and legs, as those mangy pups in the back yard were for every scrap I threw to them. No father would've been kinder—or more helpless—than Vin, getting between me and the bed when one of them wanted to throw up, spilling the luke-warm soup Miss Ryder sent up over the one good counterpane I tried to keep spotless for Doctuh Willie's calls, leaning against the doorjamb sucking on his corncob and scowling, trying to remember the point of jokes he'd heard time he ran away and worked as cabin boy on a blockader. Made me sad just looking at Vin, slouching round the house like the caged animal Miss Ryder'd made of him since the day he'd married that poor-white Mattie at the point of her pappy's old army rifle. When I could make myself look at his eyes the color of Miss Ryder's I was always surprised to find Grandpa's kindness in them. Vin loved those boys all right. Told me many a time that week he'd never forget what I'd done for them and if ever in this world there was any favor he could do me, I just had to let him know it.

Slippy came over that Tuesday with a basket he said Miss Ellen and Old Lady had fixed up and when I took off the cloth and saw the edge of a letter, tucked between a fruit jar of cream and a bowl of custard, was all I could do keep from snatching it out. I said it all looked mighty good, maybe the boys could eat a little of the custard now the rash was out and the fever down a little, and told him to tell Lucille she was to go on and finish up that soap making. Said he'd tell her to do that very thing soon's she finished helping Miss Ellen pack. . . . Yesum, I'd certainly have to ex-cuse him. Miss Ellen told him to tell me first thing she was going to town to visit with Miss Charlotte two, three days. Was there anything he could get for me when he drove her in after dinner? I said, "No," then, "Wait a minute,

146

maybe this letter needed an answer." I set the basket down and pulled out the letter. Slippy asked did I think it had bad news in it, way I looked at the en-velope? I said of course not, was from Cousin Sudie, and why was he standing there waiting?

Miss Ryder opened the crack in the back door she'd been peeping through, asked who I was getting a letter from, and why didn't I read it, give her something to think about besides misery? I dropped the letter in my apron pocket, said it 'ud have to wait till I tried to tempt the boys with a little bit of this custard, but she could have all else in the basket. Didn't think of the letter again till it fell out of my pocket when I started to lie down on Ma's death-bed after dinner while the boys slept. Was dated three days after Ellen'd left Savannah. I remember it word for word.

"Dearest Cousin Ora," it said. "You'll be surprised to receive a letter from me right after Cousin Ellen's arrival with all the news about us but I feel I must write now so that you can take up the responsibility I must relinquish. As you know, I have always felt that you two girls are my own daughters (in spite of the little we see of you) and I can't bear to see one of you do a foolish thing. Mr. Graham tells me *I'm* foolish to think for a minute Cousin Ellen will refuse Mr. Stephen Clay's hand but Cousin Ellen's as close-mouthed a little prattler, if you understand what I mean, as I've ever known and I can't help but be nervous. When she upset me so saying she had to go home three weeks before her visit was out, I asked her right out why she wouldn't say 'yes' to Mr. Clay. She laughed and said a girl has a perfect right to dangle men on her line since they have every other advantage. Now Cousin Ellen's a coquette like every other pretty girl but she's not heartless and that statement wasn't like her—she was just trying to throw me off. Surely it can't be that young Mr. Williams from whom she received a few letters when she was here! She told me she was mighty fond of him but admitted, when I let my manners go with the wind and pressed her, that he has nothing but what he can scrape together from his shrimp business. Now don't think me callous, Cousin Ora, I'm as romantic as they come. But putting aside all that Mr. Clay has to offer (he inherited from his Uncle Stephen who went North years before the war and made a fortune he left up there), he is handsome and charming—and so generous nobody holds it against him that his money wasn't here to be lost with our Cause. Of course old Mrs. Clay dotes on him and would continue to live at The Crescent after his marriage and I can appreciate you girls' wanting homes entirely your own after all you've been through at Brookside but I can't believe that is what's bothering Cousin Ellen. She loves you devotedly and maybe she has given you her confidence but whether she has or not, I do hope you will use your influence to help her make up her mind. Mr. Clay's as much in love as any man I ever saw but these girls down here won't let the grass grow under their feet now that Cousin Ellen's left the pasture clear. . . ."

Well, Cousin Sudie's at ease now, I thought, and skimmed over the insistence that I write her as soon as I could. She'll be the first to know when Mistuh Clay gets Ellen's acceptance, even if Ellen didn't tell her in *her* letter.

It poured Wednesday, Thursday, and Friday, was cold and damp as only that old house could be. But Vin kept a fire going for us and I kept the boys amused cutting out hats, boats, and dancing-dolls from the copies of *The Argus* I'd found in the gardenhouse. Amused me cutting the print so that an account of Mistuh Humiston's marrying a country couple, baptizing an infant, conducting a funeral, preaching from this or that text, came exactly in the middle of a tri-corner hat, a boat, or a lady. Friday Doctuh Willie was mighty apologetic bout asking me to stay on till Sunday but said he didn't feel right either leaving scarlet fever convalescents in inexperienced hands in such weather. I told him it was all right, now that we couldn't have the League lawn-party, if I could go early Sunday in time for church. He scratched his beard, cleared his throat, said that gave him two hard things to say, patted my shoulder. Said he wasn't actually worried bout my having caught the fever—thought all that iron in my system from drinking rusty-nail water he'd prescribed during the war'd toughened my system enough to resist smallpox and lesser diseases—but he did think it best for me to stay home the next ten days. And, I mustn't be alarmed now, but he did want me to keep an eye on Benton, not let him work too hard, see that he got plenty sleep, plenty buttermilk and eggs. Now, now, might be he just *looked* puny, but he couldn't help noticing, stopping at Little Brookside Wednesday, that Benton's clothes hung too loose on him and he seemed to lack the get-up-and-get you'd expect in a prospective bridegroom. Lacked it, that was, till he'd tried to thump his chest, then got mad's a hornet—if a young man could do that and still be polite to an old one. Kept telling me not to cry, might be nothing atall, nothing atall but spring fever. But when I told him bout my worry all spring, he said he'd look Buddy over on his way back that day if he had to get Slippy to hold him.

Halfway down the stairs, he turned and came back, gave me a handful of pretty, colored Bible Scene cards Mistuh Humiston'd sent the boys and a message for me. He was praying daily for their quick recovery and my release from the strain of nursing.

❖

First thing I asked Buddy when we started home Sunday after dinner was whether Doctuh Willie'd stopped by Friday. He said he had but was while he was in town and he wished Doctuh Willie'ud wait till patients came to his office, not go running them down. Said if it would ease my mind, he'd confess he *had* gone, few days before popping the question to Mary Sue, because he hadn't felt up to scratch those first hot days, but Doctuh Willie must've been out scouting then. He'd waited an hour in that musty old office. No, he hadn't gone in the house and asked Miss Katy anything. If Doctuh Willie was taking a nap, was his hard luck losing a half-dollar. And no, he hadn't gone back since because he felt fine now and if he looked skinny, how'd that okra and that potato field look and how much Spanish moss could I find on those swamp oaks?

I asked him if he'd gone to prayer meeting Wednesday night and he said no, Mary Sue wouldn't't've expected him in all that downpour. After a minute he said Ellen and Charlotte had gone and there was such a handful, the Parson had invited them all to the parsonage to have a responsive reading around his fire and then they'd all gone in the kitchen—Miss Parker, Sistuh Wendel, Old Dummy Sayer, and all—and had a candy pull. Seemed Parson'd just got a keg of molasses from his old home. Ellen'd brought a few pieces of the candy home for us to taste and wasn't bad, considering all the cooks. Funny, after all the high-faluting shindigs Ellen'd been to in Savannah she should enjoy a parsonage candy pull but said she had.

"Sistuh"—Buddy slipped the reins to his left hand, put his right on my knee—"you mind telling me—I don't like asking. Think you'd tell me a thing like that quick's I told you bout Mary Sue and me. Maybe it's because I have got Mary Sue, I feel extra responsible for yours and Ellen's happiness—has the Parson asked you to marry him?"

"Not yet, Buddy. And I will tell you soon's he does. He told me Saturday he was just waiting for God's voice and asked me to bear with him."

Buddy took the reins in both hands and slapped Madam to a trot.

"You needn't be concerned bout me any more than about Ellen. I reckon we're both taken care of." I remembered Cousin Sudie's letter and took it out of my reticule. "Here's more about Mistuh Stephen Clay than Ellen's bothered to tell us. Let Madam walk, I'll read it to you."

❖ ❖ ❖

I got out at the hitching post and went in the front way. Ellen's old maroon cape she wore in the rain was thrown across the ladderback chair in the passage—just where she'd dropped it when she'd come home yesterday. I ran a finger down the table leg and it left a bright streak. I could hardly see the bouquet in the glass bell. Suppose Mistuh Humiston should come out today —and I supposed he would. Surely God wouldn't keep him waiting long's *he'd* kept me!

I heard Ellen's laugh, set my grip down at the foot of the stairs, and went to the shutter-door. Blades wide open to let in the flies! I peeped through.

"Thought you told me Joel had been baptized." Ellen on the kitchen stoop, still wearing her white dotted swiss, the skirt turned back and pinned up around her waist to take the place of an apron.

"Were, Miss Ellen, were, but hit didn't take. He ma say he been badder, anything. So's I'm aiming get him under onct more, Jesus willing." Old Lady decked out for meeting, began clapping her hands, singing, "Chicken in the bread tray picking up the dough, Granny, your dog bite? No, child, no" and Joel did a double-shuffle, bobbing his head and putting on.

"Well," Ellen said, "don't you let that preacher drop him. He's black enough now without any river mud on him, aren't you, Joel Jefferson Evans?"

150

"Yesum, reckon is." He pranced up and down rolling his eyes, showing off.

"My preacher ain't uhgoing drap Joel Jefferson, Miss Ellen. Baptist preachers they knows how. Be that Methodist beau-preacher come round here, I'd find me a rope and holt on to my boy-baby, he hist him down to the water." Old Lady's thin body bent like a wire with her cackling.

"Better go on then or that Methodist beau-preacher'll be here using my sprinkling can." Ellen waved the dish towel and went back in the kitchen.

Now why hadn't Buddy told me Mistuh Humiston was coming? He must've taken the message. Or if Ellen had, she could've taken the pains to tell Buddy to tell me. All that dust in the passage. I felt like calling Lucille to get right out of that wagon, come back and do her work. What had Old Lady left for supper?

"Sistuh!" Ellen set the kettle back on the stove, ran and put her arms round me. "I didn't hear you come in! Saw Buddy drive to the stable and thought you hadn't got away. I've missed you like everything! How're the boys?"

I pulled away from her. "You'll muss your dress more than you have already, pinning it up like that." I got a clean apron from the cupboard drawer and handed it to her. "Boys'll be all right now I reckon. Doctuh Willie says I saved them from complications."

"From death itself maybe! How was it over there?" She lifted the kettle again and poured water, barely steaming, over the dishes in the pan.

"Just as ever. Nothing plentiful but rain water." Wash them anyway you like. I've got to get at that passage.

"You must be starved. Sit down here at the end of the table. I'll get you some chicken and rice and everything while these things soak." She started for the safe.

"No, you go on with the dishes. I couldn't eat a bite. Still feel the sick room all through me." I took off my hat and rubbed my hand over my forehead.

"Sistuh, *you're* not getting it! You feel feverish?" She lifted her dripping hands, reached for the towel. "Let me feel you."

I waved her away. "Doctuh Willie says I'm tough. Puny's I was as a child, I slept with a case of smallpox and didn't catch it, I'm not going to—"

"What on earth're you talking bout, slept with a case of small-pox?"

"You were too little to remember time Miss Ryder put that child, all broken out, right in bed with me."

"Why, Sistuh, even Miss Ryder'd never do a thing like that. Must've been one of your nightmares."

"I know the difference between bad dreams and what happened!" I snapped. "That sorry old overseer of Miss Ryder's in Florida came by one day right after the surrender. Had his wife and a wagonload of children going back North. Miss Ryder took thum all in to spend the night and put that child—"

"But she couldn't've known it had smallpox."

"She knew it had a high fever and was broken out all over, poor little thing. I was up all night getting her water she'd throw up again right away."

"Sistuh, please." Ellen made a face.

"I'm just trying to prove to you I'm not telling a story. Ellen, do be careful with Ma's Blue Willow."

"I believe you. And I'll be careful if you'll go on upstairs and take a nap. You'll feel better."

"Not till I've dusted the passage you should've got Lucille at yesterday. Nice day like this again, can't tell who'll be dropping in."

"I can tell you one who's coming but he won't see the dust."

I stared at her like I didn't suspect a thing.

She looked up from the plate she was *polishing*. " 'Brothuh' Humiston, silly."

"Oh. Baby, I think you should stop calling him 'Brothuh' *that way*. He doesn't like it." I took the towel from her arm and the cup she'd just rinsed.

She bit her lip and I waited. She laughed. "Course Charlotte-and-Mercer may come too. After their drive. I'm beginning to think I'm a better matchmaker than Cousin Sudie. Worked hard all week, complimenting Charlotte to Mercer and getting nowhere. Then I sicked two gay-dogs—drummers staying at Miss Winnie's she brought to the League social—why, what's the matter?"

I swallowed. "League social?"

"Didn't Buddy tell you we had it? Bessie said we'd have to, all the cakes made and the ice coming on Friday's boat. Sistuh, don't look like that. Nobody thought it'ud rain *all* week and you sent word to go on with it. Had to have it inside the Garrison. Filthiest place you ever saw. Think we gave it the first cleaning since the Occupation used it for a court room. Pushed back all the benches and 'Brothuh' Humiston conducted a mock trial—old Sistuh Wendel told him just how that Yankee officer acted when he called her up because she wouldn't give his men her pet rooster they took anyway. But what I was telling you—I sicked those two drummers on Charlotte and she led thum a chase! First thing you knew, Mercer was on their heels. I tell you, Sistuh, men are sheep. Let one start after a girl, all follow. Last hour we played games, Mercer was Charlotte's partner and before we left—"

"You take the drummers?"

She handed me another cup. "No, I fixed one—named Sharpe and looking it—up with Bessie Davis. I told him he'd get a big order from Mistuh Brax, he was nice to his daughter. Other one with that youngest Carroll girl. She's grown up since I left! Dress touched the floor. And—"

"Who was your partner?"

"Oh, Mistuh Dade, Mistuh Jim, 'Brothuh' Humiston—I certainly made myself the odd one."

"Well, I don't reckon you cared—little old League social." I flung the towel over her shoulder and started for the door. If she didn't think Mistuh Humiston's message was important enough to tell me, I certainly wouldn't ask her.

"Mistuh Humiston tell you after church—bout coming out today?" I turned around at the door.

"Um-m." She glanced up at the clock and began drying knives and forks. Fast. "I hate to get caught washing dishes."

He's coming early then and I should take a nap! "When's he coming? Just what'd he say?"

"Heavens, Sistuh, I don't remember his exact words. Something bout having to conduct one of those Methodist class-meetings at half-past six and asked if I'd mind his being unfashionable and coming out between two and three." She lifted the plates and carried them to the cupboard.

"*You'd* mind?"

She closed the cupboard and began untying the apron strings, "Well, he said *you,* speaking to *me.* But I know he'll want to see you too. Asked if you were expected home today and said he must give you a verbatim account of the social."

"Now, baby, why couldn't you've told me that?"

"Just didn't think."

"But you spoke 'sthough he was calling on *you.*"

"Why not on me?" She dropped the apron on the chair.

153

"Why—why—because you're an engaged girl. Because—"

"But he's a preacher and I'm a church member. Just back from a long absence. Maybe he wants to inquire into my spiritual state. Might even want to pray with me." She grasped the dishpan handles.

"Well, maybe." I stepped across the threshold. No time to wait for more hot water. I'd just sponge off in cold.

"Sistuh!"

"What is it now, baby?" I looked back. Her hands were still on the handles but she hadn't lifted the pan. She was gazing down into that greasy water 'sthough it was a pretty pool.

"I was just wondering—was it you told 'Brothuh' Humiston I was engaged to a rich Savannahian?" She looked up at me but her eyes weren't accusing or anything.

"Why, baby, I—I—"

She laughed. "It doesn't matter. He thinks I'm a worldly little hussy anyway."

It sounded like a question so I told her I didn't think he thought that exactly. Just that she was full of spirit. More likely he wanted to talk to her because of Mercer and did he know she *had* told Mercer.

"He certainly does and a lot more than that. He knows I'm not playing 'ducks and drakes' with that rich Savannahian's heart!"

"Well, I'm glad you've come out with it. Couldn't see any point your keeping it a secret, so much to be done between now and next April. Hope you told Cousin Sudie, that letter you wrote her. You knew I had one from her? Asked me to use my influence—"

"She would! Poor Cousin Sudie. All her dreams gone up the chimney. Sistuh! I've got it! Les both of us go visit her this fall. She can double matchmake!"

I just stared.

"Oh, I know I should've told you right away. But I get so tired being probed about everything, you and Buddy acting like my mother and father." She left the dishpan where it was, picked up the towel, wiped her hands, flung the towel at the apron dangling on the chair, and faced me defiantly. "I *did* write Stephen Clay I'd marry him. But I tore it up and wrote him I still wasn't sure. Friday at Charlotte's I wrote him I never could. That's right. Look astonished. Shocked. But don't ask me *why*. Because I don't *know*. He's everything I told you he is."

154

She laughed in a funny way, fished in her sleeve for her hand-kerchief, dabbed at her eyes. "I *don't* know—unless it's because his nose is too little!" She ran past me, across the entry, and the shutter-door banged.

I knew. Knew more than she did and the truth seemed to split me in two, way Slippy's ax split a pine log.

I got up from that chair finally, picked up the crumpled apron and dish towel and hung them on their pegs.

Must've been an hour before I left the kitchen. I didn't look at the clock. Didn't look at what my hands were doing. My feet moved from stove to table to cupboard to safe, following the de-pression Old Lady's mother'd outlined on new pine boards when she cleared up after the first meal she cooked for Ellen Benton Fanning. I emptied the dish water on Ellen Evans Fan-ning's petunia bed. If I'd carried it fifty more paces I could've thrown it over Bonny hitched to the post. I heard me laugh. Imagine them driving off, strings of green sallet festooned in that shiny harness, a wishbone caught in the crowpiece, garden-peas peppering Bonny's slick coat. I took the pan of scraps to the chicken yard, watched roosters and hens and fryers stop their aimless scratching and run to my feet, heard their Sunday-quiet cluckings become everyday squabbling. I went back through the kitchen and saw it as spic and span as Old Lady'd ever left it.

I tiptoed across the entry. I opened the shutter-door without making a sound. I tiptoed down the passage. I stopped at the foot of the stairs. I listened. I heard the wall clock's ticking. I heard no voices. I tiptoed to the front shutters. I put my finger beneath the end of a rod and I tilted the blades.

A foot to the right or the left and I couldn't have seen. Not between those thick-leaved branches. I did see because of the leaves that had been bruised and broken when that limb had come down. I saw Ellen's head. It was tilted backward. I saw Mistuh Humiston's face. It hovered over Ellen's face.

I closed my eyes. I *tried* to keep them closed. I *tried* to move away.

I saw his hand, white against green, slip up to the back of Ellen's head. I saw Ellen's hand spread on his shoulder, white against black. I saw light hair against dark. I saw lips pressed to lips.

They say hearts throb and break. My hands clutched at my stomach.

❖

Mocking birds sang and fluttered above me and a twig fell on my cheek. I didn't brush it off. Let more fall. Let all the leaves of oaks that never shed fall now. Let them cover me. Let me never be missed. Never be found. Let me not be.

Am I now? The few in all this world who sometimes know there is an Ora Fanning residing at Little Brookside on the old road to Shallotte, sistuh to Benton and Ellen Fanning, do not know it now. Benton, his arm around Mary Sue's waist behind the smilax, does not know it. Ellen and Mistuh Humiston, driving fast for the willow screen at Ship's Folly, do not know it. If the twins are not fretting, if my name is not mentioned between two rocking on some veranda, if my image does not glide in and out of somebody's Sunday dozing, I am not. If I could press harder, maybe this earth would open, enfold me, close over me, and this long grass Slippy never remembers to cut would wave over me, forever and forever.

Why didn't I think, oh, why didn't I think? I could have crept around that way as well as around this. I could have stretched out in *that* long grass, just outside the gate. Hoofs and wheels went right over it, way he turned. He wouldn't have seen me in time to stop. He would've had to lift my bruised and broken body. . . .

When I stood up, my shadow stretched far ahead of me and I followed it between the magnolias to the steps. I passed him and me sitting there. He opened the shutter-door for me to come out and I went in. I *had* to get in now as a long time ago I had had to get out to hide in the long grass behind the summerhouse. At the top of the stairs I shook off Ellen's hand but I agreed with her. Agreed with her in a shout that rang through the silent, empty house: "No, he's not my preacher! He's not my preacher! He's not my preacher! Oh—oh—oh—"

"Sistuh, please come out of this hot old room. Let me help you back to yours. It's cool in there, all that mag—all the shade that side of the house."

"Oh—oh—oh—oh—"

156

"Why, you haven't touched your coffee! I'll go get you another cup. Molly's keeping it hot, not a one of the girls down yet."

"No, no, no, just leave me alone, oh—oh—oh—"

"But, Sistuh, you'll smother in here. I wish you felt like coming down to the porch. It's real cool out there. And not much passing yet. I think I'll take the snaps and butterbeans out there to do, give Molly a little help with all the fresh vegetables were sent in yesterday. Just let me—"

"Go away, away, go away, oh—oh—oh—oh—"

"Well, if I can't do anything to ease you—I'll leave this door open, let in a little air."

"No, no, no, close it, close it, oh—oh—oh—"

Just like the first time. Ellen always coming, going, coming. Twenty-five years, talking, talking, talking, never saying what she means, what she's thinking . . .

"Sistuh, get up, it's late," she said that Sunday twilight. "We drove to Ship's Folly. Brothuh Humiston wanted to see it. Sistuh, you asleep? Wake up. He has to go and he wants to see you." She put her hand on my head. "You're sick! Your head's hot." She lifted my hand. "Your hand's cold as ice! Sistuh!"

I didn't move or open my eyes.

"I'll go tell Brothuh Humiston to get Doctuh Willie. You stay right still. I'll be right back, help you undress."

Running down the stairs, running up. "Sistuh, he'll go right away. Says he'll find Doctuh Willie wherever he is. But he wants just a word with you first, you feel like seeing him. He's mighty upset."

But I lay without moving a muscle. She shook my shoulder gently. She lifted my hand again, felt my pulse, and laid it back on the counterpane like she was afraid she'd break it. Then she ran downstairs again. Away from me like I was poisonous. Poisonous to her happiness. Way she's running downstairs *this* day.

6

I couldn't get up that Tuesday and Buddy came in the house in the middle of the morning and straight upstairs. He tilted the shutters till he got some light on my face, took my arm from across my eyes.

"I'm going in town for Doctuh Willie again. Hush, not a word. How do you think I'm going to run this place without you? Not once since we moved here have you laid down on me. Not once had an ache or a pain you'd admit to, no matter how hard you worked. Yesterday I was ready to agree with him it was nervous exhaustion, all you needed was twenty-four hours rest. Now I'm damned if I know what ails you but it's *bodily*— you pale's a ghost and your eyes look sick. Just like Betsy's calf when that wildcat got through with it. And when I get Doctuh Willie here, remember your manners. Don't keep your mouth tight's a clam's and don't stare at this footboard like you're hypnotized. Let him see your tongue. Tell him right out where you hurt and whether your bowels've moved, he asks you that again. And if he doles out a dose of calomel, you take it, you hear?"

"I'll try, Buddy," and I looked him straight in the eye.

He knew! I wanted to raise my arms, put them around him, put my head on his shoulder, and tell him how it hurt. But for all his bossy talk, he had to shift his eyes. He reached down and squeezed my toes under the sheet and counterpane, and walked out, his shoulders drooping way I'd never seen them.

Doctuh Willie didn't give me calomel. He had more sense than all the other doctuhs Ellen and Brothuh David've called in since. He just kept coming out once or twice a week, sitting by my bed, stroking his beard, telling me bout other sicknesses —cases he was curing, cases stumped him—patting my hand, saying he would keep right on coming tiring me out with his talk till day he came I met him at the door and shooed him away. Time he told me when I felt strong enough to get up, I must help him get Buddy down for a rest in bed, I thought for a minute I was coming back to myself. I didn't, much as I wanted to. Another minute and his words were just sounds, no meaning in them.

Ellen was in and out all those weeks that weren't divided into days and hours, just light or dark. Bringing me this and bringing me that somebody'd sent or brought out or Old Lady'd made to tempt my appetite but I didn't say a word to her I didn't have to and what I had to say was "no." No, I can't touch it. No, I don't want it. No, I won't see him.

At night when Mistuh Humiston'd finished his courting and gone, Ellen'ud come tiptoeing up the stairs, stand in the oblong of light from the bracket lamp in the passage, and stare at my

158

head on the pillow, trying to see if my eyes were open, trying to pretend she thought I was asleep. If there'd been a thunder storm or if a breeze'd sprung up, she'd tiptoe to the bed like she was walking on broken glass. She'd lift the summer quilt from the footboard, spread it over the counterpane up to my waist, and go out again, still on tiptoe but like she'd crushed all the glass and wasn't afraid of its cutting any more.

And every night she came that way, the same horrible thought came in my head like a dream you dream over and over again and can't get rid of no matter how hard you try. Always the same words like something I'd memorized for school way back there when I'd been *happy* living at Brookside. Suppose one night I should lie absolutely still till she bends over me spreading that quilt and then suppose I should jump at her, grab her soft white throat in my two hands, pull her down, twist her backwards across my knees, hold her there till she's black in the face, and say to her what I cannot say in daylight or lamplight. If she did not die of fright, she would live to know what I think of her and of her simpering pretensions of not knowing what she'd done to me.

Was during the light time, must've been a Sunday, Ellen and Mistuh Humiston, Mary Sue and Buddy, were down there on the veranda, end nearest my room, and I heard Ellen say plain's could be, "Les have a double wedding!" Says to this day she never even thought of such a thing because they'd all put wedding plans out of their minds till I was well, or a lot better. But I know I heard it. I don't make things up no matter what they say. And I knew Buddy's leaving me for Mary Sue was more than I could stand then, more than any mortal woman should be asked to stand, and I felt like I was in a deep pit I couldn't get out of but had to. And then something seemed to push and I pulled and pulled and after a while I held my right wrist in my other hand to steady it and managed to get the saucer Ellen'd left on my table on to the side of the bed. Was syllabub and was full of Captain Ives' old brandy Miss Callie and Mary Sue tasted only on his birthdays when they drank a toast to his memory. I ate it all and was the first thing I'd tasted except kettle tea and dry toast since I'd left Brookside.

Wasn't long after that, one July day after dinner, Mistuh Humiston came. I was sitting up, in my wrapper. He wouldn't listen to Ellen any more saying I was too sick to see him. He ran up the steps and came right in and he had a little white

package in his hand tied with a white ribbon. He knelt down
by my chair. I told him to go away. I told him he couldn't pray
with me because God wouldn't hear him because he wouldn't
hear God when He had tried and tried to speak to him. He said
he didn't want to pray. He said anybody who could accept God's
will as I had, without complaint though it had led me into the
shadow of death, was a saint and didn't need the prayers of a
miserable, stumbling sinner such as he felt himself to be. And
he untied the little package and took out a gold thimble and
put it on my right forefinger. He said Ellen had told him I insisted I was strong enough to begin her sewing and only gold
would do for such unselfish fingers. He said I mustn't call him
Mistuh Humiston any more, but Brothuh David. Said I must
think of his and Ellen's home, in whatever parsonage, as mine
as much as Little Brookside was. Then he put his arm around
me and kissed me and if that was a brothuh's kiss . . .

———————◆———————

"Oh—oh—oh—"

"Deeda, you mind if I leave this door open just a little so I
can see to bring you this coffee?"

"Oh—oh—oh—who is it?"

"Me—Ann Wesley. Here, Deeda, take this spoon. Molly said
be careful, it's still boiling hot. Oh!"

"Baby, I didn't mean to burn you, oh—oh—oh, didn't mean to
knock your hand away. You know your Deeda wouldn't hurt
you, don't you, baby? Oh—oh—oh—"

"Yes. Deeda. It'll be all right. I'll put some soda on it. Can't
you take a sip even?"

"No, no, I don't want it."

"I'll put it here on the floor by you. Maybe you can just
taste it after while. It didn't all spill. I have to go take a book
back to the library. I hope you'll feel better."

"Oh—oh—oh—baby, wait a minute. What day of the month
is it?"

"It's the twenty-fifth, August the twenty-fifth, nineteen hundred and nine, Mama's and Papa's twenty-fifth wedding anniversary. We're all so sorry you didn't get well so we could—"

"No, baby, your Mama and Papa're not sorry. Oh—oh—oh—
they'd rather have me off up here in this stinking old storeroom
out of their way. Oh, oh, oh, I knew it was August twenty-fifth.
I don't know how but I did. Oh—oh—oh, baby, my life'ud make

160

a book if I could write it all down way I can see it . . . Oh, oh, oh, nobody'll ever know what I've suffered . . . oh—oh—oh—"

"No. Deeda. I'll have to hurry now, library's just open in summer nine to ten on Wednesdays. I hope you'll feel better, I come back."

"Oh—oh—oh—baby, wait. Your Papa home yet?"

"No, Deeda, but he will be this evening. I hope he won't have prayer meeting, though, now the reception's— Good-bye, Deeda. I'll come up again soon's I get back."

Yes, he went off to the District Conference two, three days ago. Just came to my door, carrying his valise, said he hoped I'd be feeling better when he got back, but I could hear him down there in the hall telling the others good-bye, kissing *them,* promising to be home early's he could on the twenty-fifth. Ann Wesley, just now, scared she'd said something wrong, mentioning the reception. I know they're accusing me of putting a stop to all their big plans. I don't want to interfere with their good times. That's why I came way off here across the porch, this old blood-stained storeroom nobody ever comes to, where they can't hear me. I know they can't no matter what Ellen says.

They think I cry this way out of meanness, say I've got no consideration for them. It's they've got none for me, no understanding all I've been through. I can't help it when all the suffering gathers up in one big wave and pulls me under, washes away such moorings as I've got. Always makes me feel like that little old sailboat, nobody knew whose, used to be on Brunswick Sound, floating round aimlessly every high wind because nobody bothered to tie it up properly after they'd had the use of it. Girls were little things, seemed like they were my ties. Now I've got none atall, Ann Wesley and Gladys growing up, getting indifferent as the rest. Ellen's turned them against me, all I've done and do for them. Couldn't be content being Mama and Mrs. Humiston, having Brothuh David to herself at night. Had to come between him and me some way I'll never understand, take away the little I did have, turn him against me too when he finally heard God's voice and knew the mistake he'd made. I was as mean Ellen thinks I am, I'd have told her long ago . . .

"Oh—oh—oh—oh—"

"Deeda—"

"Oh—oh—oh—oh—" Now they'll all come, asking how I feel, poking that old nervine at me, get me quiet so they can forget I'm living.

161

"Come, let me help you back to your room. Your bed's all made up with clean, cool sheets and I've got an ice compress in there to put on your head. Then I'll shave some ice and make you a pineapple sherbet—your throat must be parched. Just let me—"

"No, no, no, Beth. Have some mercy on me. Oh—oh—oh—I can't rest in that room, those old magnolia leaves tap, tap, tapping gainst the screens, making me see and remember—"

"They're not tapping this morning, Deeda. There's not a breath of air stirring. Come, let me help you—"

"Oh—oh—oh— Your Papa home yet?"

"Not yet. I hope Mistuh Jennings' machine hasn't broken down."

"Oh—oh—oh— I didn't want you to give up your plans for the reception. Many's the time your Mama and Papa've gone on with whatever they wanted to do, no matter how sick and helpless I was."

"They're not tonight, Deeda. Mama said there'd be no pleasure in it, your feeling this way."

"Oh—oh—oh—that's not what she said to me yesterday—or the day before. Said she did think I'd have some consideration for you if I hadn't any for her and Brothuh David. Your giving up your visit to Boston, coming straight home from summer school just to help thum celebrate. Oh—oh—oh— She'll never learn I can't help these times any more than I could help breaking my wrist or having that awful carbuncle or getting burnt time that vapor lamp exploded when you children had whooping cough. Oh—oh—oh—why I have to bear all I do—"

"Come now, Deeda. When you're in bed, I'll rub your back with alcohol and you can tell me everything. That's right, hold to my arm—"

"Deeda—"

"Fair, for heaven's sake, get out of here!"

"I just came to show her my ring. Mama said—"

"I don't care what Mama said. Get out! How can I—?"

"Oh—oh—oh, there you go, talking above my head like I was a stick of wood. Come back, baby. What ring?"

"My engagement ring. Can you see it? From Bob. I just got it last night."

"How long've you known him, baby?"

"Just since I came home in June, Deeda. You remember him.

162

He was around a lot first of the summer. Came here in the spring. He's a lawyer. From Henderson."

"A whirlwind courtship, just like your Mama's. Oh—oh—oh— you're more like your Mama used to be than any of the rest. . . . Oh—oh—oh I'm so glad it's a ring, not a thimble. Oh—oh— oh—what'm I saying . . . you all mix me up so, running in here—oh, oh, oh . . ."

"You're exhausted, Deeda. Please come with me now. Fair, you get on that side. Maybe we—"

"No, no, no, leave me alone. Oh—oh—oh— Leave me alone, alone, alone. There's something I've got to do today I can't think, you children tugging at me. . . . Oh—oh—oh—"

PART TWO
ELLEN

CHAPTER I

1

NICE RIPE WATUHMEL-ONS TEN CENTS. CANTALOUPES FIVE cents, two for five. Nice ripe— Whooa dere. Nice sweet watuhmelon, lady? Ten cents—"

"No thank, you, Uncle. We're well supplied today."

"Yes, m'am, thank you kindly. Get up. Nice ripe watuhmelons . . ."

Now how many times will I have to leave my chair to refuse to buy something this morning? I didn't think I could be seen at this end of the porch. My moonvine's thinning faster than I thought. Still, it's more peaceful out here, looking between the holly trees at the old pink brick of the Wright mansion across this shady street, hearing all the summer morning sounds— hawkers calling, little boys shouting and running after the ice-wagon, little girls practicing their scales all down the block— than it is inside, hearing Sistuh's moaning. As I have heard it for fifteen years . . . Ann Wesley, always the first one down. No shining morning face but looking right nice in that light blue cambric, dark blue hair ribbons on her looped-up braids.

"Well, baby. Where're you off to? Don't bang the screen door!"

"Library, I suppose. I'm going to get another one of George Eliot's novels. Beth says Miss Arundel's antediluvian saying I shouldn't read thum because George Eliot was an immoral woman. Besides, Miss Arundel won't be my English teacher next year."

"Did you take some coffee up to Deeda?"

"Yesum, but she wouldn't drink it. She pushed the cup away and spilled a lot of it. Burnt my hand. It's all right now though —Molly put wet soda on it."

"Well, if she wouldn't drink it for you, she won't for anybody. Unless Beth—"

"Beth's up there now. Fair, too—showing her her ring. Oh! I

forgot something I meant to do. I'll leave the door open and you listen."

And be glad to. I don't want to think today—unless I can think of happy memories. That was the trouble with Sistuh when she was young, always remembering sadness. Ma's death, Miss Ryder's meanness . . .

Dum dum de *dum,* dum dum de *dum,* da, da de *dum,* dum de dum dum de dum . . .

Why the child should know better than to play that today! Who knows but that Sistuh's well aware what day this is? There's no telling what she thinks about, shut off to herself week after week. But all the girls know she won't go to a church wedding, won't even be a witness for a hurried parsonage marriage if two others can be found in the house or neighborhood. No. I won't stop the child. She's got her foot on the soft pedal. Had it there too much of the time all her life. Sistuh hears the piano now, I don't know what difference it'll make. She can't be much worse than she's been the last five weeks. Besides, Ann Wesley's playing it for me and I should have some pleasure this day.

Wedding March from "Lohengrin." I thought it was beautiful the two or three times I heard it that winter in Savannah, played on a pipe organ by a real musician, but it never sounded so sweet as it did the day poor little Miss Taffy—Miss Daffy-Taffy—pumped it out of that squeaky thing in the Bayport church. I heard every note and my feet wanted to dance, not march, but I didn't see a face in all that crowd but David's. David standing *in front* of the chancel, his blue eyes dark and shining with love for me. Not for Christ and His church that day. No handsomer than he is now but young. Not resigned, not patient. Impatient.

Halfway down the aisle I saw him move forward a little and I pressed my white-gloved fingers into Buddy's arm, quickened my steps to get to him before he rushed to meet me. If I could've turned my head just a little as I passed the first pew, I would've seen Sistuh's face. Wouldn't have made a bit of difference if I had. I would've misinterpreted whatever expression was on it just as I did the hard, cold stare I happened to catch at Charlotte Berry's reception for me. Poor Sistuh, I thought, trying so hard not to lose control, not to cry because she's losing me, she looks like she hates me. How could she have sat there not six feet from David, looking right up at his face—face Old

166

Lady way up there in the gallery said "looked like a angel's uhlistening to God's voice"— hearing, "I pronounce you man and wife" and not, considering what she's done since, screamed in her agony?

Or had a fit as they said poor Miss Taffy did the night David told about Mistuh Adrian in prayer meeting. Or fainted. She could've fainted and not a soul would've thought it was anything but weakness first time she'd been out since her summer-long sickness. There must've been something soothing for her in the finality of those words, because right up to that minute there must've been hope beneath her misery. I might've got typhoid fever or consumption and died. Or I might have changed my mind—she'd seen me change it twice in a few months. Then too she had some control over herself then, not making a sound all those months she was so sick. She was young then and life was long. Finality had nothing to do with it.

The hope that sustained her for the next ten years must've come to her that morning—hope that I'd die in childbirth. She still hopes. Now it's that I'll die before she does. Some way. Her spells have got harder and longer the longer and longer she's had to wait. As though if I died now David wouldn't be pursued and caught by a young, pretty woman! She's afraid of that. She picks her rival in every town we live in, hates her actively two or three years, adds the memory and the hate of her to the accumulating list and every spell she has, leaves the new one, like Daphne Day Ashley here, for a few minutes to snip at the old ones. I don't like to think it but her talk always reminds me of a turkey buzzard circling fresh prey, then swooping down on yesterday's carrion to be sure he's missed nothing. Only Sistuh never gets through with a one of them, remembers every smile David gave Miss Mabel Herring in Wilmington twenty-odd years ago as well as she remembers Josie Pugh in Raleigh and Daphne Day's raving bout Brothuh Humiston here on the porch this June.

Well, I've got *that* to thank Sistuh for at least—seeing how ugly her jealousy is, I've never been able to show a trace of it the few times I've ever felt it because of other women. Maybe I've got more than that to thank her for. Maybe if it hadn't been for her those first years, still young and better looking than she had ever been, waiting on David hand and foot, he might've got mixed up in a scandal in spite of himself. But Sistuh, in the parsonage, had the advantage over all the other pining women and kept his infidelity "in the yard"—as they used to say before the war about men who went to their slave women.

Yes, thanks to her during those years, such things as Miss Wylie Randolph's going to the church study too often in Cypress City, Betty B. Middleton's giving up card-playing and dancing and joining the church in Doddsville, just made "the sisteren," as Cindy calls them, raise their eyebrows and smile behind their fans. And not at David. They thought him the saint he almost is. Even if McCall is his middle name, these Scotch women here in Cameronville have still got to learn how close he comes to sainthood. I wish Mrs. MacMillan had learned it before she laughed and said what she did before Sistuh here on the porch five weeks ago—about not envying me being the wife of a preacher as handsome as Brothuh Humiston, accessible in a study four blocks from the parsonage to dissatisfied wives and unsatisfied old maids. Soon's she said it she glanced at Sistuh, her face crimson, and it wasn't five minutes before Sistuh excused herself, said she had some work on the machine to finish. Mrs. MacMillan began apologizing to me for her slip-of-the-tongue and I told no story when I said that what she'd said about old maids hadn't bothered Sistuh, that that'd happened many a time and if there was an apology, Sistuh always said, "That's all right—I'm one by choice." As she certainly is. "No indeed, lady," I said. "you must think no more of it. Sistuh really wants to finish Fair's dress in time for Dixie Roe's party next week. It's one of those all-over lace things, so tedious and trying on the eyes." No, I didn't tell Mrs. MacMillan a story but I didn't tell her the whole truth either. Imagine my saying, "No, lady, it wasn't your mentioning 'old maid' did it. Was your calling attention to the women running in and out of the study."

Did it! I wasn't sure it had. Soon's Mrs. MacMillan left I went in the house looking for Sistuh. I didn't hear the machine but I hoped, every step I took down the hall, I'd find her there in the back room getting *ready* to stitch. She'd been polite to Mrs. MacMillan, she hadn't just got up and walked away. But she wasn't sewing. She was upstairs, sitting on the foot of her bed, her back to those magnolias, her elbow propped on the footboard, one hand covering her eyes, her handkerchief, already wet, balled up in the other. I tried to reason with her as best I could but when I finally gave up and went out, she was crying aloud. No, I still wouldn't've told Mrs. MacMillan the

168

whole truth if I'd told her about the jealousy. That was just the last straw. This spell was on its way.

It may've gone back to Daphne Day's chatter about how stunning Brothuh Humiston looked in that new suit Miss Claus made for him as her quarterly assessment to his salary— Sistuh's said more than once what she thinks of a woman tailor. Then David might've been unusually absent-minded, failed to hear a question she asked him or been abrupt in his answer. As though I wouldn't be in tears most of the time if I didn't realize how inconsequential we all are compared to his God and his work! It's always David in the end who starts or prevents a spell or brings her out of one. I should know that after fifteen years of them. But behind David's actions there's something makes her liable to one —sitting alone sewing too long, thinking about herself, getting tired and nervous, having a bad dream or one of her nightmares. David says if she'd married a drunkard, had somebody weaker than herself to worry about, she'd have been a fine, strong woman. I think if she'd married any one of the three men she could've married, had a home of her own, she'd have been all right.

I never understood her yearning for a home of her own as I did that day this spring when we went out to the Murchinson place to spend the day and she lifted a little Dresden shepherdess from the what-not and dropped it. "Oh, I thought I'd broken it!" she gasped and her hand was shaking so I had to pick it up from the thick carpet. Gracious knows, it's been bad enough for me all these years trying to protect parsonage possessions but I do have a few things of my own and a feeling of ownership, for the time being, in what belongs to the parsonage. Poor Sistuh hasn't got a thing but what's in that big old trunk of hers she used to begin to pack every time her feelings got hurt. I haven't got one bit of patience with David's other idea, one he's fondest of, that all her suffering, and mine and his, are a part of the Divine Plan which we mustn't question or rebel against and that if Sistuh'ud only accept God's will, she'd be cured. I just can't blame her for being rebellious. It's such a man's plan—giving me David when if I'd never met him, I could've been content with Stephen Clay. And giving me, with David, a whole string of houses I detest having to keep. No wonder Sistuh hates me. I've got everything she ever wanted. . . .

"Mama, did you hear me playing the Wedding March for you?"

"Yes, baby. Was mighty sweet of you."

"I thought maybe it'ud make up a little for your not having the reception tonight. You want me to finish snapping those beans for you?"

"No, baby. I couldn't sit out here in the cool if I didn't have something to keep my hands busy."

"Mama—"

"Ann Wesley! Don't sit on the steps in that clean dress. Molly's just swept but that doesn't help much, this dry weather. And Aunt Mehaley said Monday if our wash gets much bigger she won't be able to do it for a dollar and a half in summer time, all my girls home. And with your Papa down in the mouth again about the bills, I declare I don't know what—" Now that's a fine way to talk when she's trying to be helpful this morning!

"Oh, Mama, I didn't come out here to hear all that old stuff! I came to ask you if you'd been happy—*happily married*—all these twenty-five years."

"Why, baby, what a question! I didn't think a one of you ever thought—"

"I never did till last night. Over at the Wrights'. All those grown girls were talking about love and marriage and Lola Wright said sure thing she wanted to get married if she could be's happy as her mother'd been. That skinny, gray-haired Mrs. Wright and that fat, bald-headed Mistuh Wright!"

"Well, they were young too, once."

"That's just it, Mama! When Lola said that, I nearly jumped out of the chair-swing. Because I'd never even thought of you and Papa's ever being young—and, oh, well, any different from what you are now. Or whether you'd been happily married, or anything. I couldn't go to sleep for the longest time last night, trying to see how you must've looked twenty-five years ago. Papa's still good-looking—I realize that when I see him in the pulpit or on the street. And you're right pretty still, Mama, when Deeda's all right and you're talking to people and have on a pretty dress. Your hair's not gray and I can see you and Papa a lot better than I can the Wrights. But—well, I was right ashamed last night. Lola talked about her mother's wedding like—'sthough she'd been there, then she remembered Elner and I were in the swing and she said, 'Why, tomorrow's your mother's and father's silver anniversary, isn't it, Ann Wesley? Would your mother've worn her wedding dress if Miss Ora wasn't sick and you could've had the reception?' All I

170

could say was I didn't know. I never was so embarrassed in my life. I *wish* I was like Fair and could've made up—"

"Baby, don't stamp your foot like that. That's too childish now you're thirteen years old. Bad's gritting your teeth in your sleep. Besides, I don't know why you'd want to be like Fair. Fair never got on the Honor Roll every month way you do."

"Who cares about an old Honor Roll! Fair got there a lot of times and I'd rather be pretty and have everybody crazy bout me and be able to make up a story quick when I don't know the truth. That's what Fair would've done last night. She'd have described the most beau-ti-ful wedding dress anybody ever heard of, with the most lace and the longest train—"

"Well, baby, mine *was* a beautiful dress. It didn't have any lace and it didn't have a train because your Papa and I were married at eleven o'clock in the morning—we had to catch the three o'clock boat for Wilmington. But it was made of the sheerest French organdy and in place of lace, it had row upon row of little tiny ruffles all hand-whipped. Sistuh sat up night after night working on it by oil lamps while Lucille—colored girl worked for us—fanned her to keep the mosquitoes away."

"Where is it now? Didn't you keep it?"

"I kept it several years. Wore it to two big lawn parties when we lived in Wilmington. But when Sistuh'ud come to visit us, she was always looking for something to make dresses for Beth and Fair and when she couldn't find remnants in the stores to suit her, she'd pull my wedding dress out of its box and show me how she could get two little dresses out of it by hiding the seams with those little bitty ruffles—it had a tight, looped-up skirt and a bustle so there wasn't much material in it. But Sistuh always was smart's she could be, so finally—"

"Tell me about the wedding. Was it a great big church wedding with bridesmaids and ribbons at the pews and white satin cushions for the bride and groom to kneel on under a bower of smilax like church weddings now?"

"Was big for little old Bayport. It had to be. Your Papa was 'the popular and esteemed young pastor' and I 'the fairest flower of young southern womanhood with a host of friends throughout the county'—old Major Galloway wrote it up for his paper just the way editors write now. Yes, I had bridesmaids, Charlotte Berry she was before she married Mercer Williams and Claiborne Faircloth whose husband was governor when you

171

were a baby. I wanted Sistuh to be my maid of honor but she'd been sick all summer and couldn't."

"Well I wish you'd told me before I got caught in such an embarrassing situation last night. You never talk about your girlhood way other people's mothers do. They're always saying, 'Now when *I* was a girl, we *didn't*—' if it's something we want to do, or 'Now when *I* was girl, we *did*—' if it's something we *don't* want to do. I'm glad you're not that way, though. I remember once I was little and Deeda was making a wedding suit for my man-doll and I asked her about your wedding but all she said was she made your wedding dress and a coat for a little colored boy who rode on the front seat of your carriage putting on airs like he was a coachman."

"Yes, that was Ace who lived at Grandpa's old place but Sistuh'd made that coat long before I had any *i*dea I was going to be married that summer. You off now? Remember to hold up your shoulders, you walk downtown."

"Oh, Mama, I *wish*—"

"Now, now, don't *stamp*. I just said it because your hair looks so pretty right after you've washed it and—"

"That's just it! 'Ann Wesley, you've got the *bluest* eyes.' 'Ann Wesley, I declare your complexion's beautiful.' But nobody's ever said I'm *pretty*."

"The very *i*dea. Why, you're as pretty as you can be. So much character in your face. And with your braids tied with those big bows, you—"

"There you go, spoiling it! I know it's my nose and my mouth. They're too big."

"Why, you've got your Uncle Max's nose and I always thought Max mighty handsome and you must remember you're not finished yet. Why, by the time you're Fair's age, you might be a lot prettier."

"Well, I hope. Good-bye."

"Good-bye, baby."

Poor Ann Wesley. Wouldn't make so much difference her not being pretty if she wasn't so aware of it. She and Beth both are too self-conscious about their looks but I reckon they can't help it, three pretty sistuhs. Beth's a lot better looking than she was at Ann Wesley's age. Everybody speaks of her now as being "*so* attractive." Maybe Ann Wesley'll be too. But girls don't have to marry this day and time to have a life of their own. They can go to college and teach or become librarians or trained nurses. Or maybe Ann Wesley'll be the foreign missionary her Papa's always hinting at to her—I do wish one of them would gladden his heart by doing some kind of religious work, and Ann Wesley's the one most likely to. That's why he insisted on having Wesley in her name even when she wasn't a boy. . . . And if what happens to a woman carrying a child can influence a child's character, of all of them, she's the one who should be serious-minded. *And* irritable. Maybe she'll outgrow that too. Or at least show it only once a month when she begins to "demonstrate" as Molly calls the monthly periods. Lots of women, as well as Sistuh . . . Ah, Gladys. Face as bright as sun-sparkled dew.

"Mama, can I—Mama! You're smiling!"

"Am I, baby? Don't bang the screen door! I was just thinking of some of Molly's talk."

"Well, I like you best smiling. You don't much. I don't see how you can smile today when you can't have your party. Know what Bob just said to me on the telephone? Told me not to wake Fair if she wasn't, just tell her for him he wanted her to wear that all-over lace dress tonight if there's *not* a reception because he has to decide whether it was the dress or the girl first attracted him! Bob's funny. I like him better than any old beau Cindy ever had. They slobber all over me. Mama, can I go to Tom T's for dinner? He just telephoned too and invited me. They're going to have calves' brains right fresh from their farm and I love thum and after dinner we're going to set us up a cold-drink stand in front of their house where all the tobacco wagons go by. You think country tacks'll buy ice-cold lemonade?"

"Country tacks! Why, baby, when I was a girl the best people lived in the country—or had before the war."

"Can I, Mama?"

"Why I suppose so. But it's mighty early to be going out to spend the day."

"Oh, I'm not going yet! I've got a hundred things to do first. You see Hallie Wills and Mildred and them go by?"

"Yes, I did! It slipped my mind. They stopped soon after I came out. Said tell you they'd meet you on the church steps. Gladys, wait a minute! Have you been in to ask Deeda how she feels this morning?"

"Yesum, but she was crying so she couldn't tell me. Just grabbed my hands and rubbed um over her face and got um wet. Good-bye. Let me kiss you. Don't work too hard on your anniversary, Cutie—that's what Tom T's father calls me."

"No, I won't."

Look at her skipping off down the street like she owns this town and we haven't lived here a year yet! But I knew she'd be just as she is—pretty and lovable and full of fun. Knew it that April afternoon I stood at an upstairs window, parsonage in Raleigh, and saw a new rubber-tired trap go by under the new green of the trees, heard the lady driving call back to a little girl bouncing in the trap, "Gladys, sit down!" What a pretty name, I thought. Pretty's this day. If this baby's a girl, I'll name her Gladys.

Yes, I was happy most of those months I was carrying Gladys, Sistuh in Savannah nursing Cousin Sudie in her last illness. Hope springs eternal. I didn't want to think her letters were so cheerful because she was hoping I'd die *that* time and I should've had more sense than to tell her when she came back a week sooner than we expected her, day after Cousin Sudie's funeral, and found me in bed, that Gladys's birth'd been harder than the others and Doctuh Powell said I mustn't have another child. Then we *were* in for it! But I had the sweetest little blonde girl anybody in Raleigh had ever seen and even if Sistuh'd tried to adopt her as she had the others, I wouldn't've let her—certainly wouldn't've turned Gladys over to her as I had Ann Wesley. Every chance she gets, even now, Sistuh implies I love Ann Wesley less than the others. A lot she knows about it! One child may give a mother more satisfaction than another, be more congenial, but no mother's happy unless all her children are. . . .

Here I am off on Sistuh and *her* emotions again. If only for one day out of one year, my anniversary day, I could be as unaware of her as I was for twenty-three years! I was young, she was just a mother to me, no more of a *person* than I am to my girls. Why, I never once thought of her as having emotions. I thought she was just a quiet, self-effacing, unselfish kind of girl so close-mouthed that even when she talked she hardly ever said what she meant. Bossy, yes. But like a mother she had my best interests at heart and I loved her. Even Buddy, devoted to her as he was, resented that bossiness in her. It got the better of him sometimes. That first fall after David and I were married Buddy used to steal away, when she was out of the house trying to take his place with Slippy, and drive in town to see Mary Sue and me, looking for a little peace. He never got it with Mary Sue, begging him to marry her so *she* could look after him, but he did when he came to the parsonage.

After that day in November he came with a sack of Irish potatoes. I insisted he leave it in the buggy for David to bring in later, insisted he lie down, insisted he drink a glass of sweet milk and eat a slice of Aunt Merry's light-bread. "Shut up, Ellen, shut up! I live with that day in and day out. I'm sorry. You excuse me. But you can take an explosion and Sistuh can't. Cries if I don't eat the last spoonful of pap. Says I don't want to get well and what'll become of her if I don't? As though I don't want to get well! Lord God Almighty, every time I turn in at the gate, the *i*dea of not seeing Mary Sue waiting for me on the veranda's almost more than I can bear." He paced back and forth across that little parlor. "I've even decided to be beholden to the Judge, let him take a mortgage on the place, and go live in Miss Ryder's patch of Florida jungle with the crocodiles if Doctuh Willie decides it'll help me." He sat down in a straight chair by a window and I saw more than the thinness Sistuh'd tried to make me see when I'd first come back from Savannah, saw how big and bright his eyes were, how sunken and flushed his cheeks. "Sistuh's the best sistuh ever lived," he went on, and fixed those eyes on me a way I'll never forget, "and you ever remember it, Ellen, *ever*. But she's like a mother who can't see her children've grown up. She's got to have her way with them." Right then and there I had to bite my lip, keep from asking him if Sistuh was the one who'd decided he mustn't marry Mary Sue till he was well. I didn't and I'll never know. "I still have a brain to direct a good man like Slippy," he said, "even if my arms're too weak to lift a load of kindling and I can't sit in that armchair all the time. That was one thing about the farm Sistuh gave me bad advice on—not letting Slippy take more responsibility from the first. Had, I wouldn't want to follow him about now, telling him a lot of things he would've found out for himself long ago."

I remember bursting out to him one day that December just before he and Sistuh left for Florida and I was waiting for David to come home from Conference and tell me whether we'd been read out for another place or would stay in Bayport. Sistuh'd been in the day before, telling me how to pack in case we were moved and showing me how to fold David's clothes, underwear and all. Telling me a lot I needed to know but doing it in such a way, I didn't care whether I learned or not, and I said things to Buddy I wouldn't't've said to anybody else, not even to David now. But he didn't look as sympathetic as I'd expected after all *he'd* said and when I'd finally finished and felt better, he just sighed and said in a tired way, "Ah, Ellen, you won't be in Bayport close to Sistuh much longer even if you're not moved this year, and you must be patient with her—she's had a tougher time than you'll ever realize." Ah, Buddy, if only you'd *made* me realize it then. . . .

No, I don't want Ann Wesley to please her Papa by being a missionary—unless she marries one too, any more than I want Beth to go on teaching in girls' colleges, going up to Columbia University every summer working for more degrees. Proud's I am of her, I'd rather she'd never graduated at Miss Poole's Academy in Cypress City even than that she should never marry. With all her education and ability to take care of herself, I can't forget Sistuh was considered the brightest pupil Miss Tempy ever had and that she turned down two proposals and discouraged another. And if a rising young architect or a professor in a northern university isn't good enough for Beth, who will be? . . . Lord, give me David's faith that *my* prayers about that will be answered! I couldn't help but think it here on the porch the other night when she and Bob got into such an animated conversation about New York, shows and sights and things, they seemed to forget Fair was sitting there. Light from the parlor was right on Beth's face and I never saw her so interested in what any man she's met in a town down here was saying. She looked *real* pretty there for a few minutes and I wanted to slap her hand away from her throat, way she has of fingering it when she's got the attention of people. . . . Too late now, though, but Bob's old enough for her and Fair's never lacked for beaux. I can only pray Beth's not attracted to *him.* . . . Now who is that in that old ramshackle buggy?

"Howdy, Sistuh Humiston. Brothuh Humiston home?"

"Why, no, Mistuh—" Rawboned, loose-jointed, red-faced, might be any one of them.

"Smithson. Out McNeill Township way. Brothur Humiston, you an your two least girls come et Sunday dinner my place while back, Brothuh Humiston preached at our chapel."

"Why, yes, of course. How are you all?"

"Aye, I thought you'd recollect. You took on over the old

woman's flowers, made her proud's a peacock. Most of us well enough, thank you, ma'm. Leastways we're all up and about excepting for Flora Dell, next to the oldest. That's what I come in town for—wouldn't uh left my tobacco this kind of day nothing less sickness and death."

"Death!"

"Well no'um, hit ain't got to that yet but looks mighty nigh. Lessen Brothuh Humiston he come forth with some of them powerful prayers of hissen. Flora Dell she's been flat on her back seven weeks come next Monday. All broken out in a rash and weak's a kitten so old woman she says to me—"

"What is it? What does the doctuh say?"

"Ain't had Doc out yet. Thought we'ud give Brothuh Humiston and the Lord a chanst first. Where can I find him? He at the church?"

"No, sir, he's in Raeford at the District Conference." And I will not tell you when he'll be home! "What you'd better do is go straight down to your doctuh's office and get him out to see your daughter. Way you describe it, it sounds like pellagra and that's nothing to fool with. You remember the old saying, 'the Lord helps them who help themselves.' I'll tell Mistuh Humiston when he comes home. In the meantime—"

"Well, I don't know what that air disease you mention might be but I reckon I'd just better go get some kind of remedy at the drug store. Trouble *is*, we give her a dose and then Brothuh Humiston he prays, how we going to know which a one cured her?"

"Look a here, Mistuh Smithson." Yes, look at me with those crafty little eyes of yours, not up, down, and around! "If you don't go for Doctuh Stewart or whoever your doctuh is, I will not tell Mistuh Humiston to go out to your place. Mistuh Humiston believes in prayer *when* it's added to all we can do to help ourselves. Pellagra's a disease that's caused by not eating the right kind of food. No patent medicine you can buy'll cure it."

"That so? Then it ain't that air sickness Flora Dell's got. We eat plenty, our place."

"Yes, I know you do. That was a mighty good dinner we had there. But has Flora Dell been eating as she should?"

"Now you hit the nail on the head, I declare! She ain't. That air age—going on fifteen—she nibble at this, turn her nose up at that, leave the table and go set on the piazza staring at the tobacco fields. Done that all spring. Say the green them young plants purtiest thing she ever laid her born eyes on. Ain't took nothing in her stomach here lately. Child, she used to love corn pone and fatback. Wouldn't eat nothing else. Well, reckon you hit the nail on the head all right. I'll look in Doc's office. Got to get me a new hampstring next door Cameron's Supply anyway. When you expecting Brothur Humiston?"

"Sometime early in the afternoon if not before. He went in a machine through the country so we can't be sure just when he'll get back. But I'll tell him."

"You got sickness in the parsonage? Or is that—?"

"My sistuh. She has nervous headaches."

"Moan like that air every time she has um? I swear I ain't never—"

"Yes, usually. They're mighty bad." Now go along, will you, please.

"I been uhstanding here talking uhtrying all the time to make out whereabouts that air moaning sound was uhcoming from. You seen me uhlooking up in these here hollyberry trees, back there in that air old magnolia. Knowed it won't in neither one though. Too close. Sound a little bit like a owl way off in the pine thicket out our way come late dusk. She been ailing thisaway sometime?"

"For fifteen years now."

"Day in, day out?"

"No. She has two or three attacks a year."

"You have the Doc?"

"In every town we live in but doctuhs say they don't know much about nervous conditions."

"You don't say! Brothuh Humiston's prayers don't help the poor soul none?"

"They haven't so far. That is, in curing her entirely. He can always help her get over an attack though. It's just as I told you about your daughter—we have to help ourselves and my sistuh doesn't seem to be able to 'cooperate with the Lord' as Mistuh Humiston puts it."

"Yes, ma'm, that air's the thing we got to do! Well, I'll hope and pray both our loved ones get over their miseries—yourn's worser than mine, I do declare. I'll be getting on now. You won't forget to tell Brothuh—"

"I'll remember. But you go straight to Doctuh Stewart, you hear me."

178

"I aims to do that very thing quick's I can. Wisht you and yours'ud come out and eat scuppernongs under our vines. They're ripening right fast."

"Thank you. I'll come with Mistuh Humiston some day. I'd like to see how Flora Dell gets along."

"Be mighty glad to have you. Mighty glad. Well, I'll be getting on now."

"Good-bye, sir."

"Bye, m'am."

Now that's a fellow I don't like. He hasn't shaved in a week. Teeth rotting away and he owns a big farm. Had the politeness to do away with his tobacco before he came up but kept spitting on the grass from habit. David'll say his faith's a beautiful thing. Faith, my foot! David's prayers are free.

I like most people, though. Rich people, poor people, white and colored. I like the humble who come to David for clothes or for something to eat, for work or for money for a funeral. The worrying ones who want only his prayers. The grieving ones, past all worry, who ask for comfort. The strange ones with wandering and wondering eyes who want prayers for their souls' salvation upset me sometimes but I've always managed to get them to the study, whether it was in the parsonage or in the church, and turn them over to David as politely as I do all others. Those stocky, dark-skinned men with long black beards and long black coats who come way down here from somewhere in the Orient, staring at me with their somber black eyes, scare me, but it's all I can do not to pat the little Chinese, Japanese, and Korean students on the head, they're so punctilious in their speech and their manners. In Wilmington I liked the sea captains and the sailors from foreign countries talking a mixture of English and something else. Very sight of their clear eyes and weathered skins made me see Bayport harbor again, smell the wind and feel the sun, feel young and carefree again. I'm sorry the study's in the church here and the church four blocks away—except at times like this when Sistuh's "off" and I don't have to hear her soon's the music stops. Never do to let the girls hear me say that, happy's they are to be out of the shadow of a church. Other times here, even with as much coming and going as there is, I miss everybody's stopping to chat with me when they come to see David. Miss it when Sistuh's well, that is. Only ones who come to this parsonage looking for Brothuh Humiston are raw-boned divinity students from a Methodist college angling for a country chapel to practice their sermons in, out-of-town preachers and book agents, the foreigners, and people like that fellow was here just now. No parishioners. So I can't hear David talking to somebody else as I used to when the study door was open for a breeze in summer or to warm the hall in winter. Always have loved listening to David being-a-pastor. When he talks to me I just hear his words but when he talks to others I hear his voice—his quiet, calm, sure voice telling them what they want to hear, persuading them to cast their burdens on the Lord, quoting chapter and verse to prove to them the Lord is their buckler and their shield.

Funny the way I used to think—when I thought at all—that a minister had an easy life of it. Preaching on Sunday, holding prayer meeting once a week, class meeting once a month, christening, marrying, funeralizing people, and just walking about town or sitting in the parsonage the rest of the time. Maybe most of them don't do any more. I can't imagine anybody's going to another preacher for the things they come to David for. Like that Crockett woman in Laurenton from that dilapidated house by the railroad tracks telling him about her twenty-five-year-old daughter loving her twenty-four-year-old son so much she wouldn't marry the smart young fellow owned a saw mill. "Seems like it ain't right, Brothuh Humiston," she said, "for a grown woman to fondle and kiss her blood-brothuh like Iris does Johnny, much's as I like to see kinfolks friendly." I don't know how David did it but he talked to the girl and to the brothuh and to the smart young fellow and the last marriage fee he handed me in Laurenton was from that couple. . . .

"Miss Mama, you through with my snaps and butterbeans?"

"I certainly am, Molly. I was going to bring thum to you on my way upstairs."

"You set right where you is. You got to have something keep you busy out here, I bring you my rice to pick over. Ain't no call you going up to Miss Orie again now. You been up twict this morning and hit ain't ten o'clock. You set right here in the cool and keep saying howdy."

"Not much passing now. The men have all gone downtown and it's too early for the ladies. And the way I feel this morning, I'd rather just bow than have to chat."

"Now don't you talk thataway. First thing you know, porch'll be full and you'll be talking and laughing same's everybody else. Come eleven o'clock, I'm uhgoing to bring out some of

180

them pretty little cakes Miss Beth she ordered for the reception you can't noways have and some *ice* tea. And twixt now and then, soon's I get my snaps and butterbeans on the stove, I'm uhgoing up there that nasty old room and rub Miss Orie's back for her. Seem like that soothe her some. And me! I loves to hear her go on bout how much more you all's thinks of me than you does of her. Lord, eff'n I was sick to my head and somebody come every two, three minutes uhasking me how I does, what I wants, lemme do this, lemme do that, make you feel better, I'd think I was something on a stick! So's eff'n you all's thinks more of me—"

"We think a lot of you, Molly. You know that. I don't know what we'd have done without you these past weeks."

"I knows hit. You shows hit. Miss Fair uhletting me take her red silk parasol to my church last Sunday. Miss Beth uhgiving me her black voile skirt and silk petticoat what swishes like new. Miss Cindy uhcoming in my kitchen telling me all the jokes she hears like we was personal friends. Yes, m'am, we all's mighty happy together spite of our troubles."

"The girls down yet?"

"They's up but not exactly down. Miss Beth she come and make a pineapple sherbet for Miss Orie but say she ain't got her back to her bed yet. Wisht she could fore I goes up. Might be you all is right bout there's being no ghosts most places but they's in that murder-room! I feels um and hears um every time I goes in there. Poor Octavia Warren—that were her name, same's her old master's Pastor Gillespie bought her from— uhmoaning and uhdying under that white giant-man. Say he were the biggest white man folks ever seed round here them olden times. Yesum, I hears him uhbreathing and uhgrunting in there. And I hears little old Parson Gillespie uhtipping acrost that porch and uhcreeping in with his Bible in one hand and a fire poker in the other, just in case what he heerd downstairs here were that Mistuh Will Warren's overseer come back again. Lord, anybody told me I'd ever work in *this* house, much less go in that slave-room, I'd've left this town running, faster I ever run past it I was little and hit all boarded up."

"Well, you're a brave girl, Molly, feeling that way, and we appreciate it. It's mighty sad, a pall like that over the biggest, nicest parsonage we ever lived in. I said, when we came here in December and heard that old story, we'd just shut off that storeroom and forget about it, but now that Miss Ora's decided it's the quietest place for her, we'll have to go in there until we can get her out."

"Yesum, I knows. Now why you getting up?"

"Just to get my sewing. I can't sit here and be idle."

"You set still. I'll get it. Where's it?"

"In the back room on the machine—Gladys's new drawers I'm working buttonholes in."

Bless her heart. Bless her busy hands and her willing feet. Bless her chunky body and her glistening-black round face. I knew the minute I saw her, helping out in the kitchen first night we were here, she was more than the good cook the ladies praised, knew she could be the friend I'd need in a strange town. Don't know what I'd done without her before these past weeks. Wintertime, the big girls all away, callers all day long, house full of children "rushing" the new preacher's little girls, was Molly who told me the gossip and who was kin to who so I wouldn't make any breaks. A servant-friend's always made the difference to me between living and just existing. I have to laugh—keeping one used to be my only real worry. Was Rose the summer of our tenth anniversary, in Doddsville. I was happy *then*—except for the fear of losing Rose. Yes, I was. Make no mistake about that. Happy in spite of all my wants. Ignorance is bliss, deafness and blindness a blessing. I was a woman in years, still a child every other way. Only happier than I'd been as a child or even as a girl. I was still looking forward in terms of years, not simply wondering how I could get through the next few months or weeks or hours. I wanted a lot more than just peace then but I was sure I'd get it all eventually—a parsonage with electric lights and a bathtub, a husband who would be a Presiding Elder, then a Bishop, a fur tippet, and a son. Up till then Ellen Fanning'd always got what she wanted. Fifteen years ago I was still Ellen Fanning with the Humiston added for good measure. . . .

"Thank you, Molly. Now you go on about your work or you won't get your rest after dinner."

"Yesum, I aims to."

Yes, I remember one day of our tenth summer when I was happy as distinctly as I remember some that followed when I wasn't. Seems to me life goes by like a landscape from a train window, telescoped so you can't separate the days any easier than you can the trees, but every now and then the train stops at a station that's a little different from those behind you. You're

182

passing from one section of the country to another and all the differences as well as the similarities are stamped indelibly on your memory. . . .

2

David, look! There's cotton. A whole field of it, knee high."
"Um-m. Exactly as high as it should be. Farmers may forget to pay their church dues but I never heard of one forgetting to plant his cotton the twenty-third of April." David glanced at the field on my side of the road, "When Ora and Cindy drove out this way with me for that child's funeral at Rollins' Crossroads last month—first day you were feeling sick—they were giving it a final chopping. Lots of it already in bloom. They'll be picking about this time next month."
"That soon? Oh, David, what'll I do!"
"What'll you do about what?"
"Rose's going! I told you she's going to Warren County to pick soon's the season opens."
David wasn't listening again. Just holding the reins lax, his elbows on his spread knees, and staring ahead at the road stretched like a yellow tape measure between fields of tobacco. The surface of green rippled like Brunswick Sound on a quiet day and seemed to reach to the horizon too. Only the long curved fronds nearest the road were separate leaves, breathing-in the light breeze, soaking up the July sun. I sighed but David didn't ask me why. I laughed.
"*Now* what's so funny?" He didn't turn his head and I couldn't tell from his profile whether he wanted to be amused or whether this was a time he'd think me flippant.
"Oh, you. Me. Everything. Have I ever told you why I married you even though you're a preacher *and*"—I poked my toe at the pamphlets, tracts, and colored Scenes-from-the-Bible cards stacked against the footboard—"a book agent, something I'd always said I'd never marry?"
He looked at me then and a little tiny smile dented the corners of his mouth. "You've told me. Truth of it was, you loved me and I asked you."
"Well, yes. But I wouldn't have loved that combination—spite of your fine figure and handsome face—if you hadn't been a silent man. Comparatively. It was your quietness. Oh, I'd

183

known handsome men, charmers, men with laudable characters, but never, never, a man who could ever be silent."

"Then why do you laugh about that? I haven't changed."

"Oh yes you have! Here lately you've been *more* silent. Sometimes I can't get a word out of you for love or money. Reckon
I'd never get it for money if I had it. But I laughed because I
don't like silence any more. Your silence. I get right tired of
woman-talk all the time. Yesterday at Mrs. Southerland's I
thought if I had to listen to one more recipe for bell-peppers,
brandied peaches, or—"

"You shouldn't listen to recipes for brandied peaches."

"Why? Oh. You and your Prohibition business." Another
Don't. Don't accept syllabub or tipsy-cake for dessert. Don't
drink a glass of scuppernong wine. Don't . . .

"Look over yonder." David nodded toward the field on his
side. "Beginning to barn that tobacco. Day Ora and I drove out
they were just tapping it—pulling out the buds to stop the
growth."

I watched a line of dots, long dots, short dots, with great big
flat heads, moving from the center of an emerald field to a drab
barn at the far end. "Um-m. David, why don't they raise more
cotton up this way? That field of it back there looked flourishing enough."

"That little patch belongs to a Baptist brother. Named Watson. He can't read the writing on the wall any more accurately
than he can interpret the scriptures on baptism. This county's
going to be the bright-leaf tobacco market of the world. Brother
Gibbs was telling me just this morning when I dropped in the
bank to deposit Father's check. Said his bank used to depend on
the carriage and wagon factory and the cotton gins here but
now with farmers making four times as much on an acre of
tobacco as they ever made on cotton, bank wouldn't miss the
other industries if they closed down. Yes, there'll be a lot of new
people here this fall in connection with the tobacco sales at the
new warehouse. Expect we'll see new faces in the congregation
every Sunday."

I smiled to myself. Some Sundays I knew there was a stranger
in the congregation the minute I stepped inside the wide doors
and saw David in the pulpit chair, his shoulders a little more
erect against the red plush, his chin just a little bit higher, the
expression on his face a little more other-worldly. If I couldn't
find a stranger while old Brothuh Chadwick ushered me down

the aisle or couldn't locate one from my pew near the chancel, I could always tell by watching David's eyes while he repeated the invocation or read the first stanza of the first hymn whether there were strays from other flocks in the side pews, drummers in the back row, or visiting ladies sharing center pews. I was glad David was aware of them. I liked for him to show off a little on occasion. It kept him from getting too informal in the pulpit, his fourth year in a town. Already people were saying, "Well, Brothuh Humiston, when you're a Presiding Elder—" Once he was that, with no one church of his own to get used to, preaching in a different town every Sunday in a quarter, he'd keep on his toes for that step into a bishopric.

"Well," I said that day, "I won't see strangers or anybody else much this fall. If more farmers round here were as blind as that Watson man, I might go to evening service right through October."

David sniggered. "If the whole congregation were blind you mean. Not many farmers come in on Sunday nights."

"I mean if more farmers couldn't read the writing on the wall about tobacco, more of them'ud still be raising cotton."

He gave me a blank stare. "What's that got to do with concealing your condition?"

"Silly, if they raised more cotton round here, Rose wouldn't be going off every August-to-November. She could at least come back to the parsonage to sleep if she could pick close by."

"You talk like Rose's the only colored woman anywhere about."

"She's the only one'll sleep in. Even if I could find another one who feels safe from a dead man only in the parsonage, she'd get brave about the middle of August and take off in a Warren County wagon."

"Aunt So-and-So going?"

"David, how could Aunt So-and-So go! She'd have to have a wagon all to herself even if she could be hoisted into one. Besides, she won't do a single solitary thing but wash. Told me Monday seemed like she got no peace in her soul lessen she was bent over a tub. I asked her why that was. Said she reckoned was the way the Lord made her. I think it was the way old Sistuh Chadwick made her. Aunt So-and-So told me several times bout how it was her duty, she was seven or eight years old, to wash Little Miss's doll's clothes. Imagine that old stiff-neck ever having played dolls! Anyway, Aunt So-and-So said one Monday she

185

forgot and ran off to watch a hog-killing and Little Miss was so mad she wouldn't give her the pair of black velvet shoes with red buttons and tassels she'd promised her for Christmas. So now, I think, she's afraid she won't get her reward in Heaven if she doesn't wash everything in sight. Why, she even takes the clothes off the children's backs Monday mornings if she sees the tiniest little spot, stuffs thum in the big wash I always give her."

David wasn't listening again. Had been, he'd've reproved me for being uncharitable about a devout Methodist like Sistuh Chadwick who came to church every time the bell rang and paid her assessments on the dot. Or maybe he was silently rebuking me. About Sistuh Chadwick *and* about my complaints about help. Well, he needn't have. Not about the help part. He sold Bonny first year we were in Doddsville, after all it'd cost to freight her from Wilmington, because he couldn't find a stable boy he could depend on on winter mornings. David hates to work with his hands just as much as I do. Loves horses, makes a bosom friend of every one he hires or has the loan of, but feeding, curing, and hitching-up's as much of a task for him as feeding, washing, and dressing the children ever was for me.

We drove past a barn that day so close to the road the dots were men in overalls, women and children in tow-sack dresses. I nudged David's arm. "Now look at that! Darkies could carry baskets on their heads without holding on to thum. And not stumble either. Why don't *they* work in tobacco? At least they'd be within reach all year round to kill and dress a chicken. David! Why don't darkies work in tobacco?"

"What's that? Oh. I don't know, Ellen. Never thought. Just custom round here probably. White tenants must've got to it first. Yes, I expect you're going to miss Ora this fall."

"I know I am. When I have Rose though—" I bit my lip. No use trying to explain to David that when I had good colored help, I missed Sistuh in a way was a pleasure to miss her. No man would ever understand what goes on between two women in a house, sharing the work and the children—though what I did when Sistuh was with us couldn't be called sharing. I did only what Sistuh'ud let me do, exactly as I used to at Little Brookside. Besides, I wanted David to keep on liking Sistuh, because unless she hurried up and got married, she'd stay an old maid and be with us a lot of the time. . . . "What did you say, David?" For once he was talking and I wasn't listening.

"Just saying I expect it gets mighty lonesome for Ora down

there at Little Brookside so much with only the darkies around."

"Why, she doesn't stay out there long at a time! She always spends some time with Charlotte and Mercer and stays with the children when they go off on a fishing trip. Visits poor little Mary Sue a lot too. Seems she can't do enough for Mary Sue now. Insists on doing all her sewing when she's teaching with Miss Tempy."

"Still, they're not kin folks. I think people wonder why she's not with us more. Several have said to me how nice it'ud be for you if Miss Ora could make her home with us, she's so helpful with the children."

"If they knew—" no, I mustn't say that—"how things are down there, only a colored man to run the place, they wouldn't be implying we neglect our kin."

"Slippy can run it. He's kept the interest paid up on the mortgage and paid off a fourth of the principal, made a living for himself and Lucille, and passed on to Ora more spending money than she had when the three of you were living there. I'm wondering whether it wouldn't be a good *i*dea for Ora to let him take over the place in his own name when he clears up the rest of that four hundred dollars, relieve Ora of the responsibility."

"How could Slippy take it over in his own name? He's got no money to buy it."

"Why, he's paying it off as rent now. That done, he could take out a new mortgage—expect that place is worth a thousand now —use it for purchase money to Ora. I could invest it for her at six percent, and she'd be sure of a certain amount every quarter."

"Who'd take a new mortgage even if Sistuh wanted to sell her home?"

"Brothuh King or Brothuh Davis—if the Judge didn't want to again. They know that soil's the best anywhere around for Irish potatoes and they know Slippy's smart and dependable. Then Ora could make her home with us, visit around when she wanted to."

"I can't believe Sistuh'ud sell Little Brookside. Used to think sometimes she loved it more than she loved Buddy and me."

David turned to me then and there was that kind of sly, whimsical expression on his face that always masked his greediness for a third slice of apple pie or the urge to make love to me two nights in succession. "Be a big help to you to have her with us permanently."

He didn't say "wouldn't it" but it sounded like a question. Like Cindy's wanting to put on a new dress the minute it was finished, darky fashion, and pretending to take it for granted she could but, at the same time, having to be sure I agreed. I usually agreed with Cindy—I wanted my little girls as well-dressed as others—and usually I agreed with David. Now I didn't know what to say without telling him Sistuh could be as much of a trial as a help.

"Would mean you'd be free to go to Conference with me every year, go anywhere any time. There'll be a lot of lecturing for me in big towns when the Anti-Saloon League gets organized in this state. And with our growing family—"

"Yes, Sistuh'ud be a godsend in a lot of ways but—well, it's just your salary being what it is and the extra expense every time we have to move."

David laughed right out. "Little Ellen! when you try to be economical you never hit the bull's eye. Don't you realize Ora saves us enough in a month, when she's with us, to cover train fare in a year—even if I were so unpopular we had to move every year? No dollar to a dressmaker here, quarter to a scrub-woman there. Why, we might even save the dollar and a half we pay Rose every week!"

"I wish Sistuh could hear you. She'd know how much you appreciate her. Oh, I know you do! I don't hear any 'pshaws' when you get up in the mornings when Sistuh's with us. Every sock darned, every button sewed on, both suits pressed. But don't you say one word bout my giving up Rose! A new baby coming, I'll have to have a nurse too. Besides, if we didn't have Rose, Sistuh wouldn't have time to be your bodyservant. And if I had six smart sistuhs living with us, I'd still want a servant. It's not the work they do, though, as much as it's the—the—why, whoever heard of nice people *not* having a cook!"

David shook his head in that unconvinced and unconvincible way he had. "Worldly little Ellen. Don't you know a minister's family's 'nice people' no matter—"

"They certainly are *not*. You were the only preacher I can ever remember in Bayport who was made a lot of socially except old Doctuh and Mrs. Cunningham. Look—"

"Here, wait a minute! You told me once not to be conceited about my popularity there, said it was because I was a bachelor.

Now you imply was because I had rheumatic old Aunt Merry cooking for me."

I laughed and took it back. "No, Aunt Merry didn't do it. It was just because you were you. But what I started to say, look at what they said when we first came to Doddsville—how good it was to have nice people in the parsonage again. If I've been told once, I've been told a hundred about Mrs. Dean's father having been a carpetbagger and how for all her being sent up North to school, she didn't have sense enough to see why she wasn't 'accepted' in Doddsville."

"Why wasn't she? Because her father—?"

"Certainly not. Not in this day and time. Mrs. Gerald Willard in Wilmington was a Union officer's granddaughter. Was because Mrs. Dean kept right on being as Yankee as her mother, doing 'her own work' as she called it. Even the washing! They say it was a shame and a disgrace seeing clothes flapping in the parsonage back yard every Monday rolled around because she wouldn't have a 'shiftless Ne-gro taking her laundry to a filthy cabin.' As for having a 'black woman' in *her* kitchen— The very *i*dea, a lady's being possessive about a kitchen! Only good cooks are that. It's the last place I'd want to call mine."

David laughed a good man-laugh, way I liked to hear him.

"When Sistuh's with us," I said, "working like a Yankee, it's all the more important to have a cook, you see. Then her doing all the time's simply a peculiarity of hers. People know I'm never without a servant if I can help it. I don't know where Sistuh gets her energetic ways. Grandpa Evans used to say was the Fanning Yorkshire blood coming out in her."

"That's as bad as Yankee blood, eh?"

"Certainly not. Anyway, now that I know your family, I can see it's as you say—it's more the mountain air than your grandfather's ancestry makes the Humistons energetic. Besides, Miss Elspeth and your sisters've always had servants even if they do work like darkies themselves."

"Have them because they're there and must have work. Not for social prestige." He started to flick the reins, held them taut, and laughed suddenly. "Feel more at ease driving with you than with Ora. With her, every time a horse has to have an action, she fidgets and calls my attention to something way off yonder on the horizon. Always wish for a constipated animal when I take her out. You'd think, being in the family now, she'd get over her false modesty."

189

"Not Sistuh! She was born prissy. But going back to servants. The Humistons don't need thum to build up prestige. They've been high monkey-monks up there three generations. It's different with us. We're cut off from our roots. And with so many young men from poor-white families going into the ministry because they don't want to work on a farm—"

"Nobody'ud ever accuse you of being poor-white!"

"Nor you of being a share-cropper! Still people in this part of the state don't know who my people were. Unless I tell thum. In Wilmington they knew. Even if they hadn't, there were Cousin Evans and Cousin Clare Rutland to tell thum. I had a time of it, we first came here, getting it across to the first callers that I had a plantation background—even it was mostly *back*. I get right tired now whenever I think of having it all to do over again next January—and every time we have to move."

" 'Pride goeth before a fall and a haughty spirit before destruction.' "

"If we fall, it won't be my fault! But I wish you'd stop teasing me about my worldliness. When we were married I knew you thought I should stop caring about anything but the church and good works but I told you when I said 'yes,' I didn't think I'd make much of a preacher's wife."

"And I told you I wanted you for *my* wife. And God wanted me to have you or He would've told me differently."

"Yes, but now you want me to be both, everything you need, just like all the other husbands I've heard described since I've been married and have known wives. Now, even if I wanted to, I couldn't go to church every time the bell rings, teach a Sunday School class, hold office in the missionary societies, run the parsonage, have babies—"

"El-len!" David was looking at me in a baffled, worried kind of way. "You mustn't think I expect miracles from you. You're a loving wife and mother and they come first on any woman's agenda. What's upset you?" He pressed his hand on my knee.

"I don't know. I'm tired riding, I reckon." But I did know. Was the very thought of Sistuh's being with us always and the leash I'd been holding on my tongue to keep from telling him how Sistuh was at times. She would be no burden to *him*, financial or otherwise. Just a great big help.

"We'll be there pretty soon now and you can rest. Turn off at the next side road and then it's just about a quarter of a mile." He touched the mare with the whip. "And besides being the

190

wife and mother you are, you're helpful to me in less obvious ways than those you mention. You know I agreed with you that going driving with 'the best people' in the church is as important as visiting the—the lesser ones with me."

"But I don't think you've ever admitted how much I've helped you at the Conferences I've been able to go to. I saw, first one I went to, that the preachers who were noticed by the Bishop, put on committees, read out for the biggest churches were the ones whose wives weren't tacky. Or tactless. They say Brothuh Jessup missed because Mrs. Jessup was too outspoken, said exactly what she thought about every town she lived in. You got to be friends with Bishop Titus at that six o'clock dinner the Richardsons gave in New Bern, when we were one of four couples invited—and that was because Mrs. Richardson remembered meeting me at Camilla once."

"You leave me mighty little."

I leaned over and kissed his cheek. "I leave you everything, 'Brothuh' Humiston, that's really essential. No matter what I am and do, it wouldn't help if you were not all you are. But I know too there're some capable men whose wives are dead weights. I just mean that to Bishop Titus from Virginia you were just another young preacher till you met him socially."

"All right, you're right again." David leaned toward me and kissed *my* cheek, something he hardly ever did in daylight any more—but that was my fault. "Haven't I just been saying I want you to go to Conference with me every year?" Then his face tightened. "Yes, I'm sorry I've had to learn there's as much political chicanery in the ministry as in the legal profession, learned a lot in eleven years I never expected to learn in the Lord's vineyard. I need your help in what should be secular matters, God knows."

We came to the turn off, rattled over some loose planks spanning a shallow ditch, and followed a rutted road zigzagging through pines and scrubs. Suddenly we bounced over roots spread like tentacles from the base of a great big oak. I put one hand on my stomach, grasped David's wrist with the other. "Look! Stop a minute!"

David pulled up. "Eny, meny, miny, mo." He counted the little darkies running from a cabin tucked under the branches of that old tree. "And two to carry."

"If those two'd been carried more often they wouldn't be so bowlegged." I leaned across David's knees and motioned to a

191

tall, lanky coal-black girl with a snuff-brush hanging from her lower lip and a pickaninny from her hip.

"Yasum?" She set the baby on the hard dirt, took the snuff-brush from her mouth, and started toward us. "Get behind me!" She lurched forward and pulled back a toddler making for the horse's hoofs.

"How old're you?" I asked.

"Going on thirteen, Mammy reckons."

"Ever worked out?"

"Chopped cotton for Mistuh Josh Watson way down yonder some."

"You going to pick for him?"

"Noum, not's I knows of this year."

"How'd you like to come in town and help me? Next month when my girl goes off to pick. You could sleep right on the place and I'd pay you fifty cents a week and give you some dresses."

"Ellen—" David muttered but I pressed my hand hard on his knee.

"Yasum, eff'n Mammy say I can." Her black eyes were bright as new pennies.

"Could you ask her now—or let me speak to her?"

"Noum. Mistuh El Gideon done took her off, see do we all want to live on his land. Wherebouts you live?"

"Right next door to the First Methodist Church. In the center of town. You'd have a real good time sitting on the church steps with the other nurse-girls in the afternoons. Or walking my baby girl up and down Main Street. I'd give you some white aprons too."

She grinned from ear to ear.

"When'll your Mammy be home?"

She shook her head.

The next-sized one, a bright-face, still clutching her pickaninny, came closer. "Don't never come till sundown, she go off with Mistuh El."

"Shet your mouth!" The lanky one slapped at her.

"Well," I said lamely, "maybe we can drive out again some day."

"Yasum."

David reached down and took some cards from the manila envelope, held them out to the girl. "You read?"

"Nawsuh." But her pink-lined fingers closed tight on the cards. "Thankee."

192

"You'll like the colored pictures anyway. Jesus and His disciples little Moses in the bulrushes, Joseph and his brethren."

"Yasuh." She held the cards above her head, out of reach of the swarming children. "Go get washed and I show you, hear?"

"There now," David said as we drove on, "maybe you'll believe Elwood Gideon's not the man you'd like for a brother-in-law!"

"I'd have liked that girl for a nurse. She knows how to manage children." Then I tried to laugh. "Think of my being more credulous than you about a good church member! It's mighty hard to believe, a clean-looking fellow like El Gideon. And just as clever as he can be! Came all the way across the street after that rain the other day to help me over the puddles. Asked me then when Miss Ora was coming back. Said he'd written her twice but she hadn't answered his letters. I told him she was kept mighty busy in Bayport, so many old friends to see, but that she'd be here for Christmas with us." I drew a long breath and released *that* dream.

"That's a pair you'll never match. Don't know why women're so restless when there's an unmated male around. Or why you're so anxious to marry off a sister like Ora."

"Wouldn't be very flattering to you if I weren't."

"What do you mean by that?"

"Why, if I didn't find marriage with you—"

"Oh."

"Besides, I may be selfish but I'm not that selfish—trying to hold on to Sistuh because of all she does for me. Don't you think a woman who loves a home and children's much as Sistuh does should have her own?" I straightened my fingers and spread them wide. Funny, the way they curled up in a fist every time here lately I thought about Sistuh and our children.

"Yes—when the right man comes along to provide them."

"The one with wings better hurry. Sistuh'll be thirty-six her next birthday."

"By the way, what'd you mean back there saying Ora doesn't think I appreciate her?"

"Oh, just that she's said several times it's hard to know how you feel bout her paying us such long visits. Said you never seem to notice the little things she does for you. I assured her you do appreciate thum, it's just your silent way."

"Yes, I expect I say 'thank you' mentally too often. I'll try to remember to speak out next time she comes. That's our destination—low white house beyond that tobacco field. Maybe I should be the one to mention to Ora this *i*dea of ours of selling Little Brookside."

"Ours! It's yours. And don't you mention it yet! I want to think—"

"Preacher Humiston! Howdy, Preacher Humiston!" Two little tow-headed boys in faded overalls jumped from the tall weeds at the roadside. "Preacher Humiston, you got room ride us to the house?"

"We'll make it if we haven't got it," David said and they squeezed in between us, one on top of the other. David began chatting with them about all the fun you could have on a farm 'sthough he was no older than they were. They smelled of hot sun and watermelon and I wanted to hug them. Right then and there I knew I'd have a son this time!

❖   ❖   ❖

"Mighty good people," David said when that old grandad finally stopped stroking his tobacco-stained beard and ranting about the Dukes and the tobacco trust and let us get away. "*And* mighty sweet watermelon."

"Yes it was, but you'd better drive fast or I'll have to step in the bushes."

He slapped the reins, his farewell smile to that family back there still hovering on his lips. One thing that's always made me love him is the modesty that goes right along with his self-assurance. Never seems to take adoration for granted. Some people in Bayport thought he was conceited when he repeated a compliment he'd got. Maybe some in every town since have thought so—being his wife, I don't hear criticism any more. Except what Sistuh says she hears. But I knew almost as soon as I knew him, it was just surprise at himself for affecting people as he does, great and small.

When he says "mighty good people" he means country Methodist who go to chapel the one Sunday afternoon a month he preaches to them, pay their mites, bring us produce, and ask him to conduct family prayers when he makes them a visit. He always has a better time of it than I do. There's always some man around, like that old grandad, wanting to talk doctrine or politics and David can take more interest in politics even than I can in querulous sing-songs about the births, miscarriages, wasting diseases, miraculous recoveries or lingering deaths of

194

strangers. Sometimes, as on that day, they're so tiresome I have to amuse myself by repeating all the funny incidents I can think of. It's worth doing when I can amuse them too, see one of those hopeless faces twist in what's meant for a smile or those lack-lustre eyes gleam with a little life. I don't believe David enjoys them as people a bit more than I do. I remember once when a sanctified woman rushed right in the house and in the dining room, waving her arms and shouting Halleluiah, scaring the children and taking David away from the table. Remember his saying, when I protested while he ate a warmed-over dinner, that the parsonage was open to all Christians whether they were on my calling list or not. I know it's his goodness, his determination to be sincere, to practice what he preaches, that's always kept him from drawing the line anywhere but as long as I'm nice to everybody in church and chapel—I used to think—I've got a right to make friends only with those I enjoy being with.

I used to do it too. Keeping up the prestige we were talking about that day was about all I could do during what David called my fruitful years. Going out when I was presentable, welcoming ladies upstairs when I had to hide up there. No young married woman's ever nominated for missionary society office or asked to take a Sunday School class so I didn't let him down there. I haven't been active in the church since Gladys was born either but that's been because of Sistuh. When she's well, she resents my being out, being helpful or sociable, and when she's off, it's all I can do to go to church.

Was because of Sistuh I'd burst out at David the way I did that day fifteen years ago. I was exasperated with her for being able to take over the house and the children and do church work too, felt envious of her virtues and wanted to add them to mine. Certainly that wasn't fair because I was the one who'd started her off being active again. Doing substitute teaching. *First* year we were in Doddsville, before Cindy was born. Remember it like it was yesterday.

David was resting on the lounge in the sitting room one Sunday after morning service and telling me who'd spoken to him after the benediction and what they'd said. He snapped his fingers. "I knew there was something for you besides inquiries about your health! Sister Lathrop wants to know whether you'd feel equal to taking her Infant Class four Sundays in June while she's away at Seven Springs."

I shook my head. "I haven't felt sick all week but look at this morning—I couldn't go to church, much less to Sunday School. David! Maybe Sistuh would."

"That's so! Ora'ud be good with those little tots."

"Be good for her too. She's been right shut-in since she came this time, my feeling so uncertain. I don't know how she keeps so cheerful. When I told her about another baby's being on the way, she said I wasn't to do a thing but take care of myself and she sees to it I don't."

"Well, if our having babies keeps her happy—"

I leaned over, slapped David's face, kissed him quickly on the forehead, and said I'd go ask Sistuh right away. She hemmed and hawed till I told her David thought she'd be just the person for it. Then she said she supposed she could, Beth and Fair 'ud be at Sunday School anyway and I could stay in bed till she got home.

Now that was the third time I'd been pregnant and still I was so wrapped up in myself and so blind I didn't see why it was she was so sweet to me all the time I was carrying a child, so irritable and touchy soon's I was safely over the birth. There was a morning in Wilmington, when Fair was the baby, should've made me blink my eyes at least—was the first of many such a scene, acted over in almost the same words when I was nursing each one of them. . . .

I'd heard Fair cry and had gone upstairs. But Sistuh'd already picked her up, was walking up and down the passage—hall they say now—patting and shushing her. I held out my arms. "I'll take her, Sistuh. I expect she's hungry."

"She's all right. She can't be hungry again already—I heard Brothuh David getting her from her crib and taking her to your bed a little after seven and it's not ten yet." Then bouncing and patting, "Fair loves her Deeda, doesn't she? Yes, she does. We listen, we'll hear her *say* Dee-da before she says Ma-ma way Beth did."

"I think I'd better take her, Sistuh," I said, meekly as I could.

Sistuh pushed her at me so fast I had to lean against the banister to keep from falling backwards. "I just don't see why it is, Ellen, that you always think you have to nurse her the minute I pick her up. Besides, some of the ladies were saying to me after church Sunday they thought you were nursing her too long. Said she's nearly a year old and could take a bottle and said you look pale's a ghost."

"I'm going to wean her soon's the weather's cooler. But I

wish you'd stick your nose in the air and walk off when those old pussy cats start meowing bout me."

"Why, Ellen Fanning, very *idea* your talking like that about ladies in the church! What would Brothuh David say!"

"I don't care what he'ud say," I lied. "I'm tired hearing—"

"There you go finding fault with me again." Sistuh raised her voice above Fair's hungry cry. "I can't do anything right. But I don't repeat such remarks I hear except for your own good."

"Why, I didn't mean *you*'ve done anything wrong. Just meant—"

"Don't try to explain it away, Ellen. I'll try to bear your ingratitude what time I'm here. If I didn't think you needed me, I wouldn't stay another day. But with Beth and Fair on your hands, and that lazy girl in the kitchen, I know I'm a big help to you."

"You certainly are, Sistuh. You always are."

"Well, I do try to relieve you all I can, let you be free to run around and have a good time way you've always liked to do. You tell that girl what to have for dinner?"

I shook my head. She said she'd think of something, then, and went on down.

I carried Fair to the rocker by the window in my room. I hated to wean Fair much's I hated having to leave a tea sooner than I wanted to or cut short a nice drive with somebody in order to feed her. Nursing the children seemed the only thing I could do for them Sistuh couldn't.

That morning—and a hundred times afterwards, I reckon—I had the baby on the bed, gurgling and clutching at my hair while I changed her diaper, when Sistuh came back talking.

"Ellen, I told that girl to candy the sweet potatoes the way Brothuh David likes thum. That all right with you?"

"Any way suits me. David's getting so finicky about food here lately, I can't keep up with his whims."

"Well, Ellen, all men're finicky. You must expect that. Or thought of it before you got married."

"I'm not complaining. Just meant I can't keep up with his whims."

"You don't think I try to keep up with thum, do you?"

"Why, Sistuh, I'm mighty glad you're here to try—if you do."

"Well, it's just that it's another way of smoothing things for you."

I fastened the last safety-pin and Sistuh picked Fair up and carried her to the window. Fair said, "Goo-goo."

"Listen to that, Ellen! She's saying 'Dee-da'!"

And Sistuh stood there, talking baby-talk, and pointing out all the pretty-pretty flowers in the front yard. I asked her if my red asters were in bloom this morning and when she didn't answer, I looked over her shoulder and saw David at the gate, reaching in his pocket and talking to a poor old man, another beggar.

"Point to David," I said. "See if she can say 'Papa' any plainer than 'Deeda.' "

"Oh, we don't want to 'turb your Papa, do we, Fair? We mustn't be 'interruptous' when he's talking to the poor old man, must we?"

"Why, I reckon he's hearing all the chattering and cooing you're doing!"

Sistuh whirled around and pushed Fair at me for a second time that morning, picked up the wet diaper I'd dropped on the floor, and left the room. I stood there, unsuspecting innocent that I was, wondering what I'd said *that time* to upset her.

I was still an unsuspecting, self-centered innocent when Fair was seven years old, that summer day driving back to Doddsville with David. Passing that lopsided cabin under the big oak, I waved to the lanky girl. She'd turned the iron wash-pot upside down and was sitting on it holding the two toddlers in her lap and still showing them, or maybe just again, those Bible cards. A curl of smoke was rising from the chimney and the other children were nowhere in sight. Now their Mammy's home and I can't speak to her. But I felt as sorry for that capable girl whose hopes I'd raised and dashed as I did for myself—whose hopes *she'd* raised and dashed. Sometime before we went up the country I must get Mary Lassiter to drive me out with some old clothes and magazines for her.

"Shame you can't take time to teach those babies to walk," David said. "I'll never forget the picture you made sitting on the steps at Little Brookside holding out your pretty arms to that little Mister. 'As ye have done it to the least of these,' I thought, 'ye have done it to me,' and I realized in that minute that maybe God didn't have to *speak* always, He could *show* me what was right. No matter if Miss Ellen is light and gay and worldly, I argued, she's a Christian at heart and it was the spiritual as well as the physical so attracted me the instant I looked

198

up and saw her face at the window. In spite of what Ora'd told me about that Clay fellow, I felt right then that you must be God's choice for me. I was confused, though. Confounded as I've never been before or—ah, well, I learned then that all a mere mortal can do at such times is pray and wait, 'wait, I say, on the Lord.' "

"Well, you wouldn't've had to wait so long that time if you hadn't been so faint-hearted. Minute you and Sistuh walked off, I tore up that letter to Stephen Clay saying 'yes' and started another to hold him off till I could find out whether *you* were already engaged. I hope Beth and Cindy'll fall in love at first sight but I don't believe it happens often."

"No, most young people're too impatient, not willing to ask or wait for God's directive. They let the mind rather than the heart dictate. What time'll we have supper tonight?"

"Soon's Rose can get it. Shouldn't take long. She'll have the biscuits ready to go in the oven. Why? Is there a meeting or something tonight?"

"Nothing tonight." He slapped the reins as we turned into the main road, "But go a little slow on supper. Before I take this outfit back to the livery stable, I'm going round to see Brother Gideon. He should be in his rooms by now."

"No, he won't be. That girl said—"

"He'll be there. Sleeping off his debauchery. He passed the Johnson place with that woman while you were in the house getting your hat. No one of the men said a word but that old fellow spat a long stream of tobacco juice at the back wheels of Gideon's new buckboard. Glad Gideon saw me. He'll know I'm not acting on hearsay."

"You're not going to him about that thing now! After all this time!"

"As surely as the sun's going down in glory ahead of you. I'm his pastor, what else can I do? If every minister in the South'd been doing his duty these past two centuries or more, white people would be white and black black as God intended them to be. I'll not stand there in my pulpit and preach against doctrinal sins—dancing, card playing, gambling on cotton futures, breaking the Sabbath—against drinking and smoking, then wink at the Seventh Commandment. Adultery's adultery whatever the woman's complexion."

"You—you won't preach about it!"

"No. Not right now at any rate. If I can save one guilty soul by private prayer and counsel it's worth more than preaching at random to the ninety-and-nine. I think I've learned that."

I hoped he had. That sermon in Wilmington about the hostility against able colored men who held public office had stirred up some mighty hard feeling and done no good either. Going to see Mistuh Gideon was bad enough. I realized then I hadn't given up that dream about Sistuh and Mistuh Gideon. All the time I'd been listening to those farm women whining back there, I'd been arguing with my conscience about it. Why, plenty men who were good husbands today had carried on with colored women before they married and people forgot all about it. Look at Miss Taffy in Bayport. She'd regretted all her life she hadn't overlooked Mistuh Adrian's behavior as a young man before the war. She'd realized too late she might've had all that love that kept mounting up for that slave-girl after she'd jilted him. Could've kept him from being a traitor to the Confederacy, been a happy woman herself if she hadn't been so high and mighty when she was young. If David could just ignore what he'd heard and seen this afternoon, felicitations for Sistuh and congratulations for Mistuh Gideon would've come thick and fast soon's we announced the engagement. But if David went to Mistuh Gideon now, Mistuh Gideon would never come to the parsonage again, never walk home with Sistuh from church or a social—leaving me the pleasure of walking alone with David.

David's never known how to live in a *town*. In the eastern part of the state anyway. Up the country people seem to live on a higher level in more ways than one. May be the mountain air and the distance between farms. Down here, in town and country, everybody knows all about everybody else and the only way to get along is to keep your mouth shut—when you're not paying compliments.

"When the right man comes along," David had said. The right man—I knew that *then*—would be the one David stamped with his approval. Sistuh looked up to David as she'd always looked up to Buddy, thought both their mouths were prayer-books. But David wouldn't approve Mistuh Gideon any more than he'd approved James Wiley in Wilmington. Was during her first long visit to us there after Buddy's death she had her first beau—or so I thought then. I used to stand at the window and watch her drive off with James behind those two spirited horses of his and I believe I felt as happy for her as I'd ever felt

200

for myself on such an occasion. Astonished me the way she'd come out of her shell at the supper table and repeat the compliments she'd got from James, cutting her eye in David's direction, hoping he wasn't thinking her conceited—or so I thought then. One day I came upon her at the back door reading a note and heard her tell the Wiley's yard-boy there was no answer. I waited till she went upstairs, then slipped in the study. David was writing at his desk and I sat down till he twirled himself around in that first swivel chair he was so proud of before I told him I wished he'd advise Sistuh to give James some encouragement, said she needed a man to look out for her now that Buddy was gone. David said we mustn't press her, that she'd have to come to her own decision a thing like that. Then said he'd made up his mind, if Sistuh mentioned it to him again, to tell her it was a question her own heart would have to answer. Said he would've told her that the first time if Brothuh La Grange had told him earlier that that story about James's sleeping with one of those bad women from Norfolk, in a tent at the County Tournament, had never been proved for a fact. That if *that* was a lie, there wasn't a straighter young man in town than James Wiley. I was more exasperated with David that morning than I'd ever been—and stayed so whenever I thought about it till I realized that Sistuh'd never had the slightest intention of marrying James, had just gone to David to let him know she *could*.

Way down by that cotton field that day, David began talking again 'sthough my mind were part and parcel of his, keeping on with the same thoughts. "If ever I feel I must preach such a sermon," he said, "I'll quote what old Colonel Creecy in Elizabeth City said in '89—about history's showing amalgamation's the only solution to the race problem. That'll get them! I'll point out that all the ranting politicians're doing now about White Supremacy and passing Segregation Laws is a waste of breath so long as such amalgamations as Gideon's and that woman's are countenanced."

"Why, David, back there in Bayport when you spoke out in prayer meeting bout Mistuh Adrian, Charlotte Berry told me you told her father—"

"Yes, I know. I did. That was a bona fide common law marriage. Whether the courts of this state recognized it or not. Mister Adrian took a husband's and a father's responsibility—fed, clothed, and educated those boys. Look at the older one, teaching at Shaw University now. Never fails to send me a Christmas greeting. But Gideon's just taking his pleasure where he finds it. Most of those children're too dark to be his but he could at least give them decent clothes. It's irresponsibility and unadulterated adultery I'm talking about now."

"In Wilmington people used to say such things were dying out, said you turned to look again when you saw a mulatto baby."

"That was true of Wilmington. Colored people there've held on to a lot of what they gained during Reconstruction and developed a kind of pride in themselves. White people there've had to show them some respect no matter how much they resent doing it. Up here colored people're as lowly—more so—than they were in slavery and white scoundrels take advantage of it. In every way."

"People seem to act a little differently toward darkies in different towns and counties, don't they? I've noticed that, living in Bayport, Wilmington, here, and seeing your part of the state. In Bayport we knew thum all by name, what colored families'd belonged to what white, and treated thum like old friends. Miss Ryder was the only slave-owner I'd ever heard of was mean to her negras. In Wilmington it seemed there were two races in one—the humble ones to love, the uppish ones to hate. Here some people seem to think they're no more than horses or mules, be used for all the work they can get out of thum and not thought of otherwise. But—"

"Plenty money in this county but not much real aristocracy left."

"But up your way where there're so few—I don't know, I can't put my finger on it—but I have a different feeling when I'm up there. They don't come in the front door or anything like that but—well, they seem to be people like us. Why're you looking at me like that?"

"Because you'll never cease to surprise me, one way or another. With your mind—when you take the trouble to use it—or with your beautiful face."

"I'm glad of that! Sometimes here lately I've thought I was just another *soul* to you."

"No, never," he said—fifteen years ago.

Still I was disappointed he hadn't said *body* instead of face. I might've had a pretty face or a winsome face but only Stephen Clay'd ever called it beautiful before. Only David knew my body was beautiful and he wouldn't say so! If just once he'd admit that he was as—as carnal as I! Just once accept that what went on between us in the night was nothing to be ashamed of in the day!

" 'The heavens declare the glory of God and the firmament showeth His handiwork,' " David quoted and I saw what I'd been looking at—the edge of town in the afterglow of that sunset. All the little old darky and poor-white houses looking less shabby, less like shacks, more like homes, smoke curling from the chimneys of kitchens where women were cooking supper, men lounging on stoops waiting to be called, children—white, black, mulatto—playing hop-scotch or rolling barrel hoops on the hard-packed dirt of unfenced yards hoping they wouldn't be called yet.

When we were on Church Street bowing and waving to ladies rocking on porches, gentlemen walking among flower-beds with sprinkling cans, children in white stockings, white dresses, white skins, rolling store-bought red-and-white hoops or riding tricycles, David said, "You haven't told me what you think of suggesting to Ora—"

"I'm still thinking. I reckon I'm selfish but I do like to feel the house belongs to me—and I belong to you. Not to her. You needn't look surprised. Sistuh's never got over the notion that she's got to bring me up. That I'm her child she's responsible for. Oh, I know she doesn't want to be that way but habit's mighty strong. David, les wait till we're settled in the new place after Christmas and see how things are. We'll be going up the country the end of August now and, when we come back, I can't go out anyway—maybe I won't miss Rose's much's I've been thinking I will. What's worrying me now is the trip up there and back. It'll be the first one we've made with three children. David! Why don't we ask Sistuh again to go up with us! She's refused every time we've asked her. Of course, there's the extra expense. We couldn't let her pay her own way."

"That phase of it's all right. Father sent me thirty dollars. That's ample for all of us with my preacher's discount. If you don't insist on parlor car seats."

"Oh, I can stand the daycoach with Sistuh to help with the children," I said and laughed suddenly.

"Now what's funny?"

"Just thinking how much fun it'll be hearing Sistuh tell Miss Elspeth and Kathy how to do something better than they've

203

been doing it! Maybe this time, too, I can see A View instead of the children's dirty feet and red-bug bites. You sit right down tonight and write Miss Elspeth. Ask her if it'll be all right if we bring Sistuh."

"I don't have to write Mother. Ora has a standing invitation. But I'll get a letter off to *her* in the morning mail—unless you want to write it."

"No, you do it. It's *your* old home."

You see! It was my selfishness that time, and that time was the beginning of all time since. I didn't know how things'ud turn out because I was deaf and blind. Didn't know then that Ellen Fanning couldn't have what *she* wanted without giving somebody else something of what *they* wanted. I wanted to take Sistuh to Humiston Hill with us for my convenience and to show her off to Miss Elspeth and Kathy. Then I wanted her to go on back to *her* home.

Funny how I remember little details of that July day fifteen years ago when I hadn't the faintest idea of what it all meant. Must've known deep inside of me if not in my mind because it's all etched on my memory like that murder scene in *St. Elmo* was etched on a windowpane by lightning.

David was gone a long time that evening seeing Mistuh Gideon. I told Rose to give the children their supper, they were hot and tired, playing around the church corner till nearly dark, and I'd get them to bed. I'd heard their prayers and kissed them goodnight, and was on the porch again before the gate clicked. The light from the hall lit the path and I watched David, head high, shoulders straight, looking twice as tall as my tall dahlias in the borders on either side of him. And when he mounted the steps, I saw that his face had that triumphant expression it always has had when he's brought a sinner to repentance. He strode past me, sitting there in the shadow.

"Here I am."

"What's that? Oh." He felt his way through the circle of chairs, sat down next to me. "Well, I found him. Sound asleep, just's I'd expected. Saw that buckboard out front so I knew he was back and I knocked on his door till I awoke him. Should've seen his face. You'd've thought I was his conscience personified. But he pulled himself together, invited me in to his sitting-room, and came back from his bedroom in a few minutes with his hair brushed and his coat, collar, and tie on. Have to agree with you, he's not a bad-looking fellow. Hair getting a little thin I noticed, and waist line a little thick. Never did like black-eyed men though, especially when they have a shifty way—however, that's beside the point. Maybe hereafter he'll be able to look his pastor in the face!"

"David, stop tapping that chair arm and tell me what happened!"

"Oh. Well, he tried to pretend he didn't know why I was there. Asked how the fund for the Infant Class room chairs was coming on, reached in his pocket and handed me two dollars—been meaning to give it to me all week, he said, sorry I'd had to come for his donation. I took it and thanked him but told him my errand had nothing to do with contributions but with his soul's salvation. Didn't mince my words either. Said in my eleven years as a minister I hadn't had to put many out of the church but as God was my witness, I'd put him out if he didn't mend his ways. He got red in the face, clenched his fists, but he kept his eyes on the floor. When I'd finished, he gulped and spluttered about having been a good church member, attending services regularly, the men's Bible Class every Sunday morning, paying his assessment on time, ever since he'd come to Doddsville, but he was a man and lonely. I told him none of that made any difference in God's sight if at the same time he took advantage of a poor darky woman. Said he wasn't taking advantage. She was lonely too, working in the field all day, coming home to all those children, nothing in her life to brighten it. Said this very day he'd taken her to see the little farm he's bought where she can live free in a four-room house that doesn't leak, feed her horde from her own vegetable garden, have chickens and pigs and all the cash she can make from selling eggs and watermelons and cantaloupes."

"Have to admit he's not sinful as you thought, being generous as that."

"Yes, but how long would it last? And he'd still be breaking the Seventh Commandment every day of his life. And first time—"

I had to laugh. "What a man! As Buddy used to say about you."

"Ellen, do be serious. You know as well as I do, first time a white tenant farmer offered him a good rent, he'd put that poor woman out and take up with a young girl with no family to support. Anyway, I commended him on his generous impulses but asked why, being willing to support a family, he didn't get

205

married and lead a respectable life. Said he reckoned was because he'd always been too shy with the ladies—seems he was raised on an old plantation in Dare County, played with darky children all the time, and—"

"Shy with the ladies! Why I've never met a more affable, courteous—"

"That's the way he appears. Has nothing to do with the way he feels inwardly. I've heard enough confessions these past few years to keep me from judging from mere appearances again as long as I live." David's hands clasped the chair arms. I thought he was going to get up and started to myself when he blurted out suddenly, "Here's something'll surprise you though. He said he got his tongue untied, after two or three attempts, and proposed to Ora."

"When, David, when?"

"Said was that evening in May he escorted her to the Ladies' Aid lawn party—at Sistuh Lassiter's, not long before she left. Said Ora gave him 'the gate' or some such expression."

"He's too faint-hearted! Doesn't he know enough to know a woman like Sistuh 'ud have to say no twice before she said yes? She wouldn't think it proper—"

"Not so faint-hearted's you think. Says he's written her twice begging her to reconsider but has had no answer at all. They were the letters he mentioned to you."

"Well, I reckon she meant it." I sighed and kicked off that dream now like an old worn-out slipper I'd put on for the last time. "What surprises me is Sistuh's not asking your advice before she refused him."

"Does she always ask my advice?"

"She certainly does! Every little thing. 'Brothuh David, you think I'll need my *um*brella today?' 'Brothuh David, you think this letter'll get to Bayport day after tomorrow?' Things I'd never think of interrupting you about. Reckon it's just habit—she used to run to Buddy 'sthough his mouth was a prayerbook too."

David sniggered that way I'd given up trying to break him of and said there was more justification for his mouth's being one but that he hadn't noticed Ora's coming to him that way. Right then and there I should've got a glimmer of his feelings for Ora. One thing I'd learned about a man when I was young was that no matter how conceited he could be about most girls liking him, he was always humble and doubtful about the One

206

Girl. Stephen Clay brushing off all the Savannah butterflys so arrogantly and overcome with gratitude when I gave him a smile. Mercer Williams perfectly sure of himself with Charlotte and grovelling in the dust at my feet. I didn't get it. I was still the only pebble on the beach. In my own eyes.

Rose called us in to supper then in no uncertain terms and David held open the screen door for me. "It's just as well Ora didn't ask my advice this case," he said. "I would've had to tell her marriage with such a man was out of the question and you'd've blamed me."

"Suppose he reforms and persists about Sistuh?" I could feel my toes groping around for that old slipper.

"Let's say no more about it." David hung his hat on the rack 'sthough he meant it to stay there. "If after his prayer and penitence this evening—and I've never seen a man seemed more sincere—*if* he follows my directions, clothes those children for the winter, leaves that woman where she is—and leaves her alone—he'll be able to find him a good wife, now he's broken the ice with Ora. But Ora's too fastidious for him and her own sister should know it."

David was rough-and-ready *that* night, not waiting for me "to rise to the occasion," as that flighty grass widow in Wilmington used to say about her itinerant husband, and I annoyed him by laughing. Better to laugh then than in church the next Sunday when I'd see him in the pulpit clothed in the spirit and begin wondering what people'ud say if they could see him in bed full of the Old Adam. Was that night I dreamed about being up in the belfry in Mistuh Gideon's arms looking down at David searching for me among the tombstones.

3

"Mama, how does it look?"

"Step away from the door—don't bang it!—and turn around."

"Don't bang it! Deeda can't hear a sound but her own moans, way up there."

"Just habit with me, I reckon. Why, it looks fine, Fair. Didn't need any fitting after all. That's one middy blouse nobody can say makes a girl look pregnant."

"Must say *enciente*, Mama. French and nicer. I told you if I ordered it ready-made from Moxwell's in Norfolk it wouldn't look that way. Now I feel right for tennis—it's exactly like the one Cadence Rountree had on the other day."

"You let Sistuh see you?"

"I went in there to show her this and my ring. She actually looked at my ring. I don't want to worry you, Mama, but I think Deeda's losing her mind. She didn't seem to remember who Bob is and said she was glad it was a ring and not a thimble!"

"Her mind's all right."

"Then it's the worst attack she's ever had and she's delirious."

"Ah, Fair, you haven't seen what I've seen. You've been away most of the time the past four years and you don't remember some—"

"I remember them since I was five or six—"

"No, they didn't begin till you were nearly eight, year we were in Lynnboro."

"Yes, that's right. Was coming home from Miss Fay Dosier's school one hot October day I saw all the windows closed and wondered why. I remember opening the front door and hearing that awful moaning and I thought you'd died suddenly and the world turned upside down and I hung on to the doorknob to keep from falling."

"I remember. You did fall—or sat down limp on the floor— when you saw me coming downstairs. You cried and cried then, begged me to do something for poor Deeda and I had a hard time explaining it was a headache the doctuh didn't know what to do for."

"I don't remember anything but that first awful feeling. That day. Then when it went on and on, I can remember Beth and me lying in bed at night whispering about it, saying it must be true what Deeda told us, that you and Papa didn't love her and wanted her to go away and how we wouldn't have any more pretty dresses or doll clothes if she did. Oh, Mama, I didn't mean to make you cry!"

"I'm not going to cry, baby. I'd've cried my eyes out long ago if it could've done any good. It's just thinking about poor Sistuh, up there remembering— Don't lean against that banister, Fair, it's dusty this dry weather."

"Mama—have you and Papa ever considered sending Deeda to the asylum? Bob asked me if you had. Said the doctuhs there know more about nervous conditions than general practitioners do and that she might be helped. Why're you looking at me that way?"

"Makes me want to smile— Sistuh's said more than once we'ud never dare send her to Raleigh because no young man would want to marry one of you with an aunt in the asylum."

"Then you have—"

"No. But Doctuh Bradford in Lynnboro, that first attack, thought she should go and some of the stewards came to your Papa about it, said it'ud ruin his career having insanity in the parsonage. Your Papa told them if Sistuh was insane, everybody was one way or another. Said his career was preaching God's word and he could do that in the open if all churches were denied him and that in the meantime he could manage his own household without advice. Sistuh got over that spell and we all thought it'd been just another nervous breakdown—she'd had one, without the moaning, the summer we were married— thought, if we were careful with her, she'd never have another. But the Lynnboro stewards never forgave your Papa for being so independent and outspoken, and we were moved way down to little old Queenston at the end of the year."

"Mama, I *know* she won't be over this attack any time soon. I'd certainly like to wait and have my announcement party at home as it should be but Bob's family and all those Henderson people are sticklers for form and I'll have to have it as soon as I come back from visiting up there next week. Now Mama, please don't look hurt. Dixie says of course you'll be hostess exactly 'sthough we were having it here."

"I don't feel like being hostess anywhere right now."

"Oh, Mama, *please*. Think of me *now*. You can't help Deeda by losing interest in everything else. If you'd only care more about your clothes than what we're going to have for dinner, you'd feel a lot better. You should go out more—you told me yourself you hadn't returned half the calls you had last winter. I can just remember when I used to think you were the prettiest lady I'd ever seen. I wanted to be just like you when I was grown. And you taught me etiquette with my stick-dolls. You could help me a lot now. I have the whole burden of keeping this family in the swing socially. Beth's so darned highbrow she shows she's bored to death with everybody who hasn't been to New York or abroad and she doesn't want to go with anybody but whatever northern people there are in a town running a mill. Like that Mistuh and Mrs. Eastbrooke here she calls artistic because they live in a bungalow and have mission furniture. Nice people're bringing out family furniture now, antiques that've been stored in the attic. And Cindy! I declare if I meet her downtown just once more with that La Fayette Street crowd—"

"Why, Cindy was saying the other day you can't say a word to her bout the girls she goes with here because every last one of thum comes from an old family!"

"Too old! Run down. Miss Maybelle Grimes says La Fayette Street was *the* street when she was young but her father sold their house there when they built that cotton mill at the end of it, says now family tradition has to be held up by a little money at least. Why that Madelaine McRoberts Cindy's so crazy about *works*! Clerks in Heller's every time they have a sale. But that's not as bad as all of them being *fast,* meeting the train every time a ball team comes in. If Cindy should decide she'd rather be married than just engaged all the time and marry Bill Harrow, nice as his family is, I'd try to persuade Bob to go back to Henderson to practice. I simply could *not* live in the same town with her and be embarrassed *all* my life. It's going to be bad enough living here where I've been a preacher's daughter. Bye, now. Don't forget to have Molly put on her white apron and cap before anybody comes. Oh! I forget to tell you—I met Mrs. Charles MacNeill in Heller's yesterday. She asked me how Miss Fanning was and whether you were receiving. Said she was coming around one day real soon if you were, even if you hadn't returned her call, because she'd just had a post card from some ex-governor's wife who's abroad. Said she was an old friend of yours—"

"Claiborne Faircloth! One you were named for in a way."

"Mama! I wish you'd tell me these things. You never talk about the important people you used to know."

"Do I look all right—if she comes this morning?"

"Um-m. You've got on your new corset, haven't you? And that old lavender lawn's still mighty sweet on you. Be good to yourself today. If Bob calls again, tell him it's still one o'clock he's to meet me. On the Grimes' court."

She looks like a Gibson girl, walking off swinging her tennis racket. She'll keep her figure too, maybe, all the active things girls do nowadays. Hard to believe I ever looked as she does now but David and Sistuh say I did. Her features are better than mine ever were but maybe there's more resemblance in personality and expression than in noses and mouths. Fair's always seemed more my daughter than any of the other girls. My eyes were just the color of hers before too many worrying days and sleepless nights drained the blue away and put lines between them, pockets beneath them. Fair's and Gladys's eyes are deep set like David's and that makes them more beautiful than mine ever were but my lashes were as thick and dark once. And my hair as light and fluffy. Ann Wesley's being proud my hair's not gray! I wish it was. Gray hair makes a middle-aged face more youthful, seems to me, than faded blonde.

If only I could tell my girls what life can do to a woman if she's not careful, doesn't see the first danger signal. I don't mean about looks. They're just by-products. If she's so wrapped up in herself she can't see anybody else, much less try to understand them. Trouble with me was I wasn't selfish enough with all my egotism. I wanted to be kind to everybody, even when I was a girl—if I remembered to think. These girls're selfish enough. Each one of them thinks of nothing but what *she* wants. No, Beth doesn't. She insisted on going off to New York three years ago to get her Master of Arts degree, goes back to every summer school, but when she's home, she thinks of me and of all of us. Gave up her visit to Boston to be home today! She tries to be a kind of extra-mother to Ann Wesley and Gladys, doing things for them I should do if I wasn't so distracted by Sistuh. Maybe it's because she's the oldest like Sistuh. No, I mustn't think that. Beth doesn't work for them hand and foot way Sistuh did for Buddy and me, has gone on doing for David and the children and me. Beth's concerned about Ann Wesley's timidity. Says she's going to take her away to school wherever she's teaching year after next and try to bring her out of herself.

Sistuh's never been able to see there's something more important than keeping the house spic-and-span and having plenty to eat and wear. She can't see it's more important what you *are* than what you *do*. She knows we don't love her as we say we do but she honestly doesn't know why, after she's worked her fingers to the bone for us. Even when she's all right I can't think of anybody but her. I walk a tight-rope all the time trying to see her feelings don't get hurt so she'll be off again. No wonder I couldn't blend the children into a family, make them think of each other a little bit. Have to laugh thinking of my egotism. Why, Sistuh and David, with all his goodness, are about as self-centered and egotistic as people ever get to be! Theirs has increased as mine has diminished. Disappeared. Sometimes I feel like a worm being crushed between two stones.

If only I'd had an inkling of their real selves when I was young. I thought Sistuh lived to do for me. Thought David loved me more than himself. David's selfishness isn't obvious and ugly, though, as Sistuh's is. On the surface he's so quiet and gentle and sweet-natured and patient, never aroused, out of the pulpit, except when he sees injustice done to some poor-white or darky; so unworldly, so generous with what money he has, it's no wonder most people in every town we've lived in have called him Christlike, loved him as few preachers have been loved. I'm the only one who's seen his selfishness because I'm the only one who's suffered because of it.

David wasn't entirely responsible though. Least I can do, being honest about him and Sistuh, is be honest about myself. If fifteen years ago I'd been as selfish as I was self-centered, I'd have held out against Sistuh's selling Little Brookside and coming to us, might've gone on being as happy as I was then. Trouble was those first ten years when she was coming and going, I never did decide whether it meant more to me having her for what she did than not having her because of what she *was*. My wishy-washy attitude was as much to blame as David's selfishness. I couldn't make up my mind whether I was happier being tied down and running the parsonage my hit-or-miss way or happier having Sistuh there for housekeeper and nursemaid—and pastor's assistant. In the end, I gave in to David because I wanted her more than I didn't want her. Nothing unselfish about that! Oh, yes, I wanted to please David too, I grant you that. But if I hadn't felt as much to blame as he did, I'd have steeled myself and tried to be as stern with her as Doctuh Bradford advised that first time, not gone on for fifteen years handling her with kid gloves. When you come right down to it, it's a guilt David and I shared and we'll carry the burden of it as long as we live. If only I could go back to that morning fifteen years ago . . .

❖ ❖ ❖ ❖

I sat on the porch of the Doddsville parsonage with my sewing, watching Rose go off up the shady street pushing Cindy in that perambulator she was too big for but still loved to ride in. Watching cooks or yard-boys stop sweeping sidewalks to chat with Rose, ladies with rose shears lean over fences or boxwood

212

to take on over Cindy, as big-eyed and sociable then as she is now. It was three or four days after that afternoon ride with David, and I expect I pushed a baby-petticoat down in my sewing bag when Fair came running from the yard.

"Mama, please make me a stick-doll dress out of this. Quick!"

"Why, baby, where'd you get this Nile green silk? It's a scrap of Deeda's last Easter dress."

"Deeda gave it to me herself. When she was making that pretty dress. Now I've got to have one for Miss Annabelle Graham. She hasn't got a stitch to her name and she's in a big hurry!"

"So it's Miss Annabelle Graham this time?" I folded the scrap in a square, cut it round, cut a little hole in the middle.

"Yesum. She has to be 'piscopal so she can dance. But I won't tell Papa. Look at her—all green and strong. Beth cut her from your tea-rose bush. Give me her dress. Yep, it fits. Now cut this blue linen for her to travel in."

"Where's she going?"

"Seven Springs. With Miss Honey Isley. Nancy Lassiter's Miss Honey's chaperon. We don't call ourselves mamas. We're playing like the Springs're under the mimosa tree. Beth's digging um now. That'll do. But it's just a skirt. I wish you could make little bitty shirtwaists like Deeda can."

"Deeda's fingers're nimble enough to make clothes for a flea but—"

"There comes Nancy Lassiter now! I got to go!"

I pulled out the petticoat again. Funny. I didn't mind sewing so much when Sistuh wasn't around. She admitted my handwork was all right but she'd look over my shoulder a lot anyway trying to find a flaw she could correct. I didn't like sewing on baby clothes in her presence though, ever. Always started her off on The Nevers. Never stretch, Ellen, when you're carrying a baby. Never stoop suddenly. Never lift anything heavy. Never look at a disfigured person. Never take a hot bath, never a cold. Never laugh heartily. Heaven knows, I heard those things enough, *sotto voce,* from all the Old Wives without having Sistuh repeat them aloud every whipstitch. And I was no novice at that time. I knew by then that pregnancy's not an illness. It was a natural state for a woman of my years and I felt fine every time. What interested me about it was the different way I felt with every child. With Beth it was all curiosity and interest, astonishment at nature's provision for peopling this world. I was proud that *I,* who'd never given it a thought, had a body

213

equipped for the job. At least, I was proud when it was all over and I knew that I had. Used to wonder, in the early months, how the baby would get out, was always telling myself it had to, somehow. Used to look around the congregation and be consoled that all those Methodists had got here the same way. And when I felt Beth coming, wriggling out all arms and legs like an octopus, I laughed aloud in that burning pain at the ridiculousness of it. I was still interested with Fair but it was like rereading a book you like—you keep watching for some detail you've missed in your first hurry to get to the end of the story. With Cindy I was bored most of the nine months. That was like being shut up in a dark room after you've been dancing in a sunny meadow, peeping through a crack at freedom. Nature didn't mean it to be that way. It's prissy people acting like it's a disgrace to be seen in public after the first little bulge shows. Only Mary Lassiter had any sense about it. She never thought of calling it a delicate condition. Always said women make a big to-do about it to get even with men for having none of nature's handicaps. . . . Wish I could see Mary this morning, talk as carelessly to her as I did then. . . .

"Well, lady," she said, coming up the steps, "you're up bright and early this morning!"

"Why, Mary Lassiter! I didn't hear you drive up."

"I didn't. I walked. Started out with Miss Honey Isley's chaperon but she was too fast for me."

"Sit down. I was just thinking how this summer's passing, and wondering what I'll do next without you."

Mary shook her Japanese fan at me and pulled a chair close. "Ellen Humiston, you stop such talk right this minute, you hear? Told you the other day if you so much as mention it in my presence another time I'd cut your acquaintance. I mean it. Not sure I shouldn't anyway—make it easier for me to see you go next January. Everybody's going to miss Brothuh Humiston but just me'll miss you." She teased but her eyes were browner and brighter than ever, with tears.

"I'll miss you more. You're the only Best Friend I've had since I left Bayport. In Wilmington I was trying so hard to be a good preacher's wife. I went with all the important older women, never once let myself be intimate with any woman my own age. Never felt myself quite real's I do with you, more like I was just playing lady the children's way."

"Now you've learned to be a gracious preacher's wife with

214

one hand and have the other free for such as me, you'll never lack for bosom friends."

I shook my head. "There'll never be another like you. Charlotte Berry in Bayport comes nearest but she misses by a whole lot. You and Charlotte're the only two I've ever known who always say what you think and I admire that trait more than anything in the world. Other women are so much alike—in Wilmington, here, and I expect in every town I'll ever live in. Different names, different faces, different houses, different clothes attached to the same personalities. Be fun, though, picking thum out in each new town, waiting for This Kind to say just what I know she's going to say, That Kind to do—"

"Oh, go long with you. Everybody's full of surprises as a grab-bag." She laughed. "Just wait till This Kind and That Kind here hear you won't be going out this fall! All I can do to keep my face straight when I hear them wrangling. 'But I want Brothuh and Sistuh Humiston for Thanksgiving dinner, you can have thum the Sunday after.' 'Now which do you think little Sistuh Humiston'ud like better—a five o'clock tea or a six o'clock dinner?' "

"Don't talk about it. I'm disappointed enough all ready, much's I want a boy."

"Well," Mary said and I can see her right now, pushing her lustrous brown hair up beneath her hat brim 'sthough a strand of it was ever out of place, "you wouldn't take my advice."

"*I* would have but you know David."

"Not that way!" The chair rocked with her laughter. "Did you tell him why I have just two—a full three years apart?"

"Yes, and he said maybe you thought it was your doings but it was simply God's will."

"What's God's will got to do with the way you've managed not to have one every year? You've gone nearly three years this time. My method's a lot more fun than watching the calendar and using restraint and when you get David, Junior, here you'd better persuade David, Senior, to try it. Even if a bishop's salary would be big enough to support a dozen, you don't want to spend half your days upstairs."

That happy, happy morning. Like most summer mornings on my porch or Mary's, hearing the children's busy voices—happier, whether they realized it or not, when Sistuh wasn't there calling and motioning to them not to show their little bottoms when they leaned over, going in their room on scorch-

215

ing nights, pulling down their nightgowns and pulling up the sheet because nice little girls didn't sleep stark naked. Happy sitting there seeing a Future, breaking off my dream to chat with This Kind and That Kind dropping in, swapping compliments. Had no idea when I left the porch *that* morning to walk through the churchyard to the study, tell David it was dinner time, that there wouldn't be thousands more like it.

David wasn't in the study. I came back through the cool, dim church, sniffing that stale, weekday odor, and stood under one of the old cedars between the side door and the gray tombstones feeling sad for all the people who weren't living any more. That "Beloved Daughter of James and Maria Whitcomb" they said hadn't died with acute indigestion. Trouble was she'd been secretly meeting a Yankee government agent when the county was overrun with them in '67 and that when he went away without marrying her, she'd eaten nightshade berries and died to save her family embarrassment. All those wives who'd died in their twenties and thirties, leaving their children to stepmothers. All those little tiny tombstones you could find cherubs on if you traced your finger through the lichen. Better to have died yourself than to see your child die. How did all those mothers stand it? How do mothers ever stand it seeing those little bodies they've loved, as I love my children, laid out in coffins, stiff and white, a flower in a cold, clean hand instead of a June bug in a hot, dirty one? Oh, I hoped then, as I have ever since, that I'd die before any one of my children did! Dying after you've lived a full life can't be too awful. Only thing I think I'll resent, whenever it comes—I was thinking that morning—is the idea of lying in front of the altar speechless while a preacher goes on about the virtues you maybe never had—"an earnest and devout Christian," "a faithful servant of the Lord," —and never once mentioning, because he can't possibly know, the virtues you did have—the hurting words you'd bitten back, the selfish acts you hadn't committed, if, a few times in your living, you'd thought in time. No, nobody understands you when you're alive, so you can't expect them to after you're dead. Everybody who knows you, knows a different kind of person and there's no piecing together, even in a crazyquilt pattern, the square, triangular, or round yous each of them sees with their different eyes. That's the sad thing about dying—you yourself as you have known you is gone forever. Getting my soul to Heaven can't console me for the loss of my body and mind.

David never seems to realize he'll be a nonentity there, lost in a crowd of angels exactly alike. Every good person who's died can't sit at God's right hand but David's as sure he'll be as close to God there as God is to him here.

There he was, that morning, threading his way between the graves, cutting through to the parsonage from Elm Street. I called to him.

"Why're you standing here smiling like that?" he asked me.

"Just thinking bout a dream I had the other night. You were walking among the graves just as you are now, looking for me behind all the tombstones."

"You must feel guilty about something, dreaming of death. Better tell your pastor what's on your conscience."

"Not when I live with him! He knows too much already. You get the mail?"

"Yes and here's a letter from Ora. Says she'll try to be here by the twenty-first to help you with the packing," and he separated Sistuh's letter from a handful of other mail and handed it to me. "She seems mighty pleased at our invitation."

I took that letter 'sthough it was any letter from anybody at any time, skimmed through it walking toward the parsonage, David holding my arm. Only feeling I had was relief that Sistuh'd be back a week before we had to leave and I wouldn't have to make a mess, trying to cut down Beth's blue reefer to fit Fair. . . . Why, here's the La Fayette Street crowd right now.

"Good morning, Mrs. Humiston, how're you this morning?"

"I'm fine, thank you, Madelaine. Come in, girls. I declare you all look like a big bouquet, those white dresses and different colored hats."

"Mrs. Humiston! You're the sweetest thing in the world to say that because a flower garden's just exactly the *idea* I had, I saw these straws all on a table reduced first morning I went to help Mistuh Heller out at the summer sale. I hid five of thum and telephoned the gang fast's I could. You like Cindy's blue one?"

"Yes, it's mighty pretty but she didn't say how she happened to have it. Sit down all of you. I'll run see if Cindy's ready."

"Noum, you sit right down again. I telephoned her we were on our way. She'll be down in a minute. We'll perch right here on the chair arms. We sit down on this cool porch, we might

217

stay too long and we promised to be at the depot when the Shoo-Fly comes through. Doris's cousin from Wilmington's coming through on her way—"

"Why, Doris, I didn't know you had kin down there! We lived there four years, you know. Mistuh Humiston's second pastorate. Who is she? Maybe I know—"

"Madelaine's the craziest thing in the world, Mrs. Humiston. My cousin's not from Wilmington. She's from—"

"Well, wherever she's from, it's dead loads of fun being at the depot when that Shoo-Fly whizzes in and I couldn't go down one single solitary morning last week—to meet anybody's visitor or anything—because I was a Working Girl. You know, Mrs. Humiston, Mama put her foot right down on my clerking for Mistuh Heller—said she'd never show her face in this town again if I did—till I showed her a piece in the *Ladies' Home Journal* commending girls who wanted to help pay for their own clothes. Said there were so many ways boys could earn a little extra but hardly any *nice* way for girls, said most positions had unpleasant and undesirable associations, so I just pointed out to Mama what a gentleman Mistuh Heller is even if he is of foreign descent and I said it isn't like people here don't know who we are, and course I'd never even think of going to a strange town so she finally gave in. And except for having to get up with the chickens and missing my nap after dinner and running round with the gang, I declare it wasn't bad atall. Only the very nicest people come in Heller's. Golly, Ann Tate, why're you punching— Oh! Mrs. Humiston, there's something we want to ask you. I certainly hope you won't think we're forward or anything like that but—well, I had a lot of time to read last week, after dinner when there'd be just a few country people in the store looking around scared to death and not buying a thing, and I came across another piece in the *Ladies' Home Journal* called 'The Right of Every Girl' so course I had to see what *that* was. It compared a 'distorted, vicious explanation of the meaning of life' to a glass of muddy water but said the story told by a mother is like a glass of clear crystal water. Said both are true but one is foul, the other pure, and said the right of every girl is to have her mother for her confidante and then she'll never go wrong. So—"

"I'm sure that's true, Madelaine."

"But you know, Mrs. Humiston, it's *mighty* hard to ask your own mother personal questions like that and we all were talking, way over here, and Ann Tate got the *i*dea we should ask you."

"Why, I'd be glad to answer anything I could, girls. You all come back some day real soon—"

"Oh, it's just one, Mrs. Humiston, and we thought it'ud be appropriate to ask you because today's your twenty-fifth anniversary. What we want to know is, do *you* think a girl's happier married than single? Here's that Cindy!"

"Cindy! I declare that hat's the most becoming thing you've had on this summer! And that peek-a-boo embroidery shirtwaist's simply darling!"

"Just wait till that Wilmington team—"

Ann Tate putting her hand over her mouth 'sthough I don't know their plans!

"Thank you kindly, as Molly says. What took me so long was, I was looking for this post card of Niagara Falls to show you all before I put it in my album. Prettiest thing I ever saw in my life. You hold it to the light, you see the sparkle on the water. Thad Creech sent it to me and I've barely met him. Pass it around and les go! It's half past ten right this minute."

❖

I don't think that big floppy hat's so becoming to Cindy. Doesn't show enough of her pretty face. It's certainly strange she should look so much like David and be less like him than any of them. I'd like Ann Tate's red one better on Cindy. It'ud set off her dark hair. Now there's not a nicer looking or better mannered crowd of girls in this town than the La Fayette Street one, I don't care what Fair says. I don't believe they're actually fast. Just high-spirited. And I'd never deny them that! They'll have to sober down soon enough. Far's Cindy concerned, I'd rather she went with them than with some of the flighty married women she's taken to since she was fourteen. And they to her. I couldn't find her in Laurenton, I'd run across to that Mrs. Harold Brown's and there she'd be, curled up on the fancy sofa-pillows behind the bead curtains of that cozy-corner like a pet poodle, listening to I don't know what.

Happier married or single? What do they think marriage is? The ceremony a conversion like David's, making a new person and a new life out of an old? Removing all doubts and fears, fixing it so that you live happily ever after? Or miserably? Why, marriage is no more of a piece than anything else in life. Some-

219

times you're happier than you've ever been and sometimes you'd give all you have just to be yourself again. I was as happy as any woman can be from the day I knew David loved me, wanted to marry me, right up to the day seven months later we knew Buddy had to die. And for long stretches afterward, Sistuh or no Sistuh. For most of those first ten years. No matter how clearly I remember now how she used to bother me, I could forget her the minute I got out of the house. And except for a dutiful letter every now and then when she was at Little Brookside, I didn't think about her any more than I had before I was married.

Those first months of marriage I used to laugh at myself when I remembered what *I'd* thought marriage was like. Sitting in the Bayport church that fall before I got Cousin Sudie's invitation, I'd look at Mercer's ginger-colored head two pews down and wonder what difference it made who the man was when marriage was just like death, just standing up in front of the altar instead of being laid out beneath it. All the fun's over and done with in either case, I thought. All the primping and the flirting, all the man-compliments, all the not-knowing-what-next. Saying "I do" and wondering what it meant. That's the catch in it! Just for an answer to "What am I promising to *do* when I promise to *love?*" has made many a girl marry a man she didn't really love. I had a pretty good idea what it meant but, hadn't been for Cousin Sudie, I'd have promised to serve, honor, and obey a boy like Mercer to experience it. From all I could see in Bayport, marriage was darning socks, getting up the wash, having children, thinking about what you'd have for dinner and how you'd keep a cook to cook what you finally decided to have, sitting on a veranda with other ghosts of dead girls talking about the ones who weren't there or about the clothes you'd have—this to be turned and made over the stylish way, this to be bought new. And from all I saw in Savannah, marriage with Stephen Clay wouldn't be so very different. Just more luxurious. My cake would be made with thicker white frosting by a permanent cook but I'd have to eat *it* and no other. My bed made up with pure linen sheets by a permanent house-girl but I'd have to lie on it. With Stephen Clay. Then in the very next spring I saw David ride up to our hitching-post that Sunday, listened to the friendly sound of his voice talking church to Sistuh, and realized *he* was the bachelor minister! And when he looked up at me 'sthough I was an apparition

220

from Heaven, I was sure marriage-in-a-parsonage wouldn't be like other marriages. Why I'd live with *that* man in an old cabin like Slippy's and Lucille's! Be as happy as Slippy and Lucille loving each other, having nothing but each other.

Was the thought of Slippy and Lucille consoled me that first night when the answer to the question wasn't all I'd thought it would be. Lying awake there at dawn in our room at the Cape Fear Hotel in Wilmington while David slept, the first light seeping through the lace curtains at those long French windows. Being disappointed. Why all the fuss and furor? The solemnity of married women whispering behind their fans? The open laughter of colored? It's no more than I saw peeping through the cracks of the barn time Buddy borrowed a bull from Camilla to freshen Katy. No more than seeing a rooster on a hen. No more than seeing Slippy and Lucille rush together stark naked down by the brook that summer day, sun shimmering and glistening on yellow and brown skins. No more than? Why, not nearly so much as! Seeing those two slim bodies flatten, crush the tall reeds, become one on a bed of green, I saw something beautiful.

Till then I'd thought beautiful was just a word you said when you saw a face or a picture or a white-columned house like Camilla. I wasn't more than six that summer but I knew I was seeing beauty because I couldn't understand why Lucille and Slippy looked so ashamed when they sat up and saw me standing astride the stile above them. They must've realized, though, by the way I looked that they had nothing to be ashamed of as far as I was concerned. Because when Lucille'd pulled her old rag of a dress over her head and Slippy'd stepped in the sewed-up sacking he used for pants, they helped me float the blockader Uncle Ram'd made for me and acted like nothing had happened. But David's jumping at me in a featherbed in a stuffy room wasn't beautiful and what he did hurt. Then I saw what the trouble had been—Slippy hadn't jumped at Lucille, they'd seemed to melt together. The lace and ruffles of my nightgown and David's buttoned-up nightshirt would've kept us from melting together if we'd known how to. I hadn't suspected it was going to hurt and had thought there was something wrong with me. That hadn't been a first time for Slippy and Lucille even though they weren't much more than children then. They'd learned! Well, we will too, I thought, and dozed off.

But I did see something beautiful in the Cape Fear Hotel that morning. Something more beautiful even than David's sleeping face. David opening his eyes and seeing me there beside him.

No, no, I can't feel it now just thinking about it! After twenty-five years! Why, I'm forty-eight years old! What would the girls think? But there's my needle and thread dangling and here's my hand at my throat! Exactly as it was that morning. But now, after all the children, after all the meals I've thought up, all the clothes, all the hubbub of all the parsonages, all the movings, all the little irritations of David's little everyday ways! In spite of Sistuh, of feeling crushed between two capital I's, in spite of growing up so suddenly after I was a woman, of growing old so fast since, here for the first time in I don't know when I feel it again—that love for David draining through my whole body, gathering in a lump in my throat. Not even that day on High Brighten when . . .

"Mama, Frances Eastbrooke just telephoned—why've you got your hand at your throat? Your neuralgia bothering you again?"

Beth opening the screen door a crack, clutching her kimono together.

"No, just nervousness I reckon. You get Sistuh back to bed?"

"I did *not*. I give up for this morning. She ate a little of the sherbet though. I wish you'd lie down and try to get a nap. Heaven knows when you've slept."

"I slept some last night. Maybe because your Papa wasn't here I felt a little relaxed not worrying bout his being kept awake."

"I'll dress and come on down. Help you entertain if anybody comes. I started to tell you—Frances Eastbrooke just telephoned and invited me for lunch. Said she'd just heard my aunt was no better and the reception called off, asked if I'd come eat Waldorf salad with them—if I can bring myself down to that after two weeks of midday dinners. But I'm not going till after twelve. Ralph'll pick me up in the machine on his way from the mill."

"Ah, me. All those vegetables I've been fixing and three of you not here to eat thum. Gladys has gone to Tom T's again."

"I'm not invited out so often. Thought I'd better go for a change. But if—"

"No, it's all right. Be all the more left for Molly to take home. But hurry down. I certainly don't feel like entertaining atall. I think if I have to say one more time that Sistuh's no better, that these headaches just have to run their course—"

"But, Mama, what can you expect when you insist on keeping up the fiction that it's physical?"

"That's a lot easier for me than saying it's psychological, as you call it. A lot easier to say she has these attacks because she *will* work too hard, gets run down, than to say she has thum because she thinks she's not appreciated, and treated like a dog. There've been queer people in every town I've lived in but I've never known anybody kin to thum to tell the truth about thum. It's easier for everybody to cover up. You'd better shut that door, you don't want Colonel Ryal to see you. Old fellow's coming up the street. Now *he*'ll have to stop and pass the time of day."

❖

I have to laugh, idea my trying to tell Beth why I had my hand at my throat. Neuralgia in my throat! When I have it it's in the back of my neck. Thoughtful and helpful as Beth is, she does think she knows it all. Every one of them does, so far's that's concerned. I did too when I was young. The less we know the wiser we think we are. Life seems mighty simple, just a matter of getting what you want. Sad thing is, now that I know better, I can't tell them a thing about it. Just have to sit by and watch them get hurt finding out for themselves. I remember what Aunt So-and-So used to say, "You makes out you got worry now the chilluns is on your toes, you waits till they's on your heart then you'll know what worry am."

As for trying to explain their Papa's still a man to me—well, it's my fault they can't see he is. The Wright girls see their parents as people. Not many children do, in the best of circumstances. Unless it's acted out for them as Mistuh and Mrs. Wright seem to have done. If I hadn't stopped David's putting his arms round me in front of Sistuh first year we were married, he might've done it in front of our children. All they've ever seen is a dutiful peck on the cheek when he goes away on a trip or comes home from one. Day I ruined everything was that spring in Wilmington when Sistuh was with us for the first time. I heard David's step on the porch and opened the shutter-door for him. He dropped his hat on the little table, grasped me in his arms, kissed my face and neck, lifted me off my feet and squeezed so hard I was afraid he'd hurt the baby I was carrying. I didn't protest though. I squeezed back hard's I could, till over his shoulder I saw Sistuh standing in the parlor door. Her eyes were bigger than I'd seen them since her sickness and actually shining with pain. Her lips began to quiver and she looked like she wanted to run but couldn't. I pushed David away, laughed and said something about his acting like he'd been away a month instead of an hour, talked fast above his astonishment. Later when I got him alone I told him he must remember not to behave like that when Sistuh was around till she got over grieving about Buddy or found somebody to love her. Said maybe he'd just better try to treat me in as brotherly a fashion as he treated her. In the daytime at least. And brotherly to David didn't mean being demonstrative.

No wonder after a while Sistuh didn't know that David and I loved each other as much as ever, began noticing and even mentioning his forgetting to take my arm when we went down steps or crossed a street, his sitting down at the table occasionally before I did. Such absent-mindedness never bothered me. I knew he was too absorbed in his work to remember little politenesses but Sistuh couldn't see how unimportant such things are. She wasn't in bed with us at night. At least she wasn't in bed with us at night! And that's where a third person would have to be to understand whether a marriage is happy or unhappy. Makes me tired hearing somebody say glibly such and such a marriage's not happy when they have to judge by what they see and hear in the daytime.

Took us long enough to learn how to be happy in bed. On our wedding visit up the country when he was keeping me awake night after night and I was getting no bodily pleasure, so sleepy all day I could hardly be polite to the hordes of kin kept pouring in, I tried to talk to him one morning about Intimate Relations as he said it was called in legal papers. He seemed embarrassed, murmured something about marriage being God's plan for begetting children, and went downstairs to breakfast without waiting for me to finish dressing. Later in the morning we went to see Uncle Hope and Aunt Tennessee across the creek and when we were leaving Aunt Tenny leaned out of her invalid's chair, grabbed David's coat-tail, and said in a stage whisper, "Mas' David, don't you play too hard on this here sweet-stringed harp the good Lord done give you, she look kinder puny to me." David didn't say much on the way back and when we went upstairs to get ready for dinner, he opened his Bible, handed it to me, his finger on verse twenty-two of the fifth chapter of Paul's Epistle to the Ephesians—that's one scripture I've been able to spot!—kissed me on the forehead and left me. Was a good thing he did. If he'd stayed in the room I might've thrown the *Bible* at him I was so mad. *Wives, submit yourselves unto your husbands, as unto the Lord,* and all the rest of it about the husband being the head of the wife and wives being subject to their husbands in everything as the church is subject to Christ.

As though I needed the Bible to tell me to love him. As though if I didn't want to love him and make him happy, what some old man said way back yonder could make me. I was so mad all through that long dinner I wouldn't look at David, wouldn't speak to him, and when we went back upstairs for our naps, I told him he was a coward to run hide behind the Bible when he didn't know the answers to my questions. He just stood there by the open window, against the green of that old cedar, his hands in his pockets, his eyes on the floor, as though he'd been made a fool of in school. I felt so mean I began to cry a little and begged his pardon. He shook his head, said I was right to call him to account but just try to bear with him till he got straightened out in his thinking. I said he didn't have to *think* about how to love me, just come lie down and put his head on my shoulder. But he said he thought he'd better take a walk up to that high pasture, to that big old gray rock where God first revealed Himself to him, and where, he added as he was going to the door, "I always ran to as a boy after a tussle with my earthly father." Then I did cry, up there in that high four-poster in that big square room. Cried because I'd hurt him and because I didn't like feeling more of a mother than a sweetheart. Didn't like feeling there was something I knew more about than he did. I just wanted to *be*. And be happy.

I was too, before another day dawned. God must've talked pretty straight to David that time. When we went to bed he just kissed me gently, turned on his side away from me, and after a little twisting and thrashing about, began to breathe evenly. I went to sleep finally but I had a bad dream, a real nightmare for the first time in my life. Remember it now clearly as I remembered it the next day. Slippy and Lucille were in their grass bed, locked in each other's arms and legs, lost to the world. I was astride the stile smiling down at them. Suddenly the sun went behind a black thundercloud I hadn't known was there and as it did, Sistuh came running from that abandoned rice field across the brook, brandishing a big stick, her hair flying wild and her eyes big as saucers. Her feet didn't bog down in that marshy ground and she jumped right over the brook, ran through the waist-high grass as though she could see through it and knew exactly where Slippy and Lucille were. I tried to cry out to warn them but I couldn't make a sound. I kept trying till David shook my shoulder. "Wake up, Ellen! You're having a nightmare." Then I heard my moans and clutched at David. "Too much stewed corn and hot bread for supper," he said sleepily. "Better lie on your stomach for a while." "No, no," I protested, "I want to lie close to you. Put your arms around me." "Oh, my darling," he said, wide awake, and he held me as he hadn't held me in those two weeks. No tighter but as though he had a right to, not hurried as though he was afraid somebody was coming after *us* with a big stick before he'd had his way with me. "You *want* to love me?" he asked. "Yes, yes. But let me take off this old nightgown first." And when I sat up and began undoing all those little tiny pearl buttons, he sat up too and pulled his nightshirt over his head. "This is right," he whispered, his mouth hovering over mine, "nothing between us. Oh, Ellen, let's never have anything between us again!" And we never did. Not at night . . . Now who's this lugging something in?

"Morning, Mrs. Humiston, how you all today?"

"Why, good morning, Red. We're all well, thank you, except for Miss Ora. She's no better. What've you got there?"

"Just a little something from the express office. I'm making me some pin money, the mater calls it, while the regular man's away taking him a vacation. Believe *me,* pin money's exactly what it is. Girl from Four Oaks got my Kappa pin somehow, commencement house party, and she's never sent it back. Now I hear she's sporting an A.T.O. Ain't *that* something, nice a fellow's I am? Looks like there's nothing for me to do but get me a new pin and a new girl. Can't get the girl till I get the pin and the pater's mighty tight since I ran the Steamer up against that colored guy's ox-cart. You sign right here, please, m'am."

"I the one to sign? Is it addressed to me?"

"To you *and* the Reverend. And in-sured. Came from The Old Dominion Jewelry Company in Richmond. Didn't I hear something bout it's being your Silver Anniversary today?"

"Yes, I expect you did. But I wish nobody'd done anything like this."

"Can't be sure, thing like that, till you see what you've got. Thank you, m'am. Well, reckon I'd better be moving on—less you want me to undo that cord for you?"

"No thank you, Red. Just push the box up against the banister there out of the way. One of the girls'll open it."

"Yes, *m'am*. Glad to. Yessir, I got to do a twenty-three skidoo and no mistake, I don't want old man Ryal on my neck. Got a whole crate of vanilla extract deliver to his house. Way he's been down at the depot this morning personally supervising those two coons loading for us, you'd think it was a case of Scotch whisky. Now I ask you, what you think *he* wants with all that much vanilla extract? Can't flavor cakes with it. Hasn't even got a cook now. Takes his meals at Miss Irma Irington's. It beats me." Lolling against the banister, scratching his red hair, frowning.

"Why, I can't imagine. Passed here this morning, said Miss Irma sets a mighty good table. Maybe it's for—stop that laughing, Red Griffen! I see what you're driving at! Good thing Mistuh Humiston's not here to hear you."

"You think I'd told on the Colonel before the Reverend? Not me! Never have forgotten that sermon of his the mater took me to, time he came from Cypress City to lecture for the WCTU in the opera house here. Mighty graphic. Used to stare at the Colonel, at every man I knew took a nip occasionally, and think what was going on inside thum. Stomachs all curdling up just like that egg did when the Reverend dropped it in a glass of pure alcohol. Whew! Thought I'd never in my life let anything like 'at happen to *my* stomach. By the way, Cindy home this morning?"

"No, she's gone downtown."

"Having a coke with that swell-head of a Bill Harrow! He thinks he's something, out of college selling in-surance. Lissen, Mrs. Humiston, you my friend, you tell Cindy I've got me a ten-buck a week job now and I can pay for cokes 'swell's the next fellow. You do that for me?"

"I certainly will, Red."

"So long now."

"Good-bye. Come again—without your wagon."

"I'll do that thing, I can beat that sorry Bill Harrow to the steps."

He won't, if he walks up as lazily as he's walking away, swinging those long arms, whistling.

Yes, I could sit here the rest of the day, look at that big box and not lift a finger to see what's in it. There's nothing I want now—except peace. "Trouble with you, little Ellen," David used to say those first years, "you'll never be content so long as you crave material blessings. No sooner does such a heart get one thing than it begins to want another. It never stops to thank God for what it has, just feels impatient with Him for what's denied." I reckon I did complain about material things then. And more than I realized. Expect the first time David gave me that little lecture was when we got electric lights in the Wilmington parsonage, almost as soon as anybody else got them, and I said, "Now if we just had running water, I wouldn't care how dirty Beth and Fair get or how hot the weather is." And believed it. But soon's we got a tap and a sink in Doddsville, I wanted a bathroom. I would've had it too if I'd known the Ladies' Aid had raised the money for it before it was meekly handed over to David for a new Sunday School piano.

Every time I had to go out to the gardenhouse that winter I was provoked with David for putting the material needs of the church ahead of his family's physical ones and thinking that because he liked wearing a hairshirt, I should too. That sleety day all three of the children had diarrhea, I wished he'd been a woman-hating hermit. Then we had a bathroom in Lynnboro and I'd think, sitting up there in my new-parsonage room convalescing so innocently, that now we had all modern comforts—spite of it's being gaslights in Lynnboro still—maybe we could get a few of the luxuries, a silver water pitcher and goblet for the hall table and a lady's writing desk with a mirror in it for the sitting-room. Yes, David was right about me in that respect, knowing me as little as he did in others. If he'd ever suspected how often I'd wished he'd come to Bayport to practice law rather than to preach, he'd have had me on my knees as quickly as any other sinner.

But he never did know how I used to pine for a big house with a cupola and bow-windows, lace curtains upstairs and down, Brussels carpets, red wallpaper in the hall, the statue of a goddess, draped and gilded, holding a gas or an electric light on the newel post. I'd break the tenth commandment in every such house I was invited to in Wilmington and Doddsville and, for the first ten months in Lynnboro. I wanted to be the hostess leading the way up softly padded stairs to a bedroom full of furniture bought for it, not of things given to the parsonage because nobody else wanted them. *I* wanted to be the one to say, "Now just lay your wraps here on the bed." A bed made up with drawn-work pillow and bolster shams and counterpane, with drawn-work bolster and pillow cases underneath the shams—I always peeped if I had the chance. "You'll find the bathroom right at the end of the hall," they'd say and I always went whether I had to or not. Stepped inside and closed the door and admired the long bathtub on clawed feet, white and smooth inside, colored porcelain decorated with gilt scrolls and flowers outside, the matching commode with a flower-shaped handle at the end of the long chain. . . . It's certainly a kind of joke on me that here in this old mansion we've got a bathroom was once like that and I don't even care how cracked and discolored everything in it is now.

But I was happy those first years in spite of my wants. Wilmington was so much like Savannah I felt I was going forward all the time, finishing the social education I'd begun in Savannah as surely as Ma'd finished hers at St. Mary's in Raleigh. Even adding little French phrases I'd pick up from Mrs. LeGrande who'd come to Wilmington from New Orleans. Stepping out of a victoria at the parsonage block in summer twilight or winter dusk, exchanging farewell compliments with those fashionable older women, sitting on the veranda or before the fire with David, hearing Alvinia singing the children to sleep upstairs, telling David where I'd been—to see Whittier's mother's house, Cornwallis's headquarters, the Dram Oak, or just calling and leaving cards from the maroon leather case with Mrs. David McCall Humiston on it in gilt, Miss Tempy's wedding gift. I'd repeat all the compliments I'd heard for him, feel his arms around me when I was sitting straight up in a chair. That first winter while Sistuh was in Florida with Buddy. And David'ud tell me what he'd been doing and thinking—way he's never been able to do with Sistuh and the children around. I remember one evening there like a link brighter than the others in a necklace. . . .

❖   ❖

"So you're back before dark today!" I grasped David's arm as he opened the front door and laughed when he jumped.

"So *you're* back before dark today!" He threw his hat at the rack, dropped the mail on the table, and took me in his arms.

229

"Why don't you ask me if I had a good time?" I ran my fingers up and down his coat sleeve.

"Because I know you'll tell me without my taking the trouble to inquire. Let's sit down first though. I've walked all the way from the Navasea Guano Works."

"Why'd you go way out there on foot?" I went ahead of him to the sitting room, full of flickering shadows from the fresh fire Alvinia'd made.

"Bonnie needed a shoe and I thought I'd just make a visit at the Soldiers' Home while Lambert took her to the blacksmith's shop. Found an old fellow out there had lost both legs at First Manassas and he began telling me about the fossiliferous rocks they bring up from the great marl beds near Charleston. Grind them up here at the works and make fertilizer. Said they contained pieces of vertebrae and the teeth of prehistoric animals!"

"Um-m. Cousin Sudie uses the petrified vertebra of some old monster for a doorstop. Said it was dug up there in the savannahs. But how could an old man with no legs get to the Works to see all that?" I pulled my skirts up a little and stretched my feet to the fire.

"Ellen, don't do that. You know it distracts me. Right away I begin wondering—"

"What?" I leaned toward him across the hearth, trying to get him over his word-shyness.

"Never mind that. Just pull down your skirts."

"But my feet're cold. Mrs. Willard forgot to have Moses put the foot-warmer in the carriage. I thought my toes would freeze."

So David used one hand for a blinder but went on. "One of the Daughters had driven him over and he'd got about on his crutches. That was why I walked on out there. Was ashamed not to use the legs God'd let me keep by ordaining my birth in '57 rather than earlier. Mighty glad I went too. I found just the illustration I need for my sermon on 'The Flaw in the Theory of Evolution.' The scientists' theory disputing the Old Testament won't even nibble at my faith again! It's as clear as day now: God made Adam out of the dust exactly as reported in the Book of Genesis. But the dust was full of bits of prehistoric animals and people today are nourished by food grown with fertilizer made from lime stored eons ago, by God the Father, in those bones and teeth! Of course all animal life that went be-

230

fore is in us and by it we live and breathe and have our being! How powerful is God, how puny man!"

But God made the scientists too, I wanted to say. Made that man Darwin. And his ideas you were telling me about seem more miraculous to me than that sleight of hand trick in Genesis. Meant a lot more trouble for God. I didn't say it. David and everybody else took it for granted I was as religious as he was and I didn't want to be prayed with. I know there's a God but I've never thought anybody understood about Him or that He was any more interested in us humans than in any other of His creations. I'd never have been so bumptious as to express an opinion about Him and certainly not to David. The God everybody I knew—except Miss Ryder—worshiped seemed to belong to David as much as David belonged to Him. Seems sometimes David thinks he's God's Other Son and after I met old Mistuh Humiston—Mistuh Andrew—I could understand why David felt the need of a father he could love and twist around his finger.

That evening he left his chair and walked back and forth between the center table and the hearth, berating the puny scientists who tried to undermine Christian doctrine, arguing with himself and practicing his sermon at the same time. "Faith is greater than logic. Logic's useful for handling legal matters, man's temporal affairs, but it's a snare and a delusion when applied to the spiritual. If any one of these fellows who think man can live by mind alone had ever felt God's presence as I've felt it, as the prophets of old felt it, they'd put logic behind them and stop wasting their time exploring the mystery of life by devious paths—paths that lead straight back to God the Infinite beyond the comprehension of man's finite mind every time."

I said "Amen" to that and might've got up my courage to ask him why he didn't let the Old Testament go and just preach applications of the Sermon on the Mount but I saw Alvinia standing in the shadow of the dining-room door, her white teeth shining because her mouth was open in awe. She waited till she was sure David'd finished, then said in a church-whisper, "Got you a nice hot supper to put on soon's I take up the hominy."

"All right, Alvinia. Just tap the bell when you're ready for us."

David turned suddenly and strode to the hall, came back

231

holding out a letter, "Slipped my mind, so taken up with eternal truths."

"From Sistuh?"

"Yes. Hope she's saying she's coming for that long visit she promised us. I need some new shirts."

You see! Every happy time I can remember with David ended up with Sistuh! Seems I married her twenty-five years ago today surely as I married David.

❖ ❖ ❖

"Yes, Mrs. MacNeill, I certainly will. Just as soon's the weather's a little cooler." Or warmer. Or it clears up. Anything but just as soon's Sistuh's quiet and I can hold up my head when I don't absolutely have to.

"I know! Nothing could've got me off my porch this morning but wanting you to have Claiborne's message. Thought it'ud mean a lot to you feeling in touch with one of your bridesmaids today. Do hope she'll keep her word and come to visit me before Mistuh Humiston's four years're out so you can have a real get-together." Going toward the steps at last, opening her ruffled Nile green parasol, lifting her ruffled white skirt.

"Yes, I'd certainly enjoy it." Very last thing I want to happen, seeing Claiborne "beautiful's ever, slim as a girl." "Was like old times, reading her handwriting again. Be sure to give her my love when you write."

"I certainly will. Good-bye. Good-bye, Miss Beth. Don't you forget now. You're coming to see me real soon and bring me *The Old Wives' Tale*. I declare there's not a thing in the library but books I read as a child and the Tuesday Afternoon Book Club won't buy a novel unless it's by Robert W. Chambers or George Barr McCutcheon or some man like that." Neat little face wrinkling in disdain.

"I'll come, as soon as I've finished it, regardless of the weather! Good-bye."

Beth and I lingering at the steps, smiling till she's passed the gate.

"Well, Beth, it'll please Fair—your striking up a friendship with Mrs. Charles MacNeill!"

"I'd strike it up with any others like her I could find in town. But I saved you in the nick of time!"

"From what?"

"From making up some flimsy excuse for not having opened

232

that package! Now I'm going to be as good as my word and hide it from you till Papa comes and you can open it together!"

"It wouldn't've made any difference to this Mrs. MacNeill what I said. She's Presbyterian."

"Don't fool yourself. She might've mentioned your lack of interest to Mrs. Angus MacNeill and any woman staunch enough a Methodist to've taken a MacNeill from the Presbyterian church—Whew, it's heavy! Bet it's a whole silver service."

"Just set it there behind the front door, here's your Mistuh Eastbrooke roaring up right now."

"Himmel, he's early! I'll be right back."

Walking up on pins, lifting his hat, bowing.

"Good morning, sir. Won't you come up and have a seat. Beth just stepped in the house a minute." He hears Sistuh! Doesn't know what to do or say.

"Er—Thank you very much, Mrs. Humiston. My time's limited today. I had to leave the mill a half-hour before noon in order to be back for a—a directors' meeting at two." Mincing kind of voice, as precise as his manner.

"Why, you should learn to take things easier the hottest part of the day. You know they say Southerners never get sunstroke because they know how to behave in hot weather."

Beth hurrying out, "Now, Mama, don't try to break down Yankee morale. Hello, Ralph. Let's go. If I stay around here another minute, I'll have to answer the telephone again for one of my popular sistuhs. 'Bye, Mama. Remember now, you're going to take a nap after dinner. I'll try to get back early enough to see that you do."

"Good-day, Mrs. Humiston."

Tips his hat like a mechanical doll. Eyes set too close together. Nose too sharp. I agree with Fair. I don't see what Beth sees in *him*. His wife's a right attractive woman. Or would be if she weren't so tactless. Telling me here the other day I looked tired. Idea anybody's saying a thing like that to your face! No, I don't see why she married him. Unless it's as Beth says—northern girls're not like southern. Don't have nearly so much attention. One man makes a "date," they hold on to him till he's proposed. Romance's just something they read about, I suppose. Beth says they don't have anything like as many clothes as southern girls either, and their dinners are just one meat, one starchy vegetable, and one or two green . . . "Yes, Molly?"

233

"Miss Mama, you better come wixt me upstairs. Miss Ora she's uhbanging on the floor up there in your room like she's uhcoming splank through the dining-room ceiling!"

4

She ain't lock hit. Hit gives a little bit when you pushes. More like she got a chair wedged in under the knob. Ain't nobody but Miss Orie coulduh do that so tight. Miss Mama, you got no strength. Lemme."

"Mama! What on earth's happening now? Came in the front door, sounded like the house's coming down. Telephone ringing. That crazy Bill Harrow. Just left him downtown few minutes ago. Could hardly hear a word he said. Going to the picture show with him tonight though so reckon I'll find out. Deeda in your room! That's awful. Baptist Hendricks'll hear her this side of the house. Lord, I'll be glad when we've lived here a second year and everybody stops asking me how Deeda is—or Miss Ora or Miss Fanning. Here, Molly, lemme help push. May not be's fat as you but I bet you my bottom dollar I'm almost as strong."

"*Miss* Cindy. Your little bitty toothpick arms! Come on then, you push when I pushes."

"Oh—oh—oh—oh—oh . . ."

"Listen, Mama, she's getting weaker. Must've pulled that big old wardrobe down on top of her. Must be dying all by herself in there. Poor Deeda. Deeda! Let me in if you can. It's Cindy. Deeda, please—"

"Cindy, don't you tune up now. One's enough."

"I can't help crying. It's so pitiful."

"Both you push now. I feels that chair uhgiving."

Little brass knob coming off in Molly's hand, door flying open, chair skimming, and all of us landing in a heap on a barricade of mattress and pillows.

"You hurt, Molly?"

"Noum, mattress save me. Lord, Miss Mama, how she do hit?"

"Look at that, will you? Tore the lace smack off one shoulder. Now, Mama, you'll be happy. I can't wear this peek-a-boo waist any more. Don't see why you say it's not decent, though, everybody's wearing thum. There she is! The other side of the bed.

Curled up like a little bitty baby. Look a there, Molly. Did you ever? I declare. . . ."

Not like a baby. Tighter than a baby. More like that picture of an unborn, old Doctuh Lipcom showed me to prove I was grieving over something not a baby when I lost my boy. Poor skinny legs drawn up, knees under her chin, arms folded over what used to be the handsome bosom she was so proud of, head tucked in like a sleeping bird's."

"Oh—oh—oh—oh—"

"Deeda, I'd be ashamed myself lying there, nightgown up to your neck! You'd ever caught me like that when I was *little,* I'd never've heard the end of it. Spose Papa or Doctuh Stewart'd been here!"

"Cindy, stop that chattering and go telephone Doctuh Stewart. Ask him to bring a hypodermic."

"Yesum.

"Honey Boy, I hate to see you leaving,
Honey Boy, you know my heart is grieving,
When you are sailing . . .'"

Pulling a pillow and sheet from under the mattress and pushing my way around the bed. "Here, Sistuh, just let me put this pillow under your head and a sheet over you. There's a draft—"

". . . oh . . . oh . . . oh . . . don't touch me, Ellen . . . oh . . . oh . . . don't touch me . . ."

"Sistuh, let go my legs! You'll make me fall!"

"Catch aholt my arm, Miss Mama. Now you leaves her to me. Me and her uhgoing get long all right now. Uhgoing back to her own bed, get her back rubbed again way she likes and her head scratch. Come long with Molly, now, Miss Orie. I'm uhgoing make you feel better."

". . . oh . . . oh . . . oh . . . they none want me to feel better, Molly. Want me off to myself out of their way . . . oh . . . oh . . . oh . . . Brothuh David and Ellen lie here night after night talking about me . . . oh . . . oh . . . oh . . .'"

If I could laugh, I would. What David and I have had to say about her in criticism we said long ago. But her concern with our bed will go on till one of us is laid out on it dead. I wonder if she's got any satisfaction, tearing it up like that at last. Must be what she's wanted to do every time she's made it up and she's done that every morning she's been with us, when she's been well, if I didn't do it the minute we got out of it. "Ellen," she'd

235

say if she saw me start it, "do don't make up your bed this morning, it needs airing. I'll take care of it later." Or, "Ellen, I do wish you'd tell that girl she's not to make up the beds. Negras always pull all the covers up to the head."

In the hall not knowing which way to turn. If Molly's cajoling, in that speech of hers so like Old Lady's, does get her back to her own bed she hasn't been in for three weeks or more—and then only after we've got a dose of nervine into her and carried her there—it won't do for me to be here holding on to the banister. She might spring at me when she passes, topple me down the stairs.

Let her do it! Provoke her to it! Tell her you know, have known for fifteen years. Tell her you stopped being stupid, self-centered little Ellen that February day in Lynnboro she left to wait on Miss Ryder for the last time. Tell her she's pulled no wool over your eyes once since. Not a thing she's done, not a word she's said, but has screamed the truth at you. Yes, let her push. No pantomine this time, Sistuh. No holding back once you've raised your arm. Please, I pray you, put an end to it all. I'm so tired . . . so tired . . .

"Mama! Lord, you scared me. Can hardly breathe. Thought you were going to fall right down the stairs. Why're you holding your head? You feel faint?"

"I'll be all right, baby. Something just came over me. Feel like my head's bound round with wire. I don't know how I'm going to stand it one more minute."

"You've stood it all these years, don't see why you have to break down now. I telephoned Doctuh Stewart. Said he'd be up soon's his office's empty. Has to make a call out at McNeill Township and'll stop on his way. You better fix up a little. Mrs. Angus MacNeill and Mrs. Pris Courtney, Glad calls her, just drove up in the MacNeills' new electric. Cutest little horseless buggy I *ever* did see."

"You'll have to invite thum in. Keep thum on the porch. I'll be down in a few minutes."

Mama they call. *Mama* David says. That's why I've stood it. Why I'll go on standing it. And keeping up appearances . . .

❖ ❖ ❖

"Noum, Sistuh's no better. In fact a little worse this morning, I'm afraid. We've had to call Doctuh Stewart to bring a hypodermic. After a long siege like this, the nervine from a bottle

236

doesn't seem to relieve her. Let me pull your chair over this way, lady. Sun's coming right through the holly branches now."

"Thank you, I'll do my own pulling. You've got enough on your hands without thinking of me, I declare you have. Why don't you let Henry Stewart give *you* a little something?" Mrs. MacNeill's voice as maternal as her enormous bosom, as understanding as her blue eyes.

"Oh, I'm all right."

"I declare, Mrs. Humiston, I can't see to save my life how you keep looking so well, nursing an illness in such hot weather." Mrs. Courtney pursing her thin lips the way her Kind always does. "We had Mistuh Courtney's mother with us of course for years—she passed away three years ago last April. She was subject to migraine headaches too and I declare, sometimes I'd think I needed to be in bed more than she did. Of course she didn't moan in her pain the way Miss Ora does but—"

"Migraine has different effects on different people, I expect. Some come on right suddenly and others're gradual."

"That's right, Mrs. MacNeill. Sistuh's come gradually. I can always detect the first signs. She *will* do too much, get all tired out and despondent, and first thing you know, she's crying with pain."

"Yes," Mrs. MacNeill drawing in her breath sympathetically, nodding her head and emphasizing her double chin, "you know I dropped in one day early in July—remember distinctly was then because I was just driving home in the old trap. I'd been down in Cattail Row collecting rents—chicken feed, Mistuh MacNeill calls it, and I declare it's not much more than that and smells like a chicken yard too, toted round in a darky's stocking two, three weeks. But as I was saying, Fair'd just got home from that houseparty at Wrightsville Beach and Miss Ora was stitching lace on a tissue paper pattern, making that all-over lace dress—"

"I wish to goodness Fair'd never got the *i*dea for that dress, from wherever she did get it! There's been not a minute's peace in our house since Lassie Courtney saw her in it at Dixie Roe's party. But I absolutely refuse to go to all that work such weather as this. Or ask Miss Lizzie Cramer to do it. It's *so* tedious and hard on the eyes." Looking down a little guiltily at the hand-tucking on her shirtwaist.

"You will before the summer's out, Annie Courtney! Never saw you deny that daughter of yours anything yet. But let me

237

get on with what I was saying. Miss Ora was trying to keep Fair on the other side of the machine holding the stuff straight and Fair had to go to the telephone two, three times. Finally poor Miss Ora's fingers began to shake so she couldn't do a thing. She stopped right in the middle of a row and turned to me, 'You see how it is, Mrs. MacNeill,' she said, 'I do and do for them and they haven't the slightest consideration for me. Fair's just like her mother was at her age.' I laughed and said that was the way with all young people but—"

"Why she must've been crazed by pain then, thinking our quiet little preacher's lady's anything like that butterfly of a Fair!" Leaning over tapping my knee with her fan, "Not that we all don't love you just as you are but I can't see a little home-body like you ever having been on the go all the time. That Fair's a sugar-plum, taking the best catch in town and still keeping all the girls devoted to her! Met Maybelle Grimes in Heller's this morning—ran in to try to match some ribbon scraps I'm using on a boudoir cap for Emma St. John's trousseau. Couldn't of course and had to buy it all new. Anyway, Maybelle said she didn't see anything for Fair Humiston to do, console these girls for taking Bob Alexander out of the running, but to have a big church wedding with a dozen bridesmaids!"

"Yes, Fair wants a big wedding but I told her this morning I couldn't even think of the announcement party till Sistuh's better."

"You don't have to, lady. The Roes say they're going to do that for you if it's the last thing they do in this world. Why, look what Molly's bringing us!"

In her white apron and I forgot to mention it to her!

"Yesum, Miss Annie, thought you and Miss Isabelle'ud like a little refreshment. Hot, ain't it?"

"*It* certainly is. Don't know what we'll do we don't get a shower soon. Thank you, Molly. Why, what delicious looking little cakes! Don't tell me you made thum!"

"Noum, wisht I coulduh though. Miss Beth she ordered these *ready*-made. From Richmond, Virginia. For the re-ception we can't have tonight. Seem like they ought to be et whilst they's nice and fresh."

"By the way, Mrs. Humiston, have you seen Red Griffin today?"

"Now, Mrs. MacNeill, stop your beating round the bush! Of course I've seen him! Came here early with a great big package.

238

I was going to mention it before you left. But I haven't the slightest *i*dea what's in it. Beth insisted on putting it away till Mistuh Humiston gets home so we can open it together. It's mighty sweet of you people—"

"Nothing atall. Just a chance to let you all know what we think of our preacher and you."

"Well, we certainly do appreciate it— Thank you, Molly. Did you take some up to Sistuh?"

"Yasum. She taken one sip the *ice*-tea. And I got her back— I means I *rub* her back. There the doctuh right this minute!"

"Yes, it certainly is. Now you ladies sit right still and drink your tea. I'll just run up with him."

❖ ❖ ❖

Doctuh Stewart drinking tea, finishing up the little cakes, listening to Mrs. MacNeill's and Mrs. Courtney's diagnosis of the illness of every one of his *nice* patients, following me upstairs, I apologizing over my shoulder for having had to call him at such a busy time, saying I realized there wasn't much he could do for Sistuh—all the old rigmarole I wish I had a dollar for every time I'd repeated it going up some parsonage stairs. Wish all the doctuhs had had their two for. If only a preacher could pay for their calls I'd feel a lot better about having to ask them to come. In Cameronville I'd thought we could, all of them being Presbyterian, but David's been to Doctuh Stewart's office any number of times last spring about his heart and we'd called him twice the first weeks of Sistuh's spell but he'd refused to send a bill.

"Yesum, but it's always a busy time. You mustn't hesitate on that account. I manage to get in a little hunting in the fall but that's about all. Winter there's grippe, diphtheria, pneumonia, scarlet fever. Spring, scarlet fever, measles, whooping cough, chicken pox. Summer, typhoid. And always consumption, malaria, hookworm, and pellagra. Understand you sent me a case of that this morning. At least I think your diagnosis of Jeb Smithson's girl's complaint is more accurate than some of those Annie and Isabelle've been giving me. Now which room—?"

"Sistuh's in hers now, Doctuh. Right down the hall. She doesn't like to stay in it when she gets one of these headaches— says that old magnolia outside her window depresses her. As a girl she used to hate thum."

"Well, these old Victorian houses give a family room to

239

move about, don't they? Lot of thum in this town, remodeled from ante bellum mansions like this one or built new. Tobacco money came in just in time, before the plan went out of style. Always thought was a lucky thing for the Methodists nobody'd buy this place after the last Gillespie died. Better be careful you don't exorcise that old ghost or those Gillespie cousins down in Currituck'll be able to sell it and put you out of a parsonage. Now, you just let me try that door, Mrs. Humiston."

"There! I have it. The knob's just loose and hard to turn."

"Good-bye my bluebell, farewell to you,
One last fond look—

"Lord, help us, I didn't know Doctuh Stewart was here yet! Good morning, Doctuh, how you?"

"Fine, Miss Cindy. What's this I hear bout you? Giving up school and stepping on the carpet before your two older sistuhs step off."

"Fair's stepping off real soon and if I wait for that Beth to, I'll never get on! Mighty glad I don't have to be cooped up in that Greensboro Female Academy another year! Want me to come in with you, Mama?"

"No, but I wish you'd run down and entertain the ladies till I can get back."

"Yesum. 'Good-bye my bluebell . . .' "

". . . oh . . . oh . . . oh . . . oh . . . oh . . ."

On the floor again, huddled against the foot of the bed. But Molly's got her into one of Beth's pretty nightgowns. Always something to be thankful for! Times I've had to usher a doctuh in and blushed with shame. Close and hot in here, all the windows closed, and the sweetish smell of that Happidine. Why she's taken a half a bottle this morning! Better than the smell in that old store-room though—charred pork, chitterlings, rags, and blood burnt into the bricks of that fireplace forty years ago. . . .

"Sistuh, here's Doctuh Stewart, come to give you something to relieve you. Let me just help you back to bed."

". . . oh . . . oh . . . oh . . . leave me alone . . . don't touch me . . . I beg you . . . oh, oh, oh . . . have some mercy . . . oh . . . oh . . . oh . . ."

Sistuh pushing at my knees but I holding on to the bed post and nodding to Doctuh Stewart. "Come in, Doctuh, and have

240

a chair. Oh, Molly must've taken thum all out when she cleaned and forgot to bring thum back."

"Never mind, hardly time to sit down." Bending over Sistuh, putting his hand on her shoulder. "Miss Ora, I'm mighty sorry to find you no better. Doesn't speak well for my doctoring, does it? But you let me help you get on the bed now and I'll give you a little something to relieve your pain."

". . . oh . . . oh . . . oh . . . oh, Doctuh . . . they none care how I suffer . . . oh . . . oh . . . oh . . . just so long's Brothuh David can get . . . oh . . . oh . . . oh . . . up there in the pulpit and preach Christian kindness . . . and . . . never . . . oh . . . oh . . . oh . . ."

"Yes, I understand, Miss Ora. Preachers're not a bit better than the rest of us, are they? But we just have to put up with thum and get along the best we can." Straightening up, filling the little syringe.

Sistuh raising her head, looking up. "No, no, no, not that thing again! Oh . . . oh . . . oh . . . you want to kill me . . . put me to sleep so I'll never disturb any of thum again . . . oh . . . oh . . . oh . . ." Clutching at the mattress, trying to pull herself to her feet.

Doctuh handing me the syringe, putting his hands under her elbows. Can't lift both her and the mattress, she clinging to it like a life-preserver, so grasping her left wrist, pushing up the half-sleeve. "You hold this sleeve out of the way, Mrs. Humiston, and give me the syringe."

Handing it to him but Sistuh twisting about, sending it spinning across the bed.

". . . oh . . . oh . . . oh . . . I'm helpless and you torment me . . . oh . . . oh . . . oh . . ."

"Doctuh, is it broken?"

"No, didn't hit the wall." Dropping on his knees, clutching Sistuh's wrist again. I trying to push up the sleeve and Sistuh's right hand striking back at me. Striking me across the face, that bump of misshapen bone at her wrist hammering at my nose.

"Mama, Papa's here! You want *him* to come? Ladies've gone, Said tell you—Mama! Your nose's bleeding! Here, let me—"

"Go tell your Papa to come!"

"Yesum!"

"Ellen, don't let him come up here . . . oh . . . oh . . . oh

241

. . . I've told you and told you I won't see him . . . oh . . . oh . . . oh . . ."

Doctuh dabbing at my nose with a piece of gauze. "Hold it just here. Press hard. It'll stop soon. Pain you much?"

Shaking my head, looking down at Sistuh's poor shoulder blade sticking from the low-neck gown like a sawed-off wing.

Doctuh looking at it, shaking *his* head. "Afraid I'm a poor hand at this sort of thing. I've seen some suffering women this time of life but never anything like this." Motioning me aside. "How old's Miss Ora?"

"She'll be fifty-one next December." That's all, believe it or not.

"Been having these attacks fifteen years or so, I think you told me?"

"Yes. And they seem to be getting worse the last few years. Not any worse than when they first began but worse than they were ten years ago. Or so it seems sometimes. I don't know—there've been so many—three or four bad ones a year."

Patting my shoulder. "No, I shouldn't think you would remember. Marvel to me is *you* haven't broken down some way. Wish you'd come down to my office, let me check on you. Call me on the telephone some day right soon and—"

"Oh, I'm all right, Doctuh." But don't be sympathetic with me or I'll be crying too!

"You ladies in middle-life can't be too careful. I'll expect you. Nose better?" Taking away the bloody gauze, tilting my head, looking in my nostrils. "Don't believe you'll have any swelling. Put ice on it if you do." Turning back to Sistuh.

I grasping his arm. "Doctuh, you think this is—physical?" Nodding at Sistuh, her face pressed against the mattress, her moans muffled.

"Um-m. Could be. Menopause starts early with some women. Sad thing is we've got nothing to treat it. Case like this, seems to me, maybe an institution—Oh, good morning, Mistuh Humiston."

"Good morning, Doctor. Mama, you sent for me?"

Walking in on eggs. Walking forward, wanting to walk backwards. As tall and straight as Doctuh Stewart and at least ten years older.

"Yes, David. Looks like you'll have to help Doctuh give Sistuh a hypodermic."

"Well, I—" Inching to the bed, bending over Sistuh, touching

242

the tips of his fingers to the tangled mass of hair Molly hadn't been able to braid, "Sister, I'm sorry to find you no better. Anything I can do to—"

. . . oh . . . oh . . . oh . . . My heads hurts so, Brothuh David . . . but I didn't want Ellen to . . . get you away . . . from your work . . . oh . . . oh . . . oh . . ."

"Well, now, that's all right. You just let Doctor here give you something to ease the pain."

Raising her head, shaking it from side to side. "No, no, no . . . he'll just put me to sleep and I'll never wake up . . . oh . . . oh . . . oh . . . I'd be glad . . . but I don't want you to have murder on your conscience . . . add to everything else . . . oh . . . oh . . . oh . . ."

Straightening, stiffening. "Sister, I've told you enough my conscience is clear!"

"David, Doctuh's in a hurry." Nudging his arm, pointing to Sistuh's left arm. His conscience now!

"What is it you want me to do, Mama?"

As though he's never done it before!

"Drop on your knees, Mistuh Humiston. Put your arm around her shoulders and hold her right arm down, if you can. Lift her left and keep it steady."

"Come now, Sister. I'll see to it you don't get too much. Just enough to . . ."

It's working again! Sistuh's head on David's shoulder, nestling under his chin, her body going lax against his. Scene I hate and welcome—that old woman's face, mouth open for the moaning, eyes closed for the ecstasy, pressing up against that *young* man's. No lines about the eyes, no touch of gray at the temples, no resignation around the lips—young to her in every way. No change in character, no growth in spirit. Not Brothuh David now. *Mistuh Humiston. David* if she dared.

Doctuh stooping to inject the needle and Cindy just inside the door again! A big audience of one. Hands spanning her little tiny waist, head bending forward, eyes round and dark, dark blue, missing nothing. A child's face still but her tongue quiet for once, her lips pressing downward in disgust.

"There now, Miss Ora. Now you'll be able to rest a little." Doctuh looking about on the bedside table for a place to set the syringe. Pushing aside the bottle of smelling salts, the spirits of ammonia, the damp washcloth, the glass and spoon, all the paraphernalia of the sick-room. Picking up the half-empty bot-tle of Happidine. "Miss Ora take much of this stuff?"

"Yes, Doctuh, she does. Not only when she's this way but says, when she's up and about, she can't get through a day without several doses."

"Hasn't killed her yet, I reckon it won't. Now, Mistuh Hu-miston, if we can make her comfortable on the bed, she should sleep for a few hours."

❖ ❖ ❖

David going on downstairs with Doctuh Stewart, talking about some poor woman who's dying with pernicious anaemia. I to the bathroom splashing cold water on my face. Thinking about the night last December we'd come to Cameronville and how I'd hoped again things might be different here. After the welcoming committee had gone, David, Sistuh, and I'd sat around the sitting-room fire commenting. "Why I don't see how you can think *she's* so much," Sistuh said about whoever it was I'd mentioned. "She has those simpering ways I can't stand." I'd never learn, it seemed, to keep my mouth shut about any-body I like though I know perfectly well Sistuh'ud decide then and there that she didn't. Ann Wesley was sitting on the sofa looking 'sthough she'd lost her last friend and Gladys came running in. "Ann Wesley, you're a mess, crying bout having to go to a new school when we've got a bathroom here big's the parlor nearly! Come see it!" Ann Wesley wouldn't budge. "Then you come with me, Mama," Gladys begged. Sistuh was fumbling in her handbag for a soda mint for David and hadn't seemed to notice Gladys's not inviting her, so I went over the tenth home I'd had in twenty-five years—a spacious house on a corner, not built for a parsonage, filled with furniture that'd been bought for it, no overpowering shadow of a church on one side. Here, I thought, maybe we can live like people at last. I'll die hoping. . . .

Was that night I discovered something about Sistuh I'd missed all these years. When I went back to the sitting room, I said with all these bedrooms, we could have a real company room, always ready for whoever came. Sistuh said, no, better let the children have a room of their own if there was one extra—Ann Wesley could tack up those Gibson Girl pictures she was collecting and Gladys could keep her paper-doll house set up in a corner out of the way. So she's giving up the children at last, I thought. Going

244

to let them go to sleep without having their legs and backs
rubbed, going to sleep at last herself without a hand on her face.
Then she said, "Company comes when the house is filled up at
Christmas and in summer, you can sleep with me and Brothuh
David can have a cot in the children's room." "Why that's—"
I started to say *foolish in this parsonage.* Nobody so foolish as I!
All these years I'd heard her planning every time company was
coming and never once'd seen that her sole idea was to separate
David and me for two weeks, one week, a night! Anything had
seemed logical in a parsonage with only three or four bedrooms
but when we had one with six . . .
    "Mama! Where *are* you? Oh. Be all right if I ask Bob to stay
for dinner? Cindy says Deeda's had a hypodermic."
    "Yes, she's getting quieter. But, baby, I'd thought you should
ask him for supper—Beth wants to do something a little extra
tonight."
    "I spose that would be better then. But will you come ask
him?"

❖   ❖   ❖

Company for dinner, though, anyway, Ann Wesley's bringing
Elizabeth Oats and Tiny McKinnon home with her. All sitting
there on the porch steps, giggling and eyeing Fair and Bob in
the chair swing, Molly ringing the bell, Bob tearing himself
away for a few hours but Elizabeth and Tiny not moving so
nothing to do but invite them to stay. And Ann Wesley's saying,
"Beth's not here. She's out for *lunch*. After dinner we can go in
her room and try on all her New York clothes!" Such excitement! Hearing them telephone their mothers 'sthough they'd
never had a meal with us before.
    Ann Wesley looking right pretty, face flushed and eyes shin-
ing, and all during dinner acting mighty important because
she's Fair's sistuh, has got something Elizabeth and Tiny with all
their money and curly bobbed hair haven't got—a grown sistuh
engaged to be married to a tall, dark, and handsome man. Why,
listen at her! Coming right out and asking Fair to let them all
try on her ring, making a face at Cindy, Cindy asking what's got
into her, riding a high horse instead of ʌitting under a willow.
I'm mighty relieved to see her coming out of her shell at last.
Maybe she'll get married after all. It doesn't have to be a missionary. A school superintendent or one of David's protégé
preachers . . .

All this giggling and chattering's a good thing today, David having so little to say, looking absent-minded instead of quietly benign, way he usually looks when there's laughing and talking around him he doesn't have to be drawn into. Now why's he looking at me with that foreboding expression? Enjoy this while you can, he's saying plain's can be, but when you know what I know— Well, what can it be but that the Presiding Elder's told him he'll have to resign from the Conference because of Sistuh? We've got callous, thinking that because it hasn't happened it never will. Was his being given good towns again, after that little old Queenston and *Second* Church, Raleigh, that's consoled me for the dead hope of *his* ever being a presiding elder or bishop. Was his eloquence and popularity as a prohibition lecturer that brought him back to salaries we can live on—bishop. couldn't ignore a preacher who'd been asked to run for governor on a dry ticket. But that movement died almost as soon as it flared—some politician's remembering the blight on our home—and now the state's dry, Conference'll take less pride in a preacher's eloquence than feel shame at what goes on in his parsonage. Now David's got me so upset I can't eat a bite of Molly's sweet potato custard I've been looking forward to . . .

". . . so all my bridesmaids'll be in mauve-pink, and, Elizabeth and Tiny, if you don't sit right up there within the ribbons and keep your eyes stretched as wide's they are now, I'll never forgive either one of you, you hear? Mama, may I be excused? I've got to go shut mine tight. Three sets of tennis've made me feel like a rag."

"Excuse me too, Mama. Excuse me, please, Mrs. Humiston, and thank you ever so much. Excuse me, please, Mrs. Humiston, and thank you ever so much," and all three trailing after Fair. Cindy stretching and yawning, hoping "those silly little galoots won't keep her awake first chance she's had to sleep in the daytime in a month of Sundays." But waiting to ask Beth, coming in, what you have to eat when you're invited out to *lunch* and Beth making a face at her, kissing David's cheek, congratulating him on our anniversary, asking, that facetious way that so annoys him, if he had a soul-stirring district conference, turning to me, asking what happened to quiet Deeda.

"She had a hypodermic and's dead to the world, thank the Lord, before she could kill Mama!" Cindy going on, spite of all my efforts to stop her, telling about Sistuh's tearing up our bed.

246

"You didn't tell me anything about that, Mama." David pushing back his chair, playing a nervous tattoo on its arm. "If I'd
known—"

"What time've I had to tell you, David? I'm glad you had
your dinner before—"

"Doctor Stewart know about it?"

"He knew about the accident to my nose. And it was an
accident."

"Accident my foot! I would've told him bout all of it, I'd got
a chance, but Mama sent me down to talk to Mrs. MacNeill and
Mrs. Courtney—said, Mama, they'd come back after supper, pay
their respects to you and Papa both."

"I hope you had sense enough not to tell them all about it!"

"You lie low, Miss Beth Humiston. You're not here with
it much's I am. One reason I'm sorry I'm not going back to that
female penitentiary this winter. You better thank your stars I
didn't tell thum what's the matter with Deeda!"

"Well, if you know, let's have it. Maybe we can do something
constructive." Beth picking up my spoon and dipping into the
custard.

"I know all right. Have known since I was knee-high to a
pup. . . . Deeda's so in love with Papa she can't see straight."

David's face white—and ugly with his suppressed fury. Hands
gripping the chair arms, holding on, to keep him from lunging
at Cindy. "Don't ever let me hear those words again."

Cindy bursting into tears. "Papa, you—you never spoke to a
one of us in—that tone—in all your life." Pushing back her dessert plate, putting her head down on her folded arms, sobbing
like her heart would break.

"I'm sorry I had to now, my child." Getting up, walking to
the bow-window, looking down at my potted plants, his head
shaking like an old man's.

"Himmel!" Beth gulped, cleared her throat. "Why pay any
attention to Cindy's crazy notions? She's just not all there."

Cindy sucking in a sob, lifting her blotched, tear-streaked
face. "I knew you'd say that!" Glancing at David's back, taking
a chance. "But I've got two eyes in my head for seeing more
than what's printed in a book and I get tired hearing you all
talking all the time and never saying anything. I know what I'm
talking about. Dee—"

"Cynthia, *that will do*." David starting toward her, his arm
up-raised.

247

Cindy crouching in her chair, her face as full of horror as it was the night the steam laundry in Queenston exploded and they all thought Judgment Day'd come.

David's hand falling heavily on the chair back, flinging that big chair to one side like a stick of light wood. "My God, have mercy upon me!" Striding from the room.

Beth starting after him.

"Baby, come back. He's gone off to pray."

Telephone ringing and Cindy jumping up to answer it, patting the row of puffs across her forehead, and humming one of her popular songs. Beth letting go the chair back she'd been clinging to, coming and putting her arm around my shoulder. "Mama, you come upstairs now and get some rest before Deeda wakes up."

"Yes, I'll have to. She may be worse tonight."

Passing the closed parlor door, wanting to go in, kneel with David, comfort him, but going on up the stairs with Beth, passing her closed door.

"Now what in the name of heaven's going on in my room?"

"Ann Wesley's crowd trying on your clothes. You'd better see what—"

"Let thum have fun. I'm flattered, my wardrobe not being exactly a southern belle's. Frances was certainly right, saying at lunch how fortunate it is that we live in the South. Said up North with a case like Deeda's we'd live behind closed doors, be isolated as a family, and probably every one of us would be queer in some way. She can't get over the charming fact that all misfortune down here's glossed over with pretty talk. Says we live on two levels—a real and a social, the whole idea being that 'never the twain shall meet.' Everybody knows the truth about everybody else but they'd die before they'ud mention it to anybody's face. She thinks it makes life very pleasant."

"Why, that's exactly what I was telling you this morning! It makes things easier, endurable, for all of us. Seems to me, though, you were being mighty frank."

Beth stooping, picking up the little brass knob, pushing my door open. "Ye gods! How could Deeda've done it? I almost had to carry her to the bathroom this morning—but then, she fought like a tiger when I tried to take her on to her room."

"Sistuh's superhuman these times. Every doctuh who's ever seen her's said she's bound to creep down to the ice-box at night. She never has. The sound or the silence would give her away."

"You sit down, Mama, wherever you can. I'll go get Molly and we'll fix up the bed for you. Maybe Massy can get this knob back in place."

"No, Molly's had a morning of it too. I want her to get through the dishes and go home for a rest herself, coming back to cook supper tonight. Massy'll be here when he gets through at the church. To cut the grass. We can get him to lift this mattress too. I'll just drop down on it where it is for a little while."

"Undress, then, and stay here till I call you. I'll close the shutters."

"Beth—"

"What were you going to say?"

"Nothing. What's the use?"

"There 'ain't none' unless—but you go to sleep now." Pulling the mattress flat on the floor, laying a pillow at one end, and going out, closing the door as well as she can.

❖ ❖ ❖

Getting out of my corsets is some relief for my body but there's none for my mind.

What's the difference whether Beth knows the "psychological basis of it," as she would call it, whether she meant what she said to Cindy or not. Cindy's never had the book-sense of the others, no judgment of what's right to say or do, poor child, but she's got a sharp eye for seeing right through people and the way they behave. Wonder is she hasn't burst out with this before. For all her lightheartedness, her nerves must be on edge today too to let her come out with a thing like that she's managed to keep bottled up I don't know how long. Poor David, having to hear those words spoken by one of his children after all the years we've thought we were keeping the secret! Poor David? Poor *me*. David's got his God. Down there right now casting *his* burden on Him. He'll get up from his knees, hold his head high's ever, go off to pray with that old woman with anaemia 'sthough he hadn't a care in the world. He'll give her the sacrament and leave her waiting for death with a smile. I don't believe there's another man in the world like him. Twenty-five years his wife and today's the first time I ever saw him lose his temper. Almost lose it. First time I ever heard him speak sternly to one of the children. Good thing it was Cindy. She can throw it off her way surely as he can his. I don't know why but I felt a kind of pleasure right along with the pain of that scene. Hearing Cindy's words, seeing David be human that way was the next best thing to having Sistuh act out her hatred of me. Was like a gust of fresh March wind when you open the windows to air a winter-sealed room. Maybe if David'd spoken sternly to Sistuh fifteen years ago, she might've controlled herself the first time and there'd never have been a second. Reckon that young Doctuh Powell Sistuh detested so, in Raleigh, was right. "Miss Fanning's just a spoiled child," he said. "If you'd given her a hard slap first time she behaved this way, she'd never've tried it again."

Mighty easy now to see what should've been done the first time but if I had to live that time again, I'd do exactly the same. I could no more've been mean to her that fall in Lynnboro, knowing what caused it all, than I could've flown. I felt nothing but sympathy for her, kept thinking how I'd've felt if David had gone on with his idea of marrying *her* after *I'd* fallen in love with him. Oh, I'd've got over it, married somebody else, but the world would've been mighty black for a while. And I wasn't poor Sistuh, afraid of my own shadow, scared to be myself, pretending all I wanted to be was a self-sacrificing "mother." No, I couldn't have slapped her and certainly David couldn't have. The "loud sickness," we thought, would pass as the "silent sickness" at Little Brookside had. Was the reaction of going back to that gloomy old house she hated, nursing Miss Ryder's last illness, remembering everything on the spot, coming back to Lynnboro and finding David had changed toward her, hearing his "Sister" spoken in a brother's voice instead of "Ora" in a—a lover's. So I held out, gave no sign of my knowledge or of hers, because I was pregnant again and this time it just might be me, rather than the baby, who'd be lost. I could see that she had to give way the second time David had blighted her life as she had the first and I had nothing but admiration for her come-back the summer of my wedding—now that I knew what she'd been up against. I could stand the disgrace of her moaning for a while. Better for her to get her suffering to the surface at last. And then Ann Wesley, the prettiest *baby* of them all, came into the world the easiest . . .

Maybe if I'd told her then I knew the truth at last, had it out with her, said "well, here we are, these're the facts, let's see what we can do to make the best of it," we might've saved her

250

and ourselves. I couldn't have. Already we'd lied to each other too long. David to me silently, I to him in words—at least I didn't tell him the whole truth about how I felt having Sistuh with us—and both of us to her in every way, she to us. All three of us lying so fast and furiously that August fifteen years ago we'd forgotten what truth was.

There we were going up the country together, at the end of August, 1894, Sistuh with us because she wanted to help me (be with David), because David wanted her to help me (be with him), because I wanted her to have the trip (be a help to me). Makes me mad right now to think of my deafness. I've forgiven David, I've forgiven poor Sistuh, but I'll never forgive myself for being so dense. So complacent. Why, I do believe I like not forgiving myself! It makes me feel something again—like that love for David welling up in me this morning. Even Fair's engagement to a man she's in love with, a man with position and money—all I've dreamed of for my girls—has gone over my head like water over a duck's back. I've taken it as a matter of course.

I was alive that August fifteen years ago even if I didn't have all my faculties. . . .

5

As the train pulled out of another little station, I fixed the third of David's clean handkerchiefs against the grimy red plush, leaned back and shut my eyes to keep out the cinders. Was better when we were in motion. The puffing of the engine and the rumble of the wheels better than the crying of babies, the hot, dirty breeze better than the smell of greasy fried chicken and soiled diapers. My eyes closed, I didn't have to make soundless answers to Sistuh's soundless questions from diagonally across the aisle, nod and smile every time she pointed to Cindy asleep in her lap; to Beth, her nose pressed against a closed windowpane, not missing a hog wallow or, to her, a poor untravelled child waving from the door of a log cabin; to Fair, dressing and undressing paper dolls from a shoe-box trunk. Now who but Sistuh would've thought of cutting out ladies in chemises from all her old pattern books, cutting off the heads of those in stylish dresses, cutting shoulder tabs on the dresses and slits in the hats, so that Fair could dress and undress Miss Annabelle Graham to her heart's content? Last time we'd come

251

up Fair'd been the pet of the Pullman but without Sistuh in this daycoach with three to handle I don't know what I'd have done. Rather have her than a Pullman any day.

We could've had the Pullman this time too even with Sistuh's extra fare if David hadn't given the fifteen dollars Brothuh Mason'd handed him "for extra comfort on the vacation" to that Yankee impostor. I knew the fellow was a rascal the minute I saw him at the door, bowing and simpering. "I come to ask for nothing but your prayers, Brother. Only your prayers that our Heavenly Father will provide for my return to an anxious wife and ailing child far away in Pittsburgh, Pennsylvania." And I wasn't a bit surprised when we heard that Doctuh Lathan had had him arrested when he got around to the rectory drunk on David's money. But David'll never learn to detect the scamp in any tramp claiming a speaking acquaintance with the Lord.

"Papa!" Fair's wail pierced through the train's noise. Fair clutching at paper dolls, at dresses and hats fluttering like butterflies from the upset shoe-box. David half standing, half siting, reaching across Sistuh, clutching, closing his fists on air. Sistuh smiling around at everybody, trying to help Fair without disturbing Cindy. All up and down the aisle, necks craned, people looking and laughing. Even the sad old fellow whose wife's body was in the baggage car reaching out and catching Miss Annabelle Graham in nothing but her chemise, turning her over in a hurry, printed side up, leaving his seat in front of me to hand her to Fair, patting Fair's curly head.

I half rose, sank back. They were managing all right now. Fair, pleased at all the attention, ostentatiously trying a coatsuit on Miss Annabelle, holding her at arm's length, frowning just as Sistuh does when she tries something new on me. David leaning toward Beth, pointing out sights to her, talking close to her ear. I couldn't see Sistuh's face now but I knew how she looked. Proud as Punch. Except for those close around who'd heard us talking at all the stops, people certainly thought those two seats she'd had David make face each other belonged to a happy family Sistuh was the mother of. Probably thought what a good-looking and young-looking mother she was too. I'd never known her to look so well and be so lively as she'd been this last week, since she'd come from Bayport. Salt air'd done her a lot of good, I thought. After church Sunday she'd greeted everybody like old friends, said glibly how nice it was to be back, accepted invitations without hemming and hawing and waiting

252

for me to. There was something about her I couldn't quite put my finger on—a softness in her eyes, a kind of purr in her voice. Of course I couldn't, any easier than a blind man could put his on a button! I was just glad she was coming out of her shell at last because it left me free to be my natural self.

And when we get to Humiston Hill she's going to be a mighty fortress between my natural self and the Humistons! She'ud be overcome if she suspected there's one place she's a big help to me socially. One place where I feel at a loss. No bishop's wife or town's reigning matron has ever made me feel small but Miss Elspeth and Kathy can. Neither of them'll faze Sistuh. She's too much like them. Round the house at least. She won't be able to argue books and politics and religion way they do but they'll never notice that lack, each fighting to hold the floor. Now they'll find out it's just me, not eastern North Carolina, that's to blame for my slipshoddiness. And they won't feel it's their bounden duty to try to make a good housewife out of me. This time their exasperation won't come out in "Now, Pretty One, you just let me pat that butter smooth," "Now, Pretty One, you go sit on the porch and entertain the men folks."

But I can't tell Sistuh that any more than I could tell David, the second summer we were planning to come up, that I didn't want to come. Not want to be in that big house set on a hill overlooking the valley of the Catawba, "commanding a view of some of the highest peaks in the Blue Ridge!" Not want to be with his family and kin, the God-fearing, industrious, well-to-do, hearty, healthy Humistons and McCalls, Herndons and Callaways! Not want to get up with the chickens and eat hot rolls and biscuits and cornbread, stewed apples and corn, eggs, ham? Drink hot fresh-roasted coffee with thick cream? Not want to go with Sister Kathy to gather more new-laid eggs from the nests of hearty, healthy Humiston hens? Or with Mother to the smoke-house to cut down a big, perfectly seasoned roast?

No, no, no. My nays rolled with the rocking of the coach. I come because David loves "the old home" so—now that he's got from under Mistuh Andrew's heavy thumb, away from Miss Elspeth's and Kathy's management. Come because the children love being out of the coop of a town, on a farm where all sorts of exciting things are going on. Love riding the horses to water, drinking warm milk squirted from the cows' tits, wading in the creek, riding on hay wagons, watching the thrashers thrash wheat. It's an education for them and they don't even squirm

253

during long family prayers, or fuss and fume when company fills even that house and they have to wait for second table. But I don't love it. I'll never feel at home there. Never feel I'm Ellen Fanning Humiston most other people I know seem to like and admire. Even feel sometimes they think David took a step down marrying me instead of my taking one down to marry a preacher from up-state. No, it's foreign country to me. As foreign as that ancestral Scotland-in-Ireland Miss Elspeth brags about.

I reckon if the North hadn't invaded the South, Mistuh Andrew and Kathy (not Max!) would brag about their Connecticut ancestry. As it is, they keep mighty quiet about it. But they can't hide it. It's there. Like bluing. Like a little bluing seeping through their Georgia's tub of clear creek water. It dissolves, disappears, but the clothes dipped in it come out whiter than if they'd been rinsed in plain water. Those Scotch-Irish must be like Yankees because everything David's little mother and big strapping sistuh do is done with more care and skill than any cooking, preserving, sewing, and weaving I ever heard of down-state. Kathy likes to brag about the slaves and their descendants still there. "Grandpa and his sons didn't go to auctions to pick up bargains," she says. "Every slave they bought was to fill a particular need. When they needed a good extra farmer, a cattle-man, blacksmith, tanner, a cook or nurse or weaver, they read up in a book Grandpa had about the various skills of the various African tribes and advertised all over for what they wanted. Why, yes, Pretty One, they usually got it. Got smart darkies always." I had to admit Grandpa, they say, never picked his slaves as carefully as he did his horses and he would certainly've wondered how fifteen men slaves could've farmed all those acres of wheat and barley, corn and flax.

Maybe it's because they didn't have so many slaves up-state as down that people up there don't think it's a disgrace to work with their hands. Love to, as much as they love to think with their minds. Fact, they do nothing seems natural to me but talk a lot—where *did* David get his silence?—and go upstairs to rest after dinner. Miss Elspeth doesn't even go upstairs, just stretches out on the parlor sofa. And Kathy doesn't put on a nightgown. Puts on a Mother Hubbard, right over her corsets sometimes. And never sleeps. Reads. *Christian Advocates,* the Charlotte and Greensboro papers, Mistuh Daniels' *State Chronicle,* the county weeklies, Shakespeare's plays, Sir Walter Scott's and

Dickens' novels. Thinks the modern novels somebody always lends me to take on trips are trash. And she talks. Addresses me from the foot of the bed like men I hear on a courthouse green when I pass or in a post office when I step in to mail a letter. Mistuh Bryan and Free Silver. The Farmers' Alliance. The Populists. Free schools for all. Railroad scandals. Tobacco trusts. Kathy always makes me think of a baby regurgitating too much milk. Nothing else to do with more food than body or mind can absorb. I told her one day it was a shame she couldn't vote. She said never mind, she would yet. How the ladies in Wilmington laughed when I told them we had a Woman Suffragist in our immediate family. I asked Kathy once why she didn't get married. Said she'd never seen a man good enough for her. Always a suitor around though, no matter how strong-minded she is. She's just never fallen in love. And she's happy. Remember what Miss Tempy said to Charlotte Berry and me once. "You girls learn this lesson by heart: if you're not smart enough to get your man, don't you fall in love with him. Marry him or keep your fancy free as I've kept mine or you'll be as silly as Parker Piver or daffy as Taffy."

David always says it's the invigorating climate and the fewer darkies up there make his people so different from mine. What I want to know is whether the two who married brothuhs and went to live in Mississippi have lost their domestic virtues in *that* climate, with all those darkies! All I can say for knowing the Humistons on their home ground is, I understand David way I wouldn't've if I'd never gone up there. "David's not inclined to be demonstrative," Miss Elspeth said very first conversation we had alone, "but I expect you've found him affectionate enough beneath his reserve. He's a chip off the maternal block—loves his home and family and's loyal to kith and kin. When he angered his father insisting on reading law instead of coming back to the farm after college, I bided my time. I'd promised him to God when he was a wee babe and only God could save him from death. Had diphtheria. So when worldly ambition called, I knew he just hadn't realized how deeply religious he was, how thick the blood of the Old Covenanters flowed in his veins. *I* wasn't surprised when he astounded everybody else by throwing aside his early-won laurels and entering the ministry. Didn't even mind it was Methodism he chose. I had a hard time hiding my joy from his father, twice disappointed. Yes, David's independent, self-reliant, brave, *and*

255

opinionated like the rest of us but he is too sweet-natured to become bigoted and narrow-minded. He might be crushed—many's the time his father's crushed him to earth but he's never subdued his spirit. One thing I've noticed about him since he was a lap-baby—more than most males he hates to be caught in the wrong about anything. Once he's made up his mind he's got the tenacity of a turtle in holding on to his decision."

I love Miss Elspeth, though, in spite of my awe of her. Want to pat her still bright, red-gold little head sometimes, forget that a woman as tiny as she is can be so powerful—but then, I've noticed, most little women are like that, making up in spirit what they lack in body. I love her sweet, strong mouth so like David's. I think she loves me too, careless as I am about what she thinks is important. Kathy tolerates me because I'm an audience for her. All of them laugh good-naturedly at my helplessness, repeat my polite questions about things so they can laugh at them again. They'd be surprised if they knew how often I know the answers. They weren't taught to pretend ignorance so that other people'ud feel wise and pleased. Even Mistuh Andrew has a kind of grudging affection for me because I can make his stern old face crinkle in a kind of smile now and then. Only Max loves me—reckon I should say *likes* there—for what I am as I like him for what he is.

Thought of Max, my eyes popped wide open. What'd I been doing, worrying about Mistuh Gideon 'sthough he was Sistuh's last chance? Why, if I used my wits, in another few years Sistuh might be on this very train going back to Humiston Hill surrounded by her own children, after a visit to us. Talking to her own husband as she was talking to David now, her head turned sideways against the plush, David's bent forward, listening. Beth looking through the new picture Bible again now that there was nothing but red clay banks along the track. Fair fast asleep, her head a yellow splotch against the blue of Beth's sailor-suit.

I stood up but the train rounding a curve sat me down again. Must be getting well into the hills. I waited until we straightened out, then crossed the aisle, held to the seat behind Sistuh's head, bent over to speak to her, and caught Miss Annabelle's trunk just as it slipped from Fair's lax hands. Sistuh clutched at my waist.

"Why, Ellen, what're you up to? Thought you were sound asleep."

"Just trying to save the paper-dolls."

"What?"

"Just wanted to catch this box before it fell."

"You shouldn't take such a risk, getting out of your seat in all this motion. I was keeping an eye on everything. Here, give me the box. Brothuh David, you help Ellen back."

David was already on his feet. He squeezed between the girls' legs and Sistuh's skirts, grasped my elbow. "Been waiting for you to wake up. We'll be slowing down for Charlotte in a minute. Want you to come with me to the next coach. Found Brother Harrington and wife in there—Presiding Elder in the Western Conference. They want to meet you. Let's go over to your seat till the train stops."

He sat on the arm, leaned over to peer from the window. "Yes, there's that new dye-stuffs factory northern capital's building. Be at the station in a matter of minutes now."

"David, you think Max'll meet us tonight?"

"Expect so. He always has. Why?"

"Then you sit in the back of the surrey with the children and me. Let Sistuh sit with Max. He can point out all the peaks to her."

"Be too dark for that. However, I expect Ora's had enough nursing for one day. Be a pleasant change for her. There! The last jolt. Let's go before the aisles're full."

❖   ❖   ❖

Sukie was on her knees tying Cindy's sunbonnet strings in a fly-away bow. In the mirror I saw Sistuh come through my door. She had on her black piqué skirt and white linen shirtwaist. Her trim little black straw was set just right on her brushed-up hair. Why, she looks just like that picture in *The Queen of Fashion*, July issue—"The Correct Costume for a Summer Picnic!"

"Why, Ellen! You letting Cindy wear that batiste to play in round here today?"

"It's not real fresh, Sistuh. And she's just going for a walk with Sukie." I thrust a hatpin through the crown of my old sailor, anchored it to the knot on the top of my head.

"Not real fresh! Why, I looked it over when I undressed her last night and there wasn't a spot on it! That was because I covered her with one of Carolina's big aprons when we ate

257

watermelon. All it'll need before next Sunday is a little pressing. Come to Deeda, baby. Let her take off—"

"Miss Orie, she *mighty* sweet in this here frock. I wisht you'd let her wear hit. I can do hit up again fore next Sunday. I aims to walk her real slow. Just over to Miss Tennessee's. Miss Tenny can't get enough looking at Mas' David's seem like."

If Sukie'd looked up at Sistuh's face when she interrupted that way instead of at Cindy's starched bonnet strings, widening the loops, smoothing them flat, she'd 've known she'd have it all to do over again.

Sistuh unpressed her lips. "Through a corn field and a melon patch! I should say not! Come here, baby. Let Deeda fix you so you can run and play and have a good time." She sat down in the big rocker and held out her arms.

I searched through the rosewood box lined with purple velvet 'sthough there was one special handkerchief for an August Monday on a mountain.

Cindy stood solidly in front of Sukie. "Les we go, Sukie. I want to wear this very same dress." And she started past Sistuh 'sthough she'd settled the argument.

But Sistuh reached out and caught her. "Now, baby, don't you treat your Deeda that way. Deeda just wants to keep you looking pretty."

Cindy looked doubtful. "Beth and Fair got on spanking clean dresses."

"But not their Sunday best. Deeda'll get you a spanking clean everyday dress—one you like with the rickrack braid on it."

"Lawd, Miss Ellen, you going to take a fancy lace handkerchief like thataone! Hit'll get tore to pieces on blackberry bushes. Yes, ma'm, that plain hem-stitched one's a heap better. Now you come clost to me, let me hist up your petticoat, top or bottom one *one* showing a little tiny bit."

Sistuh was putting one of her "bugs in Cindy's ear." Must've been a tickly one because Cindy was laughing. "There's my baby!" She lifted Cindy on her lap. "You do love your Deeda, don't you? You know she'll make you a pretty dress out of every remnant she can find." She tossed the sunbonnet up on the high bed, looked over Cindy's dark curls at Sukie. "You finish with Miss Ellen, Sukie, you go on down and help with the picnic basket. Ellen, I never saw such a variety, not even at Camilla. Chicken, fried and roasted, ham, savory eggs, and I don't know what."

"Miss Elspeth say whilst Mas' David's here my onliest job's helping Miss Ellen and them," Sukie mumbled around the safety pin in her mouth.

So that's why she's been sticking to us like a plaster these four days!

Sistuh pressed her lips and went on undoing all the little buttons down Cindy's back.

Sukie stood up. "There, Miss Ellen, reckon that'll hold hit. Want me to fetch Cindy's other frock, Miss Orie?"

"You go on downstairs. I'll finish with Cindy."

"Yesum."

"Impudent," Sistuh said when Sukie was out of the room. "I don't hear her talking back to Miss Elspeth and Kathy like that. But if she's been waiting on you every time you've been up here—"

"She hasn't, so I haven't spoiled her."

Sistuh set Cindy on the floor. "Run in my room and get your rickety-rackety dress, baby. It's right on the bed—where I thought that girl would see it." She looked at me accusingly. "Which one *has* been waiting on you?"

"Not a one of thum. I couldn't believe my ears when Sukie said she'd been appointed. I've told you how much I've missed you up here—that way, well as others."

Now why, this summer when I had Sistuh, jealous of anybody and everybody who did anything for the children, did Miss Elspeth have to hand me Sukie on a platter? David must've said something to his mother. If he had, he'd made things worse instead of better. Fixed it so that Sistuh'ud be free, when she wanted to be, to go everywhere he and I went. Men were always putting their foot in it. But it was mighty thoughtful of David to try to help me. Meant he did hear when I complained about being more tied down up here than I was at home. . . .

"Step back, Ellen. I can't get at this drawer."

"What you want in there?"

"Just want to see if I remembered to pack two stiff-bosom shirts for Brothuh David—wasn't sure he was going to preach both Sundays up here. Why, how can this be? I put his socks and underwear in the top drawer!"

"And I changed thum. He has his shirts in the top drawer at home and I get tired telling him every time—"

"The middle drawer in this bureau's only one deep enough

for shirts. I do declare I don't see how he finds anything—socks, handkerchiefs, underwear all which-a-way in here!"

"Sistuh, you haven't got time to straighten out that drawer now."

"Deeda, here am's my dress. Here am's my dress, Deeda. Hurry, hurry. Lissen at Beth and Fair out there right now!" Cindy ran to the window. "They getting a ride in the surrey! I want a ride in the surrey!" She ran back to Sistuh, pushed the dress in her hands, jumped up and down in impatience.

"All right, baby." Sistuh took it with fingers that itched to get at that drawer. "Be still now, you want Deeda to get it on you."

I stepped to the window. "Jeb'll give you a ride in the buggy, baby. He's just leading Prince out of the stable."

"Buggy?" Sistuh said. "Where's that going this morning?"

"Why, to High Brighten." I dropped the curtain.

Sistuh stared at me, standing there holding the dress while Cindy bounced up and down begging her to hurry. "Who's riding in it?"

"David and I." I picked up my smelling-salts bottle, dropped it in my reticule, and went back to the window. "I do hope Jeb didn't forget to mend that side-flap. Be windy up there today."

"When was that fixed up?"

"I don't know that it has been. I said I hoped—"

"Do don't wriggle so, Cindy. How can I get this on you? Ellen, I mean when was it arranged for you and Brothuh David to ride in the buggy? Last night the plan was for all of us to go in the surrey."

"I arranged it when David came up to bed. Seemed to me six of us'ud be mighty crowded, three on a seat. I told David how dizzy it makes me going up those steep narrow roads with hairpin turns, in an open surrey."

"Why, those surrey seats are plenty wide enough for three and this's the first I ever heard bout your getting dizzy—anywhere, any time." She laughed in a superior, teasing way. "Miss Elspeth'll think you're mighty picayunish. She was saying yesterday—when you jumped up and went running down the steps after Brothuh David, going off to watch the sunset from that rock he loves so and I called after you to be careful, Miss Elspeth laughed and said, 'Miss Ora, you're worse about Ellen than a ewe about a lame lamb.' I said 'I just can't help it, Miss Elspeth, she's all I've got left in the world.' " Sistuh turned her head to one side and groped at her belt for her handkerchief.

"Now, Sistuh, you've got the children and any number of good friends." Why the tears right after that laugh?

She sniffed, looked at me reproachfully out of those wide, lustrous, greenish-gray eyes before she went on buttoning Cindy. "But you're the only close blood-kin left. I haven't been able to get Buddy out of my mind since that gentleman on the train stopped to speak to Brothuh David, asked for his prayers. Said he was going up to Asheville to find a boardinghouse for his daughter's got consumption. Said doctuh down there in little Washington advised mountain air rather than a warm climate. If only I'd brought Buddy up here instead of taking him to that Florida swamp! Owls hooting all night keeping him awake, so many big snakes and crocodiles he couldn't sit in the sun in peace. Oh, I'll never forgive myself—"

"Don't cry, Deeda." Cindy reached up and hugged her around the waist. "Those nasty stinking old snakes and 'diles and things didn't eat you up. Tie my bonnet, please. I'm in a mighty big hurry."

Cindy trotted off and I tried to think of something to say, distract Sistuh's thoughts before she actually cried. I bent over the bureau, blew a film of rice powder off the polished surface, managed a laugh as at a joke on me, said, "You haven't told me what Miss Elspeth said—why she'll think I'm picayunish."

"Oh." She tucked the handkerchief in her belt. "She said carrying babies never stopped her from doing anything she had to do or wanted to do. Said time all those soldiers from Stoneman's Raid came in April '65 just before one of them was born, she worked's hard's the darkies getting hams out of the smokehouse and toting thum up to the attic to hide under the floor. Said she had every one of her eight with nobody to help but old Tennessee."

"Tenny wasn't so old then—but three of those babies didn't live."

"Well, Miss Elspeth did and plenty mothers and babies too die at such times with doctuhs and nurses to help." Sistuh stepped to the looking-glass, put her hands on her hat brim 'sthough to straighten its straight line, but her eyes were on her shirtwaist fitting so smoothly over her firm breasts, drawn in so neatly at her narrow waist.

There's certainly something to be said for not marrying! When I've seen Sistuh's figure outlined against the light or've watched her picking out a pattern for a new dress, I've thought how nice it must be to be sure of your size and of wearing the dress when it's finished. And when I've heard her say she was going to do this or that next spring or fall, or *I* think this or *I* think that, I've realized that in many ways she's more of a person than I am. She's just herself while I'm less than myself, being a preacher's wife supposed to have no thoughts of my own, having to preface most statements with "Mistuh Humiston thinks," most plans with "if we're not moved this year."

She walked to the bed, picked up Cindy's batiste, and folded it. "I wish I could feel easy bout your taking this trip today. Brothuh David said, when it all came up, that maybe you'd feel it was too much for you."

"When did he say that?"

"At the breakfast table yesterday morning before you came down."

I bit my lip but not hard enough. "Some day, maybe some day, David'll learn he can't speak for me in every thing. About church and preacher's wife doings, yes. About my soul if he must. But not about my body or my personal life—what there is of it. Come on, les go down."

That laugh again! "*You* getting touchy! Never knew you to give a snap of your fingers bout what anybody said about you."

As though David were anybody! But I laughed too. "It's just my 'delicate condition.' That's all can be said for it—nobody expects a pregnant woman to be quite sane. I've never taken advantage of it before but I made up my mind to go on this trip no matter how I felt this morning."

"You sick this morning? Thought you were past all that." Voice reluctant, eyes out on stems with that curiosity she always had about any detail of pregnancy.

"Yes, first time in more than three weeks. Was all that delicious stewed corn Mistuh Andrew insisted I eat. I overdid my politeness. Didn't even have time to get to the gardenhouse. The children came out with Georgia when I was right in the midst of it, behind the grape arbor. Georgia told thum I must've swallowed a fly and Cindy began holding *her* stomach and gagging."

"Well," Sistuh said. "Such things're to be expected when a woman's that way. They say, though, early morning sickness is a sign of a safe delivery. If you just have that, I'll be mighty thankful, way *you're* running about."

262

"Hooray up there!"

Sistuh darted to the front window, leaned out. "We're coming right now!"

"Time you were! We want to get started before the heat of the day." Max's voice. I hoped he was noticing how nice Sistuh looked. If he wasn't, sometime during this day I'd see that he did.

"Brothuh David!" Sistuh called, leaned farther out.

"Yes, m'am!"

"Did you remember to get a sofa pillow for Ellen's back? Oh, yes, I see you did. All right, we'll be right down."

She caught up with me in the hall and took hold of my elbow. "You be careful on these bare stairs. They polish thum with goose grease."

If I'd been one of the children, I'd've sat down on the top step and refused to budge. I thought she meant it all for my good but I was getting tired of it. I'd never even thought about dying in childbirth after Doctuh Cobb in Wilmington told me I had the right maternal build for delivering babies easily. Until this time. But early in the summer when I'd be working around my flowers against the church yard fence, in view of all those old graves of young mothers, the possibility had popped in my mind and it was nothing in the world but Sistuh's eternal harping on my being careful. Rose or no Rose, I was mighty glad she insisted she'd have to go back to Bayport the first of October. All I had to do was just keep from insisting she stay and help me move. And keep David from bringing up the subject again of her making her home with us.

Why, what a time and place for David to be preaching! I heard his pulpit voice when we were halfway down and when we stepped out on the high veranda nobody noticed us for all Max's calling. David held his family as rapt as he could hold a congregation of strangers and in spite of his standing on the flat stones at the base of the steps looking *up* at some of his audience. It all made a beautiful scene—dark blue mountains against distant light blue sky, sunlight pushing through the foliage on Humiston Hill, making shadows dance on horses, children, darkies, and white people. I stood still in the doorway looking and listening. A circle of sunlight fell on David's uplifted face and I felt ashamed of my exasperation with Sistuh. A woman fortunate enough to be married to a man like David should be above such meanness.

I glanced at Miss Elspeth's little wrinkled face and it seemed to glow like her bright hair. I wondered whether some day I'd be as proud of my son as she was of hers. Looked at Mistuh Andrew, next to her in a chair drawn close to the steps, stroking that long gray beard and nodding his head approvingly—as though all those thrashings he'd given David had made him handsome and eloquent! Looked at Kathy sitting on the top step and her handsome face was more like an adoring little sistuh's than a statuesque woman's. At Sam Winston on the step below, that fat, tongue-tied bachelor farmer was this summer's suitor, and felt right sorry for him, envy of David written all over his blunt features. Max was standing at the team's head, his hand on a cheekpiece, and I was struck for the first time by his resemblance to David—was like a rough, unfinished copy that'd been left out in all weather, the skin browned by sun, the dark of eyes and hair washed nondescript by rain. He seemed simply interested in what David was saying, as he always seemed to be in my remarks, inconsequential as they were. Beth and Fair, perched up there on the front seat of the surrey, and Cindy in Jeb's lap in the buggy, her little bitty white hands clamped over his great big black ones holding the reins, were gazing wide-eyed at their Papa. Carolina and Georgia, holding their aprons up around their waists 'sthough they felt they were in church in the wrong clothes, Sukie staring open-mouthed, three strong young darkies leaning on scythe handles, looking pleased school wasn't keeping yet, were grouped together in front of the big cedar.

". . . Yes, I felt God's presence then as surely as I'd felt it once before. August twenty-seventh, 1886—eight years ago today. Seemed as though the first tremor was the direct touch of His hand bidding me be of good courage. My sermon the next Sunday was 'The Earthquake and Its Lesson.' My text, Isaiah 13:13: 'Therefore I will shake the heavens and the earth shall remove out of her place, in the wrath of the Lord of hosts, and in the day of His fierce anger.' I quoted too from Psalms 18:7: 'Then the earth shook and trembled; the foundations also of the hills moved and were shaken because He was wroth.' There's no doubt about it—God brings about catastrophes in nature to show men the might of His hands and their helplessness when He devises a punishment for their sins. That sermon brought two elderly backsliders back to the fold and one young sinner—worldly young woman too fond of dancing—to the altar. There was a quickening of spiritual feeling along the whole length of the Carolina coasts."

I had to smile at David when he'd said all he had in mind—he looked so at a loss, not being able to add, "Let us pray," as he always did at the end of a sermon. But Sistuh piped right up.

"We certainly felt it in Brunswick County." She shuddered, then stammered, "The spiritual awakening and the quake itself, I mean. I was all by myself at Little Brookside and I thought that old house was coming down on my head, put me out of my mis—" She broke off in the middle of the word, walked to the steps and asked Max if he'd got all the shawls and cushions under the back seat.

"No cause to worry, Miss Ora," Mistuh Andrew thundered before Max could answer. "Maxwell's fussy as any old woman comes to looking after the ladies' comfort. Only wish he'd find one particular one to concern himself about, that's what I wish. Time to get started now. Let's have no more standing about."

He stood up suddenly, strode down the steps looking neither to the right nor to the left. If he'd been God descending a cloud there wouldn't've been more bustle and hurry. Max, his face redder than with sunburn, jumped to lift Beth and Fair out of the surrey, Kathy hurried to take Cindy from Jeb's lap, Sam Winston grabbed Prince's bit rein as though he was preventing a run-away. Sukey ran to take Cindy from Kathy, Georgia took off down the hill to the wash-house, Carolina to the kitchen, and the three colored boys shouldered their scythes and did a quick-step toward the fields ahead of Mistuh Andrew.

". . . says she's not feeling so well this morning. I'm worried about her attempting this rough trip," Sistuh was saying to Miss Elspeth.

Miss Elspeth laughed. "There you go, bleating about your wee lamb again!"

David heard, came up the steps. "What do you think, Mother?"

I walked past Sistuh and straight to him. "I think I'm the one to be consulted in this case. I'm going!"

"Good for you, daughter! Don't let them make a namby-pamby of you," and Miss Elspeth patted my shoulder before she went in the house.

❖

I felt tired time we finished that picnic dinner but I was glad I'd come. It was worth the effort just to see David so carefree. If

265

there'd been any young girls around, I'd've thought he was showing off a little on his vacation—as any man would any time. Then I laughed to myself, sitting a little apart on the surrey cushion, my back against the sofa pillow and a fallen pine tree. Why for him this summit's full of girls, I thought. Just listen to him!

"Yes, here's the first. June ninth, 1870. I was thirteen then and this was as high as I could reach." He traced the letters and figures cut into the bark of a big oak. "D.McH.—L.W.M. Lucy Wells Monroe. She rode up on a mule between her two brothers. I can see her now as plainly as I see you, Ora. Come to think about it, you must've looked like Lucy Wells when you were thirteen. Neat and trim."

"Why, Brothuh David, I don't know that I can claim that compliment!"

"Lucy's not neat and trim now I can tell you!" Kathy laughed and said. "She married that sorry gold-panner came here from West Virginia. Lives in a shack on Lower Creek with a house full of ragged children."

"Well, now," Max drawled in his slow way, "they all couldn't marry David." He wandered over to another tree. "Who's M.E.J.?" He pointed to what I could just make out was a heart pierced by an arrow. "You certainly dug that one deep—can hardly see the others around it."

"What's the date?" David moved along, Sistuh, Kathy, and Sam Winston trailing after him. "July 12, 1880—my first vacation from the bar."

"Mary Elizabeth Jackson," Kathy said. "First time you met her too! You brought me along on *old* Prince that day and we kept so close to Judge Jackson's carriage I had bruises all up and down my limbs."

"What was *she* like, Brothuh David?" Sistuh asked teasingly, as frisky and gay as anybody.

"All airs and graces," Kathy answered. "Frothy and light as whipped-up cream. If I hadn't showed her up, though, time David had her to visit at Humiston Hill, you and Sister Ellen wouldn't be here today."

"*You* didn't show her up to me. This is the first I knew of your trying," David said.

"Why, that must've been the one—" Sistuh began, stopped to listen to David.

"As beautiful a girl as ever I saw. Married now to a lawyer

who's in the legislature and's been mentioned for governor. Might be too if he keeps in with the Populists."

"What beats me, Brother Humiston, is how you recollect um all." Sam Winston peered up at David, gimlet eyes as full of admiration for the beau as for the preacher.

"I can't in detail." David laughed. "Sometimes 'in sessions of sweet, silent thought' faces long forgotten appear momentarily —blurred, though, like faded tintypes. Mixed up too—the winsome smile of this one on that one's rosy lips."

"Don Juan Humiston—that's what they used to call him round here before he went off to Vanderbilt University," Max said.

Kathy turned around. "Sister Ellen, you have any idea you were marrying such a one?"

"Doesn't bother me, Kathy. I'm glad he got it all out of his system."

"Yes, there's no soil in the pulpit for wild oats. Come on, let's go to the cave!" Kathy started ahead, Sam at her heels.

Sistuh came over to me. "You feel like going?"

I shook my head. "I'm going to stay right here."

Sistuh didn't seem to know what to do, David still behind her looking for initials he might've missed in the tree trunks, and Max beside her but making no move to follow Kathy. "Well," she said finally, "I don't care anything about it, if you'd like company."

Before I could think of a tactful way to get her started with Max, Max dropped down on the pine needles by me, leaned against my log, stretched out his long legs. "You go along keep David company, Miss Ora. I'll stay here and scare the bears away from Sister Ellen."

"The very idea, Max!" I pushed on his arm. "More likely to be bears in that dark old cave than prowling round in the open."

"Nope. Too early for hibernation and they love all these ripe berries out here. Besides, m'am, I'll need all my strength for the brakes going down the mountain."

"Why, I'd be ashamed, a big, strong man like you!" I pushed at him with both hands but he reached around suddenly, grasped my hands, and laid them firmly in my lap.

"You couldn't find a sweeter spot to rest, Ellen." David walked over to the break in the trees and looked down at the world spread below us. " 'The mountains shall bring peace to the people, and the little hills—' "

"Stop your quoting and go along," Max said lazily. "Sun'll be getting low mighty soon now."

"All right, Ora." David turned and took Sistuh's arm. "Let's go find the tallies bushwhackers made in the rock at the entrance—for all the cattle they stole during the war."

"Don't you keep too close to Kathy and Sam now," Max warned as they started off. "Father's going to be almighty mad if Sam doesn't get the word out soon."

"You think it'll do Sam any good when he does?" I asked Max when David and Sistuh had walked on without answering.

"That I do not! But Kathy'll take her raking over the coals then and we won't have Sam hanging round like a sick bull-calf all fall. Good solid farmer, no nonsense about him, Father says. Can't make Father see the other girls're doing all right married to gentlemen. Easy enough to think of his fighting for *States'* Rights way he holds on to his own, but hard to believe keeping his darkies had anything to do with it. Even says now the war was fought to rid the South of cotton royalty. Reckon he's always felt uncomfortable on the fence—old slave-holder in this small-farm country."

"What about you, Max? Hasn't Mistuh Andrew picked a good solid farmer's daughter for you?"

"You heard him this morning. Never misses a chance to berate me for living the way I want to live. Nearly as I can. I wanted to get out and be a surveyor but no, my place was on the farm. I stayed but I've got some will of my own, much as the others have, and I won't be pushed into matrimony."

"Of course you won't! But if you fell in love, you'd slip into it happily. Nothing in the world could hold you back. I think you should look around. You'll be lonesome when the old people pass on and you're left with just Kathy."

"Kathy's stimulating company enough and I reckon I'm not the marrying kind." He scooped up a handful of pine needles and let them trickle out between his fingers.

"Well, I just don't see what the girls up here're thinking about letting a handsome fellow like you run around untethered. And you can't tell me you haven't ever been in love!"

Under the sunburn, his face flushed redder, right up to the roots of his hair—the texture of his mother's, thick and wavy like David's.

268

"So you have been in love!" I teased. "Now why didn't you marry her?"

"Never had a chance." He scooped up more pine needles.

"You didn't try! What *did* you do? Stand aside politely and let her marry somebody else?"

His Adam's apple moved up and down and he threw the pine needles so that they fell in a shower. "Trouble was, she'd married somebody else before I ever saw her."

"Oh. That's mighty hard. But she's not the only pebble on the beach. Why, I could point out—"

"Only one for me, I reckon." He leaned forward and peered into the branches of a hickory on the slope. "Flying squirrel in there somewhere." He looked at me, looked away. "I'm not like David. I mean to say—not like David before he met you. Or maybe before he was converted and went off to study for the ministry. Never saw much of him after that. Lawyer days, though, he was the catch of the county. Trouble was—or good thing was, since he waited for you—there were too many after him. Reckon he got confused, debating between this one and that one."

"Yes, I was mighty lucky."

Max didn't seem to want to say anything more and I couldn't think how to say what I wanted to. He watched the branches a minute, then reached for a cone and threw it at the squirrel flattened now on the hickory trunk. It scuttled away and Max settled back again, folded his arms across his chest, and stared into space.

May as well give up trying to make a match for Sistuh if he felt that way, I decided. Was funny the way you could know somebody for years, *think* you knew him, but unless a conversation like this got started, know nothing beneath the skin. I'd never've thought Max was romantic but here he was, preferring not to marry atall if he couldn't marry the One. I wondered who she could be. All the young wives I'd met up here seemed too much alike, concerned only with their butter-and-baby making, for him to have selected *one* for a life-long, silent passion. I couldn't imagine David's doing a thing like that. He and Max must be as different inside as they were alike outside—except for Max's coloring and his nose, high and bumpy like Mistuh Andrew's. Both of them had Miss Elspeth's beautiful brow and firm, sweet mouth. Max's shoulders were broader than David's and his arms stronger—I realized that every time he lifted me

269

out of a conveyance and swung me to the ground. His hands—
I glanced down at the one clasping the arm muscles nearest me,
so close the tips of the oval-shaped nails were caught in the fuzz
of my shawl. Tanned and capable-looking hands. Not white and
gentlemanly like David's. Hairier but the light hairs didn't
show so much. Shame no woman would ever feel those strong,
gentle fingers on her body, never be held breathless in those
strong arms, never . . .

I gulped, put my hand to my throat, coughed.

"You catch a gnat?" He looked down at me, concerned.

"No—just a frog in my throat."

"Little thing like that's nothing to worry about. Swallow the
pest and let's walk down that slope over there a little piece. If
you feel equal to it. I'd like to show you Adam and Eve." He
sprang to his feet, grasped my hands, and lifted me like a
feather.

"I knew you all thought a lot of this mountain," I laughed
and said, "but I didn't know it was the Garden of Eden."

"Wait till you see that patch of bellwood and trillium. They
call thum Adam and Eve because you always find thum together."

He held both my hands, guiding me past the rocks in the
path, and when we stood in the cleared place on the mountain-
side, alone above the world, he stooped and picked two fragile
little blossoms on tender green stems. My fingers trembled as I
took them and I looked up to say something inconsequential.
And I looked into his eyes. There was more than passion in
them, thank God. There was a tenderness and a restraint that
gave me time to get hold of myself. I felt mean and I felt denied
but I pulled my eyes away and looked at Blowing Rock Mountain way off there in the distance and managed to ask him how
far away it was. He turned his head and looked for a long time
before he said it was twenty miles or so. Then I said we'd better
go back, the others would be coming, and walked on up the
slope till he could get control of himself.

❖

" 'A horse is a vain thing for safety, neither shall he deliver
any by his great strength,' " David quoted, when we were halfway down High Brighten, 'sthough he agreed with whatever
Biblical character had said it.

It was the first time he'd opened his mouth since we'd started but he hadn't seemed to notice my silence and I hadn't chided him about his. He had a right to be silent now, all his attention on the driving, holding Prince back to keep a good space between us and the surrey. Suddenly I laughed but he didn't ask me why. I couldn't've told him if he had. It just struck me as funny—a husband and wife riding along together, side pressing side, years of life shared between them—and their thoughts as far apart as the poles. If I should blurt out mine . . .

"Yes, that's my sermon!" On a level strip of road David loosened his grip on the reins.

"What is? What sermon?"

"For Humiston Chapel next Sunday. Man's happiness the end of all God's creative thought. *Idea* struck me up there today. Look at what God did for us. Perfect weather, congenial company, every one exhilarated by the mountain air, every one happy—an evidence of God's goodness to us unworthy sinners too prone to think only of the imperfections in our lives."

I was an unworthy sinner if anybody was, I thought, maybe more undeserving of God's blessings than anybody else there today. Married to a man I loved, carrying his child, and yearning for another lover! It wasn't the first time either. There was that dream I'd had about being in Mistuh Gideon's arms on the belfry while David searched for me among the tombstones. But there was no accounting for dreams and I hadn't felt anything for Mistuh Gideon when I was wide awake. Was just that look in his lively black eyes had made me feel young and giddy and like Ellen Fanning again. I hadn't felt guilty when I'd remembered that dream. Just amused. No? I hadn't shared that amusement with David. Still, any guilt I might've felt then was nothing to what I felt now.

I was wide awake today when this thing happened with Max. I wanted to lie right down on those pine needles with him. No use trying to beat the devil around the stump—that's what I wanted to do. There was no "premeditation or malice aforethought," though, as David would say. Was just the Eve in me. But I conquered her with will power as surely as David conquers the devil with prayer. It hurt and saddened me but I'm glad it happened. Hurt because I'd had that feeling in my throat for somebody other than David, had understood in a flash that marriage was man's plan, not nature's. Saddened me because I couldn't be two women and make Max happy. Glad because hereafter I'd have more sympathy when I heard gossip about

271

some married woman who'd "carried on" with another man. Who knew but that the other man wasn't the right man for her? That was what had given me will power—knowing I would've chosen David if I'd met him and Max at the same time. My wanting Max too was just plain greediness and I was almost as sinful as any fallen woman who did in fact no more than I in my heart wanted to do. Yet men talked about the purity of good women!

"Hold tight," David said as the buggy bounced over the stones Prince's heels were kicking right and left on a steep descent.

If a big one should roll on down under the team's hoofs . . . I grasped the supports and shut my eyes and I didn't know I'd screamed till I heard the echo come back at me from the mountain's side. The violent lurch as David pressed on the brake doubled me up. Prince's forefeet were pawing the air but the buggy grated to a stop as he got all four on the safe side of the road.

"Don't look, Ellen!" David commanded through clinched teeth.

I did look. Was better to see the surrey on its side now, wheels still spinning, than seeing it teetering on the edge of the cliff, finally tipping to the right, dropping Sistuh on the embankment. Neatly, 'sthough that was what it'd had to do, why it had overturned.

I saw it all but I felt suspended somewhere above it looking down, curious, not particularly concerned. I saw Sam in a heap on Kathy's lap. Saw Max leap over the dashboard, land near Sistuh but noticing her no more than the quiet stones around her. Saw him grasp the back half of the broken shaft, pull to right the surrey before the struggling team dragged it over the drop on the left. Or kicked it back to the right. On Sistuh!

"Hush, Ellen. Sam and Kathy can help him now."

I heard my pleading then, heard David soothing Prince as he'd soothed me, felt the reins thrust in my hands. "Not too tight. Just steady. He won't move now."

David scrambled on all fours around the surrey, clutching at berry bushes, sending red earth and rocks cascading down on three straining backs. He got to Sistuh at last, pressed his body against the bank, slipped his hands under her head, lifted it to rest on his legs, pushed the crushed straw back from her head and the loosened hair back from her face.

272

I can't faint. I've never fainted. Whatever's happened to her I'll have to know the rest of my life. May as well know it . . .

"There, there, Pretty One, you'll be all right now." Kathy between the wheels, rubbing the back of my neck with one hand, holding smelling salts under my nose with the other. "Caught you just in time. Keep your head down."

"Sistuh?"

"She's all right except for a broken wrist. Must've landed with her full weight on it. Fainted too." She thrust the smelling salts in my lax hand. "Keep your head down a little longer. I've got to help the boys."

"I've got to get to Sistuh."

"You stay here. David's looking after Ora. You have a miscarriage—another miscarriage—it *will* put us in a pickle," and she sniggered. "We've got to get the team and the surrey— what's left of it—down to that wider space round the curve so's the buggy can get by to take Ora to town. Behave yourself now."

I sat straight soon's her back was turned. Surrey's left shaft dropped with a thud, the right still sticking straight up. Max undid the last buckle of the twisted harness and waved Kathy ahead with the team. I could see Sistuh's face now, clean of blood and red clay, and I heaved a long sigh of relief when I saw it move on David's lap.

Max and Sam leaned over the wheels, pushed and held back, pushed and held back. When the road in front of Sistuh and David was clear, I told Prince to "Get up" and he moved forward, cautious as a person.

David looked up. "Just hold on, Ellen, till the men get back. No use moving Ora till we can keep going. You over your faintness?"

"Baby, you—all—right?" Sistuh raised her eyelids, let them close again above the criss-cross of red scratches.

Baby! Her mother-voice I hadn't heard for so long, speaking to me. Tears spurted from my eyes. "*You* asking bout me! I'm not hurt."

"So—glad. So—thankful it—wasn't you. So—sorry—make—all this trouble."

"Sistuh, do don't talk that way."

She didn't try any more, just lay there, looking so white, so peaceful, so At Rest, I would've thought they were fooling me telling me she wasn't dead if I hadn't heard her speak. Was then I looked below her poor face and saw her arm and hand.

273

In her lap like an arm that'd been thrown at her, the hand at an angle with the wrist.

That right hand! Love for her such as I'd never felt before surged through me. Love such as a child must feel for its mother, forgetting all the do's and the don'ts, remembering all the yes's and the smiles. Why, I'll spend the rest of my life being a good sistuh to her, I vowed. A good *child* . . . Now she'll have to think of herself for a while, not so much of my "condition," maybe it'll be easy to be good-natured with her again! My head went down in shame at the thought and I turned away.

The stars were out and the reiteration of all details of the accident finished and done with. For a while. Kathy and I sat huddled together on a surrey seat, our heads protruding from jackets and shawls, our feet drawn up out of the dew-wet grass. Max and Sam paced up and down the road watching for a light. Every time the dark blur of them moved out of sight the wildcats' howls seemed closer and I shivered and shook with more fear than chill. Finally we heard the crunch of wheels, then saw the glow of a carriage-lamp.

Was a colored man from the livery stable in town, towing a whole surrey behind his buggy. He didn't know much about Sistuh though. "Reckon she resting at Doctuh Soddy's house," he said. "Doctuh Lipcom he gone to the Con-federate Rally over Morganton way."

"That's too bad," Kathy said.

"Why, Kathy? Isn't Doctuh Soddy reliable?" I asked.

"He's all right, I expect. Young man just started in. But all of them must know how to set broken bones."

Worrying about Sistuh all the time they were hitching up, I didn't remember I had a body. Didn't feel a thing till Max came, stretched out his hands and lifted me to my feet. Then such a pain shot through me, I grabbed his arms like they were ropes tied to bedposts and groaned through my clenched teeth. . . .

CHAPTER II

1

THUMP THUMP THUMP THUMP THUMP THUMP . . .
Teams of big black stallions pounding across my pros-
trate body whirling pounding back again coming to a
halt hoofs on my stomach on my breasts rearing stomp-
ing coming down one two three four five six seven eight and
more of thum far's I can see I'm smothering can't take any
more of it can't take any more can't can't can't. Push then push
hard harder harder *harder* can't push if only could raise my
little finger show David and the girls I'm still alive why don't
they do something to help me why why why not just stand there
staring. . . .

"Mama! Mercy guide me, old Aunt Mehaley used to say.
Why you lying here on the floor? Why didn't you come in and
bunk with me? You got to get up from that mess now though.
Couple down in the parlor waiting for the Reverend to marry
thum. Country tacks if I ever saw any. Came in a mule-wagon.
You won't get enough of a fee to sneeze at. Groom's a big loose-
jointed fellow looks like he lacks the sense to pee a hole in the
ground. Bride's ugly's a mud fence dabbled in monkeytails.
Must be bout five months gone. Got on a pink shirtwaist and
a—"

"Cindy?"

"Well, I'll be—who'd you think it was?"

"Where's your Papa?"

"Went to the court house bout an hour ago. Beth with him.
Search me what for. Asked, they just walked off without answering. It's nigh on to five o'clock old fellow at the depot always
says. You been sleep nearly three hours. I had me a good nap
too—till Ann Wesley and her crowd woke me up. They used
every drop of the hot water taking a bath together. Good thing
Deeda's still sleeping it off or she'd've given thum Hail Columbia—if she'd been well I mean. Then they put on kimonos and

275

pranced up and down the upstairs back porch like those bad women in MacDonald Alley. Seems to me it's bout time you gave Ann Wesley *What a Young Girl Ought to Know* to read. She might learn more from it than I needed to. Should learn *something* from the Bible she gets up early every morning to read. *If* she reads it stead of just holding it open in front of her to impress Papa. Notice she hasn't been up any sooner than the rest of us last two mornings when he's been away. Think I'll fotch out the Bible, 's Molly says, when the Reverend's around. He never compliments me on going to church every time the bell rings, singing in the choir since I could peep a tune, going up to the altar and shaking his hand so he won't feel bad when he asks for penitents at revivals and no other sinner'll go. Golly, it's dark as pitch in here. Better let in some light on the subject."

Going around opening all the shutters, leaning from a front window, calling down some foolishness to somebody passing, laughing. Going to the looking-glass, patting her puffs, picking up my chamois skin and dabbing powder on her little nose. Coming back to stand at the foot of the mattress, dainty and pretty as a princess in that white all-over embroidery made Princess style.

"Thought I'd kill myself laughing at Fair flaunting down the hall, carrying her sacred bath-salts she won at Katie Stewart's Rook party, coming back mad's a wet hen cause there wasn't any hot water. She poured half a bottle Violet Sec Toilet Water in the basin in her room and took her a sponge bath. Was 'sitting all over' Glad, they say at GFA, for taking all the water. Wouldn't believe me I told her was Ann Wesley. Don't see why you all think she's such a saint—much of an imp of satan as the next one, she gets with her gang. Told Fair not to sit *too* hard on her, though—she doesn't want to fall off her pedestal. Heard Elizabeth or Tiny one tell Ann Wesley she was getting pimples on her face. Ann Wesley asked her what difference that made, said Fair'd had thum when she was her size! Fair's gone off with Bob in his machine. Should've seen him trying to crank it. Had to get Massy come and help. Wonder all that banging and thumping didn't wake you up. Glad and Tom T hopped off a tobacco wagon just as they got started and begged to go with thum! Should've heard the polite excuses Fair made.

Here, take my hand. I'll hist you up, Molly says. You don't look wide awake *yet*. Better go splash in cold water and get dressed.

Got to be two witnesses, the Reverend ever gets back to tie the knot. No telling what Miss Beth's planning to do. Dixie Roe comes in time, though, she can be *one*. Always cussing cause she's never been here when a couple came. I'm going driving with her in her phaeton. We going to split this town wide open. Reckon with Dixie, Fair wouldn't raise the dickens if I *walked* right past the livery stable or the barber shop or right *in* the hardware store. But just let me get on the wrong side of the street with one of my crowd and I never hear the last of it. Forgot to tell her Doris said wasn't a word of truth that story going round bout her going up to Doctuh Hough's office by herself to keep an appointment. Said her cousin Somebody from Raeford was up there having a tooth pulled and she just went up to be with her. Like to know what difference it'ud make any way, I don't care how good-looking Doctuh Hough is, he's an old married man. Dixie telephoned for Fair of course. Couldn't get Fair, she asked me to go. Said she was so lonesome since that Cadence Rountree was visiting her left she didn't know what to do. Why, Mrs. David Humiston, just look at that puddle of perspiration your head's been in! And you haven't got a dry thread on you."

"I didn't mean to go to sleep. Reckon I was more exhausted than I realized." Standing there, still dazed from that awful dream, pushing the damp hair back from my face, not knowing what to do next.

Cindy going to the washstand, coming back with a wet cloth. "Here, rub this over your face, might 'fotch' your eyes open."

Handing the cloth back to her, listening. "Why I don't hear the lawnmower! Run catch Massy before he gets away. Want him to get this mattress back where it belongs."

"*Massy's* gone. Bob gave him a quarter and he walked straight off down town. Don't know whether he finished the grass or not. Wait till Dixie comes. Three of us can do it."

"Let Dixie Roe in on all this havoc! I should say not! It'll just have to wait till Molly comes back. I don't want your Papa to see such a sight on his anniversary."

"Don't see what difference it makes, he knows all about it. Oh, I knew there was something I forgot to tell you! Papa called me down to the parlor before I got settled for my nap. Told me Deeda's a burden the Lord put upon us and it's our Christian duty to bear it patiently, not question or try to explain it in the Devil's language. I said, 'Yes, sir, I'll remember next time.' But ask me, I'll tell you the Devil's language's got some sense to it at least. Just's I said at the dinner table—I've known since I was knee-high to a pup what's the matter with Deeda and today it just popped out."

"Well, I hope and pray it hasn't just popped out before." Going to the bureau and starting to take the pins from my straggling hair but my arms so heavy having to ask Cindy to come do it for me.

"Just once before. You need a shampoo, Mama. Tomorrow's a nice sunny day, I'll help you. Hand me the brush. I'll give it a dry-cleaning now. Don't see why some of us besides Fair didn't get long thick hair like yours. I've got no more than Grandma Humiston had. Glad, though, when it comes to washing. Sit down in that straight chair and bend over, I can't get at it this way."

"Cindy, when did what you said about Sistuh's trouble 'pop out' before?"

"Was one day when we lived in Laurenton. Talking bout that Brooke girl's hanging herself when her sistuh married Clem Seffert. On the Cramers' porch. I just said was a pity Deeda hadn't killed herself when you married Papa. Hold up your head a little or it'll take all the dust off the matting."

"How can I hold it any way but down, your saying a thing like that to people? Why, you weren't more than sixteen when we *left* Laurenton!"

"Had eyes *and* ears when I was born, didn't I? Could see Deeda hop up from the table every time the door bell rang, pretend like she had to get more biscuits or something, and go peep from the back hall to see whether it was a *woman* asking for Papa. Could see her eyes glitter every time company was coming and we had to shift beds. 'Best thing'll be for one of you girls to sleep with your Mama let Brothur David have the sitting room sofa'—so she could tip in at daybreak with an extra blanket or something! Saw her do it once and I reckon she did every time—tucked the covers up under his chin like he was a little bitty baby. I never heard of any woman's being jealous of a man unless she was in love with him and Deeda's been green-eyed of *any* female Papa speaks to ever since I can remember—young, old, white, black. Doesn't even want him to go in the kitchen to get shaving water from the kettle if a cook's there. Reckon the truth is, it's you she is really jealous of and tries to hide it by taking it out on anything wears skirts. Can't

278

hide it from Yours Truly though. All I have to do is translate what she says backwards when she's this way and it comes out straight. Always did flunk that old Latin but I'll bet I'd get a hundred, anybody give me an exam on Deeda's talk. Said the other day when I was in there fixing her a dose of Happidine, said, 'Baby, I never thought about it one way or another but there were people in Bayport said they couldn't tell for the longest which one of the Fanning girls Brothuh Humiston was courting.' Never thought about it one way or another! Must've begun eating her heart out for him first time she saw him and she's still at it, old's she is now. Makes me right sick seeing her cuddle—"

"Cindy, please. Les don't talk about it."

"Yesum. Just let me ask you, though—did you ever hear anything bout people saying they didn't know which of you Papa was courting?"

"No. But they may have. I'd've been the last to hear it after our engagement was announced and that wasn't long after I got home from my Savannah visit. But Sistuh did know your Papa before I did, got to be a real church worker, president of the League and pastor's assistant that spring I was away. But at that time I was as wrapped up in my doings as you girls are now, couldn't see my hand before my face so far as anybody else was concerned. There, that'll have to do, Cindy. Felt mighty good."

Laying the brush on the bureau. "Well, you and Papa both've admitted I'm right about Deeda whether you know it or not."

"I can't see that that helps the situation any. And I want you to promise me as you promised your Papa you'll never mention it again."

"Yesum. Glad I got my hundred on something though, keep me up with the know-nothing bookworms in this family." Running to the window. "There's Dixie now! Letting the Reverend and Beth out of the phaeton! Must've saved thum a whole block of walking. I'll go tell Papa about that poor couple. Bet they've forgotten what they came for, sitting down there one on one side of the parlor, other on the other, like they've never been introduced. You can take your time bout dressing now, three witnesses on the spot."

Off down the hall . . . Back at my door again. "I hear Deeda. She's making that little whimpering sound, way she does when she's coming out of it.

"Roses, roses, roses, bring dreams of you, dear,
White is your soul so pure, dear . . ."

Running down the stairs, calling to Beth, "Go right back out there and tell Dixie to come in! Couple in the parlor and she can be a witness."

I tiptoeing to Sistuh's door. Quiet now. May be another hour. May be two. Better get a tray ready though. Try to get a little something to eat in her before she's awake enough to know what's happening.

❖ ❖ ❖

Starting downstairs finally just as the "wedding party" comes from the parlor. Leaning over the banister looking down.

"God bless and keep you both." David shaking hands with the bride, with the groom. "Now wait just a minute. I have a little present for you." Going to the hatrack and opening the boot-box.

Dixie's hands, soft and white as mine used to be, glittering with rings, squeezing that poor girl's red coarse ones. "I declare you're one of the prettiest brides I ever saw in my life! And I know you're going to be mighty happy with this great big strong good-looking husband. I can see how you got him but there must've been right much of a scramble out your way—"

Cindy choking, her handkerchief to her mouth, her head down on Dixie's shoulder, her body shaking with suppressed laughter.

"All those other girls after him I mean!" Dixie blushing, lifting the groom's hand he didn't seem to know what to do with, doing her best to shake its limp weight, "Yes, *sir,* you're real lucky and you be just as sweet to this little girl as you know how to be, hear."

"Yes, ma'm, I aims to be thataway." Gulping, fingers pulling at his stiff collar, red skin reddening, "Shore did have us some mighty purty bridesmaids what you call um."

"Why, aren't you nice! Cindy, you hear? Well, I just can't tell you how glad I am *I* was here. I *know* it was one of the very sweetest weddings I *ever* saw, in there with all Mrs. Humiston's beautiful flowers and the sunset and all."

David handing a gilt-edged Bible to the chunky, sallow-faced bride. "Read a passage every day and you'll find consolation for life's unavoidable sorrows."

"Don't know, sir, as I kin spell hit out but hit'll shore look mighty nice on our *center*table we git hit." Clasping the Bible to her big loose breasts 'sthough she'd never had a thing of her own before.

Dixie impulsively lifting her silver fan-chain over her black puffs, "Duck your head, honey," dropping the chain over that girl's droopy rummage-sale hat, opening the silk-spangled fan, fanning them both. "There!" Pressing the fan in the girl's hand. "I'm so glad I had a wedding present right with me. It's new, too. 'Something new, something blue' brings good luck, you know."

"You mean I keep hit!"

"Of course you keep it! I'd rather you had it than anybody in the world. Now when you get out on that hot old road, you fan with it, hear."

The bride looking down at the folded fan swinging over her bulge, then up at that scarecrow of a man and smiling in a way made me blink back tears, "Hit don't make no difference bout the ring now, honey," and reaching for his hand.

Dixie and David following them out on the porch but Cindy running back through the dining room calling Beth. Has to tell her about Dixie's "break." Will repeat it to me, to every girl or woman she meets the next few days, and to all of us again hereafter every time a country couple comes to be married. With all the details of her nearly disgracing herself laughing. "Now wasn't that something! Dixie talking about there having been a scramble and that girl ready to pop with a baby!" That's Cindy, a regular graphophone. But I love her light-heartedness. She's made me laugh many a time when I've felt more like crying.

"Here's your fee." At the foot of the stairs David handing me a worn dollar bill. "Told him it wasn't necessary but he seemed hurt, insisted I take it."

"I'm sorry you had to. Looks like they'll need it mighty soon. I can't help wishing, though, we lived in Cypress City right now —Fair's wedding coming off—and had big fees from all those Norfolk couples running away across the Virginia line."

"Lord'll take care of that expense as He has of all others. Sister still sleeping?"

"Yes, but she won't much longer. Just hope we can get through supper with things quiet for Bob."

"Bob coming for supper? If I didn't have so much else on my

281

mind, it'ud be a good time to mention that matter of church affiliation."

"Not tonight, David! If you must atall. Seems to me that's something they should decide for themselves. Besides, you've always said if any one of your girls ever left the Methodist Church, you hoped it'ud be for the Episcopal because it was the mother-church and like the Methodist in doctrine. Bob's been an Episcopalian all his life and—"

"Fair's been a Methodist and there's my position to consider. However, the essential thing is that they worship together and the Episcopal church here certainly needs new blood. That reminds me—heard an interesting story in Raeford about the origin of Methodist strength in this Scotch community. Seems a freed slave, converted by Bishop Asbury down near Bath, came through here preaching to plantation darkies. He was so eloquent crowds of white people—of the planter class —began going around to hear him preach. He converted them. They organized the first Methodist congregation and had *him* preach to them till they got a white circuit rider. I tell you, individual conversion's the only way—"

"Step off the rostrum, sir, and go make your ablutions." Beth coming from the dining room, smoothing strands of fine straight blonde hair up from her flushed face. "Table's all set in festive style—why, Mama, you look scrumptious! So glad you felt like putting on that frock."

David turning and looking at me. *At* me. Not through me. Eyes not glancing off 'sthough I was a piece of furniture not actually seen unless needed. Saying, "Yes, I've been admiring it past few minutes. With my inner eye. Didn't realize it was new though. Same color as the one you used to call your second-day dress, isn't it?"

"No, this is orchid crêpe, that was maroon watered silk."

"Just as becoming." Hesitating, I thinking he was coming back to kiss my cheek, but "ho-humming" in an embarrassed kind of way, going on up the stairs.

"Now, Mama, you go sit on the porch. Soon's I've helped Molly pack the ice-cream freezer, I'm going up to have a quick bath."

"Is the tank hot again?"

"I didn't feel it. Usually by this time it's had time to recover from Fair's and Cindy's draining."

"It's had more draining than that today. Cindy said Ann

282

Wesley and her friends used every drop early in the afternoon. Why don't you run over to Mrs. Hendrick's? She told me yesterday, again, that we're welcome any time we ran short. Only two of them there and always more hot water than they can use."

"Oh I hate to bother. I'd have to make a social event of it, take all my clothes—"

"No, you won't. Put on your kimono and slip through the side gate. Grape trellis'll hide you all the way. You're as finicky as Sistuh—tying her nightgown up around her waist when she gets in the tub."

Beth laughing. "How do you know that?"

"She told me. When we first had a bathtub. In Lynnboro. She thought I was shameless saying how restful it was to stretch out in a long tub."

"How does she wash the rest of her anatomy?"

"Slips the gown down *to* her waist and stands at the basin."

"Wonders never cease! Will you telephone Mrs. Hendricks for me, be sure the way's clear? Nothing I'd like better right now than to stretch out in a long tub after—" Breaking off, starting off upstairs.

"Beth! Wait a minute. What in the world were you and your Papa doing at the court house today in all the heat?"

"We'll tell you when we have time to talk. You telephone Mrs. Hendricks, then go sit on the porch—and hold on to all the Humistons as they appear. We're having supper at six-thirty sharp!"

At that old telephone fifteen minutes, first accepting Miss Bertie's congratulations on our anniversary, then, when she finally rang the Hendricks' number, listening to Mrs. Hendricks' apologies for not having been over today, her commiserations about Sistuh, her pleasure that we were accepting her invitation to bathe at last, her assurance that drawing off a tub of hot water would save their tank from blowing up because that trifling cook she had now *would* use coal in summer time to save her bringing in a few armfuls of wood, and what was going to happen to all of us anyway, negras charging two dollars a week to cook, taking home every scrap of food left from a meal, and getting so out-of-hand in every way? Sometimes she declared she wished every last one of thum had been sent back to Africa where they came from. Her Grandfather Warren down in Pasquatank County used to quote Mistuh Thomas

Jefferson's remark, "We've got a wolf by the ears and we can't hold him or let him go," meaning, of course, *slaves,* and Grandfather Warren used to say, "We've got to train thum, never let um get careless and shiftless, and hold on with all our might." What she wanted to know was who's going to look after *us* when they've eaten us out of house and home? "Now tell me all about Fair's wedding plans. How I envy your having such a daughter! Was saying to Mistuh Hendricks this very morning, I declare I've never seen a prettier or a nicer girl than that Fair Humiston. Of course you'll have to have a big church wedding, popular's Fair is, and I want to tell you right now even if we are Baptists if there's anything in this world I can do to help you—extra rooms for out-of-town guests . . ."

Hanging up the receiver, rubbing my aching ear, David standing at my elbow. "Mama, come in the sitting room with me. There's something I want to discuss with you. Beth means well but she's a little inclined to take a conversation out of my hands—and this is a matter for you and me—and God—to decide."

"Yes, David. I've known there's something I don't want to hear—ever since I saw your face at dinner, but I can't hear it now. I've got to get a tray ready for Sistuh before she wakes up." Whatever it is, I'll put it off long's I can.

"Mama! Mama!" Gladys running in the front door, banging the screen after her. "Mama, where's an old stocking? Tom T and I're going to stuff it and when it's dark we're going to pull it *real* slow across the sidewalk and scare all the cooks going home! You mind if Tom T stays for supper?"

David frowning. "Now, now, how'd you like to be scared, going home in the dark, tired out and—"

"Oh, Papa, we won't scare thum *much.* We'll be hiding behind the fence and if they act *real* scared, scared's Beth and Fair and Cindy were they thought Judgment—"

"You're not going to scare thum atall, baby. You're going right upstairs and put on a clean dress. Bob's coming for supper."

"Oh! Then I don't believe I want that silly Tom T hanging round. I'll run tell him you're *mighty* sorry but there's just not enough room for him *tonight.*"

❖ ❖

A reception after all. Twelve stewards and their wives just dropping in separately to congratulate us quietly and all stay-

284

ing nearly three hours. Standing around the table Beth'd reset with the silver paper decorations she'd brought from New York, drinking coffee I poured from the new silver service they'd given us, finishing up the fancy little cakes, munching mints and crystallized fruit, going on about Ma's rat-tail spoons Molly'd polished like new, about Beth's being so artistic, Fair so lovely, Cindy so pretty and lively, Ann Wesley so smart in school, Gladys so adorable, and what brand of coffee was this so delicious, and David and I certainly didn't look like we'd been married a quarter of a century, and no wonder Miss Ora broke down, sewing the way she did but must make her mighty proud everybody saying there were no better dressed girls in town than the Humiston girls. On and on till for a little while they had me feeling like somebody again, even laughing at Brothuh Simpson's old coon-jokes, not even hearing Sistuh's moaning like a low wind rising. David telling about the old Irishman up the country drunk on moonshine, stumbling into the cemetery during a funeral, listening solemnly to the service till the preacher said there's no peace this side of the grave, then roaring out, "Faith and bejabbers, Parson, come this side, there's no distarbance over here!"

Then before the laughter'd died down, David putting on his ministerial expression, saying now that he had his board all together informally, this was as good a time as any to sound them out on extending an invitation to the Annual Conference to meet in Cameronville in December! Seems the brethren in Rocky Mount had had to recall their invitation because the new church there wouldn't be finished in time and at Raeford this morning the Presiding Elder'd suggested Cameronville, Conference not having met here in twenty-three years. Above the chatter of the ladies as to who should entertain the Bishop, the men were having a hard time voicing their approval of the invitation. Spite of Fair and Bob, Cindy and Bill, creating a new clamor coming in from the picture show, the Bishop, Presiding Elder, and most prominent preachers got settled in homes, David insisting, in spite of all my motioning and frowning at him, on our taking two at the parsonage! If he once thought of the year Conference'd been invited to Laurenton and called off to Durham at the last minute "because of sudden illness in the family of our prospective host and brother in Christ, Reverend David McCall Humiston," he was giving no sign of it.

Was after eleven before David, Beth, and I were alone in

the sitting room, the door closed on Cindy's and Bill's low laughing and talking in the parlor, Fair's and Bob's silence on the porch, Sistuh's old grief, regular and cadenced now, from upstairs. David, not hearing my question, sitting down in front of the jardiniere of red asters on the cleaned-out hearth, sighing, putting his fingers on his pulse. "Don't believe this heart of mine can take another such strain as it's been subjected to today. What was that you asked, Mama?"

"Whether you remember when Conference had to be called off in Laurenton?"

"I couldn't forget that humiliation. Brother Thomas hadn't forgotten either. Took me aside before he called the morning session to order. Complimented me on my quarterly report, said he knew the church here was prospering under my ministry but how was it with me and mine in the parsonage? My sister-in-law's health? Didn't seem surprised when I told him it'd failed again this summer—expect he heard about this attack when he was here filling my pulpit the fourth Sunday in June. Said he was sorry to hear it because this question of finding a host for the Conference'd come up and personally he felt Cameronville was the logical one, but of course with severe illness in the parsonage, some alternative would have to be found."

Listening to him and watching him—leaving his chair, striding to a window, making blinds of his hands and looking out on the dark lawn—and his murmur that we were going to have rain at last seemed as consequential as his repetition of Brothuh Thomas' remarks. Why, I feel removed from all this. Feel like one of Molly's ghosts looking in on people living. And have all day. I see and hear, note the comings and goings, but it's not even as real to me as a story in a novel. I've got to get back somehow as I had to get from under those fire-horses' hoofs. . . .

"David, wasn't it Thomas Bishop Rollins picked instead of you, time your name was first on the list for Presiding Elder of the Washington District?"

"Yes." Turning around, going to the table, picking up *Everybody's Magazine* and dropping it with a thud on *The Review of Reviews*. "But that's neither here nor there. Ashamed to say I felt a twinge of animosity at the time but I haven't nourished it for fourteen years. No, I just stopped there on the Raeford church steps and looked him straight in the eye—not easy to do either, wall-eyed as he is—and I told him he needn't

286

worry about finding an alternative. Told him to go right ahead and put it to a vote with the Cameronville District preachers. If they wanted it, I would lay it before my stewards. And if *they* were ready to extend the invitation, he could notify the Bishop. Never saw a man so taken aback. He stroked that gray goat's beard of his, said of course cognizance had been taken of the fact that our parsonage is at some distance from the church and if I felt satisfied it would cause me no embarrassment or lay an undue burden on my good wife—now, Mama, don't look like that. Let me finish."

"No, Mama." Beth leaving the sofa, coming and standing behind my chair, running her fingers through my hair as she did through her own when she was upset. "There's no use to go on playing ostrich, pretending we don't know people talk just because we don't hear thum."

"Went on to say he was sure everyone concerned would understand if the parsonage did not offer hospitality. With God's help I restrained myself till he finished, then I told him as unmistakably's I told that pompous Armstrong in Lynnboro —only other time any fool ever rushed in talking to *me*—told him I could manage my own household and he could rest assured my good wife would do her share in providing hospitality."

I laughing right out and it was a sickening sound. Beth's hands slipping to my shoulders, pressing them 'sthough she was holding me together. "It's going to be all right, Mama. Just wait till Papa says all he has to say."

David at the door now, opening it a crack, putting his ear close. "Time those young men were going home. Storm's coming."

"Himmel, don't break up Cindy's tête-à-tête, have her coming in here with her clairvoyant insight!"

"I'd feel better about it if I could hear a tête-à-tête. Just hear Cindy giggling." But he was closing the door, pulling a chair close to mine, sitting down, reaching in his pocket, unfolding a long legal-looking paper. "Mama—" then looking up at Beth as beseechingly as a child— "Beth, maybe you'd better—"

"First, you tell Mama what Doctuh Stewart said."

Holding out my hand for that paper, David holding it back. "Just a minute, Mama. Today when Doctor and I came downstairs, he asked for a word with me. We stepped there in the parlor and he said he didn't know just how to say what he had in mind, but first he wanted me to understand he was speaking only as our physician and not as an interfering friend—friendly as he felt toward all of us."

"Go on."

"Well, the gist of it was that he sees no way to help Sister out of her misery for the next few years. Feels, however, after what he saw today, that she'd suffer less, be better off generally, separated from us. Says she's in the worst period of a woman's life—fact is, he's more concerned about the effect all this will have on you—at this stage—that is—"

"Concerned about *me*! Why, I'm strong's an ox. Have to be. Have had to be. How else could I be alive now?"

"Yes, I told him you never complained. Always seemed well. More concerned about others than about yourself. He said, nevertheless, there's a limit to the nervous strain anybody can take, a breaking point physically—"

"Well, Doctuh Stewart—or you either—needn't worry bout my going to pieces this late date."

David leaning over, laying a hand on my knee, I wanting to brush it off. No sympathy, no understanding *now*, please! I *might* break if you show me that after fifteen years! Only reason I've been able to go on as I have is because you've been like a rock. Unseeing, unheeding. Coming in the house to groan and sigh about what Sistuh's spells do to you and to your work, walking out to peace and quiet in your study, or into sunshine and admiration on the street. Putting it all out of your mind, leaving me to bear her crying and her talking, her moaning and her hate. And the children took their cue from you. Thank God. Yes, thank God, they've been able to throw it off too. Off on me. And because you all have, I've been able to take it. Expecting nothing, wishing for nothing but peace there's only one way to get, I've been *willing* to go on half-alive, carrying the burden for you and for the children who taste what you eat, sleep when you lie down, have hope and ambition. . . .

"You may not be as strong as you think. Physicians' eyes are sharper than ours. Doctor Stewart wants you to come to him for an examination, then have a change of climate and a rest. Told him I was at low ebb myself, planning to go up to the old home after the first Sunday in September and had been trying to persuade you to go with me, only a brother and a sister there, bracing air, plenty of fresh vegetables, eggs, milk, and fruit. Said he would order you—"

Shaking my head—as I'd shaken it in every such August conversation for fifteen years—making Sistuh my excuse now as I'd usually been able to. "How can I go and leave Sistuh this way?"

"Let Papa finish, Mama."

David getting up suddenly, pacing to the window and back again, standing in front of me, holding out that paper, tapping it with his forefinger. "Here's the means for carrying out Doctor Stewart's recommendation—for the good of your health and the continuance of my work."

Waving it away. "I can't read it without my glasses."

"Where are they?" David going to the mantelpiece, fumbling among the ornaments.

"I don't want to read it. I know you've done at last what you've thought about and hinted at a long time. But I'll never consent to sending Sistuh to the asylum for the good of my health. And as for your work, it seems to go on no matter—"

"Then for Ann Wesley's and Glad's sake, Mama! Give them a chance to grow up normally. It's too late for the rest of us." Beth's hands leaving my shoulders, Beth's feet stumbling over the hassock, Beth standing at the window now, rolling up the shade, staring through the upper panes at the lightning flashing.

"What do you mean, baby—too late for the rest of you? Seems to me every one of you has had a good life so far in spite of it all. You were saying today Frances—"

"Good life?"

"Why, baby—?"

Turning suddening, her eyes, blue as her Alice Blue dress, filling with tears. "Oh, Mama, can't you *see* what it's done to me?" Then, her voice quickening with impatience. "I know you hoped I'd marry Davidson Broderick, then Milton Sellers. You may as well stop hoping I'll marry anybody." Looking from one to the other of us staring at *her,* not understanding, waiting. "Well—" her wide mouth twisting wryly as at a bad taste— "if you must have it in a word—*sex.* From the time I can remember, Deeda's made the—the relations between men and women something nasty and unnatural. I like men, like to be with them, talk to them a lot more than I like to talk to women. But as soon as one of them shows a personal interest in

me—and there've been more than those two persistent ones—
I shy off. And can't come back!" Her face puckering, her teeth
biting at her lip, giving up, dashing for the door.

David standing there, his arms at his side, *his* shoulders
drooping a little, I reaching over for that paper at his feet,
feeling embarrassed for Beth as I'd felt when she'd shed a
child's tears, because crying made her ugly.

Cindy throwing open the door. "What's struck Beth? Ran
right past Bill and me in the hall—what's this anyway, a
funeral? One of you come to and tell me where Papa's *um*brella
is. Reckon you don't know it but it's raining little nigger babies
and Bill's got to go."

❖

"Let's don't discuss it any more tonight, Mama. Should try
to get some sleep while it's still raining hard and we can't hear
Sister so plainly. It's got to be your decision—nearest relative
must sign the commitment papers. And if you can't find it in
your heart to put your husband and your children above your
sister, then we'll go on as we've been going."

"Oh, David, how can you?"

Fingers reaching, touching my shoulder. "I don't want to
make it any harder for you, Ellen, wasn't easy for me to make
my decision—to go as far as I could with it—but now I have, I
can leave it in God's hands to do what is best. I feel He's been
with me. If I'm right, then you'll have peace too when . . ."

"But you're leaving it with *me* and I don't know what's right
or which way to turn."

"Then just leave it all till morning, maybe it'll be clearer
then. You mind turning on your right side so I can get this
sheet up over my shoulder? Wind's blowing a little through
that east window."

He'll be going off to sleep now easily's a cat, with no more
feeling of guilt maybe. Sometimes I wonder if he even remembers . . .

2

Much as I'd hated having to leave Doddsville and Mary Lassiter and as worn out as I was, I was sure I'd like Lynnboro.
Felt it, as surely as I felt the ache in my head and my legs and

arms, the minute we stepped off the train in a sleety drizzle and all I could see in the gaslight were the welcoming faces of two of the stewards.

"Well, well, well, so we have you here at last!" The round-faced, clean-shaven, substantial-looking one was squeezing my hand. "Hope you had a comfortable trip. Parlor car warm enough, porter attentive, everything up to scratch? You'll have to give me a full report on it, Sistuh Humiston. You all the first regular passengers in the new parlor car on this now up-to-date line."

"Oh, you're Brothuh Woodruff! Why I don't know how to thank you for all your thoughtfulness! I never enjoyed a train trip more! If Lynnboro hadn't been our destination, I'd've wished there'd been miles and miles more of it."

He laughed heartily and said there was no use putting your bottom dollar in a railroad unless your friends could enjoy it free on occasion. Patted my shoulder. "Yes, m'am, I see you're going to be's happy in our little city as we're happy to have you and that's a fact. Now les see bout your hand baggage." He turned and motioned to a young darky there in the shadow.

"Ellen"—David touched my arm—"this is Brother Armstrong you remember meeting at Conference last year."

"Why, I certainly do!" If I hadn't remembered those coal-black side-whiskers I would have the bare touch of cold fingers that was his handshake. "It's *mighty* nice to see you again, sir. I was *so* grieved to hear of your sad loss last summer. I remembered your telling me Mrs. Armstrong's health wasn't good but I'd no *i*dea—"

"Yes, the Lord giveth and the Lord taketh away, blessed be—"

"Brother Armstrong, I want you to meet my wife's sister, Miss Fanning. Ora, you've heard me speak of Brother Armstrong, chairman of the board of stewards." David tightened his left arm around Cindy, perched on his shoulder, and freed his right hand to urge Sistuh nearer.

"*Miss* Fanning did you say, Brothuh?" Bowing to Sistuh, holding out his hand. "It's a pleasure, ma'm, I assure you."

Sistuh bowed stiffly, kept her hand pressed against her side. "You'll have to excuse my not shaking hands. I have a lame wrist."

"Yes, Sister Ora broke her right wrist in a carriage accident last August and it still gives her trouble. Setting wasn't what it should've been," David explained.

"Now I'm right sorry to hear that, Miss Fanning. We'll have to get Doctuh Bradford to take a look at it. One of the most prominent physicians in the state and lives right here in Lynnboro."

"Come, children!" I stepped back to Beth and Fair and stood with them a minute watching the red lantern on the train's end dwindle to a red speck in the darkness. A widower. A rich widower. If only Sistuh could and *would* like him! "Come on now and meet these two nice gentlemen who'll take us to the parsonage."

Fair ran right up between Sistuh and Brothuh Armstrong, pounded his overcoat with the little white muff Mary Lassiter'd given her, asked if she could ride on the engine of his train tomorrow.

"Why, baby!" Sistuh put her hand on Fair's white felt bonnet. "You mustn't act like a tomboy. Be Deeda's little lady now and shake hands with Brothuh Armstrong."

Fair did.

"How old're you, little lady?"

"I'm seven years old. Beth's nearly ten though."

"Well now, let me tell you. I don't own that big train but I do own a cotton mill and I've got some mighty smart little girls working in it not much older than you are. I'll tell you what— when you're a *little* bit taller, I'll let you card cotton for me, how'd that be?" He cut an eye at Sistuh, smirked, and turned to David. "No lack of good hands here, Brothuh Humiston. More mountain folks coming down every week. First thing we've got to do, now we've got an up and coming man like you, is build thum a chapel before the regular congregation at the First Methodist's pushed out of their pews. The ladies've been complaining for some time now. I've been telling thum just to wait till we get that young—"

"All right, folks"—Brothuh Woodruff hurried up—"baggage's all taken care of, les go." He held out his arms and Cindy bounced into them. "That's a girl! I'll take care of this babydoll and either one of you ladies wants to ride in my buggy."

"Ellen, you go. You're shivering. I can get in anywhere."

As though a closed carriage, two big seats, wasn't waiting three feet in front of her! I didn't try to say yea or nay, my teeth chattering way they were, just went along with Brothuh Woodruff's clever talk and jovial laugh. I pulled back the storm-curtain and he helped me in with one hand, then pulled the

292

robe up over my knees. I held out my arms for Cindy but he kept her, carried her to the hitching-post and let her stroke the horse's wet nose. Cindy's face, bright's a dollar one minute in the shimmering gaslight, dimmed and wavered and I had to shut my eyes. Oh, but I felt sick! Now there'd be bed again and Sistuh hovering over me, doing more with her left hand for my comfort than anybody else could with her right, tiring me out with her devotion. *Now* if I have to go to bed with grippe, she'll say she warned me about all that running around the last six weeks before I'd got my strength back.

I'd had to run around, be made a lot of by those Doddsville people. I couldn't have stayed in the house till Christmas, grieving over my loss, over David's loss, and putting up with Sistuh's crankiness that'd begun the minute I was out of bed. Refusing to go out to suppers with David and me, refusing to go spend the day anywhere, even when the children were invited, because "she could get so much done toward the moving when she had the parsonage to herself and Rose." Then acting like she'd been slighted when we came home, asking a thousand questions about who was there and what was said and whether Brothuh David'd seemed to enjoy it. . . .

Brothuh Woodruff reached over, set Cindy in my lap, climbed in himself, and set her between his knees. He put her hands on the reins, closed his hands over them. "Now say 'March, General.'"

"He can't hear me through the curtains," Cindy said.

"Then we'll have to whack the reins. He never starts without orders."

Cindy prattled away about the horses at Grandpa's and I didn't have to talk. Just sitting upright seemed as much as I could do.

Suddenly all the pleasure and excitement about coming to the new town that'd won David in a kind of competition was gone. How could I've thought it'ud be fun again? Made me tired just to think of getting new people sorted out, fixing names on their rightful owners, picking out the ones I wanted for friends, isolating them from the parsonage habitués—those earnest women, plain as old shoes, who loved all preachers' wives on sight and whose sugary words reduced me to a simpering nonentity; learning who was kin and whether it was loving or hating kin so I wouldn't say the wrong thing; learning to walk past just what I was looking for in a Presbyterian or Baptist store window, waiting in a Methodist (a Methodist paid up in church dues) while a skinny Miss Somebody rummaged in shelves and drawers for "the *i*dentical thing, Sistuh Humiston, though it may not look *exactly* like what you saw in the Bee Hive, it'll wear longer *and* you get the ten percent discount"; standing downtown on a cold winter day waiting till the streets stopped merry-go-rounding and the post office its silly puss-in-the-corner game with the bank so I could walk with dignity in the direction I wanted to go. . . .

"Oh, excuse me, Brothuh Woodruff, I must've dozed off!"

"Mighty tired, honey, I know. And still feeling mighty weak." He cleared his throat. "Don't mind my mentioning it—I'm an old man with grown children—but Mrs. Woodruff went through just such an ordeal once. Said she'd rather have had triplets any day. But what I said just now was, you're lucky to have your sistuh with you while you're getting your strength back. Lucky a handsome woman like Miss Fanning hasn't got a family of her own to do for."

"Yes, sir. I certainly am." I thought I couldn't but I went on. "I'd be all right now but for the stress and strain of moving. And all the farewell hospitality of those Doddsville people right around Christmas time." I even laughed. "I do wish the church fathers hadn't thought it best for a pastor to begin new work with the new year. Moving in spring or fall 'ud be a lot easier."

"Often thought of that myself. Still they changed one thing we Lynnboro people mighty glad they did—that *i*dea of Wesley's preachers should be bachelors. Hadn't, that little lady Mrs. Woodruff and I heard so much about at Conference last month wouldn't be riding with me now! I tell you we all here don't know whether to be prouder we got our man or his wife! Yes, m'am, Lynnboro's going to love you and you're going to love Lynnboro."

All I could see of Lynnboro then through the isinglass windows of the storm curtain was its fuzz of sleet and rain but I knew it had paved streets because every clank of hoofs on brick resounded in my aching head. "Yes, I'm sure I will. First thing Mistuh Humiston said when he came home from Conference was if all the Lynnboro people were like you and Mrs. Woodruff, we were going to hate leaving here much's we hated leaving Doddsville."

"We'll see that you do, we'll see that you do. Les pull the

reins this way, doll-baby, turn this corner. And here's the church and there's the parsonage!"

New church, new parsonage, they said, with all modern conveniences. I pressed my nose to the isinglass—church close to the sidewalk, lights from the parsonage windows glittering on the frosted grass strip separating church and parsonage. Certainly would have to keep the children quiet during services!

"Now you sit right still, Sistuh Humiston." He set Cindy on my lap, reached under the seat, pulled out an umbrella, unbuttoned the curtain and stepped out.

Holding tight to Brothuh Woodruff's umbrella arm, holding my skirts high, I got over the smooth bricks between gate and steps. Oh, I cried silently to Cindy perched again on Brothuh Woodruff's shoulder, if only your excited chatter were ladytalk and all those people inside that door paper dolls, what a relief it'ud be!

They might've been for all they meant to me, their faces beneath the dim yellowish light of the pineapple-shaped bulb on the swinging gas lamp so much alike it seemed that one smile stretched from one end of the receiving line to the other. And their voices blended now in a chorus, now coming in separately like the repetitive antiphony of an anthem. "Sistuh Humiston how glad we are to see you how glad glad glad we are how glad I am what a night for you to be travelling and this is the baby child I declare she's just like her father how glad I am so sorry the weather the rain the sleet three little daughters now isn't that nice little Fair's pretty's a picture so this is the oldest one Beth the oldest one cat's got *her* tongue has to be a shy one I always say mighty glad so glad do better bout the weather tomorrow no, no, Maria, *this* is *Sistuh Humiston* pass it on pass it on all of us made the same mistake up this end this is *Sistuh Humiston* pass it on pass it on that was *Miss Fanning* no not Brothuh Humiston's sistuh Sistuh Humiston's sistuh no, no, *Miss* Fanning the little girls are Humistons. . . ."

❖ ❖

One cool hand on my forehead, cool fingers feeling for my pulse between cuff and glove. "No, Brothuh Humiston, you can trust her to us. She's coming to now. Maria, run tell Phoebe to take that washtub up to the *bathroom* and fill it with hot water. Katy Lynn, tell Mistuh Woodruff to get right back in that buggy and go for Doctuh Sam. Miss Fanning, you let me handle this. Those children're famished and you and Brothuh Humiston must be too. You go right in the dining room before that supper gets cold. Yes, Cam Derickson, you certainly can. You're young and strong and she's light's a feather. Right on upstairs, room at the front."

Away from the faces, curious, concerned, concerned, curious. Stair carpeting not matting. Big bedroom. Blazing fire. Soft bed. Warm blankets. Cold, cold, cold . . .

"There now, honey, stop that shivering." Blanket tucked up under my chin. "Hope I didn't blister those little tiny feet. No bigger than a heathen Chinese. 'Feet'll tell,' my mother always said when we went to The Springs summertime and didn't know who was who. 'Quality never wears more than a size two.' What'd those Doddsville folks mean, letting you travel on the verge of pneumonia?"

"Didn't—feel badly till—we got on the train. But I'd've come anyway, Brothuh Vann's family waiting for the parsonage. So sorry—to put you ladies—all this trouble."

"Honey, don't you dare say such a thing's that! We're pleased's Punch have you in any condition. Now all you've got to do is lie still. Nothing atall for you to worry your pretty head about. Got a good cook in the kitchen for you. Phoebe used to be my girl and she's one you can depend on, she'll be here bright and early every morning rolls around. And I live just around the corner— Come in!"

"Just thought she might taste this chicken broth. It's piping hot. Was the only nourishment Mistuh Slocum could—"

"Shush. Yes indeed, Alice, les see if she can sip a little." Going to the door. "Rest of you go on back downstairs. No, wait a minute! Katy Lynn, see if you can lay your hands on that old flannel I brought over for dust cloths. Doctuh Sam's going to order a mustard plaster and I know it. Mrs. Maddox, you come help me take this tub out."

Lady in widow's weeds bending over me. Big sorrowful eyes, low sorrowful voice. "Think you can take a few spoonfuls this nice hot broth, dear one? No, I'll hold it. I'm Alice Slocum, your next-door neighbor. Feel real capable nursing pneumonia too—I lost my dear husband with it two years ago next month."

I had no more idea of going downstairs that rainy morning, first Thursday of February, 1895, than I'd had any morning in the last week of a bright, cool January. When Phoebe'd taken my breakfast waiter, compliments to herself on my appetite floating back to me as starched calico and white apron rustled to the door, and when Beth'd shown me her new *History of the Old North State,* "a whole lot bigger than the one she'd had in Doddsville," and gone off with Fair to Miss Fay Dosier's Select Academy for Young Ladies, I reached in my darning-bag.

Empty again! Sistuh must've slipped in here when I was asleep yesterday and taken the socks and stockings Phoebe'd managed to wash and bring to me. Why have a needle-point bag on polished bamboo legs if it has to be folded and set against the wall? "Dear One," Mrs. Slocum'd said. "*You* must have this now. Every time I look at it, my eyes fill with tears to think never again will I darn a hole those precious toes of his've made." Be the last thing I'd cry about if David should die. And I certainly won't cry now because Sistuh's emptied the bag.

I reached behind the pillow in my chair for the novel young Mrs. Cameron Derickson'd brought me yesterday. "Yes, I know," she said when I told her what David thought bout the modern novels he hadn't read. "He told us in prayer meeting last Wednesday night we'd find the works of Shakespeare, Scott, and Dickens on the parsonage book shelves but no works of living authors. 'Why, how do we know,' I said to Cam walking home, 'that such modern authors as Mistuh Henry James won't be classics some day?' Hide it if you must, but read it. I'd like somebody in this town to talk books to." I was hungrier for novels, now with time on my hands, than for chicken broth, blanc mange, syllabub, lemon cheesecake, and all the other dainties the ladies brought in. And already more absorbed in Isabelle in *The Portrait of a Lady* than in any heroine I remembered. Maybe it was because her determination to improve herself in every way and her refusal to marry till she fell in love made her seem close kin to me in spite of all the differences in our lives. Now I found her in that beautiful old garden in Florence, Italy, where I'd had to leave her when David'd come upstairs last night and I settled back in my chair happier than I used to be even hiding down by the brook with *The Wide, Wide World* Buddy'd given me for Christmas while Sistuh made jelly or something in the hot kitchen. Sistuh knew where to find me now if she thought of a thing I was capable of doing.

I must've heard the front door open and close, voices in the passage, but if I did, the sound was far, far away, across the ocean, and I hardly had time to thrust the book behind my pillow before Phoebe opened my door.

"Miss Elnuh Woodruff here to see you. Say she won't stay long, just want to say howdy."

"Tell her to come right up. Wait a minute, Phoebe—I look all right?"

"You knows you do, that blue wrapper. Mind I brings up your sweet milk whilst she's here? Miss Elnuh get talking she got no sense of time and you won't eat your dinner eff'n you drink your sweet milk too late."

Mrs. Woodruff pushed past her. "Phoebe, you hush telling stories bout me and get on back to your kitchen! How're you feeling, honey?"

"Lawd, Miss Elnuh, I thought you stay down till I announced you like you yourself teach me to!"

"Good morning, lady." I held out my hand. "Phoebe, go tell Sistuh we've got company."

"Miss Orie ain't here. She taken Cindy to the church, do something nother."

Mrs. Woodruff ignored my hand, put her arms around me, pressed my face against her long brown furpiece, my nose in the bunch of violets pinned on it. "Fresh violets! Don't tell me spring's here!"

"Is in the sunny corner of our ell. I picked these yesterday." She unpinned them, handed them to me. "Daffodils coming up too." She took a little vase from the mantel, filled it at the washstand pitcher, and set the violets on the table at my side. Then she stood off and looked at me. "You're a lot stronger, I declare you *are*. In the face, at least. Better get downstairs, exercise your limbs or you won't be out in time to do all that gardening you want to do. Never had a preacher's wife here who thought it worthwhile to raise flowers for some other preacher's wife to enjoy and a little color gainst this new white house's just what we need." She leaned over, put her fingers under my chin, tilted my face to the light. "Your color's *real* good, considering. Why doesn't Doctuh Sam let you go down? When was he here last?"

"Day before yesterday. Said I could go now, first morning I really *wanted* to. But the very thought of a relapse makes me feel right weak. If you knew how I hate being so unsociable!"

She laughed, the round brown eyes in her round big doll-face twinkling at me. "I *do* know! Knew you were just my kind minute I saw you, pale's you were. But we'll make up for this retirement, you just wait!" Then, seriously, "Pneumonia's a touchy thing but I don't think you're in a bit of danger now, honey. You're getting some flesh on your bones and your voice's lost that tired sound." Suddenly her eyes were as bland and expressionless as a doll's. "I declare I'm surprised. I asked Miss Ora about you Sunday after church and she said you were getting on well's could be expected. I thought I'd find you looking as peaked as you did a week ago I was up here—came two other times, you know, but Miss Ora said you were sleeping and I wouldn't let her disturb you." She took off her fur and threw it on the bed. "It's mighty nice you have a sistuh and three little girls to hold down the parsonage pew but we want to see *you* in it. First thing you know, there'll be whispers that you're a permanent invalid. Lynnboro's my home town and I love it but it's a mighty gossipy place too. Listen, honey, let me run downstairs and see how the sitting-room fire's doing, then help you down. You can be sitting there big's you please when Brothuh Humiston comes in. Be a *mighty* good surprise for him. All right?"

"I'll certainly try."

She unpinned her fur-trimmed hat and threw it on her fur and started for the door just as Phoebe came in with my sweet milk.

"Now, Miss Ellen," she said, "I can tell you just what Miss Ora's doing over to the church do you want to know."

"I certainly do. I don't trust her."

Was Mrs. Woodruff's quick intake of breath made me glance from Phoebe to her just in time to see *too much* expression in her eyes—surprise, curiosity, pity. But Phoebe knew just how innocent my words'd been, knew exactly what I'd meant, and her flat chestnut-colored face crumpled in a silent laugh and her talk gave me a chance to get my balance again.

"You tell me Monday not let Miss Ora do up all Beth's and them's dresses again cause some could go in the wash. Tuesday you say don't let Miss Ora press Mistuh Humiston's frock coat, it's too hard on her lame wrist. Yesdiddy you say bring me the darning before Miss Ora gets it. But this morning you don't say,

299

don't let Miss Ora go over to the church and show Jeff how to clean hit, so when I sees her wrapping up herself and Cindy in shawls and things, putting on rubbers, I don't waste my time trying to stop her doing whatsomever it is she aiming to do. So that's what she's doing right this minute. Just sent Jeff over here to get my turkey-feather duster and all my rags. Yasum, Miss Ora she's a going to heaven the hard way!" Phoebe handed me the sweet milk. "Whyfor your hand shake so today again?" She took the glass and set it on the table." You lean over and sip," she said.

"Miss Ora's making the trip a step at a time, anyway, Phoebe," Mrs. Woodruff laughed and said. "It's just the study this morning. I stopped in to give Brothuh Humiston the list he asked for of young people old enough to join the church and I could hardly get in for all the books and stuff piled on the floor—oh, honey, I meant to tell you first thing what little Cindy said! Found Miss Ora and Brothuh Humiston laughing when I went in. Seems Cindy'd been up to some mischief and her Papa'd reprimanded her. Told her if she wanted to be a good little Christian she'd have to ask God to give her a new heart and Cindy'd looked up at him with those great big blue eyes of hers and asked, 'But what'll God do with my old one, Papa?' Yes," she went on when we'd stopped laughing, "the study's getting a spring cleaning a month ahead of time. Hope the stewards'll appreciate it, their meeting tonight."

"That's right. It's the first Thursday in the month here, isn't it? Depend on Sistuh to remember things like that." I managed to lift the glass steadily and I sipped a little milk.

"Now, Phoebe"—Mrs. Woodruff bustled to the door—"you find me a dark quilt and bring it on downstairs. We're going to fix Miss Ellen up in that big chair by the sitting-room fire. You've been pampering her long enough."

"Say you is! Now if that ain't the *best* news I heard since freedom come!"

"You hush bout your freedom and get me that quilt and two nice pillows."

Minute the door closed I clasped my hands over my stomach. If I'd drunk that milk, I'd have vomited, every organ inside me turning a somerset at the awful realization that there was gossip about Sistuh and David.

After a while the pain subsided and I got up and walked

300

about the room. Not feeling weak, not feeling my body atall. All mind and soul—or whatever it is makes us more than animal, not content when creature comforts are satisfied—shattered, wounded beyond any doctuh's aid and skill.

I stopped at a front window and looked out through the mist of fine rain at the white of the four big houses on the block, the green of soaked grass, the black of wet tree trunks, the dark lacework of bare twigs against the gray sky, as vivid and strange as when in the dark of night a flash of lightning unexpectedly reveals the daytime familiar. That flash of insight when I'd caught Mrs. Woodruff's expression had cut through familiar pictures in my mind and memory revealing a fact that was new and strange to me. But none the less real. Other people in the house with me had an existence *of their own* apart from mine as surely as the people in those houses across the street had. They'd had it two months ago before I'd even heard their names and they'ud go on having it after we'd moved to another Church Street. Everybody in the world had been and would go on being themselves. Only I—suddenly, unexpectedly—was *different*. Humpty Dumpty sat on a wall, Humpty Dumpty had a great fall, all the king's horses and all the king's men couldn't put Humpty together again. . . . Why, all this's happened to me before, sometime, somewhere. Where? When? When *had* somebody I thought I knew through and through twisted like a divining rod in a dowser's hand to indicate water beneath what looked like solid ground? I doubled my fists and beat them against the window frame trying to remember, sat on the edge of my bed a minute, walked back to my chair—and there it was before my eyes like a picture flashed on a blank magic lantern screen.

I saw myself fifteen years old standing at a window of Ma's old room at Brookside, room I'd wheedled out of Miss Ryder for a birthday present. I was in my petticoats waiting for Sistuh to finish my new dress with a sailor collar. Sistuh sat on the upstairs veranda, in the old chair without rockers or arms, taking the last stitches in the hem and I put my hand over my mouth to keep from calling out to her to hurry. Claiborne was sending the carriage for me. We were going sailing on the bay from the Faircloth dock with some Faircloth kin who'd come up from Charleston in a real yacht. I watched her bite off the thread, lift the dress to shake it out, opened my mouth to say I was right there, hand it through the window. I never said it. Never said a word, she did it so suddenly. Picked up her scissors and slashed the skirt straight up the front. Everything inside me turned a somerset *then*. The dress slid from her lap to the floor, the scissors fell with a clang, her hands covered her face, and her shoulders shook. She hadn't meant a word of what she'd said bout not minding she hadn't been invited, excusing Claiborne, saying even if Claiborne *was* nearly seventeen, as near her age as mine, she'd always been my friend, not hers! I stood there too shocked to move, hearing her choked sobs. Then feeling again, and feeling cold with anger, trying to think of the meanest thing I could do to her. But when she finally dried her eyes with the hem of her apron and stood up, I saw her face. Thought I saw courage in it. Thought she was coming to tell me the truth and beg me to forgive her, and I ran to my bureau and rummaged in a drawer 'sthough I was looking for something. "Baby," she said to my back, "I've ruined your dress. My hands were so slippery with perspiration the scissors slipped when I started to pull out a basting. I'll run press your old picnic pinafore and you can wear it over your Sunday lawn. Oh, baby, don't look at me like that! I couldn't help it. I can fix this tomorrow, got a whole length of material left." Pity for her, shame that I'd seen what she was trying so hard to hide, left me. I ran to the wardrobe, snatched the pinafore, and threw it at her, told her to hurry because I was going on that sail if I had to go in my shimmyshirt. Young as I was, I reckon I was as disappointed in Sistuh as in the loss of my dress, but somehow I knew enough to know that if she didn't tell me, it'ud never do to let her know I knew something about her she didn't want me to know. Best thing was to forget it and I must've pretended so hard I *didn't know*, I fooled myself. Made myself forget Sistuh was jealous of my good times. Because they wouldn't have been such good times any more if I'd remembered. She certainly helped me. If she'd ever let her jealousy get the best of her before or ever did again, I never saw an evidence of it. All my clothes for Savannah, my wedding dress finished to perfection— But scissors slashing *at her heart* then? She *did* give evidence again! That illness that had no name! Evidence of jealousy but not jealousy of my good times! Blind, blind, blind. Willfully, determinedly, selfishly blind, blind . . .

"Ready, honey?" Mrs. Woodruff opened the door, big doll-face like a mother's on Christmas morning. "Everything's cozy, just waiting for you."

❖

Nothing'll ever be cozy again, cozy again, cozy again.

The clock on the mantel above me ticked it, renewed rain on the windowpanes tapped it. But I sat there huddled in an armchair trying and trying to pretend it could and would be. I've been jumping to unwarranted conclusions. Ha, jumping from self-delusions to an external reality that's been waiting for me more than ten years. Deep inside me I'd known it was there. I'd refused to see it as I'd refused to remember Sistuh's capacity for jealousy. Nothing else could explain my wholehearted acceptance of a fact on so slight a hint.

But it can't be true of David, I argued again. And if it's not true of David, it can't be true of Sistuh. Not to the extent I've been imagining this past half-hour. Why, if Sistuh'd wanted David, she'd had plenty time to get him before I ever saw him. It's gossip, pure and simple. Lynnboro's no different from Bayport or Wilmington or Doddsville. I haven't lived in four towns without discovering that people are alike everywhere. They never say to your face what they say behind your back. Yes, but they do! Say the same things in different words. If you know the facts, you're not fooled by the disguises. If I'd known these people were gossiping about David and Sistuh, I'd've known exactly what they meant when they said to me, coming upstairs since I'd been sitting up: "I declare you're lucky, Sistuh Humiston, having a proxy-mama for your little girls! Miss Fanning laughs and says they can't tell one of you from the other." "Never in my life have I seen a more considerate brother-in-law than Brothuh Humiston. Isn't every man, I can tell you, who'ud go out of his way to be so nice to an in-law, I don't care how helpful she is." And Mrs. Derickson just yesterday—just *yesterday* to that smug, smiling child sitting up there in a lady's wrapper, her hair done up on her innocent little head—laughing and saying, "I came in, Brothuh Humiston said, 'Yes, Mama's upstairs still.' *Mama,* a slip of a girl like you! Course I know nothing could be farther from Brothuh Humiston's thoughts, but it's always seemed to me when *some* husbands drop a real name for a generic, or whatever the word is, they're rubbing their wives out as sweethearts. You'll have to tell

Brothuh Humiston what I tell Cam—when he begins calling *me* Mama, I'm going to call *him* Grandpa."

I sat up straight and looked around this new sitting room I'd pretended to see and admire when Mrs. Woodruff'd led me in. "*Your* sitting room," she called it, and gone on to point out the new platform-rocker over there, the new matting on the floor, the velvet-chenille table cover she'd got for a Christmas present and couldn't find a place for. My sitting room! Another parsonage sitting room. The Ladies' Aid's sitting room! Only things in it belonged to me were Ma's walnut lowboy—that wouldn't be here if I hadn't defied David about it every time we'd moved —and my rosewood lap-desk, Ma's once too. Yes, Sistuh's appropriated that along with David and the children. Lid back, ink well open, sheet of paper on the blotter. Not like her to leave anything that way. Must've been a sudden notion of hers to clean the study. Sistuh's sewing basket on the center-table. Looks like a new black satin four-in-hand she's making for David. Sistuh's green and white hug-me-tight on the back of that platform-rocker. Sistuh's sitting room "cozy and waiting."

I leaned over, lifted the edge of the quilt, reached under the chair I was in, and came up with one of David's felt houseslippers.

Every evening I've lain upstairs in bed, not knowing whether I was alive or dead, Sistuh's sat *there*—between trips up and down to see whether I was asleep. David's sat here. My husband's been her husband, my children her children. And what she'll be explaining to me first thing will be the crack across the drawer of the lowboy, how it happened on the freight car, or when the men were bringing it in, 'sthough a piece of furniture was the only thing important to me. Ha, now I know why I— who's always *tried* to treat *her* like company—have *felt* like company since the first day I sat up in bed.

But isn't it better to have her this way, asserting herself, running the house and the children, being *happy*, than have her as she's been *whenever I've got safely over a confinement*? Touchy about every little thing, belittling herself, going out of her way to find something to feel hurt about, getting me so I'm afraid to show the least affection for David or the children because she looks so left out in the cold. There's no telling how long she'll be with us now. She hasn't mentioned going back to Bayport, not even last month when Slippy sent her only fifteen dollars instead of the usual twenty. I can't make her out about that poor wrist. Unless she's using it as an excuse to stay on! Till I began to get better she never complained about its hurting, seemed to enjoy telling every lady who came upstairs just how it'd happened, how kind the Humistons were, how tender David. If I heard her say once, I heard her a hundred times, "I declare, Brothuh David couldn't've been more tender if I'd been his *own* sistuh." Lately since I've been sitting up, I see her pulling her sleeve down over that lump, pulling up her glove, supporting her right wrist in her left hand when she stands and talks, explaining how delay and an inexperienced doctuh have marked her for life.

If she does love David in a way she shouldn't— Stop shuddering now and say it again. Face it. *If she does love David as a man and not as a brothuh,* that's the reason she seems to think only of me when I'm sick, only of herself when I'm well. So long as there's a chance of my dying, she has something to live for, look forward to. If you do face a fact, not turn your back on it, *of course* you see.

But I can't be an invalid just to make Sistuh happy! I'm not that generous. Maybe if I could just let her run things— But without the hope she wouldn't *be* happy. I don't know. I simply do not *know*. Could I be sitting here making all this up? It's certainly true that if I'd stayed in bed as long's she wanted me to last fall, I wouldn't have got pneumonia. Doctuh Bradford agreed with her was because I got up before I had my strength back after that long trip home from up the country, agreed I should've listened to her and gone back to bed for a month instead of a week. I reckon I knew it too but I felt I just had to see all I could of the old Doddsville friends before I . . .

The doorknob turned and the door opened a crack. "Expect he is, baby. Sitting right in here by the nice warm fire." The crack narrowed. "But don't you want to run upstairs and show your mama the shiny new penny Papa gave you for helping us?"

"No, *m'am*. I want to see Papa. He's got horehound drops for me."

"All right then. But first promise Deeda soon's you get thum you'll run upstairs to your poor sick mama. She'll help you take off your leggings and things. Promise Deeda?"

"Yesum."

Door opened wide and Cindy ran in. "Papa, you got my— Mama!" She threw herself on my lap, tried to hug me and the quilt.

But Sistuh just stood there. Stood as still and as rigid as a statue once that kind of muscular spasm had passed from her shoulders to her hands. To the curled fingers of her right hand Cindy's breaking away had exposed. To the fingers of her left clutching the doorknob, squeezing them white. Beneath her dilated eyes the smile warm for David froze to a grimace for me.

"Sistuh, don't look so!" I laughed a little. "I'm not a ghost—and I won't be just because I came downstairs."

She *must* know how she looks. How can she?

My eyes took refuge in Cindy, swinging on the chair-arm, clamoring for Papa and horehound. "Papa hasn't come in yet, baby. He'll be here pretty soon. Stand still and let Mama undo your reefer before you catch cold in this cold—this *warm* room."

She lifted her chin high. "Mama, reckon what Deeda and me's been doing? And Papa and Mistuh Jeff both? Every single one of us's been cleaning—"

"Not *Mistuh* Jeff, baby. Deeda's told you." Her voice was shaky but she went on. "*Mistuh's* just for white men." She looked at me accusingly. "I didn't know you were expecting Doctuh Bradford this morning. I wouldn't've gone over to the church. If you'd just tell me these things—"

"Doctuh hasn't been here."

"You should see Papa's study, Mama. Papa likes it clean. That's why he's gone to buy chocolate and things for Deeda to make a lot of little bitty cakes for the stewardsmen tonight and when Beth and Fair come home we all're going to have us a tea-party and Deeda said—"

"That's mighty nice, baby"—I threw aside the quilt—"but you climb up on my lap now and I'll undo your leggings."

"Then who helped you downstairs?" Sistuh's voice sounded tired.

"Mrs. Woodruff and Phoebe. Sistuh, you take off your cape before *you* catch cold."

She walked to the table and put David's new four-in-hand inside her basket. "What right did Mrs. Woodruff have, getting you down here before Doctuh Bradford said it was all right? He told me last time he was here to see to it you got plenty of rest and I've tried to. But the study's been on my mind ever since Sunday when I stepped in there to get the February Sunday School Quarterlies and noticed what a mess it was. And with the stewards' meeting tonight I just thought—"

"I'm mighty glad you got to it. And Doctuh won't blame you. He told *me* I could come down just as soon's I felt equal to it and this morning I realized I did. Mrs. Woodruff didn't have anything to do with it—except maybe saying if I didn't hurry and let people see me about, there'd be gossip— Yes, baby, I see. It's a spanking-new penny."

"Gossip about what?" She stooped for Cindy's leggings.

"Why, that I'm a chronic invalid." I laughed a second time. "Or, for all I know, that maybe I'm in 'a delicate condition' again!"

I saw her clutch at *that* rope now, plainly 'sthough she was struggling in water over her head. "Are you?"

"Not that I know of." Now that's mean. I know perfectly well, for once, that I'm not.

That old left-out, hurt, *inquisitive* expression slipped over her face. "Well," she said, turning away, "I always thought you'd tell me a thing like that but here lately I never know what to count on from you."

Already! I hadn't heard that note in her voice since she'd come back in August. Then she surprised me, saying briskly, "I'll go get my things off." Holding out her hand to Cindy, swinging on the arm of my chair. "Come on, baby, les hang up yours. Show your mama how you can open the door with your hands full."

Her lips twitched with impatience but she waited while Cindy dropped and picked up her reefer, opened the door, turned to see the effect on me, then followed her out. That was a lesson to me. ("Ellen, you do too much for these children. You should let them learn.")

"Why, Brothuh David! What kept you so long?"

Her words floated back. Cindy hadn't closed the door tight.

"Now how many times have I told you to hang your overcoat on the top peg so it won't drag on the floor?" Reproach, loving reproach, at the hat rack.

She must've heard David's step on the porch, been at the front door when he opened it. I hadn't heard it and I'd been listening for it. Love may be blind, it certainly isn't deaf.

"Yes, ma'm." Not the *pshaw* I usually get now few times I ever correct him. A little-boy meekness and a grown-up intimacy in David's voice. "You should commend me too, though—I left my *um*brella on the porch, wide-open to dry."

"I commend you, sir!"

How long has this been going on? Since he was so "tender" when she broke her wrist? Since— My head fell back against the pillow and I let the Fact have its way with me. He's never wanted Sistuh to marry. All that talk about asking her to live with us for *my* comfort. No. NO. If he'd loved Sistuh from the beginning, he could've had her. It's not a Fact. It's Jealousy. Jealousy making me see what's not there. What couldn't be there. Jealousy's more than an ugly word. It's delirium. It's horrid. I've never felt it before for anything or anybody. . . .

"Run give your mama a horehound drop, baby. Not upstairs! Don't you remember where your mama is?" *That* laugh. "Ellen's in the sitting room, Brothuh David! Got Mrs. Woodruff to help her down."

I couldn't hear what David said because Sistuh talked right over whatever it was, 'sthough my being downstairs for the first time in a new parsonage wasn't of interest to him. "You get everything on my list?"

"Yes, ma'm! Had to go three places looking for the cheese. Hope it's right—it's Presbyterian, not Methodist."

"I don't care bout its denomination just so it's good."

"And that applies to more than cheese." David sniggered. I *wish* he could laugh aloud way Max does.

"Got a letter for you too."

"Hold it for me. I'll take these things to the kitchen. You go on in and welcome Ellen."

You go on in and welcome Ellen. Why, he's been coming upstairs first thing soon's he comes in the house. Maybe she's been sending him up! Maybe . . .

"*Mama,* how many times I have to tell you please have a horehound drop?"

"Oh!" And how long've you been standing there telling me? "Thank you, Cindy. Don't you eat too many, you'll spoil your dinner."

"Ellen!"

He hurried to me like a long-absent lover. He fell on his knees by my chair. He kissed me hard on the mouth. He kept his arms tight around my waist. He said, "It's a direct answer to my prayer this morning, 'Lord, give her strength to be with me soon again.' "

My head down on his shoulder, *I* prayed. Prayed forgiveness

for having doubted him and his love for me. Prayed for strength
and wisdom in going on living with Sistuh—whenever I must.

❖

"Davis and Sons, General Merchandise, Farm Implements,
and Notions, Bayport, N.C.," Sistuh read, staring at the envelope before she inserted the mother-of-pearl paper-knife Mrs.
Willard gave me when we left Wilmington. "It's Vin's scrawl.
Must've been in there waiting for something when he took a
notion to write."

"That's the place to get notions." David laughed out loud,
took the knife Sistuh held out to him 'sthough he was there to
wait on her, walked with a springy step to the lowboy and laid
it *in its place.* "By the way, where's Fair? Noticed Beth walking
home with some other little girls but Fair wasn't among them."

Sistuh looked up. "I told her she could go home with Sibyl
Timberlake for dinner. All the to-do bout Ellen's being down,
it slipped my mind." She unfolded the single sheet of store-
paper.

David moved to the hearth, studied the lay of the fire, poked
a burnt log together, lifted a new one from the basket and set
it exactly right to catch the flame. Only thing he does well about
a house, I thought, is make a fire. And not only in the fireplace.
In the hearts . . .

The sound came from Sistuh's lips was half-sigh, half-moan,
and she sat down in the straight chair by the table 'sthough her
knees'd given out under her.

"Sistuh! What is it?"

She pressed her knuckles over her mouth, shook her head,
answered me finally. "Miss Ryder. She fell and broke her hip
and's begging for me." She turned her head to one side, pressed
at her mouth again.

Right then and there I knew the meanness I was capable of.
And the deceit, hearing my halleluiahs behind my words, "Why
the very *i*dea, her asking you to go down there in this weather!"

David stepped to her side. "Let me read the letter, Ora."

Sistuh handed it to him, took her handkerchief from her belt,
and wiped her eyes, sniffed back other tears. "I'd have to go,
Ellen, if there was snow on the ground, much's I hate to leave
you now. We're the nearest woman-kin she's got and *you* can't
be at her beck and call." But she looked up at David, standing

there so straight and sure, his back to the fire. "What do you think, Brothuh David?"

"I agree with you, Ora, hard as it is. It's your Christian duty as well as a family one. Oh!" He saw my hand outstretched and put the letter in it. "Doctuh Willie must think it imperative or he wouldn't've told Vin to write you. However, it'll be mercifully short—Miss Ryder's an old, old woman, must be over ninety."

"Ninety-two her last birthday. Born the year of the Louisiana Purchase. Always bragged bout her father's going out there and picking up a bargain in slaves to add to her inheritance. Said he got thum from a Creole family moving back to France. Strong, healthy ones. Few of thum he couldn't resist maiming one way or another because he'd got thum so cheap he felt he could afford—"

"Ora!" David's jaw clinched like a dog's after an angry bark.

It stopped Sistuh short. Her breath caught in a sob way one of the children's did when David made a rare, mild correction. He lifted his hand 'sthough he was going to lay it apologetically on her shoulder, then it clasped her chair's back. "Don't take it to heart, Ora. I—well, the fact is, I expect I was using you as a scapegoat for my conscience." His voice trembled a little. "A conscience that for eleven years has groaned under the burden of that infidel's sins." He snapped his fingers. "I see it! At last God's heard my prayers for her immortal soul! You'll be His means of bringing her to her knees!"

Sistuh looked up at him, her face so full of hope I wondered whether she *was* more of a Christian than I'd ever given her credit for. Then she frowned questioningly. "*I*, Brother David? But you were the one to make her grovel—make her see the error of her ways, that is."

"You know how miserably I failed eleven years ago." His face lit up. "I'm not sure I would now, though. With God's help I've grown in grace and persuasive power. My first impulse just now was to say I'd go with you but with the stewards' second meeting tonight—"

"Oh, Brothuh David, if you only would! Couldn't you postpone this meeting a week?"

He shook his head. "No, Ora. This is God's plan and we mustn't interfere with it. You're delegated to work in the field. If I'm needed to gather the harvest, you can count on my coming. You must find time to write me—"

"Mama, I'm opening the door for Phoebe. She's bringing you your good dinner." Cindy stood aside importantly.

"Why, I can go to the dining room! I've had enough waiting on for once in my life."

"Miss Orie she say bring hit in here to you." Phoebe set the waiter on my lap. "Miss Orie, Mistuh Preacher, you all come. Everything's on the table and I hears Beth at the front door."

❖ ❖

Such a rush and a hurry as there was, getting Sistuh ready to catch the four o'clock train. She had to catch it or she'd miss the boat for Bayport tomorrow. Meant getting into Wilmington at eleven o'clock at night but it wasn't like getting into a strange town alone at that hour. Both the hackmen at the depot knew her and one of them would drive her right up to Cousin Evans Rutland's.

A rush and a hurry for everybody but me. I felt right foolish sitting there by the fire cutting and folding wrapping paper into walls for the paper-doll house Cindy was setting up beneath the windows. Now if it was me going away, Sistuh'ud be darning my best stockings, running ribbon in my chemises, washing handkerchiefs, matching gloves. But Sistuh kept her clothes in such apple-pie order, was just a matter of doing a little pressing and of packing. Phoebe the pressing, Sistuh the packing, David the fetching-and-carrying up and down the stairs. If it'd been a fair day, some of the ladies would be in chatting with me.

David opened the door, Sistuh's dark-green chenille over his arm. He stopped short. "What're you smiling at?"

"At you. Being the man-about-the-house."

"Not going to be any more. Going down now to send a telegram to Cousin Evans and on to the livery stable to order the hack. Think you can keep Cindy amused down here? Had to send her out of Ora's room—fast's Ora'ud get an article in her valise, Cindy'ud take it out."

"I should be able to do that much." And I motioned to David to look at Cindy now, setting tables and chairs here and there against the paper walls, tip of her tongue between her lips, scowl between her eyes, little tiny face thoughtful as a woman's full one, obeying that urge to rearrange the furniture in a room.

He looked from Cindy to me and when our eyes met, we smiled that mutually possessive, proud smile of parents the world over. I felt as warm and happy—and ashamed of myself—

as I'd felt this morning when David's lips had pressed hard on mine. How *could* I, having all I had in David's devotion and in the children, begrudge poor Sistuh's loving him hopelessly? Sistuh's flesh and blood, isn't she? And what woman flesh-and-blood could be in a house with David day in and day out and *not* love him as a man?

"Yes"—David nodded, the smile still making his mouth sweeter than it was strong—"Ora and I commented—silently this way—after dinner last Sunday when Beth was reading *The Lamplighter* aloud to the least ones, little Cindy sitting on the floor at her feet, her hands squeezed together, gazing up at her big sister in admiration and awe. We had peace for more than an hour."

I brushed walls and paper scraps from my lap to the floor. "Give me that dress!" I snatched it from his hand. "What does Sistuh want done to it?"

David stared at me. "Why, what ruffled your feathers so suddenly?"

"Nothing—unless I'm tired being useless."

"Then finish tacking down—that the phrase?—the last row of braid around the bottom of the skirt. Ora said you'd find black silk thread, whatever you need, in her sewing basket." He stepped to the table, opened the lid of the basket. "Ah—new four-in-hand for me. Wouldn't tell me the other night *what* she was cutting out of those black satin scraps she had."

"Hand me the thread, a thimble, and a needle."

He laid the tie on the table and looked at me. "Mama, why're you so impatient? You can't feel as well as you pretend to. Better let me help you over to the sofa, rest awhile. I've been looking forward to sitting here by the fire with you. I've been denied your company a long time."

You needn't've been denied it much's you have! You could've sat upstairs with me a lot more than you have. You've preferred being down here having Sistuh cater to your every whim, flattering you with her adoration, sharing the children with you.

Every bit of my jealousy and my fury must've been in my eyes because I hadn't taken them off of him all the time he was talking but he didn't *see* a word of it, just stood there looking baffled and helpless when I pushed away his hands, said the last thing I wanted to do was lie down again. "And please stop calling me *Mama*. My name's *Ellen* as Sistuh's is *Ora*."

"But I've been calling you *Mama* now and then—as a term of

312

affection. Seems mighty sweet—and still new and strange—to me to hear children calling *you* Mama."

"Yes, I know you have—but I've decided I don't like it. It makes me feel like a—a piece of furniture."

He bent over and kissed my hair. "Wouldn't do that to a chair," he whispered. "But I'll try to remember hereafter."

"Bro-thuh David!"

He hurried to the door and on to the foot of the stairs. "Yes, m'am?"

"You haven't gone for the hack *yet*? It's after three."

"Going right now."

"Ellen finished my dress?"

"Tell her almost—soon's I pull out the bastings," I called and began to sew fast.

"Almost she says. Want me to wait and bring it up?"

"No, *sir*! I'm not presentable. Tell Phoebe to."

Sistuh didn't sound sad any more. Sounded happy.

And looked happy, spite of her effort not to, a little while later when she stepped in sitting room ready to go. "How do I look?" she asked, shy as a sixteen-year-old wanting affirmation on her first party dress.

I bit my lip on *happy*, said, "Why, you look *mondaine* as Mrs. LeGrande used to say. *Real* elegant." And she certainly did, that chenille fitting so close over her slim hips, black plush cape swinging jauntily from her shoulders, green velvet ribbon on her hat standing up like a feather above that veil draped just like the picture in the latest *Queen of Fashion Magazine*. "You make me mighty impatient to get out of this wrapper."

"Well, don't you hurry it. Take care of yourself. If you should have a relapse now, I'd never forgive myself for heeding this call to Miss Ryder. Now, Ellen—don't let Phoebe forget the children's underwear I left soaking in the tub. And don't pay her but a dollar Saturday—she borrowed fifty cents yesterday. And oh, yes, remind her she's to kill and dress that hen the farmer brought us yesterday. Shame about the refreshments I'd planned to make for the stewards' meeting—cheese straws and coffee and cookies—but it can't be helped. And there's Beth's new coat, all cut out and not a seam basted! Be next winter before she can wear it."

"She can manage with her old one. Don't you carry any worries with you, you'll have enough when you get there."

She shuddered. "I'd rather be boiled in oil than go down to that old place now—more dilapidated every time I see it." She glanced at the clock. "If Brothuh David doesn't hurry with the hack, I won't get started today."

"There it is now!"

She rustled over to Cindy, stooped and hugged her, told her not to forget her Deeda. She bent over, kissed my cheek, told me to tell Beth and Fair good-bye for her soon's they came from school, stood straight, patted at her eyes. "Oh, Ellen, if you only knew how I feel, leaving you with so much on your hands and not feeling strong!"

"I'll be all right, Sistuh. But I'm certainly going to miss you."

"And I, you."

Then, like the lines in a play memorized to be spoken at a certain time, "Come back soon's you can."

"I don't know, Ellen. Don't know how long it'll be for Miss Ryder." She turned toward the door, turned back. "Sometimes I feel like it might be best if I just lived to myself all the time," she said and her big, lustrous eyes fixed on mine like a hungry, hopeful dog's.

"Now, Sistuh," I said obediently, "you mustn't talk like that. You know we couldn't get along without you 'all the time.' "

"All right, Ora." David opened the door. "Valises in the hack. Not much time."

"Why, I'm ready and waiting, sir!"

4

I was mighty tired of my thoughts by four o'clock and it certainly made me feel better seeing Beth's and Fair's faces when they came home and found me in the sitting room. Surprise and pleasure made Beth's pretty and Fair's beautiful. Wasn't till all three of them clustered around me to hear the first chapter in *Elsie Dinsmore* Sybil'd lent Fair that any mention was made, by them, of Sistuh's having had to go away so suddenly. Then Fair, sitting down emphatically on the carpet-stool at my feet, said, "Now Deeda's gone, all those girls at school'll have to stop asking me how I like having *two* mothers. I say 'don't *you* wish *you* had two?' But I don't like it a bit—when nobody else's got two."

"You mustn't say that, baby. Just think of all Deeda does for you I can't do. Making a real suit of clothes just like your Papa's for your man-doll and—"

"Yesum, but Deeda's as bossy as Sybil's stepmother. I like you for my only mother."

Beth stopped gazing solemnly into the fire. "Hush now, Fair, and let Mama read. I've got three solid pages of fractions to do before I go to bed."

"*You* hush bossing me! Besides, Deeda's not here to hustle you off to bed before you finish studying, so there!"

I heard the front door open just's I finished the chapter and much's Sistuh'd been wanting the children out of the room it seemed, I wanted them out now. I needn't've worried. Fair bounced right up, said she was going in the kitchen and make that doughboy Deeda wouldn't let her make last night and Cindy trotted after her. I held my breath but after a minute Beth picked up her books, said she was going to spread out on the dining-room table till Phoebe was ready to set it, and brushed past David as he opened the door. David grunted a kind of greeting and Beth said "Papa" as a kind of statement. It wasn't right for a father to be so shy of his older children or they of him and I wondered whether was because they never got over in the week seeing him in the pulpit on Sunday or whether there was something else I'd let Sistuh's presence bring about. If *that* was it, while she was gone this time, I'd try to remedy it—along with the other thing.

David strode to the mantel, took a spill from the vase, and stooped toward the low flame licking at a new log.

"Don't light the gas yet. It's just getting dark enough to enjoy the fire light."

David started, and the spill dropped on the hearth. "Why, I didn't notice you sitting there! Thought Phoebe would've got you back in bed by now." He picked up the spill and put it back in the vase. "Have to be stingy with these things now, Ora not here to keep a supply on hand."

"I reckon I can roll paper into spills as well as fold it for doll-house walls. You'll be all right, Phoebe to cook, Dora to wash—she's better at it than Sistuh'll let you know. And you've got enough socks darned to last a month! You pay Phoebe and Dora just the same whether Sistuh's doing their work or not and I won't put out any sewing. All I want is to wear some of the clothes I've got—they're all new here—and without Sistuh to keep me shut off upstairs, I can."

315

I said it all in an even, matter-of-fact way, looking up at him standing there, half in light, half in shadow, and except for the ticking of the clock and the burning of the fire, there was no sound in the room.

"What do you mean—Ora keeping you shut off upstairs?" It came slowly 'sthough he didn't want to ask it and when I didn't answer it, he sighed, sat down on the edge of the platform-rocker, and reached for the poker. Charred crusts fell from the old logs, and in the spurts of new flames, I saw his face.

I wanted to hide it on my breast, away from my sight. I wanted to stroke the back of his head, tell him I hadn't meant anything. "Just what I said. Sistuh's been keeping me upstairs so she could have the house and the children and *you* all to herself."

He set the poker in the rack without a clatter. "How could Ora keep you upstairs if you didn't want to stay?" It was a simple interrogative sentence, asking for an answer. It might've been, "Is supper ready?" or "Where is my *um*brella?"

"By persuading me I was too weak to come down. Telling me of all the deaths she'd ever heard of from pneumonia. Reminding me I got up too soon last fall after my miscarriage."

"Mama—"

I made a little mooing sound.

"Ellen then. You're doing Ora a grave injustice. The last thing she said to me when I put her on the train was to take good care of you, not let you overdo. She's solicitous of you whether she's here or not. Your imputing—"

"I'm imputing nothing. I *know*. I've had the wool pulled over my eyes long enough. Sistuh loves you and not as a sistuh!"

My words, like the quick flick of a whip on a horse's un-suspecting back, jerked David's head up and I saw his eyes. Blue, triumphant, *male*. For just one instant in the bright blaze of the fire. I shivered from my head to my toes, pressed my teeth together to stop their chattering.

All moorings gone, I seemed to swing in space, in the dark, in the cold, looking back at David in a chair, in a room, in a house, on a street, in a town, warmed by more than a fire on a hearth. Warmed by the love of *two* women. For just one instant. Then his head was back against the antimacassar, in the shadows, but his hands clasping the chair arms were in the light, flesh colored, and the fingers were busy, pressing and releasing the plush like a cat's claws "making biscuits."

316

"You're wrong, Mama. You've been upstairs too long," he said finally and 'sthough we'd have no more of *that* foolishness.

"I've been enjoying myself up there till today. But do you think I'd've sat up there meek's a lamb these past two weeks if I'd had the slightest *idea* of what Sistuh was up to? I've got more spirit than that. It didn't once occur to me what was going on till Mrs. Woodruff came up this morning, said there was gossip, and opened my eyes."

His fingers were still, pressing down hard. "What kind of gossip?"

"About my being a chronic invalid. Don't smile yet! *That's* what she *said*. Not what she meant. Was the *way* she said it, way she looked, told me—"

"There! I knew it! It *is* all in your imagination. The devil can find employment for idle minds as for idle hands. Now, now, just a minute—let *me* talk. I *know* you're wrong. Not three days ago, right here in this room, Ora told me—I was teasing her in a joking way bout Brothuh Armstrong's seeming to have business with me only when he knew he'd find me in the parsonage—and she told me she wouldn't marry that old blackbeard if he were the last man on earth. And went on to say she'd never been able to seriously consider marrying anybody because she couldn't leave you with a parsonage and the children to cope with alone."

I shouted accusations silently, my tongue paralyzed. So that's the way you ask her if you're the only one and that's the way she answers you! Using me for a sounding board to throw back truth your cloth and Sistuh's timidity won't let you speak! But beyond the shouting something else in me spoke. You three, it said, are bound together so long as the three of you shall live. Don't strip David, leave him naked, exposed, defenseless. . . . "Sistuh told you that and you believed it! How can *you*—trained to be a lawyer—be so simple? Can't you see the feeling Sistuh's—*begun* to have for you? Absence making the heart grow fonder's a lot of nonsense. It's propinquity. If you could've seen her face when she opened this door this morning, expecting to find you and finding me, you'd realize you've got to put a stop to it—if such a thing's possible."

"I'll put a stop to your—your blasphemy! I won't listen to you, saying things you'll regret the rest of your life." He jumped up 'sthough the spring in the chair suddenly tightened and bounced him. "You're sinning against yourself, against me,

317

against the best sister a woman ever had, with every word you say!" He snatched a spill from the vase, lit it at the fire. "No wonder you wanted to sit in darkness! A little light—"

It came with a snarl and a splutter from the swinging lamp above the table. He threw the half-burnt spill in the fire, watched its black ash float up the chimney. "No," he said and shook his head, "Ora's not the woman to love a man unasked."

I heard a queer sound. It was my laugh but it might've been Eve's. With the use of those silly words—and he knew how silly, his head bowed in shame like a schoolboy's hearing his own wrong answer—he'd said, "I love Ora and because I love her, I can't believe she loves me."

But I've got to have it in the *right* words. And from David. I've got to know all that's gone on between them from the very beginning. 'Sthough I could ever know that! Not even if each of them could tell me every word, describe every act. But there's no stopping now. I've gone too far. I can't be the compliant sistuh and the considerate wife. Or the protecting woman for the man I love. I am still *an I* too, not a sightless, nerveless earthworm to be stepped on heedlessly in their path. To be cut in two.

"David, are you—what do *you* think and feel about Sistuh?"

"Why, Mama, what a question for you to ask." He tried to laugh aloud and he made a gurgling, idiotic mess of it. "I don't know how to answer it, put to me suddenly in that tone." But his hand, fumbling for his watch, shook and he turned his back to me, stepped close to the mantel, and looked at the clock. "Supper be on time, you think? I can't keep the stewards waiting."

"Supper'll be on time. Even without Sistuh here to nag Phoebe for you. Phoebe's a woman too, with a family of her *own* to think about, get home to." Something struck me as I said that, something I would've clung to if the idea of David's loving Sistuh as a woman had come to me slowly, as nothing more than a possibility. "Why, how can you be so inconsistent! *You,* who's said time and again that the touchstone of a Southern Christian's his—*her* attitude toward darkies—putting Sistuh up on a sacred pedestal! Why, just last summer you told me again was seeing me teaching that little Mistuh to walk made you know *I* was the right one."

"Ora's praying every day that God'll take out of her heart

318

that one obstacle between her and full grace. And He's hearing her! Never in my experience have I seen clearer evidence of it. I don't hear her nagging Phoebe and just yesterday she made a fresh pot of coffee for that old colored preacher waiting for me in the kitchen. Yes, she and I've had many a talk about it. It's a strange thing. Only explanation occurs to me as to its inception was her tendency when she was a girl—she told me that herself—to belittle herself and the lowlier a white person is, in possessions or spirit, the more he's inclined to look down on the lowlier darky."

"That's ridiculous! Makes some lowly people more sympathetic with thum. And look at Mistuh Jim Barry in Bayport and others I could name in every town who—"

"They put it on deliberately for political reasons and you don't know any more about politics than you do about your own sister! Why, going down in the hack this very day, I apologized to her for having thought I detected a kind of *relish* in her beginning to recount Miss Ryder's father's treatment of those slaves. Told her I'd realized I'd been wrong the instant I stopped her, remembering the change of heart she'd had. And she said, yes, that was what'd hurt her, my not seeing it was her horror of Miss Ryder's sins'd made her say what she had, and went on to tell me that even before she had my guidance, she'd tried to make up to that little Ace for Miss Ryder's meanness, had made that coat he wore to our wedding with as loving care as she'd made your dress. Now let's have no more maligning—"

"Sistuh made that coat right after I came from Savannah. And I know now she made it for you, not Ace. She wanted to impress you. She was in love with you then." I looked down at my hands lying like dead things in my lap. "David, are you in love with Sistuh?"

He sighed, sat down again, put his head back, and looked up at *Christ Blessing the Children* on his side of the clock. Now it was all I could do not to rush to him, clasp his miserable beautiful gullible face in my hands, kiss the twitching lips he was trying to hold firm. I sat still, saw one cold hand clench the other cold hand, felt cold all through. But he seemed the one off in space now, I in a room in a house on a street in a town in an hour that was eternity. I in good clothes in a courtroom probing a tattered culprit in a dock!

319

"Mama—"

I started. The earnest, the solemn, voice he used at the altar, at the graveside. Whatever he was going to say would be the truth as he knew it. The "Mama" might've been "God."

"Mama," he repeated and brought his eyes on a level with mine, "God never intended for a man to be blessed—and tortured—with the presence of two women like you and Ora. Not in this day and time. Unless He deliberately devised the situation—the blessing *and* the torture—to test my strength and my will. If that's the Divine motive—I don't know. I don't know." His head drooped and he looked down at *his* hands, clasped tight between his spread knees 'sthough he was suffering physical pain he mustn't cry out against. "I've tried to fathom His purpose, plead on my knees for an understanding of it. If He did design it for a test, I am fighting as He would have me fight. In time He can't fail to recognize it—and give me peace."

"Then you do love Sistuh?" It was a whisper but he heard it.

"I don't know," he whispered back.

They say when you're drowning, or think you are, you live your whole life over in a second or two. They mean when your body is dying. I've never heard what happens when your soul, your *self*, the I, me, mine goes forever and your body remains intact. And doesn't go happily as it does in one of those religious conversions such as David loves to describe. Oh, no, that's not the death of self. That's a rebirth, they call it. The You's not killed with one blow, it's just "washed in the blood of the lamb and reclothed in the Spirit." Then you have "life more abundant." One minute I was a living, breathing woman, chastened by my fall from the wall of selfish insensibility this morning but still living, breathing. The next I was nothing. And as I was becoming nothing, I seemed to see every minute of my life from three o'clock on an April Sunday in 1884 to a quarter to six on a February Thursday in 1895. My life with Sistuh and David.

It was like a play I had a part in and was watching from the audience at the same time. I recognized the gay, careless, heedless, self-centered girl in the first act and the gay, careless, heedless, self-centered wife in the second only because she looked exactly like the reflection I saw when I looked in the looking-glass. And when the play'd rushed to *this* scene I knew that the

320

culprit in the dock was my client, that I hadn't been probing for truth but for a lie. A lie I could hide my suspicions behind, go past without seeing, go on being gay, careless, heedless, self-centered, laughing at the very idea of David's loving a woman as different from me as Sistuh was. Why, I couldn't even've believed he could've loved Sistuh if he'd never seen me!

"You want me to tell you the truth and the truth—if I were taking my oath on the Bible in court would be what I am telling you now—*I don't know*." He was looking straight at me but the misery in his eyes kept him from seeing the agony must've been in mine and he went on, "Seems strange now but I can't remember—in that first spring, in those months before I ever saw you—that I ever felt drawn to Ora as a *woman*. I saw her as a preacher's wife and helpmeet, not as the sweetheart I craved. But the more I saw of her, the more I felt she was the one God'd chosen for me and I listened patiently, then impatiently, for that still, small voice. I wanted *a* wife and I deluded myself into thinking God'd answered my prayers by His silence. Was on the point of proposing to Ora the very day I saw you for the first time. *Your* face at the window was my sweetheart's face and when your inherent Christianity was made manifest over the flippant girl's airy ways, instantly Ora became nothing to me but *Ellen* Fanning's sister. And that's what she's remained—till just here lately. A sweet, self-denying, *remarkable* sister. She's changed in the past year though. Something's come over her that—"

"You don't know what that *something* is!"

He didn't even hear me. He snapped his fingers. "Yes, there *was* one occasion when I saw her as—as I do now. Was a rainy afternoon when we sat in the parlor at Little Brookside. She had on a tight-fitting dress without trimmings and I was surprised I'd never noticed her womanly figure. Yes, if she'd encouraged me then—one gesture, a touch of her hand, would've clinched it. Never once did she give a sign that spring—*nor has she since*—that she cared particularly for me or had an inkling of my intentions. Fact is, her indifference made me feel foolish when I flattered myself I owed her an explanation and told her, day we were driving to Camilla, that I was only awaiting God's voice." He stared at me and *I* was not a woman then, just an audience with no personal involvement, there to hear his belated confession. A confession *he* was enjoying.

321

"Trouble was she didn't *feel* herself to be the woman she was and is!"

"No, it's taken your admiration, devotion, *flirtation* to convince her! But you're not being honest with yourself yet, David," I went on in a dead kind of voice, not heeding his efforts to stop me. "You must've looked into her eyes at sometime in that—that other-worldly courtship and Sistuh might lie in word and deed but if you *want* to see truth, you look—"

"Mama, stop it I say!" I thought he was going to spring at me, slap or shake me, but he grasped the chair arms and held on to them.

"Stop calling me Mama. I *won't be* a mama to you. Somebody to run crying to when God turns His back. Call me Ellen. I'm a woman if I am your wife, here to make the parsonage respectable while you carry on with Sistuh!"

"Stop it!" In a flash he was bending over me and his hands were pressing down on my shoulders as they had on the chair's arms. "I won't let you perjure your soul with lies." He jerked his hands back 'sthough I was a hot stove, stood straight. "Before my God, I can tell you I've never sinned with Ora. Never even hinted to her what I've told you. I couldn't keep my pulpit if I didn't feel as innocent of wrong *doing* as mortal man can feel." He lowered his voice. "As for anything I've unwittingly done, I've asked God's forgiveness—and I'll receive it. In His good time. Evening after evening, I've left Ora here alone by the fire, gone to my cold study to wrestle with the Devil. And I'll conquer him too!"

He strode to the table, reached up, turned the gas higher, turned to face me. "Look at me. Do I look like a guilty man? Could I look you in the eye after what I've said here this night if I didn't feel innocent of all carnal sin and didn't believe absolution is waiting for all—all lust of the mind?"

I looked at him. What a handsome saint! "What a man"! A man who should have as many women as he wanted. For the glory of God and the good of the world. Was his need for God, as for women, made him what he was.

"Why're you smiling at me like a mother if you refuse to be one?" he asked softly.

"Is that the way I'm smiling? Like Mother Nature then—*I'm* not feeling like a mother. Few minutes ago I didn't even feel like a woman. Now I seem to be all women who ever lived or ever will." I rubbed my hand over my forehead, held it over my eyes, blotting out his face, trying to come back to myself, trying to think of *me.*

"Ellen, you're tired." I didn't hear his step but his hand was on my head. "All this would've been too much for a strong woman. But how could I help but tell you? Come, let me help you to bed before I have to go."

I dropped my hand and I fixed my eyes on the black cloth of his coat. "There's something else you must tell me now," I said, hardly hearing my own voice. "What's to become of me if you don't love me?"

"Don't love *you!*" He dropped on his knees, put his arms up around me, held me tight, and his head was on my breast. "Why I've loved you, my darling, since the first minute I saw you. And I love you more every day that I live. Thank God, there's never been any doubt in my heart or mind about *that.*"

I struggled to get my hands on his face, and when I did, I held it there just below mine. And when our lips had parted, all the strength I had flowed to my arms and I held *him* tight.

"Oh, David, David, David," I breathed, and the rhythm sang on, "I love you, love you, love you. . . . I don't understand you. All I can do is love you, love—"

"Maybe that's all I need, my darling. My *Ellen!*"

"Doctuh didn't tell me—didn't tell me not to—" my lips mumbled under his.

He clasped me so hard, so quick, I thought my ribs would break. "Then with your help and God's, I'll put Ora—*Sister Ora*—out of my mind and heart."

Now that I'm well and Sistuh's gone! But David was *there* and in good health that day on High Brighten I felt this way about Max!

"Oh, it's the sweetest music I ever heard, your laugh. Your happy laugh."

I pushed him back so that I could look *him* in the eye. "Maybe I can understand you after all, my David. But—I'm not sure I can keep it up day in day out, Sistuh here. David, Sistuh must never, never come to live with us. You know that, don't you? Tell me you know that."

"Let's don't talk about it now. Let's don't ever talk about it again. Let's make a covenant between God and us that we'll never mention this again. Here on our knees, let us—"

He jumped to his feet and when Beth opened the door to

323

say supper was ready, he was standing in front of the fire, hands clasped behind him, chin high. . . .

❖   ❖   ❖

"Mama?"

"*You* awake still! You've been mighty quiet."

"Been an effort. Thought you were getting some sleep."

"No. I've been lying here trying to make some sense out of all's happened to us these twenty-five years. But just keeping on, way I've been doing all day, living it over and—"

"There's sense to it—a clear example of what can happen when a living soul pits itself against God's unalterable will." He turned on his side.

No use pitting my opinion against such faith. No use saying what I'd been thinking ever since I'd seen that legal paper down in the sitting room—that there'd be more understandable human justice in sending us to the penitentiary than Sistuh to the asylum. We deserved it, thinking back there in Lynnboro that we could brush Sistuh off, have each other . . .

"David!" I reached out, touched the back of his head. "Listen— Sistuh's leaving her room! You'll have to go. She'll get soaked crossing the porch."

Throwing back the sheet, fumbling for his pants on the chair. "Come with me."

"I'll just make her worse. Anybody can get her back it's you. Wait, I'll open the door. Hall light's on."

"Be careful of that knob, Mama. Not sure I could fix it a second time."

Sistuh creeping, *sliding* along the wall way down there, her head so low I couldn't see it. More like a bundle of clothes moving than a human being.

"Mama, please, don't you come. I'll get her." Beth slipping her arms in her kimono sleeves, two long thin pale-gold braids getting in her way.

"I'm not. Papa is." Standing aside for him to pass, feeling my way back to the bed, sitting on its edge.

❖

Poor little Beth, her hair in braids for the first time, trying her best to help that spring in Lynnboro when Sistuh'd come back. That May Sunday, "You go to church, Mama. I'll stay with

Deeda. I'll rub her head and maybe she won't cry so much."
Was about the last Sunday I'd be able to for a long time and it
might be better for Sistuh if I did dress up and go out, act like
everything was as usual.

The sight of David—of that *man* I'd been having a second
honeymoon with—in the pulpit as usual, as quiet, composed,
and other-worldly as usual, sight of still newish faces smiling
a kind of holy welcome to Fair and me settling down in our
pew, sight of fans waving, passing the soft scented May breeze
from one to another, all seemed to soothe the week-old tumult
within me and I stood up and sang *How Firm a Foundation*
'sthough I felt it beneath my feet. And when David'd opened
the big Bible and in a voice as sure as usual had given his text—
and Fair her cue to take off her bonnet and put her head in
my lap, I looked down and smiled to think what she'd say if
I told her her head was nestling against another head, a little
brothuh's head whose name was Wesley.

Sistuh's going to be all right. Of course she's going to be all
right. If she *hadn't* broken down visibly, begun to cry, to sit
off upstairs by herself, refuse to speak to David or me, she
would've gone on disguising all her disappointment at the
change in David till her touchiness and irritability made the life
we've got to live with her unbearable for all of us. Yes, I thought
that morning, not knowing what was bearable and unbearable,
I'm *glad* she got to snooping and eavesdropping on David and
me. Glad she heard David tell *me* his hopes for her. Was nothing
anybody else would've considered "an insulting, backhanded,
deceitful plan" to get rid of her. Why there were two unmarried
women right in this congregation would've been overjoyed if
it'd been one of them Brothuh Smith had told David he wanted
to take back to China with him as his wife and fellow missionary.
Brothuh Smith *was* skinny and bald-headed but he was just
as clever as he could be and he'd packed the church the two
times he'd lectured about heathen customs and showed all
those curios he'd brought back with him. Sistuh herself'd got
real sociable with him first night he was at the parsonage,
fingered the silk and satin tablecloths and pajamas, asked questions about the Chinese women who'd worked all the exquisite
embroidery. When David'd first mentioned the possibility of
his being a husband for Sistuh, I said if I wasn't already Mrs.
Humiston I wouldn't mind a bit being Mrs. Smith, seeing

strange sights and meeting strange people, crossing the United States and the Pacific Ocean—in spite of the creepy, faraway feeling I had looking through Brothuh Smith's stereoscope at a sunset view of it.

David was preaching away and I'd just got my attention on what he was saying when it came. Through the open windows of the parsonage, across the grass strip, through the long open windows of the church. For a second I thought it was Phoebe. *Phoebe* gone crazy, her mind skipping centuries back to those African jungles, remembering a savage chant for all dead children, and moaning it out oh-oh-oh-oh-oh-oh . . . Next second I knew who it was and what it was. Sistuh humiliating me, slashing at my pride as she'd slashed at my new dress. I forgot Fair, would've dropped her to the floor if Mrs. Slocum hadn't caught her, drawn her head over to her lap, motioning me past, pulling in her skirts, murmuring, "Dear One, if there's *anything* I can do . . ." I walked as fast or ran as slow up the aisle as I could, between the rows of craning necks, the staring, the nodding, the whispering, till at the door I heard David's sharp command, *in the middle of his sermon,* "The Lord is is in His holy temple, let all the earth keep silence before Him."

PART THREE
DAVID

CHAPTER I

1

YES, CHURCH IS FILLING UP AS USUAL, USHERS HAV-
ing a little trouble finding seats for latecomers.
Can't believe our Presiding Elder's the drawing
card though. Expect it's due to Miss Myra's an-
nouncing her musical program in *The Silverboro Clarion*.
Whatever the cause, it's your congregation today, Brother
Mixon, and I earnestly hope you'll give my people a stronger
sermon than you did last Quarterly Sunday. Hardly expect
you will. You're too much of a simple pulpit-and-parlor
preacher. Most of you younger men are sinecurists. We of
the preceding generation at least had one evil we could fight
openly, strengthen our spiritual muscles on, but I can't see
you or your ilk of this second decade of the century going into
combat as we of the first decade did, accepting such a challenge
as came to me when Elizabeth City's better element was cam-
paigning for a dry town.

There I was on a Saturday morning, summer of 1903, being
escorted to the depot, having to stop every few steps to receive
congratulations on my Battle of the Bottles lecture the previous
night, when up struts the bloated proprietor of a notorious bar-
room looking like a cartoon of himself. He grasped me roughly
by the arm. "You get outuh this town on the next train or
you'll wish you had," he spluttered. "I'll leave when I'm ready,"
I replied. "Not a minute before." He pulled me around, put
his ugly face close to mine. "Ain't nothun saving you now, Long
Tails, *but* them tails." "Don't let my cloth stop you if it's a fight
you want," I said, and in spite of the protests of my escorts, I
removed my coat and handed it to one of them and looking
into that rascal's bulging, bloodshot eyes, said calmly, "Now
that there's nothing between us, come on!" His heavy jaw
dropped and he backed away amid the jeers of the crowd . . .

"The Lord is in His holy temple, let all the earth keep silence before Him. Come, let us worship the Lord in the beauty of holiness. He who hath ears to hear, let him hear what the Spirit sayeth unto the churches."

Now I'll take a back seat. I'll never like taking a back seat in my own pulpit whether it's for bishop, presiding elder, lecturer, or evangelist. Come to think about it, I've had to do it only once for a bishop. That one time my church was host to the Annual Conference. In Cameronville, December, 1909. Ten years ago. I expect I minded it least on that occasion. It was more than three months after Sister had gone—been taken—to the asylum but God was still hiding His face from me. And if I couldn't see Him, how could I interpret His word to my people then? Yes, I was content to have a respite that one Sunday, to sit in the shadows. Every sermon I'd preached that fall had come from the head, not the heart. . . . Ah, the "concord of sweet sound" Miss Myra can draw from that organ!

> "I come to the garden alone
> While the dew is still on the roses,
> And the voice I hear falling on my ear. . . ."

That sensuous "In the Garden" for a solo again! Voluptuous as Miss Sara's bosom . . .

> "And He walks with me,
> And He talks with me,
> And He tells me I am His own . . ."

Tune's like waltz music. Words like those popular love songs Cindy used to sing around the house all the time. I'll have to mention my feeling about it to Miss Sara. It takes the thoughts of every woman under sixty-five off sacred subjects, puts them on the level with those girls and boys who come to revival services, sit up there in the gallery to sing phrases of hymns back and forth to each other. Uncle Silas brings me the hymn books the next morning to show me how marked up they are: *close to Thee, Thy head upon my breast, lost in His love.* Sometimes, even the sacred name of Jesus scratched out and Bill, Pete, or Joe written in. As for the thoughts of the men in this congregation—better not think about where it puts them. If I'd known it was to practice "In the Garden" Miss Myra had to go out to the colored school, honk Whoops out of his classes in the middle of the morning to come pump the organ for her, I wouldn't have told her where she could find him. Now, now it wasn't for this solo. She told me. Was for the new anthem the choir's going to render this morning. They're certainly putting it on for Brother Mixon today. Look at him. Head back, eyes closed, relishing every word. I know *his* thoughts all right. I was a young man too once, subjected to such temptations few men— unless it's doctors—are. Presiding Elder at forty-two! He's not as young as I was, though, when that honor hovered over my head. . . .

"You get right in, Brothuh Humiston, and I'll take you anywhere you want to go," Miss Myra said, stopping that electric bird cage of hers at the curb. "I'm just cruising round trying to get hold of that Whoops to do a little pumping for me. I called Williamses' and Mistuh Bob said he was out making the last of the early morning deliveries. Said I couldn't miss him if I just kept driving round."

I looked at my watch. "It's ten o'clock. He's through delivering. You drive out Gaston Street. Whoops goes to school two hours before his twelve o'clock rounds. You couldn't practice after supper tonight?"

"I certainly wish I could, Brothuh Humiston, but I just can't tonight. I've got a date with My Papa to go to the picture show. They're showing 'The Birth of a Nation' again and My Papa can't get enough of it. You think Whoops minds getting out of school a half-hour or so?"

"Well, he's trying mighty hard to graduate this year. Wants to go to college in the fall. Ambitious to be a preacher. Colored people need educated young men in their pulpits today to hold their interest. You know, Whoops is the most attentive listener I've got—every time I glance over toward the choir loft during my sermon, never fail to see that little door to the pump open a crack and Whoops' black face pressed in the aperture. Mighty bright boy, his teachers tell me. And he's saving every cent he can—the two dollars a week he gets from the church, the five from Brother Williams, all he can pick up mowing grass and toting coal—to pay his tuition at the Greensboro college for Negroes. I've been intending to mention it to you, Miss Myra—do you give him a tip when you pick him up this way for extra practice?"

"Why, Brothuh Humiston, I never thought of it! I don't pick him up often though. I wouldn't today if the choir hadn't had me stumble through this new anthem at practice last night and I just can't make a mess of it next Sunday, can I? Brothuh Mixon here and all. But I'll certainly do something for Whoops hereafter, after what you've just told me." Turning that bright-eyed kitty-face to me. "You don't agree with my Grandpa Pennington bout overeducating negras, do you? My Papa never fails to quote him, every time the subject comes up—and it comes up real often now since the war and everything—bout what my Grandpa Pennington used to say bout that brillant colored orator round here before the war—*the* war, I mean—who used to hold white audiences spellbound but died in his early thirties, said 'Naturally he died young. No negra can master a college course and devote himself to study *without* shortening his life.'"

"No, Miss Myra, I don't agree. I—"

"Yes, 1 know you're mighty liberal-minded. Everybody says so. As for little me, I honestly don't know the least thing about it. But if *you* think I should give Whoops a quarter for extra pumping, I'll certainly do it and I'm just's glad as I can be you mentioned it. And I want to tell you something, Brothuh Humiston—Whoops is not one bit more attentive to your sermons than Myra Pennington is and that's the truth! I declare I never miss a single solitary word of what you say. Doesn't make one bit of difference what your text is, there's always a message in your sermon aimed straight at little me. Now, you needn't smile that way. I declare it's the truth. Why, right in that one on Practical Christianity you preached last Sunday night, bout the need for patience and forbearance in the home, course I know that was just the by-the-way part of it but right there you said, 'Miss Myra, you stop nagging at your poor Papa for leaving his dentures on the bathroom shelf. You just drop thum in a glass of water for him and say nothing about it.' I declare I've been doing that all week and every time I do I hear your voice commending me. Honestly I do, Brothuh Humiston. I declare we've never had a pastor at St. John's so easy to listen to. Everybody says so. Or so easy to look at. You'll just have to excuse me, giving a *man* a compliment like that right to his face but, honestly, except for My Papa, I believe you're the handsomest man I ever saw in my life! And so distinguished too, everybody says, that touch of gray at your temples and those *intellectual* looking rimless glasses you put on now and then to read fine print, just like President Wilson's!"

331

Pshaw! I'll look mighty distinguished up here if I forget to announce the first hymn. . . .

"Now let us stand and sing hymn number twelve, the first, third, and fourth stanzas, 'O Thou to Whom in Ancient Times—' "

Miss Myra's a fine organist. As fine a one as I can remember at any charge I've served. Seems miraculous a little thing like that can manipulate a big pipe organ. I like to drop in at choir practice when I can just to watch her little feet dance over those pedals. She puts life in these good old Methodist hymns too. Even Beth, when she's home, has no adverse criticism. The My Papa talk disgusts her, though. Says she can't see how Miss Myra ever stayed away from home four winters studying music at Converse College in South Carolina. I don't believe I'd want a daughter as devoted as Miss Myra is. Sometimes wish though— now, now, count your blessings. None of the things Mama used to worry about has ever happened to a one of the girls. Even little high-strung Cindy's put away childish things and become a woman—well, at least she's married and settled down. Learned she couldn't go on to the end of life collecting new beaux, engagement rings, expensive Christmas presents every town we lived in. I miss her, though. I'd rather hear her sweet voice singing those silly songs than hear what I have to hear when I'm in the parsonage now. Glad she's still child-hearted, feeling "like she'll just curl up and pass out if she can't come home every so often." She was the best home secretary I ever had. Never forgot to give me a message and always gave it word for word, with a little illuminating comment added. Not like Mama, being careful to edit every message—from a woman—so there'll be nothing in it to start Sister off, and sometimes leaving out the very crux of it. Not like Sister, "forgetting" to give me this or that number to call if the caller's on her Black List or asking me so many questions. . . .

" '. . . Shall temples rise and praise be sung.' A-men.

"Please remain standing now while we repeat the Apostles' Creed: 'I believe in God the Father Almighty, in . . .' "

All right, Brother, you take it over. I won't compete. Should think you'd want to save your voice for preaching, for even the twenty-minute-by-the-clock, please-the-young sermons you preach. I never had to depend on brevity for my popularity. Admit I like the way you lead the Creed, though. You recite it like a solemn reiteration of your faith, not something you're mouth-

332

ing from habit. It is, though. Habit and the elocution you were taught at Vanderbilt, Trinity, Emory—whatever your alma mater is. Your class was more up-to-date than the class of '83, used more than the Bible and the Church Fathers for textbooks. Was taught to steer a middle course, a modern course, between old-fashioned sanctification and hell fire. Men of your generation go into the ministry as I went into the law. To most of you it's a genteel profession, not a calling. But the Church of God isn't something you can choose. It's got to choose *you,* if you're going to be worth your salt in it. And you can't sincerely believe in Jesus Christ,His only Son, our Lord, unless you believe in what Christ Himself believed. In what Wesley believed. In saving the individual soul whether from hell fire or from doing evil in the flesh. Men of your ilk'll never suffer the disappointments, heartaches, I suffered when I discovered my eloquence couldn't bring a whole congregation to its knees simultaneously, to its feet with a solemn determination to do right. You'll never have to learn patience, taking the members of a congregation one by one . . .

"'. . . forgiveness of sins; the resurrection of the body; and the life everlasting.' Amen."

"Brother Mixon, will you lead us in prayer?"

"Thank you, Brothuh. . . . Oh, Lord, we pray Thee on this brightest of May mornings that Thou wilst cause Thy face to shine like the sun above on each and every one of those dear people gathered here in Thy sanctuary to pay Thee homage and on the President of our fair country and on the Governor of our great state and on the lesser officials who maintain law and order in this thriving county and in this hospitable town. May each and every one of thum feel the inspiration . . ."

I'd like to have the exact figure on the number of prayers like this being said this brightest of May mornings. They get no higher than the roof of the church. If they did get to Heaven, they'd be filed from God's sight by the recording angels on the lowest rung of the ladder. They're mighty smooth, though. Can't offend or change or help one soul in a congregation. I'm sorry I'm missing a Sunday getting in my weekly list of unchristian dealings that've come to my attention in this community. Would've had old Brother Waters on it this morning. And Sister Tyler. And young Ashe. There's no more effective way of bringing wrongdoers face to face with their misdeeds than by mentioning them to God in public prayer. Flatters them to be singled out even if I do disguise my presentment of the case so that the accused alone recognizes himself and his misdemeanor. Ah, Lord, if I could enumerate on my Annual Reports the number of persons who through my prayers and counsel have rectified old wrongs and walked more uprightly, maybe that feeling of frustration comes over me when I can't sleep would disappear. No, it hardly ever fails—such a prayer as I would've made this morning. The ones I single out usually come tapping at my study door before I can get to them in office or parlor.

". . . in the name of Him who taught us to say when we pray, 'Our Father Who art in Heaven . . .'"

❖

An anthem's a mighty pretty form of music, voices coming in unexpectedly, bass, tenor, alto, soprano. I can't remember titles and composers the way Beth and her Musical Appreciation friends do, but I like to listen to the music of an anthem just the same. Best trained choir here I've ever had. And I like the loft's being over there on the side where I can see the singers. Yes, every member of this choir has a right to be in it, not a one of them up there to show off her clothes. That's due to Miss Myra's and Miss Sara's making the right use of their talents. I expect it's true that Miss Sara could've stayed up there in New York and been a paid soloist in one of those big churches if she hadn't been so homesick for southern cooking. Well, her figure's loss is the church's gain. I've noted many a bosom but hers has got the mightiest rise and fall I *ever* saw. Makes that bunch of flowers pinned to it shiver and shake. Expect I'll get the name of them at the dinner table. Don't know why but I remember Mama's saying to Sister after church one Sunday recently, "Did you notice that corsage of lilies-of-the-valley Miss Sara had on today? Made me think of the bed of them we used to have at Little Brookside." Um-m, you've got flowers on your hat this morning, Mama. Crown covered with them. Must be the new hat Beth insisted you buy when she was home for Easter. I heard the discussion about it and made a mental note to mention your Easter bonnet. . . . Sister here today! First time in several Sundays. That means I'll have to watch myself at the chancel after service, shake hands as briefly as possible with Miss Blades—she'll want to tell me how much the high school students enjoyed my conducting devotionals last week. But I can hold old Sister Newell's hand as long as I like while she berates the Lord, through me, for not better attending to the functioning of her kidneys.

Lord, give me grace to bear Sister's innuendoes today as you've given it me the past twenty-five years. With one exception. You stood aside that night ten years ago, Lord. Left me dependent on frail human strength. It wasn't enough. It's never enough. My fault, Lord, for not going on my knees and pleading for extra strength before such an ordeal. By not doing so, I left a vacuum for the Devil to fill. I'd been going on feeble human strength all that hot August day, thinking that I, having got Mama's signature to a legal paper, a *secular* paper, could rid myself of a burden You had seen fit to put upon me. I've always wondered why, after denying the You-in-me as I did *that* night, You let me assume, for more than three years, that I'd dropped my particular cross. I took it up again, Lord, took it up meekly, to bear till the end. Now more than ever I need Divine strength. More and more of it, Lord. Sister seems to try my patience in every way. Was hard for me in my study last Thursday to listen quietly to young Brother Ashe, earnest, hesitant, eyebrows twitching, begging guidance in the matter of his wife's unfounded jealousy. I advised patience, forbearance, and positive action in loving her. But what I wanted to say, Lord, was "My brother, thank God every day of your life that you're not afflicted with a jealous sister-in-law." A man can make up with a wife after a misunderstanding—a minute's show of jealousy can become an hour's sweet forgiveness in physical reunion and communion—but there's no quieting a sister-in-law with words or—silence. At times, as much as I've appreciated and reverenced Mama's never showing jealousy of other women—if she's ever felt it—I've wished since I had to suffer it, it'd come from her. Yes, yes, but was because Mama never showed it, Sister's used to flatter me. Well yes, yes, it still does. Expect I'd feel my sixty-two years more than I do if Sister wasn't convinced that every woman who looks at me isn't ready to forsake husband and children—grandchildren now, in Sister Tyler's case—and come to me. Or that I'm not ready to forsake my All, God—church, and Mama—for every smile from a young and pretty woman. It's a mighty big price to pay for feeling younger than I am. Believe I'd rather be blind and on crutches . . .

"On earth His Church doth me sustain, and after death I
    look to reign
With Christ, my Lord, in glo——ry."

Beautiful, true. Beauty is truth. Pshaw, should've asked
Brother Mixon if he wants to read the lessons. Can't remember
whether he did here last Quarterly Sunday or not. . . . No, I
reckon not. Still sitting with his hand over his eyes. He needs
inspiration if he's going to do any better with his sermon than
with his prayer. I don't know his text. Can't choose scripture in
concordance. I'll open at random:

"Our lesson from the Old Testament today is taken from the
thirty-first chapter of *Job:*
    *I made a covenant with mine eyes; why then should I
    think upon a maid?*
    *If my step hath turned out of the way, and mine heart
    walketh after mine eyes, and if any blot hath cleaved to my
    hands;*
    *Then let me sow, and let another eat; yea, let my offspring
    be rooted out.*
    *If mine heart have been deceived by a woman, or if I
    have laid wait at my neighbor's door;*
    *Then let my wife grind unto another, and let others bow
    down upon her."*

That for you, Brother and Sister Ashe. And for you, Sister
Ora. Now, Lord, turn the page, point Thy finger. . . . yes, yes,
right here. . . .

"And the reading continues with the Thirteenth Verse:
    *If I did despise the cause of my manservant or of my
    maidservant, when they contended with me;*
    *If I have withheld the poor from their desire, or have
    caused the eyes of the widow to fail;*
    *Or have eaten my morsel myself alone, and the father-
    less hath not eaten thereof;*
    *If I have seen any perish for want of clothing, or any
    poor without clothing; if I have lifted up my hand against
    the fatherless, when I saw my help in the gate:*
    *Then let mine arm fall from my shoulder blade, and
    mine arm be broken from the bone."*

That for you, Sister Tyler, Brother Waters—and you, Brother Pennington, just in case. . . .

"Thus endeth the lesson. There are no announcements of church activities to be read by your pastor today. Each of you has found in the pew rack a leaflet, which gives the Order of Worship, for the convenience of those among you who may be strangers, and the Apostles' Creed, for those who may have faulty memory. You will find the Notices your pastor heretofore has had to announce by word of mouth: date and hour of the meeting of the Epworth League, the Young Men's group, the Bright Jewels, the Foreign Missionary Society, the Home Missionary Society, the Ladies' Aid Society. Please note the fine print at the bottom of page three: 'Notices of Special Entertainments and of Cake and Rummage Sales must reach the pastor's study *in writing* not later than Thursday noon of each week.' Please take these leaflets home with you each Sunday and tack them on your calendar. I'll miss your inquiring voices on the telephone. Be glad, however, to have a social call at any time."

Now, now, that's enough laughter. Save it for Brother Mixon.

"And now I suggest a rising vote of thanks to Brother Q. K. Waters for his generosity in covering the cost of the paper and the printing of these leaflets for the remainder of the year. May God prompt some other member of our congregation to assume the burden for 1920."

Yes, Brother Quentin Kenton Waters, you looked like an old toad when I was reading scripture at you, but you're beaming like Foxy Grandpa now. You didn't expect me to chastise you one minute, laud you in public the next. Shouldn't be surprised if you doubled your contribution today. Dig in, collection plate'll be coming your way now. . . .

"Give, and it shall be given unto you; good measure, pressed down, and shaken together, and running over, shall men give into your bosom. For with the same measure that ye mete, withal it shall be measured to you again."

Four earnest young men taking collection, four earnest young men singing a quartet for the offertory. I wonder if my son'd lived, he would've been less worldly than my daughters. Maybe I wouldn't've been as shy with him as I've been with my girls, might've made my influence felt in a way I haven't been able to with them. I've never been able to understand, Lord, why You denied me a son, another *man* in a house of women. The preacher's world of women seems enough to have to put up with. I know I draw more men to church than most preachers do, but look out over this congregation now—three women to every man. Young Men's Group and Board of Stewards only masculine organizations compared to five for women.

Trouble with the church is it's gone to petticoats. Only sins I can get at are petticoat ones, usually. I do get at *men's* petticoat ones though. Less than formerly, now that most towns're cleaning up their red light districts at last. What I mean by women's petticoat sins, I suppose, is best illustrated by Miss Myra's feeling virtuous showing patience about her father's false teeth while she clings to her grandfather's attitude toward Negroes. Yes, it's the men I have to reach to make a dent in political and social sins. Have to reach? I haven't reached them in thirty-five years so what can I hope to accomplish in the few left me?

The last time I addressed the Kiwanis Club, some one of them asked, "How many towns were you responsible for drying up before state-wide Prohibition, Brothuh Humiston? We were having a little argument as to the number just before you came in." Yes, men worked with me those years, hated the Republicans enough to do it. Maybe if I could've run for governor on the Prohibition ticket back then, I might've—no, no. At least as a minister of the gospel I've been allowed to speak my mind. Whether or not any body listened. As governor, I'd've been muzzled and hamstrung at every turn. I've been allowed to speak my mind in the pulpit because *words* can't get at the roots of evil, dig them out, burn them. My young days I thought they could. I learned better.

Learned it finally after I preached that sermon against lynching in High Mount, time that poor darky was strung up back in the county. That was the only lynching I've ever been close enough to to get the facts of and the only comment on my presentment of those facts to Christians was three threatening anonymous letters. That very same Sunday the Baptist preacher sounded off on antivivisection, basing *his* sermon on an article he'd read in a Chicago, Illinois, newspaper, and on Monday it was printed in full in *The High Mount Sentinel*. I came into the ministry with the conviction that the salvation of the world lay in the salvation of individual souls and that, when my mission was accomplished, I'd be able to present to God the population of eastern North Carolina—the enlightened, by me, Methodist population at least. I was a mighty self-confident young man then, freed of worldly shackles, not yet fettered by domestic ones, blissfully ignorant of time-consuming parish details. . . .

"Let us stand and sing Charles Wesley's hymn, number thirty-six, the first and last stanzas. 'Come, let us who in Christ believe—' "

". . . . . A-men."
"Now, may God bless the message Brother Mixon has prepared for us."
Glad to sit down permanently for a while, even back here.
"Thank you, Brothuh Humiston. May God, indeed, bless my message.

"It gives me great pleasure, this brightest of May mornings, to stand here again before you good people of Silverboro, in this ancient pulpit from which the Word of God has been so oft interpreted and brought to you, to your parents, to your grandparents, yea, to some few of you, your great-grandparents, and to humble and devout slaves in yon gallery, where now I see the shining faces of the younger generation—ah, it warms the cockles of my heart to be vouchsafed the application of that phrase, *The Younger Generation*—now so bandied about in our great cities in reference to flask-carrying flappers and hip-bulging lounge-lizards—to clean-minded youthful church members expressing their liberty in no more flagrant a way than in worshiping apart, chum with chum, outside the confines of the family pew—hum-m-m—"
Better cough into your handkerchief and start again!
"Yes, the Word of God interpreted and in this antique edifice giving consolation to boys in gray leaving mothers, wives, and sweethearts to fight the glorious albeit the *lost* Cause of Southern Independence; to boys in blue leaving mothers, wives, and sweethearts to fight the glorious *and* victorious war against tyrannical Spain's attempted domination of our fair country, and last but not least, to you young men here today who donned the khaki, leaving mothers, wives, and sweethearts, to fight to make the world safe for the democracy we in America enjoy.

"Today it is for the mothers, wives, and sweethearts themselves I would interpret and to whom I would bring an especial

Word of God. And for my message to you dear, good women I take my text from the Epistle of Paul to the Galatians, the fifth chapter, the twenty-sixth verse: 'Let us not be desirous of vainglory, provoking one another, envying one another.'

"Now as my good wife so often tells me, a mere man . . ."

Petticoat sins. Don't you get enough of women, going from town to town, being entertained in this home and that, saying, "Yes, yes, Brothuh, I know you're a man of business, don't let me keep you. I'll sit right here and talk to the little woman a few minutes, you trust me, ha, ha." They say you're a ladies' man and I noticed you in the vestibule before church bowing and scraping and complimenting right and left. Don't know what any woman can see in a bandy-legged, bald fellow like you. They must see something or you wouldn't be Presiding Elder over this District now. If only women, now they've got the vote, could use some of the interest and energy they devote to church politics in putting good men in secular office, preachers —*sincere* preachers like many I could name in this Conference— wouldn't lie awake at night. I can't see you, Brother Mixon, missing the world of men as I have these past twenty-eight years.

It may be that *a* wife and no daughters make you feel starved for feminine society. If only Mama and I—now, now, who's failing to accept God's will? I can't help but think, though, Lord, if there *were* only Mama and me—if You had seen fit to grant us a normal married life, I wouldn't be lonely for the companionship of men. Mama liked people, still likes them, men, women, young and old. And people certainly liked her. Would still if they had much of a chance. But Sister seems to be a damper on them, whether she's up or down, and since all the girls have been away and she's been back with us, the parsonage's mighty quiet. It's Sister's presence more than the girls' absence, come to think about it. Mama never lacked company, three years Sister was in Raleigh, whether it was summer, Christmas, or mid-term, and she was getting to be more like the *young* wife I remembered, accepting all invitations again, issuing many. . . .

Any man but a preacher, afflicted in his home as I've been, could go stand around the drugstore or the post office, sit on the courthouse steps. Now, now, Sister's not responsible for the barrier my cloth makes. I used to feel envious when I was a young and free man—in Bayport, Wilmington, Doddsville— of laymen sitting around the stove in a general store or lolling back in tilted chairs, summer days, in front of the livery stable.

At first it'd seemed natural to stop and join them, so soon after my lawyer days. I learned better mighty quick. Conversation always stopped too. Men old enough to be my grandfather getting up, offering me their chairs, putting away their pipes, spitting out their quids, waiting for me to say something they hadn't been talking about. I felt as shy and awkward and out of place as I did the first day I went to the Academy and the big boys pushed me up against the fence and demanded I tell them who shot Abe Lincoln.

No, all I can do to be a man among men, talk with a man about secular matters, is to drop into a church-member's office or place of business, chat as long as I can after I've done my real or pretended errand. Then all that's left is my visiting. Visiting homes where there're only women and children, the men off at work—or off talking to other men. I go back to work in my study then—there's always something awaiting my attention there, thank you, Lord—or into the parsonage, either too quiet these days or too noisy with some garrulous old sister or two gossiping away. The plain old shoes, Mama used to call them. Now, she says, they give her a little relief from Sister and never seems to remember a time when they wouldn't've dared "run in" a parsonage on young Mrs. Humiston because *young* Mrs. Humiston knew just how to hold them at arm's length without hurting their feelings or my reputation as a pastor. Used to feel I had to remonstrate with Mama sometimes but I expect she knew some of them bored me as much as they bored her. Never thought of it before, but the parsonage is to them what the general store and livery stable used to be to old men. . . .

"That true, Brothuh Humiston?"

"Just occurred—yes, yes, I'm sure it is, Brother." Bad form to turn your back on your audience.

"Thought you'd agree but I didn't hear your Amen."

Ripple of laughter. I'm sure I don't agree, whatever it was. I don't like such informality in the pulpit. Don't like being used like the end man in a minstrel show either. Puts the church right down on a level with moving picture shows and off-season skating rinks and ball rooms in every tobacco warehouse. Don't like it any more than I like present tendency to apply Better Business Methods to the House of God. God doesn't need such "boosting." Christ said expressly, "Render therefore unto Caesar the things which are Caesar's; and unto God the things that are

341

God's." I felt disgusted with that twenty-three-year-old evangelist the papers've given so much space to, *advertising* his conversion under shellfire in France, bouncing into my study Wednesday two weeks ago, bragging about the souls he'd saved in Lynchburg, number he was going to save in Atlanta, like an Indian flaunting scalps. "Just got a hunch, Brother, the porter called Silverboro, these folks here 'ud fall like a ton of bricks for my Sky Pilot sermon, so I hopped right off the train. They call me the Eddie Rickenbacker of the Pulpit. Got my poster advertising right here in my display case. 'Come one, come all, hear him soar in the Spirit of Christ.' You and I get a move on, we got time to set um up in all show windows before noon. We'll call it a One-night Revival and pack your prayer meeting, be turning um away." I've learned, though, you can't judge from first impressions and offered him my *lectern with no collection.* I felt mighty sad when he began to hem and haw, finally backed out the door, saying he had a hunch might be better after all to catch the three-fifteen and go on to Atlanta where a *generous* welcome awaited him.

There's one thing to be said for sitting back here. I get a view of my congregation I don't get from the pulpit chair. Can't take, at least. It's too close. Just let my eyes travel over all those faces from *there,* there's sure to be one in every other pew waiting to catch my eye and accuse me of some neglect. "Broth*uh* Humiston, you promised me faithfully you'd come to see my mother before she had to go back home and you never did." "Broth*uh* Humiston, I've got a crow to pick with you. You didn't announce the Ladies' Aid rummage sale for next Saturday. Now it'll have to be postponed a week so we'll have something to sell. Now don't you forget it *next* Sunday or the Presbyterians and Baptist'll have every negra in town outfitted for spring before we get a chance at thum." "Broth*uh,* what about the dedication date you promised for the new recreation hall at my mill? Told me you'd set it this week. Don't want the walls plastered with Coca-Cola and tobacco ads before it's consecrated." Their eyes say it all louder than their tongues do after service. Well, I'll not be bothered trying to keep all such things on my mind hereafter, now these little leaflets're out. Another advantage in sitting back here. I don't catch Mama's eye and wonder whether my tie's crooked or a vest button's undone or whether I'm playing a tattoo on the pulpit chair's arms. I expect she's right in saying I feel as much at home in that chair as I do in a rocker by the fireplace. . . .

Ah, Brother Waters, you got it! Look as solemn as an old owl now. Giving it to you in scripture reading's as effective as through prayer. It's mighty hard for me to believe the gossip I hear about a man who's as generous to the church as you are. I went to the courthouse and found out for myself that you'd sold those little houses at the edge of town long before the lattice fences were built and the red lights installed. Thirty years ago the gossip would've been that you lived with a colored woman. When white women can't get a bachelor married they take it out on him in gossip the rest of his life. Had to pin the disgrace of Silverboro's Red Light District on you as though there haven't been houses of ill repute in every town I've lived in since 1900. They began to flourish in a big way same time the Democratic Party did down here.

I've always wondered whether there was any connection between them and the Segregation Laws going into effect. Biggest mistake the legislature in this state ever made. If politicians'd let things alone, the two races might've learned to live together tolerantly and peacefully. And it wasn't only the politicians! Only time I ever agreed with Miss Ryder's definition of a Methodist preacher as a namby-pamby, pussy-footing, nincompoop hypocrite was during the fight for White Supremacy in 1898. Was sorry I hadn't thought of that definition myself when I read in the papers that prayer a so-called brother-of-mine-in-Christ made right here in this town at a political rally. Quoted it so often in denunciation I've never been able to forget it: "Dear Lord, let us feel this day the vibrations of our coming redemption from all wicked rule, and the *supremacy of the race destined not only to rule the country but to carry the gospel to all nations and maintain civil and religious liberty throughout the world. Amen.*" Fellow couldn't think any straighter than that shouldn't be allowed to be the sexton in a church. Yes, white people cut off their noses to spite their faces that time.

Best neighbors I ever remember having were that colored couple in the neat white house around the corner from the Queenston parsonage. Best shave I ever had I used to get at a colored-white barber shop in Raleigh, dual-owned and patronized by the better class of both races . . . well, poor whites know now how high the politicians raised them once they'd

been used to vote the black man down! That's a see-saw weighted
down on both ends now. It's hard to believe, Brother Q.K.,
that you've added your brick to the white end, a man who puts
a five-dollar bill in the Collection for the Poor on Communion
Sunday and more than his assessment in pastor's salary envelopes every Sunday, who never fails to give me more than I
ask for any good cause. But I know for a fact that the gossips
are right in saying that it's all conscience-money used to white-
wash your "sorry meanness" in under-supplying and over-
charging your tenants.

Yes, I had to get Miss Reeves to drop me at that farm of
yours on the new highway when she went her demonstration
rounds last Tuesday. I didn't have to ask any prying questions
of that poor Haskel woman. I've learned enough about raising
cotton my years in this part of the state to know what the yield
per acre is. I know what price cotton brought last year and I
know that family should've had enough to eat, decent clothes,
that those nine children should've had nine pairs of shoes to
wear to school. "If I have withheld the poor from their desire
. . . seen any perish for want of clothing . . ." I don't want
your arm to fall from your shoulder, Brother. I want your hand
to fall on that big ledger you have on your desk in your Grain
and Feed Store, want you to open it, and make corrections in
the so-called accounts of every share-cropper on every one of
the five farms you own. . . .

You got the lesson aimed at you, too, Sister Tyler. Despising
your maidservant. I haven't seen you smile once at Brother
Mixon's quips for you ladies and you've got a smile that erases
the years from your essentially kindly face. I knew you'd feel
ashamed of your overzealousness, your new cook spending
three days in jail before you found the Foreign Missionary dues
you'd collected still locked in the safe on your closet shelf. *So*
positive you'd put that money in your bureau drawer because
you'd come home in such a hurry last Wednesday . . . Wish
I could be sure young Sister Ashe, Sister, and Brother Pennington caught the references to them. I can't see Brother
Pennington's face behind that big hat some lady's wearing but
Sister Ashe keeps glancing at the choir, trying to see, I'm afraid,
whether Brother Ashe's chair is any closer to Millicent Allen's
than it was. . . .

Sister's staring at that little black hat with the slick bird's
wing on the side. In the Stanhope pew. There's something mighty

344

familiar about the face. Pshaw. She's somebody I know or have known somewhere. Caught her looking at me, smiling a little, while I stood down there waiting for the ushers to bring the collection plates back. Black eyes, graying hair. I can count on my fingers number of decided brunettes I've known in this bue-eyed, tow-headed Old North State. Now with automobiles running up and down improved roads, I can't step down town without meeting some friends from a distance stopping at Robinson's Drug Store for a Coca-Cola. Withered faces that were smooth as rose petals the last time I'd seen them; grown-up faces on little girls I'd brought into the church; great pouches on skinny boys I'd helped go to college. Leaning out of their shiny machines, stretching out their hands to grasp mine. "Broth*uh* Humiston! I declare it's just like old times seeing you walk down the street, head high, back straight's ever. Now if you don't remember *me,* I'm going to be real mad and that's the truth. Why, you married me in Lynnboro!" Or "I joined the church under you in High Mount!" Or "I declare I used to *live* at the parsonage, you all were in Cypress City!" . . .

Why, that face belongs to Josie Pugh from Raleigh! Mrs. George Stanhope, Jr., she is now. Lost her oldest boy in the fighting in France. She wrote me a mighty sweet note in answer to my letter of condolence. Lives in—pshaw—some little town in the Piedmont section. Well, I can't blame myself not recognizing her immediately. It's hard to see the sparkling girl I used to know in that sad-faced woman. She played the piano in Sunday school in Raleigh and if I needed a musician for a cottage prayer meeting or a country wedding or funeral, Miss Josie was always ready to help me out. Little surprised Sister Stanhope didn't invite me to dinner today or at least telephone and tell me Josie was coming. She's mentioned several times that George's wife always asks about me. Well, I'll be mighty glad to shake her hand after service. . . . Mustn't forget Sister'll be watching though. I can't recall the details but was something in connection with Josie Pugh started Sister off once, a long, hard spell. Dear Lord, when You were a man among men, did God the Father stand ever by your side, give you patience and forbearance to accept without complaint the *little* impositions on the spirit as He surely did your great agony on the Cross? I know that every day He seals my lips, keeps back the unkind word I myself could not restrain. It's the meditations of my heart I want pure and undefiled, as positively devoted to His service as are my tongue, my hands, my feet. . . .

"Brothuh Humiston, will you lead us in a word of prayer?"

"Dear Lord our Father, be with us as we begin another week. Let us not only refrain from doing evil, in our minds and hearts and in our contacts with others, but let us actively search for some good that we may do in behalf of our fellowmen. Let us expand patience and forbearance toward members of our own families and kindliness toward those in our own walk of life to include all those akin to us in Thy great family in every section of this town. Prompt us who are Thy instruments —the eyes, tongues, hands, and feet of the Almighty will—to comfort and aid last week's unfortunates; the sorrowing widow and fatherless children on Pennington Row and the colored family bereft of its home by fire in Dandytown. Help us, Oh Lord, to deal fairly with those dependent on our bounty. Restrain us from hasty suspicion of those who serve us. Cleanse our hearts of jealousy of those we love and our minds of censure of those who have surpassed us in whatever profession we follow. This we ask in Thy name, Amen.

"We will close by singing hymn number thirty-nine: 'Lord, dismiss us with Thy blessing, Fill our hearts with joy and peace, Let us each, Thy love possessing, triumph in redeeming grace.' "

Yes, Lord, I pray you now in my own behalf: Cleanse my mind of censure and of prejudice. I'd not like to be Presiding Elder now. It's hard enough in these latter years to accept invitations to speak or preach away from home, my heart as likely to sudden failure as it is, and Mama's feeling she can't go with me and leave Sister alone. . . .

"Praise God from whom all blessings flow;
Praise Him, all creatures here below;
Praise Him above, ye heavenly hosts;
Praise Father, Son, and Holy Ghost. A-men.

"And now may the peace of God, which passeth all understanding, keep your hearts and minds in the knowledge and love of God, and of His Son Jesus Christ our Lord; and the blessing of God Almighty, the Father, the Son, and the Holy Ghost, be among you, and remain with you always. Amen."

346

Ellen, you getting up the clothes already? That Lamie never comes for thum before eleven o'clock and many a Monday not as early as that. I thought you came downstairs to telephone the fish market, see if they got in any shad roe this morning."

"I did telephone, Sistuh. Said it's too late. They haven't had any for some time now."

"I was afraid so but did want Brothuh David to have one more taste of it this spring. What've you thought of for dinner then?"

"Why, there's plenty cold chicken and did you see the garden peas Mrs. Tyler brought us? The first from her garden she said. Stopped in on her way to the study to speak to David."

"She still over there?"

Ah, Sister, I can see you, right through the wall. Eyes full of quick suspicion the glasses you wear now seem to accentuate.

"Why, I don't know. I hope not. David said he was going down to the post office before the morning mail closed, get that check off for Gladys's commencement fee."

"Well, you better let me finish getting up the clothes and you telephone Smithson's, see if they've got a nice piece of beefsteak for Brothuh David's dinner. He's said several times here lately he doesn't want Sunday chicken again on Monday. Rather have something else then, chicken again on Tuesday."

"It's all right with me—but I've about finished the basket. Why don't you call Smithson's?"

"Ellen, I've told you time and again I don't like telephoning for meat or groceries. I always have to explain it's not Mrs. Humiston speaking, it's her sistuh."

"Why bother to explain it?"

"Why, because that fellow answers the telephone always asks who's speaking, makes me feel they think maybe you and Brothuh David're away and I'm trying to get something charged just for myself."

"Why, Sistuh, what a notion! Of course he asks if you don't tell him. How does he know where to send it? But if you just said in the beginning, 'This is Mrs. Humiston—' "

"There you go, Ellen, trying to make a numbskull out of me! But I've never told a story like that all the years you've been

347

married to Brothuh David and I'm certainly not going to begin now. Why, what would people think, I taking—"

"They couldn't think anything if they didn't know. I can't imagine that Skinny's they call him doubting you or running round saying—"

"That's neither here nor there. Important thing now is to get something to tempt Brothuh David's appetite."

"All right, in just a minute. Let me get the towels out of the *downstairs* bathroom."

Have to smile. Mama says "downstairs bathroom," as some ladies say "my automobile." I do believe she's just as proud, having a bathroom downstairs as well as up. Shame we could not've had two when there were eight of us waiting turns. It used to try my patience, face half shaved, hearing, "Papa, you mind letting me have the bathroom just one second?" Second used to stretch to ten, fifteen minutes sometimes. Soap drying, pulling at my cheek. Tries my patience now, having this downstairs one opening off our bedroom. Can't get a nap for Sistuh's tiptoeing through. "Don't let me disturb you, Brothuh David, just have to get a little something out of the bathroom cabinet." As though she doesn't function the way all humans have to. If I ever have a say in plans for a new church again, I shall certainly insist the architect make some provision for the women to relieve themselves between Sunday School and Morning Worship. Changing my shirt last Communion Sunday after I spilled the wine I was measuring, a whole bevy of girls opening that door there, starting through, gasping, turning back. Was mighty embarrassing for all concerned. Pshaw! Forgot to ask Sistuh if she got that stain out. . . .

"Sister, did you have a chance to work at that wine stain in my new shirt?"

Now you'd think she could hear me through that open door's well as I can her.

"Ellen, why're you putting Beth's bedspread in this week's wash? It'll just collect dust being on her bed from now till she comes home. And you've got that newest stiff-bosom shirt of Brothuh David's he spilled Communion wine on! I left it soaking in a basin upstairs behind the tub!"

"Why, I thought you'd forgotten all about it. The stain was out and I dried it so it *could* go in. I wish you wouldn't pull all those things out of the basket. I haven't put in a thing doesn't need to go. Gladys'll be home a week before Beth, everything she owns dirty, so I thought we should get Beth's spread out of the way. Lamie in the condition she's in I don't want her to overdo when the hot weather comes. Beth's spread can stay folded away far's that's concerned. And speaking of hot weather, it seems to me we've got to be looking round for some help in the kitchen, house full of—"

"Well, if I'm not help enough, I'd better pack my trunk and get out, let you try to do better. I try to help you all I can. Save you all I can. But you none appreciate it. But just let that bad Lamie do a little extra for you and—"

"We do appreciate it, Sistuh. I don't know how I'd get along without you. But there's no reason for not having a cook all the time now, Gladys out of college. Why, even when David's salary was the lowest, in Queenston and Second Church Raleigh, and you not strong enough to do much, we managed to keep a nurse for Ann Wesley and Gladys as well as a cook!"

"Well, if I'm not saving you anything—don't need to save you anything now—I had just better go off to myself somewhere."

"Now, Sistuh. . . ."

Have mercy upon me, O Lord, heal me, for my bones are vexed.

"I've never been able to be extravagant any time. I saved all I could for you and Buddy when I was young and strong, and I've been trying to save for you and Brothuh David and the children ever since. And there's still need for it whether you can see it or not. If I hadn't persuaded you to let that lazy What-youcallum go after Christmas, Gladys certainly couldn't've had *two* new evening dresses for Commencement. But you none think I've got any sense—"

"Sistuh, the very *idea!* Why, you heard me telling old Sistuh Stout yesterday how Gladys says nobody but Deeda can made a dress without a pattern, look at a picture in *Vogue* and copy—"

"And if you think just because Vin's gone, there's nobody else in Bayport'ud take me in, you're just as wrong as you can be. There're the twins in that big old house alone, trying to housekeep for themselves, and there's Mary Sue, sending me a Christmas card every year, asking when I'm coming down to see her."

Ah, Sister, the twins know what their father got into, taking you out of the asylum! Telegraphing Mama to come get you when he found he had more than he'd bargained for. Better not count on them.

349

". . . said the first time she came to see me after I got out of that awful place, said, 'Ora, you know Benton's beloved sistuh has a place in my heart always and one in my home whenever she wants it.' She meant it too. No, I don't have to go round begging for . . ."

But Mary Sue issued that invitation before Vincent had to drive in town in the middle of the night, wake her from a sound sleep, tell her she'd have to come help him or *he'd* be ready for the asylum. Yes, breaking down the way you did at Brookside was the kindest thing you could've done for Mama and me. *Then* people down there understood why there was a limit to human patience.

". . . and you heard that Mary Lassiter you think the sun rises and sets in, heard her say right there in the sitting room two weeks ago, when I was showing her Beth's old Alice-blue crêpe-de-chene I'd turned and made over for you, said, 'Miss Ora, you're a genius! I'd never be able to do a thing like that in all my life.' Laughed and said, 'If Ellen and the Reverend David don't treat you right, you just telephone me long-distance and I'll hop in my machine, come and take you home with me. You remember that, hear?' They were her very . . ."

He that keepeth his mouth keepeth his life; but he that openeth wide his lips shall have destruction. But I'd like to step to that door and remind Sister that when Mary Lassiter knew her in Doddsville she was—No, no, I don't like to think of the young woman Sister was when Mary Lassiter last saw her. The day we left Doddsville for Lynnboro. I can see her right now, straight and slim and trim, sure of herself and of—Lord, Lord, help me to keep that time out of my mind, as surely as it's out of my heart. But Sister's got sense enough to know that "don't treat you right" is just a manner of speech. I doubt if the people in Doddsville have any idea what's gone on in every parsonage we've lived in since we left there. Driving us to the Silverboro Hotel for dinner two weeks ago, Mary said she'd heard that Sister's health hadn't been good since we were in Lynnboro, understood she'd had nervous prostration and had had to go off for treatment. Mama said, "Yes, Mary, Sistuh's been subject to migraine headaches the last twenty-five years and when they come, they make her nervous and despondent." If people'd had telephones and automobiles back in those days, they'd've known in Doddsville as soon's they knew in Lynnboro about that first attack.

350

I had to admire Mama, answering Mary's inquiry so calmly when she must've been remembering that third sleepless night for all of us, after the loud moaning began on Sunday morning, making me dismiss my congregation halfway through my sermon. Remembering the dawn *after* that third sleepless night when she was startled from a light doze to find Sister crazed, bending over her, her hands on her throat. I'd gone over to the study, in the first light, to pray again but I knew by the state I found Mama in a few minutes later, crying, vomiting, that she hadn't exaggerated her terror and horror. Yes, I would've thought if the Devil was ever going to get me in his power, he would've that morning. Instead of waiting fifteen years. Ah, but waiting made his triumph the greater, as it would've been if Jesus had capitulated on the *fortieth* day. Devil wasn't working in Sister that morning either as he was that night in Cameronville, night before she was taken to Raleigh— Now, now, how do I know he's ever actually worked in poor denied, afflicted Sister? There's a big difference in refusing to accept God's will and in being the Devil's avowed instrument.

I'm the sinner about whom there's no doubt. If I'd been blessed with sufficient grace that early morning in Lynnboro when Sister, contrite, pled with *me* to save her from herself— "Oh, Brothuh David, help me as you help others! Save *me*, save *me*. Don't know what'll become of me if you desert me. Just know something, somebody must save me from what comes over me at times. Have pity, Brothuh David. Stay with me, pray with me!"—and the tears streaming from her wide, wild eyes. Yes, Lord, if I'd been blessed with sufficient grace that morning, I might've brought her rebellious spirit in line with the Divine plan. Was because I was more man than preacher . or brother then so far as Sister was concerned and in spite of my fears for Mama's and the coming baby's—Ann Wesley's— safety, I felt more pity than censure for Sister and knelt there by her bed, helpless and dumb. Felt, along with the astonishment, a kind of Old Adam pride that a woman, a timid woman, could love me enough to so forget and debase herself. Her pleading and her tears called forth all the chivalry in my nature and I wanted only to protect and comfort her. I felt that if I could put my arm around her shaking shoulders, kiss her quivering lips, let her cry it out like a child on my shoulder, then—and only then—would my prayers help her. And maybe— no, no, Lord, You were right in sustaining me. If I had followed the dictates of my human will, all the coldness I'd affected for the past six weeks would've been but to affect again and with a weakened will.

"... it's not only your and Brothuh David's enemies know what my life with you has been. There've been people in every town you've lived in who've said to me they didn't see how Brothuh Humiston could have the face to stand up there in the pulpit and preach to them about loving kindness when he didn't show it himself in his own home. If they only knew the half of it! Hush, Ellen, I'm not through. When the Bayport people heard that Vincent'd gone up to Raleigh, claimed next of male kin to me, and got me out of that awful place, they all came right out to see me—all the ladies who used to 'just love Brothuh Humiston.' Even that high and mighty Mrs. Layton D. Baker from Philadelphia drove out with Charlotte and Mercer—"

"Why, Sistuh, not—why, you've never mentioned *that* before! What does she look like now—I mean what did she look like then? What was she doing back there in Bayport?"

"There you go again, Ellen, implying I make up these things. I don't know what she was doing there—yes, seems I did hear she'd brought her husband down for his health that winter—anyway, everybody was making a lot of her and I saw her with my very own eyes. And heard her. I'm not making up a story. She said if she'd had 'the remotest *idea*,' that Yankee voice of hers, 'that that saintly young man could be such a monster, she'd never've urged his overcoming his scruples about marrying a worldly girl like you.' They were her exact words. You ever know she had anything to do with Brothuh David's proposing to you?"

Lord, Lord, help me keep my patience. Hold me in this chair!

"I knew she *thought* she had but David said it was just conceit on her part."

"Ay, law, you can't trust Brothuh David's memory. As for me, I never knew any more about *that* than I did about anything else went on behind my back that spring. Everybody in town, seems, knew more about you than your own sistuh did. But it wasn't only the ladies had harsh things to say about Brothuh David. Mercer Williams said he'd like to get a horsewhip—"

"Mercer as sleepy-looking and wide-awake as ever?"

I had on my hat, I'd take it off to you, Mama!

"Ellen, do stop trying to throw me off what I'm trying to say, being so conversational while you sand-fiddle to the door. You'll stand out there on the back porch and listen to all that disgraceful Lamie has to say but just let me try to talk to you and you—"

"But, Sistuh, I simply asked if old Mercer was as always when you saw him three—no, four years ago?"

"I didn't notice whether he was or not. They say he's made Charlotte a mighty fine husband. Gives her anything she sets her heart on. Was a big automobile just before I went down there, the first in Bayport. And he's enlarged and improved the old Berry house till you wouldn't know it. Say Mercer's got the biggest shrimp business on the coast and that son of theirs, Mercer, Junior, is as handsome a boy as Charlotte was a girl. The two girls're nice looking too but both of thum're more like Mercer than Charlotte. And they couldn't've been sweeter to me the two times I was invited there for supper—when I felt like going out. Wait, Ellen. Let me tuck that sheet in round the clothes. You never get it in tight enough. Felt ashamed, I saw Lamie going out the gate last Monday that basket on her head and one leg of my drawers hanging over her shoulder."

"Well, Cindy's always telling you you shouldn't wear Mrs. Noah's drawers."

"I certainly wouldn't wear those butterfly-pants the girls wear! And the last ones I made for you're not much better. Well, I'll take Beth's bedspread back upstairs. You'll see I'm right about it. Put it on two weeks from now, it'll be nice and fresh when you want it to be."

Ah, Mama, you did it this time! It'll come soon though. Never knew anything to head off, for more than a few days, an attack that's on the way. Thank God, though, for a little reprieve. Was your even tone of voice getting her started on the Williamses again did it. Thinks now she's made you sorry you didn't marry old Mercer. Hope I'm not overestimating myself, but I don't think you've regretted . . .

"Why, Brothuh David, you in here! How long've you been back? Thought you were in the study with that Mrs. Tyler. . . . Better pull your chair away from that window or you'll get a stiff neck."

"No, I've been downtown. Just sat down to glance through *The News and Observer.* Oh. Slipped my mind. I've got a letter

353

for you. From Ann Wesley. Somewhere here among these others. There!"

"Who did you hear from?"

"Nothing personal. Church matters and bills."

"Well, I didn't mean to be inquisitive. Just thought you or Ellen one might've heard from some of the others."

"Read Ann Wesley's. I'm a little impatient to know if I'm going to have my five here for my birthday."

"You open it for me while I take this bedspread back upstairs. Ellen was about to put it in the wash unnecessarily. You could open all the mail I'll get the rest of my life and never catch up with all I used to open for you! You used to say I made you feel like a big city pastor with a secretary. You remember?"

"Can't just recall—"

"Well, I'm not making up a story. You said it right there in front of the fire in the sitting room in Lynnboro."

I'm sighing like a woman. I need good clean May air in my lungs after a session like that. Poor, poor old soul. She would've liked to straighten those shoulders, gone from the room haughtily. Too many hours of crying, bent over a chair's back or a bed's footboard, to e-rectify that once erect spine. . . .

"David, what *did* you say to Sistuh this time?"

"Um-m, can't recall my exact words, Mama—something about opening letters. Why?"

"She passed me there in the hall, lips trembling, head turned to one side. Do be as careful as you can today. I thought she was off a few minutes ago there in our room, standing over me while I sorted the clothes, objecting—"

That's right, Mama, bite your lip, keep back the useless repetition.

"—but I got her side-tracked telling me all about the Mercer Williamses again."

"I heard it."

"Why're you looking at me that quizzical way?"

"Just wondering whether you've ever regretted not marrying Mercer."

"Won't hurt you a bit to keep on wondering! Might even make you remember I'm still here, well's the Church, your Work, the Poor and Needy, the—"

"Why, you're talking with more spirit than I've heard in many a year! Except the day the Lassiters took us out to dinner. Certainly did you good, seeing Mary again."

"Certainly did do me good seeing Mary! I felt *alive* for the first time in many a year, seeing somebody who remembered when I *was* alive. And lively. Made me feel fine—even if I did look dead and laid out compared to Mary, nothing but that streak of light gray in her hair she dresses up to in gray to make you know she's twenty-six years older."

"You didn't look 'dead and laid out' that day, Mama. Talking away, laughing, your eyes had a spark of life— Why're you looking at me *that way?*"

"Go on, I can take it."

"Take what?"

"*Your* compliments."

"Well, I know I don't pay you as many as I should. But I gave you one yesterday. On your pretty hat."

"That's right. You said it was becoming. I wish you'd remember to say something bout Sistuh's too. You would've if you noticed her expression when you mentioned mine."

"I didn't know hers was new."

"Wasn't. Was a last spring's one she retrimmed. Asked me two or three times if she had the ribbon bow just right. Then you told *me* the one I was wearing for the third time was pretty's a bowl of violets. They're pansies, by the way. I was afraid she was going to leave the dinner table then. And again when you looked so impatient with her when she was apologizing about forgetting to give you the Stanhope invitation."

"I *said* it was all right—said I'd rather sit behind Brother Mixon in the pulpit than face to face at a dinner table. If I looked impatient—and I didn't mean to—was because if Sister forgets one message, she's likely to forget another might be more important."

"Her memory depends on who telephones. And what about. Was the thought of your getting a chance to talk to Josie Pugh—"

"*You* be careful now. I hear footsteps."

"I'm thankful for that! Afraid she'd stay up there, begin packing that old trunk. Any news in *The News and Disturber*, Cindy calls it."

"More strikes up North, laboring men trying to organize into unions. They'll be organizing down here if men like Brother Lassiter and Brother Pennington don't stop luring northern capital with the promise of cheap labor. I hope they do. Laborers as well as other men've got a right to protect themselves and their families. Good basis for a sermon here in a story from Massachusetts—"

"Come in, Sistuh, and sit down a little while. No hurry about anything now, clothes up, dinner planned. Smithson's said they'd get the order up by eleven o'clock."

"Why, the front porch hasn't been swept! I went over this room—"

I may as well be in Massachusetts when Mama and Sister begin talking.

"Thought I'd have Lamie sweep out there when she comes. She'll be glad to make an extra dime."

"I have to laugh, Ellen. As many times as you've been without a cook and you still cringing bout sweeping the front porch and sidewalk. Lots of ladies're having to do things now they never did before, all the negras running off up North. And Fair's just like you. Used to close the kitchen shutters in Cypress City, cook didn't come any morning, to keep the Sheppards next door from seeing her wash dishes. It's a mighty good thing she's been able to hold on to Molly down there in Cameron-ville. Brothuh David, you open Ann Wesley's letter? Where is it?"

"Right here—I slit it with my pen-knife but I haven't read it. Now where did I—oh, here!"

"Why, I didn't know there was a letter from the child!"

"La, Ellen, it'd been from Fair or Gladys, you'd've seen it under that newspaper! Ladies used to say, every town we lived in when Ann Wesley was little, she seemed more my child than yours. She wanted to go wherever I had to go—Seven Springs, back to Bayport—and she never went to sleep without putting her hand on my 'pace,' she called it. Times of my bad headaches, she'd leave her playmates and run upstairs. 'Deeda, you want me to rub your head!' And she always has seemed to have more sympathy and understanding than any of the rest, unless it's Beth. Brothuh David, do hand me her letter."

"Yes, she never would take the nickel or dime I used to offer to any one of them to get a dose—" All right, Mama, I see you.

"What's that, Brothuh David?"

"Just saying Ann Wesley's less—mercenary than the others. Never would take the nickel or dime I used to offer to get a dose of medicine down their throats."

"Why, that's news to me—your offering any one of thum money to take a dose of medicine. Way I remember it—whether it was quinine in malaria season, iron for a spring tonic, kerosene-and-sugar for sore throats, calomel for summer complaint —every time, you'd stand there and say, 'Want Jesus to help you get well, you must *help yourself* get well,' then walk out and leave Ellen and me to hold their noses or poke a capsule down their throats. Well, les see what Ann Wesley has to say. Um-m, she's getting real smart, typewriting inside too.

"City Room,
Saturday Afternoon

"Dear Deeda,

I hope you and Mama are out driving with somebody this beautiful day or at least rocking on the porch. It's nearly five o'clock and I'm still in the office finishing writing up an interview I had with a woman from New York who's here to plan a School of Social Work, the first one in the South. (She tried to sign me up as a first student but I told her I'm a Feminist and committed to writing about *all* the new careers for women.) As soon as I type the last page of *that* and finish this letter, I'm going out to Seven Pines Battleground on a picnic with some others from the staff. Tell Papa I wish he could go with us and show us where his Uncle Lucien lost an arm. I should have that diagram he has of the battlefield with X marking the spot. It helps my prestige up here, having had grandfathers, uncles, and cousins in so many battles of *The* War. If you talk to anybody over fifty in Richmond, you forget that peace hasn't reigned steadily since 1865.

"I can come home for Papa's birthday because it's on Sunday this year but I'll have to 'break the Sabbath' and leave on the nine-ten Sunday night. Will Fair and Bob and the boys be there? Last letter I had from home, you all weren't sure. Cindy wrote me one of her chatty post cards, said she and Hal would stay with some of 'the sisteren' if 'all the tribe' came. I've written Glad that if she wants any company for that weekend, I'll go sleep at Louise Daughtry's —I'd rather do my social duty that way than any other. Or Beth and I could go to the hotel as we did at Christmas. Oh, by the way, ask Papa to let me know if it's necessary to make a reservation at The Silverboro at this season.

357

The Book Critic on the paper, from Vermont, says he
wants to take a look at North Carolina and may just come
down when I do. I suppose we should invite him for Sunday dinner if he does—but don't have it on your minds.
If he does come, he'll be delighted with the usual chicken-
bogged-in-rice.

"Now I must hurry to Miss Kate's, swallow the iced tea
she always has set out for me, and meet my crowd at the
Jefferson. Be good to yourself, Deeda, and don't get 'run-
down.'

Lots of love,
Ann Wesley

"P.S. Deeda, if I bring some black taffeta with me, could
you make me a bathing suit? I'm invited to Virginia Beach
for a weekend next month. I don't swim well enough to
wear an Annette Kellerman and don't like any of the others
at Miller & Rhoads.

"Well, I don't see why she's concerned about all sleeping here.
Gladys certainly won't have *three* visitors this time. And if you
and Brothuh David, Ellen, give your room to Fair and Bob,
there's plenty space in there for a pallet for the boys, and you
can sleep with me, Brothuh David here on the sofa, and—"

"Yes, we can manage. What I want to know is, what's got
into Miss Ann Wesley, being so sociable—picnics, Virginia
Beach—all of a sudden. Let me see her letter, Sistuh."

"Here—but I read every word just's it's written."

"I know you did. Just thought I might read something 'between the lines.' Now, where *did* I put my glasses?"

"Here, take mine. Pity you don't wear yours all the time.
Brothuh David, what does Baby mean—saying she's a Feminist?"

"Women's Rights. She's more than a suffragette, though, the
way she's explained it to me. Wants to live her own life, support herself, not marry—or continue to support herself if she
ever should marry. It's interfering with God's plan but maybe
for a girl like Ann Wesley—"

"Ay, law, a girl doesn't always have the say-so. But I've said
to Baby many's the time it looked like she was going to be one
to herself 'sI've always been, not having the beaux the other
girls've had, and maybe she'd make a little home for me some-

where. We could get us one of those apartments she's described in Richmond and—"

"Yes, and I'd feel easier about her having a chaperone, working in a newspaper office, meeting all sorts—" Now, Mama, why're you shaking your head at *that*? "Thing she should do, though, is take this training in Social Work. It's the next best thing to doing the Lord's work directly, as a missionary."

"Well, Brothuh David, if you think I'd be more useful up there looking after Ann Wesley than helping out here, maybe I'd better go."

"Sistuh, the very *idea*! David's talking through his hat. He didn't mean to imply—"

"No, no, any girl can cold-shoulder young men way Ann Wesley can is safe anywhere. If it were Cindy now, or Gladys or Fair—"

"I'm wondering right now whether this Yankee Book Critic she talks about isn't a kind of beau. Seems funny he'd want to come down just to see the state. And a bookish fellow'ud be the only kind could interest Ann Wesley."

"I doubt it. *Book Critic* sounds—well, I picture him with a long beard and eyeglasses on a black ribbon Like the New England Poet Group Kathy has on the parlor wall at the old home."

"Must be an elderly gentleman or Baby wouldn't be telling us not to have him on our minds for Sunday dinner, all the *young* men friends of Gladys's dropping in, taking pot luck."

"There's that old telephone!"

"You sit still, Ellen, I'll take it."

Mama leaning toward me, whispering, "David, I warned you she's right on the verge and your talking about her *leaving us* to take care of Ann Wesley!"

"What I say's no more dangerous than your shaking your head, holding up your finger, winking."

"I'm careful to do it behind her back. It makes me shudder —very thought of Ann Wesley's being 'one to herself' like Sistuh. She's always been more like Sistuh than the others. Sensitive, not putting herself forward. I wish you didn't feel so positive this Book Critic's in his dotage."

"Now, Mama. You used to worry bout Beth the same way and look how proud you are of her now! I never hear you talking to the ladies without bringing in Beth's name in some way. Dean of Abington Women's College in Tennessee. To hear you, anybody'ud think you'd rather she had that Ph.D. than a M-r-s. any time."

"Yes, there's a lot to be said for a girl's not marrying this day and time—if she doesn't have married sistuhs. Always have felt it's good for Beth *and* Ann Wesley that they have their Aunt Kathy, know a woman doesn't have to be queer if she *is* an old maid."

"Yes, they'll both be all right. They'll have their work. That's why I wanted all my girls to have a good education."

"But suppose Beth and Ann Wesley lose their health—after we're gone? What could they do but go live with a married sistuh?"

"Why, they'll have their share of what Father left me, after you've come to join me in Heaven!"

"I'm not concerned bout my needing it, but what'll be left when you've finished contributing to mill chapels and country churches, helping educate worthy young men for the ministry? I used to hope Cousin Sudie'ud outlive Cousin Louis and leave—"

Chance to hold up my finger at Mama!

"Brothuh David, that was Mrs. Stanhope again. Said Josie'd made up her mind to stay till tomorrow 'if she can have a little talk with Brothuh Humiston.' Wants us all to go for a drive in the country after dinner, then have supper with thum."

"Why, that'll be mighty nice!"

"Don't know how much chance Josie'll have for a talk with me, all you ladies gabbing away! However, you tell Sister Stanhope, Sister, that we'll—"

"Well, *I* don't have to accept, Brothuh David. That'll make one less."

"Sistuh, the very *idea*. David's just joking."

"Well, Ellen, I don't want to put myself forward when I'm not wanted."

Now, now, can't even make a little joke when I feel like it.

"David included me in that remark and I'm not thinking of giving up such an outing."

"Yes, but you're *Mrs. Humiston,* expected to go wherever—"

"Sister Stanhope still on the phone, Sister?"

Pressing her lips, looking from the window, nodding.

"Then forget my little effort at a joke and tell her we'll all—"

360

"You better tell her. Or you'll be thinking I forgot some of the message."

❖

". . . always this way. Just let somebody think enough of me to specifically invite me too, and he never fails to make some cutting remark. Besides, if she wants me so much, why couldn't she've asked me when she called Saturday? To come to Sunday dinner."

"Why, she didn't ask me for Sunday dinner either! She explained that—after church yesterday. Said was because she'd invited the Gays—Mrs. Gay's Brothuh Mixon's third or fourth cousin—and with all of George, Junior's, family, said she honestly thought we'ud be too crowded at the table for comfort. Said she just thought she'd wait and have the three of us another time."

"Yes, Ellen, you can make excuses for everybody but me. But let me make a mistake and I never hear the end of it. Mrs. Stanhope laughing and saying—soon's she heard my voice— she hoped my memory was in good working order today. It's always in as good working order—"

"Why, Sistuh, she was just showing you it wasn't so important she couldn't laugh."

"—as Brothuh David's any day. Here last week he carried that letter of mine to Fair in his pocket three days and I waiting to know whether she wanted the sleeves in the boys' summer shirts long or short."

"I'd hate to count the letters of mine he's—"

"And it's not only things like that. Sitting back there behind the pulpit yesterday, looking over the congregation, recognizing this one and that one, smiling, then coming home saying he was glad I'd felt like going to church yesterday, first time in several weeks, wasn't it? And I was right there Sunday before last, Communion Sunday, and he passed me the cup himself. I remember that because you and I were at the middle of the altar where you never know who's going to reach you first—Brothuh David or whoever's assisting him."

"Sistuh, do come here to the window a minute! There's Louise Daughtry right now. I want you to see that new spring gingham she's got on, four big tucks in the skirt. Girls can call her poky all they like, but she's as well-dressed—"

"And yesterday that Miss Sara Creech looking straight at

361

Brothuh David every time she lifted her eyes from her music, like she meant every word of that religious love-song for him. And he staring back at her till I thought everybody in the church would notice. It doesn't matter to me how much he takes on with every organist or choir-singer . . ."

Don't know why I stand here listening, running the risk of losing my temper. *He that is slow to anger is better than the mighty; and he that ruleth his spirit than he that taketh a city.* Better go on to the study, put my mind on my work while I can. When Mama's and Sistuh's voices begin overlapping that way, there's no stopping what's coming. . . .

"David!"

"Yes?" Should've gone past that door atiptoe.

"Step back in here a minute, please."

"Not more than a minute—got some letters to get off in the noon mail."

"I just wanted to ask you what time the Stanhopes'ud be here for us."

"About four I understand—whenever Brother Stanhope can leave the office."

"Well, Sistuh and I'll be ready. Be nice getting some country air a day like this, everything so fresh and green."

I see, Mama, I see. Just trying to decide what it is you want me to say. "Yes, there's plenty room in that big Cadillac. Brother Stanhope, Josie, and I can sit in front, you ladies the back and gabble all you please. Well, I'll be in the study if—"

"Brothuh David, you needn't crowd yourselves because of me. I'm not going."

"May change your mind, Sister, the day gets warmer. Hope you will. Yes—well, I'll be in the study if anybody wants to find me." Hard to leave you, Mama, your eyes pleading with me like that. If I could help you one bit, God knows I'd stay with you. But I always seem to make things worse, this stage of the thing.

"Don't know how they'll fix it, I not there, but Josie'll manage to sit next to her 'Brothuh Humiston' somehow. If I could've put myself forward instead of holding back—and giving up to —others—but I've tried—to do—the best—I knew—how—"

"Now, Sistuh, do don't cry. We all know . . ."

Oh, Lord, *terrors are upon me; they pursue my soul like the wind; and my welfare passeth like a cloud.*

3

June 2, 1919. Next Sunday, June the eighth, my sixty-second
birthday. Tear off another May of my life. How many more
years, months, weeks, days, Oh Lord, hast Thou allotted me?
So much to be done, so little accomplished. Look at the nota-
tions I made in these big squares of days when I stood at this
calendar on May the first. How few there are I don't have to
carry over to June! Many of them I'll have to carry on to July,
all the turmoil there'll be around here this month. Lord, give
me grace to bear the joyful noise as You've given it me to
bear the wailing and the lamentation of the past two weeks.
Yes, Lord, I pray Thee let it *be* joyful, let us have peace in the
house of Thy servant. I delight in having my children and
my grandsons around me. "Children's children are the crown
of old men." I long for my girls when they're gone from me.
It's just that they stay so long, Lord, when they come.

Walking from room to room above my head, talking, laughing,
far into the night. And Mama with them. Mama knows I can't
go to sleep till she's lying quietly beside me, but she's not solicitous of my comfort when her girls're home. I heard her at
Easter, Cindy calling out from the room she and Hal had, "Mrs.
D. Mac, you better stop that carrying on with Beth and Glad
in there before the Reverend gives you Hail Columbia," and
Mama calling back pert's a jay-bird, "Your Papa's foot in the
bandbox, I've got to hear the end of Gladys's story." No respect,
any of them, for me or for my work. Now, now, Beth and Ann
Wesley have some. At least they're interested in the incidents
I tell them about, the injustices I see done to mill folks, share-
croppers, darkies, the rarer evidences of Christ's spirit working
through some fortunate white man or woman. Ann Wesley,
though, seems ill-at-ease when I tie up remedies for social evil
with Christianity and Beth wants to argue Fundamentalism at
the drop of a hat. I don't care what she calls my Faith, it's mine
and nothing she or anybody else can say, thinking with their
brains instead of *feeling* in the souls, can shake it. Prophets of
the Old Testament may have described their communions
with God more literally than I would mine but I *know* I've
been with God many a time as surely as Moses, Joshua, Job,
Isaiah, and all others of the great company were with Him, and

if I haven't *actually* seen Him "high and lifted up on a throne" or heard His voice *unmistakably* in the whirlwind, I've *felt* His presence close to me as surely as I feel the wood of this desk here under my hand.

As for that theory of hers that Christ didn't believe Himself to be the Son of God, that it was the Disciples who foisted divine lineage upon Him for "propaganda purposes," I proved to her beyond the shadow of a doubt, quoting Christ's own words, that He did truly believe it and therein lay His power over the souls of men of His time. If she couldn't accept the Virgin Birth, the Miracles, the Arising from the Dead, the Ascent into Heaven, then take Christ the Human and His teachings and leave the "folklore" as she calls it for those who need the finite to grasp Infinite Goodness.

Greatest miracle of all, I said, was that Christ lived in the flesh and has continued to live in the hearts of men for nearly two thousand years. Yes, Beth and Ann Wesley both are more religious than they like to admit. It's the flaws they've seen in established Christianity that's made them shy of outwardly championing the Essential. They've lived too close to the church, seen it used as more of a social than a spiritual center, a Sunday showroom for new dresses and new hats, more for gossip than prayer, and they've known too many amen-corner hypocrites even for my example to lead them—as, thank God, I know it's led others—to active Christian lives. . . .

Well, setting an example was the only way I knew how to lead my children. I felt shy of them as a young parent. Was always afraid if I remonstrated with them directly I'd lose their affection as Father lost mine by his stern discipline. I wanted them to find in me as kindly an earthly father as eventually I found in my Heavenly One. I realize now that such an attitude was wrong. There's a great difference in a timely remonstrance and a too-ready birch switch. There're fashions in bringing up children as there are in clothes, and some are "becoming" to children, emphasize their best features and some obscure them beyond recognition. I wish I could live to see what present-day parental laxity will do. Every playmate I had got from his God-fearing father what I got from mine and some are ne'er-do-wells and drunkards today and some are prominent professional and business men. Such harshness seared my very soul as it must've the souls of the failures, but by some miracle I was turned to the Bible rather than to the bottle.

Mother always claimed it was her faith and her prayers and I expect it was, though on the day of Revelation for me I felt I needed no intermediary between my God and me. . . .

Yes, the unsparing use of the rod was the fashion of those times. I'm inclined to smile, reading a northern writer's indignation at slave-whippings. As though slaves were the only ones who got them! White boys got as many, from fathers *and* school-masters, and in an owner's eyes black men and women were but children. The shame was not as much in the treatment as in the fact that an institution belittling the dignity of man, Christ's brother, could flourish in so-called Christendom. And to berate a Southerner, victimized by geography and by his co-partner in the North into the *handling* of the human implements by which both grew rich, is nothing but the pot calling the kettle black . . . I know for a certainty that Father never whipped but one of his slaves between 1860 and '62, time he joined the Cavalry and rode off to war, a restraint he never showed toward his son in later years.

I was four years old that October day in '61. I can remember the tang in the air. Can see the leaves all-colored on the trees, way they never are in this part of the state. Jeb'd taken me rabbit hunting—was a make-believe rabbit hunt but I didn't know that till five, six years later when he began waking me every fall morning, chattering like a squirrel beneath my window, to go on a real one. That day he was toting me home on his shoulder, "not kase you is wore-out, Mas' David, kase I ain't got no rabbit to sling acrost." Anyway, we loped up through the flax field and into the hickory grove. The sun was low and everything under those old trees looked red. Everything but the gray bark and the black faces in an awesome circle and the two figures in the middle of that circle—one stripped to the waist, knees and elbows and forehead deep in the leaf carpet of gold and crimson, one clothed in Sunday coat, ceremonially, arms high to swing the cowhide strap. I heard Father's voice, ". . . three . . . four," and I quivered and let out a wail. Jeb started trotting but Father called out, "Bring that boy back here. Time he saw me pay the wages of sin. Five . . . *six*. There. And that's all, you rascal, one for each peck of corn you filched from my crib. Tenny, take this son of yours to the barn. Arnica's on the shelf. Spread it on thick," turned, and strode off.

Far's I know Al never stole anything again.

Maybe if my sins'd been breaking any of nine Commandments,

such wages would've cleared my account, but the hickory stick had no effect in subduing my spirit to Father's will. I never felt I was breaking the Fifth—being as true to myself as Father was to himself. And it wasn't till I was Al's age, seventeen, and saw Father lift that cowhide from its nail by the loft ladder and raise it for my bared back that I openly defied him. Leaped like a panther and tore it from his grasp and glared at him as he glared at me. He never lifted hand or hickory against me again. . . . Yes, children're as different, one from another, as adults are. Now Father never had to do more to Max than look at him sternly and tickle his legs with a switch to keep him under his thumb and he left the girls to Mother—except for verbal chastisements when they grew up. It's hard to believe the story old Captain Harcum used to tell, about the time when he, a boy of seventeen, and Father were on cavalry duty between Petersburg and Richmond. In a schoolhouse all night at Wyatt's Mill and Father praying from dusk to dawn to bring him "into fellowship with God." "I've heard many eloquent prayers in my life," he used to conclude, "but never one to equal, in length *or* eloquence, the one your Father offered that night." *Fellowship with God* was a favorite phrase of Father's and one I could understand. The picture I got of God at family prayers was of a twin brother of Father's. Beard trimmed as neatly, chin as determined, eyes the same intense, penetrating gray. I marvelled there *was* a being Father considered his equal in intelligence, consulted with about the weather, the crops, the family's health, and the heathen, local and foreign. But I never felt drawn to *Him* any more than to Father. I had no idea, though, Father's concept was fallacious till God revealed Himself to me directly that Sunday on the hillside—as an all-loving, all-protective, all-forgiving *Father*. I knew instantly that I had found the true and eternal God. I could never've got an inkling of that kind of paternity from anything I'd known up to the time . . .

Now I wonder. I just wonder if Bob tipped into little Davy's, my grandson's, my namesake's, room on a cold morning and found him burrowed under the bedclothes, he'd throw back the quilts and blankets all of a sudden and leave little fellow and his Sin exposed, helpless, backsides already bared for repeated, resounding slaps. If ever I see Davy or Bob, Junior, either going around all day with a cushion to sit down on when they can't stand any longer, I'll—now, now, I've thought more than once my son-in-law's the kind of father I hope I might've been if I could've had a Davy without skipping a generation . . . I know now that Father acted according to his lights for what he thought was my good but I was twenty-nine years old before I could accept him for the friend he wanted to be.

Never once in my childhood did I get over the fear that he'd come tipping into my room again, on one of those mornings when I was dressing at dawn to go hunting with Jeb. And being scared he'd stop my hunting with Jeb was as foolish as some other actions I used to be afraid he'd object to. Because I knew he knew I slipped off with Jeb. He used to be at breakfast when we got back, made no comment when I slid into my chair, and was mighty pleased a minute later when Jeb displayed ingredients for rabbit or squirrel stew. I can see him standing in the door, grinning, holding them up by the ears, and Father nodding, saying he was as good a shot as his daddy. Yes, and I can see Jeb's brown fingers clasping the muzzle of that old flintlock as I can see his daddy's sureness and competence the day Father handed it to him for Mother's and my protection before he mounted old Prince and rode off to join the cavalry. "I give this weapon, for use when necessary and at his discretion, to the best overseer *and friend* a man ever had," he said, and the voices of all the darkies gathered around were raised in *"A Charge to Keep I Have"* . . . .

Pshaw! Where'd I put that letter from The American Bible Society? You'd think those fellows up there in New York City'ud be able to read figures. Writing back to ask me whether it was thirteen or fifteen little red Testaments I required! They won't be here by Thursday now, time for me to deliver them, and next Sunday those children out at New Town chapel're going to be mighty disappointed. Yes, yes, here it is, in the waste basket with the Month of May. No ink in my pen again! A fountain pen's a miserable invention as well as a misnomer. Always inkless or clogged. Hope one of the girls'll give me another new one for a birthday present. . . . There. *Fifteen* in the biggest figures I can make in the body of a letter. Should be able to make it out this time. . . . Now, a stamp. A stamp, a stamp, a stamp. Just one little red stamp. Mama must've been over. That's all right only I don't see why she had to take that whole book I bought yesterday . . . Excuse me, Mama, excuse me. Haven't the slightest recollection of putting them in that drawer.

367

Yes, I'll be mighty glad when Beth comes and straightens me up in here. Next to Sister, Beth's the only one I've ever trusted to clean up my desk and study. I don't trust Sister now, when she's well and comes over, because I know she reads every scrap of writing she can lay her hands on, hoping to find something compromising. Must be disappointed when there's no evidence about of my carrying on a lover's correspondence with every woman she's been jealous of the past thirty-five years. If it gives her any pleasure hunting, I shouldn't complain, little as she has in life, but I just don't like anybody knowing the amounts I contribute to charities and to the furtherance of God's kingdom on earth and there're usually thank-you letters here, from Brother Smith's Mission in China, from Korea, Japan, Brazil, Jewish Mission in New York City. She reads them all, as well as the confidential comments pastors often write on people whose church-letters they're transferring to me, and the grateful replies to the letters of condolence I write to those in sorrow. No, I'd rather have layers of dust as thick as they are now, wastebasket full and two weeks' accumulation of advertising circulars piled up—hymnals, Bibles, Sunday School chairs, pew cushions, Ford automobiles, and Little Liver Pill glorifications—than have Sister come over, curiosity camouflaged by carpet sweeper and duster.

Yes, yes—but it was different twenty-five years ago. She didn't pry then. She felt sure then of her place in my affections and didn't feel the impulse to pry. I can recall handing over to her, across the hearth in the sitting room—the fall we lost our boy, the winter Mama had pneumonia—appreciative letters from men *or* women, invitations to lecture throughout the state. Her face used to light up and she'd say to Beth and Fair if they were around, "Listen, children, to what so-and-so says about your Papa and be as proud of him as I am." Yes, Sister was mighty close to me then. She filled a need in me for a confidante in spiritual and professional matters, Mama at that time more concerned with worldly ambition for herself—through me as a future bishop—than with eternal values. Now that I understand the wellsprings of Sister's interest in the church I know they were as selfish as—no, no, I must not question Mama's sincerity. From the first I realized that the Truth had never been made manifest to her as it was to me but she's conformed through loyalty to me and at heart she's a real Christian. . . .

Ah, Lord, I can't deny that for a few years back there the two of them seemed to satisfy every aspect of my dual nature and I used to wonder whether Your Old Testament plan of multiple wives wasn't the right one and whether it might not be made applicable to life in the nineteenth century. I felt a sympathy with the persecuted Mormons in the State of Utah I'd never felt before and one night there at your altar in the Lynnboro church, when I got up from my knees unappeased, I felt anger toward the self-deluded Know-It-Alls in the government who'd tampered with their Faith. Thought that if they had been let alone, Utah might've become a haven for Mama and Sister and me, a peaceful refuge for my tortured body and soul. . . . Mama would've set me right about that, if God hadn't through her. Not till that evening by the fire when she drew from me, so relentlessly, all I could tell her of my feeling for Sister, did I suspect the possessiveness in the woman who was my wife. It pleased me and in it—until I saw Ora again— I found peace. She had me wondering, though, that day two weeks ago when I watched her happiness with Mary Lassiter, whether if it'd been Mama, *Mary,* and me. . . . Now, now, I always was a little bit jealous of Mary Lassiter. . . .

"David! So relieved I found you. Was afraid you were still at Preacher's Meeting."

"No, I got back a few minutes ago. Just stepped in here to get off a letter. Sit down, Mama, and get your breath. Why will you hurry so, weather like this?"

"Sit down? Where? Every chair piled up with papers and things. You'd think, much as you like to be in your study times like this, you'd have Uncle Silas keep it clean. No, I don't want your chair and that sacred cushion. These Quarterlies'll be all right if I can keep my balance on thum. It does seem to me, though, it's a sexton's business—"

"Yes, it is. And Uncle Silas considers it his business—and mine to expound the scriptures to him while he works. He listens for my footsteps in the vestibule, Mondays and Fridays when he's in the church, and comes in here bowing and scraping, trailing his paraphernalia behind him. 'Lawd,' he says, 'if hit ain't de preachuh, an me jes' acoming in to clean up a little bit so's he can do Gawd's business. I got an *im*portant question to axe you dis mawning, Reverend. Bout Elijah. I axe my pastor but he jes squint an grunt an back an fill so I comes to you kase you is full of the sperit an takes yo words right outer Gawd's own mouf, yesuh.' No, I have to tell him I'll take care of my study. Rather look him up somewhere in the church, hear

369

what's on his mind, give him a thought or two, and walk away. If he gets in here, it takes an hour sometimes. I'll be glad when these colored folks get a young educated man like Whoops they'll have respect for. You can't expect a colored congregation today to listen patiently on Sunday to an old fellow who drives an ox-cart collecting trash during the week. He comes to Preachers' Meeting every month, sits as far back in a corner as he can get, agrees with both factions in an argument, nodding and 'amening brother' right and left."

"Well, but do you suppose a young, educated one'll be welcome at Preachers' Meeting? Even the old-fashioned ones haven't been in many towns, even when they come in the back way and sit in a corner. But that's not what I ran over to—"

"They will be in time. Southerners've got to learn to distinguish between the servant class we've always known and what *The New York Christian Advocate* calls the 'New Negro.' Not going to be possible much longer to lump all colored individuals—"

"That reminds me! Something I meant to tell you last night, I'd been able to think. I sat down on the porch a few minutes yesterday afternoon to get a breath of air and Mrs. Colonel Spiers saw me—was driving past in her little electric—and came in. Said she wanted to know when Beth's coming. Wants to have The Book Club meet at her house while Beth's here and have her give a little talk on the new books. Said it'ud be good for them all to hear somebody who's got a cosmopolitan outlook. 'And speaking of cosmopolitan outlooks,' she said, she'd just been to the Altar Guild meeting and'd shocked thum talking about going to the colored Episcopal church when she went back home—to Davisonville—last weekend to hear the bishop from Liberia preach. Said—"

"Why should anybody be shocked—?"

"Wait a minute. Wasn't her going to the colored church shocked thum. Was what happened after the service. Seems this bishop is the grandson of one of her family's slaves and when some old colored friends brought his wife up to meet her, they said, 'Miz Spiers, this is Catherine, the Bishop's wife.' Said she shook hands and said, '*Mrs.* Langston, I'm *so* glad to meet you.' 'Why,' she said, 'if anybody, white *or* colored, thought I was going to call *her* by her first name, they were mighty much mistaken—a woman better educated, more useful in the world than I am, and just as much a lady in every sense of the word!' Said she was going to send round some oysters, tempt Sistuh's appetite, next time Colonel's regular shipment—"

"Glad you told me that incident. Mrs. Spiers'll be another one to give Whoops some real help."

"Well, try to think bout your own children now, what they're coming home to if we don't—"

"Not so much concerned about them right now as about you and me—how're you going up to Gladys's graduation with me Thursday, Sister doesn't improve?"

"*How* am I going? Why, I'm *not* going. I gave all that up two weeks ago, day this spell started. Hadn't the faintest *i*dea you hadn't too—I mean, expecting me to go with you. Unless— that's what I came over here to talk about. I felt at my rope's end this morning, third time I came downstairs after trying to get her to eat a little breakfast, and the thought just struck me, maybe we could persuade Ann Wesley to come down tomorrow if we telephoned her long-distance today. She'll be coming Friday night, seems like she might get three extra days off in an emergency and maybe get Sistuh quiet before the others come. Now, why're you shaking your head?"

"Because I don't feel we have a right to interfere with Ann Wesley's work that way. I'd rather give up the Commencement entirely, as much as I've counted on seeing my fourth 'sweet girl graduate.' "

"I wasn't even thinking bout that. I'd already given it up so completely I'd forgotten just which day it was. I just hate for Hal and Bob and the little boys to be here at such a time, say nothing of all Gladys's friends in and out from morning till night. And there's that Book Critic fellow! I wrote Ann Wesley she'd just better tell him right off that there's sickness in the house and maybe he'd decide to come some other time when we can be hospitable."

"Worrying about all the social side of the question, but do you ever give a thought to me and my work?"

"David, how can you!"

"Now, Mama, don't get upset. I was just thinking a little while ago how it's always the girls with you—"

"If it hadn't been for the girls, I don't know what I'd've done all these years! Think sometimes now if I have to live another winter like these past three since Cindy was married, shut up here with Sistuh day in and day out, I'd rather—"

"Why, you've got me!"

"Got you! I'd like to know when! Always out hobnobbing with some of the men, visiting homes, having people make a to-do over you, or off over here reading or writing, out of sound of it. If you hadn't been in such a hurry to get to this musty-smelling old study two weeks ago this morning, we might've held this attack off till after your birthday."

"Ah, Mama, you'll never see it as something beyond our powers. Something *in* Sister—like the rash of chicken pox or measles, or the swelling comes with the mumps—something that has to come out because the germ of the disease is there. If she'd only given her heart to God—"

"How could she when she'd given it to you!" . . . "David, I'm sorry. I'm worn out, the way she's been going on this morning, telling me things I never—"

"Yes, Mama, remember we made our covenant a long time ago never to speak of—of that phase of it again. God forgave my selfish, thoughtless behavior and I've been—well, if not continually *at peace,* at least able to leave it all to His wisdom. If you would pray as hard as I have—"

"For what? More endurance to bear it? I'm not sure I want it. I've kept going all these years because I felt my selfishness and blindness about Sistuh made me as guilty as your ignorance of women made you. You may've been ignorant but you certainly weren't as innocent as you pretended to be—being 'so tender,' as she calls it, after Miss Ryder's funeral. Sitting by the brook—"

"Mama! Not another word of this!"

"—sitting there in the twilight, telling her she mustn't feel lost and homeless because *Miss Ryder'd* gone! Poorest excuse I ever heard of any man's using to get a woman back in his home. I suppose you thought she wouldn't see through it. Suppose you expected her, after that evening, to come back and be a sweet, self-sacrificing sistuh to you!"

"I said nothing to her then about coming back."

"No, you just tactfully reminded her that she wasn't homeless. You didn't need to say it again. Oh, she told me. Less than an hour ago. I reckon she's told me before in some back-handed way I didn't get but now she came right out with it. After all this time! Hush, David. Not another word till I've finished. She said it wasn't her fault she has nothing to her name now but her trunk and the quarterly pittance from the sale of Little Brookside. Said she'd never have thought of practically giving it to Slippy if you hadn't advised her to *that day she was packing to go to Miss Ryder*. While I sat downstairs, my eyes opened at last, waiting to tell you Sistuh must never, never come to live with us! Yes, you'd given her her cue then and when you went down there three weeks later to get Miss Ryder's deathbed repentance—or so you said—*you didn't tell her not to sell*. What happened between you and me there by the fire may as well not've happened, all it meant to you. With all the confessing you did, you didn't tell me—"

"No, Mama, you're wrong. It was because you and I *had* had that—that time together, I felt strong enough to stand by what I had already said to her, if she should decide—"

"Yes, *I* remember what you said to *me*, 'With God's help and yours, I'll put Ora out of my mind and heart.' They are words I remember exactly. Words I lived on a long time. I had to repeat thum to myself, like a litany, the day her letter came, telling us—telling *me*—what she'd done with Little Brookside. I wish I could remember what you said or how you looked then. I must've been blinded and deafened again by—by my love for you. But how you, who knew all that was behind it, could've thought for a minute that Sistuh could come to live with us permanently and you could treat her as *the sistuh she'd never been to you*—well, never at all from her point of view—and have her accept it, I'll never understand. No wonder she tried to choke me first time she rebelled. The wonder is she never tried it again. And succeeded. Ruined the lives of you and the children— Oh, David, what've I done! David!"

"It's all right. Just my heart. It can't stand—"

"Pulse is fast but it's strong. I'll run get you some water, the Baptismal Font. You lean back."

"Mama, no! Come back. That water's stale."

"I wasn't getting it for you to drink. Just bathe your face."

"No, no, I'll be all right, fluttering'll just stop."

"I'll run to the house and get the pills Doctuh Odum—"

"No, you stay with me. Faith—and a soda mint'll get me through. Now where—?"

"Here they are. Under your Ritual . . . Now. David, I'm sorry's I can be, bringing up all this. Nothing was farther from my thoughts when I ran over to ask what you thought bout telephoning Ann Wesley. Reckon, though, there're some things I still can't stand, no matter how strong I think I am. . . . Wish

373

we could get those windows up, get a little fresh air in here . . ."

"Mama, stop! You'll strain yourself. The sashes stick tighter than ever after such a rain as we had yesterday. No, you can't do it. All I can do to raise them when I feel stronger than I do right now. Open the outside door in the vestibule, that'll help."

"Yes, that lets in a little breeze. . . . David, it was true then, what Sistuh told me you said—?"

"Mama, Mama, I thought you regretted—"

"Regretted bringing it up. Now I've started it, I'd like to know the truth."

"How can I remember every word I said to her or to anybody else a full quarter of a century ago?"

"She expects you to! Every word, gesture, lift of your eyebrows even! As she seems to."

"She's had nothing else *to* remember, poor soul. Wonder sometimes, though, if most women don't hoard emotions, the memory of emotions, as some men hoard facts. Hal, for instance, reeling off makes and speeds of every automobile on the market and not remembering Cindy's birthday date. Now, Mama, I'm not trying to get off the subject. Just be patient. Seems what I remember clearest about that time of Miss Ryder's passing— passing to meet her Maker unrepentant, defiant as ever—is what I *didn't* say. I recollect Old Lady's being there and getting supper on the table and nobody's being able to find Ora—*Sister*. I volunteered to look for her and I came upon her down by the brook, sitting on a log—a sweetgum Vincent'd felled and never bothered to use, for whatever purpose he'd had for it. She was crying and—"

"For Miss Ryder!"

"For her dying in sin. Said she'd always thought she could persuade Miss Ryder to let me pray for her salvation, now realized it was too late ever to see her on her knees. Said she felt lonely too—more of an orphan than ever—even as miserable a grandmother as Miss Ryder'd been. Said—"

"Why, I was as much of an orphan as Sistuh and I shed no tears for Miss Ryder. And I'd never feared and hated her as Sistuh had!"

"Yes, but you had me—husband, protector, friend, and lover!"

"I had a husband and lover then, I remember that. As for protector and friend—Sistuh still had Vin."

"I don't suppose she felt—at that time—she could ever call on

374

him for anything. But let me go on now you've started me. The fact is, she was crying, her arms on her knees, her head on her arms. I sat down beside her. Put my arm around her shoulders—"

"Yes, go on."

"Don't look at me 'sthough I'm a prisoner on the witness stand then! I wish I *could* remember my emotions, you want all the truth, the whole truth, nothing but the truth. Know I must've tried to make my attitude purely brotherly because I certainly was remembering then, as I've remembered ever since, the weeks of renewed love and understanding you and I'd had. Maybe I didn't succeed— I'd purged my soul of my feelings for Ora at that time, in my confession to you. Or maybe she just didn't take it that way. Anyway—"

"She wouldn't've been a human woman if she could have!"

"Anyway, she lifted her head suddenly, threw her arms around my neck, pressed her cheek against mine, and—well, kissed me. Or I kissed her. I don't remember— Why, Mama!"

"I feel like shouting! I'm so glad she did something positive in her life! Some happy thing. So glad there was one positive act for *herself* in all the talk, talk, talk I've listened to all these years. I expect you kissed her but I hope she kissed you first. And—yes, I do—I mean I'm *glad you* kissed her—glad for once— the preacher, the saint, got—all mixed up—"

"Mama, don't cry. Here, take my handkerchief. You want me to go on? That means yes or no?"

"Ye-es."

"Well, was then, I think, she said something bout being all alone in the world except for you and the children and I reminded her she'd always have a brother in me—yes, they were my words—and a home in my house and heart. I meant it not as—"

"Hush! I don't want to hear any more words."

"I admit it was a mistake. I admit it. Was just that I felt I owed her something—*protection*. After— Mama, please don't cry. It tears me up, way it did Beth and Fair those months it all started. Come, Mama, put your head on my shoulder. I'll kneel right here— That's right. There's just one more thought—"

"You sound like you're getting to the end of a sermon."

"Just beginning one. Text is, *God is love*. Was my love for you, our renewed love at that time, made me feel so—so generous toward Ora. You can't break love up into bits, say this goes here, that goes there. You have the same feeling inside you whatever its direction. Or its motivation. You can understand what I'm driving at if you'll think back and remember the way you've told me you used to look for a letter from me when I was away at any time in the first years of our marriage. I don't believe you felt one bit more impatient for a letter from me then, a love letter, than you feel for an ordinary letter from one of the girls now. Or were more disappointed when you didn't get one. Was noticing your face, your disappointment or delight, when I didn't hand you one, I came from the post office, and when I did, was *that* gave me an understanding of the various manifestations of *God's* love in human beings. I believe as surely as I'm stan—kneeling here, that we first become aware of the depth and intensity of God's love for us when we're young and feel that first surge of love for one of the opposite sex. Term—"

"David! I never knew you felt that! I know *I* felt religious when I fell in love with you, but you've always talked about your conversion as being—"

"I felt God's love more intensely when I saw your face at the window. But you've taken the words out of my mouth. Was just going to say, the term *falling in love* means more than we realize. It takes the physical to reveal the spiritual in us. To release the universal love pent up in us. Free it to flow in a single mighty stream. Through the one first loved who in turn loves us, we satisfy our physical longings—you, Ellen, did that for me, rid me of shame—and it passes on through the Beloved, as wife or husband, to children, back to mother and father, sisters, and brothers, neighbors, friends, *all* peoples. Why're you smiling?"

"You called me *Ellen*. I don't know why I still mind being *Mama* to you. I know enough now to know that what every man wants when he marries his sweetheart is a new mother to fill all his needs."

"There, you see! The sweetheart's not dead, actually living more abundantly in wife, mother, friend!"

"Oh, David . . . you haven't kissed my poor old face like that in I don't know how long!"

"Almost did this morning when I got up at six o'clock. I knew you were getting your first sleep, though, and was afraid I'd disturb you."

"If you had, maybe I'd've been able to control myself, Sistuh bringing up that crucial period in our lives again. Seems to me since she came back this time, after the asylum and Bayport, she's deliberately tried to provoke us, because she knows we can't get her back there again. Not me so much as you. This morning's the first time she's been so—so brazen with me. But I hear her reminding you of this you said and that you did— before I ever knew you and in those first years before I suspected there was anything between you."

"Yes, I know she wants to—" Wants me to use physical violence again. That's right, hold it back, keep it off the tongue. There was relief Mama knew the perfidy I was guilty of in respect to her. The Other Sin *that* night was against God and my cloth. "Wants to torment me. Thank God, I *can't* remember all—"

"Hush! What's that!"

"I don't hear—"

"It's Sistuh! She's coming over here! Listen. . . . She *is!*"

"Oh—oh—oh—"

"Mama, wait!"

"Let me go! She *can't* come across the front lawn. She'll be *seen!*"

"Oh—oh—oh—"

"Be seen more if we meet her out *there*. Come, stand here in the vestibule till she gets in. . . . Lean against me. Don't want you fainting."

"Never fainted but once in my life. There's a machine going by right this minute and she's got Beth's old kimono on!"

"Bushes'll hide her."

"Oh—oh—oh—oh—OH—OH—OH—"

"Let me go, David."

"Why, Sistuh, what're you doing coming way over here? Watch out, you'll stumble on that old kimono, these high steps. David, you take her other arm."

"Oh—oh—oh—you and Brothuh David off over here . . . oh, oh, oh . . . to yourselves . . . talking . . . bout me . . . oh . . . oh . . . oh . . . and that old telephone ringing . . . oh . . . oh . . ."

"Come here in the study, Sistuh, out of the draft."

"Oh . . . oh . . . oh. I *tried* to answer it . . . oh . . . oh . . . oh—"

"There, Sistuh, sit down. On Bishop Asbury's cushion. Remember old Sistuh Jerome gave it to David, time he preached at Bath? Said her grandmother made it from the featherbed Bishop slept on once."

"—oh . . . oh . . . tried to answer it . . . so weak I couldn't get the . . . receiver . . . off the hook. . . . Oh, oh, oh . . . didn't want to be accused . . . not taking . . . a message. . . . Oh . . . oh . . . oh. Ellen, do don't . . ."

"Just trying to pin up your hair a little."

"Oh . . . oh . . . you stood there listening . . . to me . . . then . . . oh . . . oh . . . oh . . . ran right over here . . . repeat to Brothuh . . . David . . ."

Lord, cleanse my heart. Let me hate the sin, *not* the sinner. Let me look on that poor ravaged face with *compassion*.

". . . I wasn't telling a story . . . every word of it . . . oh . . . oh . . . oh—"

"Why, I just came over to ask David to write to Ann Wesley, tell her you're sick and need her. Come on, now, let's—"

"Yes, Sister, let me help you back to the house."

"Take your hands off me, Brothuh David! Oh . . . oh . . . oh . . . A minister of the gospel who'd strike . . . and . . . shake . . . oh . . . oh . . . oh . . . a sick, helpless woman . . . oh . . . oh . . ."

"I'll carry her, Mama. Through the Sunday School room and basement. In the back way. You go ahead and open the doors. Come, Sister. Put your arms around my neck and hold on. I won't drop you."

"Yes . . . do drop me, Brothuh David . . . oh . . . oh . . . oh . . . drop me . . . here . . . in your church . . . stomp on me . . . oh . . . oh . . . oh . . . kill me this time . . . oh . . . oh . . . oh . . . make me the sacrifice . . . I am . . . oh . . . oh . . . oh . . . put me out of my misery . . . oh . . . oh . . . oh . . ."

Clutching at my neck like a drowning kitten, holding on for dear life, in spite of her renunciation of it. Poor old face like a crumpled rag.

". . . oh . . . oh . . . oh . . . please don't look so disgusted with me, Brothuh David . . . oh . . . oh . . . oh . . . I can't help how I look and am . . . oh . . . oh . . . oh . . ."

4

A joyful sound—my grandson and namesake calling for me on my birthday. So like me in features and in coloring, I can only pray that God will grant him an awareness of the spiritual in his mortal life and leave him unhampered. . . .

"David Humiston Alexander, here's your Grandpa! Still sitting in the middle of all his birthday presents. You help him pick up all that tissue paper and ribbon, he'll tell you stories bout when he was a boy. I'm going to take Bobbie over to the church, see can we find us some change folks dropped under the pews getting out their collection money. Just telling Fred Stiles out there on the porch, only thing ever made me feel like a poor preacher's daughter *I* was little was not having's much spending money as other children. Had's much of everything else but never saw a nickel or a dime less I found it under a pew. Come on, Bobbie, take Cindy's hand and 'les we go' as you say."

"You go halves with me, Bobbie, you hear? Don't, you know what you get!"

"He will, Davy, won't you, Bobbie? Les we go."

"Well, now, Davy, what do you want Grandpa to tell you?"

"Bout the War Between the States. *You* know I studied history third grade last year? Well, I did. *Elmentry History of the Old North State*. Next year fourth grade we gonna have a bigger one. Big's my rithmetic book. And in the fifth grade, gosh, Grandpa, it's big's a jogphy book! Sixth grade you get a little teeny-weeny *Elmentry History of the United States*. Took home a big boy's in the sixth grade's books—Hunt Whitaker—one day he had to stop an' play crap behind Joe's Barbecue Stand and gosh, I coulda got *that* little old history in my pocket I'd pushed real hard. Go on, tell me."

No, no, don't ask whether he ever gambles. That's Bob's responsibility. Here's my opportunity to be as pleasant a memory to my grandson as my grandfather was to me, telling me tales he remembered about the Revolution.

"Well now, Davy, I wasn't as old's you are when the war broke out, just about your age when it ended. But I expect I remember a lot boys four years old now wouldn't remember, so much moving about now, so much to distract them. I never left the old home place to sleep over night till I went away to college. Had plenty to distract me right there but it was different somehow—everything 'stayed put.' I saw the same faces, heard the same voices, every day. Saw the same sights—according to the season. Men on the place making brick, cutting and hauling lumber, killing hogs and cattle, shearing sheep, tanning hides, thrashing wheat—all as interesting to me as moving picture shows, skating rinks, graphophones, trains, automobiles, aeroplanes are to you. I expect *more* interesting because I could have a hand in it all when I wanted to. Didn't like it so much, I got bigger, and Father *made* me take a hand in it. Yes, I can remember the sunset hour as a mighty busy time. After the war Father had some white tenants on the place as well as the freed slaves—good farmers who'd lost all they had—and after the day's work white and black'ud gather in the back yard to get their rations of meat, corn, flour, household remedies if any in their families were sick, and their instructions for the next day's work. The men listening to Father, the women to Mother—about bleaching, weaving, dyeing, and putting up fruit. But I must tell you— your great-grandfather was as resourceful a man as I hope you'll grow up to be. When *he* came home from the war, the Yankees'd taken every horse and mule on the place but Father took a twenty-dollar goldpiece he'd hidden away and walked forty miles, caught up with them, and bought back one of his best mules and what he did with that one mule, that spring plowing, made him one of the richest men in the county in a few years."

"But, Grandpa, I want a story. Look, there's a pyramid all your boxes of presents, your fountain pen's a steeple on it! Now you tell me a story, you remember one."

"Yes, I remember several. Wasn't as long ago as you think when I was a boy. Thought on my fiftieth birthday how short a century is. Why, I'd lived half a one and it was no time atall! Well, the *very* first thing I remember is, is playing with all the little darky boys and girls on the place. And with two big boys. One named Jeb I loved the best. Then there was Al—that was short for Alabama because old Aunt Tennessee named all her children after the states. Very first memory I have of the war was a day in the spring of '61 and Aunt Tenny took me with her to carry water to the men in the field. They'd been eating their dinner under a persimmon tree at the edge of a field and they were talking about the war and laying Abe Lincoln out. He was to blame for the whole thing. They couldn't give him enough hard names because he wanted to send them all back to Africa. Suddenly Jeb or Al one jumped up, ran to the creek, and cut him two sourwood sprouts. One about four feet long and the other shorter. Came back rubbing them together, making the bark loose so he could slip it off. Made him a gun right then and there, long piece for the barrel, short piece the butt, and he tied them together with long grass. Then all the boys, big and little, ran and cut *them* sourwood sprouts, and before work-bell rang, they were all marching round and round, saying what they'd do if the Yankees got hold of *them*. Then—"

"Grandpa, did you ever see any Yankees? I saw a little one one time. He was visiting the Eastbrookes."

"I expect you've seen lots of Yankees, all ages. They look just like other people, you know. Fred, Ann Wesley's friend here's a Yankee."

"Well, but this was the only little one I *ever* saw! Us guys teased him and he ran home squawking he didn't want to be a Yankee, wanted to be 'a soothern' person. Gosh, he couldn't talk right *anything* he said."

"These I remember didn't talk right either. They were soldiers. Was Easter Sunday, April the sixteenth, 1865, after the Surrender. I'd been over to Cousin Sarah Calloway's to get my share of Easter eggs she always dyed for all the young kin. I had five. One in each hand and three in my pockets. I was about halfway between the Big Gate and the house where the—but you don't know the old home. You must make your Mama keep her promise and take you up to visit your great-aunt Kathy and your great-uncle Maxwell and see—"

"Yep, but you go on bout those Yankees."

"Yes, well, I was halfway to the house when I heard horses coming, galloping along the ridge road. Presently they appeared at the Big Gate and came on, loping up the lane. About a dozen of them. I saw their blue uniforms—first time I'd seen *blue* uniforms—and I lit out for the porch fast's I could. Got *almost* there before they came through the Small Gate. Just one horse at a time could come through *it,* so I was on the top step when a soldier grabbed me. I held on so tight to the two eggs in my hands I crushed the shells. One was pink and one was blue, I remember. Soldier took the three out of my pockets and dropped them in his. 'Two's enough for any little Rebel to eat,' he said. They all came up then and went through the house but they didn't find the silver because Aunt Tenny'd buried it in the potato hole underneath her cabin. They didn't find any hams because Mother'd hid *them* under the attic floor. They cut down some shoulders in the smoke-house but they didn't take any middling meat or lard. One of them asked Mother if she could spare one of her two hundred-pound bags of flour, and she said she could. The officer in charge said, 'Don't take anything else from this good woman, her husband may never get back.' Little later one of the men sneaked back and took the other bag, but that officer saw him dragging it to his horse, and made him put it down there on the ground and leave it."

"He was a *real* good man, wasn't he?"

"Lots of them were good men, Davy. You must always remember—there were good men and bad men on both sides. It's the *man* you must look for, whether he's Yankee or Southern, white or black, Episcopalian or—"

"Go on, Grandpa. What happened next?"

"Well, next they went on to Aunt Cindy Herndon's—my father's sister's place. Aunt Cindy's husband, Uncle Marion, had lost an arm at Gettysburg—"

"I know bout that! That's where the North Carolina troops were the bravest of the brave!"

"Yes, they were mighty brave. Anyway, Uncle Marion was back home then and sheriff of the county. He'd got word of the Yankees coming and he and his two boys had driven all their horses and mules off into the mountains. So when the Yankee officer asked Aunt Cindy where the Sheriff was, she said she didn't know, said 'he wouldn't tell me because he knew you'd ask.' Then the officer sent a man to the barn for a rope and they looped it and put it around her neck and the officer said, 'Now if you don't tell, you'll live just long enough to get to the edge of that woods over there.'"

"Gosh."

"Aunt Cindy said, 'That's all right. If I told you where the Sheriff is, you'd kill him. I'd rather it was me.' So they started off with her. They stopped under a big sycamore tree. 'Are you going to tell now?' officer asked. 'No, I'm not,' Aunt Cindy said. 'Then you're too brave a woman to die,' he said and told the men to take the rope from around her neck. The least child was clinging to her skirts all the time and crying."

"What were *you* doing?"

"Oh, I wasn't there. I've just heard the story so often I know it by heart."

"Tell me more, Grandpa."

"No time for more now, young man—"

Beth in the doorway, smiling at her nephew.

"Look, Beth! I've got all the paper folded and the ribbon wound up and me and Bobbie're going to play store after dinner!"

"Then you find Bobbie and go eat your dinner right now. Deeda has it all ready for you—set out on a little table under the chinaberry tree in the back yard!"

"Yea, I gotta find that Bobbie first, see how much money he's got! See you later, Grandpa!"

"Papa, if you have enough breath left, I wish you'd go out on the porch and tell Fred your reminiscences of Humiston Hill. Intelligent as he is, he's got the impression most Northerners have that the South was all big plantations with Simon Legree overseers, or benighted poor whites. Little time he's here, I think he should have some conversation too. Glad and Fair've been holding forth out there ever since we came from church. Impression he has of us now is just as erroneous—all frivolity."

"Well, I'll see what I can do—take a lot of breath to compete with them, though. Where's Ann Wesley?"

"She's out there—not getting a chance to get in a word."

❖

Happy, happy birthday scene! Tablecloth as white as on other Sundays but not such a lonesome expanse of it showing as there is when only three of us're here. More silver at each place today and more flowers for a centerpiece. Sweetpeas. Remember hearing Mama say yesterday she'd picked her fill in Sister Allen's garden. They're no more pleasing to my eyes, though, than the sight of my five daughters gathered here. Nor more varied in color than their summer dresses. Pale yellow for Gladys, soft pink for Fair, rose—I think they call it—for Cindy, white for Ann Wesley—and Mama. Beth's outside the picture in her dark blue and Sister's hardly noticeable in that black-and-white check, in spite of all that frilly lace thing at the throat. . . . Wish I could wear my palm beach suit on Sunday, feel as cool as my sons-in-law and Ann Wesley's friend look. Yes, it's a joyous occasion and I'm appreciating every minute of it. Their chatter and their laughter music to my ears . . .

"Be quiet, you all. The Reverend wants to ask the blessing."

"Thank you, Cindy."

383

"You're welcome, sir. Everybody quiet now but that Gladys over there, gabbing cross the table to Fred. She always could talk the ear off a brass monkey. Scuse me, Fred! Didn't mean to say you're a—"

"Why, I haven't said a word!"

Ah, Gladys, if you were as innocent of all wrong-doing as are your eyes!

"You hushed just this minute, telling Fred—now, Mrs. D. Mac., you stop wagging your finger at me. I'm the best behaved child you've got if I do have to say so myself. Go on, Papa, it's quiet's it's going to be—quieter, if Hal doesn't stop pinching my knee."

"Lord, we thank Thee for watching over us when we were separated one from another and for bringing us safely together again. Grant the visitor in our midst a pleasant stay in The Old North State. May each of us, after this reunion, take up again the duties of our daily lives refreshed in mind and spirit. Bless this food set before us, let it strengthen us for Thy service, we ask in Jesus' name. Amen. . . . Now, just a few quotations from the scriptures—"

"I don't see anything set before us but little old fruit cups. I'm hungry's a bear, driving forty miles through the country. Hal and I had our breakfast at six—"

"We'd like to hear about your journey, Cindy, but first, I have just a few scriptures appropriate—"

"Fred, Bob and I were wondering whether you've *ever* gone in church in Vermont in such a procession—"

"Fair, could I interrupt? Just a few verses from the Psalms—"

" 'Be interruptous' you used to say, Brothuh David."

"I don't believe you have, have you, Fred? Beth says you don't have such big families up North as we have down here. I do hope you'll tell us all about your life up there. The girls—Beth and Fair, at least—have been to New York—"

"Mama, could I have the attention of all of you for just a minute? I've selected two or three scriptures—"

"Glad, please hush a minute and listen to me! Who on earth were those two girls came in after the Voluntary this morning? Both of thum in white linen, *Vogue* patterns. They *knelt* for prayer—way Bob thought he'd never teach me to. Honestly, I declare, my arm used to be black and blue. Whoever they are, they—"

"Good thing you've got a husband to call *you* down occasionally, Miss Pris, way you've tried to make me walk the chalkline since I was knee-high to a pup!"

"And never got you near it! Glad, who did you say they were?"

"Fred, you must think my girls're are *mighty* rude to each other. It's all in fun, though. They go on like this every time they get together."

Mama smiling, enjoying it all, paying no more attention to me than her girls pay. But I'll get attention and respect at this table if I have to hurt the feelings of every one around it. I will be heard in my own house as in the House of God! "Now, let's have quiet. I want the attention of every one of you."

"Glad, who *did* you say those girls are?"

"Bob, will you please lean real close to that deaf wife of yours and shout that they are the Truwell girls. Just moved here from Norfolk. Their father's a cotton-seed oil man. Clair Belle Strong introduced Fred and me in Robinson's yesterday. We had to push our way through the crowd—every boy in town was hanging over their table."

"I noticed Glad remedied that situation pretty quickly!"

Laugh, laugh, laugh. I feel like applauding, one man at this table getting a word in. Fred's a quiet fellow too but when he speaks they listen. I'll get my word in if I have to dash every dish to the floor. "Quiet now!"

"Depend on Glad to get the beaux these days! She's never had any more than I had, though. Fair either. Why even Doctuh Elspeth Fanning Humiston had two or three, the books-and-flowers kind, but I declare you could've knocked me over with a feather, Deeda told me soon's I got here this morning that *Ann Wesley—*"

"Cindy! I meant to ask you—you remember Mrs. Lassiter in Doddsville used to think so much of you, you were a little thing? She came to see us in April—"

"Why, Ellen, it wasn't Cindy she took on over so! Was Fair. I remember distinctly. Fair and Nancy Lassiter had stick-dolls they called Miss Annabelle Graham and Miss Honey Isley and they—"

"That's right, Sistuh! Fair, did you know your Miss Annabelle, who could've married any man in the State, married Mistuh Elwood Gideon, an old beau of Sistuh's?"

Sistuh simpering. "Now, Ellen, you mustn't tell tales out of school!" But as pleased as she was when Fred came, handed her a box of crystallized fruit twice as big as the box of candy he gave Mama.

"I remember, Deeda. Remember your bribing me with rock-candy to stay in the parlor with you every time he came to call, and he'd say, 'Now isn't it this little Fair one's bed-time?' "

"It's usually the other way around, Miss Fanning—the beau doing the bribing. You must've needed protection badly."

"Yes, Fred, I've always said I'm Miss by choice. But you must call me Deeda as the children do." Fingering her lace, looking as coy as an old lady can.

"Yes, 'm'am,' I'll remember."

"Now isn't he just the cutest little old southern boy you ever heard talk! I declare he *is*. And before he goes way off up North to Richmond again, I'm going to have him saying—"

"Gladys! I'm going to say something now. I've been patient as long as I intend to be. I have a few—"

"Yes, Papa, let's have a little intelligent conversation. I've been trying to ask the Book Critic of Virginia's leading news-paper a few questions for the past ten minutes."

"At your service, Doctor Humiston, after your father's—"

"First, I should like your opinion of James Branch Cabell—before I address Silverboro's exclusive Tuesday Book Club next Thursday!"

"Then you must say something about his forthcoming book, *Jurgen*. To be published in September. It's—but let it wait. Your father—"

"Why, is Thursday the day, Beth? I thought it was Friday."

"*Ellen,* do look at Brothuh David. He's about to lose his temper, trying for the longest to get everybody's attention before Annie serves dinner."

Ah, it takes Sister to get the attention. I wish they were as afraid of hurting my feelings. . . . "Thank you, Sister. I just wanted to quote a few passages from the Psalms that seem partic-ularly appropriate today. First, from . . ."

"Pipe down now, you all. The Reverend's got the floor. You can't hear yourself think in this Humiston Hotel, can you, Mistuh Fred Stiles?"

"*You* pipe down, Wife."

"You call me *Wife* again, Hal Gray, I'll drown you with this glass of water. He got that from an old fellow he's been trying to sell a Model T to. Out in the country from Richton. Rich-

386

ton's where *we* live, Fred. A *mighty* pretty little town. Do wish you could come to see us next time you're—"

"*Cindy.*"

"Yes, sir. I'll keep still now. Would've before, you'd spoken in that tone of voice."

"I've selected a few Biblical quotations appropriate to this occasion. First, the last three verses of Psalm one hundred and twenty-seven:

"Lo, children are a heritage of the Lord . . . As arrows are in the hand of a mighty hunter, so are children of his youth. Happy is the man that hath his quiver full of them . . .

"And the third verse of the hundred and twenty-eighth:

"Thy wife shall be as a fruitful vine by the sides of thine . . ."

"That old telephone!"

"Sit still, Sistuh. Annie'll answer it."

"I'm up now. Excuse me, please. Go right on, Brothuh David."

". . . by the sides of thine house; thy children like olive plants round about thy table.

"And from—"

"Gladys, it's for you."

"Excuse me, please."

"May's well give up, Papa. That olive plant'll take root out there, she gets to that talking-machine, old cook we had in Laurenton used to call it. Never would let *me* leave family prayers, we used to have thum every morning, to answer the phone. You and Mama getting mighty lax in your old age."

"Why, Cindy, you were a mere child, the phone began to ring for you. Fred, all this must be *mighty* confusing for you. Ann Wesley says you have only one brothuh and if he's as quiet as you are—"

"I'm enjoying it, Mrs. Humiston."

"Now, Mama, how can we know whether Fred's quiet from habit or necessity at *this* table! How is he in Richmond, Ann Wesley?"

Time Beth or somebody called attention to the fact he's Ann Wesley's young man. Don't quite like the way Gladys has appropriated him or the way she looks up at him from under her long black lashes every time she catches his eye. He looks at her as though he can't believe a girl can be so pretty. As though he's trying to find a flaw in her . . .

"He's quiet. That's why I like him. He lets *me* talk."

"Lord, listen at Miss Ann Wesley!" Trust Cindy to break a silence! "First thing in pants I *ever* heard her say she liked. Always turned up her nose—"

"At the pills Mama picked for me at home!"

"The truth is, Ann doesn't give me much chance to talk—in Richmond. I've been surprised to discover she wasn't exaggerating, telling me that she's the quiet one in the family."

Fair leaning toward Fred, chin cupped in her palm, "Fred, do you actually *mean* to say that *Ann Wesley* talks a lot up there? I simply can't believe it. Why, I've known her to go for weeks, literally, without saying a word she didn't absolutely have to. I told Bob if she ever came to Cameronville to visit us again, I was going to hide every book—"

"That's all right, Ann Wesley. You come to visit us, I'll find thum for you. I believe you and I could have some conversations now as interesting as some Beth and I have, when she comes. How about it?"

"Thanks, Bob. I'll remember."

Now I don't remember Bob's ever noticing that Ann Wesley was around before. Must be true what Mama says, a girl has to have *a* man to attract other men. I hope Mama noticed, all that chattering down at that end of the table, that Bob wants to talk to Ann Wesley as well as to Beth. Bob's a fine-looking man, that straight black hair, those straight-cut features, but I don't believe Beth's ever felt sentimental about him, spite of all those postscripts he tacks on to Fair's letters, telling her he needs her, is tired hearing about clothes, parties, salads and scandals. It's a shame, Fair's good mind has gone to seed. She's always had to keep up with the crowd, do and say what "everybody does and says." Does it, though, in her own way. She's a pretty woman and a lovable one—when she takes time to be— and Bob's a happy and a proud husband in spite of his teasing. . . .

"Brothuh David, you better begin carving. Annie's ready with the vegetables I expect."

"Well, Miss Gladys Katherine Humiston, it's about time you

hung up! Seven and a half minutes by my new wrist watch. Said you were *one* olive plant going to take root out there."

"Annie! You took my fruit cup and I hadn't even tasted it!"

"*Miss* Gladys. I'm just as sorry's I can be. I'll bring it right back quick's I put down these plates."

"That was Clair Belle on the phone. Had a compliment for every single one of us. Said everybody she'd seen since church this morning'd said what an impressive sight it was, nine members of the Humiston family walking in together. Said they all wanted to know who the good-looking stranger was between Ann Wesley and me. That means you, Yankee, just in case you're too modest to recognize your lean and lanky self!"

That coy glance again. Fred returning it too, brushing back that lock of hair—fawn? No, not enough color for that, just house-mouse—way I've noticed his doing when he doesn't quite know what to say.

"Thanks for the compliment. I'd've said I met *everybody* after the service."

"Why, you haven't begun! That's what Clair Belle was calling about—"

"Baby, Clair Belle notice I wasn't in the procession?"

" 'Scuse me, Deeda—had to swallow that grape. She certainly *did*! Asked me where *you* were this morning."

"Tell her I was right here, helping Annie with dinner. Somebody's got to be the Martha—that's what Brothuh David used to call me, the Martha of the parsonage." Looking around, at Bob, Hal, Fred, lips pursed that self-conscious way she has when she's feeling fine and "puts herself forward."

"That's a very important role, Miss—*Deeda*."

Now you deserve all white meat for that, young man! Bob and Hal looking uncomfortable, not knowing what to say.

"Now, let's see if I remember which part of the chicken each of you prefers."

"You don't, Papa, I do. Beth and Fair white meat, Ann Wesley and Glad the drumsticks—"

"Just one apiece for them today. I served two to the little boys. Fair, they did seem to enjoy their dinner."

"Deeda, I know they *did*, you fixed it!"

"Um-m, wish I'd been born in this generation. *We* were little, we always had to wait till grown people'd finished, big crowd like this. I'll never forget going up to Grandpa's with Papa all those summers. Thought I'd cave in, waiting for all the

Humiston kin hanging round the table and arguing politics while their dinners settled. Both wings for me, Papa, so I won't fly crooked. Second joint for Mrs. D.Mac. and the back for Deeda, *in*cluding the bishop's cap!"

"Yes, Cindy, that's right. Sistuh always insists that's the sweetest meat."

"Well, Ellen, time the children began coming to the table, one big hen was still enough if I said I preferred the back. Wasn't that—"

"But, Sistuh, you still insist on it, only three of us here! I had no *i*dea—"

"You've cultivated a taste for it by now, haven't you, Miss Ora? Way I've had to do for a supper of Fair's left-over party salads."

"Well, I don't know, Bob. Reason I ask for it these days is because Brothuh David likes a pie made with left-over chicken and white meat's best for it."

"Wish Wife and I had a sistuh—"

"Cindy!" A full glass of water straight in his face. I'll put a stop . . .

"Hal, you're drenched! Better run to the downstairs bathroom!"

"No, Hal, you sit right still. I'll run get you a towel." Sister *laughing.* Sounds rusty, but it's a laugh.

Laugh, laugh, laugh. Talk, talk, talk. Hal pushing back his chair, pulling Cindy from hers. Across his knees. "Now, now, enough of this! Young man, stop that! I'll not have my daughter spanked!"

"David, sit down. Very *i*dea." Mama laughing, shaking all over.

"It's exactly what she needs." Beth even!

"There! Now see if you can behave yourself." Hal getting up, pulling back Cindy's chair, seating her again politely. "Sorry, Mistuh Humiston, but you can't let thum get the upper hand of you like *that.*"

Fingering that sprouting mustache, looking mighty pleased with himself. Now, now, Hal's all right. Must make me envious, his doing in fun the sort of discipline I'd require righteous anger for.

"Thank you, Miss Ora." Mopping face and neck, proud as a turkey cock.

"Ellen, ring for Annie. She's standing there in the entry holding two vegetable dishes not knowing which way to turn. Fred, let me give you a stuffed bell-pepper and some of the sweet pickle relish."

"Thank you, Deeda."

"Mama, why haven't we a salad today instead of—"

"Your Mama wanted to serve the lettuce, tomatoes, and cucumbers as a salad, Fair, but I thought Fred should have thum old-fashioned Southern style today. Just put thum all on your salad plate, Fred, add a little vinegar, salt, pepper, and sugar."

No, Fred wouldn't believe it. I wouldn't myself if I hadn't seen her last Sunday at this time. Heard her. Question I'll never be able to answer—does she have to make a heroic effort to be well again, be solicitous, managerial, positively egotistical, overpleasant, or does it come back to her naturally once a spell's spent itself? Does it ever spend itself? When the girls were too little to help and the sight of Mama made her frantic, used to be I was the one had to stand over her, listen to all the hard things she had to say about Mama and me, keep my patience, pat her shoulder. Till one day, no different from any other that I could see, she'd creep downstairs again, like a child who's been locked up in a dark closet for some mischief. Creep down, neat, timid, tentative, ready to slip away again if we said too much or too little.

Well, I've been relieved of that part of the burden since Fair was ten or twelve, old enough to take turns with Beth. Always told Mama it wasn't my particular ears she needed. Give her any till she got that verbal bile out of her system—she must know the exact amount has to come—then my standing in her doorway, commenting on the weather, asking her how she felt, whether there was anything I could do—exactly as I'd done every day for a week or a month, or more—and suddenly the trick was turned. She'd answer me reasonably. And that would be the day she would come downstairs. Ah, Lord, it's always her accusations about my behavior with the women in my church that's hardest for me to listen to silently. If she only knew, as You do, what fortitude and spiritual tenacity it has required to keep myself blameless in that respect!

Was in the Bayport cemetery Easter Monday, 1884, that I got the first inkling of the lengths to which a professing Christian woman would go to lure a minister to destruction. Mrs. Baker meeting me—by chance I thought at the time—as I was leaving the post office, saying she was out for a little walk, asking me to join her if I had no duties pressing me at that hour, leading me —by chance I thought—to the willow-draped Williams plot, sitting down on the iron bench there, sighing, telling me of her girlhood, of her efforts to be a devout Christian woman, then gradually—and reluctantly I thought—of her suffering as the wife of a man too fond of wine, women, and song. I listening raptly, flattered by the confidence of a woman of the world, tongue-tied, eyes glued to her face, awed by her beauty. Finally the pressure of her hand on mine, lightly—unconsciously, I thought, in the intensity of her emotion—then her fingers tightening, till I felt her rings denting my knuckles, and her brown lashes fluttering, lifting, brown eyes revealing a physical longing and urge that matched my own. I shifted my gaze, looked down —at her lace-covered bosom, saw its rise and fall. I forced my eyes to the soft green grass around us and saw it as stiff yellow stubble, the graves as mounds of sheaves, felt that once-known pagan rapture rise like sap in my veins. A moment's indecision while the conflict raged within me, then the encircling headstones were crossroad signs: To God and my future in Him. To the Devil and eternal Damnation. I sprang to my feet and left the lady sitting there.

She never tried her wiles again but I was skittish as a colt whenever I met her till I received a sweet-scented note begging forgiveness for having been "temporarily aberrant" on first meeting a truly Godlike man and promising exemplary demeanor if I would but grant her my friendship and guidance. She kept her word, won *my* confidence, guided *me* in those few days of wavering in my choice of a wife. Winning that first battle against Eve the Temptress made it easier thereafter to turn from the coy, beseeching eyes, release the clinging hands. No, Sister has no right to provoke me about sins of which I'm guiltless. Was her accusing me of meeting Miss Daphne Day secretly in my study in Cameronville, because she'd found her there on choir business one day when she and Mama stopped in for something, and getting bolder, less shameless when that Miss Claus tailored a suit for me. . . .

"What's that? Somebody speak to me?"

Laugh, laugh, laugh. Absent-minded Papa! Thoughts always on his sermons! "Brothuh David's mind in the clouds, his father used to tell him!"

392

"We *thought* we'd get your attention by a one-minute silence! Even Cindy succeeded."

"Well, Beth, you have it now." Wish they'd tell me how to get theirs when I want it.

"Afraid I'd get spanked again, I didn't keep quiet! I'll tell you all right now what I'm going to do to Hal Gray, I get him home. Very next time *my* Annie—going to have to ask my Annie what her last name is now we've got two Annies working in the family. Anyway, first time my Annie makes a peach pie again, I'm going to put strychnine in it, way Mrs. Albert Long in Richton did, time sugar was short during the war. Fred, you haven't heard that story. You stop listening to Glad half a second, I'll tell you. This Mrs. Long in Richton made a pie herself for Mistuh Long one day and when he came home for dinner she said, 'Albert, honey, I made you a mighty good peach pie today, I sweetened it with strychnine.' Meant to say *saccharine.* Said Mistuh Long turned white's a sheet and wouldn't eat a bite of it no matter what Mrs. Long said. Said—"

"Fred, can't you just imagine what Mistuh Long said? Well, you just think real hard about it and while you're translating all those Yankee cuss-words into southern, I'll tell you—"

"Beth, what was it you wanted to ask me?"

"It wasn't my question, Papa. Was Glad's. You get *her* attention now if you can."

"Gladys! I'm waiting." Got attention of all with that tone. But I'm tired seeing her monopolizing Fred.

"Oh! Papa, I asked you whether you'd mind if Ann Wesley and Fred didn't go with you to that country chapel this afternoon. Clair Belle—"

"I did not invite them to go to 'that country chapel' with me. I gave them old Brother Waters' invitation to drive in his new Oldsmobile—I think it is—to the Bentonville Battleground. They'll drop me at New Town Chapel, go on and let an ex-Confederate show there's no hard feeling any more—by showing a Yankee round the battlefield. And I'd hate to hurt the old man's feelings, state of grace I've got him in now."

"But, Papa, how could his feelings be hurt if he's going to take you anyway and doesn't even know yet whether Ann Wesley and Fred've accepted?"

"Gladys, why not ask Ann Wesley and Fred what *they* want to do? You mustn't be so high-handed, baby, with your invitations, whatever they are."

"It's just one, Cutie. Clair Belle wants us to come round to her house. I've hardly seen the crowd yet and I *know* Fred wants to meet everybody he didn't meet this morning. Time that crowd gets through with him, he won't know there's an 'r' or an 'ing' in the language. And, Fred, you just can't go back up No'th without even tasting one mint ju—"

"Yes, baby, you'd better put your hand over your mouth and let Ann Wesley and Fred decide! I thought you said you had a date with *Wilbur* Strong today."

"I have, Cutie. That's why it'll be fine for me to stay with the crowd—I won't have to hear about the riot at Chapel Hill commencement again."

"What's happened to that New Bern fellow, Whit Somebody, gave you such a rush at Easter?"

"Hush, Cindy—they're coming out of their huddle. Ann Wesley, what'd you say?"

"I said Fred wants to go to Bentonville. We've been collecting battlegrounds round Richmond and I think he *should* see Silverboro's. Maybe we could stop at Clair Belle's house on our way home."

"Now, I declare I'm just as disappointed as I can be. Fred, you sure—"

"Yes, I should like to see it very much. That was Sherman's army's last engagement down here, wasn't it, Mister Humiston?"

"That's right. Fought March nineteenth to twenty-first, 1865. If I didn't have some prizes—little red Testaments—to give out to those children at New Town chapel, I'd let a layman hold the service and go on with you myself. Yes, the Union lost a hundred and ninety-four, killed, one thousand—"

"Papa, you give Fred statistics on the way out. Ann Wesley, I don't see why you can't get back in time for one—"

"Fred, won't you have some more butterbeans? Or garden peas?"

"No, thank you, Mrs. Humiston."

"More snaps, or rice and gravy?"

"No, thank you, Deeda."

"Then some new Irish potatoes?"

"I really couldn't, thank you."

"Then ring for Annie to pass the hot biscuits again, Ellen. Maybe he'd—"

"Fred, you ever hear bout that other Yankee came down here? Got back up North, somebody asked him how he liked hot biscuits. Said he didn't know, he never tasted one—every time he got ready to bite into one, the hostess'ud say, 'Have another biscuit and butter it while's it hot.' Bet you think—"

"Hush, Cindy. Then that's just as fine as it can be, Fred and Ann Wesley! I'll run call Clair Belle before—"

"Just a minute, Gladys. What was that you said you wanted Fred to taste at the Strongs?"

"Why, Papa, did I say we'd have anything there? I don't know how in the world I could've because nobody ever knows what that sweet, crazy old Clair Belle's going to serve. I've got to run catch her before she goes to sleep!"

"She did say something, David—a mint drink of some sort the Strongs' butler has a reputation for, I think. I'm sure it's all right—they're good Methodists."

"I hope so. That's one thing I *will* put my foot down about. After the stand I've taken in this state on Prohibition, I'll not have my daughters—"

"Bet I'm the only daughter you've got hasn't—"

"Hush, Cindy. Your Papa's speaking."

"Ellen, if we can't persuade anybody to have any more of anything, may as well ring for Annie to serve the ice cream and birthday cake. Brothuh David, I expect it's just some mint lemonade they're going to have at the Strongs, and you remember how you used to enjoy that I made—on the porch at Little Brookside."

❖ ❖

"Papa, you come right on in here and make yourself comfortable. You're all worn out, I know you *are,* preaching that good sermon and 'keeping your patience' through all that dinner time. Now you sit right down here and rest yourself just as long as you want to."

"No, no, Fred, keep your chair. I didn't know the parlor was occupied. Thought Gladys would've gone for her siesta."

"I'm on my way upstairs. Just came in to show Fred *The Chanticleer* because I want to know whether those college annuals up North're a lot better than ours. But what we've been talking about's the difference between northern and southern girls. Believe what Fred says, a boy up there's afraid to make two dates in a row, fraid he'll find himself engaged before he knows what's happened to him. Now aren't you sorry you're not a northern Methodist preacher? Were, you and Cutie would've had every last one of us married and gone by this time."

"Well, now, that gives me one more reason for being glad I'm *not* a northern Methodist. Gets mighty lonesome round here sometimes, just two of you married."

"Yes, Mister Humiston, there's safety in numbers, isn't there? Glad tells me she's worn three fraternity pins at once, two concealed and one on display. I'm not surprised dueling was such a popular sport down here."

"Yes, dueling was like war. It's easier to fight than to think your way out of an altercation. Believe, though, there was more sense in dueling. It's harder to compromise about a girl than about States' Rights or the Freedom of the Seas. On the other hand, hatred, animosity between peoples has to be artificially worked up. It isn't real as it is between two men wanting to possess one tangible, indissoluble entity. Just thinking about old Brother Waters, hot-headed a rebel as there ever was, wanting to take you, as much a Yankee as any he shot to kill fifty-four years ago, in all friendliness to the scene of carnage."

"But, sir, after fifty-four years, don't you think that two men who'd been in love with the same girl would wonder what the fight'd been about?"

"Not down here, Yankee! We're just's romantic as we can be. More old bachelors and old maids down here than you ever saw in your life because of unrequited love." Gladys blinking, twinkling at him.

"Go on! There's as many where I come from. It was the generation, the Victorians, not the place. And judging from my experience in Richmond, I'd say Mister Waters is an exception to the rule."

"Say 'go on' again."

"Why?"

"It's so funny—'go *an,*' *you* say."

"All right. You say 'knife and foulk' and I will."

"Well, I think I'll go find a place to take a little nap."

"Papa! You want this sofa! I declare I meant every word I said bout going upstairs. I can't lose my nap, much's I'd like to have that Deke pin from Dartmouth College! See you later, Fred. Now don't you go poking all over that old battlefield so long you can't get to Clair Belle's, you hear?"

"Here now, wait a minute! If a pin doesn't mean any more down here than you say it does, you can have mine!"

"Why, I wouldn't take it for anything in the world after such a cold-blooded presentation as that! You should be ashamed of yourself, I declare you should. At least we *pretend* a little bit."

Smiling at him, walking backwards, then flaunting airily out the door that way. Airily's she can in that hobble skirt. *He* smiling, looking after her. I just don't like it. If she'd met him first, Ann Wesley not involved, it'ud be all right to carry on such a flirtation if she must. Seems a fine young man, much's I've seen of him, and no worldlier than my present sons-in-law. Still, I can't see that Ann Wesley's disturbed. Other hand, can't believe she'd've invited him down if he's no more to her than other members of that newspaper crowd. If there *is* anything between them, now's as good a time as any for him to speak to me. . . .

"Haven't seen Ann Wesley since we left the table."

"Ann's upstairs, sir. Packing."

"That's right, no other time for it, you leaving on the nine-ten train. I'm glad she has an escort, getting into Richmond at midnight. You can see her safely to her boarding-house."

"Yes, I shall. But don't let Ann hear you say she needs a protector! Ann's very independent—or maybe you know that, sir. She's not at all like the other southern girls I've met. But I mustn't stand here keeping you from your nap."

"No, no, sit down if you will. Looks like southern hospitality peters out this time of day. I'll just lie here on the sofa and relax a little. Always feel let down after preaching, need to rest but don't often sleep. Good chance to get acquainted—unless you'd rather join Bob and Hal there on the porch?"

"If you're sure you don't mind, I'd rather sit with you."

"No, no, mighty glad to have you."

Got an engaging smile, whether it's for me or for Gladys. Fine face but I wouldn't call it good-looking, like Bob's. Rugged. Virile. But he doesn't make a show of his masculinity way Hal does. Now what's that inane word Beth uses to describe a worldly man? Tweedy! Yes, he's that even in a palm beach suit. Glad he's putting that pipe away, though. Glad he smokes a pipe instead of cigarettes. Or those cigars Hal puffs away on.

"Yes, it's the quiet time of the day around here. Something on your mind you'd like to say to me?"

"Matter of fact, there is. I wanted to tell you I got quite a lot out of your sermon this morning. Wish I could hear you again this evening. I've been trying to decide whether it's you-the-

397

preacher per se or you-the-preacher in this environment that gave your sermon more content and impact than sermons I've dozed through other places. Well-behaved rural New England and well-heeled city congregations anywhere don't, perhaps, give a minister either insight into social problems or stimulate an urge to look for them. But what you see at first hand here in the mills must carry your interest on—to read about what's happening in Massachusetts. Any case, you worked out a sermon that, it seemed to me, was a masterly exposition of the rights of labor. Everywhere. How'll it strike the capitalists in your church?"

"Just graze them. Make no dent. When I was a young man, I thought all I had to do bring about the millennium—in eastern North Carolina—was rise in my wrath and the people'ud refrain from doing evil and learn to do good. Learned better as I've grown older. I know now the little I can accomplish toward establishing God's kingdom on earth'll come from my concentration on individual souls. Seeing this state go dry in 1908 was a great personal satisfaction. I certainly had a hand in that—sorry some of the other hands, the selfish political ones, weren't so clean."

"But you still 'rise in your wrath' on occasion?"

"Yes, some seed may fall in fertile soil. Then, too, you know, a preacher has to preach as a dog has to howl."

"Wouldn't say either 'wrath' or 'howl' are descriptive of your logical approach. Have your pastorates always been small towns?"

"Ten of them were—in the thirty-five years of my ministry. Wilmington was my second charge—but that was a small town in 1886 and in Raleigh I had the Second Church. Twelve pastorates in all."

"Should've thought you'd've had a bishopric or some other over-all office—don't know what you call it in the Methodist Church. My family's Congregationalist."

"Well, I was headed toward a presiding eldership—our Conference is divided into districts with a director chosen by the bishop from the ranks of active pastors—but there were—" Now, now, mustn't go into that. "Real reason was I lost my ambition. I didn't want to play church politics any more than I'd wanted to play secular when I was a young lawyer. I don't regret it now. I was thinking a minute ago, your mentioning rural and city preachers having no urge to look for social evils—small towns down here that have mills are small worlds unto themselves. There're three distinct social-economic levels: 'nice people'; mill hands and share-croppers; colored people. And lots of social gradations in the 'nice people' class I make no effort to understand. Girls could tell you about them. It's no effort atall to see mankind and his conflicts in miniature. In cities sections and classes are too separated. You don't *hear* economic greed using White Supremacy as its mouthpiece—supplying such whistles to ignorant men—on every street corner every Saturday or feel personal shame when you step in the County Clerk's office once a year to pay tribute to political chicanery through that Poll Tax this state levied when so-called Democrats got hold of it again, end of the last century. That's the only tax a preacher has to pay, by the way. You don't *see* capital outdoing labor as I saw it just yesterday—visiting a new-made widow. Husband killed a few weeks ago, crushed in a piece of machinery because a lever was faulty. Superintendent at the mill says the accident was due to the man's carelessness and won't allow that poor woman a claim. She's got five children. Leaves the oldest, eight years old, in charge while she goes off to work ten hours a day as a doffer—changing loaded spools of cotton for empty ones—for twelve dollars a week. Superintendent's a Baptist but I'll get at him someway! Often think if just *one* southern town would work out its salvation, make Christianity a living thing, it could be a model not only for other southern towns but for the world at large."

"If one industrial northern town did that, it would be as applicable. We're just beginning to get the 'Negro Problem' up there but we've had others you've never had down here. And prejudice against the foreign-born's as prevalent and ugly, though they have citizen rights, as prejudice against the Negroes—" Glancing around, jumping to his feet, proffering his chair to Beth. "Come join us!"

"Don't get up, Fred. I'll perch here on the sofa arm, run my fingers through Papa's hair—little extra birthday present."

"Yes, yes, Beth, that's mighty soothing."

"What're *you* doing, wandering around in the heat of the day? Thought it was a social misdemeanor for the feminine South to be up and dressed at this hour."

"Oh, I'm a maverick! I've been in the kitchen helping Annie shell shrimp for supper. Had an interesting conversation with her. I thought I might get in another one at last with another functioning mind—meaning yours. Stood there in the front door trying to inveigle Bob to join us but Hal and the boys've got him cornered. Trying to sell him a Ford to drive the two blocks to his office so Fair can have the Haynes for her party-going—without having to walk two blocks to get it. Davy says in two years his legs'll be long enough to drive and that seems to be the only license he'll require!"

"What about this conversation you've been having with Annie? Your father and I've just been discussing the 'Negro Problem.' I noticed she doesn't talk like the Negroes I've heard on the streets. Is she educated?"

"Um-m. A graduate of Hampton Institute. By the way, Papa, she told me old Judge Hyde lent her the money for her tuition and she's paid most of it back. She teaches the sixth grade here in the winter—and those little darkies're learning a lot more than white 'chillun' are under that little flapper who's making her debut here and teaching 'on the side.' Annie's been reading John Dewey and really going in for progressive education in a big way—lack of strict supervision of colored schools has its advantages!"

"Still she works as a domestic in summer, has no social privileges, comes in the back door—"

"Don't your domestics do that in the North?"

"Well, yes—yes, of course—but they're not college graduates and professionals."

"*That's* the point! But I'm surprised at you, ready to berate us for having the conventional attitude toward *servants*—adding that to our burden of guilt—"

"It'll be added, more every year from now on, till we learn that *all* darkies aren't hewers of wood and drawers of water. Scratch behind my left ear a little, Beth."

" 'Yesuh!' Two agreements with one word! You should hear Cindy come in the kitchen and 'carry on' with Annie as she does with all other colored people she knows! But Annie's a smart girl in more ways than one—catches her cues and plays thum right back. Except for her good grammar, you'd never know she's 'different.' But I must tell you about the visiting professor and his wife from Boston we had in Abington this winter, insisting that their cook and laundress, who'd never thought of being anything *but* cook and laundress, come in through the front door, be addressed as *Mrs.* to show us benighted heathens how to treat colored people. Of course, if that's their enlightened attitude toward their *white* servants at home . . ."

❖ ❖

Must've dropped off, Beth scratching my head that way. Don't know when she and Fred went out. Must be nearly three o'clock, company on the porch. Folks move around a little earlier on Sundays. Um-m. Beth's company out there. "High brow talk" as Cindy calls it. Talk about things of the mind is next best to talk about things of the spirit, a high degree above chatter about people and clothes and parties. I always like it when Beth's home—particularly at Christmas when she keeps a fire going here in the parlor all day, every day. I come in from a round of visiting at poor little cottages, noting families the Ladies might've overlooked making their list for Christmas baskets, and find Beth serving Chinese tea with a piece of lemon and a clove in it. It tastes mighty good. I'm never at a loss what to say to Beth's friends as I've always been with Cindy's and usually with Fair's and Gladys's. That young fellow who practiced law and was more concerned with things of the mind than of the spirit always comes to my assistance in here on such afternoons. His stories about The Browning Club he used to be president of and the plays of Shakespeare he had leading roles in get real appreciation from Beth's friends. That day last Christmas when they got away from modern novels and on to the classics, they were mighty interested to hear how I'd read Scott and Dickens in serial form, in old magazines stored in the attic at the old home.

If Kathy ever agrees to visit us again, now the girls're grown, and comes when Beth's home, she might not cut her stay so short for fear of "brain atrophy" as she did the one time she ever visited us. In High Mount. "Small town talk sets my teeth on edge, David, and as for Ora's deterioration into mental and emotional debauchery . . ." Mama never got over the humiliation of Kathy's superior manner in that visit. I could never persuade her to even consider going up the country with me again. Not even to Mother's or Father's funeral. If Mama ever felt shy of anything or anybody when she was a young woman I never knew it. Never seemed in awe of Father even and made him smile many a time. Now she doesn't seem at ease except with young people and the "old sisteren." Even makes excuses to Beth about coming in when her friends're here, says she's been too confined to Sister's humdrum talk these last seven years to have anything to say that would interest anybody and doesn't like to sit like a bump on a log. Those three summers in Burlingham, while Sister was in Raleigh and Bayport, Mama got to be a little of her old sociable self again, going to Chatauqua three times a day, helping Beth entertain the lecturers at dinner and supper, reading the books recommended. . . .

Must tell Fred that little incident of Ann Wesley and the minister from a big church in New York City, lectured two summers in a row. When he came for supper at the parsonage, Mama was introducing her girls, telling the place each one had in the family. When she came to Ann Wesley and he was shaking her hand, he said, "So you're the penultimate one!" Ann Wesley sidled up to me, asked what *that* word meant, and when I defined it, her face clouded over 'sthough she was going to cry. "Oh," she said, "I thought I was something important at last!" Yes, that'll make Fred laugh out that way he has. Always did like a fellow can laugh, quick and short, be through with it, go on listening or saying something. Used to practice trying to laugh out loud like that myself but never did quite get the knack of it. Second thought, maybe I'd better not mention that little incident. If he's interested in Ann Wesley, it won't do to emphasize her shyness. Enough of that was done at the dinner table. I don't know quite what to make of his comment about Ann Wesley's being so independent. Sounds more 'sthough he's thinking of her as a friend, not a sweetheart. Not making use of his opportunity to speak to me about his intentions makes it appear that way too. If that is the case, I hope Ann Wesley's not letting herself be fooled. Fooling herself, rather. Can't believe an open-minded, straight-thinking young man like Fred could play the cad. Can't tell about young men, though, these days, such free and easy manners and morals as are countenanced.

In my youth, any fellow sowed his wild oats in an open field was looked down upon as much as a fast girl was. Well, almost as much. Greatest injustice was in society's welcoming him back to decorous behavior while it cold-shouldered a girl, who'd taken one false step, for the rest of her life. Father's coming upon me and that itinerant thrasher's big girl—named Juno and rightly—behind the stacks of bound wheat gave me a never-to-be-forgotten respect for the force of public opinion, an understanding of its total lack of sympathy in regard to unhallowed sexual rela-ᵗions. There was I under the August sun, all-powerful one minute like a pagan god, like Jupiter himself, the next no more than a dumb barnyard "creetur" cowering under Father's wrath. Sight of Father's face was enough—made more impression on my mind than that cowhide would've made on my bared back if I—the new man in me—had let it come down. Yes, was the fear of public opinion kept me on the straight-and-narrow during those worldly years of my young manhood, temptations on every side. To this day I feel the blood rising to my face when innocent, bright-faced children in Sunday School sing "Bringing in the Sheaves." . . .

Yes, I hope Ann Wesley's as heart whole and fancy free as she appears to be. Mama used to say of all the children Ann Wesley was most like Sister in disposition, getting her feelings hurt, crying easily. Seems to've got over that tendency, though, far's I can see. Developed a kind of aloofness. I noticed her glancing around the table today with the expression I used to see on the faces of people watching the chattering monkeys in the Raleigh zoo. She seems at ease with Fred—with Bob, too, for that matter —in a way she's never been with men. Expect we made a mistake in the choice of colleges—she should've gone to Trinity, got used to men, and Gladys to Abington with Beth. I've heard Beth say more than once, defending Ann Wesley against Fair's and Gladys's complaints, "Why, she's one of the most popular girls at Abington. It's just at home she goes in her shell." She certainly talked to Mama and me with a lot of animation when she got here last Tuesday morning, told us about her work and her good times in Richmond before she shut herself up with Sister. I'd like to know what magic she used to get Sister well in such record time. Never've known her to recuperate quite so fast. Or be so outgoing to a stranger as she's been to Fred, asking him to call her "Deeda." She's let Bob and Hal know she wants to be "Miss Ora" to them, says their calling her Deeda makes her feel like a servant when they call Mama and me "Mistuh" and "Mrs." . . .

"David, you awake?"

"Come on in, Mama. I've just been dozing."

"No, don't get up. It's not much after three. I want to talk to you a minute if I can find a little peace and quiet in here."

"Better close that window on the porch then as well's the door."

"Yes, I reckon so. They're all out there now. Miss Myra, Miss Sara, those two musical guests of hers from New York she brought around to meet Beth. Fair and Bob at this end of the porch with *them,* Gladys, Wilbur, Ann Wesley, Fred, and Louise Daughtry at the other. Gladys is outdoing herself, mimicking everybody in town. Pity Louise is here, she can't mock her prissing down town. I've been in the sitting room peeping through the shutters, getting a little laugh."

"Where're Cindy and Hal?"

"Oh. They took Sistuh and the boys off in their machine for a little ride. First time Sistuh's been out of the house in three weeks. I feel like a bird out of the cage. Or would if—"

"You look refreshed. White dress, white slippers, white—um-m, *silk* stockings again! Yes, sit right there where I can see—"

"David, do hush, sixty-two years old and's aware of ankles as Hal is! Fair brought me these stockings. But what I started to say was, I'd feel like a bird out of the cage if it wasn't for this situation."

"What situation?"

"What do you think I'm nodding backwards at, at the porch out there, if it isn't at the way Fred's taken to Gladys? I've been watching him. Doesn't seem able to take his eyes off her face!"

"Hard for any young man to do, I reckon, a face like Gladys's."

"I hardly slept a wink last night, worrying about it all. Got right exasperated with myself, Sistuh quiet and I lying awake. But I think I just can't stand it if Fred decides it's Gladys he—"

"A man doesn't decide a thing like that."

"Falls in love with Gladys then, when he's the only beau Ann Wesley's ever had and Gladys can take her pick when she's ready to."

"You said anything to Gladys?"

"No. What could I say? 'Now, baby, you mustn't let Fred fall in love with *you.* It'ud do about as much good as it would've if Buddy'd tried to remonstrate with me about you, way back yonder! Gladys'ud say, looking at me innocently's you please, 'But, Cutie, I'm not *trying* to make him like me. I can't sit back on my fanny and be mum just because he's Ann Wesley's company.' And she can't. She's treating him exactly the way she treats all other young men."

"And that's just what she shouldn't do with Ann Wesley's 'company.' "

"Well, the child can't change herself. I know that. But she didn't have to take him off downtown a few hours after he got here yesterday. Of course she was speaking to both of thum when she said, 'Come on down to Robinson's with me,' and Ann Wesley said she couldn't, Deeda was just ready to try her bathing suit on her. She didn't seem to mind Fred's going but it was so like the kind of thing Sistuh would've done when *she* felt slighted, it made me shake in my boots. What was Fred talking to you about in here after dinner? I hoped—"

"No. Just telling me how much he'd enjoyed my sermon. We got off on social problems. Never enjoyed a conversation more. He's a fine young man. Strong face, strong mind, strong character. I'd like him for a son-in-law no matter which of my daughters—now, now, Mama, I think you're overanxious. After all, Ann Wesley's like Beth—a better-looking woman than she was a child. That bobbed hair makes her a little conspicuous maybe but it's becoming to her—straight like that, not frizzed up any more way she used to wear her hair, trying to look like every other girl. I like the color of it—"

"Ash blonde they call it."

"Whatever it is. And she's got clear blue eyes like Benton's and a slim figure like—like—"

"Sistuh's used to be, slim *and* straight-shouldered. But Ann Wesley's as flat-breasted as I was at her age."

"You got me in spite of that! Fooled me, though, with those ruffled things. All you needed to swell you out was a baby."

"I asked Ann Wesley once why she didn't wear a ruffle. Said 'Oh, Mama,' that impatient way she has with me, 'those things went out with bustles.' But there's no use sitting here listing the poor child's good features. She's just not pretty and I've never seen the man yet—except a devoted father—who'd stand off and take inventory of a girl's looks. If she's got a pretty face—or gives the impression of having one as I somehow managed to— nothing else matters."

"I don't believe you know as much about men as you pretend to. These days of shorter skirts, men're not so likely to begin at the face. I was young, we considered it a lucky day when we got a peep at a pair of pretty ankles, regardless of what was above."

"David, do be serious a minute. I came in here to try to think of some way you might handle things on this trip—"

"What's this solemn conference all about?"

"Sh-sh, Beth. They'll hear you on the porch. Close the door. Your company gone?"

"Just left. Now maybe I can get out of this tricolette and into something cooler."

"Come over here and sit down a minute first. Your Papa and I—"

"Needn't be so hush-hush. Fair and Bob've joined the young-sters now and when Fair and Glad begin competing—"

"I'm glad there's a match for Glad around—even if Fair is an old married woman. I've been trying to get a word alone with you all day, Beth—bout the way Glad and Fred're taking to each other. . . . I don't see why you have to laugh."

"I don't see anything else to do. What in himmel's name could you and Papa and I do about it if they are!"

"Just what I was telling Mama—"

"Now, David, you're as concerned as I am, whether you'll admit it or not."

"There's no reason for any of us being concerned. Ann Wes-ley knows what she's doing. Fred's either nothing to her or she's so sure of him she doesn't have to worry."

"Ah, Beth, when you've lived as long as I have you'll know there's no such thing as being sure about anything!"

"Why, Mama, you sound cynical! What on earth has Papa been doing!"

"Let it pass, Beth, let it pass. Your Mama's genuinely upset."

Smiling at us that way, she the parent, we the children! Sad thing about growing old, you can't make your children under-stand that you still have personal emotions, any emotions not connected with them. I don't suppose it's ever occurred to a one of them that Mama and I're still people in our own right. Come to think of it, Sister's assertion of self has given them a con-sciousness of her as an individual they don't have of us. They'd be surprised that this situation between her and Mama and me is as vital and painful to us as it was twenty-four years ago because Sister won't let it die.

". . . not sure I'd've brought one of my beaux home, sub-jected him to Fair's charms. But the way you've been telling me Ann Wesley's worked over Deeda this week, makes me fairly sure she's engaged to Fred. I can't see her coming home a week early—"

"She's not wearing his fraternity pin!"

"Wouldn't mean she was engaged to him if she were. What amazes me is his wearing it, grown-up as he is in other ways. Still, he told me he didn't get out of college till last June—had

406

to finish after he was released from the army. But, as I started to say, I can't see Ann Wesley's giving up a week in Richmond and coming home to work on Deeda for a guy she just likes. I tried to find out a little about it from her, when we were dressing for church, but she shut up like a clam. Then Fair came in and asked her if she and Fred were engaged and she said, 'You're a fine one, thinking I have to be engaged just because I have a man around!' "

"I thought surely, her coming out like that at the dinner table, saying she liked him because he was quiet, meant they were engaged, that he'd be speaking to your Papa at the first opportunity, but—"

"Mama, I've told you—Ann Wesley's no shrinking violet away from home. And having two here—Fred and me—who know that, she must've felt 'away from home' for a minute."

"Mama thinks a man wants just a pretty face. Why, I could count any number of downright homely married women in every town we've lived in!"

"You'll have to admit, though, Papa, if you think it over, every one of thum had money. *Or* intelligence enough to know that prettiness isn't important unless you're brought up to think it is. As most girls are in the South. A few I can remember in every town escaped such indoctrination and developed a personality that compensated for their snub noses or buck teeth. They're the ones *I* used to envy. I—"

"Why, baby, you haven't got a snub nose or—"

"No, but I haven't got a patrician nose like Glad's or perfectly even teeth like Fair's, say nothing of Cindy's Scotch lassie beauty. Neither has Ann Wesley. But what *I* used to envy were the girls who didn't care. I knew I couldn't be pretty but I couldn't see why I had to care so much that I wasn't. I had to get away from Fair's shadow before I could lose my self-consciousness and have a beau. But that's another thing might give you hope for Ann Wesley—northern men don't think prettiness is the only requisite in a girl."

"Maybe not, but as you said, you didn't bring your beaux home!"

"No, but I'd've had to chance it if I'd wanted to marry one of thum."

"Chance it! Then you *do* think—"

"Himmel, Mama, I don't know! But let's stop worrying about it. There's no danger Ann Wesley'll be another Deeda even if

407

she should lose—even if she never marries. She's capable of taking care of herself. Look at what she's done already—going off to Richmond on her graduating money and getting a job *not* teaching. There's something we *can* do something about I want to talk about, now I've got you two together. I want you to have a vacation together this summer, away from Deeda."

"Yes, I've been trying to persuade Mama again to come with me up to the old home in August. It's mighty embarrassing explaining to Kathy and Max every summer—"

"Now, David, how can I go and leave Sistuh alone!"

"You don't have to leave her alone, Mama. I'll be home—"

"Thought you were going to the University of Chicago this summer?"

"I am, but I'll be back the middle of August. Next summer I'm going abroad, hell or high water. That's why I want to do something for you this one. You look tired out and a rest at Humiston Hill with Papa is just what you need."

"There's Brothuh Waters, tooting out there right now! We'll have to talk about all that another time. David, you'll have to go comb your hair. It's all on end."

Talk about it another time! Give her time to think up another excuse for not going up with me. Why, Mama, why? If only you could give me a reason, I'd try to accept the loneliness of a vacation without you.

CHAPTER II

1

A<small>LL SO QUIET AND PEACEFUL AND FAMILIAR. IT'S HARD TO</small>
believe the year is 1922—if I don't look at that new
highway over there."

"Another half hour, Brother David, you'll know it's
there without looking. Little after five the trucks and automobiles'll be roaring past."

"Here on Humiston Hill though, Max, it all looks just as it
did twenty-eight years ago. Except that the foliage is thicker.
I see you keep it thinned out in places for a view of the mountains."

"Of Grandfather and Blowing Rock, Ellen. We've lost High
Brighten. Nothing I can do about the trees on that far hill. Yes,
was 1894 you were here last. As long a time between your visits
as between—"

"Oh, but I've wanted to come! Just seemed there was something every August to keep me at home. This summer's the first
I could—girls all away and Sistuh visiting Cindy. I wish I could
sit right here with you all now and wait for the sunset but,
Kathy, if you'll excuse me, I think I'll go upstairs and lie down
a little while before supper. I just saw Sukie go round the back
with an armful of corn and a basket of tomatoes I'd like to feel
rested enough to enjoy."

"Why, yes, Sister Ellen, you do just what you like. It's your
vacation as much as it's David's. Anything I can get for you?
Glass of nice fresh buttermilk or cool, spring water?"

"No thank you, Kathy. You're mighty thoughtful but that
nice fresh cool bed's all I need right now. Now, Max, don't you
get up! I can slip past."

"Ellen's kept her sense of fun all these years, I see." Max closing the screen-door, coming back to his chair. "It's the only
thing reminds me of the Ellen we used to know."

"You should've come to see us at some time during these

years, Max. Used to say you'd come if we ever lived in Raleigh, to see the State capitol, but—"

"Just as well he didn't—if he wanted to see the Ellen he used to know!"

"Now, Kathy."

"I wasn't going to say anything, 'now Max,' except that Ellen didn't have any sense of fun when I visited in High Mount. In 1903. And I doubt if she'd had it in Raleigh, Miss Ora's 'health having failed' as Ellen calls it, in Lynnboro. Thought at that visit, I'd never seen a woman change so in less than ten years. Of course, Ellen's prettiness was the kind that fades early—all due to her bright hair, bright eyes, and high spirits, and you couldn't expect any woman to keep those characteristics long, a creature such's Miss Ora'd become on her shoulders. Like the Old Man of the Sea."

"Kathy, if this is my vacation—"

"You just heard me say it's Ellen's too, and looking at the two of you, it's obvious she's in greater need of one. We women have to stand together and if I'd had any *idea* Ellen'd failed as she has, I'd've gone down and brought her up summer of '19, when she backed out of coming at the last minute."

"She went to visit Fair then. Sister Stanhope was driving down to Wrightsville Beach through the country and offered to drop her in Cameronville. Mama said she thought that'ud be more rest for her than taking the long train trip up here."

"Well, last summer you should've brought her, spite of—"

"She would not leave Beth alone with Sister, state Sister was in last summer. Said was enough, Beth having to give up her trip abroad."

"Well, Brother, I hope you've realized if you'd taken my advice nineteen years ago, gone back to the law, and handled this thing sensibly as a man of the world, Ellen wouldn't look so—wasted. That's the only word to describe it!"

"Kathy, I told you then nothing could make me give up God's ministry. And I'll tell you now I've never regretted ignoring your gratuitous advice nor that of anybody else. And that's the only kind of advice I've ever received!"

"Don't doubt that for one minute! Stubborn as ever you were. You'll admit, though, you did follow my advice eventually—in committing Miss Ora."

"Not until it was *my* decision. And it turned out to be wrong, advice *and* decision."

410

"To my way of thinking, after all Beth's confided in me the last few years, the authorities at the asylum were wrong."

"That's your way of thinking. Has nothing to do with the facts. You weren't there to see her, sensible as the nurses, making herself useful helping with the other patients. There wasn't anything the authorities could do but release her when Cousin Vincent—"

"Release her to cut her monkeyshines again—nobody but her sister and brother-in-law'ud put up with! It's a pity that 'Cousin' Vincent, as you call him, hadn't ever visited you, seen what I saw. Had, he wouldn't've acted in so cavalier a fashion!"

"Now, Kathy, let's stop all this. You're upsetting David. His hands're shaking. He comes up here to get away from it all. If I didn't feel so sad about it, I'd have to laugh at you two, making the feathers fly again. David, you should've taken that trip to Mississippi with Kathy and me last fall. We had a mighty good time, four of us together again, recalling our childhood here— you and Kathy always at loggerheads, both of you determined to be right, and Father—"

"Trouble with me then was I thought the sun rose and set in my big brother David. I didn't like having that feeling about any member of the masculine sex, even as a child. Had to fight it and him. Believe it'll surprise you, David, but I used to wish you weren't my brother so I could marry you when we were grown!"

"It certainly does. You covered up mighty successfully. Did notice, however, that you became respectful when I began reading law. Didn't think any girl was good enough for me."

"Of course I didn't! You were going to be governor some day and I was going to live in the governor's mansion and help you run the state. The way it should be run . . . Well, I've always been honest with myself. That's why I'm so healthy in mind and body. Now as I grow older, I find I'm prone to be honest with others. Now, that's a beneficial thing when it's a matter of foresight, but I want to beg your pardon for rushing in on angel-ground just now. I promise you, I'll not mention that subject again the next three weeks. I'll concentrate on building Ellen up on nice fresh eggs, rich milk, and—"

"Yes, Kathy, do that and we'll let bygones be bygones."

"David, *I* don't want to distress you but I know it's hard to see changes in a person you see every day and I noticed soon's

411

you stepped off the train that Ellen's not looking right well. Her skin's got a kind of gray hue. Has she been sick lately?"

"Why, no, Max. She has that chronic neuralgia. It comes and goes. Hasn't mentioned its bothering her lately, however. No, I'm wrong. Come to think of it, she did complain of it a little on the train. Had the porter close the window nearest her chair, thought there was a draft on the back of her neck. She enjoyed the trip though. She began talking to two girls had chairs near ours. It turned out they were old school mates of Gladys's—sorority sisters—going up to Blowing Rock. They wanted to know if Gladys was having as good a time being married and living in New Bern as she'd had teaching there and Mama went on to tell them about all her girls. Showed them those foreign postcards from Beth and the snapshots of her first granddaughter she was showing you."

"Ann Wesley hasn't brought her down for a visit yet, you say?"

"Not yet. Says she will in the fall, weather gets cooler. They have a little apartment way 'up town,' she says, overlooking the Hudson River where they get a good breeze and little Evans is thriving on it. Now that's one trip Mama's promised to take with me—up to visit New York City next spring!"

"I've written Ann Wesley I'm coming too—whenever the Woman's Club holds its convention there. Told her I hoped she hadn't lost interest in women's activities now she's started a family."

"No, but she says she's not determined to support herself any more, now she has her hands full domestically. Says she just redefined a Feminist as a woman who does her woman's work and something on her own besides."

"I'll have to go to the mat with her on that, far as some of us're concerned. If *all* women'd put themselves under men's thumbs, there wouldn't be any Feminism for her to redefine. Have to laugh, though, every time I think of her stealing such a march on you all, bringing her *husband* down, not even admitting he was a beau, because she 'had to prove marriage didn't have to interfere with a career'! I'd had the luck to've been born to this generation, I'd've gone her one better—proved that marriage and a dozen children didn't have to interfere with what *I* wanted to do!"

"You'd've had to pick your man mighty carefully even in this generation, get you one with no backbone, to do that." Max's

412

backbone stiffening, eyes fixed on Kathy's smooth and placid face. Expect those two make the feathers fly these days.

"Well, Fred's got plenty of backbone but he raised no objection when Ann Wesley kept right on with her work, right up to two months before little Evans was born. Seems a lot of northern women do that these days. . . . Ah, here they come! Rattle, bang, clatter, spoiling the peace of this countryside! Wasn't anything you could've done, Max, keep them from building that highway eighth of a mile away?"

"You've asked me that both times you've been up since 1920. Told you Kathy wouldn't even let me raise a protest."

"I would not. There's no sense in trying to block progress. The world's changing and we're in it. Nothing to do but go along."

"Father wouldn't have gone along, no matter if the county did have a right-of-way through his property! I can't get used to seeing old Grandfather Mountain lying over there serene as ever in the sunset and hearing all this racket."

"Every one of those conveyances, David, is filled up with neighborhood men—sons of boys and girls used to go to the Academy with us. They're coming back from work in the factories in town. Your quarrel should be with the inventors if you've got to have a quarrel. Not with folks who have to adjust to new ways of life the inventions bring. Automobiles made young people restless, got them away from the farm, but because of the automobile, they can still live in this community—"

"Sad thing is, all the big farms we used to know around here are breaking up. Can't get hired help any more unless you pay wages high's these furniture factories pay. Look at me here, able to cultivate less than half of what Father used to. And I couldn't do that, it wasn't for Sukie's boys having had enough travelling when they got out of the army, and for Jeb's middle one, bringing his family back from Philadelphia to where living's cheaper —no rent to pay, food 'all found.' "

"He wouldn't't've come back, though, David, in spite of Max's generosity if it hadn't been for my Ford and that highway. I promised him I'd see to it that the children got to school every day, rain or shine. And we've got good colored schools in this county. *I'm* on the board. By the way, how are they in Hertford County? Noticed somewhere those northeastern counties have the largest Negro population—"

413

"Miss Kathy, you all, supper's on the table. *Mistuh* David, do seem natural seeing you setting there. Where Miss Ellen?"

"She went upstairs to lie down a little while. I'll go tell her."

"Nosuh, you go right on in the dining room. Lemme go get Miss Ellen. Ain't had no time to carry-on with her way I used to. Look like she need me, too, make her laugh out big 'swell as fatten her up. Yesuh, I'll go get Miss Ellen."

❖　❖　❖

"Mama, you still asleep?"

"I haven't been asleep."

"I thought you were, I tiptoed up about an hour ago to ask you if you felt like coming down and you didn't answer. You mind if I turn up this lamp a little, see how to undress? Glad Kathy thought more of this old house than of electricity."

Yes, Lord, you've given me restraint if not the forbearance I asked you for. Mama'ud never guess from my tone how I'm seething inside. Now, just help me control the seething, the resentment. . . .

"You're not going to bed this early!"

"Why, it's eleven o'clock! Moon's up. Max and I walked down to the creek, to that site near the bridge where the panther sprang me, time I was riding out from town, fall of '81. Hard to believe wild animals ever roamed—"

"What'd you do with all the company?"

"They'd gone. Cousin Kim's family left round nine and Cousin Robert soon after. All sent their love to you. Made Kathy promise to bring you to spend the day sometime this week. I was afraid Cousin Robert trying to crank his machine, cussing like a trooper, would wake you up. Now that's one way to work off your wrath—if you're not a praying man!"

"No, I didn't hear a sound. Can't believe I was asleep though. This pain in my neck and head's kept me from even feeling drowsy."

"Any better now?"

"A little—right now."

"Remember where you put my nightshirts?"

"Sukie unpacked for us when she brought up my tea and toast. They must be in one of the bureau drawers. That bureau. I remember some old argument with Sistuh bout your clothes and those drawers, last time I was up here. Clearer memory, though, is of the pain I suffered then in this very bed."

414

"You remember anything else about the last time you were here?" Now, now . . .

"Nearly everything it seems. Coming back to this room, not a piece of furniture or an ornament changed, it's almost 'sthough I'd never left it, never lived all those years between my visits. Think I'd even feel young again, it wasn't for this neuralgia. Couldn't expect to look as young as Kathy, carefree life she's—"

"I wasn't thinking so much of this room. Or of the house. What I'm curious about is that day we all went to High Brighten. Day Sister broke her wrist in the surrey accident. Do you remember anything else about that day?" Too late. Devil's in me. "I mean anything not connected with your own pain and our loss?"

"Wish I could forget it. My blindness that day. If I'd been able to see your attentiveness to Sistuh was a lot more than brothuhly solicitude then, we might've been saved twenty-eight years of— Why're you standing there clutching that nightshirt that way? I wish you'd get into it and come on to bed."

"Not sure I am coming to bed. Way my heart's palpitating, I can't rest if I do."

"Too much excitement, getting back to 'the old home.' But let me be the invalid tonight and get some sleep—if I can. I don't think I've ever felt so played out. David, what has got into you! Standing there in your underwear glaring at me that way."

"Speaking of blindness, it seems you were not the only one handicapped by blindness that day. Kathy's just been telling me about you and Max. You—"

"Why, what does Kathy know bout Max and me?"

"—weren't blind for twenty-eight years—or more maybe—as I've been. Yes, it must've begun the very first time you came up here. A bride! I never remember hearing of Max's sparking a girl after that, for all of Father's prodding. Ha, I see now why Max never would come to visit us, why he was always writing and insisting you come up here with me. A lot more opportunity for carrying on a flirtation up here or whatever— Ellen! Stop smiling that superior way! Stop it! I've had about all I can stand in one hour. *Now you tell me the truth about you and Max as I told you, when you asked, about Sister and me.*"

"Well, don't stand over me that threatening way. . . . I wish I had something to tell, David. I like to see you mad like a *man*. Mad about something you think *I've* done. So mad you call me Ellen—have to realize at last I'm not just a part of you. Why,

415

I never had any *i*dea how pleasant it is to have a husband jealous!"

"Laughing's more than I can do right now. All I could do to control my anger while Kathy was talking. Couldn't have, maybe, if she hadn't taken it for granted I'd known all these years. But all I know now is what she's told me. I want to hear from your lips what went on between you and Max."

"Then stop that pacing up and down and I'll try to make up something worth this deceived husband act you're putting on. David, I didn't know you had it in you! Taking me for granted every day since I said 'yes' and now—all right, I'll be serious. If I can. Maybe you'd better give me a cue, though—tell me what Kathy said. And why."

"All began with Kathy's telling me about the will she wants to make. She wants to leave Humiston Hill to that Civic Club she's president of. Make a kind of community center of it with a library and lecture room, picnic ground, and so forth. Max won't agree to have his share go that way. Says if he passes on before you do, he's going to leave what he has to you in trust for the girls. Says they've never had as much as the Mississippi nieces and nephews and *you've never had the kind of life you deserved!*"

"Why, if Max wants to be clever's that, he could sell enough land to fix the girls up and still leave the house and grounds— David! You're shaking like a leaf. Come sit here on the bed, let me put this quilt—"

"No, Kathy wants the money from the land to go for the up-keep. Wants me to persuade Max our girls're well enough off now. I'll persuade him of a lot more in the morning! I'll tell him— It's a good thing he and I had that walk alone before Kathy—"

"You'll tell Max nothing. None of it's of any consequence. I'll be dead a long time before a strong, healthy man like Max is and I reckon Kathy can handle him far's the girls're concerned. I'm surprised she even brought up the subject, shocked's she looked when I got off the train today. Max, poor fellow, didn't seem able to look at me at all—after the first glance."

"Well, we all get older. It's your health they're concerned about. Think you don't look well. Want to—"

"Shush. Tell me *all* Kathy said bout Max and me."

"I wish you wouldn't couple your names that way! It's not

416

pleasant for a husband to feel jealousy I can tell you. Makes my blood boil, my own brother—"

"Was my own sistuh drained all the blood from me, seemed, that night you confessed how you felt bout her. You should be mighty grateful I'd discovered—and not till that day on High Brighten—Max loved me and that if I hadn't been married *to you, could've loved him*. Now, wait a minute—was realizing that made me understand how you could be—be attracted to Sistuh and love me at the same time. Was why I was sympathetic that night in Lynnboro. Why I was willing to start again. Thought if Max and I'd lived in the same house day after day maybe I couldn't've behaved as well as you did!"

"Ellen, *what happened between you and Max on High Brighten?*"

"Nothing happened. I told you nothing did. Was just that I caught Max looking at me *passionately* little while after he'd been telling me he'd never marry because the girl he loved was already married."

"You didn't—"

"Didn't what?"

"Well—kiss him?"

"No. But I wanted to. And if I had, it might not have stopped there—you and Sistuh off—"

"Ellen!"

"Now don't be such a simpleton. That's right, kneel here and hide your face. I didn't see the difference in a woman's kissing a man, *wanting* to lie with him and not actually doing it. Unless such behavior can hurt others concerned. Now, do be quiet a minute. I was shocked at myself thinking such things when it was you I loved. Had loved for ten years. Knew it was too late to love Max *that way*. And I understood men better than you did women. Didn't underrate my power over thum. At that age. I pretended I didn't see the expression in Max's eyes and turned my back till he could get control of himself. . . . Now will you tell me how any woman with no more intuition than Kathy has could know anything about *that?*"

". . . Seems she came—"

"Hush groaning, I can't hear you."

"Seems she came across a handkerchief of yours with those flowers we call Adam and Eve—"

"Because they're always together. Bellwood and trillium."

"—pressed together and sewed to a card laid in its folds—both your initials and the date written on the card."

"Where'd he keep thum?"

"In the Gray's 'Elegy' you sent him. Christmas present from us the first year we were married. Kathy was dusting his books, dipping into them, reading along the way she does. So when this matter of the will came up first, year or two ago, she told him her plans for Humiston Hill and he told her his and she asked him point-blank if you were the reason he'd never married. Just waiting, I suppose, for my heart to fail, take me off, so he could—"

"You haven't had to live with *that* hope, day after day, year after year, anyway. Go on."

"Max said yes you were. Was plain Kathy thought you'd confided in me whatever'd gone on between—now, Mama, don't cry. I'll try to understand. Prayed alone there on the porch before I came up that God'ud help me let bygones be bygones but I wouldn't be mortal if I could let this pass without getting to the bottom of it."

"I . . . can't help . . . crying . . . and laughing too. Think of having been . . . so . . . young . . . and now so . . . old. Poor Max . . . treasuring me in his heart all these years, then seeing me . . . Oh, I wish I'd held out against this trip way I have all the others . . . let him keep his illusion till the end. . . . If I'd once suspected he hadn't forgotten long ago—"

"Thing made me almost's mad as this revelation was Kathy's saying, matter-of-factly, it was a pity Max hadn't visited me in Bayport before I married you, said you might've taken Max and left me for Miss Ora and everybody'd been happy. I didn't ask her where she got that *i*dea—just walked out of the room."

"She got it when she visited us—even Kathy's got enough insight for that, I reckon, being right in the house with it. Cindy was just the only one ever blurted it out. Expect Kathy and Beth've talked it all over many a time. All the children understand it now—or think they do. Talk about it among themselves. What they'd never understand is that you could be jealous at your age."

"Be jealous and know how to remedy it too! You look sweet, propped up there against those ruffled pillows, your hair in two long braids—"

"Sukie did it. Said I ought to give Miss Kathy some of what I use to keep the gray out!"

418

"—and young, in this lamplight. You just wait till I get out of this nightshirt now!"

"David, not tonight! It can't bother you too much, be denied once these days—nights. All this's exhausted me more than—"

"You'll feel better, once I get close to you. I feel I've come back after a long journey away from you, brief's it was. . . . There, now . . . no better place this old heart of mine to stop beating than pressed against yours . . ."

❖

"Mama, that you groaning? Mama—?"

"It's this pain. Never had it like this before."

"Want me to get you an aspirin tablet?"

"They're—right here—"

"Got water?"

"Yes. But I've taken . . . two . . . doesn't help."

"Let me rub your neck and shoulder. Sometimes . . . You're sitting up! Lie back so I can reach you."

"Can't lie down. Head swims. Can't breathe."

"How long's this been going on?"

"Hours maybe. Dozed off after— Get the basin! I'm—so sick."

"Don't see how that can be, nothing but tea and toast. . . . Pshaw, where're the matches?"

"Hurry. You can see. Moon's—"

"That miserable chair! I'll wake up the house. . . . Here, Mama. I'll put the basin on the floor, hold your head."

"Oh, David, I'm so—sick."

"There now. You'll feel better. . . . I'll just get a wet cloth."

"Have to call the doctuh . . . can't stand . . . Sistuh's head hurts her this way, don't blame her . . ."

"Mama, don't lie in that position, it— Mama! Ellen! Ellen!"

❖ ❖ ❖

"Come with me now, Brother David. Lie down in my room. Try to get a little rest before it's daylight. Doctor Soddy and Kathy and Sukie'll take care of everything."

"Yes, Max, do get David out of here."

"Come now, Brother. You'll have a chill, spite of my warm bathrobe. Cover up in my bed and I'll get you a cup of hot milk."

"I prayed as I've never prayed before that God'ud let *this* cup

419

pass from me. All that hour, waiting for the doctor, my hand on her pulse . . . so weak . . ."

"Must pray now for strength to bear it. That's right, come with me now."

"But the telegrams must go. The girls. Sister—no, she's with Cindy. Better address it to her though. Hope Mama's got—hope Ann Wesley's address's in Mama's handbag. Some numbered street. Beth'll be with her tomorrow. Boat docking eleven o'clock."

"Now don't you worry bout anything. I'll see the telegrams go soon's the office opens at nine o'clock. You get a little rest, then you can tell me everybody should have one. No, not in there—that's Kathy's room. This way. I still have your old room. Moved in when you left home for good. Yes, right here. Used to sneak in here to sleep, though, you were away at college. Made me feel mighty big. Now you sit here in my big chair and I'll straighten the sheets, tuck you in."

"No, I can't lie down. Just put the lamp here on the little table, hand me your Bible. Consolations I've cited for others must be there for me. *Must* be."

"Yes, it'll have to be a case of physician, heal thy self, won't it? There, that comfortable? Now I'll just see where I left my Bible. . . . Brother David, it doesn't seem to be here in the bookcase. I'll—"

"New Testament'll do."

"Now I don't think I've owned just the New Testament."

"Then I'll see to it you do own one, I get back home. Home? Where's home now? Home was where Mama was. Was her face I saw, coming back from wherever I'd been. Not this or that parsonage. I never told her that, Max. Took it for granted she knew that."

"She did, Brother David, she did. I'm satisfied of that. Now, I'll go get the Bible for you. Then a hot toddy—if you'll drink it!"

"Yes. Weak though. Been taking a little at bedtime sometimes, last three years—since we moved to Allenford. Doctor there prescribed it, heart condition like mine. Heart condition like mine. High blood pressure like Mama's . . ."

"Now, David, nobody blames you. Mustn't let Doctor Soddy's outspokenness get to you. He's got no more tact than Kathy has. You couldn't take Ellen by force to see a doctor. Now you just sit right still a minute."

"But I've heard her say, several times this summer, she felt so let down. All comes back to me now—seeing her, after dinner last winter, drop down on the sofa in the sitting room, jump up worrying bout what Sister was doing, tiring *her*self out. Reckon was because she was younger than I am, never actually complained—"

"Now, Brother, Ellen'ud never've complained about your—your not thinking bout her health. She loved you too much just as you were. Now, you just sit right still. . . ."

Sit right still. Sit right still. Could lie still there by Mama's side. Lord, why not I too? Why not I too? You heard my words. No better place . . . Forever and ever, Lord, it could've been. Rigor mortis set in. . . . *Can't* sit still. . . .

❖

"Here's the Bible, Brother David. . . . Where'd you find that?"

"Your bookcase, Max. . . . Mama writes—*wrote* a mighty pretty hand. Better than any of her daughters. 'To Brother Max, with Christmas Greetings and Love from David and Ellen.' Yes, I recall now. She didn't think Gray's 'Elegy' a cheerful Christmas gift but she liked the imitation leather binding and the steel engravings and there wasn't much to choose from in Miss Belle's stock of Christmas books. Now where's that stanza—?"

"Let me have it a minute if you're going to read *it*. Have a habit slipping odds and ends, clippings and such, in my books. You might litter the floor, thumbing through."

"It's all right, Max. *It's* not between the pages. I have it here, in my hand. Linen's turned yellow, all color's gone from the flowers. You can still see what they were, though, can't you? Bellwood and trillium. I'll never forget the names of *those* flowers again. First and last conversation Ellen and I ever had, the names of flowers came up."

"David—"

"Sit down there on the bed, Max. It's all right. I'm not your big know-it-all brother any more. Just a poor know-nothing, a blind, blundering—ass."

"I didn't know you knew—didn't know anybody but Kathy knew—and she only here lately—how I'd always felt about Ellen. Since the first time you brought her up. She was so different from all the practical, nose-in-the-flour-barrel kind of girls

Father'ud pick out for me. Once I'd known her, I couldn't even look at a one of them. Told myself was just her prettiness and liveliness. Then the summer Miss Ora came up with you all, I saw such character—such patience and forbearance and generosity—as I'd never thought a pretty woman could possess. *You* don't doubt she had all those things!"

"No. Just wonder, though, whether she'd developed them all—just at that time. Have her own word—"

"I had my own eyes and ears. Wasn't just because I—was in love with her. She was too modest about her own virtues to even suspect that. A man gets over these things, though, in time—I would've married if ever another right girl'd come along. No, you mustn't hold any hard feelings. Ellen never knew."

"She did know, Max. *You* needn't be modest. If it's only for my sake. Was because she knew—that day you picked these flowers—how you'd felt about her and how she might've felt about you—under other circumstances—made her patient and forbearing and generous time I—I confessed—"

"Now, Brother David, you mustn't talk any more. I'm going to get that toddy for you."

"Just a minute, Max. I want to get this off— Just want to say, that is, I'm glad that you and Ellen had such a memory. Was because of it, was because of *it*, she laughed at me—laughed lovingly in all her pain—way she used to when we were young."

2

Help me to bear it, Lord. I am your obedient child now—and forever. Surely you can forgive that one second's rebellion. In that instant of finality when I cried out against You. Where are the scriptural consolations that've been at the tip of my tongue or pen for nearly forty years? Infant, child, young men and women cut off in their bloom, husband, *wife*—for each bereaved I've quoted the Word, our Father's special consideration for each of His children in each special sorrow. And to each message from You I've added—thought I'd added human understanding and sympathy. Word, words, words. Hollow. No understanding in them. And, therefore, no sympathy. Only a father hopeful of a son who died before he was

422

born or adults whose parents passed away have ever received genuine, heartfelt condolence from me. And if my tendering of sympathy was hollow, then the letters of appreciation from the bereaved that I've cherished have been perfunctory. As mechanical as my responses yesterday to kin and old friends. Responses to every effort at consolation in words, at least. Only the few who clasped my hand silently, looked into my eyes with tears in their own, knew there is no consolation in this earthly sphere for the finality of a loved one's death. Just mute acceptance. *Acceptance of God's will* . . .

Ah, Sister, it's hard. Maybe *I* would have to moan aloud if God'd ordained that for the rest of my life I must see my Beloved day in and day out just beyond my reach. Yes, there must be comfort of a sort, when I can find it, in the finality of death. It's been easier to accept the burden of Sister God put upon me than to bow meekly before His will in taking Mama from me. Yes, Lord, I hear! That's right—I never tried to accept Sister days, weeks, months, years ahead. I laid down the burden at night, took it up again each morning, and carried it without visible or audible complaint that anybody save Mama ever saw or heard and Mama wasn't another person but was flesh of my flesh, bone of my bone, an alter ego. . . . Now, who—?

"Brothuh Humiston, may I shake your hand?"

"Yes, sir."

"Don't remember me, do you?"

"Face's familiar but can't just recall—" Know you're a Baptist, though. Never've been able to put my finger on just what it is but I could count the few times I've been mistaken in spotting a Baptist.

"I'd've known *you* anywhere. If I hadn't just had the pleasure —I use that word advisedly spite of the sad occasion of your presence on the train—yes, just fell into conversation with your estimable brother in the smoking car. I caught the family resemblance soon's I got his name. Yes, I've got quite a memory for faces and names. It's a big help in a preacher's public life, no mistake about that."

"You're a preacher then?" A smoking preacher!

"Gave you a broad hint, didn't I? Yes, sir. Got the name now?"

"No, sir, afraid I haven't."

"Well, now, that's too bad, young-looking man like you. First glimpse of your light gray hair when I opened the parlor car door I wished mine'ud turn evenly all over. Yes, gives a more youthful appearance than splotches of iron gray, I must admit. Kept your figure too. Ha, ha—broad hint, I said a moment ago. That's about the size of it. Time you knew me I weighed no more than a hundred and thirty, forty pounds. Wife always says I was no more than a beanpole, she cast her lot with mine. Tell you a fact, I'm up to a hundred and eighty now, scales in the Charlotte depot can be relied upon. Yes, sir, I was a mere shadow my present self when I was called to High Mount, second charge I had, the November before you were moved to—to—don't tell me. I'll get it . . ."

If you don't stop snapping those fat fingers, I'll tell you. You've got a smile like a rubber-doll, a squeedunk the children used to call it, on, off, on, off, when you press it, not a crease left between the grimaces.

"Laurenton! Right?"

"That's right. I remember you now. Came to the Baptist congregation out on Jarvis Street."

"First Baptist it is now, a big, new church, green-tinted sandstone. Right in the center of town, site of Oldman's livery stable. Yes, we turned over the old Jarvis Street edifice to the mill folks, organized a Second Baptist. Why, Brothuh, you wouldn't recognize little old High Mount these days! Progress written all over it. Trees all down in the business section, thinned out in the residential. A real city apartment building on the site of the old Rose mansion the Daughters of the Confederacy took such pride in. Lions Club and Kiwanis take the cake for bringing a town up-to-date. I'm an honorary member of both organizations, happen to think of it. But say, look ahere now, you haven't mentioned my name yet!"

"No, you'll have to excuse me. Memory's a little more faulty than usual today."

"Don't mention it, Brothuh. I came in to tender you my deepest sympathy. Going to chat, though, it'ud be convenient for you to know what to call me, now wouldn't it? So I'm going to recall it for you. It's Boykin. B-o-y-k-i-n. Reverend J. C. Boykin. Ah, you remember me now, I see. Yes, sir!"

"Yes, I recall adding your name to the membership of the Preachers' Meeting group—I was secretary that year—in place of Brother Boyd Smith's. A fine old man, was a Ba— Yes, he and I worked hand in hand my three years in High Mount, building up an inter-denominational library for the first colored public school building there. Has he passed on?"

"Yes, the Lord called him five, six years ago, if I remember correctly. Now you speaking of Preachers' Meeting brings to mind my outstanding recollection of you. Tell you why: I was the youngest preacher in the group. Would've felt right insignificant, my first attendance, hadn't been for a negra preacher sitting back in the corner. Negra preachers have their own group now. Yes, sir, we're making progress in that town. But as I started to say, you were late arriving and rest of us couldn't do anything but chew the cud waiting for the secretary to read minutes of the last meeting. You came in finally, said right out you'd been delayed because you'd been to one of those—if you'll pardon the expression—bawdy houses used to be at the end of Railroad Avenue to pray with the fallen woman the Ledbetter boy'd shot the night before. *Fallen*'s the right word there, ha, ha. More sense than one, eh?"

"Word that's wrong is *woman*. Was a girl of sixteen. I'd baptized her—"

"Hold it, Brothuh! *Sprinkled*'s the word *you* want. Yes, sir!"

"I'd *christened* her, a baby, in Wilmington. She came from mighty good people. They'd treasured her *baptismal* certificate and she'd remembered my name through all her hardships. She wanted more than my prayers that day—wanted my active help in leading a new life. You may've known that I persuaded old Sister Rose—very mansion you mentioned—to take her in as nurse-companion. The last woman in my church I approached on the subject and the only one who agreed to help. A mighty hard-headed old lady. Didn't care what anybody said about her. . . . But I must tell you, that girl today is happily married, has a family of her own. Lives out in Ohio. Never fails to send me a Christmas greeting every year rolls around."

"That so? I didn't recall the outcome. I'll never forget, though, all us preachers sitting there, subject of the shooting uppermost in our minds but 'nary a one of us', old woman says, daring to refer to it. Then you walking in, calm's you please . . ."

You remember, Mama? It wasn't the first time you'd gone with me to answer such a call. Once was a phony, somebody playing a prank, and we were mighty embarrassed. The second time was in Queenston but no good came of it. The girl had a deep cold, thought she was dying of pneumonia. We took her to the parsonage. In the curtained hack we had. Was the middle of the night and she was sobbing, thanking us for saving her from a life of shame. From dying in shame, she put it. I was always grateful to Sister for taking her right in her own room in that cramped little parsonage, giving up her own bed and sleeping on a cot two nights. And couldn't do enough for her in the daytime. Waiting on her, making mustard plasters, bringing hot this and hot that. Had her cough cured by the next day. At nightfall banging on the front door, Beth running to answer it. Fellow bellowing, "Where's Sadie?" Sadie heard him, ran down the stairs in her night dress, Sister after her, clutching at her, begging her to come back and lead a good life. But the fellow—a tobacco auctioneer—threw off his overcoat, wrapped the girl in it, picked her up bodily, and dashed out to the waiting hack before I could get from the sitting room to the front door, Fair, Cindy, and little Ann Wesley getting under my feet, pulling at my coattails, clamoring to know what it was all about. Didn't know how to tell them—you, Mama, up in our room putting baby Gladys to bed. They all ran to Sister but I didn't know till a few years ago what her explanation was—when Beth said she hadn't answered the door after dark from that night till she was nearly grown, was "so afraid a man would grab her and make her go live with a lot of men like she was married to them all." Yes, that was just another instance of the truth of what I've always contended—if Sister'd had somebody dependent on her all her life, to do for as she did for that Sadie she might've continued to be as fine a woman as she was a girl. If God'd seen fit, Mama, to let this stroke paralyze you rather than take you from me, I believe you'd've had a fine nurse for the rest of your life. No, no, it might've been harder for me to see you lying helpless. Been harder for you, never giving up to a cold, not a day in bed since Gladys was born . . . Ah, Max, glad to see you coming, stop this fellow's harangue!

" '. . . refuge and strength, an ever present help in time of trouble.' And when you meet again on that happy shore, clothed in spotless raiment, a harp—Why, here you are! Got enough of 'the foul weed' to last you awhile, eh, Mistuh Humiston? Just tendering a little consolation to my old friend here, your good brothuh. Now maybe he'd like time for mediation and silent prayer, you and I could settle down—"

"I'm going to have to ask you to excuse us, sir, for the time being. David, the dining car's open. If we go right in, porter says we can find a table at the far end where you won't be disturbed."

"Yes, I feel the need of a little nourishment now. Good-bye, Brother Boykin."

Pump, pump, pump. Pat, pat, pat. "You ever get to High Mount, look me up, the Methodists give you a chance, and I'll do the same by you I ever get to—by the way, where is it you're stationed now?"

"Allenford. Hertford County."

"That so? Think I've heard of it. Well, well, we can't keep the better-paying charges forever, can we? Age creeps up on all of us. Can't see what your bishop's thinking about, though, man looks in the prime of life—by the way, knew there was something I had in mind to ask you—your good brothuh here couldn't tell me. Your sister-in-law's poor health. Hope it's improved some these latter years?"

Yes, Mama, I see you winking. You're with me still. . . .

"Sorry, sir, I can't hear you in all this rumble. Good-bye."

❖

"Telegrams for you, sir. Handed on at Greensboro."

"Thank you."

"You comfortable, sir? Get you a pillow?"

"Yes, porter. Get him one. Might take a little nap."

"Yes, *sir.*"

" 'Appreciate acceptance our plan. All arrangements made. Continued sympathy from all your bereavement.' P. F. Doyle, Chairman Board of Stewards.

"Now read that, Max, and tell me how they knew where to reach me."

"Why, Kathy told them at the telegraph office, had it forwarded care of this car. See—car number's on it. Well, that relieves your mind—where to lay Ellen to rest."

"Yes. Me, too, in God's good time. I hated to go against Kathy's wishes but somehow—don't know just where I got the *i*dea—just had a feeling Mama'ud feel lost there at Humiston Chapel surrounded by three generations of our family. And wherever she's resting will be right for me. Allenford's accessible for Fair, Cindy, and Gladys now. They'll look after the plot when I'm—"

"What're your other two messages?"

"Oh . . . This from New York. From Beth. 'Ann Wesley

427

and I will be with you in Allenford Friday morning. Fred taking Evans to his mother in Vermont. Sends his love with ours.' God's hand in that, Max! Beth'd first planned to stay in London another week, then suddenly decided to sail with a friend coming earlier and picked up a stateroom somebody else'd turned in. I don't believe I could get through the next few days without her. Mama and I used to think Beth was just a little overbearing with us, no family of her own to fuss over, but she's mighty dependable."

"Yes, you're fortunate in all your girls, David. You can spend your time visiting around when you have to retire. I've been wondering about the immediate future, though. You think Beth'll give up her work, keep house for you? Miss Ora, I reckon, will want to go back to Bayport. Can't expect— Excuse me. Forgot you had another."

"Yes, this is from Sister again. From Allenford this time. 'Parsonage in readiness your sad home coming. Everybody thoughtful and sympathetic our great loss. Love and affection from the girls and me. Ora Fanning.' "

Ora Fanning. Now why—at this late date—should she go back to that signature? *Sister* would've been the natural— No, no, God wouldn't add *that* to my suffering! Why, she's an old, old woman.

"Here's your pillow, David. You let the porter lower your chair back and see if you can get a few winks before we have to change at Raleigh."

"Yes, sir, might just get in *forty* winks. You just sit right still, I fix this fine for you, yes, sir."

❖ ❖

Your du-ty, your du-ty, your du-ty, click-clack, du-ty, click-clack. . . .

"Your duty to your family and to the Cypress City church, Brother Humiston, as your Board of Stewards sees it, compels me to make this suggestion . . ."

Didn't dare make it to my face. Had to take cover in a letter. Never dared mention it again, either, when the letter got no answer. Got the point, though, the very next Sunday when my New Testament scripture reading was only one verse from Paul's first letter to Timothy: *For if a man know not how to rule his own house, how shall he take care of the*

428

Church of God? Got it with extra emphasis at the next Stewards' Meeting when I left no doubt in any of twelve minds about my ability to take care of the Church of God. I read statistics of my accomplishment in the two previous years. And there wasn't a dry eye in the congregation when I preached my farewell sermon the following December, and voices broke singing "God Be with You Till We Meet Again." If I could've brought myself to answer such interference with my personal life—family supported, pastorate flourishing—I would've told them all that my first duty was to my God and my conscience, that there was no meaning in any other duty if I failed in the primary one.

Some people—ladies and men in different places—have told me outright that my sense of duty to my wife's sister was an inspiration and daily help to them in regard to in-laws living in their homes. It was a help to me to know that some good'd evolved from my suffering. No, the only sin I've never felt absolved from since I took up my ministry was listening to advice from Doctor Stewart and Beth about the asylum business. If I'd been honest with myself at that time, hadn't had Doctor's concern for Mama's health to hide behind, I would never've decided as I did. I listened, not only for the sake of Mama's welfare but for the sake of my own selfish pride. I wanted to play host to the Annual Conference. And then as though it weren't enough to've got Mama's signature on the commitment papers and all arrangements made for Sister's departure, I let the Devil himself get hold of me in that awful hour before dawn on the day Sister was to leave. In that store-room where murder *had* been committed half a century before by a minister of the gospel. Yes, I got an understanding of and sympathy for murderers in a righteous cause no other Christian preacher can possibly have. What stayed *my* hand a second later was a Voice. Whether God's directly or God speaking through the spirit of old Pastor Gillespie I've never known. Makes no difference which it was. I heard, as unmistakably as I heard my Call on the hillside, "Thou Shalt Not Kill!" Words I'd repeated how many times but'd never heard before. Words meant for Unknowns the world over now meant for *me*. Thundered at *me* from the rafters of that blood-stained room. My hands fell from Sister's shoulders and she in a heap at my feet. "Yes, kill me, Brothuh David, kill me. Oh, oh, oh, kill me and have done with it all!" Clutching my knees, pressing her face against my thigh till I felt the wet of her tears through the cloth of my trousers. Begging, pleading, "Kill me for mercy's sake, Brothuh David . . . nobody'll ever know. Hold me tight again till my breath's gone . . . throw me from the window . . . nobody'll ever know . . . I didn't do it myself." Her hands crawling up to my waist, pulling me down. But I was safe then. God had me safe. Sister could've begun at the beginning of her vile accusations again, gone straight through them, from my deception in respect to her, through the names and dates of my probable deceptions of other women, right up to my *asking Miss Claus to make a suit for me so I could undress before her and do she didn't know what else.* Vengeance is mine, saith the Lord, I could've quoted then to the spirit of Pastor Gillespie, all understanding sympathy vanished for his blind and righteous rage, coming up to this room with broth and Bible to minister to the body and soul of that poor slave girl wavering between life and death, finding her whimpering beneath the heavy body of that scoundrel overseer, grasping a poker from the hearth and smashing away till brains and blood befouled the bedclothes. . . . I lifted Sister tenderly then, laid her down on the bed, stroked her head till she, as spent as I, moaned almost inaudibly. Back with Mama, though, my Sin was rampant again and I tried to tell her all I'd felt in that other room and you, Mama, stroked *my* head, and said, "The very *idea*, your comparing yourself to a murderer—why, you couldn't hurt a flea." But I've thought, Mama, the day I could bring myself to confess the whole truth of that dawn to you, I'd feel relieved. Now you've left me to bear that spiritual burden along with the physical burden of . . .

"David?"

"Yes, yes, what is it?"

"I hate to disturb you, but a lady who got on the train at Burlington just motioned me to her chair and asked if I thought she could clasp your hand. Seems she lost her husband a year ago. Named Plyer—Tyler—not quite sure which."

"Why, yes! Sister Tyler from Silverboro. I'll come right along."

3

Ah, the times I've gone from a cemetery to a home bereft of a loved one, never once suspecting the agony beneath the wan smiles of gratitude "for the comfort of my presence and my words." I've no words, no comfort, for myself now. Nor for the girls sitting here in their white dresses and hats, shedding the tears all of them but Cindy held back in the church and at the cemetery . . . here in this last of parsonage parlors that piano, pictures, ornaments and cushions made Mama's, make a kind of homelike place for me now that she's gone. She didn't seem to care about personal possessions these past years but I can remember her disappointment in those first movings when things that'd been presents to her had to be left behind. Yes, here we are all together as she loved to have us, Mama herself absent for the first time. How often I've heard her say, "All my girls under the same roof again, I know how an old hen feels, her brood under her wing."

"I declare, I've never seen so many beautiful designs in my life and I've been to more funerals than anybody else in this family—except Papa."

"Yes, Cindy, you were just a little slip of a thing, you used to beg me to take you to funerals I conducted in the country. It used to worry Mama."

"You always asked me to go along, Brothuh David, to keep Cindy from falling in the open grave, she'd get so close to the edge peeping in."

"I still go to every Methodist funeral in Richton, out of respect to Papa. Now, Miss Fair, you needn't cut your eye round at Beth that way! If you showed more respect for Papa in Cameronville, went to a funeral occasionally instead of all those card parties and—"

"Please don't talk about funerals. I never want to see another white gladiola or purple aster or smell another lily!"

Sister dabbing at her eyes. "Your Mama would've liked thum, Ann Wesley. You were too little to remember the gardens she used to have in every parsonage yard. I never did understand why she lost interest in gardening, she got older. She didn't even mention starting flower beds here, as much space and rich soil as there is around this big lawn and colored boys ready and willing to work for twenty cents an hour. But it ever was hard to get an explanation from Ellen as to why she did this or that."

"I'm inclined to agree with you, Ann Wesley, about the color of the flowers people sent today. I always remember Mama's planting bright flowers. Not many I could remember the names of, though."

"And I know just how you feel, baby, bout the cloying odor of those big lilies. Not since *my* mother died, when I was just a little thing, have I been able to bear the sight or smell of magnolia blossoms." Voice quavering, black-gloved fingers clutching at Ann Wesley's shoulder.

"First memory I have of Mama was connected with a magnolia blossom. The Sunday afternoon I met her, at Little Brookside. I'd driven out—"

"Why, no, Brothuh David!" Voice strong, censorious. "You didn't drive out that day. You rode that mare Esther you were so proud of. . . . But we'd better not begin reminiscing now. I think the ladies've about got supper on the table for us. We mustn't hold thum up—some of thum have been here all day."

"Yes, let's have the house to ourselves as soon as possible. It's been like Grand Central Station ever since Ann Wesley and I got here."

"Hush, Beth, they'll hear you. Always remember your Papa's saying, he was a young man, you shouldn't make a personal remark within fifty feet of your subject."

"I'll whisper then. Papa, we all want to hear your reminiscences when we can be alone. I suppose Fair and I're the only ones who can remember Mama when she was young but I'd like to get some *idea* of her as a girl."

"Why, Beth, Ellen was just like Fair as a girl. Brothuh David and I have always said that. She didn't have Fair's regular features but—"

"Yes, I can remember people in Lynnboro telling me how like Mama I was." Fair taking her handkerchief from eyes the color Mama's used to be. "And I used to beg her, when I was a little older, to tell me 'about when she was a girl' but she always said 'Bye and bye, baby, I will—now I must see about dinner,' or something like that."

"Yes, I'd like to recall all I can for you girls. Mama was all that Brother Simpson said she was, in his eulogy this afternoon

432

—'an earnest and devout Christian, a faithful servant of the Lord.' But he's been Presiding Elder of this district just since December and he couldn't know that in her quiet way your mother was a great woman and if I can give each of you some insight into her character—" Now, now, Mama, I'm not going to say any more, Sister listening. "I've been thinking while we've sat here talking—wondering if the most influential day of a person's life isn't the day after his—or her—death. Seems that not until then—"

"I don't like to be 'interruptous,' Brothuh David, but we should all get our hats off and be ready for supper when the ladies ring the bell."

"Yes, Sister, that's right. You must be mighty hot in that high collar and crêpe veil."

"I haven't minded the heat, Brothuh David. Least I could do for Ellen now was show my devotion and sorrow by wearing deep mourning. Was all right for the girls to wear white but—"

"Now, Miss Ann Wesley, where do you think you're going! Stairs're in the other direction, this parsonage!" Cindy's everyday voice again.

"I'm going on the porch for a breath of fresh air!"

"She's loony's they come. I haven't seen her shed a tear all day. Always did think she thought more of Deeda than of Mama."

"Cindy, hush!"

"Well, I don't know about that, Cindy, but Ann Wesley's always been more like a daughter to me than any of the rest of you somehow. Not that all of you haven't been mighty sweet to me. Now that I haven't a brothuh or sistuh left in this old world, I don't know what's to become of me."

Gladys going to her, leaning over her chair. "Now, Deeda, don't you cry. You have five nieces left. Come on upstairs with me. I'll help you take off those hot old clothes."

"I'll try to bear up, Gladys, well's I can. But what's to become of me I don't know. Wait a minute, baby, don't pull at me that way. There's something I want to say—I just want you all to know I can find a little corner somewhere. I can't get back my home I sold so I could be with your Mama, help her bring you all up, but . . . furniture from it's still stored in the attic at Brookside . . . and . . ."

"Here, Deeda, take my handkerchief. Yours is all wet."

". . . I never once thought I'd ever need that furniture again. Always thought I'd go first, Ellen's health so good and

433

mine so undependable. Long as she lived, I felt I could count on a home, but now—"

"You'll always have a home here—or wherever I am, Sister. Don't let that worry you."

Now, now, what did they expect? That I'd turn her out in her old age? Beth staring at me as though I've lost my mind, Fair and Gladys startled but looking just a little . . .

"Well, Brothuh David, you hadn't said anything. I didn't know what your plans were. But if I can make things easier for you, you know I'm ready and willing to help any way I can. . . . Yes, baby, I'm coming with you—just wonder where all the menfolks are, supper about ready. I haven't seen Max since we got back from the cemetery."

"Max went for a walk. Said he thought this little town must seem as foreign to him as anything I saw in Europe this summer. Said he can't get used to seeing so many black faces. I think Bob and Whit walked down to the station to ask if Ann Wesley's Pullman reservation had come through. Papa, let's you and me take a little stroll, see if we can find Uncle Max."

"Why, Beth, Max can't get lost and your Papa's worn out. Besides, here's Sistuh Doyle right now to tell us supper's ready!"

"It certainly is, Miss Ora. We did our best to make it as appetizing as we could for you all. Come right in now— But you'll want to take off your things! You go right along, take your time. I'll see that nothing gets cold."

A kindly soul. She was mighty fond of Mama the three years we've lived here and Mama didn't seem to class her with "the old sisteren" but I wish her eyes didn't gleam so behind those spectacles as though she enjoys a funeral as much as a wedding.

"That's mighty thoughtful, Sistuh Doyle."

"Don't mention it, Miss Ora. Seems like the least we can do for dear Sistuh Humiston is see to it that her family's comfortable as possible this saddest of nights. Now, Miss Ora, why don't you let me help you off with your things right here? No use your climbing the stairs."

"Thank you, m'am, but I'd better go on up with the girls. They get up there to themselves, there's no telling how long they'll take and you ladies must be mighty tired."

"Now don't you think about us! Just occurred to some of us maybe you all'ud like to be alone and together soon's possible so we thought we'd just do what we could and leave you. I brought my Flora along to help Maggie with the dishes. And I'll be over bright and early in the morning to get the platters and bowls, take thum back to their rightful owners. Never trust colored to do that, funerals *or* weddings, and I don't want you and Miss Beth to be bothered with a single solitary thing."

"That's mighty sweet, lady. I don't know what I'd do without you."

Sounds just like Mama! I didn't know Sister could be so gracious and outgoing, so at ease. If Mama's generous spirit can inspire Sister to more sociable living, maybe, Lord, I can get through what future years You have allotted me. . . .

"Brothuh David, you dozing over there? I'm going upstairs now, hurry the girls down. You better go on in the dining room and begin carving that big guinea hen."

"That's being done in the kitchen, Miss Ora. Brothuh Humiston, you sit right still and wait till your ladies come down."

❖ ❖ ❖

This is going to be the hardest night of the three, Mama, thinking of you out there alone. The two nights you were above ground were hard enough for me, seeing you straight and still in that narrow casket. Weren't for God's infallible word, I couldn't've convinced myself you were just sleeping, straight and still on all that white satin as you've never slept in a bed. . . . "Mama, can you unbend your knee a little? It's in the small of my back." . . . "Mama, could you turn on your other side! Your elbow's jabbing me." . . . "Mama, move a little closer, it's mighty cold tonight." . . . "Mama, move over to your side of the bed, too hot to be generous with my side tonight." . . . "Mama, you asleep? Can't get my mind off this, that, or the other thing, have to quote a few psalms aloud." Yes, now for the first time I see some point to this new-fangled idea of twin beds. When one goes, the other can't feel quite so abandoned as I've felt these three nights. And for all the girls' efforts, not a one of them can understand how I've suffered lying alone through the dark hours.

I can understand and sympathize with each of them, though, because I felt the same regrets for my behavior in the past, when Mother was taken. Believe of them all, Ann Wesley's the most conscience-stricken. Felt mighty sorry for her, she came to me

435

this morning. "Papa, I never once thought I wouldn't be able to tell Mama, some day, that all I did for Deeda was for *her!* I hated being called Deeda's child from the time I can remember—even when I loved Deeda, all the petting and spoiling I got those summer vacations I was sent off with her to Seven Springs and Bayport. But I could never tell Mama—even when I was little, I'd've felt 'two-faced' taking all Deeda's babying and admitting I loved Mama best. It used to make me furious playing hide-and-seek in the house on rainy days and Glad and I would run in the sitting room to hide under Mama's and Deeda's wide skirts where the other children could never find us. Because Glad always ran to Mama's and I *had* to take Deeda's. Just once I remember getting under Mama's. I don't know how it happened. But every time since when I've felt proud and triumphant about anything, been sure the world's a wonderful place, I've had the feeling I had hiding under *Mama's* skirts that one time—I've literally felt the silk of her black petticoat rubbing against my cheek. I have no memory of Deeda's atall— except the memory of resentment of having to hide there. Deeda never held hers out in a welcoming way, even pretended she didn't notice our coming, but Mama'ud smile and nod at Glad, put down her sewing, and hold out *her* skirts like a mother hen spreading her wings. Mama did understand about my telling Deeda I was married before I told her or you, didn't she, Papa? I hadn't once thought she didn't till Cindy said today that'd hurt her more than anything I ever did. How else could I've got Deeda normal before Fred came down the first time except by giving her an advantage over you and Mama then? All I've felt for Deeda since I was ten or twelve has been pity. She *has* been just as alone as she's always said she was."

Yes, I wish Ann Wesley and Mama could've got together at last. I doubt if they ever could've though. Ann Wesley couldn't know without being told and Mama could never've told her. But if ever a baby were handed over for adoption, our fourth was handed over to Sister. Nobody could've blamed Mama, carrying a baby in her body she wasn't strong enough to carry easily, carrying in her heart and mind the knowledge of my perfidy, sick with shame about Sister's first attack and that attempt to choke her, then, when by God's grace she'd lived through Ann Wesley's birth, seeing no way out for any of us till she came upon Sister bending over the cradle trying to coo through her tears at the two-weeks-old infant. "I'd cut off my right hand, David, if that would help her and us, but she couldn't coo at and fondle an amputated hand. Sistuh's always loved little helpless things—baby chicks, kittens, babies—so I said on the spur of the moment, 'Sistuh, Doctuh's told me I must give up nursing Ann Wesley. If you could just tend to her bottles, it'ud be a mighty big help,' and, David, you should've seen her face!" And the cradle was moved into Sister's room the very next day so that she could feed Ann Wesley at night and she didn't have her second attack for nearly three years, not till after Gladys was born. . . . Gladys coming to me grieving because she hadn't insisted harder that Mama come for that long visit in New Bern. I couldn't tell her it was my fault Mama hadn't gone, I demurring, complaining about my heart—justly, Lord, but selfishly— saying I didn't want to be left with Sister *weeks* on end. I did console Gladys a little maybe, telling her she'd given Mama more happiness the past few years, made her laugh more, than anybody else had. Fair regretting the times she'd left Mama alone with Sistuh while she went off to house parties. . . .

Tap, tap, tap. "Brothuh David, you all right?"

"No, Sister, but I'm comfortable, if that's what you mean."

"Not too hot?"

"No, there's a little breeze in here."

"I'll open your door if you want me to. I've got the girls quiet at last."

"No, it's all right."

"Did you find the milk and crackers I put there on your table?"

"Yes, they're here."

"Well—I hope you get some sleep. Good night."

"Good night, Sister. I hope you rest well."

"I'll try, Brothuh David. You call me, though, if there's anything I can do for you, you hear?"

"Yes, I will, Sister, but I can't think of anything there'ud be."

"Good night, then."

"Good night."

"I've got the girls quiet at last." Mama's own words again. I used to tease Mama when she said that, told her she was the one couldn't let the girls stop talking when she got them home.

I don't believe Sister could've had much trouble getting them quiet. Cindy's the only one who seems to enjoy talking to Sister because in Sister she knows she has a willing ear for all the odds and ends of scandalous gossip she picks up, the illnesses she knows about, the accidents and crimes she reads about in papers. . . . No, no, Lord, take *that* selfish thought out of my mind. A pledge to keep I have, the burden mine to bear. Even if Hal would consent to such an arrangement, I expect he'd rather give up lodge meetings, playing pool, or hanging around the drug store and stay home every night or take Cindy to the picture show every time she wants to go, than have an old lady like Sister in his home, company for Cindy. No, I hope the thought of passing my cross on to one of my sons-in-law never enters my head again. . . . It was mighty thoughtful of those three young men to insist they be the ones to go off to sleep these two nights and leave the girls here together. Expect Bob and Whit fixed it to go together to Sister Doyle's—they're as congenial a pair of brothers-in-law as I've ever seen. Don't reckon Hal minded going to Sister Bizzell's, whether or not Cindy decided to go with him, because it'll give him a chance "to clinch that deal" he initiated when Sister Bizzell admired his new machine standing in front of the parsonage. Oh, Mama, Mama, how I wished I'd told you of my plan! Of some day rewarding Hal's effort to sell me a Ford. I thought when we came to Allenford I could learn to run the thing on these flat open roads. Only thing made me put it off was the thought of Sister—of the fact that I'd have to remember to invite you both to take a ride, to have to hear you insist that Sister sit in the front seat with me. . . .

4

At last! I've been trying to find you alone all morning. Uncle Max get off all right?"

"Yes, train was on time. I'm sorry he felt he had to leave so soon. I enjoyed having a man and a contemporary around, aside from the fact that he was Max. Sit down. You remind me of Mama, running breathlessly to the study."

"I'm fleeing external pressure, not internal. . . . Papa, I'll never forgive myself, not noticing those signs of extreme tension in Mama when I was home in June. I wouldn't've known what they meant but I should've suspected something was wrong and called in Doctuh What's-his-name here. But I was so absorbed in my own plans, getting ready to sail, I noticed no more than that she looked more tired than usual. Did no more than make her promise she'd keep Maggie in the kitchen, Deeda or no Deeda."

"Yes, she mentioned that promise to me every time Sister complained that Maggie was lazy or was eating us out of house and home. It gave her a lot of pleasure, Beth, your getting to Europe at last. If anybody's to be unforgiving, it should be me. Right here and—"

"But, Papa, that's why you couldn't see the change in her—being here, seeing her every day, you wouldn't notice—specially when she was always bragging that she was never sick. That, I see now, was her reaction to Deeda's hypochondria. Besides, I've come to the conclusion nobody worries about anybody who doesn't worry about himself—herself. We're all so self-absorbed we're callous even about those we love. As long as they'll let us be. I suppose, too, children look upon their parents as permanent fixtures—maybe husbands and wives do too. Always having taken them for granted, we can't—"

"Ah, Beth, when you're as old as I am, you'll know that at our age nothing is taken for granted. Nothing's sure—except the youth that's passed. We're on the crest. Nowhere to go but down. The only thing keeps us moving is merciful ignorance. We don't know when we'll take the final step. I said merciful ignorance. I don't know, I don't know. Sometimes I've thought the criminal condemned to death has the advantage—man's given him information God denies the well-behaved."

"But hope of reprieve must spring eternal even for him. I think I'm getting old enough, though, to see your point. I've felt older ever since I read Uncle Max's wire. As though I belong to another generation now."

"Yes, and you'll feel it absolutely when God calls me. As I did when both of my parents were gone. It's a sobering fact we have to experience to understand. Doesn't seem possible that people who were my age now when *I* was a young man could've looked so substantial and felt so ethereal. That unsure feeling comes just after middle age, or did with me, and was the only symptom I had of growing old. You'd be surprised how

439

the strength and intensity of other emotions don't lessen much —but I'm rambling on and you've got something on your mind you've got to say. Your eyes always seem to get bluer—"

"Yes, I have, Papa. And if I don't say it in a hurry, we'll be interrupted. I want to talk to you before the others have to leave. Fair's decided she'd better go home with Bob this afternoon, after all. She called Mollie long distance just now and Bobbie has a cold."

"I'm sorry to hear that. The more of you the better for me the next few days. I'm thankful that *you*'ll be around for another month!"

"Longer if necessary, Papa. I could arrange to take my sabbatical this year and—"

"Stop right there, Beth! Your work's as important to you as husband or child is to the others. The first thing I thought— when I could think atall—was that you were not going to share my burden."

"It doesn't have to be a burden, Papa—to you or to anybody else. Not if we use a little common sense—and use it quickly before the old pattern of doing nothing, going on, enduring, re-forms. And that pattern *is* broken now, Mama's going has broken it. In spite of that declaration of yours to Deeda before supper last night! I think even she can be made to understand that it was no time for you to make decisions and promises. You shocked us all."

"I saw that in your face, but it seemed to me Fair and Gladys looked relieved, and I expect Ann Wesley would've if she'd been in the room at the time."

"They may've been, momentarily. Not a one of us has thought of anything but Deeda's future the past three days. We confessed that last night. We talked till nearly daylight— once we got Cindy off with Hal, and Deeda in her room. Huddled on my bed in the dark, whispering like conspirators. We all feel alike about it, Papa. We cannot leave Deeda here to worry and bore you. It was bad enough for you and Mama together but at least you had each other, some relief from Deeda's atrophied mind. We hit on something we think'ud work—there's Miss Mary Sue living alone in Bayport, needing companionship, writing Deeda two or three times a year asking her to come for a visit. Mama told me in June Miss Mary Sue hadn't stopped asking her even after Uncle Vincent had her down there and she knew the form Deeda's neurosis takes.

Miss Mary Sue hasn't much and Deeda's board and room'ud be a boon to her. We'll all help if—well, let that pass for the moment. I don't know what Deeda's little capital amounts to but every one of us feels we owe her more materially than we could ever repay. And we'd all go down to see her. Fair says she'd love taking the boys down there for the whole summer, stay at the old Swain house and Bob'ud come down for weekends. What do you think? I don't want to press you—just hoped the others could have some *idea* of a plan before they go."

"They have it, Beth—have had it as definitely as it can be put. Wait now! *I've* heard you out because I—well, I just wanted to know what you girls did think after all these silent years. Wanted to know each of you, as only the reaction to such a situation as this can reveal a person. . . . I may've failed in bringing you up to go in the directions I would've had you go but I see now there's nothing lacking in character. Not a one of you is vindictive or even disloyal, no matter what Sister's done to you."

"May be more in heredity than it's fashionable to think right now! No, the environmentalists'ud win again! It's the example you and Mama set us, of course. And it extends far beyond Deeda too. Comparing notes last night, it came out that each one of us has had the same experience: wherever we are, we're the ones people in trouble come to. And we're under a compulsion to pretend sympathy whether or not we feel it—because of those hours with Deeda, listening, cajoling, boosting. We out-tact the proverbial southern lady on occasion because beyond hurt feelings we see a dark corner and a huddled figure and hear that moaning. Glad says she's stuck for life with the biggest bore in New Bern—saw her sitting alone, looking sorry for herself, at the first party she went to there, and just had to go over and be nice to her."

"Well, I'm glad some little good has come out of it all for somebody. And, as I should've said just now speaking of character, not a one of you seems to harbor resentment against Mama and me for putting our duty to Sister ahead of a—a normal home for you. Except for the mention you once made as to why you've never married, I'm afraid Mama and I let our own suffering blind us to the effects Sister's affliction's had on all of you—Ann Wesley's resentment of Sister's partiality for her; Fair's spending her summers on a round of visits when she'd rather've been home reading at least half a day—now, I'm not sure you should smile that way, she made a fine record in college."

"Not sure that I should. What one's family knows—assumes it knows—of one's real self isn't worth sneezing at."

"And Gladys tells me it's given her just one ambition in life—to laugh as much as she can and to make others laugh. Says she never wants to see another tear. May God grant her wish. As for Cindy—"

"Cindy's not vulnerable. She'll be Cindy whatever her environment. And as a matter of fact, the effect on the rest of us has been superficial. Even on me. You needn't look at me that way, sir! I'm not unhappy. But do you know why I think it has been superficial? I read a new book on psychology going over on the boat—professor at Johns Hopkins lent me—and the chapter on The Child interested me immensely. The theory is that if a baby has adequate affection and protection, an assurance of being wanted, it will grow up able to take whatever life gives. Deeda never had that, but the extra mother love she gave us gave us extra stamina. Why, that's the reason we can't be vindictive now! It isn't the parental example so much after all—it's that Deeda's protected now by the love and protection she gave us when we were infants! We *can't* be vindictive. Not even about the wrong id*ea*s of sex she fostered on us. We still can't talk freely on that subject even among ourselves but from the little we've said I know Glad and Cindy were not affected but that Fair, Ann Wesley, and I have had some adjusting to do. I'm sorry, Papa—I know your generation never even mentioned the word."

"It's all right, Beth. Was just glancing at my watch because I want to get over to the house, see as much's I can of the others before they leave. But I'll have no more discussion of this plan to send Sister back to Bayport. Let that be understood. I commission you to tell them all: my word to Sister stands."

"But, Papa! You can't! You're just making a martyr of yourself!"

"I heard you out. You hear me. I am doing my duty as I see it and that's something nobody can see for me. And I haven't been doing it for twenty-seven years, sacrificing the peace of my home and of my mind, my professional ambition **an**d your mother's life, to drop it now when there's nothing

442

Sister can do that God won't grant me patience to bear. I shall pray daily for His extra help in times of her attacks—"

"That's one thing you won't have to worry about! Deeda'll never have another hystero-neurasthenic attack—not such as we've known in the past, at least."

"That's a word I'm not familiar with."

"I wasn't either until I met Doctuh Newman—the psychologist I was talking about—on the boat. I told him all I knew about Deeda's mental illness, all her physical ailments and accidents. He was much interested. Seems it all forms a picture of typical hystero-neurasthenia. As symptomatic to him as the measles. All those years Mama hedged and covered-up! I had intelligence enough to know after I was grown that it was as much an illness as—"

"This Doctor Newman told you the cause too, I suppose."

"Now don't be sarcastic about him! Of course he did: shock—*trauma,* they call it, Greek for *wound.* Excuse me, sir. I forgot you had a classical education. Anyway, a *trauma* in childhood aggravated by a mentally unhealthy environment, a feeling of inferiority brought to active hysteria by a second *trauma* later—your marrying Mama instead of her. After that, every time anything happened to remind her of her suffering then, revitalized it, activated the old pattern, and—"

"You've told the other girls all this?"

"Yes. And discovered that Ann Wesley and Fred know more about it than I do. One of the first things they did in New York was to go to a psychoanalyst about it. Thought something might be done at this late date to give you and Mama relief. But it seems Deeda's too old for the kind of treatment might've made a normal woman of her if she could've had it when she was young. But Doctuh Newman thought that if she outlived Mama—if the object of her jealousy were removed—she'd have a few fairly normal years. Whether that's true or not, there's no sense in your torturing yourself any longer, in any way. You wouldn't feel you had to nurse a case of smallpox just because you happened to be around when the victim was infected!"

"If I had infected the victim I would! No. You girls may talk in whatever terms you like, scientific or personal—and I expect ever since Cindy broke the ice that day in Cameronville there's been plenty of personal interpretation."

443

"Oh, Papa, I didn't mean to upset you so! I mentioned your role in it—an innocent bystander role—because it's high time we all faced facts and brought them out in the open. But I don't want to hurt you—"

"Go on. It's all right. Even a relief—in a way."

"Then I will. You're something of a neurotic yourself on this score. I suppose all these years you've felt guilty because Deeda's what she is when you were as innocent—"

"Don't use that word again! Innocent never! And no bystander. Stupid's the kindest word you can use and I don't deserve that! A stupid, smug, blundering, egotistical young fool thinking God'd spread his samples of young womanhood before me—as Hal spreads pictures of those Ford automobiles of his. Mine to admire, appraise, take my time over, ask advice on. Say, finally, 'Why, it's this one, of course. Your choice for me too, I see now, God. Thought for a while You felt the one over there more suitable for a minister of Your gospel. Not so pleasing to the eye and the senses but—' "

"Papa!"

" '—capable and devout. Yes, that's right, God. This one has a more pleasing personality, too, and a way with people that'll be a great help to me in my work. But just leave that one around, will You? She'll be mighty useful. . . .' "

"Papa, poor Papa. Here, let me slip Bishop Asbury's cushion from beneath you and put it here on the desk under your head. There. Now I'll scratch your head for you. . . . Cindy! Get out of here!"

"What's the matter with Papa?"

"He's feeling badly. You get out."

"Just came to see what on earth'd happened to you and Papa. Deeda's been worse than a cat with a lost kitten. *She* started over here. Told her Hal wanted to take her picture, I'd come. Hal thinks he got some mighty good ones of Mama's grave. Sun was just right when we got out there, designs look as fresh's they did yesterday. Nearly cried my eyes out, though, thinking of Mama being way down there, couldn't see all those beautiful flowers . . ."

"Cindy, don't cry any more. Go on back and keep Deeda there—if you can. But don't you dare tell her Papa's feeling badly. Say I'm helping him sort some papers and we'll be over in a few minutes."

"O.K. but don't be all day about it. I want Hal to take some snaps of us five girls all together. . . .

> "Safe in the arms of Jesus,
> Safe on His gentle breast,
> There by his love o'er-shaded
> Sweetly my soul shall rest. . . ."

"I'll just sit up now, Beth. Thank you. No, Mama was the innocent bystander. *Blind* innocent bystander, she would've said. Blamed herself for being selfish and self-centered as a girl. And I suppose she was, but no more generous, self-denying *woman* ever lived. I can testify to that."

"She was too self-denying. I don't believe in it. If she'd continued to be selfish—"

"She couldn't be that after she knew— She took the responsibility of my guilt along with what she called her own."

"Papa, please try to forget that word. You and Mama and Deeda were simply victims of circumstance. Caught in the mores of your times. Why, nobody today berates himself for being—well, attracted to two women. It can't very well be avoided, men and women thrown together everywhere as they are now. There simply is not *one* woman a man wants to marry, or *one* man—"

"That may be. But once a man's chosen *one* and married her—"

"But look at the way divorcees're accepted now as a matter of course! And I can remember when a 'grass widow' was looked at askance! As for a public divorce—"

" 'Cleave thee only unto her' is as sacred a vow now as it was thirty-eight years ago. I've got no patience with these modern tongue-in-cheek marriages."

"And I've none in your continuing to live in purgatory purging yourself of the imaginary sin of having been human when you were young! I've thought lots of times—watching you living a Christlike life, refusing to accept an increase in salary if a church wasn't free of debt, preaching against worldliness with your daughters sitting there before you—I've thought you should've been a Catholic priest."

"Could've still been a Methodist, had direct contact with God, and remained a celibate—if I'd had the strength of mind I thought I had when I heard the Call!"

"Never once thought you could've been a celibate unless the Church demanded it!"

"That a compliment or a defamation of character?"

"A compliment, sir. Hand me your pocket comb, I'll repair my damage. It's funny, isn't it? But I can't remember any show of affection in our family except our kissing Mama and Deeda goodnight, kissing you good-bye when you went away on the train, and rubbing or scratching heads. Like primates in the jungle. But I know you and Mama loved each other and us. I suppose it was Deeda's presence kept us from being demonstrative though I can't see why it should have."

"It was your mother's sympathy for Sister's 'aloneness' after your Uncle Benton's death put a stop to my demonstrativeness. And I've seen Mama many a time when you all were little take your arms from around her neck and whisper 'Go hug Deeda.' You were as likely, those days, to run to Sister first but Mama took no chances on your overlooking Sister—once she knew how sensitive she was. Yes, it was a mistake, as were most other steps we took trying to live together peaceably."

"That's why no one of us can bear having you continue to watch every move and edit every word every day from now on. I've done enough of it to know how exhausting it can be for a few weeks at a time. Oh, it makes me sick! The way we've all been so sure Deeda'ud go first, leave you and Mama a happy old age, at least! Now that there's nothing we can do for Mama, we've got to help you, Papa. Don't you see that?"

"I see the best way you can help me. And that's by stopping all this talk about sending Sister away. I am master of my own house and I propose—"

"Just let me say this—because I know you haven't felt like thinking two days ahead—"

"I've thought enough to resolve to think only one day ahead. 'Sufficient unto the day—' "

"But it doesn't have to be evil, Papa! That's what I'm trying to say. You're a man in your prime. Oh, yes, you are! Sixty-five. And look five or ten years younger. Why, if you were in politics, you'd be just of age to run for the presidency. Or be appointed Secretary of State."

"Just five more years and I'll be appointed to a back seat. Superannuated."

"Yes, of course. The Methodist Episcopal Church South—

446

all other churches and businesses so far as I know—have to be more careful of their administration than the government of the United States. All that aside, you're a healthy, good-looking man in your prime and—well, we all agreed last night that if you should want to marry again, we'd trust your good taste and welcome a step-mother. Not that our reactions should make any difference. Just—"

"No, that'ud be another thing I'm capable of deciding for myself."

"Just thought we'd like to go on record. But if you tie yourself down with Deeda, you'll— Papa!"

"Sorry, Beth. Didn't mean to jump out of my chair that way. But I can't take another minute of this. . . . I *will not* be advised. What I do or do not do is a matter for God and me to settle. He's used Sister all these years to test my submission to His will and I'll brook no interference between us—from my children nor anybody else. I know you all have the kindest motives. I don't mean to appear ungrateful for your thought of me. Maybe some day I'll be able to tell you all that's on my conscience and then—"

"I can imagine all that's on your conscience and I know it's no more than would be on that of any other young saint living in the same house with a young woman as attractive as Deeda was—if that picture in Mama's album, taken in Doddsville, wasn't it?—can be trusted. This wearing a hair shirt the rest of your life because you were aware of her as a woman and felt the—the urge any other man—"

"I'm not any other man. I'm a man of God. Can't stop you one way I will another: If I *could* marry again, I *would marry Sister.* All right, laugh if you will. But it's as true a statement as any I ever made from my pulpit."

"I feel more like crying. It just seems ludicrous. Poor, broken, old woman like Deeda, looking ten years older than you, standing at an altar—"

"You needn't picture it. It will never happen. I'll go the rest of the way alone. And by doing that, I'll keep my faith with her . . . to about . . . the extent I kept it with Mama."

"Papa, please— Come in, Cindy."

"I'm *not* Cindy. Whit and I drove down for the mail and I thought Papa'ud like having his left over here. There're enough notes *addressed* to Deeda, mostly from Bayport, to keep her

447

happy. Beth, who in the world do you know—masculine gender—writes such an exciting hand as this? Postmarked Philadelphia, sent special delivery to Abington Woman's College, forwarded here. I held it up to the sun but I couldn't make out a single word. Good stationery. Why didn't he know you were here?"

"I'd expected to go to Abington— Give me that letter, you imp of Satan!"

"Here. But pass it back to me soon's you've read it. Papa, may I open yours for you, Beth's so selfish with hers."

"I think not now, Gladys. Rather have them to console me when you all're gone. That's what they are, I see. Letters of sympathy. Written as I've so often written to others."

"Then you come with me out in the sunshine. You look all in. Les leave Beth alone with her secret. I don't like the church smell in here. Makes me sleepy. I don't mean the memory of your sermons, Papa! Not after I was big enough to listen. I mean when I was little and thought I went to church to take off my hat, put my head in Mama's lap, and go to sleep. Thought everybody else went for naps too because I never woke up till they stood up to sing the last hymn. Come on, les go over to the chair-swing. You know, Papa, first thing I'm going to do when my *little* Cutie's walking—you're going to christen her Ellen Humiston Roberts—is bring her here to this great big lawn and let her roll and tumble all over it. You know you'll be here a long time, way these people love you, now that you don't have to be moved at the end of four years. Wonder what town I'd've chosen to live in seven or eight years if Methodists had had that plan earlier. I had such a good time every place we lived. And, Papa, won't David Humiston Roberts have himself a time some day climbing over that high back fence? I'm going to leave out the McCall out of respect to Davy Alexander and call my little old brat Hummy. Now will you just look at my children's father poring over that ragged old road-map he paid a quarter for at the Allenford Garage! Told him all we have to do to get home by tomorrow night, way he wants to go, is turn in every little old dumpy, bumpy road we come to, stop at every little old cabin on it, pet the pickaninnies, eat corn pone, buy us a watermelon and a cantaloupe, get wrong directions for the next mile, and by the time we have a machine full, we'll be crossing the Neuse. Papa, when'll you come and preach a sermon in New

448

Bern that'll keep my head off Whit's broad shoulder? We've got that "Holy" Smith there now. Took his D.D. at Trinity my first year. Taught me Freshman Bible—at least he sat in a chair in front of the class and—"

"He's a mighty good man, Gladys, in spite of his delivery. I'll come whenever *he* invites me."

'Then that'll be soon. He depends on me to keep 'the gay young married,' as he calls us, 'interested and active in good works.' I can't keep thum on the straight and narrow exactly but I do get thum in their pews right often by inviting thum to our house after church for a— Papa, stop here a minute! Before we get to Whit, and I forget whether I'm coming or going. That's a fact. That's the way he affects me even yet. Looks at me out of those wistful brown eyes. . . . What I wanted to ask you, Papa, was—you like the *idea* of Deeda's going to Miss Mary Sue— Oh, I didn't mean— Please don't look at me like that!"

"Don't cry, Gladys. I didn't mean to upset you. You'd better just ask Beth to tell you what I've said on that subject. I've had all the talk I can stand this morning."

"I—just wanted to help you. We all want to help you. Cutie not here to protect you any more, she'd never forgive us, letting Deeda—"

"The best way *you* can help me is by—being your naturally happy self. The way you helped Mama. No, there's one thing you can do for me. Today. Before you leave. Persuade Sister to take off that deep mourning. Aren't there some light colors called 'second mourning' she could wear?"

"Yes, Papa, there are. What everybody wears for first mourning now, lavender, gray, and white. We're all going to wear white the next six weeks, then go back to our usual fall colors. Ann Wesley can't wear white in New York—wouldn't if she could, I reckon. She thinks a funeral's as barbaric as a big wedding. She's the one to do something bout Deeda's 'widow's weeds.' Said last night the very sight of Deeda swathed in black made her sick, and you know how she had to get away from Deeda's talk before supper. Oh, I'm sorry, Papa! I'll try to guard my tongue."

"I wasn't frowning at you, Gladys. Just realized that a week ago this morning I stood here between church and parsonage, with Mama. Looking out on this quiet, wide street. She said

449

something about the houses and the people in Allenford being less pretentious than in most other towns we've lived in but she hoped we'd stay here right up to my retirement—living here demanded so little of her and when Sister was 'off' there were no close neighbors to hear her. Now, now, Gladys, I didn't mean to make you cry."

"I'm not going to cry. I'm going to find Deeda right now and see what I can do about her mourning clothes. She'll be more influenced by my telling her what people down here wear than by anything Ann Wesley can say."

"Well, I'll appreciate anything you can do. It'll try my patience sitting across the table—"

"I know it will. Papa, you must promise me you'll visit us real soon and just stay and stay. Course you'll have to visit Fair and Cindy too but I want you first. Ann Wesley says she's going to show you New York soon's they find a larger apartment. I declare if she doesn't hurry and bring that Fred and that cute little old Evans down here, Whit and I're going up there if we have to sleep on the roof! Here comes Deeda now. You go sit in the swing with Whit a little while. I'll see what I can bout all that crêpe right now. Deeda! I've got a bug to put in your ear!"

"Baby, I don't know how you can talk so today—like it's any other day. Wait, Brothuh David! I want to ask you something. Which'd you rather have for dinner, first course, chicken soup or jellied tomato juice? We've got plenty of both."

"Why, either's all right with me."

"Then I'll give you the soup. It's better for you. I don't care what Doctuh Soddy said, I know it was eating too many tomatoes all summer killed Ellen. When I was young, they were considered poisonous, but she wouldn't listen to me. Do wait a minute, Brothuh David—did you get any letters of condolence this morning's mail? Mine're all there on Ellen's desk, you want to see thum. Just thought I'd like to know—"

"Yes, I have some. Haven't read them myself yet. I'll bring them from the study, though, when I have."

"Deeda, les us go in the house. I want to help you plan your fall wardrobe. Yes, Papa?"

"Why, baby, I don't know—"

"Just wanted to say this while I think of it. Speaking of letters, I don't know how much visiting I'll be able to do, but I promise I'll write to each one of you more often than I have in

the past—when Mama was here to keep us all in touch—and I'll
be needing—"

"You'll get thum, Papa. Don't you worry."

5

Bayport, N.C.
May 12th, 1934.

Dear Beth,

Just a few words in reply to your good letter of the first.

I appreciate your taking time out of your housekeeping
and teaching schedule to keep me up-to-date on national
and world affairs. Yes, I see your point in your sympathy
with the Roosevelt "children." I expect all preachers' children feel the same way. It's the President himself, though,
who gets my deepest understanding and sympathy, doing a
job I believe no other man at this time could do in spite of
all the petty sniping about his personal and family affairs. Maybe it's your little comments make me digest today's complicated politics easier from your letters than
from the magazines you and Martin subscribed to for me.
I never seem to get through one before all the next month's
issues come.

But they're not wasted I can tell you. I've found a little
colored boy with a goat and wagon. First of each month we
load up and take them to places where they'll do the most
good—the library Miss Tempy Williams founded in the old
Garrison, the white and colored schools, any home where
I've noticed an especially bright boy or girl. My assistant,
by the way, is Old Lady's great-grandson. It was his father
your Mama taught to walk—expect you remember my telling you all that story the first time you gathered here, for
my seventy-first birthday.

Every day I live here again I'm struck anew by the fact
that nothing much changes in Bayport but the faces of the
people who walk these oyster-shell sidewalks—and they,
with few exceptions, have the names I learned fifty years
ago. Same old live and pin oaks, festooned with ivy, same
old double-veranda houses with shutter-doors—with the
exception of the Mercer Williamses' and the two newish
ones you spoke of as looking like intruders. The few automobiles that were new fifteen or twenty years ago look very
much at home now parked between horses and mules

451

hitched along High Street. Yes, it's a sweet, stable old town. I doubt if there's another like it in the country and I'm thankful things worked out as they did and Sister got her way about my retiring to this peaceful, memory-filled spot. There's so little I can do now it's a blessing to be where there's little to be done. If the whole world could learn to live as Bayporters live—quietly, good-neighborly, unambitiously—it could live peaceably. I can't imagine, though, any but those to this manner born discriminating between what modern improvements they will have: refusing a railroad and accepting electricity and telephones and radios; refusing trucks and accepting motor boats for the ever-growing fish, shrimp, and fertilizer industries; accepting automobiles (those who needed them to get back and forth to Wilmington when the causeway outmoded the boat) but refusing to buy a new model till the old one refuses to go. More generous people never lived. They "share the wealth" that's come to them and there's no poverty among the laborers, white or colored.

I've discovered a compensation for being superannuated—laymen are more at ease in my company than when I was an active minister and it's a real pleasure to be a man among men again. Expect I should learn to smoke a pipe and take a nip in company to encourage perfect fellowship, but I'm content to be accepted for a few minutes moving from group to group on the courthouse green during court week without putting an abrupt end to an argument; walking in on a trial like any other spectator, hearing no clearing of throats, seeing no sliding along a bench to give me more space than I need. That reminds me—there was an interesting trial here in the fall term you should tell your Yankee friends about, their thinking due process of law never applies to a Negro down here: a darky was caught red-handed robbing the till in a cross-roads store down in the county, the proprietor dead at his feet, a knife in his back. The darky was brought here and put in jail. Within a week he'd broken out. There was some excitement in town for the few hours he was at liberty but no panic or talk of a lynching. When the fellow was imprisoned a second time, he was put in the steel cage that had never been used before and hadn't been thought of in the first instance. In two days he was out of that! It seems that when Brother

Jenkins, who has charge of the jail now, took him his supper he wasn't under the blankets humped up on his cot but was lying flat on *top* of the cage and when Jenkins opened the little aperture to push the tray through, he got a whack on the head that knocked him unconscious. When he revived, the darky was gone. Really gone this time. When the sheriff was satisfied he wasn't hiding in the county, he began watching the mails for a letter to the fellow's girl. In about three weeks it came, from Atlanta. Police down there spotted him and he was brought back. This time he was kept under guard in the cage, tried, found guilty, and sentenced to death. Five heavily armed men took him to Raleigh in an automobile. Not one of them had ever been to the Capital before but didn't want to admit it and drove round and round the city till the prisoner himself got tired, and directed them to the penitentiary—where he'd been incarcerated before! During the trial here I talked and prayed with him. A bright fellow, quiet and industrious when not under the influence of monkey-rum. He made his peace with God and was resigned to his fate—his soul saved but his body wasted.

Sister is finally over that deep cold she contracted in the early spring. Don't remember whether I wrote you Dr. Stevens said he'd never understand how she missed pneumonia, said she has the most remarkable constitution for a woman of her age he has ever encountered. She was telling him about all the illnesses she used to have and the accidents she'd sustained and he laughed and said she should be on exhibit. And I'm well. Still not sleeping straight through many nights but since the warm weather came, I've given up retiring at ten and take a late evening's stroll along the beach, under the moon or stars, and find that it helps me through the pre-midnight hours. And I nap in the daytime.

I'm enclosing the latest letters from the other girls. I know, from what I've heard each of you say, that you don't write to one another as often as you do to Sister and me.

My fond regards to Martin and my love to you,

PAPA

P.S. If any one of you is wondering what I'd like for a birthday present next month, it's a new fountain pen. When this one's not empty it's clogged.

"Why, Brothuh David, haven't you finished that letter yet! Sitting in here and all that good sunshine going to waste on the veranda."

"I'm going to get plenty right now, taking this down for the morning mail. Pshaw! Can't ever remember Beth's new address. Where's her last letter?"

"And they moved last December! Letter's in my sewing basket. I had it out there yesterday reading her message to me aloud to Charlotte—here bragging bout the way her children can't go off on a trip without writing her to take care of herself. Just wanted her to know your children think as much of me as my own daughters might've—if the Lord'd been willing for me to marry and— But I know Beth's address without looking. It's Mrs. Martin Newman, Sixty-two University Avenue, Philadelphia, Pennsylvania."

"I hadn't forgotten the name, anyway!"

"Well, I thought I'd better repeat it or you'd be doing the trick you did the other day—putting Cindy's name on Fair's envelope. Then, too, I always like to say Mrs. Martin Newman, thinking of Beth. Poor child had to wait long enough to find her a husband, then take a man had to get a divorce so he could marry her. Not that Martin's not just as nice as he can be, thoughtful of me when he's been here as any son-in-law I've— you've got. It's just the *i*dea of his turning his back on a woman he had promised—"

"Well, I think I'll be going along before the sun gets too hot."

Following me to the door again! Wish just once I could leave this house without having to talk all the way to the gate.

"Now, Brothuh David, do don't forget to get more stamps. I never feel safe handing you a letter to mail without stamping it myself. And I must find a few minutes today to write to Gladys, tell her the twins say she can have that old bureau of Miss Ryder's and welcome if she can get a truck down here to take it away. Say they won't take a cent for it. I think she may's well wait, don't you? till she comes down for your birthday, see that it gets moved without getting scratched. Neither of the twins'll move out of a rocking chair long enough to watch it for her. Here, wait a minute! You forgot your hat."

"Don't need it this warm day."

"You wait. You can take a cold on a warm day's well a cold one and your age. . . ."

My age. My age. One year, three months, and two days more than hers. Never seems to realize my frailties should apply to her too. However, I can't say they do. I never saw such bouncing energy in a woman of seventy-five. If she ever gets tired she never admits it, unless her constantly emphasizing my feeble memory and body is a sign she wants to hurry me to the grave so that she can follow.

"Here's your hat. Now, don't you get talking with everybody you meet and be late for your dinner! I want you to have your nap before the ladies come."

"No, I'll be back in plenty of time."

❖

Yes, it would've been a relief to've added a line or two to this letter. A relief while I was adding it, a regret now. What could I say that'ud make any one of my daughters—any woman for that matter—understand? There's always that impulse, though, writing or talking to them, to say there's more to being well than not being sick in any way. Young people seem to think all an old person wants is physical good health. I've got through twelve years now without verbal complaint, only my Father in Heaven to understand and give me, each day, the courage and fortitude necessary for the ensuing twenty-four hours. And He gives me that as generously as He used to give mere patience and forbearance—all I needed when Mama was with me. If only He could let me sleep between two and five *every* morning, or at least let me awaken *quietly* every morning when the clock strikes two. It's that nightmare, recurring about every fifth night—that thud of footsteps below my window, that shouting, that calling of names—makes me awake with a start, my heart thumping and my body in a cold sweat. Feel sure it comes on an average of every fifth morning but there seems to be no way I can get it down factually. "Brothuh David, why's your calendar marked up this way—check on it every five days for the last few weeks?" "Brothuh David, I do declare, your pockets're worse than any boy's! Every time I start to press a suit, I have a little pile of odds and ends to take out. Strings, bottle caps, bird feathers, little slips of your best writing-paper with Bible verses in red ink or with dates jotted down on thum. Folks'll be saying you're getting senile, you don't stop picking up everything attracts your eye. Now I'll bet you don't even remember why you put those dates down, do you?"

No, no privacy. Lack of it may be a small price to pay for the physical comfort I enjoy—clothes in tip-top condition, house shipshape, food suited to my digestion. Can't help being irritated, though, at her invasion of my privacy. Think sometimes I'd like to take her to court on *that* charge. This matter of my pockets, for instance. Sister knows as well as I do that I'm collecting bottle caps so that Hummy can decorate a cap, next time he comes, like the ones the Bayport boys wear he admires so much. Knows the bird feathers are for little Fred, almost as many varieties in this semi-tropical climate as in that zoo in New York. She knows the strings are for any little boy I find on the pier in need of them. What she doesn't know is that I'm trying to make up to all children for what I denied my own. "Papa," Gladys said, "I wish you'd paid as much attention to us when we were little as you do to your grandchildren. You even let them play at your desk and draw with your fountain pen!" I deserved that but I don't believe there're any words more painful for a parent to listen to than a reminder of what he might have done.

Yes, Sister knows the purpose of all my collecting, prefers finding me and fingering my lapel rather than lifting a pin from a cushion in plain sight, and was asking me just yesterday if I had a Bible verse in my pocket for Miss Bessie's—Mrs. Sharpe's—little granddaughter. But she had to take that circuitous route to get to the point of asking about those dates. It's a shame her mind hasn't had the same rejuvenation her spirits've had since she's had sole charge of me, and could be put to better use than thinking up disguises for questions her eyes and ears fail to provide answers for. I wouldn't believe it if I hadn't seen it—that a young woman as intelligent and mentally alert as she was when I first knew her could become "bird-brained," as Gladys calls Cindy. Still, she's had some return of the alertness and humor I first found in her. I have never agreed with Beth it was only her good memory that fooled Miss Tempy in school and others of us on the outside. I can't say she's had a physical rejuvenation exactly, either. Shoulders still stooped as they've been since middle-age of course, but her hair's the same mouse color it was when Mama died and her face as full of wrinkles—fuller probably—but somehow they're not so noticeable. Probably because she smiles more often now and they take a new slant. It's her eyes that're younger, brighter, larger, more definitely gray now that tears don't wash out the color. Interest in her appearance again has helped too. Always as neat's a pin, gets a permanent wave, she calls it, twice a year, and's as dress-conscious as she was half a century ago. She'd be overdoing it—wearing those bright colors that so shocked the girls when she went out of second mourning—if they didn't insist on sending her materials and patterns suitable for her age. A green dress she bought ready-made reminded me of Miss Parker Piver, the Fisherman's Luck they used to call her before she was converted under my ministry here and took the red lantern off her gate. . . .

Yes, I expect pretty clothes can make up to a woman for a lot of unhappiness. I don't like to remember those lean years of ours, when the trouble with Sister first started, when Mama couldn't even have the consolation of new dresses. Decade of my three smallest congregations and poorest charges, the bishop assuming the affliction in my home'ud affect my work, and before my share in Father's estate came to me. Mama said what difference did clothes make when she couldn't show her face because of Sister any more than she'd been allowed to show her body because of a baby. A little extra money might've helped her, though. Only temptation I ever had in that respect came in 1898 when I was at the Second Church in Raleigh. I conquered it and received the evidence of God's approval immediately. I went to the office of the Governor's private secretary, asked him to convey my thanks for the offer of the chaplaincy, Second Volunteer Regiment, and explain that my conscience forbade my acceptance of the honor. Fifteen hundred a year! Just twice as much as I was getting in the pulpit then. I felt that was the snare the Devil was using to lure me from the kind of ministry to which God had definitely called me. I was right, too. Leaving the secretary's office, my eye was caught by a red-bound volume in a bookcase near the door, *Felix Holt, Radical* by George Eliot. Glanced at the title, started on out, when with no volition of my will my hand reached for it and my voice asked the loan of it. I sat down on a bench in Capitol Square and opened the book at random. My memory failing, is it? Why, I can repeat that paragraph almost word for word:

I'll never marry . . . I'll never look back and say, "I had a fine purpose once. I meant to keep my hands clean and my soul upright, and to look Truth in the face; but

457

pray excuse me, I have a wife and children, I must lie and simper a little, else they'll starve; or my wife is nice, she must have her bread well buttered, and her feelings will be hurt if she is not thought genteel!"

Poor Felix Holt, I thought. He didn't trust God enough to know he could have a wife and children and still keep his integrity. So there was no pain at all a few years later in turning down that request to run for Governor on the Prohibition ticket. Was always sorry, though, that Mama had to know about that. She couldn't understand my other-worldliness going that far. Always thought it was because of Sis . . .

"*Good* morning, Brothuh David Humiston! You're out bright and early."

"Good morning, Miss Mary Sue. And so're you. How are you today?"

"Fit's a fiddle. And you? Ora?"

"Both well, thank you. I can't say my rest at night's all it should be. Have a habit, here lately, of waking up at two A.M. and staying awake till dawn." (Tell me, Miss Mary Sue, have you heard any malicious gossip about Sister's keeping house for me? I have a recurrent and terrifying nightmare . . .)

"You ever try a cup of hot sweet milk with a little brandy in it?"

"No, but Doctor Stevens prescribes a sip or two of brandy before retiring and I follow his advice occasionally."

"Then you follow *my* prescription every night, you hear. You get you one of those little bitty electric plates Davis-Sharpe Company has on sale at a dollar ninety-eight and you put it by your bed along side of that sweet milk and crackers Ora tells me she always provides you with and you plug it in the minute you wake up. You'll be fixed for sleeping in a jiffy. Got any good brandy on hand?"

"Half a bottle left of the one Miss Bessie gave me Christmas."

"*Good* brandy, I said. I'll see that you get some this very day. You follow my directions tonight and you won't be looking so worn and tired, Sally Swain's wedding comes off next Tuesday night. Can't have the Grand Old Man of Bayport not looking his best, standing up there in the chancel. Now that reminds me! Don't you *ever* have another thought that Brothuh Turner resents everybody's wanting you for all the marrying, christening, and burying goes on in this town. Brothuh Turner's a mighty good man but he's just not folks and he knows it. Oh, I know you've been worrying, fraid he thinks you're frying his kettle of fish. Expect that's why you haven't been sleeping. Anyway, I made a point of dropping in the parsonage the other day—it doesn't look the way it did the six months Ora was keeping it, I can tell you. But what can you expect? Poor Sistuh Turner was never out of a collard patch till she married her a preacher. But as I was saying, I dropped in, with a jar of my fresh strawberry jam to sweeten my approach, and I got the conversation round to you. Said how providential it was your being free that first half-year of your retirement to fill in for us when Brothuh Gaskill was so sick and how glad we all were when you bought Miss Annie Wescott's old place and stayed on to give your daughters and grandchildren a summer vacation spot. By the way, next time you write Gladys, you tell her I meant every word I said bout Hummy's staying with me this summer when they all come down. It's all right with Hummy—looked at me out of those great big blue eyes of Benton's, said, 'Gee, that'll be good! You'll let me play soldier with your father's sword every day!' But to get back to what I was saying. Brothuh Turner said—I'm going to quote his exact words—said, 'Sistuh Ives, it's been mighty providential for me too and that's a fact. I don't want to be blasphemous,' said, 'but every time I stand beside Brothuh Humiston assisting in a service, I get a real holy feeling like the Good Lord Himself is right there instructing me in my duties.' There now!"

"I'm glad to hear it, Miss Mary Sue. It does relieve me—somewhat. And I'll make a point hereafter to try to help him get over his awkwardness with people. Noticed he doesn't always seem to know just what to do or say on occasions of joy or of sadness. Early years of my ministry, I had Mama—"

"Mama! I can't get used to your calling that pretty, carefree girl I used to know *Mama*. Much's I love the word. I certainly should've seen her, time she came to Brookside to get Ora after that distressing illness, and got it into my head that Ellen had to grow old same's the rest of us. Never shall now, it seems. Nearly every time I'm at your house I ask Ora to show me a picture of Ellen in her later years but seems she can never lay her hands on one. Shame it's not fashionable to have a family album on the parlor table these days."

459

"Why, there's a picture of Mama right on my desk, next to the one of her and the older girls when they were little. It's an enlargement of a snapshot Hal took when we lived in Silverboro. She's sitting with me on the parsonage steps. Only really good one anybody ever got of her. Mama was camera shy. If she couldn't avoid a kodak, she always managed to get her face in shadow or turned away. I'll show it to you next time you drop in."

"You do, hear. Now you'd better stop this chatting and get along to the post office with that letter you've got or Tom Bradley'll be starting off to Wilmington without it. I'm on my way to the library, return this book called *Old Families of the Cape Fear*. Lot in it about the Evanses and the Rutlands, and the Fannings're mentioned long with the Ives. Tell the girls to get it out when they come. Come see me real soon, hear."

"Yes, I'll be by. Mighty peaceful sitting on your porch. You come."

"I'll be round this very day. Right after dinner. I made a batch of cheesestraws for Ora to serve at her shindig and I have to be there early. Bye."

"Good-bye, Miss Mary Sue."

Fit's a fiddle and spry's a sparrow. Wrinkles hide the freckles I used to wonder if I could count, bright hair's grayed over, but she's still the same little Mary Sue. A few minutes of conversation with her's like a tonic, spite of the fact that she's been lonelier than Sister all these years, living alone in that house, same vase of immortelles on the center table were there when I made my first pastoral call. Nothing changed that I can see except Miss Mary Sue's appearance—and I forget that has after I've been with her a few minutes. Now, now, maybe she hasn't been lonelier than Sister. I've never felt lonelier at times than when the house was full of people. And Miss Mary Sue's always had the assurance of Benton's love to sustain her. . . . Strange Sister can't find—*says* she can't find that picture of Mama and me. Add that verb and it'ud be strange if she could find it. I've thought sometimes if the people in Allenford hadn't known Mama my first three years there, it would've been mighty hard to get it across to them the last four that there'd been a Mrs. Humiston. Sister never mentions Mama's name if she can avoid it. I hear her talking about the children and grandchildren, to old friends as well as new, as though they're her own.

Now all her memories are of what I said to her, where she went

460

with me, those months before Mama came from Savannah. Well, better those memories than the tally we used to have during one of her attacks of our neglect and unkindness, my cruelties and hankerings after other women. Yes, Sister's had her heart's desire and her little triumph getting back here, being mistress of the parsonage awhile, and it worked a cure no doctor could've achieved. Those months in my little old Parsonage-by-the-Sea she acted more like a bride than a spinster housekeeper. Fluttering about, washing and ironing curtains, showing the ladies how she'd rearranged and improved this and that, talking about *my* dishes, *my* pots and pans, *my* bedspreads. It amused the girls when they came down that first June. Made Ann Wesley cry a little, sitting out there on that little veranda with Beth late one night after they'd had a moonlight sail with young Mercer Williams' family. I couldn't help but hear, the head of my bed —Mama's and my first bed after our honeymoon—not six feet from the window. "It's like an immaculate marriage, Beth," she said. "I don't mean physically. I mean that for Deeda the shine's never worn off as it's bound to eventually in all normal marriages. Papa's still the white-haired boy for her and will be to the end." "Yes," Beth said and I knew her hand was at her throat as it always is when she's thoughtful, *"magnificent's* hardly the word to use in connection with Deeda but it's the only word to describe such a lifelong, single-hearted devotion as hers has been. In spite of all the ugliness, all the suffering her inverted passion's caused. Martin says we needn't discuss plans for Papa if Deeda should die first. Says her Will to Live won't weaken until Papa's gone, then she'll go too. But quick!" . . .

My younger days I used to wonder humbly what there was in me could've inspired and kept alive such a love. Felt flattered by it. No longer. I've understood for some time now it was Ora Fanning's need for love and for possession incited it—any other young man coming along at the time I did and showing an interest in her would've served as well. I don't care what the psychologists say, it was her refusal to accept God's will and let me go that wrecked her life—as such stubbornness always will. And came close to wrecking mine. Ora's need for love and possession I said. I don't know . . . Having Mama and all, it would seem, any one man could desire, it couldn't've been need that made me pant—yes, *pant,* like a barnyard "creetur" in season—after Ora.

Unless monogamy is *not* God's plan. For young men. If all

the young men involved in the maze of unhallowed love and passion who've come to me for guidance could've seen into my heart while they listened to my mouthing of platitudes! Never a one has crept to my study in final desperation but I've remembered, like an old dream in sleep that will not be forgotten, those winter evenings by the fireside in Lynnboro, praying for strength to keep my arms at my side, pulling myself away from the Temptress by the sheer force of my will, fleeing to the dark church, throwing myself prone at the cold altar, and praying, praying, praying till body succumbed to spirit. At the altar. Springing for combat again, as though it lay in wait for my spirit, at the top of the stairs in the quiet parsonage, disputing every step it took past Ora's door and the intimate little sounds beyond it— Ora in a white nightgown going to bed alone. I lying *alone* tense and resentful by Mama's side, hour after hour. . . . No, I don't know. I just don't know . . . not about that time.

Only one thing I do know—the loathing and the pity I felt for her that morning in Allenford, exactly a year and a day after Mama's going, was as real to me at sixty-six as passionate love and adoration had been at thirty-seven. I'd lived that year in fear—as Sister, I discovered that morning, had lived it in hope. Fear that she'd have another attack, fear that I'd lose my temper again alone in a house with her. But hope'd sustained her till the period of mourning had passed and she had ripped the black bands from the sleeves of my coats—bringing her scissors to the breakfast table that morning to snip the one from the coat I was wearing. At dinner time she did not hurry to the front door to greet me. She wasn't anywhere downstairs. I went to the kitchen. "Say she feel like one of her sick-headaches coming on," Maggie said. "Say she going upstairs to lie down. Told me to serve you your dinner, you ready." My heart dropped like a plumb to my stomach. I didn't know what to do. Ate a few bites of what Maggie set before me, and cramped with indigestion, started up the stairs. Put my foot on the first step three times, finally turned back, knelt at the parlor sofa and asked God to be with me in whatever lay before. But not until I heard the sound of her crying, my foot on the step a fourth time, did I go up. She was sitting on her bed, her elbow on the footboard, her handkerchief to her eyes. I stood in the doorway, asked her if there were anything I could do, get her a cold compress, a dose of Happidine. She took her handkerchief from her eyes and looked straight at me as she'd never done before, times like this. "Yes, Brothuh David," she said clearly, "there *is* something you can do for me. You can tell me what I'm to call myself." I asked her what she meant. "Well," she said, "a fellow came to the door this morning, selling vanilla extract. I don't know how he got your name but soon's I opened the screen door and said good morning, he took off his hat and asked if he was speaking to Mrs. Humiston. I said, 'No, Mrs. Humiston's passed away.' Said he was sorry to hear that, I must be the lady of the house then. I said, 'Well, I don't know exactly—' And *he* said, 'You're the housekeeper then and the one I want to see,' and went on with his rigmarole. . . . Whatever title you want me to use's all right with me. I just don't want to presume, so I wish you'd tell me—" "I don't know any better title for you than 'lady of the house,' " I replied. "Don't know why you should hesitate over that." "Well"—and she began unrolling the ball of handkerchief, smoothing it flat on her knee—"it's just that *that* title's one people're accustomed to using speaking of married women, of wives. But, on the other hand, housekeeper, to my way of thinking, sounds like hired help, colored help, and I told you when you offered that I'd never take a penny for what I could do for you. I've been embarrassed like that more than once since Ellen passed and it seems no more than my due to get it straight." Then it was I saw what she was driving at, her roundabout way—two more years and I would've recognized it instantly for what it was, the number of circumlocutious proposals I had from widows like Sister Tyler, younger women who were still single like Miss Myra Pennington starting a correspondence soon's her papa died. But I understood in time and knew I had to take the bull by the horns and get it straight once for all, come what may. So I said, "Then lady of the house in your case means *my wife's sister* and lady of the house is the title I want you to use. It's yours as long as you want to keep it. No woman will ever have a higher claim to it." I wish I could forget the expression came over her face at those words. I felt I'd given a poor beaten dog one more lick than animal endurance could take. I turned away fast, said as casually as I could, "I'll be in the study, Sister, till four o'clock or so." I was halfway down the stairs when she called after me, the bare suggestion of a break in her voice, "I'll make some hot muffins for your supper tonight. You stop by the kitchen, tell Maggie not to mix biscuit dough."

You had my admiration then, Sister. You were God's own instrument in that instance, demonstrating the superiority of the spirit of man and woman over that of the beast of the field. No reminder of my impulsive statement at the time of Miss Ryder's death, that should God see fit to take Mama first, you'd be her successor in my home. I walked on light feet to the study, rejoicing in your acceptance of God's will at last. Nothing but *that* acceptance could explain your cheerful acceptance of the fact that I'd never marry you nor any . . .

"*Brothuhhumiston!*"

"Yes, yes—why it's—"

"I've been speaking and speaking to you. Grandma's been honking and honking. You please come to the car?"

"Why, yes, Mary Belle. Sorry—"

"There you go again calling *me* Mary Belle. I'm Charlotte Berry Dowd. Mary Bell Williams's my first cousin and she's a lot littler than me. I'll excuse you, Brothuhhumiston, this last one time though, hear, if you'll give me a red Bible verse."

"Well, now, let me see. Wrote out one this morning, you in mind, but which pocket—? I've got it! Now you listen: tenth verse of the Twenty-eighth Psalm. 'And he rode upon a cherub and did fly; yea he did fly upon the wings of the wind.' "

"Gol-*lee*, that's a good one! Won't anybody in Sunday School learn one good's that!"

"David Humiston, you stop doing Charlotte Berry's home work for her and come here to this car. . . . Charlotte Berry, you take that letter Brothuh Humiston's holding and run fast's you can to the post office before Tom Bradley gets that Ford cranked. Hurry now, you hear!"

Have to think every time I see her, she's as handsome a white-haired lady as she was a black-haired girl. And as devil-may-care.

"Good morning, Charlotte. I wasn't expecting to see *you* in an automobile, why I didn't hear your horn."

"You will see me in one from now on. Don't mind admitting my legs're not what they used to be, anyway you take thum, but my eyesight's good's it ever was and it ever was better than most people's. And I keep my eyes on the road too when I'm driving. I'm telling you the gospel truth, there wasn't a land turtle on it far's I could see last time I looked Thursday, then bang! Been any witnesses, they'd've testified that that sorry

464

Wrightsville soda-jerker had his eyes well's his hands where they shouldn't've been on that girl or why was he driving like a snail? Certainly not to enjoy the sunset on the sound as I was! Get in, David. Sit down. I'll run you home. Watch out! You'll wet your pants!" Laugh, laugh, laugh. "Charlotte Berry's wet bathing suit I'm talking about. Toss it over on the back seat. Anyway, I was meek's Moses and paid for that boy's old fender and that should've been the end of it." Laugh. "Was almost the end of that young upstart in the license bureau this morning. I drove seventeen miles yesterday through the deepest sand I ever got pulled out of but I found out who his people are and he was meeker than Moses ever thought of being, handing me back my license little while ago, when I got through with him. Look here, why I honked my horn hoarse at you—I've just been round to your house looking for you. You want to take a chance on a glorious, gory death by my side and drive out to Camilla after dinner? Get us a free look at a Yankee's southern garden before the old stingy opens it to the tourist trade, a quarter a peep?"

"Well, now—that sounds mighty tempting. The free look, I mean—if I live to get it. Trouble is, seems to me Sister said something—"

"Bout your being home today, help her entertain that crowd sewing for the Chinese. Told thum I had other fish to fry, they could charge a layette to me at Eltinger's in Wilmington. Yes, Ora said she was counting on your being around, be goo-ed over. I told her if she could make you count yourself in on a mess like that, all of us who'd *married* a man had made a mighty big mistake. David Humiston, stop looking like that! It was all right, she didn't whimper. She *laughed*. Laughed and said she reckoned she'd have to let you off this one time. Yessir, Ora's got a little bit of fun in her old bones. Solemn's an owl when she was young. We get on just fine now. Found her out in the side-yard cutting peonies big's a dinner plate to decorate her tea table. Never thought anybody could bring Miss Annie's neglected old garden back to bloom, but Ora's passed another miracle there. Come to think of it, never knew Ora cared a continental bout raising flowers even. That was Ellen's joy."

❖ ❖

Tap, tap, tap.
"Brothuh David?"
"Yes, Sister."

"You remember how to fix yourself another toddy, you need it in the night?"

"I'll manage—if I need it."

"Well, you manage right. Don't want you to get a shock plugging in that cord. You have any trouble with it, just call me. I'm mighty glad Mary Sue had such a notion for you, tonight especially, way you've been going today. You must be played out. Didn't think you'd go out for that walk after that long ride to Camilla. Your legs ache?"

"No, I'm all right."

"Well then—good night."

"Good night."

Now *that's* finished, Lord, let me sleep. Sleep the night through, Lord, as once I slept the sleep of innocence in my trundle-bed. Now I lay me down to sleep, I pray Thee, Lord, my soul to keep. If I should die before I wake . . . But it's not death I fear, Lord. It's . . . no, no, don't think about it! Think of the drifting into the sweetest of all sleeps . . . on Ellen's breast. . . .

❖

For him, against him. For him, against him. For him, against him. For him, against him. Board split four ways. Board! Split four ways. Four to the left side, four to the right. Four, front door. Four, back door. Unanimous now! No split jury this case. United. United Stewards, First Methodist Episcopal Church South. First Methodist Episcopal Church South, Allenford, North Carolina, *and* Bayport, North Carolina. Load and take your places. Halt! Brothuh Armstrong's not here yet. Steward in good standing, First Methodist Episcopal Church South, Lynnboro, North Carolina. Old score to settle. Yonder he comes a-galloping, just like John Wesley. Who're you, Sir? Name, James Wiley. Address? Wilmington, North Carolina. Complaint? Poisoned Miss Ora's mind against me. Take your place, load your gun. And you? Name, Elwood Gideon. Address? Doddsville, North Carolina. Complaint? Poisoned Miss Ora's mind against me. Take your place, load your gun. Don't shoot till you see the white of the peonies big as dinner plates. Ready! March! Chant!

"Thodike Stevika! Guilty man
Must yield to the order United Stewards plan, •

466

Preachers must marry same's the rest
Or give up the license they don't meet the test."

Front door. Back door. Catch him on the run. . . .
 "Brothuh David?"
 "Brothuh David!"
 "Brothuh David!"
 Who's calling? Ellen, did you call? Where are you? I can't find
you. . . .
 "Somebody called me."
 "I'm calling you. What're you doing out there?"
 "Brothuh David, answer me! What're you doing out there in
the passage?"
 "I'm looking for—I don't know. I don't know. It's so dark
and they're surrounding the parsonage again."
 "You stay right there till I can put on my robe."
 "I will *not* have you dictate to me. I will not have *you* advise
me. . . . I'm going down to the porch and I'm going to preach
you such a sermon as . . . I'm going down to look at the sunrise, Sister. Worship with God's lesser creatures. I am fully
clothed. I will not catch cold. You stay where you are."
 "Why, you can't see the sunrise yet, Brothuh David. Courthouse clock just struck two a little while ago. You mustn't sit
out there in the damp till dawn. You wait now till I turn on the
light. I'll fix you another . . . Why, Brothuh David! Walking
on these cold floors barefoot!"
 "Then I'll go look at the stars. What can man do if he look
at the stars but worship, and if he worship what can he do but
walk humbly in the sight of God and love his fellowman?"
 "Oh, Brothuh David, you're out of your head! Your hands're
like ice. Come with me. Lean on me. *David,* lean on me. I'd
carry you if I could, David. Your poor bare stumbling feet.
Lean harder, David. Put all your weight on me. I can bear it,
David . . . till death do us part."